RUNNING THROUGH CORRIDORS

ROB AND TOBY'S MARATHON WATCH OF DOCTOR WHO

VOLUME 2: THE 70S

TOBY HADOKE AND ROBERT SHEARMAN

FOREWORD BY LOUISE JAMESON

Also available from Mad Norwegian Press...

AHistory: An Unauthorized History of the Doctor Who Universe [3rd Edition]
(print and ebook now available) by Lance Parkin and Lars Pearson

AHistory: An Unauthorized History of the Doctor Who Universe [2012-2013 Update]
(ebook now available) by Lance Parkin and Lars Pearson

Space Helmet for a Cow: The Mad, True Story of Doctor Who
(Vol. 1: 1963-1990) and (Vol. 2: 1990-2013) by Paul Kirkley

Wanting to Believe: A Critical Guide to The X-Files, Millennium and the Lone Gunmen
by Robert Shearman

The About Time Series by Tat Wood and Lawrence Miles
About Time 1: The Unauthorized Guide to Doctor Who (Seasons 1 to 3)
About Time 2: The Unauthorized Guide to Doctor Who (Seasons 4 to 6)
About Time 3: The Unauthorized Guide to Doctor Who (Seasons 7 to 11) [2nd Ed]
About Time 4: The Unauthorized Guide to Doctor Who (Seasons 12 to 17)
About Time 5: The Unauthorized Guide to Doctor Who (Seasons 18 to 21)
About Time 6: The Unauthorized Guide to Doctor Who (Seasons 22 to 26)
About Time 7: The Unauthorized Guide to Doctor Who (Series 1 to 2)
About Time 8: The Unauthorized Guide to Doctor Who (Series 3, forthcoming)

Essay Collections
Chicks Dig Comics: A Celebration of Comic Books by the Women Who Love Them

Chicks Dig Gaming: A Celebration of All Things Gaming by the Women Who Love It

Chicks Dig Time Lords: A Celebration of Doctor Who by the Women Who Love It,
2011 Hugo Award Winner, Best Related Work

Chicks Unravel Time: Women Journey Through Every Season of Doctor Who

Companion Piece: Women Celebrate the Humans, Aliens and Tin Dogs of Doctor Who

Queers Dig Time Lords: A Celebration of Doctor Who by the LGBTQ Fans Who Love It

Whedonistas: A Celebration of the Worlds of Joss Whedon by the Women Who Love Them

Guidebooks
I, Who: The Unauthorized Guide to the Doctor Who Novels and Audios
by Lars Pearson (vols. 1-3, ebooks only)

Dusted: The Unauthorized Guide to Buffy the Vampire Slayer
by Lawrence Miles, Pearson and Christa Dickson (ebook only)

Redeemed: The Unauthorized Guide to Angel by Pearson and Christa Dickson (ebook only)

To Steven, for keeping the flame burning.
RS

To three special boys who'll be running through corridors when I'm in a
bath chair – Louis, Oscar and Ethan.
TH

TABLE OF CONTENTS

The thing about running through corridors is that you have to approach each corridor, each monster, each story, each situation as if you are there for the very first time. The tastes, flavours and smells must take you by surprise, invigorate, inspire and catch your breath. The aliens approached with caution, yes, but also with an inquisitive and searching curiosity.

The role of the companion in Doctor Who is one of responsibility. She/he/it is a bridge between the Doctor and the audience. Of course the writer must have someone say "What is it, Doctor?" so the story so far can then be defined and explained (or not). But she/he/it is so much more than that. The companion *is* the audience; we run with the Doctor, flee with the Doctor, investigate with him and, from time to time, rescue him. Our heartbeat is raised when both of his are, our pulses quickened and we laugh and cry with him… but *he* defines us, at least for the 25 minutes (or however long the powers that be decide) that an episode lasts.

Toby and Rob have, I know, eloquently dissected each story, and lovingly crafted a tome of knowledge for you to delight in. So I'm only going to visit my two favourite stories, and really it is a little homage to Robert Holmes. He plagiarised, I know (name me a writer who doesn't), but he wrote with wit and conviction and a certain amount of love – not just for the characters, but for the actors who portrayed them.

It is no secret that my time on Doctor Who wasn't the happiest phase of my career. Tom and I had a complicated relationship, which is now a rather blissful one, for which I am profoundly grateful. We work incredibly well together and enjoy each other's company very much (mainly due to the gentle facilitating by Big Finish). But a little-known fact is that, because of this fractious atmosphere, K9 was kept on for a lot longer than was originally intended. The brilliant John Leeson became firm friends with both of us and the atmosphere lightened.

The very lovely Robert Holmes was more aware than anyone of how difficult I was finding the process and, in both The Talons of Weng-Chiang and The Sun Makers, decided that I should perhaps have a bit more responsibility and take control of the action. This was groundbreaking for the companion, and paved the way for Ace and the current women enjoying their spin around the Universe.

Talons is a huge favourite with the fans, and often mentioned at conventions as an iconic story. The cast was brilliant! And again Big Finish have seen potential and done their Jago and Litefoot spin-off series, enabling me to work with the legends that are Trevor Baxter and Chris Benjamin once again. I suspect that story would not pass the powers that be now. John Bennett with heavily made-up eyelids pretending to be a Chinaman, the terrifying dummy that dripped blood, too many knives in evidence… But it was glorious for Leela, crashing through windows, dressing in beautiful period costumes, comedic scenes with Trevor, most notably the eating of meat! What would I do now I have turned vegetarian?! We had huge fun going away to film, a rare treat in those days, and a lot of attention was paid to every detail. It was a privilege to be part of it.

But my heart lies with The Sun Makers. I thought the script extraordinary. Of course Bob wrote it in a fury, thinking it was his two fingers to the tax inspectors and the BBC. I'm not sure of the details (I suspect Toby and Rob will know more than I do), but I do know he'd had it with authority, and this was his revenge! My particular favourite little in-joke is the P45 route!

So, there we have it… my time on Doctor Who, the gift that keeps on giving. An often-asked question is "How do you explain the longevity of the programme?" The answers are manifold. It has become a unique slice of British history. The protagonist doesn't have to be "fit"… allowing a wider circuit of viewer to identify themselves with the hero. Right always wins over wrong. Rules are made and broken and made again, encouraging playground and pub debate. Some of the most challenged and some of the most brilliant brains are attracted to the possibilities thrown up by science meeting science fiction… acorn ideas growing into oak tree adventures. The bullied are protected, the strange becomes normal, and tolerance and pacifism are eloquently supported. We are allowed to laugh at and with the Doctor and his companions; and we can, most important-ly, also learn from them and ultimately grow ourselves, both in knowledge and in spirit. I am beyond grateful to be a part of this TARDIS family. Thank you.

—Louise Jameson,
February 2016

This is a story that spans all time and space, set on worlds beyond the limits of imagination, from the beginning of the universe to its very end, and all the less grandiose bits of history in-between. And it is also the story of two fans watching Doctor Who in their bedrooms and writing to each other about it.

By 2009, Doctor Who had enjoyed four triumphant seasons of the revival, but it was time for a little break. Russell T Davies was stepping down as showrunner, and Steven Moffat was preparing to take up the reins. Bar a few special episodes along the way, we were faced with the dread prospect of a Gap Year.

Rob and Toby decided not to despair. They would fill that long gap by watching Doctor Who again right from the start. All of it. Every single episode. Even, perplexingly, the ones that didn't actually exist any longer. And just so they wouldn't feel guilty about this display of massive self-indulgence, they would chronicle the entire experience. Which, you know, would mean they weren't just being couch potatoes, but working. Sort of.

And they both made a vow, right from the outset. They were here to praise the show, not to bury it. The harshest critics Doctor Who has ever had are its own fans. Toby and Rob love Doctor Who – even when, from time to time, they don't always like it very much. So this was their quest. To champion all that was clearly great, of course – but also to find within the episodes they'd long despised something to cherish, the bits that could remind them why Doctor Who is still the best television programme in the world.

It's easy to gush over The Green Death or Pyramids of Mars. But to put on your DVD of The Mutants or The Creature from the Pit with the same generosity of spirit, you need to put aside years of fandom-established prejudices and presumptions. And in doing so you can find a greater appreciation for the series as a whole. The great joy of Doctor Who is not just in its successes, but in the ambitious brilliance of its failures. Both Toby and Rob work in television, so know that no one ever sets out to make anything bad. When Doctor Who doesn't work, it's not because of laziness. It's because the best stories are told by those who are challenging themselves and taking big risks – and by definition, not every challenge can be won, and some risks will fall flat on their face.

Doctor Who rarely plays it safe, and Rob and Toby do their level best to celebrate it in its risk-taking bonkersness. They don't always manage to do so. But, by God, they try.

So, the story so far...

Rob is a writer, and he's actually scripted an episode of Doctor Who himself, and he still can't quite believe his luck, and he's never quite dared watch it for fear it'll wake him from the dream. Toby is an actor, comedian and writer, whose show Moths Ate My Doctor Who Scarf, a touching tribute to his childhood love of the show, is touring the world to great acclaim.

Toby is getting married in the summer. Rob thinks it's nice that Toby is getting married, so long as it doesn't interfere with his scheduled watch of The Android Invasion.

The boys have finally emerged from the monochrome sixties, a decade full of episodes that have had the effrontery to be missing from the BBC archives. They have strained to hear off-air audio recordings, and stared beadily down at countless telesnaps. Now, at last, a new chapter in Doctor Who's history dawns – and it's in colour, and it exists. From now on, things can only be easy. Surely...

Come back with them now to 2009. It's a different time, it's a simpler time. David Tennant is still the Doctor – just about – and though we know something is going to knock four times, it hasn't raised its knuckles to the door yet. Silurians have an eye in their foreheads, the Master is a man, and the closest any Ponds have ever got to travelling the universe was that time when the TARDIS swimming pool leaked.

And we still have Nick Courtney, and Carrie John, and Lis Sladen, and Mary Tamm. And a whole host of actors, writers, designers and directors whose work we are going to enjoy in this volume. We can be fairly sure that Doctor Who shall live forever – but the saddest part must be the way it eventually leaves all its contributors behind. We hope this book is always a celebration of them, and what they gave us.

May 8th

Spearhead from Space
(episode one)

R: There's a whole Doctor between this diary episode and the last. And a whole book between this entry of my diary and the previous one. But it's only been a matter of hours since I played the final episode of The War Games. I woke up this morning, bereft and Troughtonless, and wanted the reassurance of something comforting. Something like Doctor Who. So I fetched down my DVD, and put on the next instalment. My God, though, it was a culture shock. Something *like* Doctor Who is what I got.

It's not that it's in colour, or that there's a new actor playing the Doctor, or that there's an abundance of film, or that everyone seems to be speaking in echoes. It's that, until the final couple of minutes, we're not actually given any *jeopardy*. It's really very peculiar. In retrospect, there's a dangerous alien killer in this episode, but you don't get more than a hint that there's something wrong until the cliffhanger, when he's been foiled bundling the Doctor into the back of an ambulance. It's Doctor Who, so we *look* for the evil – and there are certainly enough people behaving suspiciously. There's a poacher who uncovers a flashing globe – but against form, he's not possessed by it, he just wants to see if he can make money out of it. There's a creepy looking porter who's listening intently to the diagnosis of the strange man found by the police box – but no, he's not an alien either, he's just another man on the make, trying to sell a story to the papers. It's actually very clever. Because for the first time, we're invited to look at Doctor Who from a different angle – from the point of view of an Earthbound organisation which has to put up with the foibles and banal greed of everyday average men. So that when we *do* see the enigmatic Channing, it's amusingly in the background of a shot showing the Brigadier being harassed by news reporters. Without the Doctor to show us the way, the script tacitly suggests, we can't see the wood for the trees. With the Doctor lying in bed and passing out every few minutes, the show presents us with a lot of background information up front, whilst all the stuff we've come to expect is buzzing about unnoticed behind it. We need the Doctor to wake up and show us where to look.

That might sound rather dull. But director Derek Martinus rather brilliantly works so hard to make what could easily have been a rather prosaic episode visually inventive. When UNIT is under pressure from the journalists, Martinus films the sequence with a hand-held camera, so we too can feel we're being bustled about; when the Brigadier and Captain Munro walk down a corridor, they're chasing after the camera, making everything look purposeful; when the Doctor insists upon his shoes, he does it straight to us, as if we're the ones who are holding out on him – and having kept the Doctor's features something of a mystery, Martinus now lets us study the face of Jon Pertwee in clear detail. If only to appreciate how little like our Doctor he really is.

Which is the point, really. Just as The Power of the Daleks refused to reassure me after Hartnell disappeared, so Spearhead refuses to reassure me now that Troughton's popped off. You can see the palpable disappointment on the Brigadier's face when he realises the man in the hospital bed isn't the Doctor at all – and he isn't; at least, he's not the Doctor *we're* wanting. Pertwee, quite rightly, makes no attempt to apologise for this. He talks frustratingly little, he gives as yet no indication of his character, he takes no interest in the action – the most passion he shows is when he hugs his shoes like a child frightened he'll lose his favourite toy. And there's a lovely verbal joke that Robert Holmes repeats. When the new companion, scientist Liz Shaw, is led into the Brigadier's office, he smiles about the officiousness of the security: "Rather amusing, don't you think?... No, you don't." When the Doctor admires his new face, he says to the Brigadier, "I think it's rather distinctive, actually. Don't you think... No, you don't!" It's a *very* subtle point, but the same deadpan joke does form a link between the two characters, and indicates that even though they can't act as friends yet, they are on the same wavelength.

I like that bit, anyway. And I find my analysis of it very persuasive! Don't you, Toby? – Oh. No, you don't.

T: Oh, you can persuade me of anything you like, as I've just embarked on a 24-hour flight to New Zealand. I meant to get this diary entry out of the way this morning, but I had loads of packing and organising to do. I'm miles above England and massively behind schedule: I haven't yet edited my stage show down by 30 minutes, and even this is taking longer than it should because, for some reason, the S button on my keyboard is only working once every four or five presses. I think I've packed everything that I need: all the stuff for the show, some in-flight entertainment and the industrial-strength moisturiser which keeps my psoriasis at bay on the odd occasion it can be bothered. It's too late to act if I've forgotten anything now, so I'm a little stressed before I start (or treed before I tart), but I'll begin watching Spearhead from Space now, as who knows what disaster awaits...

(Twenty-five minutes later...)

Wow, this is *different*. It's can't just be my change in location and circumstances since finishing The War Games yesterday – this is a monumental sea change. There can surely be no place for comedy double takes and groovy futuristics (as we so often saw under Troughton) in this world of solid interiors; crisp, colour film; and down-to-Earth realism. There's documentary verite thanks to the jostled cameras and reflected lights at the press conference, the indoor scenes clearly take place in real buildings, and you can almost feel the bite of the outside air in the verdant forest. I know that the print has been spruced up, but it looks absolutely amazing.

And yet, I've written almost nothing down by way of viewing notes. It's a curious scene-setter of an episode, which seems content merely to tease us for 25 minutes. A load of characters we'll never see again (the porter Mullins, the reporters, the UNIT operatives) get a fair amount of attention, whilst the lead baddy doesn't say a word (although he's a weird, grimacing presence and convincingly alien). The Doctor's face is hidden from us for ages, but then gets curiously and unceremoniously revealed in the corner of the screen when

the Brigadier enters the room. This is very odd: I'd assumed they'd been keeping the new Doctor out of sight so that when the Brigadier sees him for the first time, so do we. It's an uncharacteristic lapse from Derek Martinus, who orchestrates the action everywhere else very effectively. He's relishing taking the show away from its studio-bound confines, making the most of the broader canvas available here – that protracted, uninterrupted but very smooth shot backing down the corridor as Lethbridge-Stewart and Munro walk and chat is incredible. And – bloody hell – Martinus even gets a decent performance out of Prentis Hancock!

It's not just the villain who is vocally challenged – the Doctor also barely says a word. It's clear that Robert Holmes wants us to come back next week to get our proper first impressions of the new leading man, and instead prefers to pay lip service to setting up the story... which has so many similarities to the opening of Quatermass II, this is probably the main source of Nigel Kneale's subsequent grumpiness about Doctor Who.

The cliffhanger is unintentionally hilarious, though. It gives the impression that the titles crash in not because the new Doctor is in jeopardy, but because Corporal Forbes is about to swear ("You stupid—"). Is this the only cliffhanger in the history of the series which crashes in order to prevent the audience hearing the word "tw*t"?. And boy, those closing credits go on forever! That said, the opening titles are still a bit off-putting for me as well, because I'm used to – owing to the novelisation – this story being called The Auton Invasion. Did they really have to name it pearhead from pace?

Spearhead from Space (episode two)

R: The story proper really starts only when the ousted doll designer Ransome turns up at the plastic factory, bemoaning the fact he's out of a job. And we're assaulted by some of the most unnerving images on Doctor Who ever – if you want to hear a horrified reaction, just listen to Nicholas Courtney on the commentary. It's only a production line of dolls – but Captain Munro's final line in the scene before invites us to look at *faces* – and here are baskets full of eyeless heads, and here's a worker pricking open a plastic eyelid with a needle. It's bloody weird, and that sequence of naked girl dolls just thrown so dispassionately onto an ever-winding conveyor belt suggests a deeper inhumanity than we've ever seen before in the series.

And that's only exacerbated by the scenes of that overalled dummy scouring the woods for the missing sphere. That sequence where it frightens a UNIT vehicle off the road is very nasty. Doctor Who is in colour now! – so look, here's lots of red blood over the windscreen, so fractured that we're left to *imagine* the state of the dead driver inside. It's the first time Doctor Who gives us a bit of the tomato sauce... and look at that dummy's reaction, staring at the corpse (and straight at us, for that matter), utterly impassive and uncaring.

Jon Pertwee's Doctor takes an *age* to get out of his hospital subplot and turn up at UNIT headquarters. Up until then, it's a purely comic performance – we see him singing in the shower, and wincing as he sounds the horn on the car he's stealing. But just look at how he commands the scene once he saunters into UNIT as if he already owns the place, teasing the Brigadier with his identity, showing affection for the police box in the corner, charming the first smile out of Caroline John (as Liz Shaw), and beginning a scientific analysis of the broken sphere. All that, and a truly mad gag in which the Doctor says hello to Liz by waggling his eyebrows. If this new Doctor required an audition piece, then this scene was it – and the measure of its success is that before, the story was all about a peculiar eccentric found in a forest, and afterwards it's about creepy plastic aliens. This is the Doctor, and he's so convincing that from this point on, he can busy himself with doing Doctorish things in a lab with absolute impunity.

And we're made to witness one of the most honestly frightening cliffhangers the series has done for a very long time, as Ransome is menaced by a walking dummy. (That said, I think Ransome is rather on his high horse about the way he's been sacked from the plastics company. He's been around the States getting sales for his doll prototype – but look at it, it's absolute rubbish! I'm not an expert on dolls, I admit. But it's quite the ugliest example of dolldom I've ever seen. The Nestene Consciousness demonstrates not only an outstanding skill in its use of living plastic, but, in getting rid of a designer like Ransome, exquisite taste.)

T: I know Pertwee's background was in humour, but it's Troughton who rightly gets all the plaudits for clowning, and it's frankly a relief when this new chap stops doing his silent comedy shtick and finally engages verbally with his new cohorts. I said last episode that this new, gritty style wouldn't suit whacky antics, and it doesn't really. After an indulgent start at the hospital, things improve in the lab scene – the Doctor is elegant and charming, and has an excellent, expressive face, and I love the way he testily cuts through the formality and asks if he has to call Liz "Miss Shaw". Caroline John has a nice line in sarcy quips too – the way she delivers the bit about the TARDIS having a policeman locked inside is bang on. And it's good to see that rather than being a stick-in-the-mud, incredulous military stiff, the Brigadier urges *her* to broaden *her* horizons.

We do forget about the Doctor for much of the episode, though (and when we do see him, he gets naked), as we spend time with Hibbert the neck-rubbing dupe, the mysterious Channing (almost lifeless bar his blazing alien eyes) and comedy duo the Seeleys, whose hatred for each other as a married couple is hilarious. I'm still not used to Doctor Who being done like this, and because it's all so new, I think it gets away with its slowness, longueurs and slightly choppy narrative. Corporal Forbes' demise in a Land Rover crash is remarkable – it's very adult and throwaway, giving the impression that the series thinks it's always portrayed death in such a clinical fashion. It's less *fantastical*, that's what it is, and the sight of the Auton in the woods, in ordinary garb, its face a parody of the familiar, is one of the most terrifying monster moments we've ever had. The intent here is not to wow us with the outlandish, but to terrify us by perverting the recognisable. I may be flying to another country at the moment, but in Doctor Who terms, I've just spent the past 50 minutes inside one.

May 9th

[Side note from Toby to Rob: I normally watch my episodes, read your e-mail and then compose a reply. For the next few days, however, I'll be working blind without internet access, and in a different time zone. Let's just hope we don't only notice the same things...]

Spearhead from Space (episode three)

R: In part, it feels like a collection of set pieces. But that's because of the extraordinary use of pace that this episode employs. It's not merely that the episode is *fast*, and is prepared to jump from set-up to execution in a way that's unusual even in modern television. It's that it deliberately wrongfoots the audience with that pace, elongating other sequences for dramatic tension. Take, for example, the masterful way in which Martinus shoots the scene of Meg Seeley being terrified by an Auton in her house. He ekes it out so very slowly: we hear the sound of a dog barking (and then stopping – poor Bonnie, we can only think something very terminal happened to her); we have Meg investigate the house and find an intruder inside (and how much more menacing is it that until it turns around, she can think it's just a human burglar – it's that awful ambiguity of the Autons that make them so much more frightening; it's hard to imagine this sequence being nearly so tense if Meg found a Yeti or a Cyberman rooting through her kitchen); we have her rush out, find a gun and then, crucially, *have the time to load it*, warning the Auton off before firing right at its chest. Every single second of the crisis is absolutely exaggerated... Now compare it to the death of Ransome. Channing says that Ransome will be dealt with. Quick jump cut to an Auton cutting open the back of Ransome's tent and shooting him dead. Intention to execution has taken *seconds*, and we're left reeling at the abruptness of it.

This is what makes Spearhead from Space frightening. It doesn't play fair. It lulls you into a false sense of security, saving a lot of its chills for long sequences of tension – then turns about and shouts "boo"! You can't relax with it, because it'll slow down, then speed up, then

slow down again, all the best to create its scare moments. It's extremely clever.

And isn't it great to have an alien killer that's as *agile* as an Auton? That opening sequence where Ransome is pursued is fantastic – because we're so used to monsters lumbering after their victims slowly, but this one can run like an athletics sprinter! And isn't it great too to have an alien mastermind as credible as Channing? Hugh Burden doesn't overplay his extraterrestrial nature whatsoever, seeming to be a credible businessman in his dealings with General Scobie. (And only in refusing his farewell handshake does he suggest that he's not used to human customs.) The sequence where he directs the Auton to the Seeley house, with all that eager exhaustion, is just wonderful. It's unusual for a villain to be given so much sensitive acting or direction – the scene in which the Brigadier spies Channing through ribbed glass implies more about his alien background than the usual staccato ranting could ever hope to achieve.

And then there's that moment when Channing sees the Auton in its pursuit of Ransome, and stops it with a single glare. The way that the Auton deflates, like a naughty child caught up past bedtime, is just perfect.

T: I think I lost May 9th. I certainly wasn't on planet Earth during it. I left yesterday and arrive tomorrow, so I'm in some sort of limbo. I think my battery will last just long enough to watch these next two episodes and type up my opinions, in-between the rather odd meal choices available on this plane. I'm vegetarian, so I got a salad consisting of leaves and nothing else. Lee, my producer and agent, isn't veggie... so his salad has tomato and cucumber too. I don't understand (unless it's a *beef* tomato, but come on...). I cleverly packed a portable CD player and some spare batteries, so I could use the flight to catch up on all those Big Finish CDs I've dropped behind with. Only when I'm several hundred miles above Great Britain do I realise that I've forgotten to pack the actual CDs.

Although there's not as much comedy in this episode as in Robert Holmes' later scripts, he injects some wit on occasion. His trademark black humour accompanies the truly horrible Seeleys indulging in unpleasant verbal rubbernecking about Corporal Forbes' death. Meanwhile, Scobie's assertion that machines "don't go on strike" is a nice gag, considering the industrial relations problems that gripped the UK for the next decade or so. Say what you like about the unions, though, at least they never tried to destroy the world! As someone who, on principle, refuses to use those automated tills they're trying to introduce in supermarkets (as well as getting the poor buggers they're looking to replace to exhort you into using them), the story's thematic by-product about replacing human beings with an automated workforce appeals to me. And don't get me started on those bloody "press one now" robots you get at the end of the phone. No matter what the situation, I want a human being to deal with it, not a machine. Holmes has been very canny in tapping into our disquiet about unemotional automata.

As the spokesman of these creatures, Hugh Burden is extraordinary as Channing. It is surely the single-most impressive example in Doctor Who of an actor conveying alien qualities whilst never looking stupid or hammy. Quite often, I've been impressed by thesps having a crack at trying to do something inhuman, even if they don't quite pull it off, but Burden is *perfect*. I don't know how he hit upon the choices he's made, but they work. His mannerisms are unsettling whilst having their own internal logic. He has a wonderful stillness: a quiet, unforced delivery with occasional flashes of strange, malevolent power flickering only in his eyes. He's simultaneously low key and has a burning intensity, and his control over Hibbert is emphatic and calmly controlling: "Think", he repeats when ordering Ransome's death, "think and you will see that it is necessary". Derek Martinus also elects to shoot Burden and John Woodnutt through a distorted, goldfish bowl lens to suggest that Channing has a mental link with the Auton, with Burden emphasising the mental strain with an intensity of concentration.

Talking of the direction, I bet you've mentioned the ripply shot of Channing through the glass (and used it in an essay about the recurring themes of the distorting, dehumanising nature of man-made materials in this story, no doubt), so I'll just say that it's a brilliant visual and leave it at that. This is Martinus' last

Doctor Who story, and as I suspect there'll be plenty else to talk about next week, I'd just like to mark his imminent departure. He's been a consistently excellent man behind the camera – he's paced stories interestingly, cast brilliantly and kept the science fiction on display plausible and never silly. One of the very best at his craft, this Martinus has left me shaken *and* stirred.

Spearhead from Space (episode four)

R: It's the episode with the shop window dummies coming to life! It's so good, and so deservedly iconic, that it's the sequence Russell T Davies worked into the pilot of the revival in 2005. It's much better here, though, for all that it's done on a budget, and that the smash of the glass is an off-camera sound effect. There's the way that the policeman races towards his own death, and the way that the Auton seems to try out his hand in curiosity before going on a killing rampage. Best of all, there's the comic incongruity of seeing those poor people waiting at a bus stop, bored but patient, wholly unaware that there are dummies wearing natty dressing gowns walking up the street behind them, about to blast them to kingdom come. Stylish and remarkable, it's one of the best pieces of Doctor Who ever, building to a wonderful climax of Nicholas Courtney panicking on a telephone – the tense music only coming to an abrupt end when he slams the receiver down.

Sad to say, though, it's not only the best thing in the episode – it's also one of the only truly *good* things in the episode. The clever use of pace that has previously served Spearhead so well and given it its edge now works against it. The Madame Tussauds scene comes out of nowhere, and is directed with uncharacteristic clumsiness – you can see the eeriness it's aiming for, but it's blocked so awkwardly that moments of Liz getting scared bumping into the Doctor make her look rather hysterical. Hibbert has only a few words' conversation with the Doctor, but the next time we see him he's turned into a full rebel, smashing the Nestene tank with a crowbar: there's no depth given to his sudden volte-face, so it's hard to care. And, worst of all, the Nestenes are defeated with a gadget the Doctor suddenly rigs up without any set-up whatsoever – he doesn't even bother to explain what it is until after the crisis is averted. Doctor Who is a long master at the disappointing conclusion, but Spearhead from Space is wrapped up so perfunctorily, it almost feels that we're not watching a final draft, just an early synopsis.

Jon Pertwee's rather brilliant, though. Even when he's wrapping rubbery tentacles around his face, he commands a certain authority – the calm manner with which he informs Channing that he'll defeat the Autons, and so casually refutes that he's human, establishes him utterly as the Doctor. And that last scene is charming as the Doctor holds the Brigadier to ransom and demands a new car, with all the glee of a child promised a present.

T: As you've had a dig at the new series, I'll redress the balance (because it seems fashionable to like New Who and yet hate the very first episode, but I'm very fond of it)... I hope those same people who give Christopher Eccleston his anti-plastic are behind the Doctor's magic-Nestene killing machine that just pops up out of nowhere. It's a truly horrible resolution, dismissed in a line of dialogue that facilitates an ill-advisedly comic confrontation between a gurning Jon Pertwee and some rubber tentacles doing battle by a smoking vat of silly. The sounds of shock when General Scobie awakes at Madame Tussauds are weird too – surely, they wouldn't have opened the place after most of their exhibits had wandered off?

That said, I think I got more out of the episode than you. Watching Doctor Who after reading the Target novels, or articles praising the series, I was often acutely disappointed, and only began to appreciate certain things on rewatch after my unmatchable expectations had dissipated. The much-lauded shop window dummy scene was an exception – it's terrific. Shot by shot, moment by moment, it works. And, I have to say, it's ten times better than the similar sequence in Rose (and I'm a *big* new series fan). It's so uncompromising: the slow build as the dummies start flexing their hands as they come to life, the fact that they shoot unsuspecting victims in the back, the really painful-looking final shot as the fleeing

man tumbles over and skids along the kerb. And is that a woman holding a baby amidst the carnage? Nasty. Not even the complete lack of surprise on the face of the about-to-be-murdered bicyclist undermines a truly iconic sequence that I'd happily show any modern viewer, knowing it would stand up. (Although I remember my mum seeing it, and all she could bring herself to comment on was how flat-footed the policeman was. They see different things to us, Mums.)

The Autons are a simple but effective menace. These impassive, silent killers require a mouthpiece, and Hugh Burden continues to impress as Channing – his slightly deadened, drooping features occasionally sear through the screen with a penetrating glare, and he sounds exultant without turning on the histrionics when he talks of the impending invasion. His waxwork drones look magnificent during that final battle as we see the bullets thwack into them, tear their overalls, and yet not impede their progress one bit. Martinus directs this sequence very well, proving that he can easily match the more-lauded Douglas Camfield in the gung-ho action stakes.

Pertwee is so lucky that this story was shot entirely on film – it gives his debut a grandeur it might have lacked with a straightforward studio treatment (can you imagine how flat the hospital and office scenes could have been?). There is a bit of clumsiness to some of the editing, which makes it seem like it's lurching at times, and the sound appears to have been recorded in a cupboard... but this looks like nothing else the series has done before. It's fresh, confident and stylish.

That bit before the Auton attack, where Liz yawns and muses about the rest of the world being asleep, really impacts on me as I fly through the night, dozing tourists around me, wondering whether the plane's on autopilot. And shivering.

Doctor Who and the Silurians (episode one)

R: Well, this is about as far from the style of Spearhead from Space as you're going to get. There aren't many thrills. The music builds to a climax on such moments as the Doctor finding out that someone's ripped a page out of a log! The episode sells its greatest crisis upon the shutdown of a nuclear reactor – a threat that's so high concept that the Doctor has to take the Brigadier to one side to explain exactly why it's so dangerous. It's bookended by two dinosaur attacks – one in the prologue, one at the cliffhanger – and never a mention of a dinosaur for the 20-odd minutes in between, with chat instead about cyclotrons and atomic particles to keep us happy.

I'm not complaining. Anything but. This is great stuff, building up a credible tension between all its characters. There is a world of depth to the firm but gentle way in which Dr Quinn refuses to let Dr Lawrence take control of the shutdown, or in Major Baker's thoroughly respectful resentment of the Brigadier's authority. The divide between the scientists and the soldiers who have been summoned to nanny them is full of simmering but polite hostility, and it's impeccably drawn. It's a slow burn episode, certainly, but in the best way. It's the first instalment of a serial that's going to run just shy of two months, and writer Malcolm Hulke works hard to give a world we're going to get very used to a real pressure cooker feel.

I remember this episode going out on its repeat on BBC2 in 1999. Back then, fandom was rather hoping that the intended jaunt through all the colour episodes in the archives would give Doctor Who a new lease of life, maybe even lead to a fresh series being commissioned – ha! As if that was ever going to happen! This opening instalment in particular felt very cruelly exposed, as it offered so little that would please the audience that was expecting something of the pace of Buffy the Vampire Slayer. It's colour Doctor Who at its most black and white, the show at its most deliberately low key. It's subtle stuff, and frustrating – much of the drama comes from the Doctor being unable to prove to the Brigadier that anything in the base is untoward – but that frustration is the point. Any careful viewer can see that the ordered society Hulke has taken such care to build is on the point of shattering. And it's something of an indictment against the late nineties TV viewers that the *promise* of a crisis alone wasn't as absorbing as something more blatant.

T: It's bizarre – I have very little to say about this instalment, even though loved it. It's a solid piece of television – it's mounted very effectively, and has enough going on that it doesn't get boring. But it's not wildly exciting either, and perhaps I'm helped by the subtle differences the TV version has from Malcolm Hulke's novelisation, and my foreknowledge that we have an epic to come.

Ultimately, it's the performances that get most of my attention. Jon Pertwee is establishing himself rather nicely – we first see him singing along and being an absent-minded boffin, and it's great the way he pats his car and names it whilst stuffing oversized bits of equipment into his pockets. He's pleasingly anti-establishment ("I never report anywhere, particularly not forthwith") and occasionally rather rude. (Dr Lawrence: "You're not proposing to dismantle a piece of equipment worth £15 million with a screwdriver?", the Doctor: "Well, it's not worth 15 million pins if it doesn't work, is it?")

I also enjoy how Liz Shaw has deduced that the Doctor needs to be cajoled into following orders, and so galvanises him by appealing to his thirst for exploration. Her scientific background means that she can just get on with investigating matters without needing to have her hand held, but she's not precocious; she's intelligent, capable and likeable. Nicholas Courtney's on good form too – polite and unflappable, and quietly amused by Major Baker's fastidiousness. There's a great moment after Dr Lawrence leaves, where Norman Jones (as Baker) checks that the coast is clear whilst Courtney does a mental recce of the room that will become his office, ticking off a checklist in his head as his eyes scout the area. It's also rather clever that the story's larger conflicts will stem from the polite, dutiful Major Baker and the gentle, smiling Dr Quinn, as opposed to the sneering and unlikeable Dr Lawrence.

It's all ticking over nicely, but threatening to go nuclear at any moment. And may I say how reassured I feel, in the darkness of an aeroplane at 15,000 feet, watching a group of people getting all stressed about being cooped up in a confined area.

May 10th

Doctor Who and the Silurians (episode two)

R: The scenes showing the wounded Silurian's point of view as he searches for refuge in the barn are excellent, capping the impression given by the Doctor that these new monsters should be considered sympathetically. It works well, too – the humans of the serial seem more culpable than usual. When the farmer is attacked, the last sight we are given is of him edging towards the camera with pitchfork raised; Major Baker shoots at the first thing he sees moving in the caves. "There'll be the devil to pay if he's shot some innocent potholer", says the Brigadier in one of his more subtly callous lines.

This is terrific – innovative and fresh. The Silurians, still mostly hidden from us, are being concealed not for some hideous cliffhanger as monster of the week, but to whet our appetite for a species which already promises to be more complex than usual. There is a genuine sense of wonder about the nature of these creatures, and what's so impressive is that the episode works upon *mystery* rather than shock tactics. They're hideous monsters, of course, that's a given – we get glimpses of reptile claws, and humans scream at the sight of them and die of fear – but this is a story that plays upon what this new race might stand for intellectually. It talks up to the audience; I love that. I'm not sure the series has treated an alien culture this way since the early days of William Hartnell.

Oh, and though I may be the only one, I like Carey Blyton's bizarre experimental score as well!

T: I'm in New Zealand, in a hotel. My first precious hours in the most beautiful country in the world, but I have to get my Doctor Who quota out of the way. I'm a bit woozy through lack of sleep and generous aircraft alcohol provision, but I'll do my best. It turns out my industrial-strength moisturiser doesn't have industrial-strength packaging and has exploded all over my luggage, but other than that, I have arrived on the other side of the world in reasonable shape.

Malcolm Hulke's script continues to impress in that the research-centre characters are very believable, and have subtly drawn foibles. Major Baker starts out as a helpful ally, assisting with the search for the Doctor in a decent and straightforward manner – he's not like one of the stroppy base commanders of the Troughton era, whose clashes with the Doctor had a crushing inevitability about them. Instead, the problems Baker causes are borne from his being misguided but well intentioned. He's a bit of a paranoid conspiracy theorist, but he's a believable human being, especially in the way he gives Liz coffee and is polite and acquiescent to the Brigadier. Against that, we have Peter Miles as the stiff and unpleasant Dr Lawrence, tutting his way about the place and being very uncivil. He's even cutting about his own staff, and tersely dismisses "that book" of Dr Quinn's. In Hulke's perception, Dr Lawrence's flaw of being a single-minded careerist is even greater than those of either Baker or Quinn.

It's sometimes argued that the best Doctor Who stories entail a world already in progress when the Doctor shows up, and it makes for such great drama when Hulke plonks the Doctor onto the scene, and his presence shakes up the established relationships. Pertwee seems equally at home getting down and dirty in the caves or tinkering about in the base, even though he's far more rude than the famously tetchy Hartnell ever was. It's left to poor old Lethbridge-Stewart to smooth out awkward situations caused by his scientific adviser's social gaffes.

Away from the acting, this is a terribly impressive production with excellent design work – I like little touches such as the moisture dripping from the T-rex's mouth, and the water on the floor of the caves. Director Timothy Combe gets some astonishing shots out of cameraman Fred Hamilton. So often, monster POV stuff can be a lumbering, money saving cliché, but here we're shown just enough to tantalise us, and the farm scenes are impressively staged in the murky gloom of the night. There's also a terrific moment, this time in the studio, when Quinn is walking through the caves: we're concentrating on him, and then there's an off-centre flutter of movement in the foreground corner of the screen, and it's a bit of lurking Silurian.

But, we do get a couple of clichés, as we get a woman babbling with fear and a man dying of fright. I've never stopped to think about whether those things can actually happen – but then, I've lived a sheltered life, free from the interference of prehistoric interlopers. In an otherwise believable story, these are both things that people do in drama of this ilk – much like being knocked unconscious by a karate chop between the shoulders and never needing the loo.

Doctor Who and the Silurians (episode three)

R: No sympathy from me that you're jet-lagged watching Jon Pertwee in New Zealand. I'm in London watching Jon Pertwee, and it's raining. I like Jon Pertwee in all conditions, but I think he can only benefit by geographical dissonance. You're watching a better Jon Pertwee than me.

Well, on a personal level, I'm bound to have a connection to this episode. It's the first bit of Doctor Who broadcast after I was born. Before this point, every single story has had a certain mystical status – they're as much a part of history as the Cuban Missile Crisis, the battle of Agincourt and rationing. But from now on, each review I write will be more pertinent, because I was a part of the world the episode was exaggerating or satirising – I could have been there, watching Doctor Who and the Silurians episode three, pausing from my mother's teat in mid-suck to appreciate the brilliance of Fulton Mackay.

Because he is brilliant. You can see precisely why Barry Letts later considered him as a potential Doctor. Every time he's on the screen, you watch to see what he does: the little attempts to justify himself and wriggle out of the Doctor's questions, the blatant impatience at the attentions of Miss Dawson, the way in which he'll so cheerily wave at a helicopter when he's in danger of being caught summoning a Silurian. It's a generous performance, and everyone around him shines as a result. We've seen many token female scientists in Doctor Who these last couple of seasons, but Thomasine Heiner is allowed to suggest so much more depth, always looking so hurt when Mackay patronises her or refuses to notice her crush. Caroline John gives her best performance yet in the scene where she responds to Quinn's questions about the attack, responding to Mackay almost as if *he* were the one playing the charismatic Doctor. And Pertwee is utterly brilliant when he and Mackay bounce off each other. That scene where the Doctor drops in on Quinn at his cottage uninvited, making him squirm as he looks over the man's house and offers to fix his thermostat, is the best we've yet seen of this new Doctor. He's putting every bit of pressure on Quinn to crack, but so, so politely – and what's extraordinary is the way that Mackay tries as hard to be as polite back, even returning to social platitudes after the Doctor has needled him too far and he's lost his composure. It's a scene in which two characters do their best to outface the other, and in which two fine actors raise each other's game too. It's an absolute joy.

What's so extraordinary is that this is an episode which almost plays from a guest character's point of view. The Doctor and the Brigadier seem almost threatening here, because the script is more concerned with Quinn and his increasingly desperate efforts to find the wounded Silurian without implicating himself. Over 25 minutes, we watch a man who clearly prides himself on his affable self-control lose his nerve, become rude and paranoid and obsessed. And having taken the rare step of putting a supporting player at the very heart of the drama, with the Doctor as a satellite figure – Hulke shocks us all by killing him off so abruptly. There's nothing that raises the stakes more, and clearly establishes the Silurian as a threat. It's a perfect cliffhanger: just as we're reeling from Quinn's unexpected death, we see the monster for the very first time – Timothy Combe has so skilfully delayed its appearance for three full episodes, only allowing it out at the moment of maximum impact.

This is wonderful. Doctor Who is quite clearly going to be brilliant now I'm alive. Well done, me.

T: Well done indeed, and congratulations on being brought into the world! I won't be joining you for a while yet, I'm afraid.

Really, this story is all about trust, and what happens when people do or don't allow themselves to exhibit it. Dr Quinn's thirst for knowledge is laudable, but it's tainted by human frailty and insecurity – fair enough that he can't trust other people not to nick his work, but the situation leads to his becoming greedy. Major Baker, on the other hand, sees himself as the sole voice of reason amidst a chorus of prevarication, which casts him in a heroic light, and makes him much more than an intransigent hothead. Norman Jones humanises the character by very sweetly patting the bed for Liz to sit down on when they talk, and in the manner in which he heeds the Brigadier's instructions to return to sickbay. The Doctor, at least, is as solid as a rock as the pressure mounts and characters start to crack in their underground prison. It's easy to forget that Pertwee has only been the Doctor for *seven weeks*, he gives such a confident performance. He's overflowing with charming comedy touches, dashing flamboyance, authority and a brilliantly anarchic streak, blithely breaking into Dr Quinn's cabinet as if it were the sort of thing anyone would do.

And it can't escape comment... Carey Blyton's music is a thing, isn't it? I rather like it – even if, in the opening sequence in the barn, it sounds like he's blowing through a blade of grass. There's a wonderfully scratchy, creepy piece at the end when the Doctor forces his way into Quinn's cottage at night. Fortunately, this tale doesn't just *sound* interesting – the pictures are terrific too, with Timothy Combe giving us vast sweeps of the moorland, augmenting them with hardware, loads of personnel, police dogs and a helicopter. Doctor Who has never looked so comfortably off. The farmer's barn works so much better as a genuine location than if they'd mounted it in the studio, and provides verisimilitude as Quinn rushes in from the rain all soaking wet. Even better, there's a terrific moment where the soldiers hear something suspicious and it just turns out to be a chicken.

Still, I think it's a missed opportunity that Miss Dawson didn't accompany the Doctor to find her murdered friend, because then we might have been afforded the immortal instruction "Doctor Quinn's medicine, woman". (I'm making a silent pact with myself not to inflict jokes as appalling as that on the good people of New Zealand later – it'd be too cruel.)

Doctor Who and the Silurians (episode four)

R: In the first few seconds, the Doctor meets a monster over the body of a dead human being – and tries to talk peace to it. And in a trice, the whole nature of what Doctor Who is about changes.

I don't think I can stress this too much. Was it only a season before that we had The Dominators, with its none-too-subtle treatise on the dangers of pacifism? Up to this point, Doctor Who had always seen those who wanted to treat with the alien force as naive at best, and treacherous at worst. Either way, were they Temmosus the Thal, or Storr the scavenger, they were gunned down by monsters who saw their desire to negotiate as weakness. The Doctor has largely been in a position of urging the authorities to recognise the dangers of the evil around them, not try to compromise with it. But The Silurians really does change all that. This is where the image of the Doctor as a man of peace comes from, the moral authority who's never cruel or cowardly. The brilliance of the drama is that Hulke sees the Doctor's greatest enemy not as the monster in the cave, but the Brigadier in the army uniform. It's a sudden redefinition of not only the Doctor's character, but the premise of the series – and although it's never quite as overt as this again, it's massively influential. When Christopher Eccleston approaches the Nestene blob in his debut story, and says that he has to "give it a chance", that's the direct inheritance of this moment in The Silurians. We're left with no doubt that the Doctor is the voice of reason; when Miss Dawson says so blandly, "We must destroy them, before they destroy us", it's almost as if she's parroting the credo of Doctor Who As Was, and it sounds chilling.

A word on some of the performers. Ian Talbot gives a lovely turn as the wonderfully camp technician Travis; the way in which he maintains absolute power over his own telephone provides much needed comic relief. Peter Miles has up to now deadpanned marvellously as the acidic Dr Lawrence, but now he's put in a room with a man from the ministry, and we're at last allowed to see him as someone very human and fragile – I'd be exaggerating if I said that this portrait of a man who's seeing his career slip through his fingers was poignant, but it's very real, and therefore sympathetic. And just as he did in The Abominable Snowmen, Norman Jones works hard to make sure that his character of bullish soldier doesn't come across merely as some two-dimensional warmonger. He's had a really nice rapport with Caroline John, clearly fancying Liz Shaw not a little – and now that he's the Silurians' prisoner, he conducts himself with courage and dignity. His anger as the Doctor betrays the Brigadier's troops in the name of peace is perfectly credible. Hey, had this been broadcast a year before, the story would have been squarely on his side.

T: Yes... the moment where the Doctor wanders gamely into the Silurian base and announces himself with courtesy and a big fat smile epitomises glorious, definitive Doctor behaviour. The Doctor is also us, with circumspection – he looks terrified as the Silurian enters Quinn's cottage, but instead of bowing to instinct like we would, he extends his hand in friendship. And the story highlights the tragedy that this approach only works if everyone feels and acts the same – and everyone doesn't. As you've suggested, it's doing the same thing as The Dominators, but in a much more empathic and sophisticated manner. The Dominators smugly excused tyranny and imperialism by saying, "Well, the funny-looking people will do it, so we may as well", but Doctor Who and the Silurians brilliantly says that the inevitable culture clashes when races collide will lead to awful consequences, and we must be aware of this if ever we want a decent and fair world. It's compassionate without being naive, complex without fudging the issues.

... or it's just a television programme about green aliens, take your pick.

These are *wonderfully* conceived aliens, though, with Malcolm Hulke refusing to go the alien invasion route and conceiving a race of protagonists with a very innovative and complex backstory. I rather like the costumes too – the masks, and especially the twitching mouths, are very impressive. Dave Carter has clearly worked on giving the Old Silurian a unique body language, while Peter Halliday does an amazing job at making all the voices distinctive. (He also does all the cyclotron closedown voices, with very different tones and pitches, in quick succession, did you notice?)

I am most engrossed in the character arcs, however... it's refreshing, if in retrospect, that Masters is no pompous idiot, but actually a rather reasonable man doing a job with lots of red tape and difficult decisions. Miss Dawson, meanwhile, enters at precisely the worst moment to deliver us news of Dr Quinn's death. We know the circumstances of his passing, but without access to the same information, it's perfectly reasonable for the other characters to want to go on the offensive over it. Dawson isn't being evil – she's genuinely upset at the death of her friend, and it's plausible that she'd want to lash out over it. And it's nice to see affable character actor Richard Steele (as Sgt Hart) back after only one story's break, whilst Norman Jones continues to impress with little, very believable touches. I love the second little wave he gives the Doctor and Liz from his cell as they try to escape, and before that he's so off-handedly natural when asking Hart to help take his jacket off – before giving the man one of those TV-magical shoulder-blade karate chops that stuns him a bit, but doesn't knock him out. Overall, even if we've lost a little of the fantastical from Doctor Who at the moment, I'm revelling in the novelty of this story's greater adherence to reality.

May 11th

Doctor Who and the Silurians (episode five)

R: When Dr Lawrence mocks the Brigadier's efforts in the caves, he's told coolly that a lot of men died in that little expedition. We didn't see anyone die – we see someone become a Neolithic artist, but no-one suffers a fatality – but we have no reason to disbelieve the Brig.

But it's a shocking moment, because it means that the Doctor's warning to the Silurians directly resulted in an ambush and loss of life. Malcolm Hulke specifically goes out of his way in this scene to make the Doctor's well-intentioned actions highly suspect – it would have been so much tidier (and very easy) to have simply had the UNIT troops escape without casualties. And it's this very ambiguity placed on the Doctor's behaviour that makes this episode so remarkable. One of the best moments is the look of real guilt on Pertwee's face, trying to negotiate with the Old Silurian, as he overhears Major Baker's angry jeers that he's a traitor. Because, actually, that's precisely what he is. He gives information to the enemy, and consequently soldiers die. Only a couple of stories ago, we were asked to believe temporarily that the Doctor may have sold out the resistance to the War Lord, but deep down we knew that it must all be some cunning ruse. That isn't the case here. And we're asked to question the rights of the Doctor's actions in a way we've never been required to do before.

There's a tremendous amount of subtlety on display that raises this further from simple Saturday teatime television than we've seen before. Nicholas Courtney is extremely impressive in his scenes where he's trapped in the caves, accepting the reality that he and his troops might soon suffocate with a leader's calm that saves many lives. Geoffrey Palmer ends Peter Miles' career with a little social embarrassment, and the polite performances of the two actors is hugely effective – the "thank you, Charles" that Miles delivers to himself as his old friend walks away, leaving his dreams in ruins, is so restrained that it makes him truly sympathetic. And Norman Jones is, as ever, brilliant. The dumbfounded horror on his face as he confronts his infected arm is chilling; poor Major Baker, compared to an ape on a video screen (with Jones caught in a pose that makes him look positively simian) – even as Baker tries to escape from the Silurian base, Carey Blyton's music sounds as if it's positively mocking him.

And yet – it has to be said. However great the story's aspirations, and however clever the power play between the Old and Young Silurian, a lot of this does come down to a couple of men making exaggerated movements in rubber costumes squeaking at each other. Nigel Johns, in particular, as the Young Silurian, loses all credibility by giving to his lines petulant gestures that make him seem like a silly child. There is one moment which is truly hilarious as he does a sulky double take upon abandoning an argument. It means that a lot of skilful dialogue between the Doctor and the Old Silurian about cohabitation counts for little, because this is the first episode that properly tries to *personalise* the aliens, having previously relied upon only snatched glimpses of them, a series of grunts or limited dialogue. It's not the fault of voice-actor Peter Halliday, who manages to give three creatures separate identities. If anything, it's a measure of the limitations of Doctor Who; that as Hulke's script reaches ever higher, and demands that its antagonists be now presented as individual characters, it's sold out by the trappings of the previous three episodes in which they needed to be the Monster of the Week. You almost wish that, having shown us what the Silurians looked like, the production could now ask us to take that appearance on trust – have them climb *out* of the costumes, and perform their lines as regular actors. Impossible, of course – but the complexity of Hulke's ideas cries out for that.

T: I'm now in Wellington, having just got off my fourth plane since Friday. A beautiful drive along the coast, an astonishingly nice hotel but five minutes walk from the theatre, and I've just time to keep up with my Doctor Who quota before doing the technical run...

I feel rather sorry for the Old Silurian, even though I had foreknowledge that he would die (and I love the way the Scientist looks down at the body and enigmatically shakes his head). It helps to understand that the fate of every character here was long ago ruined for me – before I could read entire books, I flicked through the Target novelisations, looking at the illustrations and their captions. Thanks to these, I knew that Quinn, Barker (as he's renamed in the book) and Okdel (as the Old Silurian is Christened in print) weren't long for this world. I often wonder how I'd view these stories if I hadn't already devoured them several times in book form prior to the video boom. Still, those Targets are such a valuable part of my childhood, and watching this provides many delights unique to the TV version. The scene where the Silurian revives Major Baker in the caves makes fantastic use of the light. The disease make-up is also excellent, and it's incredible when episode ends with Baker perishing with the stuff all over him. The Doctor's blunt delivery regarding the enormity of the devastation about to be unleashed (the Brigadier: "Is [Baker] dead?", the Doctor: "Yes, the first one") is also quite shocking. Poor old Baker – still, that odd illustration in the Target novel made me labour under the misapprehension that he was *strangled by his own sling*.

With hindsight, Major Baker's actions are neither irrational nor wrong. He's brave, and his viewpoint is understandable. Even though the narrative sets him up as the Doctor's nemesis, Norman Jones refuses to resort to playing the cliché of the reckless militarist. There's such compassion in the way he strokes the Doctor's hand, and whispers reassurances into his ear, after the Doctor has been exposed to the Young Silurian's eye-ray – this, despite Baker having been very angry with the Doctor in an earlier scene. And yes, if Baker's advice had been followed, fewer people would have died. The Doctor's way of arbitration is not without its casualties. That said, we don't *see* any of the troops die, and get no hint of a skirmish as they exit the caves. Even Private Robins has the good grace to chuck himself off a ravine in the book.

It's all so desperately sad, though. The Doctor tries to do the right thing, but circumstance and the character flaws of those involved make events spin out of control to an ultimate, devastating conclusion. Malcolm Hulke isn't really judgemental – he just sees the awful, depressing truth about our failings and makes excellent drama out of them, with the Doctor putting himself on the line in an ultimately unsuccessful attempt to bring about peace. It's a great story this. Infectious.

Doctor Who and the Silurians (episode six)

R: Dr Lawrence's death scene is embarrassing. And I don't mean that as a criticism. Peter Miles has been so good at presenting this cold and laconic director, that to see him here, his paranoia at last a ranting insanity, is genuinely shocking. He screams at the Brigadier like a little kid having a tantrum, and when he stumbles over one of his lines, it makes such an effective contrast to the man of ordered control we are used to. It's all a little hard to watch, this fussy and neat despot all askew, boils all over his face but still wearing his smart suit.

It stands out particularly because it's a sequence of such blazing fury – and the rest of the episode works precisely as something cold and emotionless. The look of disdain on the physician's face when he's informed that Major Baker is dead... the middle-class irritation of the elderly lady who walks on when the ticket collector at Marylebone stumbles beside her... the way that the police who have been chasing Masters back away from him almost dismissively when he dies. I'm not saying that any of those reactions are *deliberate*, but they all give a peculiarly distancing feel to the scenes of London gripped by a deadly plague. They're set-piece scenes of great casualties, and in that way mirror the ones from Spearhead from Space (only seen a few weeks ago) where the shop window dummies gunned down the public on the streets. But that sequence sold itself (necessarily) by being bizarre, by being almost comically incongruous – and here it's all the more disturbing by being terribly real. For the last few years, Doctor Who has specialised in the base under siege, in making its crisis claustrophobic. When it's taken that crisis to a recognisable city before, the streets have been deserted. (Only The Invasion has come close, and there the poor victims were merely made unconscious.) The last two stories have let their horrors leak outside the main cast and engulf the population who'd be watching at home. That's something that'll almost become a cliché in the new series revival, but here it's very new and unnerving.

The plague is handled with such plausible dispassion that poor old Miss Dawson doesn't even get a death scene. Poor old Thomasine Heiner. I liked her.

And something to ponder: this week is all about UNIT trying to chase Masters. Next year, the whole season will be about them chasing a single Master. Is that a budget cut, or what?

T: I don't think I could show Dr Lawrence's demise to anyone now – they'd probably laugh and say it was bad acting. But it's not, it's *brilliant*! In real life, I've never seen anger or violence the way they're usually shown on screen. Real fights are clumsy, scrappy, ugly affairs, not clean tussles where every punch connects. Anger and loss of control actually generally look rather awkward and discomforting, rather than like impressive displays of an actor's emotional range. The most realistic depiction of emotional breakdown I've seen is Roger Sloman's in Nuts in May: its brilliance is because there's something a bit pathetic and ridiculous about it. This is similar. "I'm in charge of this place!" Peter Miles hollers, his voice cracking as his disease and priggishness finally spin out of control. It's the last desperate attempt of a man to maintain his authority as his world crumbles beneath him. Caroline John is also very good – she grits her teeth and clenches her fists in all-too-real exasperation at Lawrence's self-important ranting, and looks genuinely more knackered as the test-tube scenes play out. There's a moment where the off-screen tension between her ability and dramatic purpose are mirrored when the Brig asks her to man the phones, and she protests because she's, frankly, overqualified for such mundane jobs. (Unfortunately for her, Barry Letts was probably listening.)

With regards the direction, the filmed scenes of the plague striking London give this a scope not yet seen in the series. Yes, we had the Auton attack in Spearhead from Space, but the high and wide shots make this seem more expansive. It also has a pacy mobility: note the brilliant way the camera follows the increasingly desperate Masters, with the railing zipping by faster and faster as he gets more woozy and finally expires, his dead eyes staring in ugly blankness. It's pretty damn novel, actually, to see something as ordinary as a train pulling in, and one of our characters disembarking and interacting with the bustle of realistic and everyday travellers. Canny work from Mr Combe – I especially love the shot with the flashing vehicle light in the foreground, and the many extras subtly coming into view in the background and collapsing en masse.

Speaking of the guest-cast... poor old Derek Pollitt. Instead of Driver Evans from The Web

of Fear becoming a regular UNIT fixture, he's palmed off here with a bit of bubblegum, two lines as Private Wright and a quick death by Silurian. As for Dave Carter – he's not credited despite being the body of the Old Silurian *and* the plague-ridden ambulance driver, and thus being more visible in this episode than anywhere else in the story. Still, we'll be playing Where's Wally with him for the rest of the era, so I'm sure he'll be happy enough. And there's bonus cast member fun on the DVD extras, when you notice that Peter Miles has more hair in the excellent Making Of... documentary than he does in the actual programme made 30 years before. There's either science or fiction at work there.

Oh, and there's a fab bit where the Brigadier answers the phone and gets very cross with the person at the other end – "The Daily *what*?!" he says, angrily. Well, this is a story about how bigotry prevents cultures from coexisting peacefully. The Silurians are intending to mass migrate, and they look and talk differently to us. That, surely, would be of especial interest to The Daily Mail, no question!

May 12th

Doctor Who and the Silurians (episode seven)

R: Malcolm Hulke's script still manages to be remarkably even-handed. Fan lore suggests that the wonderful last scene, in which the Doctor looks on in horror as the Brigadier blows up the Silurian base, sums up entirely his moral rightness. He unequivocally calls it murder, and just look how appalled he is when he thinks that Liz Shaw too has betrayed him. But it's not nearly as simple as that. The scene in which the Doctor tells the Brigadier how he wants to revive the Silurians one by one is extremely telling – he doesn't speak of them as a race of individuals, but only in terms of all the knowledge he can't wait to get his hands on. His eyes gleam with greed; he's become another Quinn. And we see (although, ironically, no human character ever will) that the Young Silurian hadn't been killed by the Brigadier's bullet, and had it not been for the explosion, he'd have revived his brothers and started a new crisis. Hulke gives the Doctor the last word, and clearly believes in the moral standards that last word suggests – but it doesn't mean that the Doctor's motives were pure, or that the Brigadier wasn't right to kill the Silurians. It's all really very sophisticated.

The plotting itself is somewhat more perfunctory. Having demonstrated they'll cheerfully kill any human being they see, the Silurians' decision to leave the Doctor and his friends alive, just so they can die in an atomic explosion, seems very clumsy. But even here you can sense the production making the best out of the script: there's that one Silurian who delays his departure for just a few seconds, as if rejecting the cliché, and you wonder whether he might just do the natural thing and take revenge on the humans anyway.

It's a truly great story, this. My first encounter with it was not in the maternity ward over my mother's breast (no, I was joking about that), but – as with you, Toby – via the Target novelisation. It's a good book too, but the tone of it is much more cynical than the televised version. Every character appears to me more self-serving – on screen, Dr Quinn was a foolish but well-meaning man whose desire for knowledge got himself killed; in the book, he methodically plans to murder the Silurians once he has learned what he needs. On screen, Major Baker was a sympathetic figure blinded by his own fear and patriotism; in the book, he's a xenophobe who longs for the days of the British Empire. It's tempting to say that Hulke is giving more depth to his characters here, filling in their past lives (Quinn's frustration as the son of a famous scientist, Ba(r)ker's disgrace after shooting an IRA sniper), but I'd argue that the author's view of them is so relentlessly harsh, it makes them somewhat one-dimensional. What's wonderful about the screen version is that there's a compassion to Hulke's pacifist fable, and that's so much more beguiling than the cunning and cold novel that followed it. Every character gets his moment of sympathy, even finally the Young Silurian, who willingly takes the responsibility of putting his race back into hibernation at the cost of his own life. And as the Doctor drives away in disgust from the explosions on the moors, you're left with a rare sense in the series that

you're meant to *think* about what's gone on, and maybe argue with it.

T: Hello! I think it's Tuesday morning where you are. For me it's the evening, and I've just got back from my New Zealand debut. Of course, I could schmooze and enjoy the fallout from the performance tonight (which was not bad, considering I've had to cut, rewrite and restructure the show for an audience with different reference points), but instead I've high-tailed it back to the hotel to watch my quota of episodes and e-mail you!

The problem with liberalism, you see, is the need to question, always question, and allow for the fact that you may not be correct. That is why this story is so much more interesting than the swaggering arrogance of The Dominators, in which any character who disagrees with the writers' point of view comes across as a stupid dupe who deserves everything they get. Malcolm Hulke is more brave – he has his viewpoint, but articulates its shortcomings in a very intelligently self-reflective manner. A non-liberal viewpoint tends to deal with certainties, and it's the people who are *certain* about things who frighten me. There's no point in ten people in a room deciding to take a vote, if one person comes in with a knife and is unafraid to use it. That's why I'm not sure if, ultimately, the good guys ever win. And this is why I love Doctor Who and the Silurians, and the general moral framework Hulke has brought to the series. With less sophistication, his subject matter could be boring and preachy, but fortunately, it isn't.

But within the tapestry that Hulke crafts, the supporting cast and characters experience mixed fortunes. Simon Cain needs a new agent – he's credited as a Silurian but not as Private Upton, who has dialogue and a death scene and everything. When Paul Darrow (as Captain Hawkins) spies Upton's corpse, he's terribly convincing as the professional soldier – drawing his gun without histrionics, coolly assessing the situation before withdrawing. Hawkins' own death, while saving the Brig, is quite shocking too – wherever Jimmy Munro is, he's better off! Liz Shaw once again proves the strengths of her character at the climax, supplying the Brigadier (and us) with the necessary scientific explanations whilst the Doctor busies himself resolving the drama. And I quite like the fusion of Peter Halliday's shrill, haughty tones and the prissy, wobbly movement of Nigel Johns – they give the Young Silurian a distinctive personality which really works.

As for the main man... this has been a great showcase for our fledgling Doctor. The scraps of paper Liz wades through demonstrate that he's still the scruffy boffin we know and love, whilst the Doctor's hardware-manipulation – as he's stripped down to a white T-Shirt – shows that he's capable getting his hands dirty where necessary. (An old girlfriend of mine glanced at this once, and said she thought he was sexy!) It's fantastic that he drives away the Silurians by sending the reactor into critical mode, without actually realising that the humans are all trapped because of the broken lift. Once again, in doing the right thing, he's endangered them all!

And then there's that brilliant ending, as the Doctor is all confident and purposeful, tinkering with Bessie and getting excited about the future. It's when he's in this powerful, boastful, confident mood that... he loses! His ally betrays him, and the desired peaceful resolution is never given a chance to work. In leaving our main characters unsatisfied and without the ending they yearned for, we, the audience, get one of the most impactful finales the series could ever hope to give us.

The Ambassadors of Death (episode one)

R: When I was a young fan, I assumed this one wasn't up to much. I'd been given a video recording of it, but it was almost unwatchable – the colour kept on strobing all over the screen, and I could only conclude that the plot was as hard to follow as the tracking. Others seemed to agree with me. Terrance Dicks was hell bent on novelising *everything*, but he didn't want to go near this story with a bargepole – it must have been dreadful. And in every interview, he and Barry Letts would talk about the basic failings of the seven-parter serial, how they were too long, too repetitive, too flabby – how they frankly didn't work. But everyone loved The Silurians and Inferno – and no-one had anything bad to say about

Marco Polo or The Evil of the Daleks either, come to that. So that meant they must have been talking about Ambassadors. Surely.

Not on the evidence of this. It's one of the best episodes of Doctor Who we've seen yet. The first eight minutes or so pile on the tension so thickly that by the time an astronaut, Van Lyden, opens the hatch to the Mars Probe – and with horrifying slowness – it's almost agonising; it's actually a relief that there's that moment of horror straight afterwards, Van Lyden staring straight out at us and screaming in silent terror. And it's effective simply because everything around it has been treated as completely *real*. Only five stories ago, in The Seeds of Death, we had sequences about your actual true life space travel, and they were fun – but this seems almost documentary-like in its cool precision, and it's that coolness being shattered which makes this so honestly frightening. This feels so mature, it's like a completely different series. The Seeds of Death also had lots of allusions to Mars, of course – but even the merest idea that what Van Lyden might be screaming at is an Ice Warrior would seem now rather gauche. Similarly, the warehouse battle is memorable not only for being one of the best choreographed fight scenes in the series, but because it is so grittily convincing. As Nicholas Courtney stares into the barrel of a rogue sergeant's gun and realises that his death is only a trigger pull away, you can honestly believe that his character could be written out this abruptly. The thrill of clever drama is that people don't necessarily do what they say they'll do – whereas most Doctor Who (and most television in general, to be fair) use their characters to explain precisely what their intentions are so that the audience at home will follow. Not here – when the Brigadier tries to persuade Collinson to drop his gun, Collinson tells him that he supposes he's right... but we're not remotely reassured by that. Of course not. None of The Ambassadors of Death is reassuring. That's why it's so gripping.

This reinvented Doctor Who likes to use the media, doesn't it? Back in The War Machines, it seemed almost gimmicky to see Kenneth Kendall pop up on the television screen. Journalists have hounded UNIT in Spearhead from Space and The Silurians, and here it's used as a framing device for all the exposition we need to get; the Doctor, like us, even watches the adventure for a while on his own TV set. We'll get a lot of this in the Pertwee years, most notably in The Daemons, but it's at its best here. As we'll see, this is a story which will hinge upon a television broadcast, and the hinting of that here is really very clever. And it's great to see Michael Wisher, too, in the first of his Doctor Who roles.

And Pertwee is superb. It's not an episode with room for much humour, but his irritation with bureaucracy is very funny.

T: The Ambassadors... OF DEATH!

This opening instalment has everything: an intriguing premise, wonderful direction and impeccable acting (Robert Cawdron's unfortunate accent aside, which reminds us that this is Doctor Who, and can therefore never quite be perfect!). Michael Ferguson is an outstanding director: just mark that pre-credits sequence that leads to the cliffhanger that isn't. It's moody, realistic, and then the story title *blasts* onto the screen in such an exciting and unexpectedly brilliant way, I'm flabbergasted they only did it on this story. Van Lyden being upside down, the decision to use Wakefield as an exposition buster, the superb quick cuts from character to character as the strange alien sound sears through the air... there are so many moments of little triumph in this, I'd be all day just listing them.

Just look at Jon Pertwee confidently striding in and explaining the mystery, and then standing erect and unruffled as everyone around him rocks in pain at the high-pitched message. He's got such presence, and is very funny with Professor Cornish until expedience and etiquette force him to show a certain level of respect. Also, that opening scene with the funny time-travel antics at the TARDIS console (though how the hell the Doctor got *that* out of the Ship, I've no idea) brings some much-needed fun to the rather grown-up atmosphere everywhere else.

A word for the rest of the cast, too. Ric Felgate (as Van Lyden) may well have been the director's brother-in-law, but all charges of nepotism are avoided owing to his low-key naturalism. Ronald Allen is extraordinarily good as Cornish – he's cool, calm and exudes an utterly plausible professionalism. And hoo-

ray for John Abineri (as General Carrington, wonderfully sporting a flower on his lapel) underplaying marvellously – the scenes between Carrington and his cohorts have a wonderfully stilted formality. These guys don't seem cruel or sadistic – they have a military precision, courtesy and detachment (where else do the baddies tell each other not to kill, unless absolutely necessary?) that suggests they're a different antagonistic prospect all together.

You know, I was exactly the same as you – in no hurry whatsoever to watch this adventure, even though when I *first* saw it, I waited for it to become a clunker... and it didn't. I haven't seen Ambassadors as often as I'd like since, alas, because every time I get it on video, I lend it to someone to convince them of its merit and never get it back! I've been through about four copies of it, and had to hurriedly borrow this one from a mate just before my departure from the UK. (Thank you Mr John Cooper, comedian and Doctor Who fan, with whom it's been my pleasure to enjoy many of the new-series episodes on transmission... including Dalek, as it happens.)

May 13th

The Ambassadors of Death (episode two)

R: Dallas Cavell, who entertained us in two Hartnell stories and a Troughton one, is back! And my God, he's actually playing it straight this time! If you wanted an indication of the shifting tone of Doctor Who, there's no better illustration than that.

The rest of the episode isn't quite so sure *where* it's pitching for. The set pieces are good: the re-entry of the recovery capsule is convincingly tense, and the helicopter attack on the convoy provides this week's instalment with more than its fair share of stunts and thrills. But there's nonetheless an uneasy feel about most of this; the unforced credibility of episode one has given way to something straining to take itself seriously, but which lets itself down with bits of silliness. The big fight sequence with gas bombs and stun guns is smashing, but it's prefaced by the bizarre emphasis placed upon the Doctor, in the background, unable to get his car going. The "transmigration of object" stuff is just horrible: there's absolutely no story requirement for the Doctor to make an object disappear into thin air, and as it occurs within the opening minute of the action, it completely misrepresents the style of this rather gritty drama. And only the hard of heart would begrudge Doctor Who that fun scene where he binds Carrington to Bessie by flicking a switch called an "anti-theft device" – we even get Pertwee indulging in his first comedy accent, and that's got to raise a smile. But maybe I just *am* rather hard of heart; again, the science is so wonky it feels like magic, and that just seems wrong when so much of what has made this story sing is its almost documentary realism. (Besides, I can't help but think that had the Doctor taken Carrington into custody, rather than just leaving him stuck to a car, the story's crisis might have been resolved much more speedily. It wouldn't have needed seven episodes, for a start!)

But all is forgiven by the cliffhanger. On paper, this probably didn't look very special. The Doctor decides to cut open the capsule, something that had already been raised as an option a good ten minutes previously. But without benefit of incidental music, Pertwee utterly sells the urgency of the moment. It's brilliant; you can't wait to find out what happens next.

T: Oh, it's not just Pertwee who nails it – Michael Ferguson's creeping camera, quick cutting and sound editing all build to an unbearable climax. It's one of my very favourite cliffhangers, in one of my very favourite stories!

... so with typical Doctor Who karma, this episode has to contain two of my *least* favourite moments, just show us that life is never perfect. You're right, the transmigration of object is unforgivable. Indeed, when Liz posits that the Doctor has sent the tape into the future with a flick of his wrist, you're almost crying out for him to say that he has. All right, that would have entailed resorting to ridiculous science, but it would have been a *kind of* science nonetheless. I can forgive made-up science, but I can't forgive magic. This series

doesn't *do* magic. I don't know why and I can barely justify it, but I'll accept bad science while having no time for the supernatural or fairytale – I'll accept monsters, but not gods. You can reverse as many polarities as you like, but don't even think of casting a spell, or you'll lose me. So the anti-theft device on the Doctor's car isn't quite as horrible as the "transmigrated object", but it's yet-another sign that at least one of the many writers who laboured on this story didn't quite grasp how Doctor Who gets itself out of hazardous situations. We will not see many instances like this again, for which we must be eternally grateful.

I find myself forgiving the unforgivable, though, because there's so much to admire elsewhere. The story is shaping up to be a first-class conspiracy thriller, with shady double agents and traitors at every corner. The central mystery around the capsules has broadened its scope, and we have to work out who is hiding what from whom and why. The manner in which the Doctor gets Collinson to reveal his military background (the Doctor, suddenly: *"Stand to attention when you're talking to me, and call me sir!"*; Collinson, leaping to his feet: *"Sir!"*) is a clever piece of deduction and man-management. Otherwise, though, the bad guys are admirably impenetrable – for a series where, in the not-too-distant past, the enemy have usually given away their plans and secrets in a cack-handed manner, it's fantastic to have such efficient nemeses.

Overall, and those lapses that I mentioned aside, this really works because it's a mixture of high-tech, large-scale production values and attention to the smallest nuanced detail. At one extreme, we have the impressively high interior set of Space Control and the terrific ambush sequence with its smoke bombs, helicopters, stunt falls and motorcycles (only slightly marred by General Carrington and his soldier, Grey, arming themselves with "future guns" that look like hair dryers). At the other, we have the throbbing tension of the scenes where contact is attempted with the astronaut crew and the capsule's painstaking real-time descent. It's edgy stuff that could be deathly dull in the hands of a less-skilled director, but Ferguson is rewarded by his actors working hard to keep this real – Ronald Allen's histrionic-free delivery of the line "If [the astronauts] are alive" is so much more effective precisely because of the serious, grave manner in which he issues it.

The Ambassadors of Death (episode three)

R: This borrows some of its ideas and images from the stories immediately before it. That red herring about contagious radiation sweeping the country as a plague feels borrowed from The Silurians. And the astronaut-dressed aliens, walking silently, faces expressionless, are surely a retread of the Auton dummies from Spearhead from Space. But what's clever is that The Ambassadors of Death takes these echoes, as if aware that we'll recognise them, and subverts them. Hidden behind helmets that suggest futurism and heroism, the aliens are utterly unknowable: Spearhead used its waxworks merely as something featureless and incongruous, whereas Ambassadors takes that and adds on top intrigue that is genuinely suspenseful. And when Carrington and Quinlan cook up their plague story, you sense that they may well have nicked it from recent news events themselves – it's a rare example of the series feeding off itself internally, all those victims at Marylebone station nothing more now than something that could inspire a cover story.

The joy of all this is that now the story settles down, and reinvents itself as an urban thriller. We really have never seen the like of this on Doctor Who before – conspiracies and double bluffs and car chases. And the reason the story finds its feet is because of William Dysart as Reegan. He gets the best introduction for a villain *ever*. He coolly gives orders to his men to kill two medical doctors – and they do so, brutally. And then he calmly murders *them* as well, and dumps their bodies in a gravel pit. It's not so much that the events themselves are so unpleasant, but that the episode takes its time over them – the deaths aren't quick or easy, nor is the disposal of the evidence. Dysart has a rough charm that makes him callous but efficient – and, therefore, frighteningly credible. He's a mercenary doing a job, not an evil genius, not an unhinged madman. By the time he tells Lennox that he's now been ordered to take care of Liz Shaw and the Doctor, we believe completely that this is a man who cannot be reasoned with and gets results. Our heroes seem suddenly to be under the greatest threat they've faced all season – and all from a man they aren't even yet aware exists, and who's only just this week been unleashed upon the story. Dysart energises the drama, and gives it a coherent tone.

T: Dysart is terrific, isn't he? Blunt, no-nonsense and entirely credible. The disposal of the heavies in the gravel pit is not only pretty grim, it emphasizes the underbelly of Carrington and Quinlan's neat little conspiracy. The threat seems so much more palpable when someone as pragmatic as Reegan does the dirty work, as opposed to outlandish uber-villains with snazzy facial hair or husky voices. And Reegan's little digs at Professor Lennox for being "some kind of" scientist who had his Doctorship revoked cleverly emphasise the dynamic between, and the character of, both men. Cyril Shaps is adorable as Lennox, looking like a confused mole. And a little praise for Gordon Sterne as the doomed scientist Heldorf too. His accent is so very good: it's a missed opportunity that he dies (shot at point blank range!) while Bruno Taltalian lives to taunt another day, and tell the Doctor that his father was a hamster and his mother smells of elderberries.

And *still* the mystery deepens. We don't know if Carrington is lying because he's bad, or whether he has a decent motive but just doesn't trust our heroes. The probe's radioactive interior and the astronauts' alien nature keep everyone guessing and make sure this unpredictable story appeals to our intellect, as well as entertaining us with car chases and hardware. It's a textbook melding of action, adventure and character that makes The Ambassadors of Death one of the best – and by far the most underrated – adventures we've seen so far.

May 14th

The Ambassadors of Death (episode four)

R: I've tried very hard not to be too critical so far, because it's the nature of this diary to stay positive. But as much as I'm enjoying Season Seven, I have to admit, I've been rather disappointed by the new companion. I've always rather loved the *idea* of Liz Shaw. And as one of those fans growing up who was only happy when the programme was taking itself (and therefore, me) seriously, I far preferred the idea of this brilliant Cambridge scientist to the fluffy scatterbrain who was her replacement. But watching Liz in context, I don't think she's really worked – and I can't be sure whether she's just the part of this new adult tone that seems the most forced, or whether it's because the rapport between Caroline John and Jon Pertwee seems distinctly muted.

But I think Liz comes into her own here. Separated from the Doctor, she's a far more interesting proposition. She's clever, and she's brave, and she's full of moral indignation against Reegan and the cowardly Lennox; funnily enough, Caroline John shows a Liz who seems to be finally *enjoying* herself. In the next episode, she even delivers a gag we last heard played by Troughton; grabbed by heavies, she sweetly reassures them that they mustn't worry, she won't harm them. Realistically, Liz is being written as an alternate Doctor in this part of the story – and that's why this episode crackles with energy. Because although arguably not a lot actually happens, we're passed from scenes where the Doctor challenges Taltalian to scenes where a pseudo-Doctor challenges Reegan. There's real power to these confrontations: you can sense William Dysart showing a real respect for the woman who openly despises him and isn't afraid to say so to his face. And for the first time, really, I find myself respecting her too.

The sequence where the astronaut slowly walks out of the sunlight, impervious to bullets, before calmly electrocuting a UNIT sentry, has a wonderful beauty to it.

T: I love that sequence – the alien astronaut silhouetted as the sunlight reflects in the camera lens, the haunting minimalist music, and the way the radioactive death creeps along the barrier to zap Max Faulkner. Classic stuff, and a moment that *should* be as iconic as the Auton massacre or the Cyberman day trip to St Paul's.

Alas, this episode is responsible for another fan myth that's spiralled out of control. In The Discontinuity Guide, the authors state that Taltalian doesn't have a foreign accent on film. As a result, other publications and websites have extrapolated upon this and stated that Robert Cawdron doesn't adopt his French tones "in some scenes". This is because, to sell the joke better, The Discontinuity Guide neglects to mention that Taltalian has but *one scene* entirely composed of *one line* on film. One line of four words. Four words of one syllable. And they're such innocuous words ("Get in, Miss Shaw") that even if he *was* doing an accent, it would hardly stand out. All right, I was a bit rude about the accent myself (lazy reviewers do that, remember, Toby?), but I know actual French people whose pronunciations are more outlandish, and Cawdron is actually giving a decent performance as the defensive, nervous scientist. His beard is silly, though. Beards don't flap about like that, but I'll forgive him his accent.

On the upside, Cyril Shaps was a national treasure, to be sure. As Lennox, he's so easy to feel sorry for – Reegan's line of "somebody remembers you" is a terrible dig, and Lennox's confession to Liz that he hasn't got anywhere to *go* if he escapes is heartbreaking. So I love his nervously brave decision to leave the key out for Liz to make *her* escape: it gives this fussy, weak little man a wonderful dignity. As for Reegan, William Dysart should surely be up there with the series' top villains ever. He's brilliant! The way he alters the timer on an explosive after calmly reassuring the doomed Taltalian with "Say quarter of an hour [to get clear], we can't have you taking risks..." is clinically cold and ruthless. Yet, by golly, he's a charming so-and-so with it.

And, delightfully for me as a credits-watcher, there's a quirky cast list that mixes old and new styles. They're captions, but the key guest cast are listed after the regulars in order of appearance, which means everyone gets the opportunity to receive top guest-star billing. It's a little, unimportant, trivial thing – but it pleases a little, unimportant and trivial person like me.

The Ambassadors of Death (episode five)

R: Whatever happened to Cheryl Molineaux? She was great in the opening episodes as Miss Rutherford, someone who could sit by Professor Cornish's side and come out with trajectory figures with great efficiency, and yet also communicate urgent concern. There's a moment early on in the story, when the shuttle makes re-entry, where she shows such relief that she drops her professional mask altogether; it's delightful. But she's gone, and been replaced by Joanna Ross, in what looks like a carbon-copy part. Ross, though, is a robot – no matter how great the crisis, whether the Doctor is about to be crushed by G-force, accelerate into the sun, or be slammed into by a UFO, she intones her lines with a startling monotony. There's a virtue to composure under fire, but she just seems *bored* by the whole thing. If I were in a space shuttle, and about to face my maker for any number of reasons, I'd really much prefer it if the last words I heard didn't sound quite so nonchalant.

But the Doctor's back in space! He hasn't got the TARDIS working, but there he is, out amongst the stars. It's a replay once more of The Seeds of Death, but the dangers of rocket travel are so much better depicted here. There, we had Troughton and company flail about a bit as if they were rather tipsy; here, Pertwee's entire face is wholly distorted, in what looks like agony. The comparison is unfair, of course. When Michael Ferguson directed the second Doctor flying off to meet Martians, it was for an adventure serial for kids. When he was required to direct a similar sequence only a year later, it was for a paranoid thriller for grown-ups.

Cyril Shaps' death by isotope haunted me as a kid, because it's something suggested. We never see the body slump to the ground, just the terror of a scientist who understands radiation only too well, and just what exposure of it will do to him. It's a terrific scene – Lennox dies entirely on his own; we're not even grant-ed the relief of seeing his killer, only his shoes, and this makes his murder so much more cruel and dismissive. (It couldn't be Sgt Benton, could it? He said he was going to fetch Lennox some tea. I've never trusted Benton, right from that first time we saw him shadowing the Doctor and Jamie in The Invasion; he clearly delighted just a little too much in cloak and dagger stuff back then too.)

T: This Benton thing's a bit of a myth, surely? The person who poisons Lennox is given lines, and it's clearly not John Levene who says them. And no, he's not disguising his voice – for one thing, why would he, and for another, Levene has, I'm sure, many virtues, but a chameleon-like versatility ain't one of 'em. In death, sadly, Cyril Shaps also gets dropped down the credits for some reason (yet Dallas Cavell gets executive treatment simply for lying on a desk). Oh credits, you give with one hand and take away with the other. Maybe this is why no-one else is interested in them – they only lead to heart-break.

You bemoan the loss of Miss Rutherford. Well, the male Control Assistant has changed too, as has Reegan's lackey (Tony Harwood's posture is terrible – stand up straight, man!). It would have been easy to use the same actors throughout, so I guess it's a deliberate policy of Ferguson's to keep it real (people have days off, shifts rotate). To pay for the revolving-door casting policy, they've obviously recycled the hair dryers from episode two and used them on Jon Pertwee's face to simulate G-Force. He probably nicked them, and used them increasingly during his stint on the series to make his hair more and more bouffant as he went on (copyright T Dicks circa 1990 onwards, and every convention and DVD commentary since, without fail, ad infinitum).

Much of this episode rotates around the Doctor's take-off and Reegan's aborted attempt to sabotage it. It's well-shot stuff, with William Dysart hauling himself about the complex with admirable dexterity. At one point, he kicks a technician over the railings, and we actually see him hit the ground! Dysart continues to impress all round, coldly shoving his stubby little pistol under Caroline John's chin and amusingly dismissing Liz's concern for the Brigadier's safety by reassuring her that the casualty list only contains "some of the other ranks". He's funny whilst not being played for laughs, and threatening without overegging the nastiness.

And as an antidote to the straight-faced procedural drama, we have Jon Pertwee's terrific Doctor getting impatient with all the protocols and techno-speak. The countdown scenes pass by more quickly as he injects a bit of pomposity pricking humour. "I take it you mean half an hour", he says dryly, when told that countdown will occur in "Three-O, that's 30 minutes".

There's barely been a bad moment recently. I'm in Season Seventh Heaven.

May 15th

The Ambassadors of Death (episode six)

R: After all the grit and realism of the thriller, the scenes upon the alien spaceship seem gloriously surreal. It might all be garish orange and awkward CSO, but for once that only helps the weirdness – the Doctor stepping out of the shuttle into mid-air and then gently floating down to the floor. And I love the fact that the three missing astronauts, around whom there has been so much intrigue and concern, are revealed to be perfectly happy watching imaginary football matches on imaginary television sets – it's that sudden presentation of the banal against such an unedifying backdrop that makes the whole sequence feel eerie. And then, for pure shock value, there's nothing to beat the moment when Liz sees the crumbling alien face for the first time – good make-up! The juddery stop-frame camerawork is terrific.

Best of all, though, is the growing certainty that Carrington is insane. The Brigadier is far less willing to call his superior mad than Cornish is, but what makes their confrontations so fascinating is that it recalls so exactly the Brigadier's own xenophobia at the end of The Silurians. It is surely no coincidence that, at the beginning of the story, the destruction of the caves is given specific attention – would it be too much to think that, as is so rare in the programme, Carrington's attitudes are being

used deliberately to develop the Brigadier's character?

And there I was, blathering on about the lack of rapport between Jon Pertwee and Caroline John. But that instant where the Doctor recovers consciousness, and looks with dazed delight up into the face of Liz Shaw, even reaching up to stroke her cheek, is one of the most tender displays of affection we've ever seen towards a companion. The sort of thing, indeed, that a thousand fanfics could be inspired by... if the world of online fandom could ever have the good taste to watch The Ambassadors of Death, that is.

There's a couple of odd moments, though. The Doctor's shock reaction to the word "ambassadors" is rather funny, really, considering the audience has been fed that very word in the opening credits for the last six weeks. And it's very odd to see that Max Faulkner's UNIT sentry, killed so memorably in episode four, is back at work, smiling and waving. Maybe it's his twin brother. (A rather heartless twin brother, it must be said, to be quite so cheery in the circumstances. But who knows? Maybe their sour relationship, working together in the same paramilitary force, is just something else to inspire fanfic. Or maybe not.)

T: When I was younger, I recall Doctor Who Magazine doing a Third Doctor Special in which they reviewed all the stories. The Ambassadors of Death, along with Invasion of the Dinosaurs, was the only Pertwee you were allowed to criticise in those days, and predictably the article wrote this story off as uncelebrated and muddled. I think it also claimed that later episodes ignored or contradicted some things raised in episode one, as if that were something unique that never, ever happened elsewhere in Doctor Who! I can't immediately think to what they refer, unless it's the way in which the aliens can now communicate verbally rather than by radio waves. (I think the explanation for that is straightforward: they've done what the Doctor does next week, and built a better machine – and one that also makes them do a good impression of the Cybermen from The Invasion, to boot.) Contrary to that article – and indeed, general fan opinion – I think this is expertly plotted, piling on layer upon layer of mystery and incident and populating the story with intriguing characters. The Doctor's silence in the rocket, refusing to explain things to his allies for fear of eavesdroppers, is entirely plausible, and means that his kidnapping ensures that the Brig and Cornish are left in the dark as to the astronauts' true nature. And Reegan *saving* the Doctor is also utterly plausible and not a cop-out, as you can completely buy his motives for so doing.

I spent most of Doctor Who and the Silurians banging on about the characters, and seem to be doing the same here – but these seven-parters are chock-full of really good moments for the guest cast. Ronald Allen's underplaying is beautiful, even giving the line "I think he's insane" an impressively subtle impact. General Carrington's assertion that his actions are his moral duty gives a terribly tragic angle to this single-minded zealot. And when the Doctor tells Reegan he'll need some snazzy equipment, William Dysart brilliantly pulls the chair back for Pertwee to sit down, and then tucks him in so that he can make a list. Then, when the Doctor thinks the coast is clear and goes to check the door, Reegan has anticipated this and waited for him. What a marvellous, marvellous character, and a cut above your usual bad guy. At around this time, the production team were formulating the character of the Master: a charismatic but ruthless villain who you love to hate, and who inspires fear and grudging admiration. One can easily see who might have inspired the creation of such a character.

Oh, and going to your point about Max Faulkner – I thought his character had been injured in the earlier episode, that the barrier that conducted the blast that struck him had also dulled its lethal power. Still, it's a bit early to be back at work after a zapping. Perhaps when you kill one Max Faulkner, another appears to take his place. Perhaps he's a Cylon. Or the Slayer. Or just bad continuity.

The Ambassadors of Death (episode seven)

R: If the capture of Reegan feels abrupt, then that only emphasises how good William Dysart has been. He's not been the story's lead villain, he really was just a subplot heavy after all –

and his performance was so charismatic and so exciting that we didn't notice.

The defeat of Carrington is a different proposition altogether. There's enormous dignity in the story's final moments, when he realises with genuine bemusement that he's the one seen as the bad guy. His willingness to recruit the Doctor to his cause early in the episode, and the way that he appeals to the Doctor to understand his "moral duty", sets Carrington up as that rare villain in Doctor Who: one who honestly is well-intentioned, and believes he's acting for the greater good. Essentially, Carrington is only behaving in the manner that the Doctor himself habitually has done in the days of Hartnell and Troughton – identifying the aliens as a menace, and doing everything in his power to convince the sceptics that the safest course of action is to blow them up.

With both The Silurians and The Ambassadors of Death, we see the entire series turn on its heels, and adopt a far more adult stance towards the way it engages with alien cultures. It's not hard to see who's responsible for that; we now know that the vast majority of Ambassadors was written by an uncredited Malcolm Hulke. And that's what's critical to the way we perceive the Doctor from this point on, as a man of peace, as a diplomat – that in 1970, the audience had 14 weeks of back to back of Hulke to adjust to it. Of course, the series doesn't last long like this exactly, and it won't take long before the Doctor is merrily blowing up alien invaders once more. And perhaps that's just as well, because a series that operates on Hulke's principles, however dramatic, would surely soon have collapsed under the weight of its fair play. But even if the shift in tone is softened, that shift in tone has taken place, and is long-lasting. That superb ending, with Pertwee calmly walking away from aliens and humans, leaving them to tie up the loose ends themselves, presents a very new Doctor Who altogether.

T: I guess how we approach Doctor Who depends very much on our history with it. I spent most of my time as a teenager defending it, and justifying my passion for it. Even when the show was acceptable and popular, my family still took the mickey at my level of enjoyment (or "obsession", to adopt their less flattering parlance). Later, when the general public saw fit to abandon it and mock it, I went out of my way to disprove the claim that it was childish, cheap and boring. I looked upon these Season Seven stories as the perfect potential exhibits, should I ever find myself serving as the defence barrister in The Trial of Doctor Who: they were grown-up, expensive looking and had plenty of action. Of course, they're far *longer* than most of today's audience could cope with, but that allowed me to simply rock back and bathe in the glory of how much more clever Doctor Who fans were than the lay audience, because we didn't need simple, succinct scripts to tell straightforward stories, oh no sir. We were more sophisticated. Case closed.

I'm slightly less haughty and defensive these days, but I still think The Ambassadors of Death is far from the write-off of fan lore: the weakest story of an otherwise superb season. Even this late in the adventure, the money hasn't run out and the director is still thinking of ways to augment scenes with action. The mounting tension of the TV broadcast is underscored by the gunshots outside, which increasingly distract an already edgy Carrington, and the aliens look moody and imposing when filmed against the pale blue sky. The willowy, undulating score that accompanies them is a testament to Dudley Simpson's superb work on this serial. He started the story by doing a riff of Procul Harum's Whiter Shade of Pale for the space scenes, which gave them a strange beauty. But the spare, thumping drum beats used for the scenes of tension, and the bouncy, thrilling tunes for UNIT and Bessie, just underline the man's versatility.

All the hard man stuff, however, might be a bit much were it not for the Doctor dandying about. Pertwee is great, mockingly showboating his guard, and encouragingly nodding towards the spacemen to show how he's progressing when in fact he's calling for help. This new Doctor is pitch-perfect, especially when referring to the aliens as "gentlemen". Just because they're from outer space, it doesn't exempt them from the grace of good manners from this most dignified of Time Lords. Thanks to this Doctor's eccentricity, we are also allowed that delightful moment where, because of

vehicular shortcomings, the Brig and the stunt team HAVOC (sorry, I mean UNIT, with its clone troops Privates Ware and Walsh) pile gamely into his funny yellow car.

In the end, though, it's the script and the characters that make The Ambassadors of Death into something special. Reegan tries to persuade Carrington of the Doctor's worth, but covers his back with a blithe "suit yourself, kill him", and then spends part of the episode with an ironed shirt and undone tie, as if he's waiting until he's communicated with the aliens before he can dapper up and become a gentleman thief. He then coolly tells UNIT to make themselves at home when they charge in guns blazing, and, in a moment of superb self-preservation, helps our heroes to win the day. Oh, it's only too right that this slippery customer gets to live to wriggle once more.

And then there's General Carrington, so brilliantly played by that favourite of mine, John Abineri. He's a man who genuinely believes that right is on his side, but is so engulfed by misplaced paranoia that his love for his country manifests into dangerous and all-consuming fear. Listen to the subtleties Abineri gives to lines that generally call for insane ranting. He switches halfway through a sentence sometimes, being genuinely fearful and moved when he says that "they killed [my friend] Jim" before straightening up and adopting more formal military tones, as he continues with "Jim Daniels, fellow astronaut". And for once, our lead villains aren't given the disservice of an embarrassing or ignominious death scene – instead, the shock with which Carrington greets his arrest is genuinely moving. He maintains his dignity as all of his plans go wrong, slowly and deliberately replacing his hat and stiffening to attention. He then shows a tiny speck of fragility when he asks the Doctor if he understands the motives behind his actions, and the Doctor marvellously, touchingly, reassures him. Even the Brig shows tenderness – "The Sergeant will look after you" – in this story that has been as generous to its characters as to its audience.

What an unusually deep and tragic antagonist Carrington has been, and how wonderful that the trio of central guest performances – Abineri, Allen and Dysart – have given this excellent serial an added class. In fact, it's possibly the strongest guest cast yet assembled for the series. Tragically, unlike most stories, the entire central guest cast of Ambassadors (the three I've just mentioned, plus Shaps, Cavell, Cawdron, Wisher and the three astronauts) are all no longer with us. TV Heaven indeed.

May 16th

Inferno (episode one)

R: The direction is great, and the segues between scenes are very clever (Harry Slocum beating some poor technician to death cutting to Benton hammering a nail into the wall, or even the Doctor singing Verdi in his car contrasted with Harry whistling on his bike). The dialogue is great too – Professor Stahlman's put downs to Sir Keith Gold are so good and so rude, you want to write them down so you can use them at any given moment against bullies at school.

It's all very stylish, *but*. It's an episode peculiarly without any clear jeopardy. You've got a killer on the loose, sure, and touching green ooze is doing something very nasty to him (those sequences of actor Walter Randall staggering around dead-eyed and drooling are actually rather disturbing). But it's only in the closing seconds that he offers any threat to any of our regulars. There's a strange sequence where the Doctor gets caught in some spatial limbo, which is certainly wild and different – but it's very hard to grasp (again) what the actual threat of it might be. And you've got occasional mutterings about the dangers of drilling through the Earth's crust, but as yet no-one seems to understand what these dangers might be, and the experts don't seem to have thought they were dangerous enough at the planning stage to call a halt to the project, so it's all very theoretical. The Doctor doesn't seem too bothered. Look, he's off singing Verdi, and dashing off into limbo.

And yet, it works. And it does so, I think, by telling the story sideways on. It's our third scientific base in a row, and yet this time the Doctor isn't the one who's going to be listening to the exposition, because he's been working there for quite some time. Liz Shaw is so much a part of the background too that she doesn't even make an appearance for 15 minutes. Instead, we're given a new hero, an oil driller called Greg Sutton, who comes bearing a faded Ozzie accent and rather unreconstructed views on how to chat up women. And he's great fun – he cuts through all the scientific jargon with humour and keen intelligence. We trust him immediately, and it's just as well, because unusually *he's* the character who sells the episode. If Inferno was a movie, Sutton would be the square-jawed lead, and the Doctor just some eccentric boffin in a supporting part. It's this new perspective on how to tell a Doctor Who story that makes it seem fresh – we're dropped right into the thick of things, and we spend so much time trying to understand what's going on that it's 25 minutes before we realise that, as yet, nothing much has.

Mind you, that's about to change.

T: They've done it again. They've assembled a cracking cast and given them *excellent* dialogue, with each character being perfectly drawn due to their choice of words. Olaf Pooley is magnificently haughty as Stahlman, giving the man a terse amusement at his own exasperation with Sir Keith's adherence to procedure, and what he sees as irritating "experts" infiltrating his project. Stahlman isn't a cut-and-dried bad guy – he's just an arrogant, stroppy git, but his desire to keep drilling isn't some Robson-esque stubbornness. It has a practical element, because stopping the machinery – as Sutton tells us – *would* amount to abandoning the project. Sir Keith, for his part, remains so amiable in the face of Stahlman's brusque insults, his grave demeanour has impact when he mutters that ceasing the drilling might be no bad thing.

Whilst I've enjoyed the heightened nature of much of the acting in sixties Doctor Who – it has a grandeur you don't get from ordinary drama – it really does contrast with how straight everyone's playing it here. There's no theatricality to the performances at all, and Derek Newark (as Sutton) has an appealing salt-of-the-Earth quality. He's so vital and straight-up that when he finally admits that he's scared stiff, you really buy that something of terrific import is on the cards.

But this story *also* proves that the worth of a good director cannot be underestimated.

Douglas Camfield shoots some of the scenes of Slocum staggering about with a giddy, hand-held reality, and forsakes music in favour of stark, disturbing sound effects. It's fantastic how he goes to the effort of having some scalding smoke emit when Slocum touches the earth-slime, and then increases the noise of the drilling as the camera closes in on the man's shocked face. For an episode with only a few stock music cues, sound plays such a major role – it's so much more effective dubbing animal screeches onto Walter Randall (or at least having his voice treated; you can't quite tell, which is an accomplishment itself) rather than asking the poor sod to growl. He already has to dribble and turn green for his troubles. And the noise of the drill head means that the characters have to raise their voices, helping to convince us we're not in a TV studio.

All of that said, I'm having a gloomy time watching this stuff. I can't quite shake of a feeling of sadness, looking at young, pretty Sheila Dunn – here portraying Petra Williams, Stahlman's assistant – and realising that, like the charming and energetic Derek Newark, she's dead. How gloomy and morbid am I? To the core.

Inferno (episode two)

R: In later episodes, once they've grown some fur and gnashers, the Primords will look really rather cuddly. Not at the moment, though, whilst there's still a mystery attached to them – and whilst the effect of man becoming monster is achieved through green skin, red-rimmed eyes and gollops of streaming saliva. But most feral of all is the extraordinary shrill noise they make. Walter Randall does a great job as a cornered creature lashing out, and the moment when we see the technician Bromley at the top of one of the ladders looking down at us, his humanity already lost, is chilling – it's something straight out of a zombie movie.

The scene that made the greatest impact on me, though, was the one in which – against the Doctor's advice – Stahlman takes the cracked jar containing some boiling green liquid and puts it into its box. It's such a simple mistake, and yet by that very action – by even slightly coming into contact with the substance – he's

condemned himself to death. What's remarkable is that the Doctor seems to realise it too. When there's still a chance he can still save Stahlman, Pertwee gives his warning sufficient urgency – and yet, with the deed done, Pertwee says "I wouldn't have done that if I were you" with the weary resignation of one who can't afford to waste any time sympathising with a lost cause. It gives the third Doctor a rare flash of alien disregard, the sort of thing we expect more from his successor. Pertwee's Doctor may be fractious and arrogant, but he'll spend most of his time trying to save the Earth's ecology, and becomes in later seasons a very *human* Doctor. Here, though, he seems readily willing to turn his back on us all, and his concern for the dangers of Project Inferno are just a sidestep to the power he requires for his TARDIS experiments. The manic glee on the Doctor's face as he wrestles with the shuddering console sees Pertwee utterly in his element – *this* is really what he cares about.

Caroline John's hardly in this story, is she? It's ten minutes before she even makes an appearance this week – and she spends most of her time running back and forth between the Doctor's hut and the drilling area making calculations. She's never before seemed such a minor character, nor her scientific brilliance a placeholder for any *real* personality. It's such a pity. The production team really seem to have given up on her. Is there any reason, say, why Petra Williams is in the frame, and Liz Shaw isn't? I'm enjoying the first signs of romance between Derek Newark and Sheila Dunn – the little smirk on Dunn's face as she accedes to Newark's request to call him by his first name – but wouldn't this have been more interesting still had it been *Liz* that he was flirting with? (Since it's her final story, it might even have provided a logical reason for her to leave the Doctor! Or am I totally off beam here?)

T: I love Olaf Pooley's hand-clasping twitchiness. It suggests a pent-up, suppressed rage from a man whose mind is always ticking over on his work. Note the way he taps himself with his pad and tosses his keys up and down – it's as if he's livid with everybody, and just fighting to maintain some kind of social decorum. It's an excellent performance, and I love the way

RUNNING THROUGH CORRIDORS

that we get the first, subtle indication of a green hue spreading across his skin.

Douglas Camfield clearly prided himself on attention to detail, and it's the extra little touches paid to the visuals that help to sell this as a creepy, tough adventure. The spruced-up picture on the DVD shows that Walter Randall's face, as well as being green (much to the delight of the Australian voiceover man who talked over episode one's credits, I seem to recall), has been augmented with tiny black hairs to suggest the emergence of his inner Primord. There's also blood on his clothes from where he's been shot, and he leaves a big scorch mark on the wall as he expires. I love the idea that the Primords are literally packing serious heat, which demonstrates their strangeness while tying into the central concept of tapping the Earth's core. And we get a reverse of Camfield's The Invasion, where they lost some filmed scenes and ended up in the studio. Here, we get some exposition between the Brigadier and the Doctor which could easily have been a couple of talking heads in front of a TV Centre flat. But allowing Jon Pertwee to deliver his stuff about Krakatoa atop a clangy metal stairway and on film gives it added *oomph*. That's what you always seem to get with Camfield – more *oomph*!

Inferno (episode three)

R: Jon Pertwee spends so much of his first three years trying to escape to another world – and it's wonderfully ironic that, the first time he does so, it's simply to another version of the same planet to which he's been exiled! I'll be honest – I don't normally like parallel universe stories very much. I'm not a Star Trek fan, so I'm perfectly willing to admit that I'm being unfair, but whenever I catch an episode, there *always* seems to be one of these mirror-world things going on, in which all the regular cast get to play villains instead for an hour. It never seems dramatically expedient, more a way of giving all the actors the chance to indulge themselves with a bit of camp.

The reason that's explicitly *not* the case with Inferno is that the cast aren't actually playing characters so radically distanced from their more recognisable selves on "our" Earth. Caroline John's Section Leader is not so far

removed from the colder Liz Shaw introduced at the beginning of Spearhead from Space, and Nicholas Courtney quite brilliantly shows us the crueller side of a Brigadier who had destroyed the Silurians and who has been subjected to a disciplined army life without relief. That sequence where he orders the scientific staff at gunpoint to stay at their posts, telling them that in the event of an explosion they'll all die together, isn't so radically different from that scene in which he uses his revolver to force the Wenley Moor hospital staff into quarantine. And although I have a fondness for the new series' Rise of the Cybermen, there's very little that's actually parallel about that world – the threat offered in that story, and the changes wrought in the characters, is in no way a comment upon what's taking place on the Earth we recognise. In Inferno, the drill head crisis is alarmingly similar to the one we're used to in the first two episodes – the same men have been infected by the slime, the computer's been sabotaged. And it's the deliberate use of that *parallel* that makes this all seem urgent. Yes, there's an undeniable curiosity value in seeing Nick Courtney turn around with an eyepatch, but it's what the two Earths have in *common* that gives this episode its chills.

The sadistic look of glee on Benton's face as he watches a man fall from a gas tower – great stunt, by the way – only to be replaced by comic disappointment when he realises his soldiers have shot the wrong man. The way that Greg Sutton has the same anti-authoritarian streak we've already seen, but is so much more quickly curbed by "Doctor" Williams. The fear on Section Leader Shaw's face when she realises that a stranger in fancy clothes actually knows her first name – and the hint that therefore *no-one* treats her with the easygoing affection the Doctor attempts here. These are the subtleties that make this episode sing.

Got to say, though, that I'm bemused by the way the Doctor can hide from a platoon by merely putting a dustbin lid on his head. He could at least have hidden *inside* the dustbin, rather than pretended to have been one.

T: And what a fall! The *oomph* factor just got turned to 11. I love the way Derek Ware leaps about on the gasometer and scuttles along the

34

top of it in such an unselfconscious manner, all frothing and bestial. I know that charging about on tall buildings is the sort of thing you get a stuntman for, but it's impressive nonetheless.

Mardy quibbles about the length of the chase, and the age it takes the Doctor to work out that Liz isn't *his* Liz aside, this is generally excellent. It's not all gung-ho Camfield action; there are subtle hints about the cruelty of this world. The Royal Family have been shot (!), the base is a scientific labour camp, and Sir Keith's death by motor accident appears (at this point) to be one of those banal but unfair quirks of fate. This isn't just a horrible place because some of our good characters have turned bad... look at Greg Sutton, still on the side of the angels, but with his winningly chipper personality and casual flair reduced – by the horrible regime in command – to well-enunciated submissiveness.

It's clever too, how we've been set up for this. We saw jolly young Private Latimer in episode one, just to illustrate that he was cheery and amused by the Doctor. Here, he's the first parallel Earth person we see... and he immediately starts shooting. That scene in the Brig's office in episode one allowed a little ribbing about his moustache, used Benton as a comically put-upon stooge and illustrated that Lethbridge-Stewart had a sense of humour. Here, we get action on the same set where the moustache has gone, Benton's a thug and the Brig's humour is so dark and cruelly twisted, he notes – when the Doctor states that he doesn't exist in this world – that "you won't feel the bullets when we shoot you". It's also pretty nasty when he observes that the Doctor's fate will involve being "shot... eventually". That sole additional word makes it so much more cold and threatening.

May 17th

Inferno (episode four)

R: Jon Pertwee shines as the only charismatic figure in a world full of unimaginative and frightened thugs. I'd even go so far as to say that it's here that his Doctor really takes shape – adopted by UNIT from the very first

moment he could talk, this new incarnation hasn't until now been the loner that I've identified with. But now facing interrogation and execution in a world where he's not even supposed to exist, he's at last wholly isolated, and able to contrast completely with everyone else he meets. His refusal to be cowardly, his refusal to give up, insisting on fixing the computer even as he's threatened with death at the end of Benton's rifle, returning to the drill head in a last ditch attempt to prevent penetration zero – this is what gives the Doctor his dignity. His exasperation at Section Leader Shaw's "kindness" – that she'll be prepared to suggest he's a lunatic so he can spend three years working in a slave labour camp – and the way in which he gently tells his captors when his interrogation is over, makes him seem so much powerful than anyone else, no matter how much more loudly they shout at him. It's a terrific performance.

The only problem, perhaps, with the totalitarian regime being portrayed so well is that the few scenes set on real Earth seem so... well, *bland* in comparison. The characters all seem too nice, and Liz Shaw's hair is the wrong colour.

And has there been a better cliffhanger? I'm a sucker for a good countdown at the best of times. But the stakes have never been higher. The Doctor stares down the barrel of Stahlman's gun as the final seconds tick away to armageddon. It's wonderful.

T: Isn't it? Especially the way everything cuts from shot to shot as the countdown nears zero, and the sound carries on over the closing credits, to underline that what has just started is unstoppable. Not even the end of the episode can prevent the destruction of Earth from continuing! And what a line the Doctor gets: "Listen to that! That's the sound of this planet screaming out its rage!" Terrific stuff – truly classic Doctor Who of the highest order.

And you're right... this is very different from the Star Trek/ Buffy alt-universe stories. Liz isn't a leather-clad lesbian purely designed to allow the actress to do something different – the dark-haired Section Leader Shaw illustrates that the cruel world in which she lives has unleashed the dormant sadistic tendencies already buried within her psyche. They've probably emerged out of a survival instinct – even "good" people are capable of terrible things in certain circumstances. Indeed, the section leader genuinely seems to enjoy suggesting that they let the exhausted Doctor get his strength back... so they can start the interrogation all over again. It's not just her – it's genuinely a shock to see Benton violently grab the Doctor by the hair, whilst Nick Courtney assumes an insane glint in his eye while warning Stahlman that security is "my responsibility". Superiority, authority, empowering uniforms – give them to most people and you can create a monster.

The more you think about it, the more depressing Inferno becomes – it's one of the bleakest takes on human nature that Doctor Who has yet given us. Except... we also have Greg Sutton. He's gutsy and bullish, and I desperately want to be as cool and brave as he is! He's by far the most attractive character on display, the one who doesn't toe The Party's line. It's telling, in fact, that during the interrogation, the Brigade Leader asks the Doctor whether Sutton helped him – which demonstrates in no uncertain terms that Sutton is a marked man. And the way Sutton suspects he's living on borrowed time allows him a lot of pluck and bite.

And I can't help but notice... despite all the negatives about this horrible, *horrible* society, their drilling has been far more efficient than our own, and is ahead of schedule. Perhaps there's something to be said for this kind of oppression! I suppose their trains run on time too.

Inferno (episode five)

R: Exceptional. The reality of armageddon is fully believable, largely because the Doctor is so defeatist in his assurances that there is nothing that can be done to stop the end of the world. When everyone starts deferring to him, and asking him for solutions to the crisis, we can't but help feel shocked that he so stoically can't offer any. And so the best parts of the episode focus on the characters' growing realisation that their deaths really are inevitable – Derek Newark is terrific as Greg Sutton, furiously demanding that the fascists face up to the fact that their totalitarian regime has aban-

doned them to die. There's at last a *reason* for the romance between Greg and Petra to work – she might as well join the rebels, rather than being a mindless little zombie, because in a trice her devotion to the party line has ceased to matter anyway. It's that most unsentimental of love affairs, based upon fear and the realisation that all petty differences have been dwarfed by the prospect of certain death.

And it's that same unsentimentality that makes the episode work so brilliantly. Liz Shaw was a nasty little martinet, but now finds herself becoming the Doctor's ally simply because that's what the crisis has made her. There's a lovely subtle moment where the Brigade Leader is under threat from a mutating technician, and the Doctor in concern calls him Brigadier – and because everybody appears to be working on the same side, we *want* to believe that this man can still be the friend we need him to be.

Favourite moments include Benton's stupid insistence on practising parade duty with his few remaining soldiers as he tries to grip on to some ritualised normality, or the truly disturbing scene where Stahlman rubs a hapless technician's face in the green slime, which will accelerate his decay into a Primord. Indeed, the only fault with any of this are the Primords themselves, who do resemble shaggy dogs in boiler suits. The mutation of Benton begins unnervingly enough, but ends up almost comic as John Levene sits up begging for a bone. However, the conviction of the actors and the breakneck pace ensure that somehow we still take the Primords seriously enough, and the scene where they encircle the humans before lynching Benton is surprisingly powerful.

The claustrophobia is almost perfect. Which means that the peculiar little scene of Sir Keith in a car – cheaply staged, and badly written – feels all the more out of place. For over 20 minutes, for the very first time in the series, the Doctor has failed, and the Earth is to be destroyed. And then for a minute and a half, we've got Christopher Benjamin fussing about the disloyalty of his chauffeur. I could argue, I suppose, that the scene exists just to show, to ironic effect, the cosiness of the world the Doctor has left behind, and just how ignorant they must be of the terrors that await them. But I'm not really sure I buy that.

T: Yep, apart from the interlude with Sir Keith, we're stuck entirely in the fascist world where the chips are down, and they're about to get fried. However, the nearly exclusive focus on the alternate world means that everyone is credited as their alt-Earth characters in the closing titles. It's a nice touch that makes my inner geek do a little (probably not very cool) dance.

But of course, being Doctor Who, there has to be something that lets it down – a fly in the ointment, a spanner in the works, a Giant Rat in the Talons. On this occasion, I find myself agreeing with you: it's the Primords. Still, even *they* have their strong points – they're a good concept, and having them acclimatise to the cooler temperatures cleverly maintains them as a menacing presence, but stops our heroes getting prematurely slaughtered. The really cruel thing about Benton's transformation into a Primord is that he's grabbed *and held for what seems like an age.* No sudden dispatch for the Platoon Under Leader: he has to watch helplessly as the chief Primord advances on him, and begs for his life before the inevitable finally, and horrifically, occurs. Also, notice how Douglas Camfield has the creatures stare at the camera and snarl, as if daring the viewers to say to their faces that they look like Lemmy from Motorhead (which they do, actually). Shaggy dog Benton and his fellow mutts aside, the only other blip is Caroline John telling everyone that the Brigade Leader has been given executive control – in a manner that suggests she's read episode six (which the actress has, but the character hasn't).

In this grim atmosphere, Derek Newark's Greg emerges as the heroic romantic lead. He's a pragmatic tough guy, but shows his softer side by quietly lying to Petra and thus protecting her from the awful truth that they're going to die. To her credit, she doesn't buy his reassurances – what could have become a mawkish string of this tale is pulled off very well by the two actors and some subtle writing. I also like that Sir Keith was actually successful in this world. It's refreshing to have an authority figure who isn't so daft as to unleash an apocalypse, and it's believable that their superiors

would have listened to Sir Keith because he's clearly several billion times more reasonable than grumpy old Stahlman. The scene in which the latter smothers the technician (Keith Ashley, fact fans) in slime is pretty repulsive too – though I mourn the loss of the singeing smoke effect that accompanied contact with the goo in episode one.

All in all, this is one of the most dramatic and tensely exciting episodes the show has given us. By crikey, this season is *incredible*, and effectively summed up by the starkness and uncompromising tone of the cliffhanger here, of a Primord hand smashing through a window before our heroes are ready for them. It's Earth-shattering.

Inferno (episode six)

R: On the face of it, this episode suffers too from what I shall now call "Keith Gold in a Car Syndrome". A tremendous claustrophobia and sense of doom is dissipated by a series of scenes set back on "nice" Earth, none of which in themselves are terribly dramatic. There's another fruitless argument with Stahlman, and Greg Sutton pops over to see Liz Shaw for a chat. But this time, they genuinely work wonders. The sequence with the Brigadier shouting at Benton to use his initiative and bring him Stahlman is very cleverly done – for a moment, we can see just how similar he is to his fascist counterpart – and then we see, as Benton leaves, the Brig's ironic smile and the affection he clearly has for his sergeant, and we're relieved. And if the Greg/ Liz scene is really nothing more than padding, it's padding that's impeccably well played. Moments before, we've had Derek Newark and Caroline John battle against the inevitability of death together – now they're back to square one, two colleagues who barely know each other. Newark is bumbling and just a little bit flirtatious, John polite and just a little *too* quick to jump on Newark's lines, emphasising that she isn't relaxed enough to trust him. In plot terms, these scenes count for little. But they showcase some really good performances, and remind us exactly what world the Doctor is still fighting to save.

Caroline John is really quite brilliant in this episode, no matter which Liz Shaw she's playing: the cool way in which Section Leader Shaw decides she trusts the Doctor, and devotes the last precious minutes of her lifetime to helping him, are wonderful – and precisely *because* she still seems like the ruthless fascist she was in the earlier episodes. When she shoots dead the Brigade Leader, it's utterly unapologetic, and cold, and perfunctory, not even allowing him the dignity of a warning. It's honestly just a shame that it's taken this long for Doctor Who to reveal how good Caroline John can be, because she's not been well served on the whole. And Courtney clearly relishes playing a man whose hysteria brings him nearly to the brink of tears at one point – he's a playground bully reduced to a sobbing seven year old. When the Doctor tells his unlikely new allies he'd give anything to save their lives if he could, you believe and understand him – even though a good three-quarters of them would have happily seen him dead an hour before. Even the Brigade Leader, for all his selfishness, is ennobled by his struggle to get the TARDIS powered – and that's what makes the ending so horrifying. Stock footage or no stock footage, that image of the lava flow advancing upon Greg, Liz and Petra brings to home shockingly that they're going to die, and there's no respite.

T: This is how to stage the end of the world on a famously low budget: get some good actors, spray them with sweat, shake the camera a bit, mix in some stock footage and a few well-shot bits on film, and Bob's your apocalypse. And as we leave that parallel England in the fire and brimstone of its own folly, a word about its leader. The face of visual effects designer Jack Kine may have been deemed suitable to play the Big Brotheresque despot, but the man himself couldn't have been nicer. I wrote to him as a teen with loads of questions about Quatermass, and he went to the great effort of recording his answers on a cassette and providing me with an hour's worth of reminiscences. He was very kind and funny, and went out of his way to be extremely encouraging to me at a time when I really needed it. I shall never forget his decency and positivity – he was a true gent, sadly no longer with us.

As well as the heroic characters dying as the

world ends, we also see the Brigade Leader give his last order. This is only Nicholas Courtney's sixth story, but this episode is really built around his degeneration from powerful authority figure to snivelling coward. The first thing he does as Petra (who gets increasingly braver until she shouts his bullying down) goes off to restore the power is decide to make a run for it. He also panics in the heat, whilst doling out increasingly impotent orders. It's a wonderful illustration of a man gradually losing his cool as his status and henchmen fall by the wayside. The only chink in his armour, and allowing that Courtney is a national treasure, is that he again proves less than capable of engaging in fisticuffs convincingly. As for his sidekick in "our" reality... the horror of Benton being thrown to the man-wolves last episode is superbly juxtaposed by this week's scene of comic browbeating. Put-upon is something John Levene does very well. And it occurs to me that Amiable Benton makes the perfect trusty, loyal, unquestioning sidekick – so it's only appropriate, then, that his alternative self turns into a dog.

This is a terrific episode, possibly one of the best we've ever had, with the Doctor leaving everyone to die in an edgy, intense and largely flawless production. And it shows the power of a creative team talking things through and massaging ideas, as I'm not sure I would have liked the original version of this story, Operation Mole Bore (or whatever they'd have called it), which lacked the alternative universe stuff. It would have just been lots of arguments about drilling. It would have been – oh God – like Fury from the Deep meets The Dominators.

May 18th

Inferno (episode seven)

R: This can't help but be an anticlimax of sorts. . Isn't it weird that it was *this* episode the BBC chose to release in the 1990s on The Jon Pertwee Years VHS tape? The Doctor has just failed to save an Earth from blowing up – and, into the bargain, it's an Earth run by lots of nasty fascists waving guns about. Now he's got 25 minutes to try again, but this time everybody is much more accommodating about it. The script tries its level best to give him as many obstacles as possible, even putting him in a coma for a while, but it ultimately can't conceal the fact that armageddon is averted merely by something *not* happening, and the Doctor stopping a countdown before something really interesting takes place.

But it's an example of an episode which works wonderfully, *in spite of* the plot. And it's purely because, over seven weeks, we've grown to understand these people through their blunter, more cynical counterparts. There's a certain triumph in watching Greg and Petra get it together, and particularly in Petra standing up to Stahlman and trying to shut down Project Inferno. But best of all, we get to see Olaf Pooley once again perform his rather subtler Stahlman (the one with the beard). For the last couple of weeks, he's had the indignity of romping about with false teeth and covered in hair – now it's back to basics, and he gets the chance to play a human being horrified by his own metamorphosis, and unable to do anything about it. The principle difference between the Stahlman of our world and his crueller counterpart is clearly shown in the scene around the drill head; whereas in episode five he trapped the technicians with him behind the bulkhead, and rubbed their faces in the green goo, here he forces them into safety so that he alone will be the one to mutate. It's *that* single change, rather than Sir Keith not dying in a car crash, which alters the events and prevents cataclysm. However obsessed or obnoxious Stahlman may have been, it's finally an act of humanity which makes it possible for the Doctor and Greg to stop penetration zero.

Pertwee is in his element here, smashing up the computer with fury when "our" stuffy little Earth can't acknowledge just how much danger it's in. (Which is fair enough – the last time he was in the centre, he seemed content mostly to make jokes about the boss' liver, and siphon off nuclear power for himself.) And his reflection upon free will is beautifully done.

And suddenly, that's Season Seven over! I'm not used to seasons being so short. The black and white ones used to go on for ages – and now these new-fangled colour ones come along, and everybody needs a rest after a mere 25 weeks. Bah! It's been an incredible season,

actually. It's tonally unlike anything Doctor Who has ever attempted before. The stories are complex and bursting with humanity and *point*; we're a world away from monster escapades and new planets, and it's the first time a series has aired since the very first without relying upon established baddies popping up every few stories as a crutch.

I loved it. Of course I did. I'm 39 years old. I don't think Doctor Who has ever seemed so adult. And I'm a little sad that Inferno marks the end of that... that next time Jon Pertwee pops on to our screen, it'll be in a series which feels much more recognisable, something of a fantasy for family viewing. But I also must say I'm not entirely sure where the series could go from here. I don't think it needs to be another Doomwatch, or another Quatermass – its appeal to me *is* that innocence that allows it to speak to small children as much to wrinkly old sods like Toby Hadoke. So I'm looking forward now to popping on Terror of the Autons. Where UNIT will be friendlier and make mugs of cocoa, where the Doctor's sidekick won't be an *assistant* but a *companion*. Season Seven has been a thrilling, brilliant experiment, and Doctor Who is immeasurably the richer for it. But I shan't be sad to see it get its sense of fun back.

T: Bloody hell, why is it that Press Night audiences are always the bastards? I don't understand – the two most turgid nights I've done (well, apart from Maidstone, but I'll treat that like The Feast of Steven's "Merry Christmas to all of you at home" moment and pretend it never happened) have been bloody Press Night here and bloody Press Night in London. Good old ordinary paying punters pitch in and enjoy themselves, but the sods who get in free seem to be too cool for school when it comes to letting go and having fun.

Bloody critics.

Well, if I had a first night that wasn't representative of my show, Inferno's curtain call is similarly anomalous. The Doctor spends the first ten minutes in a coma, and the drama revolves around whether or not our second tier-heroes will take the advice of this rambling Rip van Winkle. Having climaxed with the end of a world last week, it must have been difficult for them to top it. And to be brutally frank, they haven't.

It doesn't help that the Doctor, upon waking up, acts like the ranting loon Stahlman has accused him of being all story. There's a lot of talk, and it's a less-gutsy repeat of what happened in the alternative reality. Previously, when Slocum got infected by the slime (under Douglas Camfield's direction), you could *feel* and see the heat emanating from the menacing substance as the soundtrack seared, painfully, into our ears. This week, under Barry Letts, Olaf Pooley dips his hands into some swarfega and spreads it on his face a bit. It has to be said, too, that despite Sir Keith's triumph, the project still can't be brought to a halt without Stahlman's say-so – so everyone spends ages prevaricating about this until the mutated professor appears and growls at them. So let me get this straight... if he hadn't accelerated his own Primord transformation, the project would have continued and he'd have achieved his goal, whereupon Earth would have died in fire. He sabotaged his own plan! And so the moral of this story is look before you leap (into a pile of green goo).

Even so, Inferno remains a brilliant story. Yes, its final instalment has been comparatively muted, but that's been true of each of the three Season Seven epics – probably *because* they've all been epics, charting territory more complex and interesting than usual. And little touches such as the countdown stopping with 35 seconds to go show Doctor Who being almost wilful in its rejection of both the genre's tropes and its own. Inferno represents the most adult the programme has been to date, and this is a good thing. When I was a kid, I didn't want to be Wesley Crusher, or Boxey, or Luke Skywalker – I liked the grown-up characters, and the situations where cool adults did cool aduly things. So I don't think my adoration of this is down to me being a grown-up who doesn't require whimsy in the way an excitable, dreamy child might. This is the sort of Who I was *desperate* for as a kid – gutsy, exciting, believable and tough. Season Seven is like Doctor Who, but it's a slightly tougher and less compromising version: a version we'll never see anything quite like again. Perhaps it nipped over from an alternative reality.

Terror of the Autons (episode one)

R: Woooah! Now *that's* a change in tone.

Doctor Who is back! And this time, it's behaving a bit like a small child that's overdosed on fizzy drink. It's running about all over the place, pulling us by the sleeve, showing us things which are new and sparkly, before seconds later getting bored of them and wanting to show us different things altogether. We jump about from circuses! To museum thefts! To radio telescopes! To plastic factories! Jo Grant no sooner decides to compile a list of such plastic factories, than we jump cut to her getting caught spying at one, than we jump cut to her under hypnosis receiving instructions from the Master. There's a whole heap of new characters to understand, and new settings to make sense of. And, well, we *don't*, really. Because just as we begin to think we might be getting into the groove – that we're following the rules of this particular story – a Time Lord with a bowler hat will materialise in thin air, or a man will be found shrunken inside his own lunch box.

It's strange and gaudy, this new Doctor Who. But it feels too like a mission statement. Last year was composed of long seven-part epics, all of them set at scientific establishments. This time, the pace is so zippy it's almost *daring* us to keep up. We don't open at a nuclear power station or a space centre, but a *circus*, with lions and clowns and everything. And the first bit of science we see is a joke, the TARDIS blowing out smoke as the Doctor sings he doesn't want to set the world on fire. When we finally get to the radio telescope, to a setting we'd recognise from Season Seven, the first conversation we hear isn't about cyclotrons or penetration zeroes, but a man moaning about his wife's predilection for boiled eggs.

I don't think Doctor Who has ever so consciously changed its very style between seasons. And by repeating the structure of Season Seven, by opening with a four-part Auton story, it seems deliberately to be asking a comparison to be made. Katy Manning gives a performance that is so far removed from the adult companion offered by Liz Shaw, it can't but help look mannered and childish. This isn't someone who took General Science at school, it's someone who is barely qualified to walk and talk at the same time. Mike Yates is the first UNIT soldier we see who seems positively *stupid*; he's required to do two things this episode (describe what a Nestene is, and get the attention of the telescope director), and can't do either. This is a reformatting of the series' backdrop to its most juvenile. Look at the way, too, that the Nestenes finally *are* described. In Spearhead from Space, they were denied any individuality, which was quite an alien idea – here, they're big octopi. Yeah, big octopi will make the kids squirm, because they're ugly – but the original idea was so much more subtly horrific.

And yet. There's a brashness to the episode that wins me over. It has that sense of humour I've been looking for. I love Michael Wisher's pathetic factory director (he's not yet playing a Kaled, but a Farrel) – he's been called *Rex*, for God's sake, it's the name you give a *dog*. Robert Holmes will be criticised later for the way, as script editor, he takes the mystique from the Time Lords, but having one pop up dressed as a parody of a commuter is the first instance we can see of him puncturing that particular bubble – and it *works* too, it's so odd that it's actually funny. In the one sequence when she's allowed to play for laughs, when after knocking over some crates she says hello to the men she's been hiding from, Katy Manning reveals a comic timing that's charming.

And then there's the Master. With all the comic book brightness, all the rushing about, Roger Delgado is commanding and authoritative precisely because he *knows* when to stand still and shut up. Every word he says counts, every movement he makes is calculated. When he hears Professor Philips rush up to find him in the control room, he simply moves into position, he in no way tries to hide – and that's so much more powerful than anything else we see in the episode. However loud and gaudy this is, it works because it makes Delgado seem all the more sinister in contrast.

T: This was the first Pertwee story I got on video. I'd seen The Five Faces of Doctor Who repeats and the like, but this was the first third Doctor tale I could watch over and over again and scrutinise. As I think I've mentioned, when I first got old stories, they were often disappointing because they failed to match the images created by my fevered imaginings. Characters who seemed brilliant on the page were crushing disappointments on telly. Take Mike Yates, for example – "Mike" was such a tough-sounding, big beefcake army name to my nine-year-old imagination, I hadn't imagined him as this rather breezy, chipper fella with posh diction, and the least butch voice since Jimmy Somerville. It was rare that I'd finish an initial viewing of a story entirely satisfied, and it was only on repeated attempts that I'd begin to enjoy an adventure on its own terms.

Which is to say: everyone has a story whose popularity they find baffling, and Terror of the Autons was mine for quite some time. The only, *only* thing that exceeded my expectations on first viewing is the first thing seen here: Delgado's Master. He doesn't put a foot wrong – he's economical, suave, menacing and brilliant. He's such an instant presence, the episode belongs to him. He can even click his fingers whilst wearing leather gloves, which takes class.

It's a shame that it took me so long to warm up to this story, because there *is* a lot to enjoy in Robert Holmes' script. I like that the Brigadier decides that if the Doctor wants his new assistant gone, he has to sack her himself... which, of course, he's incapable of doing. Holmes also has a laugh at the perceived image of the Time Lords by presenting their messenger as an eccentric city gent (a witty turn from David Garth). And it's not just the Doctor's supposedly god-like people who are on the receiving end of the writer's iconoclasm – he even pokes fun at the show's hero himself when we discover that, back in the day, the Master beat the Doctor academically. I like that – it's important that the Doctor is clever, but not necessarily at taking tests or sitting papers. He's not an establishment figure, swotting away and sucking up to teacher – he's the flawed genius who flies by the skin of his teeth, getting through on innate talent and improvisation.

And, playing to the strengths of a TV story versus one in print, there are some neat directorial touches. The radio telescope is given an impressive sense of scale, and I love the close-up of Harry Towb's twitchy hand as McDermott makes a call to head office and asks to be put through to Farrell Sr. The CSO shot of a shrunken Goodge in his lunch box is excellent (and it's a witty piece of casting too, with Andrew Staines' bald, egg-head appearance perhaps an explanation for his wife's obsession with them), and it's a great little detail that the radio telescope director doesn't acknowledge anyone when he's first introduced (the Doctor returns him the favour later).

That said, I'm really not sure about the insult the Doctor levels at Jo ("You ham-fisted bun vendor!"), and the cliffhanger – with its stupid smoking bomb box – is nonsense. Oh, there I go, looking for fault. Everyone's a bloody critic. And you know what I think of them.

May 19th

Terror of the Autons (episode two)

R: "You've got a very distorted sense of humour, haven't you?" The deaths are great fun. The dispatch of Harry Towb by plastic armchair injects a wonderfully cruel streak of black humour into the series; the sequence works because it's both extremely nasty and ridiculously funny all at the same time. The way in which Rex judges the effectiveness of his death, or checks with his secretary for details on McDermott's unemployment entitlement, is so cool that you cannot help but laugh. And if the death by troll doll isn't *quite* as effective as it could be, it's nevertheless a sequence conceived in the same vein. You can't take the murder of Mr Farrel entirely seriously – he's a pompous middle-class windbag, whose judgment on the Master is that he "couldn't quite take to the fellow", and whose last act in life is to settle down in his armchair with his newspaper whilst his wife perkily goes to the kitchen to make some coffee. What's funny about the Farrels is that they moan on and on about the cold way in which their son Rex reacted to McDermott's death – and yet it's quite clear that the sudden heart failure of an employee who has worked as his second in command for many years is of absolutely no consequence to Farrel Sr either, and he's much more concerned about his son asserting himself against his will. It's wonderfully apt that

Farrel meets his end at the hands of a grotesque little plastic doll – and that final image of the troll scurrying away on its two little legs after it's committed the awful deed is hilarious.

It's not subtle stuff. But it's like that troll doll – it takes the form of something you'd associate with children, a live-action cartoon, but it's so warped out of shape that it feels unsettling and dissonant. As a contrast to the more thoughtful and heartfelt morality plays we saw during Season Seven, Terror of the Autons looks shallow and spiteful. It's a cruel joke of an adventure, a bad smell. And that's rather why I like it – because there's a satirical edge to its take on consumer industry that's entirely missing from the more stoic Spearhead from Space. Ultimately, McDermott and Farrel react the same way to the thing which kills them; they reject it because they don't think it'll *sell*. In Spearhead, there was a certain uncritical wonder shown towards the plastic waxworks that were being made – here, in its garish sequel, the Master plans to destroy the world by flooding it with lots of cheap shiny tat.

T: Robert Holmes displays some of the flourishes that will make him the acme of Doctor Who writers, but not always successfully. You mention Rex's funny "termination of employment" gag, but unfortunately it requires Michael Wisher to drop completely out of character just for the sake of the joke, so I'm not sure I approve. The Master's description of McDermott's demise is better ("He sat down in this chair here, and... just slipped away"), and terribly funny because Delgado plays it dead straight. The best stuff, however, is the witty exchange between Rossini and the Doctor in the caravan, which is full of one-upmanship. (The Doctor: "How much is [the Master] paying you?", Rossini: "Come, come, Doctor, gentlemen never discuss money", the Doctor: "Nonsense, gentlemen never talk about anything else.") But the circus types have brawn as well as brains: Rossini thwacks the Doctor with a particularly hefty piece of wood at one point, and en masse they don't half pile in to engage in fisticuffs. It's a good job Pertwee was mates with the Roberts Brothers and secured their services, as the depiction of these folk as a vicious mob of money grabbers is hardly flattering.

Whilst Terror of the Autons is too colourful to be the nightmare-fest promised by everything I'd read about it as a child, it still has some shocking moments – notably the way the camera lingers on Farrell Sr's kicking feet as the doll throttles him to death. Professor Philips' murder (he's hypnotised by the Master, then killed during a botched attempt to blow up the Doctor) is efficiently sold to us just by the sickened expression on Katy Manning's face and a trickle of blood on the man's wrist. And while some scenes have a bit too much talking, we do get a nifty explosion as a bomb goes off in a moat (is UNIT headquartered in some kind of castle this week?). I'm becoming wary of how taken the production seems to be with CSO, though, to look at Mrs Farrell's CSO kitchen. Nothing dates quicker than new technology.

By the way, all the reviews of my show were terribly good, so, um, ignore all those rude things I said about reviewers. And yes, I'm aware of the irony of my moaning about reviewers whilst writing a whole book consisting of reviews. For this episode, I was going to write about how surely nobody would buy something like the Auton Doll... until I remembered a mini-craze for troll dolls when I was a kid. They weren't as ugly as the one seen here, though, and they had a shock of hair that you could mould into all sorts of whacky styles. (Look, it was before computers – we had to amuse ourselves somehow.)

Terror of the Autons (episode three)

R: Of course you had good reviews for your show, Toby, because you're brilliant. But just wait until you see what they'll be writing about you in painstaking diary form forty years later...

There's a really clever bit of misdirection here from Robert Holmes: we sit through a scene in which Jo and Mike get threatened by the troll doll, so laboriously constructed that it barely offers a threat at all. And then, in the very next scene, he hits us with the sequence of an Auton hidden in a safe – there's no build-up to it, no Dudley Simpson music, just the shock of a killer coming out at you. That's the teasing nature of this story; it's all about lulling

you into a false sense of security. You think you get what tone any individual scene is playing on, and the style you take for granted comes back to bite you. Take, for example, that scene in which poor widowed Mrs Farrel tells the Doctor about Colonel Masters. As soon as his name is mentioned, Simpson starts to play his already familiar Master theme – which runs into the next scene, as we see a chipper mechanic install a new telephone to the Doctor's lab. We *assume* it's just a run-on, but actually the theme is there to tell us that this new character is really the Master in disguise.

Sometimes I think the comedy might be just a bit *too* clever. There's a wonderful send-up of the awful cheapness of seventies crap, when Rex gazes at one of the daffodils and eulogises dreamily that it's the best artificial flower he's ever seen. But I don't think that Delgado is in on the joke – when he replies in kind that his object is to show the world the skill of the modern plastics industry, he says it entirely without irony! But I do think that the best way to take this story is as a particularly skewed series of jokes. When Jo Grant starts gushing on the phone to Mr Campbell, we cut to the troll doll looking on impassively, as if it can't quite believe she's called Campbell her dolly Scotsman either.

And it *is* very eerie. Some of the special effects don't live up to the intent, but producing a story where virtually anything that's synthetic can be turned into a deadly weapon uses the plastic motif far more inventively than Spearhead from Space did. The telephone wire that tries to strangle the Doctor in the cliffhanger looks a bit ropey, but it's just one more great idea – armchairs, toys, even bits of rubbish given out free with soap, all of them are household objects that can rise up against you without warning. They're merely stooges this time for the Master, yes, and giving them crackly voices feels a bit off – but the Autons are great, nonetheless. Those opening few minutes of the episode with the two policemen trying to shoot the Doctor and Jo are extremely tense – and, best of all, having been knocked down a sharp incline by Yates in a fantastic stunt, one of them begins to climb back up the hill again without a second's pause for breath. They are impressively remorseless, and there is something disturbingly surreal about the sight of a policeman with his hand as a gun searching for victims with his unmasked brother.

T: I know we're supposed to be accentuating the positive, but the story is now making it very difficult for me to do so. This episode starts off superbly, I'll grant you – two policemen (one without a face!) remorselessly track our heroes through a quarry, with those superbly conceived (and literal) handguns. Then, the Brig arrives with Captain Yates and the UNIT equivalent of a Star Trek Red Shirt in a superbly action-packed sequence, culminating in a marvellous stunt where Terry Walsh's Auton tumbles over and over down a very steep slope. This whole section is only temporarily undone when Richard Franklin (as Captain Yates) shows that he is as accomplished at "manly running" as Nick Courtney is at fisticuffs, but I quibble.

And I must credit Robert Holmes for once again displaying great economy – he introduces the plastic flowers, then cuts straight to their distribution, and juxtaposes the smiling, oversized alien bonces of the Autons with the normality of the everyday high street. Actually, I like the disguised Autons rather a lot – they're a simple design, whose big smiles and sunny colours belie their menacing intent. Underneath their masks, the Autons' featureless, dead eyed, blank faces are more blatantly terrifying, and – to look at this – it's no surprise Russell T Davies chose to relaunch Doctor Who with these baddies, as they are timelessly unnerving (not to mention cheap).

Where things fall down for me is that we're made to endure the Doctor being totally dislikable in his clubbish, elitist trouncing of the civil servant Brownrose (whose name is, I assume, a rather funny joke). Colin Baker gets accused of pomposity, but at least the joke is on him sometimes – by contrast, Pertwee's priggish dressing down of Brownrose, who has legitimate concerns about a wave of unexplained deaths, has to be my least favourite Doctor moment thus far. I'm also no great fan of that risible scene where Jo and Yates make cocoa with the Doctor's Bunsen Burner (!) and so activate the troll doll by mistake. The horrific is now being sold to us in a wacky manner – or, to put it another way, the plausible menace of Inferno is being sacrificed for jolly japes

with Jo and Yates. It's all a bit too gaudy and, well, plastic.

Actually, I think I've just hit upon this story's problem overall: the ideas are very rich, yes, but they're *so* potentially terrifying, playing true to their nature would have resulted in something unsuitable for even post-Watershed viewers. The doll that kills, the Auton in the safe, the killer telephone flex: giving this the hard-edged Inferno treatment would have resulted in a nation of bed wetters. And, while there are a couple of exceptions, the sparse soundtrack and sweaty edginess are mostly gone. When the threats manifest themselves, Dudley Simpson's music is all zingy seventies pop, as if he's been specifically charged with undermining the horror (apart from the rightly lauded Master theme, and some spare, scratchy, clicking noises accompanying the killer Yellow Coat Autons).

One final thing: having stolen the dematerialisation circuit of the Master's TARDIS, the Doctor notes with amusement that he's stranded the villain on Earth. Great... I do hope that saddling us with a murderous psychopath provides him with endless entertainment.

May 20th

Terror of the Autons (episode four)

R: I may be missing the point – I do that – but why exactly would there be a problem with UNIT blowing up the Autons? An awful lot of energy is spent this week with the Doctor battling the Brigadier and his plan to destroy the baddies cleanly with a single missile. And there really seems to be no adequate reason given why this would be considered hasty, or ill-advised, or amoral. Instead, it just feels a bit like the production team is resorting to tried and tested stances that the characters adopt. If there's an attempt at ambiguity here, akin to the ethical struggle shown in Doctor Who and the Silurians, then I really can't see it.

So this is an episode composed of false jeopardies and false endings. The conclusion is much-derided, of course, in which the Master suddenly helps the Doctor defeat the Nestene invasion simply because it hasn't *occurred* to him that it's an unreasoning big space octopus thing. But I'm prepared to buy it, simply because the one thing this episode does well is rely upon the immediate rapport between Pertwee and Delgado. The scene where they first meet is wonderful; there's a charm to the encounter, of course, but a real danger too – we have no reason to believe that the Master won't kill the Doctor in cold blood, and we're a long way off the more cosy cliché of their being chummy adversaries. And there's such a spark between the two of them that the awkwardly plotted scene where they join forces as fellow Time Lords has a certain joyous magic to it. Or perhaps I'm just being very forgiving!

I think it's indicative of a greater problem, though. That final scene in which the Doctor beams with satisfaction at the prospect of another encounter with the Master would probably wash in a few stories' time, after the audience at home have accepted him. But at this stage of the game, he's just a one-adventure villain, a psychopath who throws a technician to his death off a radio telescope with almost feral savagery. You can't imagine the Doctor coming out of an encounter with Tobias Vaughn or Eric Klieg telling his companion that he's looking forward to their next encounter – and it seems a rather forced way of telling the viewers that the Master is someone we should have a sneaking affection for. The series hasn't earned that yet, and frankly it makes the Doctor look like an irresponsible bastard. If it wasn't for the skill of Roger Delgado, we'd be shaking our heads at this. God, they could have cast *anybody* – they could have cast Prentis Hancock.

T: There's more action in this than I remembered. The pitched battle between the Toby-jug Autons and camouflaged soldiers is pleasingly packed with explosions and flying bodies, and makes for a strange and exciting Doctor Who image. The battle also showcases HAVOC's value to great effect. And, surely, Rex Farrell's body gets crushed as the Master tries to run the Doctor over? Nasty.

I know it's unusual for me to latch onto action sequences as the key to a strong episode, but, frankly, they're a welcome respite from this story's muddled tone. Just look at the scene after the Brigadier has torn the deadly, Nestene-animated phone flex from around the

Doctor's gurning gob. Nicholas Courtney plays it dead straight, dopily apologising that "I'm afraid I cut off your connection..." I can only assume that Robert Holmes meant the line to be delivered knowingly, especially as the Doctor responds with a chiding "Oh very funny". But with both Courtney and Pertwee judging the scene completely differently, it's neither believable nor amusing.

The *other* great thing that elevates this episode, fortunately, is Roger Delgado. The production team have struck gold with the Delgado Master – he exudes such dignity and charm, he gently chides his nemesis, the Doctor, for not being more composed in the face of death! Likewise, he seems genuinely impressed upon learning that Farrell, his hitherto cowering underling, has overcome his brainwashing and discovered some backbone. It's as if the Master wants his enemies to always be at their best; otherwise, where is the glory in defeating them?

Overall, Terror of the Autons brings to mind the first time I went to someone's house and noticed they had some plastic fruit. I wondered what the point was – it *looked* a bit like fruit, but was, obviously, an overly shiny and hyper-real version of it. It was too gaudy to pass for the real thing, and too tacky to make an attractive decoration. Perhaps Terror of the Autons is deliberately aping the gaudy nature of faux fruit, and its shiny but unsatisfying style is a clever choice to echo the script's thematic concerns... but I doubt it.

The Mind of Evil (episode one)

R: This is an odd one, isn't it? "Looks like Dracula's castle", says Jo in the first scene, and then the Doctor prats about in front of a camera – and we could easily believe we were either going to be watching an atmospheric horror or some light-hearted spoof. So what we then get is a considerable surprise; that sequence of the convict Barnham being taken terror-stricken from his cell, with all the other prisoners kicking up a riot in response, and all those polite middle-class observers poised like vultures... everything is set up to suggest that the Doctor and Jo have turned up in Bessie to watch someone being fried in the electric chair. And of course that's the cleverness of

Don Houghton's script, that when Professor Kettering begins his speech, it's so he can automatically denounce state-sanctioned execution… whilst clearly offering a treatment which has all the grisly hallmarks of it. Houghton puts the idea of it squarely in the viewers' heads, whilst wagging his finger impishly and telling us we're not looking at anything so horrifying at all. When Barnham has a metal helmet strapped to his head, and the power is turned on, and he screams in fear and pain, we're the closest Doctor Who has ever come to showing us proper capital punishment. And at Saturday teatime, no less!

The subplot features UNIT's first attempts at arranging a peace conference. (Oh, yes, there'll be others.) It reveals why Captain Yates would be the last person you'd want within a hundred miles of an international summit – his views on Captain Chin Lee are enough to provoke World War III straight off… Or perhaps by calling her a "dolly", he's not actually being sexist, but instead suggesting that she's an alien threat. Maybe he thinks she's one of the Autons he fought *last* week! It's a shame, there was a missed opportunity here for a running joke, I think, with Mike Yates being this dense UNIT captain always a story behind everybody else. Whilst everyone else is fighting the Axons, he could be bemusing the Brigadier with his reports about Stangmoor Prison. How we'd all laugh! Or maybe not.

T: During this great experiment (or grand folly, take your pick) of ours, I've stuck diligently to watching Doctor Who stories in consecutive order. Doing two episodes a day, everyday, takes some discipline, and I do have a life to fit in, y'know! The Mind of Evil is an exception, however, as I watched it a couple of months ago in preparation to moderate the DVD commentary. So, it's fresher in my mind than other stories. (And, funnily enough, having dipped into Pertwee during my Troughton adventures, I've just been asked to have another butchers at The Dominators for commentary duties when I return to the UK.)

Despite the familiarity granted by my recent rewatch, however, this is much more my cup of tea than Terror of the Autons. It's a cleverly constructed script, building up its menace and mystery (how *can* a man drown in a dry

room?), in a realistic world where people refer to each other either by their Christian name or title, depending on their relationship. Lots of overlapping telephone dialogue suggests the bustle of organising the peace conference, whilst the prisoners' noisy defiance as the Keller Machine starts its work creates an effectively febrile atmosphere.

Crucial to all of this is Timothy Combe, a terrific director who – despite his only overseeing this story and Doctor Who and the Silurians – should be more celebrated. He casts good, solid, unshowy actors such as Raymond Westwell (playing the prison governor), Simon Lack (Professor Kettering) and Roy Purcell (Chief Prison Officer Powers); they lend a realism to the more outlandish ideas on display here. Combe also – rather cleverly – has his camera roving around both in the studio and on location, shooting through railings or from other interesting perspectives. There's a great high angled shot as the Keller process starts, and the machine's throbbing is overlaid onto Chin-Lee's pyromania.

By now, I can't help but note that one's attitude to Pertwee's rudeness depends upon the person he's directing it at. It's great that he calls the Keller rubberneckers a "morbid lot of sensation seekers"… but he doesn't do himself any favours with his constant barrage of snide comments at Kettering's expense, does he? Yes, it just so happens that the Doctor will be proved right about the Keller machine, but it's telling that Kettering's response to the Doctor's mocking ("For the benefit of the less sophisticated members of my audience, I shall explain in very simple terms…") uses some of the Doctor's own words to Cornish in The Ambassadors of Death!

And, a word for perennial Doctor Who guest star Michael Sheard. This is one of his least celebrated performances, probably because he gets showier turns in the likes of Pyramids of Mars and Castrovalva. This relatively humble role makes clear *why* he shows up so often – he really was a very good character actor. His performance as Dr Summers is very unassuming, plausible and pitch-perfect. Sheard may have attended every convention going, and written three million volumes of autobiography, but that shouldn't take away from the fact that he was damned good at his job, and rightly proud of his association with our favourite show. I am happy to celebrate him for that.

Oh, one last thing... I may be naive, but I too have to question Mike's "She's a dolly" line. Apart from making me want to punch him, are they seriously trying to suggest he's a heterosexual?

May 21st

The Mind of Evil (episode two)

R: The Mind of Evil fascinates because it feels very much like the synthesis of the darker and edgier seventh season and the lighter approach the series is beginning to adopt. The Brigadier is here functioning as straight man for the Doctor's jokes – and Nicholas Courtney is already perfecting his line in long-suffering facial expressions, the scene where he's ignored by the Chinese delegate being especially amusing. But when Benton is blown out for letting Chin Lee escape, it is not followed by the twinkle-in-eye-shot that will be mandatory soon. And when Yates is sent to pick up the Doctor from Stangmoor Prison, his tactless demand that the Doctor should accompany him is met with an angry display of Venusian karate. Yes, overall there is a softening of the way UNIT are presented, but at this stage they're still wholly credible as a military organisation. When the Brigadier assures the Doctor he'll blow up the Keller Machine himself if necessary, you firmly believe him.

And the Master's reintroduction is nicely done too. In his limousine, puffing on a cigar and casually ordering the death of the American delegate, Delgado suggests more authority than he was allowed in his debut story – even the way he pulls Chin Lee's face towards him suggests a brutality just beneath the surface. It's peculiar to see, in his scenes disguised as telephone mechanic (he does like playing people who work for British Telecom, doesn't he?), that this time he's quite obviously wearing a mask. It's a shame, really – Norman Stanley, who portrayed the incognito Master in the previous story, might have become something of a series regular otherwise. It oughtn't to work, but Timothy Combe shoots the scene

so that it seems there's something creepy about the mechanic's face, as if it's lumpen and misshaped, rather than being the worst disguise a supervillain has ever attempted.

There's an awful lot going on here, isn't there? Prison breaks, missile convoys and political assassinations. I love all that; it's refreshing that we get to see UNIT as an organisation important enough that it has more than one crisis at once to deal with. (Frankly, the Doctor's insistence that there's a causal link between all the different storylines makes him rather a spoilsport.)

Were we really so naive back in 1971 to suggest that Mao Tse-Tung could be a personal friend of the Doctor's? It does sound very peculiar nowadays, like the Doctor namedropping about Stalin or Pol Pot. I'm no expert on Hokkien – which is perhaps the single largest understatement I've yet written in this diary – but I'm impressed that Jon Pertwee got through it all so confidently. It's his best performance so far this season; he reveals a vulnerability in his scene recovering from the Keller Machine that is extraordinary and streets away from the dashing man of action we'll come to know. And his exhausted anger at Jo for disobeying his instructions is very believable too – she's not yet his best friend, but his mildly irritating assistant.

T: I'm feeling a bit hypocritical today... I so often laud Doctor Who because it *isn't* a formulaic, Earthbound drama, but instead offers something imaginative, fantastical and otherworldly. And yet, I love how The Mind of Evil makes its down-to-Earth elements as realistic as possible. After all, if you're going to maroon the Doctor in a contemporary setting, you need to sell his surroundings with utter realism – otherwise, I won't buy the threat level. I do buy it here, though, thanks to a number of elements such as Dudley Simpson's deep, menacing score; the moody, pulsing lighting in the Chinese delegate's room; and the presence of industrial amounts of hardware.

Once again, Tim Combe's stark, gritty location camerawork is effective, as he shoots John Levene – who looks good, returning to his cloak-and-dagger persona from The Invasion – through the railings as he collapses. The hard-edged elements are so successful, in fact,

I don't mind the odd cosy moment between the regulars, such as the Brig scolding Yates for grinning like a Cheshire Cat, and the Doctor later ribbing him for it. If poor old Nicholas Courtney's dignity is undermined by a slightly protracted stint as the comedy stooge, it's counter balanced by fellow regular Roger Delgado languidly assuming the aspect of a Bond villain. With Delgado on hand to be so mesmerisingly, charmingly wicked, any niggles vanish.

And while Don Houghton is doing some great work with the script (I love Summers' postulation that the Keller process has made Barnham become "an idiot... or a saint"), he's being a bit cheeky, isn't he? The cliffhanger's premise suggests that Houghton's previous script – in which, to be fair, a whole world was destroyed by fire – is the one that confronted the Doctor with his greatest *ever* fear. With such lack of modesty on show, it's a good job Ian Stuart Black didn't write this – otherwise the Doctor would be writhing, haunted by nightmare visions of Captain Edal, producer John Wiles, and WOTAN having the audacity to refer to our hero as "Doctor Who"...

The Mind of Evil (episode three)

R: Now here's an odd cliffhanger. The Doctor is subjected to the Keller Machine again – only this time it's not fire he sees, and a connection back a whole two stories ago to the events of Inferno. Instead, we get a whole parade of old monsters from the series' past!... Okay, you can't actually make out what most of them are, and they're just static pictures flung at the screen. And I had to look up in one of the thousand reference books to find out that one of them's Koquillion, for God's sake. But nevertheless, it's the first time in this new, bright colourful version of Doctor Who that we're given a reminder that it's the same programme in which Hartnell faced down the Daleks and the War Machines. There's a blue police box in the corner, it's true, but that doesn't travel anywhere any longer, and we've got UNIT, but they only appeared at the fag end of the Troughton years. At last we've got something to link Jon Pertwee back to a time when we hadn't heard of Time Lords, when the idea of the Doctor working for the military and

driving a car to work would have seemed impossible. Seeing The Mind of Evil out of order, the sequence doesn't seem very special. But in context, watching all these stories one after the other, that reaching back to acknowledge the past seems to me terribly moving.

Especially as it's taking place in such a very atypical story! There's an unusual grittiness to the scenes in the prison; William Marlowe's Harry Mailer has much of the same power as William Dysart's Reegan last year, inasmuch as he's a contemporary thug who's fully credible. The difference is that whereas Dysart charmed, Marlowe does anything but – and that's part of the character's impact. When you have Delgado in the background being charismatic, the contrast between him and Mailer is particularly pronounced. In a story that purports to be about evil, the depiction of a man who's basically lowlife contemptible is very welcome. I love the way Mailer seems to recoil from even the sight of Barnham, a man who has had all the evil sucked out of him and been turned into a holy fool.

Let me also add a round of applause for fan-favourite Michael Sheard, in what's become one of his rather forgotten roles. As Dr Summers, he shows the frightened courage of an ordinary man, and the only supporting character who has a shred of moral doubt as to what is taking place. With the soldiers all stamping about acting like spies, the convicts throwing bombs everywhere and the Doctor chatting in Chinese, Sheard manages to give the story the sober reflection it needs.

T: I haven't mentioned Katy Manning much, have I, or Pertwee of late? They have such a comfy rapport, it's all too-easy to take for (pardon the punnage) granted. Every time I think Manning's feisty kid's TV presenter shtick is a poor relation to Caroline John's no-nonsense scientist, Manning shoots out that winning smile or does something plucky, and I'm hooked. Jo is brave, keen and resourceful (notice how she's the one who scuppers the prison riot). As for Pertwee... he has presence and dignity alongside his pomposity, and can seemingly break any awkward situation with a twitchy, beaming grin. His treatment of Chin-Lee displays a warm, reassuring paternalism, and he pulls off the Doctor's skill with languages very convincingly.

On the side of devils, we have two *even more* estimable performances. Delgado, exquisite as the businesslike villain, is equally plausible when passing himself off as the noble Professor Keller. He's so stylish that even when he scrabbles on the floor during a skirmish with the Doctor, he immediately gets bolt upright and smoothes out his creases with quick precision. And the way in which the Master amplifies the Keller Machine's energies directly into the Doctor's brain is pretty damned nasty, no matter how courteous and low key he is about it.

Also, the chippy "everyman" colloquialisms that Don Houghton bestowed last time out upon Greg Sutton here give William Marlowe's Mailer an edgy, tough believability. Marlowe is cold and professional, staring threateningly at Pertwee and making to clobber him should he try anything. I thought Reegan in Ambassadors was a piece of work, but Mailer's quite the nastiest thug we've yet seen: just watch as he shoots down the senior prison officers and the governor (though the depiction of the latter's death is uncharacteristically muddled).

And am I wrong in thinking there must be some long-lost BBC memo praising designer Ray London's skill with right angles? From the evidence of his three Doctor Who stories, London had a little cottage industry going as the BBC's "box man". Need some boxed-shaped War Machines? Get Ray. After a box-shaped Kroton? London's calling! Now you need a Pandora's Box of alien evil? Well, guess who's top of the list?

May 22nd

The Mind of Evil (episode four)

R: This is where the relationship between the Doctor and the Master is truly cemented. The frightened concern with which the Master treats the Doctor, finding with a stethoscope that one of his hearts has stopped beating, and beating his chest until it starts once more, is the foundation on which an entire mythology can rest. It's that realisation that in trying to torture his adversary to prove he has the upper hand, the Master has simply gone too far. The

Doctor's weary defeatism, that he *can't* resist the mind parasite, is countered by the Master's urging that they withstand its force simply by dint of being Time Lords – and, for the first time, we believe in that connection between the two of them. The scene where the Master arrogantly tries to confront his slave creature, only to be presented with an image of a giant Doctor laughing mockingly at him, is beautifully done; in seeing that what the Master most fears is the judgment of our hero, we're actually made to feel sorry for him. And Timothy Combe brilliantly establishes a link between the two; that sequence where we segue from the face of the exhausted Doctor, weakened by the machine attack, to the face of the Master, painfully trying to recover from the same thing, is very smart.

And the most surprising result of all this is that a strange-looking box that makes a funny sound effect genuinely does, by the episode's end, inspire dread. It's a great twist that the machine has learned to move by itself (complete with a wibbly wobbly special effect that is so distorted it makes your eyes go funny when you look at it, and just about manages therefore to be unnerving rather than simply cheap). It really ought to look ridiculous, all these convicts clutching their heads in terror, and shooting their guns at something that looks like kitchenware bought off the shopping channel – but it's so weird that it really works.

Haydn Jones' Vosper makes for a particularly nasty piece of work. If Mailer has no charm, then his underling has neither charm nor authority, just a bullying loutishness. His amusement at the Doctor's frailty, and the callous way that he jokes with Dr Summers that he should send his medical bill, is the spiteful humour of a playground bully who grew into an adult. It's a memorable performance from a minor character.

T: *What* an episode this is! The Doctor's heart stops! The Master is so overcome by the mind-parasite, he has to lock it away! It learns to teleport! Yates gets shot! Benton gets seriously injured! They make a static phallus box seem like a terrifying abomination! This isn't any old episode four, plodding its way towards the climax; it's one of the most action-packed and dramatic Doctor Who episodes so far. Don Houghton really knows how to take the drama up a notch, even if he's not massively advancing the plot.

Such action takes its toll on the characters, though. The Doctor looks absolutely bushed; it's impressive that this most confident of Doctors isn't afraid to show us that he's not invulnerable, and that he admits defeat. The Keller Machine alien must be pretty powerful for our hero to concede that it's too powerful for him – or indeed anybody – to withstand. Delgado also skirts around the creature with a steely caution, and acts plausibly terrified without losing his dignity. I also like the way he seems genuinely approving of his muscle-bound lackeys, wishing them luck before the ambush. Marlowe remains a glowering, threatening presence, even thwacking the semi-conscious Doctor on the back of the neck as he chucks him into the prison cell.

This is such a roller-coaster of excitement, in fact, that we're also treated to the well-staged hi-jacking of the Thunderbolt nerve-gas missile (which is an actual missile!), HAVOC letting slip the dogs, loads of impressive stunts and both Yates and Benton being spattered with their own blood. What a bravura production this is... I wouldn't be surprised if Timothy Combe elects to have a scene involving the kitchen sink next week.

The Mind of Evil (episode five)

R: And as a bit of late light relief, Patrick Godfrey does a splendid turn as the boffinish Major Cosworth. Rather sweetly, he acts as a character who doesn't *know* he's supposed to be minor – perplexing the Brigadier somewhat by suddenly coming up with plans, and answering the rhetorical questions he gives the troops. So there's a wonderful moment when Sgt Benton reports back for duty, wanting to be on the assault at the prison and have a bash at the men who put him in hospital – Godfrey stands there awkwardly in the background, realises he's been supplanted, that John Levene is the *real* recurring comic sidekick, and then shuffles out of everybody's way. Aww, it fair breaks your heart.

As does the gorgeous scene in the cell between the Doctor and Jo. The way that Jo tries to make the best of a bad situation, being chirpy and optimistic, and finding some food for them to share from the floor, is surprisingly moving. And you can see the sullen and beaten Doctor warming to her, and being coaxed out of his misery – they click their mugs of water as if it's wine, and the Doctor finds the enthusiasm to tell her some tall story about Sir Walter Raleigh. And in the space of a minute and a half, you at last understand this new relationship between the Doctor and his new companion, Jo's essential goodness, and her ability to bring out the Doctor's gentler streak. It's brilliantly played by both Pertwee and Manning. And it means that the *next* time we see them, they're in their element, ignoring the bemused Master to finish off a game of draughts.

T: Major Cosworth's small contribution is delightful, and it's terribly witty how he likens attacking the prison to making a film – especially as the battle to retake the prison is quite excellent... and on film! Speaking of which, HAVOC pulls out all the stops here, with falls, deaths and a particularly painful-looking tumble down some stone steps. The sequences of the prisoners firing their guns and dying in close-up are thrilling – and all the more impressive, since cheap remounts were needed when the original footage was damaged. And, it's neat how Dudley Simpson scores these action scenes with an electronic version of his theme for The Ambassadors of Death.

But however good the action is, the principal actors' chemistry is even better. John Levene isn't the best actor in the world, but he's *perfect* as Benton, managing to be heroic, loyal, dependable and a brilliant comic foil. Give Levene a tasty vignette, as they do here, and it's a highlight of the episode. Richard Franklin gets a decent slice of the action too, with an especially nice moment where the Master tells Captain Yates he can stop pretending to be asleep. (He's very respectful and courteous to his enemies, the Master.) Later on, Pertwee and Delgado really sell us on the difficulty of bringing the mind-parasite to heel – combined with very effective lighting, sound and editing, they create some high tension from a potentially silly scene of an actor trying to put a circle of wire onto a box.

Even better than all of the above, however, is William Marlow's seemingly effortless brilliance as Mailer. He's happy enough to carry out brutality as the Master dictates, but he's also willing to stick it to his boss, insisting that the Master keep him in the loop. Mailer's tough amusement at the Doctor's offer to help if the man gives himself up is pretty funny, and an embarrassing repudiation of the Doctor's moral viewpoint. In fact, there are just too many sweet Mailer moments – such as his unease in the "reformed" Barnham's presence, and the way he nastily puckers up to Jo as he exits her cell, the horrible git.

But my favourite Mailer moment? Callous as it might sound, it's when the Master tells the Doctor that if he doesn't follow orders, Jo will be killed – at which point Mailer, every inch the clinical, professional murderer, primes his gun and points it at her. The man isn't a sadist, or some hammy braggart – he's just a merciless killer who'll chop down anything that gets in his way. He should be locked up, he should, where he can no longer be a menace to society. (Oh, wait a minute...)

May 23rd

The Mind of Evil (episode six)

R: If I've had a problem with The Mind of Evil, it's been that it's all but ignored Barnham. There's so much going on in this story – including by now a long-forgotten peace conference – but one of the most intriguing elements was of a hardened criminal who's been turned into a simpleton. It's one thing to have Mailer always order the "zombie" to be taken from his sight whenever he wanders into shot – but it has meant that his role in the story has been massively sidelined. Compare this, say, to the way they handle Tommy in Planet of the Spiders a few years later, when they take the child in an adult's body and put him at the forefront of the drama. There's a similar device used there, too; both are men of purity, and so able to withstand attack that would fell an ordinary person. The difference here, though, is that Barnham pops up as some handy way for the parasite to be tamed. On paper, he's not so much a character as a Get Out of Jail Free

Card – he's a walking, talking sonic screwdriver.

But the device works very well. And that's because of the way this manufactured simpleton makes the people he meets feel so uncomfortable. The Brigadier and Benton are both clearly irritated by his presence, and even the Doctor seems awkward around him, tapping him on the shoulder in the way that all embarrassed uncles do with kids they have nothing to say to. It's Neil McCarthy who sells this so well. He'll smile nervously at Benton over his soup, he too knows he doesn't fit in. Had McCarthy merely played the part as someone "nice", this would all have felt rather bland – but he's still threatening in posture. It's as if his brain may have been restructured to deny the man he's been, but his body won't follow suit. It's a very effective performance – and given great support by Katy Manning, who's been playing Jo Grant as something of a child in adult's clothes too, so seems to find a connection with him. When Barnham is killed, it's only Jo who seems prepared to mourn him. (The Doctor, very tellingly, snaps at her grief out of guilt, and even elicits an apology from her!) Ultimately, the lobotomised criminal is too hot a potato for the production team to let live – or for our characters to acknowledge decently afterwards.

Roger Delgado continues to excel. He seems to rise above the comic antics of this family programme (raising an eyebrow when Benton delightfully answers the phone as Acting Governor, or when the Doctor imitates Bessie in dumb show). And the deadpan works beautifully because just as he seems to be behaving as straight man, he'll shock us with a moment of viciousness, in the way that he runs over Barnham. At the end of the last story, the Doctor declares himself rather looking forward to his next encounter with the Master, as if the feud is something to be relished. At the end of this one, having undergone repeated bouts of torture in what must surely be one of the most brutal stories yet transmitted, he's a little less cheery about the prospect of a return match. That's why The Mind of Evil stands out: Doctor Who is reinventing itself as a child-friendly romp, but this is the story which refuses to follow that new brief too closely. It's a curious and slightly awkward mix of two different house styles, the grimmer tone of Season Seven meshed with something much more cosy. And it makes it all the better – a story so full of ideas, a story so jarring in tone, that it keeps you on the edge of your seat, wondering what it'll pop out with next.

T: Yes, poor Barnham. His death is very moving, especially when you consider that virtually everyone, including his fellow nice-but-dim lunkhead Sgt Benton, ignores him throughout the episode. I think it's quite clever, showing how we allow ourselves to feel threatened by something benign if it causes us social embarrassment. Neil McCarthy makes Barnham both innocent and nervous, playing upon our emotions until he dies needlessly, after showing pity to someone as evil as the Master. Some people, it seems, are just too good to get along in this world.

And isn't it curious that, even though we're finally shown the pulsing alien mass within the Keller Machine, it's atypical among Doctor Who monsters in that it isn't given verbal articulation by a third party, and cannot interact like a latex-enhanced Equity member. It's just a silent box of death, the sort of menace that needs a director such as Timothy Combe to make it seem powerful – just watch the scene where the creature's efforts to break free are illustrated with just a few giddy zooms, a brilliant combination of light and sound and some hurled chairs. Even the extremely simple realisation of the creature inside the machine is effective (sometimes we forget: less is more).

Time to wrap things up with some fannish trivia. Dave Carter's prison officer gets killed for what must be about the twelfth time this story, and I suspect that Dr Summers is the only male character to have worn a cardigan in the entire history of Doctor Who. I shall try to confirm or deny this by keeping 'em peeled for a repeat occurrence – sad, I know, but that's just how my mind works...

The Claws of Axos (episode one)

R: I love Pigbin Josh. There, I admit it. I love the fact, for a start, that he's actually *called* Pigbin Josh. Obviously, it's only on the credits – poor old Piggie (I feel close enough to the chap to call him that) is a tramp who never has

a conversation with anyone, so no-one ever refers to him by name. It'd be hard to imagine what any conversation with him could be like, though, as he resolutely fails to talk in anything remotely recognisable as English for the entire episode. Lots of grumbles and grunts, and a few actual "oo ars" of surprise as he stumbles across an alien spaceship, but nothing you'd be able to put down on a Scrabble board without being challenged.

We get used to characters like this. The hapless victims, the loners who are introduced just to be murdered by the monsters. The hiker from Image of the Fendahl. The campers from The Stones of Blood. Pigbin would fit neatly into this category, but he *demands* greater attention. He just keeps coming back! For scene after scene after scene. Watch Josh get angry with a bicycle, and kick it about a bit. Watch Josh drive into an icy pond, arse over tit. By the time the Axons kill him, Pigbin has been given so much screen time that he feels like a major guest star.

But it's that moment of death which sells it. Seriously. He's lying underneath alien tentacles, and a dispassionate voice says that he's worthless and can be disposed of. And, suddenly, all the pratfalls and stunts are over – the camera zooms in on Pigbin's face, as he realises with horror that he's about to be destroyed. In one moment, a bizarre comic caricature of a regional tramp is made real – and then thrown away. It's great. And when Benton and Yates find his body, no sooner do they bend towards it than the face just collapses. (The screen whites out, as if it's too grisly to show. In fact, the whole sequence survives uncut in location footage, and it's not that unpleasant – but the delicacy with which the production team choose to deny us the moment makes it seem much, much nastier.)

T: I see what you've done there – you've cleverly concentrated on the cult figure that is Pigbin Josh to avoid discussing the rest of the episode, and thus break our brief by being rude. Fortunately, I discovered most of my Doctor Who in isolation, so was unfettered by fandom's "received wisdom" that The Claws of Axos is rubbish, meaning I'm very fond of it. It's even become *de rigueur* to criticise Claws for things it hasn't actually done (such as the supposed CSO cloth outside Bill Filer's car, which is actually just a very blue sky), so I feel duty-bound to stick up for it.

The first thing that hits you is Kenneth Sharp's ingenious design work – Axos itself is extremely impressive, and it's very clever and fascinatingly weird how the Axons are first seen as shadows before they stand revealed in all their body-stockinged glory. The entrance to the buried vessel is impressively realised, and thematically illustrates that however much the Axons might look like golden humanoids, there's probably something altogether *alien* lurking beneath the surface. And it's wonderful that Bernard Holley (as Axon Man) accentuates this by at first speaking haltingly, as if he's getting used to the English language. Notice also how he utters the word "ship" as if it's a question, as if he hasn't quite worked out the correct phraseology.

It greatly helps, though, that director Michael Ferguson keeps thing moving so fast – the viewer can't linger too long over a potentially naff costume or bit of scenery. We're given a gorgeous establishing shot of a radar dish and a beautiful sunrise, and Ferguson's trademark quick-cutting and facial close-ups keep things trotting along in the radar room. A freak snowfall augments the location work, whilst the temporary freeze-frame of Josh as Axos lands – and the subsequent picture whiteout of Josh's decomposing corpse – lend everything a surreal edge.

And it's only now, halfway through Season Eight, that one can sense a change in tone with regards the one-off government authority figures who pop up to help or hinder our heroes. Season Seven's ministers – Masters, Quinlan and Sir Keith – were all solid figures, played straight. But Brownrose in Terror of the Autons only really existed to be brought down a peg or two, and, continuing that line of descent, the government man seen here – Chinn – is a complete buffoon. That isn't all bad, in that it gives the Doctor somebody to rail against (including his admirable disdain about "England for the English"), but it also means that the man playing the part, poor old Peter Bathurst, is forced to enact some very unconvincing blocking just so Pertwee can hit him as he opens the door. Bathurst gets some better comic moments – the Brig secures the man a

"direct line" (i.e. a phone in a different room to get him out of the way), and his request for information for "my report" is greeted by bafflement from the Axon Man (who clearly hasn't been briefed about mankind's addiction to paperwork). Still, Chinn isn't *just* present to act witless and stupid – his response to the Axons' display of their miracle product Axonite ("We must have it!"), which could give the United Kingdom unlimited food and energy supplies, encapsulates the story's theme of greed extremely well. It's as much a cliffhanger as Jo's encounter with the weird Axon-spaghetti man.

Oh, and isn't it a shame for the Axons that they didn't land in France, as their demonstration of Axonite's abilities to expand frogs to gigantic size would surely have met with more approval than it does here? And probably lunch.

On a more personal note, it happens that I spent yesterday at the house of Paul and Rochelle Scoones, two extremely nice New Zealand-based Doctor Who fans. (Paul for years was affiliated with the fanzine TSV, and helped to return The Crusade episode one to the BBC Archives in 1999.) I met them briefly in the UK, and have kept in touch ever since. They've very sweetly offered to drive me around and show me the sights – a terrific opportunity to see this beautiful country rather than just work here. Perhaps most excitingly, Paul informed me that John Hicks, who formerly played a Quark in The Dominators, and appears in Claws as "Axon Boy", lives in New Zealand. That's a potentially useful piece of information where The Dominators DVD is concerned (although the deadlines are tight for that, so Hicks contributing to it may not happen). Soberingly, though, time has marched on from the days when Hicks was young enough to stuff himself inside a Quark – he's now 53 and a father of four!

The Claws of Axos (episode two)

R: It's a little hard to credit that this is the work of the same director who gave us The Ambassadors of Death only last year. Ambassadors was a masterpiece of tight editing, provided moments of grandeur and showcased good actors sparring off each other at their best. Whereas The Claws of Axos... Well, to be charitable, it looks to me as if Michael Ferguson this time around has a different agenda. There's a scrappiness to the blocking of the scenes (just look at the awkwardness of the one where Katy Manning flounces around the set protesting that Bill Filer is alive, or the hilarious scene in which Delgado tells a hypnotised UNIT soldier to deceive a guard into helping him – only for the camera to pull back and reveal the guard is only a few feet away in full earshot!). Indeed, there's *such* a scrappiness to them it almost feels like an experiment, as if Ferguson is wanting to make the scenes more raw and fly by night than Doctor Who is used to. Why would he do that? All the better to contrast with the *real* innovative stuff he's got up his sleeve. The sequence of the Axon woman being reabsorbed, her face crumbling as the screen flashes back and forth in green, or the duplication of Bill Filer – they're all fresh, and odd, and more than a little unnerving. There's something impressively alien about the interior of the Axon ship as well, all bright colours and fleshy parts everywhere.

But I think that's the problem. That all the things that would have made The Claws of Axos look bold and new back in 1971, the liberal dashings of CSO and the louder-than-loud use of sickly orange, now seem naff and gaudy. Doctor Who hasn't looked so dated in ages – and my God, it was in black and white only a season and a half ago, so that's a pretty tall order. It's as if Ferguson has bypassed all the things that makes Who great (atmospheric music, subtle editing, good performances) just so he can showcase all the stuff that in 2009 will set our teeth on edge.

... and, by God, the performances are mostly horrible. There's a certain wit to Bob Baker and Dave Martin's dialogue, but Peter Bathurst does his very best to ensure that any potential humour is stomped all over with his gurning and his overenunciation. The scenes where he talks to the Minister on the phone, and the camera lingers on Bathurst's face in close-up for the whole thing, is like a method class in How To Use Every Facial Tic At Your Disposal – when the Minister tells him that his job's on the line, Bathurst doesn't so much as double take at the receiver as quadruple take. And it's at a telephone! You don't stare at the telephone as if it's been rude to you – *no-one in the world*

does that, it's just very bad comedy. Alongside Bathurst, Paul Grist's take on a CIA agent seems emphatically wooden; the scene where he has a fight with his duplicate resembles nothing so much as two logs in a punch-up. And it must be said: the garish setting and the stylised overacting around her do nothing to help Katy Manning's Jo, who is especially strident and melodramatic.

What's good about this episode? Honestly? Well, David Savile does small wonders with the boffinish Winser. All the scruffiness, the drawled delivery, the glasses acting – it ought to make Winser rather endearing, and yet wonderfully Savile manages to make him charmless and break the stereotype. That he dies so abruptly at the end of the episode is symptomatic of a script that is racing around with so little structure or discipline, it threatens now and again to be rather unpredictable. But for me, the best bit is a small, dispensable scene in which a soldier looking in his rear-view mirror sees the Master reflected back hypnotising him. It's a lovely idea, that – and I rather hope that children driving to school with their parents the Monday following might have had a thrill looking in the mirror for him too. Terror of the Autons may not have been a subtle story, but it worked in the way it distorted the familiar and the mundane. The Claws of Axos isn't subtle either – and that one scene is its only moment of audience recognition.

T: The funny thing about Winser's death is that it's a direct result of the Doctor's meddlesome curiosity driving him to experiment with Axonite. A manslaughter charge should be issued to our troublemaking Time Lord. Come to think of it, the Doctor seems determined to be contrary for the sake of it and actually isn't that nice a lot of the time. He was against blowing up Axos in episode one, but was immediately suspicious of the Axons' story about their planet being destroyed, and *now* he's against distribution of Axonite! It's almost as if he'll go out of his way to spar with authority, without any moral consistency whatsoever.

But whereas you seem to feel that the guest cast is letting the side down, I can find some bright spots. As Captain Harker, future star Tim Pigott-Smith wears an expression of pained apology, suggesting that he's obeying orders against his better judgment. And Paul Grist is unfairly maligned, I think – I don't think he does anything wrong in a part that isn't terribly well written in the first place. (I do wonder, though, why Axos goes to the trouble of making a Filer-double, as the duplicate makes no attempt to subtly inveigle its way into the Doctor's trust. It just tells him to come to Axos, whilst pinning his arm behind his back!) And HAVOC also puts in some good work – in addition to the well-staged Filer vs Filer fight, just watch how stuntman Stuart Fell does a terrific back flip as the Master zaps him. (It's even more impressive, by the way, when we see the Master jump onto a lorry and land face down – the viewer at first presumes it's a double, so it's a genuine surprise to see that it's Delgado himself atop the moving vehicle!)

But, yes... all of that said, I'm beginning to see why people have problems with this story. For every good moment (like the puffy faced Axon woman as she re-globulises), there's silly stuff like Winser's body turning into an animated sleeping bag of death. Ferguson does his best, selling some of the potentially clumsy or awkward-looking visuals with an apt use of slow motion, but he can't paper over all of it.

To stay more positive about this, though, I'll close by citing Roger Delgado as the best thing about this by miles. It's highly ironic, in fact, that when Axos says, "No-one is irreplaceable...", it's directed at the *one* member of the cast to whom that sentence cannot possibly apply.

May 24th

The Claws of Axos (episode three)

R: This is much, much better – and largely thanks to the efforts of one man. The script he's got to work with isn't very strong, but Roger Delgado somehow contrives to make this his best performance so far. The scene in which he turns the tables upon UNIT, and within a matter of minutes changes from apprehended felon into their new scientific advisor, is beautifully handled. Delgado's amused charm, and the ironic way in which he

recommends everyone take the useless precautions against nuclear blast outlined by the Government of the time – "Sticky paper on the window, that sort of thing" – have a real magic to them. He's so good that he can make the awkward monologues he has to deliver as he works inside the Doctor's TARDIS seem natural, and indeed his exasperation at the botched work of repair the Doctor has been carrying out there is genuinely very funny.

And it's not *just* Delgado that stands out. (To be honest, it's mostly Delgado. But there are a few extra good bits thrown into the mix.) Michael Ferguson regains some of his old verve in the sequence where the Axon Man advances upon a hapless UNIT soldier framed by the sunlight – it ought to have looked ridiculous, but in borrowing some of the composition of The Ambassadors of Death, it has a lot of its style. In fact, and rarely for Doctor Who, the monster sequences are actually some of the most effective bits of the episode – there's an element of incongruity to the film scenes of the Axon stumbling its way through a glass corridor that works very well. The visuals mostly impress; I love the way that no matter how much the Axon turns his head on the scanner, we're only ever presented with the front of his face – it's a clever reminder that this human feature that it's wearing in golden form is wholly artificial. And that scene where Jo is aged towards death has the right eeriness to it.

And although The Claws of Axos is a badly written, badly structured bit of old nonsense, its faults are much more amusing this week – and that's because the story has at least settled down and given the audience a focus. So the *dreadful dreadful* scenes of Bill Filer writhing in his coma muttering lines such as "Must not distribute, must not distribute!" are endearing.

Dudley Simpson desperately needs to calm down in a darkened room, mind you.

T: *Please*, don't talk to me about darkened rooms, because I'm stuck in one – well, all right, not a room as such, but an aeroplane – for the next 26 hours. So bye-bye, New Zealand. I saw some gorgeous sights thanks to Paul and Rochelle's generosity – Doctor Who fandom really is a unifier, isn't it? I can come halfway across the world, and yet easily fall into such company, thanks to our shared love

RUNNING THROUGH CORRIDORS

of the show. It was a bit odd to clamber around the beach, alternating illuminating and informative chat about Maori history with discussions of Anthony Ainley and Season Seventeen, but there you go!

Back in Claws of Axos-land, I love the sequence where the Axon breaks into the reactor. Slow-mo is used again as the creature walks along the transparent corridor, and a UNIT soldier's death by explosion is shocking and well realised. I also have a soft spot for Kenneth Benda, who as the defence minister infuses a dry wit into his dealings with Chinn's ludicrous buffoonery. Elsewhere, Delgado shows his comic flair rather wonderfully when dealing with Sir George Hardiman, and muttering about the shabby state of the Doctor's TARDIS. (And by the way, isn't it a neat idea to have the TARDIS scanner in one of the roundels?)

But I do worry that my initial appreciation of this story is continuing to fade. It's a pretty thin week for Katy Manning, who gets turned into an old woman but precious little else. And so much of this, I have to admit, isn't just bad, it's *hilariously* bad – even the striking Axos design is undermined by the awful bobbly armchair that the Doctor sits in whilst having a murderously lengthy conversation with a talking space penis. Moreover, poor Paul Grist surely set his embarrassment threshold to zero during those appalling talking-in-his sleep sequences, which are dramatically redundant anyway. (They're still not as embarrassing, though, as his haircut, a thing of almost heroic inelegance.)

The Claws of Axos (episode four)

R: I tell you one thing that's odd. That here we are, marching our way through the third Doctor's adventures, and yet we've barely mentioned Jon Pertwee's performance. Seven stories into Hartnell and Troughton, we were falling over ourselves to compare the different subtleties of what they were doing – but not here. And I think I know the reason. It's that Pertwee has essentially nailed his character since Doctor Who and the Silurians – that of a noble (if irritable) scientist, a man with a moral vigour and not *much* humour. There are moments of quirkiness, such as the way he'll

merrily wave at the camera of Stangmoor Prison, but they feel mostly rather contrived – the most defining characteristic of this Doctor's eccentricity is that he's frequently *rude*. There are reasons for this: it's mostly a consequence of taking the Doctor and putting him on Earth. He's no longer the bold adventurer out in the stars, he's the office worker waiting for the adventures to come to him. It means that rather than be a wild card, the force of nature that we've come to expect, he's instead the straight man to everything alien that comes to pay a visit.

I don't blame Jon Pertwee for this. If anything, I admire the way that he's so swiftly made his Doctor the reliable centre of these adventures, because that's exactly what he now needs to be for the reformatted series to work. But it also means, by necessity, that his performance isn't especially varied – it's the constant still point around which everything else revolves. This incarnation of the Doctor, quite frankly, doesn't get to have as much *fun* as his predecessors.

And that's why this episode is so remarkable. Because it requires a portrayal of the Doctor which is dangerous again. It not only needs to convince the Master that he'd be prepared to betray the Earth to save his own skin, but to convince the audience at home too. And he achieves this by playing off the same dogged determination to have his TARDIS repaired, and the same frustration that he's been exiled to one place and time, that we've seen since he first appeared in the series. Every once in a while, a story comes along which plays with the viewer's faith in the Doctor – and it's never handled as subtly as Pertwee does it here, nor as credibly. The reluctant swagger with which he says goodbye to his UNIT friends – singling out Jo for special attention – is full of an awkwardness and denied guilt that speak volumes. It feels like a particularly cruel replay of that sequence in Inferno where he took off in the TARDIS and let the Earth die; now he's doing the same thing again, and this is *our* world, not some parallel dimension.

It works because Pertwee sells it, and because Delgado believes in it. And there's real joy to be had in that scene where the Master comes to believe that the Doctor's first act of

56

freedom is to ally himself to the Axons and take revenge on the Time Lords – Delgado is *appalled* that the Doctor would go so far, and for once he's been utterly outmanoeuvred, presented with a Doctor more diabolical than he's prepared to be. We've seen Pertwee and Delgado play off each other before, of course, but it's in these scenes where they work together to escape in the TARDIS where their rapport is really established. And, touchingly, you get a real sense that this rapport is just what the Master wants – that to go travelling the universe with the Doctor by his side is his *real* ambition, and all the nasty attempts at planet destruction were just a childish attempt to get his attention.

I don't think The Claws of Axos is a success. The first two episodes are loud and garish and annoying, and quite as bad as anything we've yet seen in Doctor Who. But once the story calms down a little, and puts Delgado and Pertwee at the centre of the action, it reveals a charm all its own. I'll be honest, I've always written this off as the third Doctor's first misstep, and perhaps the greatest clunker of Pertwee's tenure. But seeing it in context, once again, I've come to appreciate that it's attempting something complex and new. It doesn't work very well – but there are greater crimes for a story than the giddy overambition of what Baker and Martin's script is trying for.

T: For shame, we've forgotten to talk about this story's unique opening credits! Have you noticed? At the end of the usual title sequence, it starts from the beginning again before the story captions are overlaid. It's a bit odd, although it's something of a shame that Ferguson didn't repeat his opening-titles trick from The Ambassadors of Death. Just imagine how surreal it would have been to see "The Claws"... pow, OF AXOS! Although it wouldn't have worked for every story – "The" *pow* "MUTANTS" wouldn't have been quite as effective, nor would "Infer..." *pow* "NO!".

Different elements about this episode please me... the genuinely cold-looking location infuses the film work with its own atmosphere. Yates and Benton have a fun scrap with the Axons clambering onto their land rover, forcing them to blow it up in a very expensive and well-realised sequence. (Let me reiterate that:

they blow up a land rover! Brilliant!) And I love the squashy membrane material throbbing about in the background of the Axos set – this depiction of a totally alien environment is, once again, complimented by Bernard Holley's calm tones, which have given the Axos-creature a distinct personality and air of menace. And I appreciate the way Delgado grills the Doctor about his apparent shift in alliance – to have accepted it on face value would have undermined the Master's credibility. Oh, and I also think that Chinn remarking, "Don't you think we ought to negotiate...", as blobby aliens burst through the door is terribly funny.

But, um... that's where the quality stops, I'm afraid, and there's no escaping that everything goes a bit tits up as the story races to its climax. Katy Manning, much as I hate to say it, fails to convey terror convincingly, and shrieks her way through most of the episode instead. Ferguson does his best to direct a half a dozen monsters terrorising a small group of actors in a not-very-large area, but with mixed results. The grenades used against the Axons result in some pretty mimsy explosions – although that's perhaps to be expected, in a story where a nuclear reactor blows up and yet causes no fallout. And the sequence where everyone piles out of their vehicles to watch the "nuclear explosion" causes Dudley Simpson to have some sort of breakdown, resulting in an extended musical sequence of random and inappropriate noises.

I know, I know... I've been extremely bi-polar throughout this story (up and down like a yo-yo, you might say, galactic or otherwise). I'm not sure that any Doctor Who adventure before now has made me veer between such extremes. For as much as I've tried to stay positive, The Claws of Axos is such a giddy mix of the impressive and the risible, I find it so hard to have a uniform opinion of it. I had fun though – and being pulled from one extreme to the other is certainly more entertaining than remaining bland throughout, so in that sense Claws is an admirable thing. I'd rather have multi-coloured than beige, and it's quite exciting that at this juncture of the Pertwee era, you never quite know what you're going to get next.

Colony in Space (episode one)

R: I'm going to cheat a little. Earlier in the year, I wrote a piece about this episode for Doctor Who Magazine, as this story's entry in its 200 Greatest Moments issue. This was the highlight I selected from this story:

Pity poor Doctor Who. There he is, he keeps saving the world, and yet no-one takes him seriously. His claims that he could travel through time and space are thought to be a joke. The Brigadier comes to smirk at him as he labours away on his dematerialisation circuit, and Jo assumes that all his efforts are some sort of pretend hobby. The blue police box standing in the lab is just an eccentric affectation to them – safe and charming, rather like his yellow car and his fashion sense. And with nearly two seasons of the Doctor stranded on Earth, a lot of the audience will have assumed that the TARDIS is nothing more than a sight gag.

And then Jo steps inside. Other Doctor Who companions get to goggle at the TARDIS some time during their first adventure. This is the only time in the series when someone we've already come to know and like through several stories gets to react to the sheer impossibility of the Doctor's ship – and so it has a power to it that is usually denied us. And she's terrified of it; here's a girl who's faced down Autons and Axons, but it takes the TARDIS to really shake her. Over the years the TARDIS has been taken for granted, and it shall be again. But for the first time since two schoolteachers blundered into the ship back in 1963, we get to see it as something alien and unnerving, and Katy Manning's performance is wonderfully real. It's no longer a sight gag. It's the gateway to a different world, and more stories than we could possibly imagine. Jo wants to go home – she doesn't want this new life – but the Doctor hasn't set foot on a different planet in years, and nor have we: a look around, and then he'll try to get her home. It may only look like a gravel pit, but in one brilliant scene the series shakes the cobwebs off, reinvents the potential of the series, the potential of the Doctor, and invites us to contemplate an entire new universe of storytelling. We've no choice but to accept.

And I'd stand by that. Although the one thing that looks especially odd in context is the way that Jo really *doesn't* know what the TARDIS is capable of – what did she think was going on during The Claws of Axos, when the Doctor and the Master dematerialised from view? I love that part of Axos, just as I love this bit from Colony. But the one spoils the effect of the other. If Jo didn't really believe the Doctor was deserting Earth last week, then that sense of betrayal has been squandered. And if she did, then much of the power of what I've written above makes no sense... I suppose I could just put my fingers in my ears, screw my eyes tightly shut, and enjoy them *both* on their own terms. Yes, go on. That's what I'll do.

I love the way too that, by accident or design, this echoes a lot of the wonder of that very first adventure on an alien planet, back in 1963. Jo picking an alien flower, the landscape so desolate... even the sound of the TARDIS doors opening is the same as the doors in the Dalek city.

T: Actually, the confusion you cite as to whether Jo should know about the TARDIS is even more pronounced in this story's novelisation (which is wonderfully, and more excitingly, entitled Doctor Who and the Doomsday Weapon). I remember being terribly confused that Malcolm Hulke felt duty-bound, for some reason, to write a brand-new "Jo joins UNIT and meets the Doctor for the first time" sequence, in what I readily knew was her fourth story. (To make matters worse, it's directly said that Jo has never heard of the Master!) In those pre-video days, when you couldn't just watch the TV stories at the drop of a hat, I was desperate for the novelisations to accurately reflect what had happened on screen. So you can see why I became so disgruntled with Hulke's break from continuity that I refused to read on and didn't finish the book until a couple of years later. (My loss as it happens – it's a great book.)

But to address the TV story in front of my eyes... the very brief appearance of the Time Lords makes this all feel quite epic, even though it's really just a short exchange between three robed actors in a room. I'll concede that we spend a little too long at UNIT HQ and in the TARDIS, but once we get onto the planet Uxarieus – filmed on location and looking suitably bleak – a really interesting tale starts to emerge. Malcolm Hulke very efficiently gives us the backstory of what's happening here, setting up this world and populating it with believable characters. The hints of the mining companies' power and evilness justifies the Uxarieus colonists being gun-toting and edgy, but mysteries and questions abound... why aren't the colonists' crops growing? The Doctor refutes the theory that giant lizards are stomping about the place, but we *saw* the monster, so what, exactly, is going on? Resolving these issues makes me want to come back next week.

At the centre of it all is the wonderful John Ringham, who, having previously been so deliciously bloodthirsty as the High Priest of Sacrifice in The Aztecs, here exudes goodness and a gentle morality as the colony leader Ashe. His compassionate relationship with the Primitives – the silent, spear-wielding natives of this planet – is a deft touch on Hulke's part. All of that said, I'm not sure why Ashe has what appears to be a picture of Tarot from Ace of Wands on his desk. Oh, and look – his daughter is very sweetly played by Gail from Coronation Street, in what must surely be about the only other acting role in her career!

Other random bits draw my interest... doesn't the TARDIS look great, battered and at a jaunty angle when it lands, and then getting all mucky while the Primitives drag it along? (It's easy to take the TARDIS for granted, but I *love* it – the fact that a tatty old thing can take you anywhere in the universe sums up, to me, what Doctor Who is about. It's not some sleek, cool, interstellar craft gliding along the space lanes; it's a juddery old box that jerks its way about the place more by accident than design.) And juxtaposed against an atmosphere of squalor and desperation is the touching domesticity of the Leesons in their habitation dome – which makes it all the more of a wrench when they're killed! The whistling wind on the soundtrack suggests that Uxarieus is a cold, inhospitable environment, and yet it seems the Leesons are *better off* here – that they didn't even have a room on Earth. Egads, it's a pretty grim vision of the future that Hulke is setting up!

And look... the Doctor's got a penknife! I remember when everyone had penknives – my dad gave each of us one during one of his rare visits, and I cut my finger on the really sharp bit used to get stone out of a horse's hooves – if you had a horse, that is, which I didn't. He'd have probably been reported to social services for that nowadays. If I were a grumpy curmudgeon, I might rail that our generation (unlike the next one, of course) could be trusted to not stab people with penknives. But I don't want to paint a grim vision of the future, do I?

May 25th

Colony in Space (episode two)

R: Ha! You're not the only one who gets to go abroad, you know. I boarded a plane earlier this morning, and I'm now in the Netherlands! That's right next door to you in New Zealand, isn't it?... Well, alphabetically, at any rate. I've got a job on a luxury cruise ship, lecturing hapless holidaymakers about Dutch and Flemish literature and fine art. I've never done anything remotely like this before, and I'm feeling slightly terrified at the prospect of standing in front of a hundred people tomorrow armed only with a microphone. And having devoured a rather extraordinary five course meal (the butterflies in the stomach interfering with my appetite notwithstanding), I've retired to my cabin to study the writings of Harry Mulisch, Hugo Claus and Cees Nooteboom. And Malcolm Hulke. Of course.

Colony in Space is one of Hulke's least celebrated scripts. And judging from this episode alone, I think that's a crying shame. What Hulke is so good at doing is subtle world building, giving the audience hints of a background to the society that lends the story a real depth. What we learn about the Earth is so jaded and soulless that Jo's perky assertion that she comes from there (deliberately) feels very jarring. I love the way that the IMC's entertainment system (!) shows programmes which are determinedly depressing; even the narrator of the little infomercial about Congestion on a Slagheap Planet sounds as if he's about to go and top himself, and Pertwee's reaction to it all is to recoil physically.

And if there's an ugly greyness to Earth, so there's the same thing to IMC. The scene where Captain Dent and the Doctor in conference come to realise they're enemies, and almost amicably toast each other, is for my money the single best bit of drama we've seen all season – it's beautifully written and performed, and ever so *intimate*, it has none of those broad day-glo flourishes that have characterised the way the stories have been told this year. Dent is rotten to the core, of course – but he's not evil as such, just brutally pragmatic, and his worst crime seems to be that he's utterly without imagination. He clearly despises the colonists because at heart they're idealists, and idealism is something eccentric and warped. There's no malice in Dent's decision that his henchman Morgan should kill the Doctor, and it's telling too that the episode ends with Morgan telling his victim that it's "nothing personal" – it's simply the businesslike way that things get done in the twenty-fifth century. We've seen the comic-book version of bureaucracy in The Claws of Axos with Chinn, all jowls wobbling and eyebrows on end like exasperated caterpillars – here Hulke is showing us its cold emotionless truth, and that's *far* more scary.

And best of all is Caldwell, an IMC surveyor. Here's a man who is clearly on the side of the villains, who'll casually threaten the Doctor with his digger robot, who'll turn a blind eye to murder for the sake of greater profits. But what's extraordinary about the character is that Hulke makes him sympathetic – he's a product of the amoral society he lives in, and however feeble his resistance to Dent, the fact that he wrestles with his conscience at all marks him out as someone redeemable. Bernard Kay is, as ever, fantastic. Just look at the way he's winded when the Doctor reveals that two of the colonists were murdered, the smug liar suddenly seeing that his scare tactics have gone too far. I love the Master, I do – but with that character safely out of the way for the moment, with his grandiose schemes for conquest and his status as a supervillain, Hulke's got the opportunity to reintroduce the same sort of ambiguity that we saw in Dr Quinn or General Carrington. And the series feels so much the richer for it.

T: Yay! It's Bernard Kay, a man incapable of a bad performance. Like John Ringham, this will be his last appearance in the series – it's odd that both of them notch up a number of credits in the show's first decade, but never crop up again, despite their being busy and respected members of the business. Kay is still going strong today (Ringham, sadly, died in 2008), so he could appear in the new series, and once again grace Doctor Who with his superb brand of underplaying. He's very amiable as the surveyor Caldwell – even when he uses intimidation-by-robot on the Doctor, he pulls off the difficult task of appearing both reasonable and threatening at the same time. And when he stands-up to Captain Dent, he displays moral fortitude tinged with an underdog's twitchy uncertainty.

On the other hand, Morris Perry is expertly cold and brusque as Dent, a man whose conscience has clearly *not* bothered him for a very long time. It's great that he does the nastiest of things with a clipped efficiency, and that he's *so* emotionally detached that even the prospect of being rich fails to fill him with glee. He does get one funny line ("All colonists are eccentric, Morgan, otherwise they wouldn't be colonists"), which is even more memorable because Perry doesn't let his inscrutable mask slip while saying it.

But what I *really* like about this story (if it doesn't make me sound too crusty in the process) is Malcolm Hulke's pessimism. The truth is, I never really bought Star Trek's (albeit very laudable) optimism about the future. I just couldn't buy a society where everyone was united and money didn't exist – to pick just one wrinkle, if there's no money, who cleans the toilets? Nobody's going to do that out of choice, are they? In Hulke's bleaker – but more morally complex – version of mankind's future, Earth is over-populated, mining companies gut planets, entertainment systems have footage of real-life violence and we hear of an Earth where people routinely commit suicide. Caldwell, whom you rightfully identify as the most moral of the IMC team, is conflicted partly because he's heavily in debt – the nasty company men have him by the proverbials, and it's difficult to afford morals if you're struggling to put food on the table.

That said, this story is in danger of becoming a bit *too* bleak, isn't it? The electrician Holden has a delightful and sweet rapport with his assistant, one of the Primitives, but even *this* bit of cheer is dashed when the undercover-man Norton murders both of them. (And it's not just their deaths that are upsetting, but the way in which Norton sullies his victims' bond by framing the Primitive for the killings.) And the cliffhanger, in which Morgan readies to kill the Doctor while offering the apology, "Nothing personal you understand, just business", aptly demonstrates how much Colony in Space is about the evil that businessmen do. Still, even if this future is a relatively unpleasant place, it makes acts of kindness and compassion stand out – as you say, Caldwell is all the more impressive because he's even a somewhat-reasonable man in a world pushing him to become increasingly amoral. He and Ashe give us hope in humankind's inherent decency, and keep this story from being so dark that you want to despair for the future.

[Toby's addendum, written June 2016: Bernard Kay sadly died in 2013, well after this was written. Whilst he never did get to appear in the new series, I am pleased to say that I got to know him rather well and showed him the snippets of Running Through Corridors, including this one, in which he received high praise.]

Colony in Space (episode three)

R: What I love about Hulke's vision of the series is that he puts the Doctor right at the centre of the story, and as its moral arbiter. It's our hero not as aimless adventurer, but as active peacemaker – and Pertwee rises to the occasion, since he's never better than when (as in The Silurians or Inferno) he plays the lone hero on a mission to save everyone from themselves. This episode is a particularly clever example of all that; within minutes of the IMC spaceship touching down, there's a war breaking out between the colonists and the mineralogists, and the Doctor is caught in the middle once again. Just as in The Silurians, there's a scene in which he actually *betrays* his friends to the enemy to prevent bloodshed – he tells Caldwell about the attack that Winton is preparing against the IMC.

It's a measure, though, of how comparatively dull the supporting characters are that the moral dilemma of this moment doesn't have the force it did last year. Winton is just another Major Baker at heart, but this time cut from a different cloth, an attractive male lead

that Katy Manning can spark off. He's another hothead, but it's hard to imagine any scene where he decries the Doctor as a traitor will carry the same weight. And in spite of John Ringham's efforts, there's a fundamental problem with the characterisation of the colonist leader, Ashe. Hulke gives him an occasional line which suggests he'll have the authority and stubbornness to have put in the hard work of making life on a harsh planet work – but every time he stands up to the Doctor and Jo, he immediately backtracks with an apology. Last year, The Silurians shone because the Doctor's actions as intermediary genuinely set divisions between different characters, all of whom had credible agendas and motivations opposing him. This time, it's really only the Doctor and Caldwell who stand out as having any complexity at all – and the scene where Pertwee persuades a reluctant Bernard Kay to help him is indeed excellent – but since it's already clear that the only supporting character of any real depth is going to be an ally, it doesn't leave much room for drama. And that's a pity, because in plot terms, the same ingredients are here as they were in Silurians – it's just they haven't been cooked very well.

I'm very fond of Captain Dent, though. He's the corporate businessman through and through. He directs his pilot to land the spaceship right on top of the colonist's settlement, simply because – as he mutters as an aside – he hates walking. That's beautiful. I used to work in an office for a man like that.

T: Ah, you know, I think I've figured out why Dent seems so, well, *effective* to my eyes... he reminds me very much of a certain British conservative columnist I could name, if I were in a mood to keep the publisher of this book awake at night, his eyes like poached eggs, worried about an impending lawsuit for slander. But the comparison is there – both Dent and the conservative-writer-who-shall-not-be-named come across as chilly, unsmiling and prone to dourly doling out unpleasantness whilst pretending to be morally justified in so doing. Dent doesn't break even his composure when forced to accede to Caldwell's threat to halt the survey unless Dent releases the captive Jo Grant – and Dent's final barb to the mineralogist, that he's just committed professional suicide, is no less threatening because of his deadpan demeanour. Similarly, Dent's look says it all when Morgan asks if the colony's security chief, Winton, should be taken alive.

Meanwhile, there's been an interesting transformation in Winton's character – early on, odds were good that he would emerge as the baddy, so hyper-critical was he of the lovely, gentle Ashe. Here, though, in getting tied up with Jo and then escaping (a flight to freedom that results in Nicholas Pennell gamely chucking himself about in the mud), Winton has all the ingredients of the romantic hero. Speaking of "gamely chucking" oneself about the place, hats off to Stanley McGeagh, who – as the IMC man Allen – picks up Katy Manning with one arm whilst firing at Pennell through a hole in the wall; that's quite a manoeuvre.

But I'm compelled to ask the most important question of all... is this the Doctor Who story with the record for biggest number of moustaches? I think it might be. It's an odd thing, the beardless moustache – it's almost entirely died out. The only person I can think of who has one these days is Andrew Cartmel... which tells you (and I say this tongue planted firmly in cheek) everything you need to know, I should think.

May 26th

Colony in Space (episode four)

R: Today the ship arrived in Nijmegen. It's taken me a good hour even to learn how to pronounce it. It sounds a bit like someone with a catarrhal cough. It's a very pretty town, though. Full of cobbles.

There's something peculiarly bloodless about Colony in Space, and it's a little hard for me to put my finger on. I think Michael Briant's direction is solid enough, the performances are fine, the dialogue is crisper than we've been used to recently. But, somehow, I don't *believe* in any of this. There's that scene early on where Leeson turns upon IMC with a gun because they killed his family, and a terrified Morgan breaks down and confesses to the colonists. It should have been dangerous, even moving – but I don't for a second think that Leeson would shoot Morgan in cold blood,

and worse, I don't think Morgan would have felt the bullet had he been shot. There are lots of deaths in this story, but they all seem rather antiseptic. We should be watching a story about two sets of extremists fighting for all they hold dear, and with nothing to lose – these colonists are *real* pioneers, who should be staring hardship and extinction in the face. But it's all too polite. In the courtroom scenes, we should feel that the Adjudicator's judgment is something worth starting a revolution over, but it has only a fraction of the fizz that you get from Sir Alan Sugar firing someone in The Apprentice. At one point, Winton urges Ashe to tell the Adjudicator about the murders. "Just leave it", says Ashe. And that's the problem. Everyone's just leaving it. On paper, and in storyline, there's a war being fought here. On screen, it looks more like something that can be settled amicably in a small claims court.

Why? Well, I think in part it's because we're led to feel increasingly that we're looking at the wrong part of the story. Now, you know I'm a sucker for clever bits of misdirection. The alien Primitives have been hidden in plain sight since the first episode, and because they're dumb, and they don't do much more than act as servants, we've quickly learned to see them as background colour. They're the equivalent of the Monoids, really. As a result, the scenes in the alien city seem like a huge twist; they *are* important, they have a history and a culture, and they appear to pose a greater threat than a bunch of bureaucrats in red helmets. That moment where the Guardian appears is truly wonderful – wizened and mummified, but bearing *such* authority; the whole lead-in to his coming out of the wall, with the throbbing sound effect behind him, is the highlight of the entire episode. But all he can do is give a warning finger wag to the Doctor and Jo for trespassing, and send them on their way. It'd be brilliant if it felt in any way that this revelation was changing the story and taking us into new areas – but after that we're just back to the squabbling of colonists and miners once again. And we're left with the nagging sensation that the really *interesting* part of the story has been tidied away and put back in its box for later.

T: I don't share your indifference to this, I have to say... all right, it's a bit low key and repetitive, but there's plenty to enjoy. For instance, what seemed like a throwaway moment in episode one (where Ashe, surely the most reasonable man in the history of the universe, asked for the Doctor's paperwork) becomes very important when the Doctor's lack of credentials prevents him from exposing that the Adjudicator is actually the Master. (In fact, to look at this version of the future, it seems that the vote on ID cards will go the government's way!) The Master's plan is canny too – he doesn't side with IMC because they're fellow baddies, it's so he can use leverage on Ashe to help him locate the Primitives' ancient city. Actually, it's curious that the Time Lords *mentioned* the Master in episode one, and yet it's still a bit of a surprise when he turns up. (It's very strange, though, that he's listed simply as "Master" in the credits – the lack of the definitive article doesn't seem right somehow. Then again, one could argue that as Roger Delgado's name is properly underneath this, the definite article is in fact present and correct.)

There are other great moments... of course the IMC guys react as most people would after such a resounding victory: they get pissed. Morgan's obviously blotto, whilst Dent maintains his composure even though he's clearly got a sore head. The use of automatic weapons keeps things believable (no futuristic lasers here), and the scene where Norton and Alec Leeson struggle to the death keeps us guessing because it's cleverly staged. And even if this puts me in the minority, I quite like the wizened design of the blind priests, and the cute little puppet Guardian. (Quite what he thinks about, though, as he just sits behind a wall waiting to tell off passing infiltrators, is anyone's guess!)

And isn't this a *cruel* story? The timing of IMC turning the tables on the colonists is deeply frustrating. Winton is increasingly driven to do bad things, even if we're still meant to like him (the way he repeats his apology to Ashe is a moment of great sincerity). Dent so expertly twists these events to make the colonists look like the aggressors, it makes the viewer want to stand up and shout at the injustice. Oh, yes, he picks on the weak, Captain Dent, and caricatures them as evil – he is indeed like that conservative writer I men-tioned, and his paper, The Mail. So it should come as no surprise to anyone, then, to learn that I'd take The Guardian over The Mail any day.

Colony in Space (episode five)

R: Yeah, I'm a little disappointed in my indifference too. For years, I've defended Colony in Space against lazy charges of it being a dull runaround – I've pointed out Hulke's thoughtful script, and the sincere way that it champions human endeavour and courage over brute force and big business. And yet... I can't help it, whilst I'm watching it, I do find it somewhat trivial. The themes aren't trivial at all. So it must be something in the execution.

Maybe it's because the Target novelisation is so good. Like you, Toby, I was irritated by the false introduction of Jo. Looking back at it now, it's just the most striking example of change in a novel which quite consciously refused to tell the story I'd read the synopsis for in The Programme Guide. Reading it now as an adult, it's quite clear that Hulke just isn't particularly interested in the "Cowboys and Indians in space" story he'd written for screen some years before, and instead wants to address other issues entirely. It's peculiar that so strangely flat a story as Colony in Space could provoke a book which is so passionate in its concerns, and so angry in the way it sometimes explains them. And he can only really write about a world so dehumanised that the Doctor has to show the colonists how to stage a funeral (in one of the most haunting chapters ever published by Target) if he ignores the idea that The Doomsday Weapon fits into a neat growing collection of TV tie-in products. This is a fully realised world in which you may meet your future wife going for a Walk (when a Walk is a moving pathway of artificial images of the outdoors), where all animals have been systematically destroyed by humanity 500 years before, where there's no space on Earth to breathe and where marriages are arranged to provide you bigger accommodation.

On screen, IMC were the villains and the colonists were the good guys. In the book, both sides are victims of the same society which has eroded everything Hulke recognises and celebrates as human. Once in a while, his anger at the futility of these people spills out unexpectedly on to the page – I was quite taken aback by the sequence in which he describes the IMC security guards chasing a victim: "They pressed on as best they could because they all had IMC living units on Earth that they didn't want to lose, and IMC wives, and their children were in IMC schools that were very exclusive... Above all, they hated all colonists because they were eccentric and didn't conform to society on Earth, and sometimes they smelt of sweat." The way Hulke keeps on listing the trivial reasons they stay alive, with "and" after "and" after "and", gives it a sneering quality. It's as if Hulke sometimes can't quite control himself. I feel at times that The Doomsday Weapon's passion almost has nothing to do with Colony in Space, and that whatever book Hulke had been working on at the time would have been invested with the same force.

It's an honest and sad book, from the way that the Doctor has to bring the colonists out of their innocence, and watch them as they abandon all attempts at negotiation and resort to war. It's a theme which was played out on screen more markedly in The Silurians – here, it's something you feel Hulke is standing back from with a resigned weary sigh. There's a happy ending of sorts. But the likes of Winton are never truly trustworthy, and even good Samaritans like Caldwell demonstrate venality, cruelty – and, in the typical cheerful wrap-up scene from the telly – complete opportunism. It's not an illustration of what was on the screen – indeed, it may be the only novelisation which follows the inspiration of David Whitaker's Dalek book, and instead writes its own story loosely based on the events shown on screen. As a tie-in product, it has its faults – Hulke all but forgets little things like Jo Grant, and the Master and his Doomsday Weapon hankerings become even more redundant than they were on screen. But on its own terms, as a piece of science-fiction prose, The Doomsday Weapon is by far Hulke's best work, and quite possibly the best novelisation that Target ever published.

It seems unfair then that my good opinions of Colony in Space are scuppered by an adaptation of it written several years later. But I don't get much of that passion in the TV version. When it is there, though, it's fantastic. That scene between Helen Worth and Bernard Kay is remarkable, as Mary rages against the way Caldwell is prepared to let the colonists leave on a wrecked spaceship. For the past five episodes, Worth has been required to play her part as if she's Katy Manning's little sister, all smiles and jokes and sweetness. So there's a real punch in the stomach feel to this, that the little girl becomes an angry woman, and Worth seizes the moment for all that it's (ahem) worth. And the confused embarrassment on Kay's face as he's chewed out by someone we'd all written off as an innocent naf is perfect.

T: Delgado is credited as *The* Master again. Hurrah, someone's clearly listening to me!

As enthusiastic as I've generally been about this story, I'm afraid it's now meandering somewhat. The Master needs to get to the Primitive city – but we're still not there by the episode's end. The desperately unfair kangaroo court delivers bad news for the colonists, but *feels* as though it's treading water. And there are a couple of outright daft moments – Jo fails Companion Academy by tripping an alarm beam in the Master's TARDIS that she struggled to avoid only minutes earlier, and Dudley Simpson seems keen to ape the comedic musical stylings of the Cushing movies when Dent's squad leaders arrive on the bridge.

But, I can still see the positives here... There's a brilliant moment of black comedy where Caldwell tells Dent that the colonists' rocket may explode on lift-off and the captain – wholly unconcerned for the lives of those aboard – orders all IMC men to position themselves out of harm's way. Dent's admission that Winton is a "very resourceful young man" is also very well done – grudging admiration for a foe is always good in a villain. And, on a fashion note, having been obliged to be drab for the colonists' outfits (check out Winton's chocolate dungarees – they're so last season), Michael Burdle had done an excellent job on the IMC uniform. It's sleek and black, and broken up with flashes of red, making it look suitably futuristic without being daft. (Had Arthur Scargill's miners been this efficiently tooled up and trigger happy, Thatcher may not have prospered so much in the 1980s.)

And huzzah – the ever-versatile extra/ monster man Pat Gorman has already been credited as Primitive and Voice (on the IMC ship, that is, although I think it was actually director Michael Briant in the end) and IMC man Long, and now he's a moustachioed (of course) colonist. Do you know, I impulse-purchased The Sandbaggers a couple of years ago, and was delighted to notice Gorman featuring in episode one as a prominent extra. (Anyone who's been reading this journal from the start will know I'm strange that way – give me a piece of exceptional and accomplished drama, and I'll start looking for the Doctor Who bit part actors.) Gorman seems to have been on everyone's books as a reliable walk-on – he worked pretty consistently for a couple of decades. He's not a bad actor as it happens, and to his credit seems happy to accept a role no matter how small. Legend!

And if I might digress, I am thrilled to report that this episode is unique in Doctor Who history. I hope I'm not wrong in thinking that Primitives' colourful body stockings are meant to be their skin – therefore, when the Master zaps one and he tumbles down a mound and his loin cloth flaps open, we see his actual bum! Surely, this is the only example of such gratuitous nudity in the show's entire history (I don't count the "Barrowman loses his clothes scene" in Bad Wolf, because we don't actually see his arse). See, even the most innocuous episodes have something to recommend them...

May 27th

Colony in Space (episode six)

R: Antwerp and Bruges today. Lots more cobbles. This time with added canals for good measure.

I don't think much of that Guardian. So he's got a job that puts him in charge of a starbursting superweapon – and the first thing he does when anyone comes around sniffing to use it is to blow the thing up, and his entire race in the process. And worst of all, he has to ask the very thieves to help him operate the self-destruct sequence! I don't think he's really thought this through very well. Wouldn't it

have been a *slightly* more sensible option to – I don't know – kill the thieves, rather than kill himself and everyone he's in charge of? It's not even as if he tries to take the Master and the Doctor out in the explosion – they alone are allowed to escape, whilst all the Primitives and priests who have been serving him for aeons, and never made the least effort to hold the universe to ransom, are the ones sentenced to death. The Doctor says the Guardian is a man of infinite compassion. I think he's an out and out loony, myself.

To be honest, all this doomsday weapon stuff feels a bit muddled. It's so tonally different from anything we've seen in the previous episodes of the story – and although Pertwee and Delgado by now are dab hands at this sort of moral sparring, it just feels as if an idea about universal armageddon has been grafted on awkwardly to what was previously a story that was admirably small scale. I rather suspect that there was absolutely no room in the main plot for the Doctor or Jo any more, and so they've been packed off into another, and rather sillier, adventure altogether to keep them out of mischief. That in the final minutes they need Winton to explain to them all that's been going on in the climax is really rather funny. They've done nothing to affect the outcome whatsoever.

And yet... I'm not so sure this is a bad thing. Ultimately, this episode works because of the little moments of humanity, and it feels right and proper that the bravery of Ashe and the determination of Winton are entirely their own and not prompted by the Doctor. This is a story about Man's endeavours after all, and it's apt that in the last reel, it's Man who wins through, and the presence of a couple of Time Lords is actually something of an irrelevance. That in the closing minutes we see Winton and Caldwell deep in conversation about ways to improve the colony, the Doctor all but forgotten, is very apt. Ashe dies not because he's prompted into self-sacrifice by the Doctor, or influenced to be a better man by example – he always *was* a caring leader, and his willingness to give his life to save his people is because of that. The scene where he talks to Dent on the monitor with studied politeness, just a minute before dying in the explosion, is pitched perfectly by John Ringham. It makes the way that

Dent dismisses him with no more than a "Goodbye, Ashe" all the more callous.

I don't know. Peculiar little story, Colony in Space. I'm very fond of that ending, where it transpires that the last few weeks of adventure have been compressed into no more than a few seconds back on Earth, and that the Brigadier doesn't realise that the TARDIS has been anywhere at all. It's light and funny, and it makes us complicit with the Doctor and Jo – we know something no-one else on Earth can do, and this entire story is just a shared secret. But because the Doctor has been so de-emphasised from the main action this episode, it also gives the more unfortunate effect of suggesting that all that we've been watching has been entirely disposable. We're meant to feel it's ironic that the Brigadier can pooh-pooh the last month and a half of japes and spills and moral dilemmas – but deep down, I can't help feeling that the Brig hasn't missed out on much at all.

T: He's a perplexing man, Malcolm Hulke. On the one hand, he dwells very much on the importance of the individual, cherishing his characters' uniqueness. He refuses to play the formulaic ball and kill his villains – Dent survives, as did Reegan in The Ambassadors of Death and Blade in The Faceless Ones. And yet, in the broader storytelling strokes, Hulke indulges in mass slaughter with few emotional repercussions; in episode four, the colonists happily killed IMC guards (and interestingly enough, the Doctor didn't try to stop them). Okay, I know we're in a grim future where a tyrannical mining company can impose martial law, but such a cavalier attitude suggests that even the lowliest IMC staff member is by definition a bad person and ranks as imminently killable, which is at odds with Hulke's moral complexity elsewhere. I noticed some internet furore over The Fires of Pompeii, and the Doctor's decision to prompt the devastation and let history take its course – here, the Pertwee Doctor allows an entire race to destroy itself (he even presses the button himself!) and his conscience doesn't seem to bother him a bit. It's perplexing.

But otherwise, there's so much that's praiseworthy here. It's been a solid debut for director Michael Briant, who has provided us with such visuals as a lovely shot of the Master's face as he looks at the frieze of the sacrifice chamber, and the extremely mucky fight between Nicholas Pennell and stuntman Terry Walsh. For that matter, the final shoot-out has some impressive looking set-ups and the weapons look reassuringly solid, with spent bullet cases flying about in the melee. Direction-wise, my only real point of criticism is that Morgan's death is botched and rather unclear in an all-too brief cutaway.

Other things that I like... Ashe's sacrifice is gallant and rather sad, although I have a slightly different take on his last communication, in which Dent doesn't look at him. Is Dent truly unfeeling, or simply unable to make eye contact with a man he knows he's condemned to death? It's a textured moment that allows for different interpretations. It's only when left alone in the colonists' dome, having won, that Morris Perry allows Dent to vent all his pent up feelings, and he tears down his opponents' now defunct maps and paraphernalia. And Caldwell, the most honourable of the IMC bunch by default, spends some time being spineless until Jo brings out his heroic side – which is too late for the colonists' ship, and Bernard Kay wonderfully displays his guilt at the resultant explosion.

Let me offer two random observations before I wrap things up... I worry that I have a one-track mind at present, owing to my impending nuptials this year, but to my eyes it looks like the Guardian is wearing a wedding ring(!). Also, it's becoming clear that you should never trust a refilmed cliffhanger – it either means the end of the previous episode was contrived to provide some last-minute jeopardy, or it's impossible to resolve without cheating, i.e. using additional material. Colony in Space has featured two of the latter in a row, with Roger Delgado being so much less dramatic when his line begins rather than ends an episode.

But, this is just me quibbling about a story that's been far, far more successful than not. I know you think Colony in Space is inconsequential, Rob, but overall I think it's been rather sweet and interesting in a subdued sort of way. There's nothing offensive or stupid about it, and its heart is very much in the right place. Its *moustaches*, however, are more likely to be found on a Village People album cover.

The Daemons (episode one)

R: This year, Doctor Who has been in a state of flux, trying to mix the earnest settings of Season Seven with reaching out for the family audience it used to have. I think that's a noble aim, but I think the results so far have been inconclusive. The credible military organisation that was UNIT last season is now something warmer and safer, which employs little girls as secret agents – and that's fine in itself, but we're still getting stories which have brutal prison breaks, and you can see Nick Courtney trying hard to maintain some continuity between the two styles. And whilst the stories have been lighter in tone, they've up 'till now still been very *earnest* in tone; The Mind of Evil was a despairing essay on the darker side of humanity, The Claws of Axos preached a bit about greed, and Colony in Space went the whole hog and showed that our descendants come from a planet choked by pollution and corporate concerns. Season Eight is more of a kid's programme – but there hasn't been an awful lot of *fun* on offer.

Until now. This is joyous stuff. It's the first time that Doctor Who has consistently tried to be funny since the days that William Hartnell rode into the Wild West – and that it's doing so under the cover of being a Hammer Horror makes it all the wittier. What's so beautiful about it is that it acknowledges right from the get-go that the black magic theme is something that doesn't really fit in the series' rationale – and then proceeds to play upon hallmarks of that theme with such giddy abandon that you've no choice but to be sucked in. Clever little scenes like the wind blowing the signpost about, so that some force tries to prevent the Doctor and Jo from reaching the barrow in time – or the way that our heroes are countered as strangers in the local pub – are bed-rocked by an episode which is all about modern-day cynicism.

If we were simply thrust into a story where a white witch casts down a spell which stops the local bobby from braining her with a rock, then this would perhaps ask us to suspend our disbelief too much. But because it's done within the framework of a BBC documentary, with journalists joking that if Satan pops up they'll simply grill him for an interview, where the lead reporter is (off camera) more concerned with the state of his make-up than in any superstition, where even the man behind the archaeological dig tells the television viewers that this is all timed as a publicity stunt to promote his new book – we're left almost reeling at the complacency of a society so hardened that it wants to play with unknown forces simply as a cheap bit of light entertainment. The BBC3 scenes are *extremely* funny – the way that the soulless journalist keeps on grinning at the camera when events get away from him on live television, or tries to offer constant editorials upon what Professor Horner is saying. And it's just wonderful too that we're led to believe that Benton and Yates are going to be all agog at the events at the barrow, but privately would much rather watch the football and argue about the referee.

And as we reach the end of this somewhat troubled season, at last it's earned the confidence to mock itself, and to just the right degree. It's spot on that the Doctor blusters into a pub arrogantly demanding directions, and it takes his young girl companion to get the help they need, simply by not being an annoying boor. Just as it's right that we can share a smile with Yates and Benton when the Brigadier gets dressed up for his regimental dinner; we're worlds away now from the edgier portrayal that we saw in The Silurians or Inferno, but this is nonetheless real and human, and (at this stage of the game) inspires affection rather than Colonel Blimp mockery. And, best of all, the Master is reinvented as an existential vicar, amiably talking about how the soul is an outdated concept. The script is warm, the gags are sharp and free of self-indulgence, and the whole thing builds to a terrific countdown climax as the barrow is opened and all hell (literally) is set loose. Earlier in the episode, as broadcaster Alastair Fergus cleverly gives us all the exposition we need, but framed in parody, he rests his hand upon a stone gargoyle; at the cliffhanger, the same thing grows glowing eyes and swings its head around. That's what Doctor Who absolutely does best – telling us that something is safe, and then bringing it to evil life just the same.

T: The opening sequence sums up the tale completely – there's darkness, the elements are at their angriest, and we witness an atmospheric death in a graveyard. The harshly whistling wind slices scarily through the soundtrack, and just *look* at that cliffhanger... the camera ascends upward from the Master, who stands erect and powerful while his coven cowers in fear as everything begins to shake around them. Roger Delgado was *made* for this sort of thing – he looks terrific both as the vicar and in his coven-leader robes, and he gives weight to ritualistic chanting even when he's spouting nonsense. (One of his "chants" is "Mary had a Little Lamb" backwards, right?)

Come to think of it, *everyone* is working so well here, and playing to the tips of their fingers. I especially love how Miss Hawthorne – the local white witch, and the kind of daft-as-a-brush but plucky English eccentric the show does so well – makes an ancient-looking sign with her fingers as the Master talks of the horn'd beast. (I've no idea if that's a genuine gesture steeped in legend or just something that actress Damaris Hayman improvised, but it convinces me.) And then, delightfully, Delgado points his index finger and little finger at Hawthorne when ordering his lackey to follow her, and melds his hand into the same shape when getting into the ritual in the cavern.

Full marks too, for the one-episode cameos of Professor Horner and Alistair Fergus. The former is brilliantly sarcy and grumpy, suggesting that the "chatty" Fergus should interview Beelzebub if the beast of darkness himself shows up. And Horner's complete unsuitability for live television ("You should have done your homework, lad", he brusquely tells Fergus when asked what Beltane means) is terribly funny. Meanwhile, David Simeon (as Fergus) channels David Frost as the upbeat but condescending TV presenter, without pitching too far into parody. That said, I've worked on ideas for BBC3 comedy pilots, and it's stretching it to suggest that either of these characters would have been allowed on screen. Fergus would have been replaced by a 15 year old with no prior experience to court the youth demographic, whilst Horner's history lesson would have been illustrated via the medium of rap so as to be cool.

This isn't *all* serious, as you say – one of the bar patrons makes a nice gag by presuming that the Doctor must be a TV presenter, owing to his "costume and wig" (I'm surprised that Pertwee let them get away with that, even if he does retort "Wig?!" at the man with comic indignation), and the UNIT scenes are quite entertainingly chummy. We even learn something valuable from them: one should never, ever ask Richard Franklin to deliver the supposedly butch, earthy line "That'll learn 'em...", as the result is more terrifying than a lap-dance from Anne Widdecombe. But so far, The Daemons is perfect teatime terror – it refutes all notion of magic and the supernatural, then gleefully milks them for all the dramatic potential that it possibly can. It has a terrific atmosphere, aided by the Doctor clearly knowing something of our ancient, occult history. Isn't it curious, in fact, how something from the dawn of time always seems more terrifying than an evil from, say, 1926? As a general rule, the older it is, the scarier it is. (Hmm, perhaps they should cast Bruce Forsythe as a villain next season...)

May 28th

The Daemons (episode two)

R: Middleburg and Veere. Cobbles and canals. In fact, so many cobbles, and so many canals, it's a little hard to see where the cobbles end and the canals begin. Today, I had my Arc of Infinity moment – I stood beside a Dutch barrel organ in a town square, and pretended to be Omega. I even looked the part. The five-course meals are taking their toll on my complexion, and I've broken out in teenage acne. I look every inch a decomposing Time Lord reverting to anti-matter.

Not that I'm watching Arc of Infinity, which is rather a shame, all things considered. Instead, it's back to The Daemons! Starring Stephen Thorne as Azal. Who will later go on to play Omega. Just not in Arc. So the connection is tenuous at best.

This is episode No. 300! Oh yes, I've been counting. And the humanisation of UNIT continues – and rather delightfully. To see the Brigadier in pyjamas, taking reports in bed and exploding with exasperation when he finds out Yates and Benton have absconded in his helicopter, is genuinely very funny... and precisely because Nicholas Courtney doesn't send the Brig up at all, and Lethbridge-Stewart behaves in exactly the same way as he would if he were in full military dress. It's the context alone that makes him amusing, and it's a subtle reminder that this man we first met way back in The Web of Fear is a real person and not just an icon. In a similar fashion, Benton's hope that Yates' mention of "first things first" is his way of suggesting breakfast is delivered throwaway; it could so easily be played as a deliberate gag, but instead it merely feels like someone all too human. Benton is never better than in this story – it's that bemused way that he finds himself as the "perfect gentle knight" of Miss Hawthorne which does the trick. And though I agree with you, Toby, that John Levene may not have the greatest range as an actor, he's ideal for straight-man duties here. We're only a year away from Benton standing up in nappies, or the Brigadier asserting that an alien world is Cromer – but at this point the comedy isn't contrived at all, and comes naturally out of characters we already understand.

I'm finding it harder to like the Doctor, mind you. The problem is that Jo is clearly besotted by him at this point. Just look at the way she hangs her head in hurt when he mocks her for not being very good at Latin; he may not intend it, but every time he puts her down, it clearly wounds her deeply. In the barrow, he'll explain to her about a model spaceship weighing hundreds of tons, and when she can't immediately fathom what he's saying, he responds with irritation. We've seen Doctors before who can be bluff and arrogant, but never before have the companions reacted this way; Hartnell's would give as good as they got, and Troughton's would treat it all like amiable teasing. Katy Manning is settling into the role now, and it's telling that just as all her UNIT co-stars are becoming more human, that she is too. But the price of it is that Pertwee looks all the more like an insufferable bully.

T: When I was growing up, I discovered that my dad had left a load of Dennis Wheatley books at our house. The occult always seemed more palpably scary than anything futuristic,

and just *looking* at the spines of those books sent a shiver up mine. I remember my brother talking about Aleister (even his name was spelt scarily!) Crowley, and his being an actual person made pentacles and ancient rituals seem all too horrifyingly real. And so I deeply appreciate the little touches here, including Bok's forked tongue, the special "æ" in the title and Miss Hawthorne's talk about a recently repealed Witchcraft Act. In particular, those aerial shots of the Daemon's giant cloven hoofs recall that story about the Devil footprints in the snow that terrified me as a kid.

I have some concerns about the supporting characters, though – it's clear enough that Horner dies in the chilly blast as the tomb is opened, but does Fergus also perish? He does in the book, and if so, his TV associate Harry seems unduly chipper (in what's been an appealing performance of soulless professional chumminess from James Snell). Perhaps the star presenter was just surplus to this episode's requirements, and sent home with a hot water bottle. Elsewhere, though, the definite fatalities include PC Groom's obliteration by towering Daemon, which is cleverly staged using just juddery camerawork, sound and a shadow across his face. Garvin's dispatch is even better – I love the spontaneously combusting bush that illuminates as he is disintegrated. Actually, *everything* catches fire quite impressively, from the exploding baker's van to the shocking but funny immolation of the Brig's swagger cane.

Time was, this story was not just *a* Pertwee classic, but *the* Pertwee classic. Recent re-assessment writes it off a bit now – nobody likes looking at other people's holiday snaps, and as the UNIT family keep telling us what a good time they had in Aldbourne, a cynical modern audience feels inclined to pick holes. You had to be there, and we weren't. And yet, I think this viewpoint is a shame – so much of this is rather terrific, and the fun is infectious. And I should reiterate: when I say that John Levene is a limited actor, it's not to criticise his performance as Benton at all. I *adore* Benton, and the pairing of him here with Miss Hawthorne – the flowery whimsy of her vocabulary playing wonderfully beside his prosaic straightforwardness – is inspired. Everything that makes Benton great is on display here – he's brave, funny and prepared for a scrap. He's, well, like a loyal Labrador. Besides, *most* actors have their limitations – Bruce Willis is no chameleon, but he's damned good at what he does, and you wouldn't expect Ray Winstone to play Bertie Wooster, would you? So yes... I may, in good humour on occasion, mock Levene, who does come across on the DVDs as someone who's been to just one too many motivational speakers and swallowed a Hollywood fake-over-sincerity pill. But I have to confess that he was perfect casting as Benton, and I wouldn't have anyone else in the role.

The Daemons (episode three)

R: Yeah, you see what I mean? The Doctor browbeats the Brigadier, because he wants to use force to break through the heat barrier. When Jo agrees with the Doctor, he snaps at her in front of everyone that the Brig is trying his best, and that she should show respect to her superior officer. It's as if he's just spat in her face. What a bastard!

He's not the only one getting testy this week. I love this image of a Brigadier frustrated that he's not allowed to join in the adventure with everybody else, and left (as he puts it so beautifully) like "a spare lemon waiting for the squeezer". With the Brig safely tucked out away from the main plot, it's as if everyone feels they can get away being sarcastic or supercilious to him. Captain Yates gets positively snide with him at one point!

The highlight of the episode is probably the sequence of the Master addressing the villagers. Roger Delgado gets the maximum comedy from it all, playing this genial vicar with a taste for totalitarian oppression. There's an effortless charm to the way he begins pointing out individuals, and amiably revealing that they're thieves or cuckolds – before losing patience with them altogether, and killing their number with a stone gargoyle. Speaking of which, I love Bok! So many fans find Bok risible for some reason; I can't see why. The opening to the episode, in which he screeches madly at the Doctor and Jo in the barrow, dancing in front of them, is so bizarre it's honestly unnerving. And I think it's extremely clever that a creature that trades in superstitious fears is beaten back by the very same thing.

T: They make no secret of the Master's politics do they? He pooh-poohs democracy and liberty, advocating instead strong, firm leadership. (He should stand in the forthcoming local and Euro elections; he'd probably do depressingly well.) The Squire, Winstanley, is actually prepared to go along with him... until he realises, the stuffy old git that he is, that a certain amount of subservience will be required. You're right – it's great fun that after all the cajoling he's deployed, the Master gives up and simply decides to destroy Winstanley instead; he swaps persuasiveness for brute force to pull the rest of the village into line, then tells them to go off and enjoy the May Day celebrations!

I'm a big fan of Quatermass, and the further I get into The Daemons, the more it would be surprising if writers Robert Sloman and Barry Letts (credited as "Guy Leopold") *didn't* have Quatermass and the Pit at the back of their minds as they crafted this – and if they did, frankly, that's no bad thing. I'm easily impressed by the idea of aliens being explanations for myths, gods and monsters, and the central idea here – that the human race has been little more than a lab experiment – really puts us in our place. Besides, whatever this story's origins, it's a good mix of drama, comedy and action – we get that exciting helicopter/ motorbike/ Bessie chase, Yates punching the Master's minion in the face to precisely zero effect, and the heat barrier keeping our heroes trapped. On the lighter side of things, we have Sgt Osgood's hapless inability to decipher the Doctor's technical jargon, and the latter's haughty response to the man's confusion. Also, the Doctor's translation of his Venusian Lullaby ("Close your eyes, my darling... well three of them, at least...") is a beauty.

And we end on *such* a cracking cliffhanger, as the Doctor tries to get the Brig and his men through the heat barrier, Jo wakes up in a panic and Miss Hawthorne claims that everyone's going to die as the camera shakes, the picture distorts and the cavern adopts a spooky red hue. Strangely, *the Master* is in the most immediate jeopardy as the Daemon looms over him – it's a testament to how much poorer the programme would be without Delgado's presence. Just look at how he contorts and twitches his face when summoning the elemental forces – Delgado does the non-naturalistic requirements of fantasy so convincingly, and suggests great power and authority in *everything* he does. Dare I say it... the devil's in the detail!

By the way, Rob, I like Bok too – it's a nice design, and Stanley Mason scampers about in the part very effectively, like a vicious terrier. I especially like the way he tries to do one more little charge after being summoned away, like the impotent bravado of a school bully who's just been dragged off by teacher.

May 29th

The Daemons (episode four)

R: The talks are going well. I'm not an expert on paintings, and I can't read Dutch, but no-one's rumbled me yet. And today we were in Delft and the Hague! Canals! And, just for good measure, cobbles too. Hurrah!

I wonder what they'd have made of this episode in the Netherlands. Or anywhere outside Britain, for that matter! The May Day sequences must seem so bizarre to anybody who's never seen anything of English village customs – all those Morris Dancers beating everybody with sticks must seem far more alien than a cloven-hoofed superbeing with designs on godhood. These scenes are the highlight of the episode, a perfect synthesis of charm and surreal menace. I love the way that as the celebrations start, windows are shut and small children pulled inside houses – right from the beginning, there's something threatening about this display of amiable festivity.

And Jon Pertwee's reaction to it all is perfect, at first showing the polite embarrassment of any sane man confronted with impromptu barn dancing: he looks almost relieved when Bert the landlord pulls out a gun and has him tied to the stake, because that's *so* much more his home turf. The beauty of the maypole scenes are that they sum up the whole style of The Daemons in miniature – they're laugh-out-loud funny (the deadpan of Pertwee forced to act as wizard, and turning to Bert after a lamp shatters and saying, "That could have been you!", and John Levene just *perfectly* timing his incredulity as Bessie comes to life with

nothing more than a droop of his pistol), and yet tonally so strange that they're quite unnerving. Bert dances around the maypole persuading ordinary people to burn a man alive, in a strange sing-song voice that borders on the messianic – that he mutters a "shut up" to the Doctor as an aside is very amusing, but the sudden burst of naturalism only highlights just how very weird this story has become.

And we see Azal! In what is one of the best reveals for a monster ever. Yeah, there's a bit of fuzziness around the CSO – but it doesn't matter a jot. We've spent four episodes building up to this moment, in a story which emphasises in true fairytale style that the creature will appear only three times. Now it's that third appearance, armageddon is in the balance – and we're presented with a giant kitted out with a saturnine mask and a cruelly sneering mouth. It's the closest to the Devil that the show will dare to get for over 30 years, and the chutzpah of that carries it through.

Got to love the Atlantis reference too. It's caused so many fans to gnash their teeth, as they try to reconcile the revelation that the Daemons destroyed the place with The Underwater Menace and The Time Monster – and it's easy to forget that it's a sublime joke. Roger Delgado's facial reaction to the exchange is priceless.

T: Doctor Who is monopolising my week. Moths Ate My Doctor Who Scarf came to Greenwich last night – in the first half of the performance, I was worried that the audience wasn't enjoying it, so I texted K (who was watching) to insult her and them (as one does) for not laughing enough! She texted back to say that no, actually, everyone was loving it – so I performed the second half with vigour (and a touch of guilt) and it was lovely. Then this morning, I did the commentary for The Dominators – which I think went well. I did slip up by referring to Brian Cant's role in The Daleks' Master Plan as a "space mercenary" when I meant to say "security" or "marine", but someone else was talking when I realised my mistake, and I didn't want to interrupt. (It's so much more important to let the people who actually worked upon the episode talk – I'm only there, I hope, to steer conversation or fill in blanks.) I know, though, that some baleful corner of the internet will clamour for my immediate execution for that single, isolated incident committed over the course of five whole episodes of otherwise (I hope) interesting and well-conducted chat. Maybe it's appropriate that I'm musing on this as I watch an episode that features flaming, a troll and a witch (well, wizard) hunt. Still, you take the rough with the smooth, and I did have a lovely afternoon watching the Star Trek movie with some friends (Steve Roberts, Sue Cowley and Lisa Bowerman) who I only know through the world of Doctor Who.

And it's this "rough and smooth" duality that's much on my mind as I watch this episode, as I vividly remember how The Daemons was shown, recoloured after years of existing only as black-and-white, when I was in my first year at university. I say vividly remember – because I was shocked that my fellow housemates (we were an arbitrary bunch, thrown together randomly in a Halls of Residence) thought the whole thing was pretty rubbish, for reasons I couldn't fathom! But, sure enough... Bok was laughed at, the ladder outside Jo's window was mocked as massively contrived and convenient (that had never occurred to me), and much hilarity ensued when the name "Rollo Gamble" rolled by in the credits. (Still, at least everyone present was reading the credits; TV companies don't expect a modern audience to do even that.) I'm sure I'm not alone in saying that old habits die hard – watching Doctor Who with other company then set much of the tone for how I sometimes feel when the classic Doctor Who DVD commentaries I moderate come out; it's excitement tinged with worry that someone will spoil it by saying something horrible about something totally innocuous. Such criticism comes from a tiny but vocal minority, but – intended or not – it can seem quite mean-spirited at times.

But you know what? I think it was my housemates' loss that they couldn't appreciate this story, as it's a terrific fusion of everything that Doctor Who does very well. It takes place on a tiny, very British locale, and makes excellent use of both horror and sci-fi tropes. It has jeopardy, comedy, action and good storytelling. Yes, all right... I agree with you about Pertwee's occasional unpleasantness and pomposity, but he's great at stuff like the moment

when the Brigadier asks the Doctor if he knows what he's doing, and the Doctor replies: "My dear chap, I can't wait to find out." Again and again, this story has so much of what I expected of Doctor Who as a kid – the English countryside, the Doctor being shot at, stunt falls off motorbikes. We even get killer Morris Dancers! (And isn't it wonderful that the locals shut their house windows and drag their kids inside as these evil jiggers appear – the suggestion being that the villagers hate them even when they're not in the thrall of an evil-devil-space-being?)

It's such a terribly good production all around. Roger Ford's design work is both interesting and practical – the pub's a homely haven, the cavern an atmospheric hideout and the Squire's house a solid two-storey abode. When Yates chucks the spellbook onto the special mark, there's a simple but nifty effect, carried off without undue ceremony, as it is torn to pieces. As director, Christopher Barry wisely shoots Azal from behind, with the camera looking down on the Master, which is visually impressive. And things I previously feared no longer bother me – I used to worry about CSO fringing, seeing it as the ultimate technical fault which bedevilled classic Doctor Who, but now it doesn't bother me a jot. And, ah yes... I no longer fear flares, which I remember my student contemporaries guffawing at. (Which was odd even back then, since they'd been in and out of fashion a number of times since this show was broadcast. I mean, I'm sure Shakespeare's garb would look silly to modern eyes, but good luck taking the piss out of him.)

All right, all right... I think I'm getting a little giddy about this episode, but so much of it makes me happy. I'm charmed to recall that the novelisation of this story has a fabulous picture of a bit of ivy strangling Jo (even if it's puzzling on screen to see such a potentially gripping moment done in long shot so that it barely registers). Better still, the Master tries to sacrifice a chicken, and Azal turns around as he grows – it's all wonderful stuff. And Benton continues to shine – forget Jago and Litefoot, I want a spin-off featuring the sergeant and Miss Hawthorne, they're a great double act!

The Daemons (episode five)

R: The Doctor enters the church, to confront Azal and certain death. He gazes up at the giant in awe – and yet the first thing he does is to say to Jo gently how pleased he is to see her. It's a tender moment which for me makes up for all the cruelty he's shown her this story – and nicely anticipates the ending, in which Jo shows her love for him back by offering her life in exchange for his.

... now, that ending is much mocked, I know. Azal cannot compute the irrationality of her self-sacrifice, and blows up in confusion – but the whole point of the Daemons, surely, is that they inspired some of the great cultural achievements of the human race, all of which depend upon imagination and celebrate such irrationality? And yet, for all its thudding convenience, it feels emotionally right. Because it comes at the end of a long scene in which the themes are so great and universal, the sudden switch back to the intimate and the personal is really rather touching. Let's face it, forget the cloven hoofs – this scene is the only time we're going to get Doctor Who having a conversation with God, and that's emphasised by the way that he cowers before an almighty hand pointing straight down at him. There's that old chestnut about how former producer John Wiles wanted to tell a Doctor Who story where the Doctor was challenged by the Almighty – and that's pretty much what we've got here. Pertwee is terrific in this exchange, all the haughty arrogance gone, as he becomes just a little man resisting the opportunity to be greater than that. This is the logical extension of the end of Colony in Space, in which the Doctor declined a share of ruling the universe, happier to see the whole infinity of creation than to rule it – so here we see a Doctor offered supremacy and prepared to die rather than accept it. Yeah, it's contrived that Azal dies so easily as a result – but Jo echoes that same compassion that the Doctor shows, and that's what saves the day. We've had a whole season built around the Doctor's feud with a fellow Time Lord, a race that on their introduction were established as being just as godlike as Azal the Daemon. How appropriate that he is at last defeated, and by an innocent expression of bravery.

And it's gorgeous, too, that after the church is destroyed that villagers can sense a change in the air – they let their children out to play once again, and they begin to celebrate. "There's magic in the world after all", muses the Doctor, and he's so right. And that magic is Doctor Who, finding its confidence again triumphantly after a fairly awkward season.

T: *Finally*, we get the Brigadier into action, and we're reminded of how much we've missed him. His "Chap with the wings there, five rounds rapid..." line is justifiably a thing of legend, as it's a fine example of deadpan comedy and unflappable stoicism triggered by a confrontation with the mindboggling. In fact, the Brigadier's first sight of Bok causes him to ask, delightfully, if the creature is some kind of ornament – and it's rather fun how, when the action's over, the gargoyle calmly sits down and becomes immobile, causing the Brig to tap it on the head to make sure it's stone.

Top marks should go to Jon Pertwee for injecting the climax with requisite intensity – he enters the coven's cavern full of piss and vinegar, selling his line about knowing he's a dead man. And it's great that the writers, via the Doctor, don't let mankind off lightly. Hitler is mentioned (and dismissed as a bounder – the understatement of the year!), and the Doctor berates Azal for advancing Man so much that he can "blow himself up and he probably will". And, once again, the Doctor refuses ultimate power – he just doesn't want the responsibility, does he?

And let me give a shout-out to the terrific job that Christopher Barry has done. I adore the shots of the Doctor, Jo and the Master filmed from the angle of Azal's outstretched arm in the foreground, and the climax is suitably thrilling before dissolving into an utterly charming coda with the maypole. The Brig's line about preferring a pint in the pub to dancing is pitched perfectly, and that final shot of the maypole dancers is a delight.

But for as much as I've heaped praise upon this story... I should be candid as to where it here falls down. Benton has an unintentionally hilarious collapse after the Master's cloak is flung on him (my favourite bit in The Naked Gun parodies moments like this – Leslie Nielsen has a pillow flung at his face, but reacts as if someone's attacked him with acid), although Benton's dignity is later redeemed when he gets to dance with Miss Hawthorne. Also, the "blast" that Azal uses to zap one of the locals is a pretty mimsy spark for such an all-powerful being. But the *big* criticism I have is that, unlike you, Rob, I think that the ending is pretty ludicrous. (Perhaps you've spent so much time surrounded by cobbles recently, you're unable to recognise cobblers!) The idea that Azal short-circuits because Jo is prepared to allow herself to be destroyed... well, I can push it out of my mind, but it just seems a great big cop-out. (I mean, it's not like the resolution of a story is important or anything like that...)

But, no matter. I have so thoroughly enjoyed this spooky, fun and rollicking adventure that I can happily forgive just one mistake over five whole episodes (do you hear me, The Internet?). From the meaty power in Stephen Thorne's Azal-voice to the storyline involving the Master embarking upon his greatest scheme yet (summoning *the* Devil, for pity's sake), to the great moment when Bok confronts the UNIT soldiers and folds his arms in a cocky manner (as if to say "come and have a go if you think you're hard enough") and so much more, this is a piece of television worth celebrating.

May 30th

Day of the Daleks (episode one)

R: In Edam today. I spent some of the day at a cheese factory. As you would. And then, having learned how Edam cheese is made, I stumbled out into the bright Dutch sunshine, to gaze out on all the cobbly canals stretching off into the distance.

And the Daleks are back! Well. Sort of.

This is a really intriguing opener to the season. Against the grain of the storytelling style established last year, the episode relies upon mystery rather than action, and raises genuine puzzles for the audience to solve rather than the typical build-up to alien appearance. What is extraordinary is that with all the ingredients that writer Louis Marks throws at us – assassination attempts, time travellers, thug mon-

sters and World War III – this does not only make coherent sense, but also is pacy and exciting to boot. Auderly House lends perfect atmosphere to this peculiar ghost story, and, as a result of that, the more character-led scenes of Yates stealing Benton's cheese and wine work. Yes, they're funny, and maybe even a little cute, but they're there because for the tension of the threat to work, the story needs to kill time and *wait*. The Doctor tucking into a Gorgonzola and declaring his tipple to be delicate and sardonic is lovely, precisely because Jo is jumping at shadows in the background. And all of this is contrasted with a sense that time is running out and we're slipping into another world war – the sequence where the Brigadier listens coolly to panicked news reports ought to feel like nothing more than expositional padding, but because we cut from that to scenes of the Doctor enjoying himself playing lord of the manor, it blows a strange chill through the proceedings. Paul Bernard directs experimentally, bravely linking all the different strands of the story with slow fades, and allowing a haunting menace to the fore in the slower scenes.

The regulars are on form as well, Jo getting a chance to display some intelligence for a change, and a real but not cloying affection demonstrated between the Doctor and the Brigadier. Indeed, the only thing that lets this down are the Daleks themselves, who in the cliffhanger appear less credible than everything that has come before. Maybe it's the slow speed with which they speak, maybe it's Bernard overplaying the camera zooms, but they're really not very threatening here. It's almost as if, after five years of the Daleks being off the screen, Doctor Who doesn't really *need* the pepperpots any more, and no-one's really sure what they have to do to give them personality.

T: Okay, I'm going to let slip one of my little prejudices here... I like Paul Cornell (he's a nice man and a terribly good writer), but there's a scene in Human Nature/ The Family of Blood that I'm very glad was cut and relegated to the DVD extras. The offence of the scene in question? The Doctor says he hates pears. My objection to that? Simple... the Doctor shouldn't ever be a fussy eater. Just look at the fun Jon Pertwee has enjoying the finer things in life – the complicated tastes, textures and aromas of sophisticated sustenance like blue cheese and red wine. This is a man who has seen everything the universe has to offer: he's too curious and full of the joys of new experiences to be picky about food. Fussiness is, I'm afraid, the recourse of someone who wilfully refuses to broaden their palette. I mean, I hated loads of food as a kid – but my mum insisted I have at least two mouthfuls of anything I didn't want to eat before I left the table, which made me acquire a liking for flavours I initially had trouble assimilating. The Doctor is a role model – he shouldn't be exposing kids to even the concept of disliking food, and certainly not pears, which are a fruit and one of your five a day.

Otherwise... this isn't just the great return of the Daleks after an extended hiatus, it's also the series' first use of time mechanics in a long while. (The last time Doctor Who dealt with such temporal jiggery-pokery was The War Games, although prior to *that*, you'd have to go – depending on how you define terms – back to The Ark if not The Space Museum, which in real time was *seven years* ago.) Indeed, the comedy scene of the Doctor and Jo meeting their cross-temporal selves moots the complicated nature of time travel very neatly, even if it's played a touch broadly. The need to keep things moving does create some wrinkles, though – I mean, it's a good job for the guerrilla Shura that neither of the UNIT soldiers he so coldly dispatches is his great-great-grandfather. Wouldn't the guerrillas have some sort of rule for this kind of thing, rather than just blindly killing every passing sentry?

All in all, it's an episode that's as interesting and fun on screen as it is on paper. Yates and Benton again have plenty to do (many accounts of Doctor Who's history sideline these two, but for now they're vital contributors), and the scene where Yates nicks Benton's food and wine (on the grounds of "RHIP – Rank Has Its Privileges") allows for more downtrodden Benton comedy, which is always a winner in the Hadoke household. You can almost hear John Levene's stomach rumbling – although if that's how Richard Franklin necks wine in real life, I worry for his liver. The person who makes the biggest impact in this season open-

er, however, is Paul Bernard – his camerawork in the studio is full of attention-grabbing zooms and blurs, and there's a great moment near the end where our view of the Controller suddenly becomes the picture on the Dalek scanner.

Where does this episode misfire, you might ask? Strangely enough, the glitches are mainly vocal. Jean McFarlane – as Sir Reginald Styles' secretary – admittedly has a wonderfully rich, 60-a-day voice, but I'm not sure about Deborah Brayshaw's waxy face and stilted delivery as the Controller's technician. More to the point, hardcore Doctor Who fans are surely familiar with the really odd bit where one Ogron talks for what seems like forever, laboriously enunciating every syllable of his report about finding and destroying some enemies, before his mate throws away the very next line ("No complications") with shocking naturalism! I love that moment, though – it makes me chuckle every time.

Niggles aside, this episode is on a sure footing. My favourite bit in this, in fact, is the wonderful juxtaposition between the sprightly athleticism of Shura's attack on the Doctor, and the Doctor's calm trouncing of the man, not spilling a drop of the wine he continues to drink throughout the altercation. The whole sequence is sublime and witty, with the mild aroma of flair and a soupcon of class.

Day of the Daleks (episode two)

R: I very much like Anna Barry's Anat, who presents here the acceptable face of guerrilla fanaticism. But what makes this story work well is that – as is now common under this production team – there is a genuine ambiguity as to who are the good guys and who are the bad. Eight years ago, remember, this little team of gun-toting killers would have been pacifist Thals; now Doctor Who is asking questions about just how far one can go in offering resistance to evil before you're tainted by it too. And whilst the Doctor is on hand to suggest that we shouldn't judge the rebels too badly until we understand them better, it's perfectly credible that Jo should have sufficient reason to betray them to the Controller on her arrival in the twenty-second century. (That's a nicely performed scene too; I love the subtle way that the Controller wins Jo's trust merely by giving up his padded seat for her.)

It'd be so easy in storyline form for Jo to look like an idiot here. But there's clearly been a reinterpretation of her character since last year, where she bungled her way through stories like a clumsy child. Last week, she correctly identified dematerialisation circuits, and now she's taking the initiative against her abductors. Katy Manning seems a lot more comfortable with playing Jo as a girl who has the wit to *learn* from her experiences with the Doctor; the scene between her and Jon Pertwee in the wine cellar where they discuss ethics, time paradoxes and escapology is played with real affection.

My inner jury is still out on the Daleks; they don't have any character yet, but they're clearly still being kept in the background of the story. And there's something rather wonderful – in their first new adventure for five seasons – that we're left waiting with anticipation for the Doctor to meet his nemeses, and that he only becomes aware they're in the story at all at the midway point. (But I'll grumble next episode if Louis Marks doesn't do *something* interesting with them, you mark my words.) No, at this stage, my only real quibble is with that image of the Doctor rushing about with a laser gun and shooting an Ogron dead. It's worrying to see that creep in; Season Seven introduced, in Inferno, the idea of his Venusian karate, and over the course of the following season it was developed into a means by which the Doctor could get out of trouble each week. But once you start putting in sequences where the Doctor effortlessly beats people up – no matter how much he's renamed it aikido, as if to suggest it's not aggressive – then it doesn't take long before the violence becomes second nature. The startling thing about seeing the Doctor zap an Ogron is that it's not quite startling enough.

T: I would go further and say that the Doctor's dispatch of the Ogron is just *horrible*, and so unusual for this phase of Doctor Who. Right from Jon Pertwee's second story, this has been the self-confessed "moral" era, where the Doctor at least has the decency to ponder, question and furrow his brow before blowing things up. So when he blithely takes two lives

whilst toting a gun – with absolutely no consideration as to the alternatives, and no discussion as to why *these* circumstances warrant such behaviour – it seems a bit of a betrayal as to what the series has been advocating the past two years. Besides, it's not as if the story desperately needed this, as the Brigadier and his handy machine gun turn up seconds later. Surely, one of the Brig's functions is to gun down monsters so that the Doctor doesn't have to? (And yes, I'm aware that this allows me to have my liberal cake and eat it...) A more complex approach to morality is welcome when Jo and the Doctor discuss the guerrillas – she condemns them as fanatics whilst he describes them as desperate rather than evil. One man's terrorist is another man's freedom fighter, after all.

This story also gives us so much to *look* at. Paul Bernard achieves some fine technical work when a close-up of Aubrey Woods pans out to become the view from the Daleks' cupboard, and there's a visual distortion when the Controller is in there with them. Woods is taller than both the pepperpots and the door, which gives a queasy disorientation to the geometry of the shot. I'm less sold, however, on the way the theme "sting" is retained during the reprise – unlike the experiment with the titles of The Ambassadors OF DEATH, I can see why this rather messy technique was dropped.

And then... yes, *there* it is! The bit where an Ogron smashes through a window, made somewhat infamous when the BBC's Six O'Clock News included this clip in its tribute to Jon Pertwee following the announcement of his death in 1996. I was utterly livid that they reported the passing of such an acclaimed and accomplished actor with the ill-informed, lazy and smug journalistic caveat that Doctor Who's sets may have wobbled and the acting may have been a bit crap, but it was nonetheless quite sad that Pertwee was dead. I appeased my rage, just a little, by writing a very angry letter to the Radio Times that I never sent... but the shoddy treatment still rankled, and I'm very relieved that I gave it a suitably fiery riposte in Moths Ate My Doctor Who Scarf.

Day of the Daleks (episode three)

R: Hmm. I probably *am* going to grumble a bit about the Daleks in a moment. But there's so much else that's happening here that's remarkable, I won't make it too big a grumble. Promise.

This started out as a UNIT story, and now it's surprised us by dropping them from the episode altogether. And instead of being a contemporary tale about peace conferences, it's instead a surprisingly subtle portrait of a totalitarian society. This clearly takes some of its cue from The Dalek Invasion of Earth, but tells the story of an invaded Earth almost entirely from the *victims'* point of view rather than the monsters'. We get glimpses of an entire world of slaves: a factory of old men and children run at the lick of a whip, their managers who tyrannise them being victimised in turn by the need to keep productivity quotas up (actor Peter Hill is left literally shaking with suppressed fear after Aubrey Woods gives him a "friendly warning"), the Controller who tyrannises them being at the mercy of an alien race who don't even dignify his constant loyalty with their trust. In one moment, the Doctor is being tortured by sadists (we don't see any lashes, but Pertwee's bemused reaction to Peter Hill's questions suggests a man who's been badly bruised by his treatment), and the next he's quaffing wine over a picnic with the Controller, and with quiet anger decrying the whole regime. There's little here we haven't seen before, but the brilliance of it is that we're seeing it here in miniature – we get a greater understanding of a Dalek-occupied world here, from the luxurious grapes with which the Controller tempts Jo, to the unpractised and rather lunatic smile he flashes at her to show her he has good news, than we did in six entire episodes back in 1964. It's done with tremendous skill.

And that's why I'm not going to grumble about the Daleks *too* much. What's being done is really rather clever, telling a Dalek tale not by showcasing the pepperpots themselves but the people that they've subjugated. The problem is, though, that it really has been rather a long time since we saw them – not since that repeat of The Evil of the Daleks in 1968. And beyond a vague assumption that the audience

will understand they're iconic, there's not the slightest attempt to explain what they are or what they stand for. By chanting the same lines over and over again, they give the appearance of being nothing more than robots. They don't show any of the cunning that we might expect, or indeed any personality whatsoever. We haven't seen them even offer any *threat* yet; they may well use the word "exterminate" a lot, but there's not been an indication to how these exterminations might be carried out. Children grow up fast; we have to presume that a fair few kids watching Day of the Daleks would never have seen anything of the creatures before, and to rely upon a few broad hints from the Doctor that he knows them from yesteryear really isn't enough. At this stage of the story, the greatest single threat has been the brute force of the Ogrons – these rather odd monsters with the staccato voices, who stay in one room and do little more than swivel about on the spot, are all talk and no balls. So to speak.

T: In a story about human guerrillas being hunted by, er, human gorillas – the latter, the Ogrons, do look pretty fearsome, their jackboots impressively filing past the camera during an unusually sunny location shoot. Less formidably, the Ogron actors try to make their "lumbering run" look responsible for their failing to catch the funky space trike the Doctor and Jo try to escape on, and which has "Jon's found something he wants to play with" written all over it, but they don't quite pull it off.

But what this story is *really* about, of course, is how people deal with occupation, and skirt that fine line between saving one's own skin and doing the right thing. To that end, it's interesting and appropriate that in a story featuring the Daleks – the most iconic nihilists Doctor Who has ever produced – *humans* are referred to as the treacherous and unreliable ones. After all, the inhumanity here is a self-perpetuating cycle: the Daleks make unreasonable demands to the Controller, who in turn gets heavy on the Manager and threatens him. In short, bullies bully others into becoming bullies on their behalf. It adeptly demonstrates that if those in charge of a society are cruel and unfeeling, such sentiment will infect the society until everybody becomes either a victim or a perpetrator of injustice.

Some fine acting accompanies the dilemmas within this moral framework. Peter Hill's tiny little shake of the head to Pertwee (meaning "Don't trust the Controller, you're still not safe...") is terrific, a lovely silent moment that speaks volumes. And Aubrey Woods has an excellent line in facial control – he's so impressive when he menaces the Manager, with his face nothing more than a controlled mask, and only his mouth articulating. Crucially, he's a plausible good guy, meaning that Jo doesn't seem particularly stupid in trusting him. (I do have to query the so-called "twentieth century" banquet that he lays on for her, though – where are the Dairylea Triangles and Pot Noodles?) Most importantly, Jon Pertwee is continually excellent, from his obvious discomfort with the sadistic guard's kinky truncheon-wielding to his brilliant ripostes to the Controller's claims that the people "have never been happier or more prosperous". ("Then why do you need so many people to keep them under control? Don't they like being happy and prosperous?") He absolutely runs rings around the Controller – in moments like this, as a seething centre of moral conviction, Pertwee is magnificent.

Let me also give another shout-out to Paul Bernard – he's learned how to shoot the Daleks (so to speak) very well, framing their top halves at the edge or corner of the picture. Overall, the sights and sounds of this are quite experimental (Deborah Brayshaw gets shot through some yellow Perspex in a rather curious moment), and whilst I still think that it's odd to reuse the theme sting in the reprise, the blending of the show's titles with the Daleks' mind probe – as well as the credits appearing over the picture for the first and only time in the classic series' colour years – is an interesting curio.

One last thing: the rebels smoke, which made me think it was terribly grown-up when I was a kid. Which isn't, I expect, what the production team intended...

May 31st

Day of the Daleks (episode four)

R: And the cruise ends in Amsterdam! Where there are no cobbles or canals at all... no, I'm joking, of course. There are *so many bloody cobbles and canals* that I fully expect when I go to sleep tonight, they'll be burned on my retina and invade my dreams. And there's a strong scent of something sweet and heady in the air. Do you know, I don't think all these coffee shops are selling coffee at all. Someone should complain.

Maybe it's the whiff of drugs in the air, but I think I can get my head around the time paradoxes here. (Well, most of them.) That all the guerrilla antics of the rebels have only succeeded in causing the very dystopia that they are trying to avoid feels like a moral judgment on them and their propensity to brutal violence, and that's exactly why it works so well; too often when Doctor Who tries its paw at all the temporal stuff, it succeeds only in being clever but ridding the whole thing of any emotional content. But this episode is brimming over with it. There's an intensity to the quiet way that the Doctor denounces the Controller and his ancestors as quislings that makes this one of Pertwee's best performances yet – and it's balanced by the humanity he shows when he dissuades the rebels from murdering the man. That this act of charity is ultimately the reason why the Controller lets the Doctor return to the past, and thus giving his enslaved race the chance of a different future, is lovely; when confronting the Daleks later, Aubrey Woods only makes the most token of efforts to convince them he's not betrayed them – he seems almost relieved not to have to bluster any more, and he stands tall with pride as they exterminate him.

I'm annoyed, though, that the *other* temporal paradox set up in episode one – that the Doctor and Jo confront their future selves – isn't resolved. It's set up, it was scripted – and then finally cut, because of (ironically!) time constraints. I remember reading the sequence in the novelisation when I was a kid, and it seemed back then the perfect neat ending to this strange story of events from the future feeding back into the past. Without it there, the story feels unresolved somehow, and a little messy.

The twenty-second century scenes work very well. The story falls apart a little back in the twentieth. Some would say this is because it's all too obvious that only three Daleks are budgeted to invade Auderly House, but I think that Paul Bernard's direction overcomes these limitations and the battle scenes work well enough. No, the problem I have is more with the plotting. Once the Doctor has returned to the present day to prevent history from being changed, the premise of the story is over and there's nowhere left to go. Saving the world from Dalek rule becomes a simple matter of persuading a lot of mute delegates to stand outside a mansion long enough for it to explode. In episode two, the Doctor has speculated that even the smallest of actions create whole future histories, but really the story deserved an action a little bit bigger to avoid being so anticlimactic.

It's a good story, though – tightly squeezed into its four-episode length, this manages to feel both epic and cerebral at the same time.

T: I have an uncle who, as a film buff, has always thought Doctor Who a bit rubbish – so Day of the Daleks was the story that I'd cite when he'd praise The Terminator. The gist of my argument was that The Terminator didn't make sense as it relied on a time paradox – and so you couldn't like The Terminator if you don't like Doctor Who, because if Doctor Who's plots didn't make sense, at least they didn't make sense *first*! I say all of that even though, actually, the resolution of the story and its temporal mechanics are sold well enough. Pertwee gives the discovery that the guerrillas created the very history they're trying to eradicate enough weight to make it come across as a major revelation, so the "chicken and egg" conundrum that this entails needn't trouble us especially. For better or worse, I'm fine with it.

Indeed, Pertwee is on form on multiple levels: his line to Sir Reginald ("Try to use your intelligence, even if you are a politician!") makes me want to see the third Doctor as a guest on Question Time! And the scene where he spares the Controller is sublime, the

Doctor's refusal to countenance murder forcing the Controller to rediscover his own humanity. Aubrey Woods doesn't resort to histrionics at this change of heart – his character has kept his emotions in check just to survive, and he's been so (forgive the pun) controlled throughout, that it has a real impact when his eyes flicker *even slightly*. The way in which the Controller then allows Jo and the Doctor to escape in the tunnel, and gets a decent parting shot at the evil pepperpots before he's eradicated, is fantastic.

Bernard's visual originality, as you've touched upon, continues and yet it's not all razzle-dazzle – the battle scenes have hardware, smoke and explosions. The Daleks and Ogrons come out in the sun on location, whilst the indoor work benefits from some impressive use of perspective when filming David Myerscough-Jones' slightly abstract sets. Look, for instance, at the final scene as the senior guard leaves the Daleks and recedes into the distance… and just keeps going. For a series where often people have been boxed in or exit off camera, it's an impressive and clever use of space.

For that matter, the nasty, power hungry, sadistic, stubbly (and slightly camp, it has to be said) guard fulfils the remit of this story – he's the sort of person who has prospered in the kind of world the Daleks create. That's why it's proper that the Doctor and his allies must never allow it to exist. As good as he's been in this story, though, I can't help but chuckle when Pertwee describes Styles as "Vain to the point of arrogance, a trifle obstinate, but basically a good man". Hmm, excuse me, I'd better nip into the kitchen where my pot and kettle are having something of a row about colour.

The Curse of Peladon (episode one)

R: In the interests of full disclosure, I have to admit more than a partial interest in this. Whilst other 12 year olds were acting out being the Doctor, or the Brigadier, or one of the monsters, I was pretending to be… Chancellor Torbis. Yes, that's right. Torbis, the rather unfortunate Pel who gets clubbed to death by Aggedor in the opening scene of this story, even before the Doctor can turn up to save him. I don't entirely know why. The adventure was broadcast in a short repeat season in the summer of 1982, and I put the whole thing on to audio cassette. And I listened to it over and over again, and there was just something about those opening couple of minutes I loved; Dudley Simpson's music has a lovely magisterial ring to it just right for marching, and so I marched around my bedroom, and the character who got to do the most marching was Torbis, on his way to tell his king that the delegates had arrived. I'd then get to mouth Torbis' lines as he argued with Hepesh, sometimes even saying them out loud over Henry Gilbert's performance – I'd even put in that smug sneer of self-congratulation Gilbert gave once the king had intervened on Torbis' behalf. And then I'd be off marching again, this time to my death, at the paw of a royal beast. Lovely. As I think of it, I get the urge to march all over again.

Typically, for that Shearman kid who got the wrong end of the stick, Henry Gilbert's performance is not the one I should have been emulating. It's perfectly okay, but of the three actors in that scene, it's not a patch on the ones offered by David Troughton (as King Peladon) or Geoffrey Toone (as Hepesh, the high priest). The acting in this episode is the most consistently good we've seen on the show for over a year – that long sequence where King Peladon reflects sadly upon his childhood, listens to the suspicions of his high priest, and then asserts his authority over him, is brilliantly played by both of them. (And considering it lasts a few minutes, and has nothing to do with the Doctor whatsoever, it's remarkable just how effective it is when it might have felt like a bit of irrelevant padding.) Troughton plays Peladon as a boy desperately wanting to be a man, almost crushed by the expectations placed upon his shoulders – it'd be tempting to think that with a father as experienced as his own, who one might think had made *something* of an impression in Doctor Who himself, that young David T had something to draw on. It's a sterling performance – I especially like that moment where he's caught listening in fascinated reverie to the superstitious cant of the legends he's trying to refute. And Toone is wonderful; you believe right from the start that he has the planet's best interests at heart, that

he sees himself clearly as the hero – and considering that he's a fanatical high priest who's obsessed with his love of hairy monsters, that he makes Hepesh so credible is quite an achievement.

What that 12-year-old me didn't understand was just how atypical this story was. It was the first Pertwee story I had seen, and it didn't seem much different from the Doctor Who template I expected; the Doctor and his companion land on an alien planet and haplessly get thrust into the middle of an adventure. But it's the first time the series has done anything like this since the days of Patrick Troughton – even the Doctor being forced to take on another identity feels very Pat, and nothing at all like the brash scientist who has the Brigadier bring problems to *him*. The last time we saw Jo in the TARDIS, she found the whole process terrifying – here, she's comically long-suffering and banters about the unreliability of the Ship. It's the first time a story hasn't used the Earth as a starting point since Season Six. It almost seems like business as usual, that we've really thrown off Derrick Sherwin's reformatting of the series; forget the Daleks last week, we've got the TARDIS lost to prevent the Doctor's escape until the end of the story (in a brilliant model effects sequence where it falls in slow motion down a cliff face), we've got characters creeping around corridors – we've even got the Ice Warriors. This feels like the Doctor Who we used to know.

And even so, it's still got something entirely new to offer. Alpha Centauri is the first deliberately comic alien in Doctor Who. (There have been a few who have made me chuckle, but let's face it, they weren't *meant* to be funny.) My wife Janie played Alpha Centauri in a Big Finish audio a couple of years ago, and I watched this story with her for research – I suggested that she copy the lovely affected laugh that Alpha gives in his first scene, even though Ysanne Churchman never does it again, just for the sake of verisimilitude. The aliens here are terrific, simply because for once they really are *meant* to seem grotesque and weird against the faux medieval setting. Arcturus is just bizarre enough, with that liquid pouring through his dome, and his funny little puppet face – if he were the lead character he'd look ridiculous, but here that's all part of the point. And the Ice Warriors are great! In colour! They're green! Of course they're green. And the Doctor seems frightened of them. That moment when they advance upon the Doctor in the throne room, long and slow and silent (save for the pumping of Arcturus' life support machine) is quite brilliant; the Doctor backs away, but there's nowhere for him to back to, and he then looks incredulous as Izlyr politely welcomes him as ambassador.

It's Katy Manning's best performance yet too. Not when she's playing the silly little girl in the TARDIS, but the haughty princess who complains about the inefficiency of her pilot. Freed from the obligation to act as a clumsy child, Katy reveals subtle comic timing, and gives a quick-wittedness to Jo that we've never seen before.

T: The Curse of Peladon hits the ground running – the flaming torches, flickering shadows, costumes and camera angles create an atmosphere that complements the neat exposition. Gilbert does a very good job as the doomed Torbis – he, and David Troughton's subsequent sadness concerning his death, convey what a loss the court has suffered, even though Torbis is just a minor character with half a dozen lines (including the words "mumbo-jumbo" – something we don't hear often enough anymore) who snuffs it in the first scene. That Hepesh, though, doesn't half push it a bit – when everyone fondly reminisces about the king's past, he can't help but repeat a few jibes about his monarch's mongrel ancestry. If I were Peladon, I'd make my reproach a bit sterner and tell him to lay off my heritage: "although the royal blood that flows in your veins is mingled with that of strangers" indeed! Still, David Troughton's intelligence as an actor shines through, and he does very well with what's essentially a drippy character.

I hate to keep going on about him, but Jon Pertwee was *born* to carry off court etiquette with élan. The current Doctor isn't an anarchist like Troughton, or anti-establishment like Hartnell, but that's fine – his eccentricity manifests in different ways. Understanding the need for formalities and observing protocol doesn't make him a creep; he's just being well mannered. It's endearing, even, how he inveigles his way into the citadel by presenting

himself as someone with official status, as opposed to an interloper who travels about time and space in a blue box. Charm and innate authority are as much tools to this Doctor as his sonic screwdriver. And when the Doctor finally appears in the throne room, it's clever how his entrance coincides with the exact moment that Hepesh prophesies doom.

But let's be honest – the real selling point here is the carnival of monsters composing the committee sent to evaluate Peladon for Federation membership. Alpha Centauri looks a bit daft, but he/ she is *meant* to be endearing. Actualising Centauri requires a wonderful dual performance from the twittering Ysanne Churchman (as Centauri's voice) and the tottering Stuart Fell (as, well, the rest of him/ her); laugh at the character being rather phallic if you must, but this delightful symbiosis of performers produces something magical. Arcturus is pretty fun too – I love how his bubbling tank is employed as a constant, throbbing presence on the soundtrack. I hope that wasn't a valuable vase that Arcturus zapped when demonstrating his defence weapon, though – surely the Federation has rules about disintegrating indigenous antiques?

If I had any complaint, it's the slightly bizarre bit where the Doctor sees the statue of Aggedor and says they can't be on Earth. The viewer has known this for about 15 minutes, yet the production tries to sell it as a major revelation, with the music echoing Pertwee's dramatic emphasis! Still, this is a minor niggle for such a well-crafted episode that – in addition to everything I've listed above – includes some fantastic model work that moulds seamlessly with the filmed scenes on the mountain, conveying the inhospitable environment of Mount Megeshra. If The Curse of Peladon can keep up this level of quality, we're in for an elegant and arresting adventure.

The Curse of Peladon (episode two)

R: Yes, I was right, it's finally happened. I've been converted! I'm a Katy Manning lover! I had hoped it would happen eventually. After all, Jo Grant is certainly one of the most popular companions. (And Katy is one of my wife's best friends, and often stays in our spare room, so I think it's only socially correct that I enjoy her performance.) In Season Eight, Jo was largely irritating – a character drawn in such broad strokes, and played as such a clumsy buffoon, it was hard to imagine she'd been allowed out of school, let alone into a para-military organisation. But there's clearly been a rethink between seasons; Jo is no longer the somewhat sheepish little girl trailing after the Doctor, but closer to his equal. The scene Manning shares with Pertwee as they ponder on who the villains might be is beautifully played – Jo not only uses her deductive powers to puzzle through the clues, she actually disagrees with the Doctor... and is right! And the whole thing is shot through with a rapport so delightful that it simply can't be faked; they *both* admit that they love the pretence of impersonating dignitaries, and so the script tacitly makes Jo as much the focus of the story as the Doctor. Manning is great when she faces down the Ice Warriors and accuses them of attempted murder – no more screaming here, but righteous anger and (better still) the ability to listen to their defence and rethink her opinion. But her best scene must be the one in the throne room where King Peladon asks her to be his friend. Lennie Mayne does something bold here – he gives Manning perhaps the closest close-up imaginable, you really feel that the camera is imprinted on her face! And that's all the better, as you see Manning assert her belief in Peladon with such enthusiasm – and then let her face fall in disappointment as she realises she's only wanted as a political ally. There's a tremendous dignity to the way Manning plays the exchange, and for my money, it makes that single scene one of the strongest in the whole Pertwee era.

It's a good story, this, isn't it? It's hardly fast moving, but it's impressively detailed. The atmosphere of paranoia is very skilfully drawn: the delegates' paranoia about the Doctor trying to maximise Earth's power in the Federation, and Peladon's paranoia that no-one believes he is opposed to barbarism. And best of all, there is the Doctor's paranoia – his eagerness to assume the worst of the Ice Warriors is the only fundamental error Pertwee's Doctor ever makes. It is rarely credited just how bold this reversal of one of the series' main villains was – or how cleverly the contrast Barry Letts and

Terrance Dicks invite with the Daleks, only the story previously. Izlyr, as the most articulate of the delegates, indeed begins to take on a very Doctorish role by the end of the episode, with his intelligent diplomacy and his practical realisation of violence as a necessary evil. There was never much depth to the Ice Warriors as characters in their last two outings, but so much more is hinted at here – the way they cling on to a constitutional monarchy, for example – and Alan Bennion does a terrific job at making Izlyr a credible character, even though he's stuck behind a mask. (And Sonny Caldinez has a good moment too. In The Seeds of Death, he memorably couldn't spot a man hiding in his direct vision; here he can find a woman hiding behind a curtain. And a *small* woman, at that, behind a *thick* curtain. The Ice Warriors have evolved.)

T: Yes, turning The Ice Warriors into the good guys really is such a great conceit, and quite a mature move for a family show that concurrently presents us with a giant green cock in a curtain and a reedy blob of snot in a box...

This story is such great *fun*, though – it's not trying to be anything other than a rollicking good yarn with twists, turns, action and monsters, and it's very much succeeding as such. The sabotage of Arcturus keeps the jeopardy simmering... *we* know that the Doctor didn't do it, but Izlyr has no reason to think that, so his suspicion of the Doctor is perfectly reasonable. Or is it because *Izlyr* is the baddy, and wants to blame the Doctor? Gaaaaaahhhhhhh... we don't know! And then Izlyr's assistant Ssorg catches Jo rifling through the Ice Warriors' quarters – it's becoming a bit like 24, where the plot gets so thick that the tension emanates (deep breath) from seeing good guys being suspected of being bad guys by people you *think* are good guys because of the machinations of the bad guys, even though you only know who some of the bad guys are! (Phew.) And then there's that great volte-face where Izlyr's knowledge upstages the Doctor, and he reveals that Arcturus wasn't as badly attacked as all that. Suddenly, this Ice Lord has become a deductive, intelligent force to be reckoned with – and I echo your applause to Alan Bennion, whose directness and poise achieve the not-inconsiderable feat of making an asthmatic lizard man with red shades into a rational and shrewd creature of nobility.

I also note that Lennie Mayne seems quite interested in offbeat visuals – there's a terrific moment where David Troughton dominates the scene even though he's the furthest back in shot, and in a different room! So far in Season Nine, no-one could be accused of just pointing a camera at the action and hoping for the best. (I mean, just *look* at the stuff here in the tiny temple set, which uses zooms, odd angles and lots of smoke – which no self-respecting high priest should ever be without.)

By the way, while I don't pride myself on being much of a lothario, even I could give King Peladon a few tips on how *not* to upset the ladies. David Troughton has to suffer the indignity of playing a man in blue shorts constantly putting his foot in it with a pretty girl, and while it's a good scene, well played by both him and Manning, I'm stifling an urge to box his ears.

June 1st

The Curse of Peladon
(episode three)

R: Most of this episode relies upon the doubt that we really *can* trust the Ice Warriors at all. Early on, Hepesh reveals that he has an ally amongst the alien delegates – and, if you can allow yourself as knowing fan to forget how this story turns out, the way in which Izlyr so readily becomes willing to fight for the Doctor's life looks *deeply* suspicious. And Lennie Mayne, as director, plays this suspicion very well; there's that lovely scene where Ssorg ever so politely invites Jo to enter the Ice Warriors' chamber – too politely for comfort – whilst accompanied by the martial score of Dudley Simpson. You can well believe that Izlyr's eagerness to prevent the Doctor from being executed hides a hidden agenda – it's the sort of thing the Master has done in plenty of stories recently, manipulating the Doctor into traps and schemes of his own. So the cliffhanger is rather clever: after a really quite superb fight scene devised by Terry Walsh, two of the delegates seem to turn their weapons

upon the Doctor. And at this stage you really can't be sure which of them is the enemy – or even, just possibly, whether *both* of them are.

This is because Brian Hayles' script, detailing the political twists and turns of no less than five different species, is easily the cleverest yet given to Pertwee's Doctor. There's that extraordinary scene in which Hepesh tries to persuade the Doctor to escape from his planet, and with great dignity (and, as we'll see, great accuracy) outlines his fear of Peladon coming under Federation rule. Or the sequence where Peladon proposes to Jo, having just condemned the Doctor to trial by combat – and genuinely not understanding why she can't see the distinction between the political and the personal. (I think if Peladon's serious about setting his cap for Jo, he'd be very wise to bump off the Doctor – she seems far too keen on him for her own good.)

T: I touched upon it before, but now I'm convinced that the king needs serious relationship counselling! I mean, I'd have trouble asking a girl on a date if I'd just spilled a drink on one of her friends, let alone if – as with Peladon here – I had just condemned them to death. Still, Jo proves as equally dim as her would-be boyfriend when she chases Aggedor off, totally ignoring the Doctor's protestations that she shouldn't. (Still, I love how Pertwee relates to Aggedor – anyone who calls a big hairy dog/ bear thing "old chap" is alright in my book.)

You know, I wasn't especially opposed to Pertwee before now, but I've increasingly warmed to him in the past couple of stories. Could it be that his old school manners and courtesy look incongruously eccentric, and therefore charming, when placed in crazy sci-fi situations? Do they look a bit pompous when cosily ensconced in twentieth-century England, but not when juxtaposed with the outlandish and bizarre? That said, I'm not sure if the Doctor's rather abrupt way of snapping Jo out of her hypnotised state would meet with expert approval – she might be traumatised for life, the poor girl.

Izlyr remains the most interesting character here – we're not sure yet whether his decision to help the Doctor escape is genuine or Machiavellian, as Alan Bennion very subtly imbues the character with ambiguity. He has some elegant dialogue too, noting that Arcturus and Alpha Centauri are respectively cowards by logic and nature. But alongside such character shading and intrigue, events build to the Doctor's action-packed gladiatorial fight to the death with Grun, the king's champion – it's a long sequence, but obviously intended as a showpiece. Mayne continues to move his camera about: there's a terrific low shot emphasising Grun's height, followed by a fantastic aerial shot of the fight arena. Repeat viewers such as ourselves tend to find such action sequences less interesting than those involving plot, ideas and character... but I remember finding all of this ludicrously exciting as a kid, and we mustn't lose sight of that perspective.

Oh, one more thing... it's worth bearing in mind that the Doctor's main legal defence is that the sacred beast that Peladon has worshipped for centuries is no mythical, extinct creature but a "solid hairy fact". So, he's essentially strode in and told them that their god doesn't exist.... or rather, *does* exist, but only as a feral creature. On balance, I think the supposedly "primitive" people of Peladon take that revelation rather well, don't you?

The Curse of Peladon (episode four)

R: In all honesty, this episode isn't a patch on the ones preceding it. But it fails for completely the *right* dramatic choices. The pressure cooker effect of paranoia and claustrophobia that gave the rest of the story its shape is lost, and the story runs with the political themes it has introduced and plays them out on a wider canvas. Peladon was just perceived as some piss-poor planet in early episodes, hardly worth the ambassadors' attention, and the Federation delegates spent much time patronising the place. So it's a genuinely clever twist of irony that somewhere so backwards and primitive so nearly becomes the pretext for the destruction of the Federation altogether, and the onset of an interplanetary war. You get the sense that it's like the Archduke Franz Ferdinand being shot at Sarajevo – that an event so small can have such shattering global repercussions. It's great to see the delegates, previously so complacent, come to realise that

everything they so primly have stood for is under threat – that this friendship between their worlds is so very delicate that it can be destroyed in an instant.

It's usually pointed out that Brian Hayles is writing a satire here of Britain joining the EEC – I think his opinion of that union is much more barbed than is often given credit. And it's fascinating to compare this to Day of the Daleks, where once again there's a big attempt at unifying separate nations, and relationships are so precarious that the world might be propelled into World War III. If Day used its peace conference as window dressing, with Reginald Styles barely appearing in the story at all, it's as if Curse takes us right into the heart of what those conferences might be like – and we're presented with a bunch of arrogant squabbling reptiles and penises in cloaks. And the irony is even better still – the *reason* why relations may break down is that the Ice Warriors were *saving* the Doctor's life. And even *better than all of that* – it's a direct consequence of the Doctor, our friendly arch peacekeeper, pretending to be someone he's not that puts the delegates into this position in the first place. It's hard to imagine Wendy Danvers as Amazonia getting herself into the sort of situation where delegates would be obliged to shoot each other dead just to keep her alive.

It's very smart, and very persuasive. And really very undramatic. The problem is that Hayles suddenly wants the action to open out onto a far greater vista – but we're stuck in flame-lit small sets of tunnels just the same, where the claustrophobic feel that the script has now discarded is really the only one the director can serve. So it means that the pacing is all awry; Alpha Centauri is taken off into conference because he baulks at taking sides in a putative civil war, and so much time is wasted that there's no dramatic payoff to be had when he finally does raise his little suckers in agreement – it's not just padding, it's not just dull padding, it's also padding that is made irrelevant as soon as we've watched it. When the Doctor tells Jo how dangerous the political situation on Peladon is, we believe him entirely; when the visible result of that situation is a rather cluttered swordfight, and a revolution overthrown simply by a short hairy beast striking a traitor with a paw, you can only feel how sad it is that The Curse of Peladon's production couldn't match its ambition. It's absolutely not the fault of Lennie Mayne's direction – he can only work with the sets at hand. For three episodes, that worked very well. Then Brian Hayles skilfully, brilliantly, refused to let the concluding instalment tread the same path as most Doctor Who adventures, and raised the stakes in unexpected ways. And no-one could follow him.

There are some great bits here. I love the way that the guard captain offers his sword to Peladon after the coup has failed; it speaks volumes about that medieval society that he not only expects immediate execution, but *accepts* it. The scene where Jo rejects Peladon's marriage proposal is played with great sensitivity by Troughton and Manning. And I can't but help love the way that, having played Aggedor as a mythical and vengeful god for three and a half episodes, how in his final scene he's recharacterised as an overaffectionate pet that follows the Doctor about everywhere. That's really very funny.

And it used to bother me there was never a scene where the Doctor said sorry to the Ice Warriors. And now I'm glad he doesn't. In a story that has tried to indulge in realpolitik as much as this one, it would have just felt trite.

T: So far in our viewing, and with Doctor Who now in the middle of its ninth year, I'm not sure I've been as moved by the death of a lead villain as I am here. Geoffrey Toone has given Hepesh such grace and nobility, making sure that he's not just an out-and-out religious fanatic whom we're glad to see the back of. Hepesh was frightened of change, yes, but he's hardly alone in that – and his motives, which entail protecting his planet, were surprisingly pure and largely without self-interest. David Troughton impressively displays the king's genuine grief when his old friend-turned-enemy dies. The laying of the hanky over Hepesh's corpse – and Pertwee's grave reaction when he re-enters – give tremendous weight and dignity to an excellent final scene.

And while I don't fundamentally disagree with your assessment of the disconnect between episode four and the rest of the story, I'd prefer to frame it that the last episode is almost a different story *altogether*, which is

certainly novel. Watch how events progress... Arcturus' instant execution cuts straight away to a post-mortem that wraps up the previous three episodes, and sets the stage for each of the protagonists' final stratagems. We're deliberately made to enter into a different phase of events, which has different concerns and leads to armed Pels storming the throne room.

Speaking of which, I think the "cluttered" sword fight that you mention is actually better orchestrated than most of the fisticuffs we've seen before now – something that's all the more admirable considering the number of people involved, and the one-level set on which it takes place. I agree with you that the scenes of the delegates stuck in a room bickering are perfunctory, but there's nonetheless a nice gag where the Martians get Centauri to vote their way by looming menacingly over him/ her. ("Carried unanimously", says Izlyr, proving that the Martians acquired a nice line in dry humour when they rejected violence.) And hilarious stuff happens later on – while Izlyr and Jo chat in the foreground, we can just see a rabbiting Centauri in the background cornering Ssorg, who can only shift around uncomfortably as the fussy old windbag babbles and bobbles about.

I'd also like to mention that Pertwee, so often criticised for being over-paternalistic and patronising, shines in his encouragement to Grun ("You're not frightened, are you? A big chap like you?") and Aggedor, whom he leads by the horns and scratches behind the ear. Indeed, the difference in attitude towards Aggedor – the Doctor being very sweet and coaxing whilst Hepesh uses fear and fire – is why, when push comes to shove, our hero survives the final showdown.

Whew! And that's The Curse of Peladon done. You know, this story has been wonderful. It uses the iconography of the genre well, reflects upon contemporary events, and even gave us a rare bit of nicely played and – given the political concerns involved – believable romance. All that and loads of monsters! If we had a referendum on this story, I'd certainly raise my suckers and vote "Yes".

June 2nd

The Sea Devils (episode one)

R: Though the definitive writer of the Pertwee era, Malcolm Hulke clearly never felt very comfortable with the concept of the UNIT family. His scripts rely upon suspicion and antagonism – most forcedly in Invasion of the Dinosaurs, where Hulke's hearkening back to the colder UNIT of Season Seven never quite comes off. It's therefore quite clever that he uses the Royal Navy in this story, and a fresh set of military characters who can be less immediately trusting of the Doctor. It makes Pertwee's Doctor more of an outsider once more, and his prickly character thrives best in those circumstances. And what's lovely is that by this stage Pertwee plays somewhat *against* the prickliness. He treats the bureaucracy of all the pass-checking with contempt, but just look at the way that as he says something impatient and cutting to Governor Trenchard, that he smiles at Jo – he came across as such a bully in The Daemons, but now that the affection he has for his companion works so well, the arrogance and petulance of the Doctor is genuinely endearing. It's a much better mix.

Though it might have been more interesting to have taken the Master's redemption at face value for a while (and one story after it had been done with the Ice Warriors, it might have worked), the scenes featuring Roger Delgado are excellent. The Master in benign mode is somehow far more unsettling than when he is being purposefully threatening, and the social awkwardness felt when the Doctor and Jo visit him in his cell is terrific. It's very clever the way that the imprisoned Master seems so much more relaxed and in control than the Doctor who is visiting him – he's so much more socially adept than our hero, who needs to mask his concern for his old enemy behind an attempt to persuade him to reveal the whereabouts of his TARDIS. Lots of good jokes here – you've got to love the way that the Master requests a second television for the cell. (In colour, of course – it's 1972, and a lot of the audience are *still* watching in black and white; this mass murderer is getting better treatment than they are!) And the Clangers scene is gor-geous. We've earned the right by now to see the Master with a sense of humour, drolly pretending that he really believes that he's watching extraterrestrials on television. It speaks volumes about his greater intelligence that he can make jokes, whilst Trenchard is a duffer who needs to point out to him that they're just puppets for children. Over the next couple of years of Barry Letts' tenure, we're going to see a *lot* of puppets for children – those who feel the need to point it out are the sort of killjoys who deserve to be manipulated by an evil mastermind.

The Clangers scene is so good that it takes attention away from the very skilful comedy scene which follows it, in which the Doctor gets a boat with a bribe. It's the way that the Doctor almost can't be bothered with the pretence of hiding it's a bribe in the first place that makes it work so well. And if we're getting a sense now that Jo and the Doctor are equals, it's emphasised here by the way that she becomes part of a running gag, bribing the same man later for use of his motorcycle.

Blink and you'll miss it, but there's a great moment where Navy officer Jane Blythe is caught by the camera doing her hair; the speedy way in which she stands to attention the moment Captain Hart comes in is great, and cleverly pays off on Hart's complaint earlier in the episode that his staff at the naval base are getting sloppy. It's little attentions to detail like that which make this episode feel so real.

T: This story revives a lot of childhood memories for me. When I was a youngster, I bought a record player for £2 from a village auction, and routinely listened to my one and only vinyl. You've guessed it: it was Doctor Who – The Music. To say I was somewhat nonplussed by the score for The Sea Devils would be an understatement, but I dutifully let it screech through my bedroom over and over again, kidding myself that it somehow repli-cated the experience of watching the show on the telly. Back in those days, of course, it was something of a novelty to actually witness a soundtrack used for its actual purpose of aug-menting a television adventure, rather than just stimulating a teenager into playing air synthesiser (I, er, nearly said "air organ" there, but didn't want to be misconstrued). Watching this story in the here and now, though, I think the score works – the scene where the Master tries to hypnotise a prison guard sounds perfectly creepy, and the composition evokes bubbly water and swelling tides.

This being written by Malcolm Hulke, it's so very tempting to go to his more-detailed Target novelisation and lament the loss of certain lovely scenes, touches and characters. When I first saw this story, I was disappointed at the absence of opening dramatics aboard the SS Pevensey Castle, which involved the mysterious sinking of some lifeboats and the massacre of a boatload of sailors. But now that my salad days are mere slug excrement, I think that this adventure begins terrifically – on Doctor Who's 1970s budget, after all, you can't have a pitched battle at sea that culminates in the destruction of a naval vessel. What we get instead, very sensibly, is one actor in a small set giving a mayday – even as the undulating camera conveys that we're at sea – before he's threatened by something half-glimpsed, and starts screaming his head off as the camera blurs out of focus.

In fact, the special brand of 70s funk in this season continues with more groovy camerawork, Citroen 2CVs with their doors removed (to give the prison vehicles a unique look), and wobbly CSO blinds representing hi-tech TV sets. As director, Michael Briant keeps the appearance of the Sea Devils under wraps, and the creepy shots of their hands being up to no good are wonderfully eerie and tantalising. In fact, all the stuff in and around the sea fort is great – the studio set is admirably metallic, resulting in echoing clangs that electrify the atmosphere.

But do you know... even though Pertwee has, as you say, become gentler and has a more twinkling humour to his exasperation, I prefer to spend time with the bad guys. Delgado doesn't put a foot wrong, and Clive Morton (as Trenchard) is just delightful as his nominal jailer. It's interesting that, for once, the Master manipulates Trenchard with reason rather than Time Lord-y special powers, and yet Morton refuses to behave as if he's in on the joke. The Clangers scene is doubly good because Morton so genuinely delivers his line about how the "extraterrestrials" the Master says he's watching

are actually puppets meant for children, and the face that Delgado privately pulls in response is a laugh-out loud punchline of effortless brilliance. Really, you can't help but to empathise with Trenchard – his colony declared independence and even he admits that his current position is "a bit of a comedown", but his upper lip is stiff, and he's still more concerned for his country than for himself.

His decision to only employ guards with moustaches (what is it with them in this era?) is an odd one, though. None of them would look out of place in a Frankie Goes to Hollywood video.

The Sea Devils (episode two)

R: There's something very odd taking place in Doctor Who at the moment. And it seems as if here is the best place to bring it up.

On the fort, as the Doctor fiddles around with the radio, he explains to Jo how the Silurians were a complete misnomer, and should have been called the Eocenes. It's rather sweet to see Malcolm Hulke trying to correct a factual error in a story transmitted a good two seasons ago – and even sweeter that Jo immediately follows it with an absolute clanger about how those "Silurians" were hibernating for billions (!) of years, and the Doctor cheerfully agrees. But it does raise a question about exactly why the production team thought it was worth correcting. After all, a mere two weeks ago, the Doctor was blithely calling the Martian delegates "Ice Warriors" to their very faces, without eliciting confusion or offence, as if somehow they'll have understood that he'll first meet them in a few thousand years' time in a different incarnation when they've been deep frozen. And that was a story which actually had Ice Warriors in it! There aren't even any Silurians on view in this adventure whatsoever, just their aquatic cousins!

Indeed, it's perhaps worth asking why Hulke felt the need to draw parallels between the Silurians and the Sea Devils at all. Yes, it's true, they share the same background – but is it really worth the effort of spelling it out? Those who get the connection will get the connection. For those that don't remember the previous adventure, it's not only a piece of backwards continuity that doesn't explain very much, it's a piece of continuity that actually *confuses* because it only raises the link to explain it was all wrong in the first place. I remember watching "The Satan Pit" a couple of years ago, and wondering whether Russell T Davies was going to give my inner fanboy a boost by ever mentioning the name "Sutekh". It's the same character, after all – he's a godlike being who goes around calling himself any number of variants upon Satan, and Russell has deliberately hired the very same actor to play the part! And, ultimately, I was rather relieved he didn't. There's enough ambiguity about the connection that the fan can draw parallels if he wants to, and yet the monster of the week can stand tall and impressive as something unique and unknowable, not just a returning (and previously defeated) villain from the 1970s.

In the late eighties, when it seemed only diehard fans were watching the series, everyone was falling over themselves to find the reason why Doctor Who wasn't popular any more. And we pointed the finger at a production team that seemed to delight in continuity and obscure references to the past for their own sake. But it's here, in The Sea Devils, where we can see it really first taking hold. By tying the Sea Devils into the Silurians, the production team aren't giving the monsters a fair crack of the whip; it's just as they did when they brought back the Autons, they're taking something original and making them the stooges of the Master. At least in Terror of the Autons, the Master himself was new – now he too is something very familiar.

Now, I have absolutely no difficulty with in-series continuity in itself, and I get as much of an inner glow as anybody else. But it has to be consistent. In episode one, the story very neatly set up that although we were seeing the Master again, the format had entirely changed. It's not just that he's imprisoned, it's that he's public enemy number one – he's locked away for the rest of his life in a special prison, after many people had called for his execution. Quite simply, even when the Master (inevitably) escaped, it's quite clear that he can't get back to his old tricks as dressing up as a vicar and changing his name if he doesn't want to be recognised. All well and good, and not a little

refreshing – you get the sense that Doctor Who isn't merely relying upon its stock, it's *developing* it into something new. By episode two, though, the Master is able to infiltrate a naval base *right beside his prison* with no greater disguise than a hat and his commanding authority. Captain Hart and Colonel Trenchard are close enough friends that they regularly play golf together – but Hart has never even heard of the Master, reacting with incredulity when his name is mentioned: what does he think Trenchard is doing in that prison of his? And within 25 minutes, what Hulke has done is to address past continuity to no great effect, and in one fell swoop rid his story of all that seemed fresh and return it back to the status quo. By the time the Master and the Doctor are having their sword fight, we might just as well be back in Season Eight again. Nothing has changed at all.

I think there's a reason for this. Just as this story was being transmitted, Piccolo Books were bringing out the first edition of The Making of Doctor Who. On the cover, Jon Pertwee faced off against a Sea Devil; inside there's an account of how the story was made. And, for the first time, there's a list of every story yet transmitted. It's the end of Doctor Who's innocence. It's the start of a time when Doctor Who can be hampered by facts. I *love* lists. When I was a kid, I compiled fresh lists of Doctor Who stories in every conceivable order. But by looking at something directly, you can't but help change what it was. It's a funny thing; when the Doctor meets the Daleks and the Ice Warriors earlier in the year, there seems a strong link between the black and white stories they evoke. When Jo Grant tells us here what happened in The Silurians over two seasons ago, the change in tone and attitude are now so remarkable that it genuinely feels like it was a product of a different TV series altogether.

T: Oh, I don't know... I first knew of Sea Devil and Silurians from perusals of books and magazines, and it was only later that I discovered that they were relatives. The idea that creatures of similar ancestry could evolve into *different looking* creatures was a neat one – it's a nice nod to the fans, but not so infused into the storytelling as to alienate the casual punter.

Besides, surely as much as anything else, the common lineage just owes to Malcolm Hulke wanting to work with some of the same themes as Doctor Who and the Silurians, and so justifying the similarities rather than crafting an entirely new monster with a strangely familiar background?

Either way, my love affair with the bad guys continues. Roger Delgado looks great when disguised as an admiral, but it's what Clive Morton gets up to whilst the Master thieves the Navy base's supplies that brings special stuff to the table. Trenchard, bless him, might be an affable bore, but it's lovely that he clearly, deep down, *knows* that he's a bore and brings out his inner dullard to distract Captain Hart. There's something rather tragic, and yet deeply poignant, about this old duffer trying to retain some form of dignity now that he's been consigned to the scrapheap. Just look at the way he smothers Jo's hand with his when they greet, and she affectionately puts her other one on top. She's genuinely fond of him (even if, by the end, she wants him to bugger off), and he's charming in an old-fashioned way. And we don't just laugh *at* Trenchard – the way he shouts "in conference!" when there's a knock on his door, and he's in the middle of playing golf in his office, is priceless.

Other moments that I enjoy... the scene where the Sea Devil melts through the door is classic Doctor Who stuff, although it's something of a shame that the creature's gait only has two modes as it chases after Pertwee: "rod stiff" or "disappointingly human". (Perhaps they should have forgiven Roslyn de Winter for The Web Planet, and recruited her to supply some "lizard movement".) It's very pleasing that Smedley, the Navy chief whom the Master tries and fails to mesmerise, is cautious and unintimidated rather than being some easily subjugated functionary. And you can't fail to love the Doctor's glee at his clever radio tinkering on the sea fort being immediately undermined when the gadget blows up on him. I was even (oh yes) *very* pleased to see one of those old metal camping cups on the table – you never see those any more, and it made me all nostalgic for spangles, Spit the Dog and the three-day week.

Oddly enough, though, it's the climactic swordfight between Pertwee and Delgado that

sums up the story so far. It's witty (the way that the Doctor munches on a bit of sandwich while holding his foil to the Master's throat), well-staged, inventive, filmed with a pleasing strangeness and full of incident. Some of the individual moments don't quite work (the bit where the action is speeded up), but you can't help but applaud how they had a go. Such a great action sequence... from an episode in which, admittedly, "Venusian karate" seems to involve doing a perfectly ordinary kick whilst saying a funny word.

June 3rd

The Sea Devils (episode three)

R: It's episode three, and all the scenes involving the Doctor and Jo *behave* like it's episode three, as well; the Doctor is locked up, then rescued by his companion, and then they run into further trouble. It's done with a certain amount of wit – the Doctor genially says, "How very kind of you", when he's released from handcuffs, and then quickly changes it to "How very unkind of you", when he realises it was only so he could be handcuffed into a more uncomfortable position. I love the way that the Master, too, has to remind Trenchard that he officially is a prisoner, and that he should be accompanied by a guard. But the plotting here is desperately slow. There's a sequence where the Doctor has to call a guard into his cell simply so that Jo can slip in, and then he has to call the same guard *all over again* so they can overpower him. This is an episode which certainly tries its best to spin out the little action it has for as long as it can – just look at how long that reprise is, containing the entire sword fight from last week!

And yet, it oddly works. And it's because outside these scenes, the story behaves not like it's episode three but episode *one*. At first all of that feels very odd. We get an entire new set of characters who are sent on a submarine into danger, and it's only at the episode end that we get to see – ta-dah! – what a Sea Devil looks like! Even though we've already seen them in the previous two instalments. On paper, it all looks like a retrograde step, but what Hulke has done is rather beguiling – he's all but ignored the fact that the audience has precious little to be intrigued about, and piled on all your usual episode one suspense anyway. It's been a good 40 minutes of screen time since we've seen what a Sea Devil looks like, and when at the cliffhanger one emerges from the sea, beautifully directed by Michael Briant, it has all the shock and climax as if we'd never so much as glimpsed one. And Malcolm Clarke's peculiar score works well too: it's so harsh and discordant that it lends an oddness to the most mundane of scenes, such as Jo running about outside the prison. Intellectually, the entire episode is one of the dullest we have ever seen: it's so rare for there to be an instalment where the plot hasn't advanced one iota. But as exercises in running on the spot go, it's surprisingly entertaining. It's like one of the Doctor's coin tricks – it distracts you brilliantly from the fact that absolutely nothing has happened.

T: We're in a submarine, we've lost power, we've hit the bottom of the cold, murky sea... and there's a clanging outside. Then something breaks in, and we hear the screams of the other crewmen as the unseen menace butchers them. It's a moment that exemplifies how Doctor Who achieves its thrills, spills and chills, with Donald Sumpter (as Commander Ridgeway) greeting the horror of this with a fixed, precise, military impassiveness, save for a slight spasm in the corner of his eye. Sumpter is a superb actor – even in bog-standard briefing scenes, he conveys his dubiousness about the whole missing ships scenario, and yet refrains from being discourteous to his superior officer. I also love the way he has his hands in his pockets in the opening submarine scene, suggesting he's a professional at ease with his surroundings. This man needs to bring his distinctive features to the new Doctor Who, as he's one of our finest character actors, and deserves more than this and being Enrico Casali from The Wheel in Space on his Doctor Who biog.

Elsewhere, Pertwee and Manning enjoy a rather lovely partnership as they silently work out a plan to free the Doctor. She also wins over the composer, who joins in with her cute wave after she's snuck into the cell. The Doctor's relationship with the prison guards, though, is altogether more chilly – when he

clicks his fingers at one of them, I was rather hoping for signs of hypnotism, which would explain why the guards have acquiesced to Trenchard's clear abuse of protocol in giving the Master the run of the prison. But no, it turns out the guard wasn't speaking just because he's surly and an extra, leaving his behaviour and that of his fellows unexplained. Are we seriously meant to believe that they're all just following orders? Maybe Trenchard secures their co-operation by getting them all tickets to The Village People...

One more thing: as Jane Blythe, June Murphy is more than a pair of legs when she shows initiative in checking up on the Doctor and Jo, questioning the bogus story about where they've gone. Strangely, though, Murphy previously appeared in Fury From the Deep – quite what how she came to only get cast in stories set by the sea, I have no idea.

The Sea Devils (episode four)

R: Trenchard's death! I love Trenchard's death. I wrote about it once for Doctor Who Magazine. I read the little article back, and I still stand by it. Well, most of it. Here are the bits I still believe:

Doctor Who *usually hasn't got the time to worry about being moving. Its job is to provide lots of ACTION! and MONSTERS! – if it gets concerned about the consequences when those two explosive ingredients meet, that's the job for the end of story coda in which the Doctor can reflect upon the moral message of the week. In no era of the programme is this more true than in the Pertwee years; the MONSTERS! are more garish, the ACTION! more thrilling, and the moral message delivered to camera with the gravity it deserved.*

When I was a kid, I devoured the Target novelisation of The Sea Devils in one sitting. And it was moving. It wasn't so much how Governor Trenchard died. He was an annoying old fool who had been helping the Master; even at that age, I recognised the fitting irony that when he decided to regain his honour and go down fighting the monsters, he forgot to take the safety catch off his gun. No, it was the Doctor's reaction to it. It was the way that when he found Trenchard's body, he secretly reset the gun so that no-one could realise that he had died a failure.

A small act. Malcolm Hulke doesn't give it much attention – he knows full well that he has to get back to describing the MONSTERS! and the ACTION! But it still seems to me one of the most truly beautiful moments in Doctor Who, of quiet dignity afforded to a flawed man. It sums up what Doctor Who – and, on top of that, the character of the Doctor – should be about. And since then, every moment I have spent in the Doctor's company has had to measure up to that act of tenderness.

A few years after I'd read the book, a friend let me see a pirate video of The Sea Devils. It was a copy of a copy of a copy, I think – whatever, it was like watching a series of coloured talking blobs running away from a set of coloured hissing blobs. I was spellbound, in spite of what it was doing to my long-term vision, waiting for that defining sequence that had helped turn me into a fan. And it never came. On screen, Trenchard blazes away at the Sea Devils with his gun. He even kills one of them – what the hell was that all about? No need for the Doctor to show compassion at all.

But in retrospect, the way that the broadcast version handles Trenchard's death is exactly right. What was so powerful and throwaway on the page would have been cloyingly sentimental on the screen. Clive Morton's portrayal gives Trenchard his dignity without the Doctor's help, as he reassures a frightened guard in the face of his own death. And in a series all about ACTION!, Michael Briant shows enormous restraint in not even showing us the moment when Trenchard is gunned down. The unspoken simplicity with which the camera reveals his dead body is subtle and affecting.

It's quite odd, I suppose, that two of my favourite Doctor Who moments are actually the same moment. I love the one for what it says about the compassion of the Doctor, and love the other for what it shows about the compassion of Doctor Who. I can look on them both now as valid and entirely non-contradictory. So everyone's a winner.

Well, everyone except Trenchard, of course. This way he gets killed twice. Poor sod.

T: Well, get you, Mr Showbiz... I too had a couple of articles in Doctor Who Magazine, way back when the universe was less than half its present size, but did I cut and paste my interview with Bernard Archard into The Power of the Daleks episode two? Nooooooo...

and yet, this is the second time you've purloined a piece of writing in lieu of doing some actual work! Not that, as it happens, I've bothered the column inches of the most recent incarnation of the august and venerable DWM. When Moths hit the West End – not a peep. When Moths got a Sony nomination – nada. I used to console myself that they're pushed for space, what with their covering a brand spanking new series an' all, so my absence – my not meriting even a line! – was warranted. But then they do a page-long interview with Lizo from Newsround... and I cry. (Sorry to go on about this, but there's an argument to be had for not turning your hobby into your living, as your joy can be tainted by proximity and the disappointments that brings.)

Anyway, as you've so elegantly discussed Trenchard's death on screen and in print, let me talk about the key moments leading up to it. While it's easy enough to mock Trenchard's old-school adherence to days of yore, tradition and etiquette... it all goes hand in hand with his calmness in a crisis, and his willingness to lay down his life for a greater good. My wishy-washy liberalism is all very well, but would I be brave enough to stand my ground and face an enemy against all odds? (Would I bugger.) This is daring stuff, conveyed through drama that refuses to rely on two-dimensional ciphers.

Then, as the tension mounts, it becomes clearer to Trenchard what he must do – "attend to the security of [his] prisoner", which he does by loading his revolver. What makes the Master such a blackguard in this adventure is that he proves the undoing of the person most working on behalf of Queen and Country, without the slightest expectation of personal gain. It's one thing to wash your hands when you kill someone from a distance, but to spend so much time with someone, to knowingly use his nobility to help you orchestrate events that will end in his death – that's cold.

And it should be said: Michael Briant once again goes the extra yard with the cliffhanger, doesn't he? Episode one was a cleverly orchestrated cheat (the advancing figure wasn't a Sea Devil, but a delirious Declan Mulholland), episode two had that stunning quick pan following the path of the knife the Master throws, and episode three had the triple jeopardy of guards, mines and a Sea Devil emerging from the waters. And here, while it's unclear about what's happened inside the Doctor's diving bell, the silence and the expression on Katy Manning's face after she looks inside the instrument tell us it ain't good. Four cracking cliffhangers in a row – how many other stories can claim *that*?

Let me finish with a handful of observations that make me happy... the subplot with the submarine ups the ante away from the prison, providing us with another melting door (I like a melting door) and a brave close-up of a Sea Devil's face during a tense stand-off. (Mind you, I'm convinced that the voice reporting to Ridgeway on the R/T is Scotty from Star Trek!) Also, Jane Blythe and Leading Telegraphist Bowman are crying out for a spin-off, aren't they? (Just watch how Alec Wallis injects a few "um"s and "ah"s into his dialogue to give it some welcome naturalism, and Jane, bless her, kindly goes to get Jo more sandwiches after some comedy Doctor-eats-a-whole-plateful business – the punchline of which seems to be that our hero is a twat.) The beach sequence is great fun, with Pertwee gallantly throwing himself on the barbed wire and then blowing up the mines. And the incidental detail that I find the most amusing in all of this? The way that Roger Delgado pushes the buttons of his signal device in such an assured, professional manner. Good lord, that man was disgustingly talented... even his button-pushing comes across like the act of a true pro!

June 4th

The Sea Devils (episode five)

R: I can't help but feel I've been a bit tough on The Sea Devils. And, really, it's very unfair. Compared to the stories we've seen recently, it's something of a stand out. There's comedy, there's tension. The direction is great. The acting is top notch – actually, there's not a bad performance to criticise. The pacing is spot on (even when the scripting is slow, the camerawork isn't). And there's lots of military hardware and honestly impressive set pieces involving diving bells and ships at sea to catch the eye.

But I know why I have a problem with it. It's because deep down, I still miss Season Seven. I still miss that rather grim and humourless start to the Pertwee era, where the series felt at its most adult and its most questing. And it's easy to watch The Daemons or Day of the Daleks, say, and just see them as being from an evolving show. They're just different. They don't remind us too much of a style that's been lost. But The Sea Devils is the closest we'll ever get to a remake of one of those stories. It's The Silurians at sea. The same moral arguments are rehearsed again, but this time in a more eye-popping comic book format. It feels (pardon the pun) somewhat diluted.

And yet, I know full well that if you showed most audiences Doctor Who and the Silurians and The Sea Devils, which of the two would be regarded as the superior bit of television. More *happened* in The Silurians than in The Sea Devils, but the running on the spot we see in the latter story is actually more pacy and diverting. It all comes to a head here in episode five, which manages to compress most of the themes and dilemmas and drama of The Silurians into 25 minutes. And it does so with better-looking monsters, Roger Delgado and a submarine. Yes, ultimately, it's more simplistic. It would be. But it doesn't mean that, on these different terms, it isn't remarkably good. Martin Boddey (as Walker) is playing a far less subtle version of a crass bureaucrat than Geoffrey Palmer did – but Boddey does so quite brilliantly. Walker is, alone of all these ministerial types that crop up through the Pertwee era, genuinely very funny. And that's what makes him all the more disturbing; that he can sit and gorge his way through meals whilst dealing death is nasty (and look at the way Briant focuses on his mouth as he chews away), but the way that he can use the National Anthem as a piece of rhetoric to justify slaughter, delivering the lyrics in childish sing-song, is truly unpleasant.

There's so much to enjoy here, not least because Hulke cuts to the chase and outlines arguments that it took weeks for The Silurians to get through. In comparison, the Sea Devil leader accepts the Doctor's proposals for peace remarkably quickly – but it's all the more effective because Man's impulse to resort to a military solution is so hasty, and stops the negotiations dead. There's not much window dressing here, and it actually serves the story well. The episode becomes a series of swift moral quandaries – should Ridgeway have shot dead the Sea Devil guarding his crew? Should he have risked everybody's lives by firing torpedoes to break free from the force field? Should Captain Hart have refused the direct orders of a superior, and resigned in protest? I love Doctor Who and the Silurians, don't get me wrong, but that story would have spent entire episodes discussing these issues, whilst The Sea Devils puts them on the line one by one, and asks the audience watching quick fire questions. Because the moral debates here *aren't* that complex, really, and shouldn't be. And it has a curious effect upon the way that we regard the Doctor. With the story all sped up like this, and with the monsters and the humans so quick to kill each other, it makes his peacemaking efforts look all the more naive. If The Silurians offered a rather pessimistic message, then it's all the more so here. And that gives The Sea Devils a surprising amount of force. No, it's not subtle. But it's powerful, nonetheless.

T: I love Season Seven too – and have always, if I'm being honest, seen subsequent Pertwees as its poorer cousins. Time and again, if I was randomly scanning my shelves for something to watch, I generally favoured Pertwee's first year over its successors. So the need to here watch the series in order makes me appreciate stories such as this one rather more.

The Sea Devils themselves are a great design, with effective guns and voices that both suit their look and are (not always a given with this series) alien-sounding and understandable. I've never quite figured out why fans make such sport of the Sea Devils' string vests – as costumes tailored for sea creatures go, they're pretty appropriate. (I would, however, question the decision to give the Chief Sea Devil a big net cloak as well, especially as it breaks when he moves his arm. Since the director evidently intended that the Sea Devils' costumes represented reclaimed fisherman's netting, perhaps another kind of sea-scavenged accoutrement would have better denoted his worth... a coral necklace perhaps, or a dis-

carded condom for a hat.) Overall, the Sea Devil costumes lend themselves to so many good images, as when one of them spasms in death, and two more are seen "floating dead" on the water.

And the comparison you bring up between Boddey's style of bureaucrat and the one Geoffrey Palmer played in Doctor Who and the Silurians is interesting – whereas Palmer's Masters was a reasonable man doing a difficult job, Boddey's Walker is part of the problem; he's an arrogant, ignorant, pompous glutton who has probably claimed the breakfast he keeps demanding on his expenses. You couldn't help but feel some sympathy for Masters, but Walker is an exaggerated nincompoop who we're meant to laugh at and be repulsed by at the same time. That close-up that you mention of his chomping lips (not to mention the noisy licking of his fingers) is an extraordinary moment, with the camera telling us what to think of the character in an abstract way.

Moreover, it's fascinating to see how the other characters react to Walker, who (somewhat infuriatingly, for those trying to argue with him) has good etiquette and addresses people with polite words, albeit in a patronising manner. Pertwee faces him down brilliantly, and ultimately it's the Doctor's guile in appealing to Walker's ego – that he'll be more fondly remembered as a peacemaker than a destroyer – that (for now) saves the day. It's worth noting, though, that our guest hero, Captain Hart, is fettered by the same adherence to the military structure as Trenchard – is Hart's inability to cross the higher-ranking Walker much different to Trenchard flying in the face of common sense for the sake of the crown? Jane Blythe, on the other hand, cements her candidacy for the Best Woman in Doctor Who Ever by being really stroppy with the unwelcome politician. You don't cross the Blythester, she'll put seaweed in your sandwiches.

The Sea Devils (episode six)

R: On the face of it, this is just a parade of shallow clichés. The military shoot at an invading group of aliens, and both sides get to perform exotic stunts involving somersaults and drops from buildings. Jo escapes from a cell up a ventilation shaft, the Doctor blows up the monsters by reversing the polarity of the neutron flow, and only after he's had a long chase after the Master using a speedboat.

It all looks spectacular, in fact. And I'm a fan, and at heart one of the self-loathing kind who can't bear it when Doctor Who isn't being wry and intellectual, but deals instead with big explosions and shiny hardware. But two things struck me whilst watching this, and revelling in it, and getting a big kick out of its Boy's Own zest. Firstly, what's so bad about being spectacular every now and then? And secondly, all these clichés I've listed – when, exactly, have any of them taken place in Doctor Who, either before or since?

It's a point worth making, I think. The only time Doctor Who has ever tried to be this climactic is in the last episode of The Invasion – and that looked great, but did make the irritating error that it forgot to put the Doctor himself at the centre of the action. If this episode's legacy is that it looks so smooth and so epic, that we think every Pertwee story is like it – then isn't that really rather impressive? Episode six of The Sea Devils, right at the very centre of the Pertwee era, seems to sum up its eye candy excesses like no other. Even to the point that it creates a catchphrase ("I reversed the polarity of the neutron flow"), only used the once during his run as the Doctor, that comes back to haunt the series like a piece of nostalgia. I know some Sherlock Holmes fans who despise "The Final Problem", because its depiction of one-shot villain Moriarty is so powerful that everyone believes he was in every story. So it is here. Watching The Sea Devils end is like watching every Jon Pertwee adventure that plays in your mind's eye; it's hardly its fault that it has summed up an entire style of Who storytelling.

When you ask viewers from the seventies what they remember from Doctor Who, it usually revolves around lots of lizards wearing string vests coming out of the sea. If ultimately episode six of The Sea Devils offers that, and not an awful lot else, then just consider how hard it is to create a folk memory. And be humbled. The biggest flaw of this, really, is that it doesn't play like an episode in its own right, but as the final reel in an action movie – it's all

climax, and no respite. But bearing in mind that the story's greatest successes was when it was repeated in compilation form on the odd Bank Holiday, even this can be seen to count in the story's favour.

T: The battle stuff you mention is pretty well staged – the use of real Naval personnel means that everyone charges about and handles the equipment very believably, and it's great to see Captain Hart leading the fight and manning the guns. As part of this, stuntman/ Sea Devil actor Stuart Fell contrives different ways to die excitingly. (There's a particularly dangerous stunt where a Sea Devil falls off a roof and narrowly misses a protruding girder.) And Jon Pertwee gets well and truly soaked in this instalment's hardware showcase, as he and someone who clearly isn't Roger Delgado chase about on mini-boat things.

Against all of this excitement, though, is the very odd (and much mentioned) plot-wrinkle that when the Doctor powers up his Sea Devil-incapacitating machine long enough for Jo and Hart to escape, the Master stands there for simply ages before attempting to shut it off. My granddad would spot that this makes no sense whatsoever, and he's been dead since 1988. The scene would probably have worked if a Sea Devil had not been present – meaning the Master might not have realised quite so fast what was happening – but when one of the creatures is right there, writhing about in agony, the Master's apparent five-minute daydream becomes much harder to explain.

Character-wise, Walker shows his true colours – not so much "red, white and blue" as "yellow", as he fears that the killer turtles will "take reprisals against the innocent" and shuts himself back in a cupboard after doing a curious dance with an agonised Sea Devil. And it's worth pondering, of course, that ultimately it's the Doctor's conscience-stricken action that destroys the Sea Devils, not Walker's warmongering. Realists would say the result is the same, and they'd be right, but at least someone who understands the moral implications of what he's doing brings about the necessary resolution, preventing the hawkish Walker from dining out on this one.

Taking this story as a whole, I've greatly enjoyed it, and found it to be a more sprightly entry into the canon than fandom generally claims. Which is to say: it's effective, it's solid, it's clever, it has memorable monsters and plenty to sustain the interest, it has higher production values owing to the Navy's participation, and its climax is another abrupt, terse affair. And yet... it doesn't ever really achieve the same league of sound, grown-up drama as its progenitor. That's not automatically a bad thing – it's just to say that a cross-comparison between The Sea Devils and the story that spawned it demonstrates how, only two years after the fact, Doctor Who starring Jon Pertwee is a very, very different series. In its own way, that's the beauty of the show – even when it looks somewhat similar on the surface, it's often altogether more interesting and complex than that. Even if the music is still from the planet Bonkers.

June 5th

The Mutants (episode one)

R: There's no avoiding it – The Mutants has one stinker of a reputation. This is really *nothing* like a Pertwee story – it has little of its cosiness, its lightness of touch or its charm. If you're hunting through your video shelves for a slice of third Doctor magic, why on earth would you go for this one, which is self-consciously depressing and cynical? In this first episode alone, we're introduced to two characters that over the next few weeks we're going to identify as friends – Ky is an arrogant rabble-rouser just a step away from advocating terrorism against humans, and who takes Jo Grant hostage and uses her as a shield, and Stubbs is a gun-toting soldier we first see hunting an old man to death. Whatever else The Mutants may be, it's not a very *likeable* story.

But seeing this episode in context, with a grimness to it that seems born out of real anger, it feels fresh and daring. A lot of the stories we've seen recently have had serious moral or ecological concerns, but the arguments have been rehearsed almost like finger-wagging lectures; it's all been theoretical, with little that's been designed to shock. Here, though, we're presented with an opening scene so genuinely callous that we're left reeling. A

lot of people make fun of it, and say that the old man coming out of the mist looks like the opening sequence from Monty Python's Flying Circus – but there's an ironic power to that, that what we see isn't Michael Palin but an elderly mutant with scales coming out of his back on the run for his life. (I wouldn't go so far as to say that the Monty Python link is deliberate, but I'd like to pretend it is – in the way that it takes the familiar and funny, and then gives it a terrible twist, it's very much showcasing what The Mutants does best.)

Because what's especially effective about the episode is the way that the Doctor and Jo cheerfully stride their way through it, expecting all around them to be just like every other Pertwee episode. The complacency they show here – thinking that the tannoy announcements refer to them, that they will be the centre of attention – is brilliantly set up by a very funny scene in which Jo reacts to a strange globe materialising out of nowhere with bored resignation. It's either lunch, or a bomb – and both seem quite banal to her. Inevitably, we try to use the Doctor and Jo as our points of reference, and watch the action from their point of view. And we can't, because the breezy way in which they act like postmen on a bit of a jolly is out of sorts with a world of institutionalised segregation and murder. It makes us uneasy. That's good. We're supposed to feel uneasy.

The acting is criticised too. But Paul Whitsun-Jones' ripe portrayal of the Marshal is just right for a man who personifies all the colonial excesses we see here. Garrick Hagon does sterling work with Ky – look at the way he quite deliberately goes into "speech giving" mode the moment he thinks he has an audience to pontificate in front of. The sequence where he so quietly starts to undermine the Administrator's speech of independence is clumsily staged, but beautifully performed. And Christopher Coll is so amiable as Stubbs that, like Jo, you find him rather sweet – even though at this stage of the drama he's playing a smiling Nazi. Rick James is absolutely horrid as Stubbs' partner Cotton, I admit – this is acting that'll scratch the glass of your television screen – but he's only *one* actor in a whole ensemble. How much harm can he do? (I'll get back to you on that.)

T: Well... I'm not quite sure what to make of this. There's much to admire – the segregation of the Solonians and the humans ruling their planet, the Overlords, is obviously inspired by apartheid (down to the use of separate trans-mat booths), and the story's colonial overtones show the writers' intent on calling humanity (i.e. Great Britain) to account. To that end, it's telling that Ky – a powerful figure amongst his own people – can get ordered about by a relatively lowly human like Stubbs. And it's a good-looking piece – James Acheson's costumes are especially impressive, with the Overlords' uniforms looking slick and futuristic without being daft, and the Solonian garb having a consistency whilst giving each character an individual identity. (I even like James Mellor's wig, but please tell me they haven't taped his eyes to make them slanty...)

All of that said, the story seems to be about taking two steps forward, one step back. As the Administrator sent to give the Solonians their planet back, Geoffrey Palmer is easily the best actor present and looks like he's going to play an important role... so it's quite shocking (and disappointing) when he gets bumped off! Only the most generous of people would call Tristram Cary's discordant sounds "music" (although it might have been insulting to credit him with "Incidental Noise"), and I really can't agree that the Monty Python bit is a deliberate homage. It's just another element of the story's presentation that's scuppered by woolly thinking.

And while Rick James is famous for his notoriously awful performance, I'm prepared, for now, to say it's partly due to his thick accent making his phraseology sound slightly off to our uninitiated ears. (However, having him say colloquialisms such as "his nibs" doesn't really help the cause.) Come to think of it, it's fairly emblematic of this entire episode – you can see the laudable intent behind it, but it doesn't quite work. I mean, for pity's sake, while it's commendable of the production team to underline the story's racial subtext by hiring a black actor, did they really have to cast him as a character called *Cotton*?

The Mutants (episode two)

R: And another addition to the cast! One of the best characters in The Claws of Axos was Winser, the acerbic scientist working for the wrong side who takes advantage of the Doctor's greater know-how. And here he is again, in the form of George Pravda's Professor Jaeger – only this time round, writers Bob Baker and Dave Martin won't squander the character quite so easily, and they'll ensure he sticks around being grumpy and amoral for another five episodes yet. At the episode's end, Jaeger even meets a similar fate to poor old Winser, blown up by the Doctor's tinkering with his equipment – but here he's just a bit stunned. (Thank goodness – it's a very odd explosion in the face that merely knocks a man out for a minute, and leaves no burns or scarring. The Doctor very nearly lost the moral high ground with his booby trap, in a story which really rather depends upon it!)

I can't but help like George Pravda. I was fond of him in The Enemy of the World, and I'll be even fonder of him in The Deadly Assassin. I'm not sure he's perfectly cast as Jaeger, but the German accent oddly suits the Solos background better than it does Gallifrey. There are so many peculiar accents, and different ways the actors are inflecting (yes, Rick James, I am looking at you), that one more just feels part of the melting pot. And although I'm sure it isn't deliberate, in a story which is as keenly concerned with apartheid issues and racial purity as this one is, the range of different nationalities and cultures amongst the cast only make the story's concerns more pointed and ironic.

T: Not shackled by humility is he, our Ky? He even *tells* Jo that his life is more important than hers! Then again, it's somewhat refreshing that one of the guest cast starts off as unlikeable. Ky is a zealot who needs to rediscover exactly what he's actually fighting for, and you can see why it's so easy for the Marshall to label this slippery (he's called KY, after all) customer a terrorist. It's such a familiar tale – we invade a land, cow its people with our superior weaponry and technology, and then question *their* morality because they fight back in ways that are, by necessity, less than entirely sporting.

We can take issue with Ky's actions, but the Overlords are plundering Solos because the good old human race has made a mess of Earth, which ties in with the rather bleak future painted by Colony in Space. For all of its whizz-bang kookiness, this era of the show is surprisingly pessimistic about the future of humanity's homeworld.

Conceptually, this story has so much going for it. And the film work is suitably drab – the misty, moody surface of Solos seems convincingly alien, and the air being poisonous to humans during daylight serves to portray the difficulties involved in one species trying to acclimatise to another world's environment. It also means the indigenous population can use their natural habitat to confound the occupiers' efforts, much like the Maoris inventing trench warfare to see off their invaders (see, my trip to New Zealand wasn't wasted).

Yeah, The Mutants has its strong points... so why doesn't this quite hang together? At this stage in the game, I think it's mainly down to the acting. I love George Pravda as much as you, Rob, but I think he's terrible here, stumbling over his words and blustering about. James Mellor (as the warlord/ chieftain Varan) adds a nice inventive piece of post-death ritual over his son's corpse, but thereafter he gives a (putting this politely) curious, ranty performance. And Mellor's escape from the Marshall is *terribly* botched – Varan seems to avoid being shot at point blank range by, ah, um, knocking a chair over and then shuffling out. Thank God, then, for Christopher Coll, whose decision to play Stubbs as a cheery scouser, amidst all the blundering, makes him a refreshingly novel and likeable character. But for him, this could have been so much worse.

I have to say, though, that the jury's back and has rendered its verdict on Rick James. The scene in which Cotton tells Jaeger to go see the Marshal witnesses James utterly mangling so many bits of inflection, it makes you wonder just how many embarrassed silences happened during rehearsals, and how close they came to recasting to the role. Lines such as "You know the Marshall..." and "He did, sir" sound as if they're being delivered by translation software. I fear I was wrong – it's not just his accent, he's genuinely terrible. Unless he's *supposed* to be playing a Sat-Nav.

June 6th

The Mutants (episode three)

R: Okay, I admit that the story is beginning to drag a little bit by this point. On the face of it, the episode exists in order to get the Doctor and Jo back together, and on speaking terms with their allies, both amongst the Solonians (Ky) and the Overlords (Stubbs and – dear God, yes – Cotton). But Baker and Martin very creditably refuse to make anything quite as easy as that. Varan is now obsessed with destroying the humans he once collaborated with – and in usual Doctor Who style, that would put him on the same side as Ky. But old enmities between the Solonian chiefs are too pronounced, and refreshingly the political consequences of it all are treated with some complexity. In the same way, Ky is certain that the Mutts are his friends, and no sooner has he asserted to Jo that in spite of their ugliness they're not hostile than they attack them both. Nothing is quite what it appears. The sequence where Varan returns to his village, only to find that it's been long deserted, and the only old man there is one of the mutants he so despises, is an example of just that. It's a very Baker and Martin trick, actually, to have a character so full of dreams of conquest or revenge that he's failed to notice that time has moved on without him – and because Varan is so much smaller fry than (say) Omega or Eldrad in future, this is much more touching and real.

... or, it is in theory, anyway. The scenes are scuppered by James Mellor (as Varan) and Sidney Johnson (as the Old Man) both acting very awkwardly, and the transition from filmed caves to poor studio set that looks very cheap and unconvincing. So many of Baker and Martin's stories over the next few years are going to be damaged by the fact they're just too plain overambitious. And so it's genuinely unfair that this, the one script of theirs that actually just feels ambitious *enough*, is just as damaged all the same. This is a good story, with interesting characters who actually develop in surprising ways, and heartfelt concerns that seem real and earnest – and the dialogue is richer and sharper as a result. And yet this looks as sloppy as The Invisible Enemy, say, or The Armageddon Factor.

There are lots of cave scenes in this episode, though, and that's a bonus, because they look particularly atmospheric. James Acheson's Mutt designs are fantastic, frankly – these are creatures that not only look repulsive, and hard as nails, but have such a doleful expression that they nevertheless elicit sympathy. And I love the scene where Jo wanders into pure psychedelia, rich CSO colours and slow-mo, and a strange featureless figure silently marching towards her. If you can watch this sequence in context, with no idea of what it means, it comes so out of left field – and feels so stylistically different – that it's honestly unnerving.

T: The visuals here are much better than fandom credits sometimes. The director, Christopher Barry, is no slouch, and on film he does great things – Solos looks genuinely non-terrestrial, as Barry uses a lot of smoke and petrified plant life to augment the bog-standard quarry, making it look quite unlike any environment (or quarry, if you prefer) seen before in the series. The cave shots are fantastic – being, for once, the genuine article – and the lighting within is excellent, providing your beloved psychedelia and giving an alien hue to the picture. The scene where the Mutants attack Jo and Ky is similarly fabulous – the creatures' design is sturdy and plausible, there's loads of fire flying about, and Barry makes great use of shadow. He then adds *even more* smoke, creating very good-looking action.

Other good things about this episode... Jaegar's intriguing info-dump about Solos' 500-year seasonal cycle sets later revelations in motion. The script bursts with genuinely inventive sci-fi ideas, and emerges as a barbed satire about colonialism. It even creates a credible culture clash between the Solonians and the Overlords on multiple levels, as illustrated when the Doctor attributes the firestorms to atmospheric disturbance, but Varan insists that it's the gods' wrath. It's easy enough to see why the two sides haven't lived in harmony.

But, I'm forced to ask again (arg!!)... why, *why* is this so underwhelming? And, once again, I think the main culprit is the acting. Garrick Hagon does his best as Ky, a character

with only one emotion (righteous anger), and Christopher Coll quietly steals the whole thing with likeable naturalism... but everyone else isn't so much bad as just, well, *wrong*. I have to strongly disagree with the common assumption that Whitsun-Jones overly hams it up as the Marshall; I don't think he goes far *enough*. Whitsun-Jones can clearly deliver a lot of colour and flamboyance (as his turn in The Quatermass Experiment proves) when needed, but here he looks out of place while bullying people who are giving bad performances. In absolute terms, he's not bad (and I like his microphone – it's like he's hosting a fascist version of Blankety-Blank), but he's got the unfortunate duty of being the dominant party amongst a bevy of banal or misjudged theatrics.

I mean, it says a lot about 1970s TV that Barry's determination to cast a black actor meant they had to hire Rick James, as he was literally better than nothing. (My understanding is that Kenneth Gardnier, Johnny Sekka and a few others turned the part down.) The normally great George Pravda is so obviously distracted as he storms about, he doesn't seem to be in the same show as anybody else. And as for James Mellor... hell, I'm an actor and stage-performer, and even I don't know what to make of him. It takes real skill (or lack thereof) to alternate between being too shouty and lifelessly flat. The scene you highlight (where Varan discovers he's mutating into the very creatures he despises) isn't convincing at all. It should be the sort of thing an actor would *love* getting their teeth into, but it seems completely beyond Mellor as he half-heartedly scratches his hand and gurns.

If there's *any* spark of life in this, though, it's when the Marshall gloriously calls Jaeger a "maundering egghead". You don't hear that insult often enough, do you? You maundering egghead!

The Mutants (episode four)

R: And we get more of the psychedelia this episode. (Man.) And once again, it's the best part of the episode. There's a certain bizarre magic to those sequences where the Doctor and Professor Sondergaard are assaulted by strange flying streaks of light in a CSO-shiny cave. And knowing what's to come, it all looks remarkably prophetic – the Doctor being knocked about by radiation and clutching an oversized crystal. Be careful, Doctor Who. Don't get a taste for this sort of thing. It could be the death of you!

But otherwise this all feels irritatingly *polite*. It's as if the anger that fuelled the opening episodes has been sapped away by mid-story ennui. When Ky makes a stand at talking down 500 years of oppression, the rest of the cast slap him down for being something of a bore. And scenes in which Jaeger seems to threaten the Marshal's authority have no power at all, as if he thinks the fascist dictator he's been working for all this time is someone you can snidely joke about to his face. No sooner has the Doctor found Jo than he sends her off again into the wilderness and certain jeopardy, as if all the bother he's spent trying to find her these last couple of weeks was of no more consequence than looking for his car keys. And it means that all the jeopardy we *do* see has a rather tired feel to it – Varan's attack on the Skybase feels so half-hearted, there's no way it could succeed; it only makes the Skybase look all the more ineffective that it largely *does*.

And yet, there's something so intelligent to those scenes where the Doctor and Sondergaard try to puzzle out the evolutionary cycle of Solos – and so wonderfully eccentric too, as they work to solve an academic problem whilst amiably commenting upon the fact they may any moment be buried by a rockfall. I like John Hollis' Sondergaard. In a way, his character is just another symptom of how passionless The Mutants has become; he's been hiding in a radiation-soaked cave for the last however many years, and yet comes across as the most socially adept man on Solos. But he's got a sense of humour, is very smart and manages to pull off a bead necklace without apology.

Mind you, if I'm rather hoping it's all a front, and that he'll go mad in episode five, and start attacking the Doctor with a hammer. Anything to get a bit of anger back in the story again.

T: James Mellor's twinkly, burly Irish persona was quite fun, you might recall, in The Wheel in Space, but... I honestly have no idea what he's trying to achieve in this episode, so

half-heartedly does he stumble about the place as Varan. It's partly his flat vocal performance, but the major problem is his body language. Remember the previous episode, where he escaped from certain death by vaguely looking like he was throwing a chair? It's even worse here, when he casually draws his sword before his ludicrous demise, and wafts it like he can barely be bothered. For the life of me, I don't understand why he spends this entire episode lumbering about as if it's a rather tedious rehearsal – I think he was a much better actor than that, and it's odd that he's so lackadaisical.

Regrettably, I can no longer claim that the story's difficulties are chiefly relegated to the acting, as so many cracks are appearing elsewhere. After all, Bob Baker and Dave Martin – and of their own volition, I would presume – have decided to write what is possibly the most ridiculous cliffhanger since Professor Zaroff registered 12 out of ten on the Fruitloop Scale. Let's break this down... the Marshall shoots Varan as the latter waggles his sword limply. Even though this occurs (the shooting, not the sword-waggling) at point-blank range, it manages to hit the wall behind Varan too. Said wall is so lacking in reinforcement, it collapses after this minor barrage, which has been perpetrated by a man *lives on Skybase*, and so might have anticipated that this could happen. It's so spectacularly nonsensical, words almost fail.

And so long as we're talking about plot holes, why did the Time Lords address their message box to Ky, who has no idea what the ancient tablets within mean, instead of Sondergaard, who has the knowledge to work it out? Besides, as the Doctor winds up doing all the clever stuff anyway, why didn't the Time Lords just tell him the state of affairs on Solos? Perhaps we're meant to infer that because the Time Lords can't interfere officially, they have to move very cautiously – but it looks for all the world like they've given their box to someone who can't possibly understand its content, just to see what the hell happens. (They do love their games, don't they?)

But, all right... in the interest of keeping things "glass half full", let me quickly list some of this episode's upsides. It's fun that Cotton gets to be brave as, with grim determination, he takes Jo's place after she spots danger. The idea behind Solos' hyper-evolution is not only a solid bit of SF, but the fact that mankind's behaviour has upset this planet's natural process brilliantly illustrates how the British Empire forced different civilisations to "progress" at the wrong rate and/ or in a different direction. And Professor Sondergaard, as you've identified, is a lively addition to the story – it's not just that he's remarkably well-adjusted to life in the psychedelic caves, he also contributes my favourite moment of the episode. As Sondergaard and the Doctor postulate that life in some form will always continue, the cave roof falls in and Sondergaard deadpans, "Let's hope so". In the real world, of course, someone in his position – bereft of human contact for years – would probably be psychologically scarred. In fact, *anyone* who saw as much death and destruction first hand as most Doctor Who characters would likely end up with some sort of complex. Watching The Mutants, I'm beginning understand how they might feel.

The Mutants (episode five)

R: This has its moments. I like the way Martin Taylor's guard disparages the sonic screwdriver, referring to it as "the other thing" – and that later, when Jo forces him at gunpoint to give it back, she seems annoyed on its behalf. And Christopher Barry directs a terrific scene on the surface of Solos, where a hand-held camera pursues the Doctor through the mist and straight into a man aiming a gun.

Elsewhere, though, this has the same insipid feel to it that prevents the script from catching fire the way it ought to. There's some great dialogue – the Marshal's witty response to the Doctor's assertion that he's mad is "Only if I lose", but in context it falls flat because everyone is behaving all-too-rationally. I agree with you, Toby, a bit of madness would help perk the proceedings up no end. Stubbs' death is more effective than the blocking should allow, partly because Christopher Coll has been genuinely likeable, and partly because it cuts against the blandness that surrounds it – Rick James looks honestly stunned that the story had the guts to kill off his best friend. You can't but help feel, though, that if the script had to gun down a Skybase rebel, then they took out

the wrong guard. And it's a feeling only reinforced in the final scene; my God, they've actually given Rick James the lines leading into the cliffhanger! You don't want to do that!

Jon Pertwee is having fun, though. The Doctor clearly enjoys telling Jaeger how in a trice they could all be blasted through to the other side of the universe as anti-matter – he's obliged to work with this unethical scientist, but he's going to have his chuckles making him feel uncomfortable along the way. (Is this one scene the inspiration for what happens to Omega in The Three Doctors?) Not so convinced by Pertwee's turn as Man on the Intercom, though. Back in Inferno, the production team edited out of the British broadcast the scene where Pertwee indulged in his repertoire of funny voices. Here it not only gets left in, it has two outings! Could this be a sign that they'll give their temperamental star what he wants just to keep him happy? Expect more funny voices next season...

T: Actually, the expression on Rick James' face upon the death of his mate comes across as "stunned confusion" rather than "upset" – he looks like someone's just asked him the directions to Timbuktu by hot air balloon in Swahili whilst dressed as a Nazi hamster. He's not just poor vocally, his face hasn't quite mastered this pesky acting business either.

... or *maybe* he's just surprised that they didn't use this opportunity to kill him off. I certainly am. I mean, I've been in shows where we've hastily had to excuse cast members – it happens in the business, and you deal with it however you can. I was once in production of A Midsummer Night's Dream that lost its Flute two weeks before press night, because the poor lad had a bit of a breakdown. I also did a radio series where the well-known leading actor clearly didn't have a comedic bone in his body, and was recast after an embarrassing day of retakes. With all of that in mind, I ask you... why did nobody involved dare to suggest that as Christopher Coll is the best thing in this, and his cohort is the *complete opposite*, episode five should be rewritten as Cotton's last stand? Are the production team just worried that the audience is now so indifferent to these proceedings that any emotion from them – even if it's anger that the most likeable character has just been killed – is better than none?

I say this even though – yes, it's true – I otherwise thoroughly enjoyed episode five. Shown this in isolation, viewers would be hard pressed to identify why The Mutants is so unpopular. After the admittedly silly cliffhanger is resolved in an admittedly silly way, we get a great shot (and I never thought I'd ever type these words...) from between Paul Whitsun-Jones' legs of the prisoners being rounded up. Now that the Marshall has gone *completely* mad, he's much more entertaining. His perfunctory trial of our heroes is brilliant, and he at least trumps up charges for the men before just smiling at Jo and saying, "Such a pity..." The more the Marshall's ego increases as he revels in his own power, the more his sanity unravels – and the more effective he emerges as a Doctor Who villain. Even George Pravda has calmed down considerably; he's so much better at chuckling sarcasm than bluster.

And it's a great showcase for John Hollis as Sondergaard, who exudes wisdom and decency despite having to spend most of the episode collapsing. He even encourages the incidental music to improve – as Sondergaard enters the caves, there's an alien moodiness to the sounds, suggesting that Tristram Cary has been trying (but hitherto failing) to recapture the effect he created with his suite for The Daleks. Katy Manning, too, has a great outing as Jo – she improvises her way around the news of the Investigator's arrival, and knows exactly what phraseology to use when radioing the ship. Actually, this whole episode feels like one of dramatic desperation – just as we think the Doctor is rescuing Jo, the Marshall reveals he's in the room with his guards, and our heroes struggle desperately and eventually lose their nicest member. Gripping stuff.

... but then! The Investigator arrives in a spaceship that seems to be a large pencil. As he does so, our heroes are stuck in the refuelling bay and this leads to – yes! – the Rick James cliffhanger! Under threat of a radioactive thesium influx killing everyone present, James utters the immortal line "We'll all be done for!!!", and conveys the import of these final moments with suitably dramatic facial expressions ranging from "shocked" to "confused" to "I'm massively out of my depth". It's a moment

of bizarre extremes poorly done – which, setting aside the improvement of this episode, rather sums up this well-intentioned but unfortunate adventure.

June 7th

The Mutants (episode six)

R: There's a bit where the Doctor turns to the Investigator, and denounces the Marshal and Jaeger as having committed the most heinous acts ever perpetrated against other peoples that he's yet come across. And maybe it's telling that I didn't find this the apotheosis I might have hoped for, but just said (out loud, to my embarrassment), "Oh, really?"

Russell T Davies said early on, when he revived Doctor Who, that he wasn't interested in setting stories on alien planets per se. That there was little emotional involvement in the affairs of the Zog people on the planet Zog. And although it's a policy he later changed for himself, it's interesting to see what happens at the *other* time in the series' history where it's been shy of setting foot on alien worlds. The problem is with The Mutants, really, is that it's a little hard to care. I think there's a great cleverness to the idea of a natural evolutionary cycle that causes humanoid characters to become insect monsters. But the ultimate upshot, when I see that cycle kick in, is that I feel a bit betrayed. When Ky was an arrogant hothead, but to all outward appearances a very *human* hothead, I could relate to him. Once he becomes a glowing superbeing with a high voice that can float through walls, a part of my brain switches off. And, what's worse, it switches off in retrospect too. The Solonians seemed fascinating when they represented an underclass of imperial society being exploited by a ruling caste that's spread itself too thin. Once you realise they were *all* just floaty glowy creatures, I find myself actively despairing of them. (And it doesn't help either, frankly, that the only act we see this superbeing make is to kill the Marshal, and then just bugger off. So they're floaty and glowy and vengefully homicidal. Lovely.)

The Mutants is a hard story, then, to get a grip on. And I wonder whether it's because we've now got so used to the Earth adventures – to caring not only about humans, but recurring human characters – that we switch off from high concept aliens. I'm intellectually impressed by what Bob Baker and Dave Martin are doing in The Mutants. And I applaud a story that, for the first time since Inferno (!), doesn't rely upon an established monster or villain as the threat. It seems genuinely ambitious. But whether it's the fault of Christopher Barry's somewhat schizophrenic direction, some of the worst acting we've seen in Doctor Who yet, or my own inability to make the leap from Earth-bound runabout to something a lot less predictable, I find it all rather resistible. The Doctor is soon to have his freedom to travel through time and space restored – the series needs to work a little harder if it wants to take full advantage of the wider storytelling styles it can offer.

T: The best thing about the episode is the Doctor's horrible dilemma. As the Marshall threatens Jo's life, the Doctor compromises his credibility and honour by lying to the Investigator about the nature of the Mutts. It's always hard to watch such injustice, and it's a relief when Jo is liberated and the Doctor can come clean. So far, so good... but then, as events sway back in the Marshall's favour, he undermines his achievements by locking up the Investigator sent to look into charges of his misconduct! Does he seriously think he can get away with this? (With bad guys this stupid, we don't actually need the Doctor...) That inane change of fortune pretty much reflects this topsy-turvy tale. Actually, check that... what *really* sums up this topsy-turvy tale is that Peter Howell, an excellent actor with a lengthy career, and here appearing as the Investigator in his only Doctor Who episode ever, gets credited below Rick James. It's enough to make a grown man cry.

I can cite other bright spots about this, sure... the idea of the crystal that catalyses the Solonians' natural mutation ties in neatly with the story's clever premise, and the shot of Super-Ky destroying the Marshall has a number of effects-processes which are pulled off seamlessly. But there's just too much off-kilter about this – I concur with you that the soprano, floaty Ky is a bit to drippy and Star Trek for

my taste, and George Pravda, after a temporary moment of clarity last week, once again behaves as if he hasn't got a clue what he's doing. Jaeger doesn't even get the dignity of a clear-cut death – given that a similar explosion merely stunned him in episode two, we're left in the dark as to his final fate. (Terrance Dicks' novelisation of this adventure, at least, cites Jaeger as definitively dead. It's a bit sad that we have to resort to secondary material to figure this out, though.)

And so we end with a callback to a door-malfunction joke from episode one, a terrible gag involving a clean sweep and a broom cupboard, and another showing for the old "Doctor... who?" chestnut. Those three comedy bits at the end suggest, worryingly, that the production team actually thinks that it's done a good job, and can now coast to the end with a bit of back-slapping jokery. In my humble opinion, the whacking great dip in quality between ideas and execution in this story suggests that they can't.

The Time Monster (episode one)

R: I have a good friend called Liz who tells me that The Time Monster is her favourite story. I'm not quite sure how it came up, actually – but now that it's out there, whatever else we talk about always somehow *hovers* around this bombshell. And it's not ironic! (Neither her love for The Time Monster, nor consequently my affection for her. She doesn't favour Jon Pertwee stories with dubious pedigrees for the sake of it, just as I don't choose friends for their freakish feelings for Jon Pertwee stories.)

She doesn't claim it's the *best* Doctor Who story. Just her favourite.

This is the first time I've watched The Time Monster since I met Liz, and I'm trying to watch it through her eyes. And it works! I've wasted years of my life despising this, but it's actually enormous fun. I never before thought I'd miss the UNIT team, but it feels like ages since we've seen them, and even in Day of the Daleks they were somewhat sidelined. They're reinvented now purely as comic characters, it's true. The Brigadier exists so he can make dead-pan facial reactions to the Doctor's rudeness about military efficiency, or his desire to track down the Master through his dreams. He can't find anyone to go on a date with him to a science experiment – and with pure sitcom timing, in comes Benton, dressed in civvies, off on leave! All of this depends on whether you see this as a betrayal of UNIT's earnest background or not, but I have to say it – Nicholas Courtney and John Levene are made for comedy, and the Brigadier and his long-suffering, put-upon sergeant make a great double act.

The oddness of the episode is that it opens with volcanoes and mythic faces, and looks desperately epic. Roger Delgado towers over us all, in full devil mode, cackling and proclaiming himself our master... And then it's all beautifully undercut by an episode which is so determinedly domestic, it can't but help raise a smile. And it's deliberate (it must be!) that the most dramatic moment in the episode is nothing more than a nightmare that before long even the Doctor can't take seriously. So when we see the Master for real – inevitably – he's not some saturnine demon, but an avuncular scientist with a crazy Greek accent. The most unpleasant thing he does all episode is hypnotise a dean – and you can see Delgado play against type so well here, clearly relishing his refusal to meet the Brigadier by pretending to be a pacifist. It's genuinely witty, that.

The Master's assistants Stu and Ruth are somewhat more frustrating, it's true. Ian Collier really *goes* for the role of bumbling pratt, and it works – of course he's irritating to watch, but he's supposed to be; there's a joker like Stu inside every single office, usually in charge of the mail room. And, in that light, Ruth's overt feminism too looks like a joke, rather than a serious attempt to reflect the changing gender politics of the seventies. She's a stereotype, of course she is – but she's *such* a stereotype, every single stretch of dialogue influenced by her bitter contempt for men, that she's established as a self-aware comic caricature. She passes from being annoying into someone who's really rather funny. And Ruth and Stu work as the Master's companions, principally because the joke is on the Master: out of the three scientists working on TOMTIT, the evil chap with the beard is the one you feel sorry for. The sequence where Ruth and Stu dance around the laboratory singing "We've done it", only to bump into the Master, is either the most cringingly embarrassing thing yet seen in the series, or a wonderful subversion of the Master, a demonstration of just how much he's had to abase himself for his latest scheme. (Or possibly both.) Either way, the contrast between *this* Master and the one in the opening sequence is too great not to have a point.

All this, and Bessie driving at supersonic speed, Terry Walsh falling off a ladder and a great gag about tea. It's not the way any serious-minded fan likes to picture Doctor Who. But it is very entertaining.

T: There are definitely things to appreciate here, such as that opening dream sequence – it's got high and low angles, giddying zooms, thunder and, better still, it's all done on film! And further to your remarks about UNIT, it's wonderful that Sgt Benton is the only person thick enough to bypass all the technical jargon and succinctly articulate how the TOMTIT machine works ("[It shoves objects] through the crack between now and... now"). Then there's Procter, an assistant who only exists to laugh obsequiously at Dr Cook's joke ("I doubt very much whether we should allow ourselves the luxury of [having] pheasants [for lunch]... or TOMTITs") – which is either a wonderfully cheeky bit of comedy or a terrible laxity with the show's budget. (I mean, to spend money hiring an actor for just one guffaw.) And since I'm veering all over the place with my analysis, let me add that I don't mind Stuart Hyde either (Collier's playing the type as written, and at least has a bit of twinkle about him) and agree that the Master posing as a pacifist (!) is a lively bit of fun.

Unfortunately, try as I might... I've now entirely run dry of good news. We can try to pretend otherwise, but some of the dialogue (including "Simmer down Stew, for Pete's sake", "a real pippin of a dream" and "all that Cretan jazz" – it sounds like somebody's been popping pills made of pure, uncut 70s dust) is a contender for the worst we've yet heard. And why is it that for all of Ruth Ingram's supposed feminism, she's given the not-remotely empowering line "Look, don't bully me, Stu, or I think I'll burst into tears"? (Forgive me for being ill-informed, but I very much doubt that's the title of Chapter Two of The Female Eunuch.) And why does actress Wanda Moore deliver that line so straight? Meanwhile, Dudley Simpson gets insanely bouncy – giving the proceedings all the atmosphere of a trip to zany mountain on the happy bus – and the cliffhanger, where the Master switches TOMTIT into high gear and screams "Come, Kronos, come!" is horribly botched. The total lack of menace surrounding the arrival of the hitherto-unmentioned Kronos means the Master may as well be yelling "Come, Timmy Mallett!"

Strangely enough, it's only here that I'm deeply experiencing the common complaint that the Pertwee era gets a little formulaic and self-satisfied – as if everyone involved is having fun, but they've forgotten that *we* need to be entertained as well. The Doctor even drives too fast, demonstrating that he might be addicted to speed. Judging from this episode, so are most of the production team.

The Time Monster (episode two)

R: It made me laugh. Sometimes at it, I admit. But quite often *with* it.

The rapport between John Wyse (Dr Percival) and Roger Delgado is lovely, actually – the Master's treatment of this poor professor (who needs his hypnosis freshened up every once in a while) is gorgeous; he thinks he's something like a pet spaniel. The gently testy way in which he tells Wyse off for interrupting him with his Einstein theories is akin to the manner in which you tell off a dog that's jumped on to your lap whilst you're trying to read a book. And the scene in which the Brigadier puts the pompous Dr Cook in his place is great fun too. It feels at first as if the Brig is just trying to deflate the playground bully, interrupting Cook in his attacks on Dr Perceval – but then after Cook goes, the Brigadier rounds on Perceval himself, which feels rather a shame. And that entire sequence, where the Master tries to outwit Benton by pretending to be the Brigadier on the telephone, is gorgeously silly – and it's just right that Benton, in his best episode yet, gets to show a bit of brains and turns the tables on him. Delgado's facial expression when he sees he's been outwitted by John Levene is priceless.

But the episode loses momentum when it goes for earnest. So pity poor Ian Collier, who's

been aged to 80 years old, and gives despair and infirmity his absolute all. It isn't just the make-up that make the histrionics out of place, it's the context of the drama – The Time Monster is throwing lots of different things at the screen, but angst is one thing that just doesn't mix well. There's one good moment which works, and that's the way in which the Doctor responds to Stu's pleas to be returned to his rightful age – the Doctor can't magic away what TOMTIT has done to him, and his very awkwardness about letting Stu down is really rather affecting. Pity poor Jon Pertwee as well, though: whilst every other regular is letting his hair down and having a bit of a chuckle, he's stuck with deathly exposition, and sincere attempts to sell to the audience the dire urgency of the situation. He seems like the one actor in a pantomime taking it seriously, saddled with all the boring bits whilst we wait for the next comedy turn. And it's an indication of just how good Pertwee is, and how much authority his Doctor has, that he all but convinces you that this isn't half as enjoyable as it is.

T: Bah! You've once again gobbled up all the good stuff to comment upon, leaving me with the crust that is the interminably long time our heroes take to realise that "Thascales" is Greek for Master. The minute the Doctor queries the name, we the audience *know* it will enable the goodies to immediately identify who they're dealing with... but they string it out nonetheless! For pity's sake, UNIT should mandate that any new academic whose name means "Master" in any language should be arrested immediately. That'd stop him. ("You're telling me that Mister Meester is the Master – I don't believe it!")

But, all right... let me list out the positives of this. You've correctly identified the heroes of this episode: Roger Delgado, John Levene and John Wyse. And to be fair to co-writers Robert Sloman and (uncredited) Barry Letts, the supposedly "stupid" characters have their own keen instinct, reasoning and intuition. It *is* lovely how Benton almost single-handedly foils the Master's plan, just as it's great that the Master remarks, "I think I know how to deal with him...", upon discovering that Benton is on guard in the first place. (Had it been an extra stationed there instead, it would've been a quick zap with a laser gun and lights out for him – the series regulars clearly merit far less terminal treatment.) Having cursed the dialogue last week, I love Delgado's exasperation as he says "Ah, the tribal taboos of army etiquette...", and Benton's mind-bendingly poetic "You're in the soup without a ladle..." And I so appreciate that Delgado affects a wonderful careworn comedy persona in his scenes with Wyse, telling the man that he's doing his "sums" (a term so much more charming and paternal than "calculations" or "maths") and playing the long-suffering straight man as he berates his stooge for his ineptitude.

None of these highlights, though, can disguise that we're taken back to the *same* research room for yet *another* fairly uninspiring cliffhanger... which this time around involves the sudden materialisation of a slightly startled old man. It's not *quite* in the same league as the Doctor hollering "Listen to that! It's the sound of this planet screaming out its rage!", is it?

June 8th

The Time Monster (episode three)

R: It's hard to hate any episode which has the line "Get on with it, you seventeenth-century poltroons!", or has a sequence where UNIT engage in armed combat with Roundhead soldiers. But, joking aside – this is almost entirely crap.

The problem is that it's stopped being comical. John Wyse has got eaten by Kronos the Chronovore, and as henchman to the Master is replaced by Donald Eccles (as Krasis). John Wyse was a bemused university professor out of his depth, but Eccles is a florid high priest who doesn't speak his lines so much as incant them. The effect it has is that all the scenes involving Delgado are no longer *fun*; there's no rapport between the actors, and precious little drama either, as they spend most of the episode either recoiling from a man in a white chicken costume (very silly), or a glowing crystal (very dull). There are long stretches in which not only does nothing happen, but the Doctor does his level best to make that nothing happen all the more slowly; the little subplot

in which he interferes with the Master's time experiments by spinning around a bit of kitchen junk might just be ludicrous enough on a kids-can-imitate-it-at-home level, if it wasn't all just a self-acknowledged delaying tactic to a story that's barely moving anyway. When you get scenes of our characters jogging on the spot *pretending* they're in slow motion, you know there's a problem with the pacing not confined to the fiction.

And the sequence on Atlantis is ghastly too. It gives director Paul Bernard a chance to give the episode a different visual style, and that's all to the good – but because nothing actually happens in this new setting either, it feels as if all the potential momentum of a fresh setting is being squandered. Sloman and Letts try to make the Atlantean dialogue sound classical, but only succeed in making it tortuously mannered. George Cormack (as King Dalios) is a good enough actor to make his lines sound occasionally natural – not so Aidan Murphy (the warrior Hippias), all mascara and ham.

There's one good thing in this episode, and it happens in the closing seconds. The Brigadier is convinced that the UNIT convoy have been destroyed by a V1 bomb, and tries to raise them on his walkie-talkie. As he gets more alarmed, he drops the formality of calling out for Captain Yates, and begins to call him Mike. That's lovely – and especially effective after an episode in which Benton rumbled the Master's impersonation of the Brigadier because he didn't understand the protocol of how to speak to junior officers.

But that aside, this is almost unbearable. It's certainly the worst episode of Doctor Who we've sat through yet. Sorry, Liz. Ouch.

T: Let me bring you up to speed on where I am. I'm moving house in about a month, I'm flying to Canada the day after tomorrow, the kids have left the place in a bit of a state and... I have to devote a chunk of my day to the middle two episodes of The Time Monster. *Whose* idea was this again?

Fortunately, I like this a lot more than you do. That much-maligned twosome, Ruth and Stu, are actually rather good – mainly thanks to the performers, who have a natural rapport that convinces you that they've known each other a while. I adore that Stu only has marmalade for sandwiches, and empathise with his scruffiness, sloppy living conditions and the fact that he's left a wine bottle's cork on the corkscrew. (Yes, I'm aware that I'm identifying with a character most Doctor Who fans regard as unfunny and annoying – the resultant complex is only a slight one at present, I promise.) I also think their exchange about the Doctor being a nutcase of "fruitcake standard" is lovely, although I'm less entertained with the Doctor's strategy of manipulating time with a conglomeration of items including tea leaves and some strategically placed forks. I'd probably forgive it in a funnier story, but The Time Monster hasn't yet earned my indulgence.

Fandom always seems to give Kronos stick too – but do you know, I think the unearthly squawking, the reflective bright white, the fact that he flies and the director's canny use of close-up and quick cuts (meaning we never quite see him properly) make him an adversary unlike any we've had before in the series. Just look at that full-length shot of him retracting back into the crystal; it's slightly abstract, but visually sound. It is a shame, though, that Kronos eats John Wyse – I liked him.

My patience *really* starts to wane, though, when the Brigadier – who has witnessed any number of alien invasions – suspects that Captain Yates is either hallucinating or hammered because he reports that "some goon in fancy dress" forced his team off the road. If you have to reduce your characters to halfwits just to get a funny line out of them, the joke probably isn't worth it. Much more effective, though, is the sickening silence as the doodle-bug cuts out, Yates' muffled cries of "It's a bomb!" and that massive explosion that lead to a jolting cliffhanger.

Sigh... as you can probably tell, I'm trying to find ways to remain optimistic. It pains me to say this, but I wouldn't put it past the production team to misjudge this story's tone *so* spectacularly, they'd actually kill off a regular character halfway through what's tried to (sort of) present itself as a zany comedy romp. Which might not be good news for Yates next week...

The Time Monster (episode four)

R: What is it with Barry Letts and his comedy yokels? What are they supposed to achieve, seriously? Here we have a farmer pop up, having just watched a *bloody great bomb* fall upon a convoy of soldiers, and he acts as if it's all just something those strange new-fangled city folk get up to. You know what the scene is supposed to provoke – a wry shake of the head, "Oh, comedy yokel, the funny things you bumpkins say!" But this is a story in which the divide between what's intended and what we're actually given is very, very wide indeed.

Take the scenes with Benton, Stu and Ruth. It's as childish as the series ever gets, pure Scooby Doo or Enid Blyton, where the kids go after the villain as if it's just part of the fun adventure. I've no problem with that in itself. (Well, actually, that isn't true, I think it's more than a little puerile, but never mind that for the moment.) It's the inconsistency of tone that bothers me. Ruth fancies a pop at an alien criminal mastermind that we've just been told is designated UNIT's A1 threat – and Benton *encourages* her, and then rubbishes Stu's manhood because, a as civilian, he doesn't necessarily feel qualified to take on a mass murderer who's threatening the fate of the entire world. Fair enough. It could happen. (Though it'd be a lot more convincing if at this stage the characters knew that the rest of the military were frozen in a time bubble, and so the fate of the planet was down to them.) But then, as they go to take on the Master – and with all the tally-ho gumption of schoolkids just *itching* to get their own back on a rotter's nasty trick! – Stu picks up a *spanner*. A heavy metal spanner. Presumably to brain the Master with. It'd crush his skull, Stu. Is that what you want? In one moment, you think you might want to leave everything to the authorities, the next you want to be wiping bits of shattered cranium off a blunt instrument.

This is what it's come to. We're watching a series that is no longer sure what level it's playing on any longer. If it wants to become a romp for kids, in which Benton gets turned into a baby, in which the Master is just a silly recurring comic book villain (and next week, we'll literally get the "curses, foiled again" line), then so be it. At least let it have the courage of its convictions. It wants to be The Daemons, which oozed family charm from every pore, and was instrumental in making UNIT feel like a bunch of bantering chums rather than a secret military outfit. But The Daemons worked brilliantly because it felt confident, and its reinvention of the series as light-hearted comedy was done without putting a foot wrong. This plays some of the same tricks – last time the occult was revealed as an alien science, this time it's mythology – but essentially it's much the same. The Master spends episode endings shouting for a superbeing to come and be in his thrall. Benton is teamed up with a comedy sidekick. Even the Brigadier gets cut out of the action (and God love him, this time around Nick Courtney gets the best end of that deal). But it's not a light soufflé as we saw last year, it's a thick indigestible porridge.

And it's so slow. If last week's was an episode of delaying tactics, this is a week of two TARDISes not actually going anywhere. I love the imagery of the two ships inside each other. But unlike in Logopolis, where it all seems surreal and disturbing, it becomes increasingly obvious that all these long conversations between the Doctor and the Master are just to prevent the plot moving to Atlantis for another week. Was Ingrid Pitt (as Queen Galleia) not yet available? I've ached this whole story for some confrontation between Pertwee and Delgado – the rapport between the two never lets me down. And even when they're talking to each other, they're doing it on separate sets – and the story focuses upon the Master simply *ignoring* his nemesis because he's a "bore". Turning the sound off, then making all Pertwee's words feed out backwards – it's padding of the worst kind, because actually Delgado is right, Pertwee really *isn't* saying anything interesting. There's no urgency to any of this – there's a lot of muttering that the universe might be coming to an end, but these middle episodes have sapped all the pace out of the story. By the close of episode four, the Azal wannabe has turned up and *eaten* the Doctor. That should be shocking! But because at this stage of the story we still haven't been given any real indication why Kronos might be a threat, it all just seems throwaway. Is the Doctor dead? Probably. What happens to Jo

now? Oh, she's said she doesn't care. Whatever. Nor do we.

I'm going against the point of this book, aren't I? What's to celebrate? Well, in the midst of all this dreadful pointlessness, just as a matter of padding, the Doctor makes his first allusions to the TARDIS being sentient. Jo can't be sure whether he's joking or not. I doubt Letts and Dicks could be either. But it's rather wonderful that, wholly accidentally, in a story that is trying so hard to be funny and sensational and epic, there's a sequence which makes the TARDIS feel like it's magic again. For the last few years, it's been a prop in the background of the Doctor's lab. Suddenly, it's the prime focus of the episode, in a series that hasn't known what to do with it, and it feels reinvented.

T: You're asking *me* what's to celebrate here? Oh crumbs... well, I do feel a swell of pity for Richard Franklin. Yates has been on this story's periphery so far, and when he finally arrives, he gets wounded and sent packing. Benton has enjoyed a far greater slice of the proceedings, perhaps because he's clearly much more fun to write. Wanda Moore, in spite of it all, makes Ruth Ingram sparky, likeable and nowhere near as irritating as she might have been. (It's a small mercy, I know, but I'm thanking Heaven for it.) And a temporal faux pas turns Benton into a baby – I love that!

But for all of the attempts here to be *whimsical*, I do worry that we could do with a little less of it in an episode where – as you say – Benton and company decide to tackle a sadistic mass murderer with all the nerves and fear of the Famous Five cavorting in a ginger beer factory. And yes, most of the episode is spent with the Master mucking about with the Doctor's ability to communicate with him – it's not exactly the stuff of high drama, is it? To be fair, Pertwee and Manning decide, admirably, to play the rather tedious situation with a lot of gravity, as if the stakes couldn't be higher. And all right – it's quite a moment when it looks as if the Doctor has been destroyed, especially when the Master's laughter echoes around as he sends Jo to her apparent death.

Overall, though, when the Doctor said, "testing, testing, testing...", into his microphone, I couldn't help but think, "Yes mate, it bloody is".

June 9th

The Time Monster (episode five)

R: What's to like? Hmm. Jo's new hairstyle is nice.
... Your turn.

T: Flippin' heck, I figured we'd have to jump ship entirely on an episode or two to uphold our positive remit, but I hadn't put The Time Monster episode five down on the list of possibles. I'd never be caught saying this is a great episode, but it hasn't exhausted my patience either. The relationships at court hold some interest, and it's *especially* fun to see the Master(!) trying to exert sexual power over Queen Galleia. All the best stuff in Atlantis, however, undeniably comes from George Cormack's King Dalios. Despite his years, Cormack is a powerful presence with a great line in iconoclastic humour – he blithely asks which god in particular the Master has come from, and what they have for breakfast on Olympus. It punctures the surrounding adventure's pomposity, and he brings colour without garishness to the proceedings.

It's telling, though, that I've mostly liked this story's comedic elements – I don't necessarily want or *need* my Doctor Who to be funny, but it's a stark illustration of how far The Time Monster's plot and drama have fallen short that I'm seeking solace in wit. The Daemons, which you mentioned, cleverly played with ideas of the ancient and mystical, which by their nature have spooky iconography. Here, the baggage of the mythic is less scary and comes beset with boringly uninvolving robes, beards and posturing. Which is to say: while our beloved Brigadier is stuck mid-sentence in a time freeze, and there's enjoyment to be had with baby Benton, we're spending our time instead with the grumpy Lord Crito, a bland member of Dalios' court.

Oh, to hell with it... I've tried being upbeat, but my inner critic is battering at the gates. If I'm being candid, Aidan Murphy, only one story after The Mutants, is giving Rick James some serious competition for the mantle of Worst Actor Ever in Doctor Who. He's supposed to be a warrior-type – strong enough to take on the Minotaur in combat, even! – but looks like an actress I vaguely know, Jayne Ashbourne (although she's *meant* to look pretty, what with, y'know, being a woman an' all). His supposed "relationship" with the Queen doesn't entirely convince – in fact, he gives the impression of playing for a different team entirely. Perhaps Lakis, the Queen's handmaiden, has a soft spot for Hippias because she likes a challenge.

Even Dudley Simpson seems to have decided that this is stupid, adding a comedy "wa-wa-waaah" when Jo suggests that the Master might like to exclaim, "Curses foiled again!" (Incidentally, Rob, I'm surprised you didn't try to pass that line off as the drama acknowledging, in a postmodern and self-effacing style, its own descent into cliché – are you feeling tired?) And how fortunate that the TARDIS has an emergency button *pre-programmed* to retrieve its pilot if a Glowing Budgie of Time sucks them into the Vortex. Does the TARDIS have other such buttons for similarly unlikely situations? ("Remember Jo, if I get stuck in an anti-matter cake five miles from Wigan, when the moon is in the sign of the ram – but only on a Tuesday in March if it's raining – press the third blue button from the right...")

If nothing else, though, it's a neat idea to have the Doctor's subconscious voice babbling away in the background during those opening TARDIS scenes. He's quite keen Jo pays no heed to them, isn't he? The dirty old sod.

The Time Monster (episode six)

R: Sorry, I'll try harder. But to be fair, it *is* a very cute hairstyle.

This episode is at its best when it's being intimate. The "daisiest daisy" speech is overwritten flab, but it's performed by Jon Pertwee very well – and the extreme close-up he's given as he narrates his little fable about optimism and purple rocks affords him the chance to play it with admirable subtlety. But the most affecting part of the scene is afterwards: "I'm sorry I brought you to Atlantis." "I'm not." "Thank you." That's charming, and works beautifully because in spite of all the cod-classical dialogue and the hammy declaiming elsewhere, you can sincerely believe in the love between the Doctor and Jo.

And it's an episode which pivots on love, very rarely for Doctor Who: the Doctor cannot complete the Time Ram which will stop the Master but sacrifice Jo in the process, so to demonstrate her faith in him and what he stands for, Jo completes the operation herself. It's another replay from The Daemons, maybe, but it's a far more effective one, because it's not just Katy Manning shouting out to a CSO effect that she'd rather die in place of Jon Pertwee, but an acknowledgement that she can face death if it's something she needn't face alone. Indeed, the sequence where she believes herself to be in Heaven with him is lovely – for once, Katy's naive perkiness is exactly right, as she resigns herself to a new form of existence altogether with the Doctor by her side to explore it. Consider too that the climax in Atlantis also hinges upon love, as Galleia realises that the husband she's ousted from the throne is dead, and turns on the Master in her grief. Yes, Ingrid Pitt is overwhelmingly awful in the role. But that final image of her, standing amid the ruins, her king dead and her city destroyed because of her greed, works very well.

The problem with the episode, however, is that it's largely not wanting to be intimate at all. The sequence with the Minotaur tries to capture a famous myth in all its glory – and is laugh-out loud funny, being little more than Dave Prowse running about bellowing and being karate chopped by Jon Pertwee. My sides were still sore by the time we got to the destruction of Atlantis, achieved by a chicken on Kirby wires flapping about. (When, later on, Jo talks soberly about the death of "all those people", the Doctor can't bring himself to comment. You can see why. It's impossible to believe that it represented not only the devastation of an entire culture, but also that it's a devastation so fabled. It'd be like watching the fall of Troy as played out with a sandcastle.) And all this self-conscious tipping towards the epic reaches a crescendo of hilarity when the Doctor gets to confront this season-climax's idea of an all-mighty god. Kronos is a literal deus ex machina – she explains that she's so very powerful and amoral that the terms "good" and "evil" don't apply to her. Which must be nice. And then sends the Doctor and Jo home like the Wizard of Oz. But not before

subjecting us all to a scene where she makes Roger Delgado get down on his knees and beg for forgiveness; it's the only time in the series we ever see Delgado ham it up, and although it'd be hard to see how *anyone* could get away from what he's asked to do without egg on their face, it's dispiriting to see a chink in Delgado's armour.

So, can I understand why this is Liz's favourite story? I suppose so. It depends whether you celebrate the kitsch ambition of it or not. It fails on so many levels, I think – it doesn't work as drama, as comedy, as adventure story, as anything moving or suspenseful – but for it to fail on *that* many levels, I can only concede that it was having a stab at more levels than the show is used to. But I hate it. I really do. It's the first Doctor Who story we've watched I can honestly say that about. Because for all its ambition, it didn't quite go far enough; it didn't have the ambition to take all these ingredients and turn them into something satisfying. A story that has roundheads fighting UNIT, has the Doctor meeting classical gods and fighting the minotaur, and has Benton revert to a baby... the last thing this should feel is lazy. But it does.

T: I remember when dramatist Dennis Potter did an astonishing interview with Melvyn Bragg, in which Potter revealed that he had a terminal illness, and his desire to see through his final project whatever it took. It was a mixture of bloody mindedness, passion, brilliant creativity and childish sentimentality – all bound up in that buckled, fiery, contrary character. I mention this because the interview's most famous moment came when Potter talked of looking outside his window, knowing his life was to end shortly, and adoring the blossom outside... as he coined it, it was "the blossomest blossom". People latched onto that as a totem for his amazing ability to conjure words and feelings – as a daring, creative talent expressing the simplicity of the beauty of the everyday. Now, I'm a big fan of Potter, but even I remember thinking, "Oh yes, clever clogs, but the Doctor said something similar 20-odd years earlier, so ner..." And the fact that the Doctor did it in one of the shittest-ever Doctor Who stories (or should I say, the "shittiest shit"?) is even more remarkable.

[Sound of crickets chirping, as Toby realises that perhaps that last remark was not whole-heartedly and 100% to the positivity standard this book is trying to uphold...]

Oh, who are we fooling? I can't say I *hate* – wow, that's a strong word – this story like you do, but I've lost the will to say good things about it. I mean, just look at the sequence where the Doctor defeats the Minotaur – the bull-man runs towards him, then runs past him, then keeps running and then *runs straight into a handy shiny wall...* and then he just dies. This, after they went to the trouble of committing the sequence to film for the extra control you get in that environment, and yet it winds up being truly risible. The only upshot is that the battle has the chutzpah to be a grand folly of some magnitude, in an episode that otherwise vacillates between being dull and horrible. I had hoped Hippias was killed off because the production team was intent upon slaughtering the supporting cast in bad actor order, and yet Ingrid Pitt survives to the end whilst the stellar George Cormack is dispatched after getting all cocky with a weapon-wielding guard. Never mind that the scene in the dungeon is only there to pad out the episode, as if the writers have self-diagnosed their need for, er, a padded cell.

I do, as it happens, admire Jo's pluck for trying to stop the Master from escaping by clinging onto him, and then bravely lighting the blue-touch paper that will destroy her but save the day. That's about the only other bit of praise I can offer. Well, that, and the fact that having forced myself to do so for this exercise... I won't have to watch The Time Monster ever again.

[Toby's addendum, written 22nd July, 2009: Guess what? I've just received an e-mail asking me to moderate the commentary for, yep, The Time Monster! So, I will have to watch it again. A lot. And soon. Still, I expect that Ingrid Pitt will be interesting to chat with, so every cloud has a silver lining.]

[Second addendum, 24th August: Ingrid Pitt can't make the commentary recording, as she's having her hip done(!). Shame. But, all is not lost, as it's always such a pleasure to spend time with Barry Letts. He's such a pro, doing commentaries with him is always easy.]

[Third addendum, 26th August: Just finished the commentary, and was very shaken to see that Barry was doing poorly. It's no secret that he's been battling cancer for some time, and while he's maintained so much vigour and energy on a lot of Doctor Who events before now, it inescapably looks as if the disease is getting the better of him. He tired easily – we took a break after episode one so he could have a nap and regain some strength – and was nothing like his sharp and lucid self. It was so distressing to see someone so learned and articulate get so frustrated with himself as he laboured to keep up with the conversation. You go forward after witnessing such things, but all I see for the moment are a lot of clouds, and the silver linings are conspicuously absent. I have the uncomfortable feeling that it might be the last time I ever see Barry, which makes me very sad.]

[Fourth addendum, 15th November: Barry passed away on 9th October, only two weeks after The Time Monster commentary was recorded. He left behind a staggering legacy in both Doctor Who and TV drama in general, and it was very pleasing that today's new Doctor Who episode, The Waters of Mars, was dedicated to his memory.]

June 10th

The Three Doctors (episode one)

R: So here's the situation. My experience fighting The Time Monster last night has rather taken the wind out of my sails. Frankly, I'm deflated. For the first time since starting, I actually don't feel like Doctor Who is fun any more. I'd like to take a breather. I'd like to cheat – *pretend* we're doing a diary, and secretly catch up with some episodes later on, when I've got my energy back.

Now is not the time I want to be around Doctor Who. To think about it or talk about it.

And so, naturally enough, it's the same day I'm sitting next to Toby Hadoke on an aeroplane. Talking about Doctor Who. And we're doing that, because we're off to a Doctor Who convention in Toronto. Where we'll be – I dare say – talking about Doctor Who.

Somewhere over the ocean, once we've been watered and given pretzels, Toby gets out his laptop. We try to watch episode one of The Three Doctors together, but it doesn't work. I'd have to get on Toby's lap to do that, and neither of us is willing to put that plan into action. We'll have to take turns to get our Gell Guard fix. "Do you want to go first?" asks Toby, kindly. "Not particularly", I grumble. Toby gives me a pained look – he's a much kinder person than I am, and so much more forgiving of a series that has just given us Ingrid Pitt and a flying chicken. And so I put on a smile, take his computer, and watch the first episode of the tenth season.

... oh, that was rather fun, wasn't it? At some point, my forced grin became a real one. I think it was somewhere around the point that the Brigadier began lamenting to Dr Tyler that his once-secret military organisation is now nothing more than a citizens advice bureau for every stray boffin who happens to be walking past. He's already had to pass the Doctor something to stir his tea with. He has no dignity left, you'd have thought. And Nicholas Courtney plays his little outburst perfectly – it's like the last cry of a character who *knows*, deep down, that he used to have proper authority on this series, and has now been relegated to comic relief. He's disappearing, this Brig we used to know, but he's not going down without telling us. I rather love that.

In an episode where the threats are either a bit of cartoon jelly, or some bizarre monster that makes comical grunting sounds as they wobble along, that image of the wildlife warden, Ollis, burned on to paper is really very unnerving. The realisation that the distorted pattern is actually a man screaming in fear has a terrific punch to it.

And the Doctor is back! I'll be honest – I loved Patrick Troughton's Doctor, but I've not properly missed him yet. There hasn't been time. It's not been 80 episodes yet since The War Games; that's less than two seasons in old money. What's peculiar is that he doesn't quite seem like the Doctor I love at all. There's an obvious reason for this. He's not the lead in his own programme, but a comic guest star to spar with Jon Pertwee. But it's also (stupid as it sounds) because he's in *colour*. Troughton shouldn't be in colour. He belongs to a different style than that. It's a bit like watching Buster Keaton with sound – it isn't quite right.

And yet – I know it doesn't quite seem kosher, but I get a tremendous rush of pleasure watching him. And it's not a nostalgic kick, it's because of the way Pertwee, Katy Manning and John Levene react to him. Either irritated, or bemused, or delighted, their reactions give this Doctor a context. That's the principle difference – once upon a time, Troughton was without doubt the dominant force on Doctor Who. And now he's defined by everyone else. It's as it should be, of course. And it's why, conversely, the sequence with William Hartnell doesn't work nearly so well. He's not in the studio with his successors. He's just acting to a camera. Yes, he looks old and ill, and he has none of the charm or the twinkle that made Hartnell so adorable. Instead, he's the grumpy old git that fandom have caricatured him as (and largely, I suspect, because of this very performance). But it's because he's just stuck on a screen, no-one to find a rapport with. He looks for all the world like he can't act, and surely makes any new viewer wonder how the series could have survived three whole years with *him*.

And yet... it's the respect for Hartnell that you can clearly see on the faces of Pertwee and Troughton that still make this work. No, these two Doctors aren't the performances we remember. They're emblems of the past. But how wonderful we can have these emblems. How wonderful the series has survived so long, and evolved so much, that this look back to the past can be so moving. Because it is.

I shall now hand the laptop back to Toby, and he can see what he makes of it. But I'm in a better mood now. Talking about Doctor Who for a weekend in Canada? You bet. Bring it on!

T: You're referring to me in the third person again – if you do it often enough, do I get turned into fiction or something? And this is doubly weird, because I'm typing something at you that I could just as easily turn around and say to your face. I feel rather sorry for Canada – it's a beautiful country, by all accounts – because we're going all the way there to watch and chat about Doctor Who. Talk about broadening your horizons.

And do you know, I've only just realised – because of the peculiar way we're watching these stories, yesterday's detritus was *a season finale*! It took me even longer to register this because – concerns about The Time Monster aside – The Three Doctors is hardly what you'd call a spectacular season opener. Rob, you've been the recipient of the odd apoplectic phone call from me, in which I've aired my difficulties with some of the new series' everything-but-the-kitchen-sink fests... but surely, at the end of a season, this lot could *at least* have given us a dirty roasting pan! Or a plug. I suppose this season opener (and anniversary celebration of the show's past) gives us a drain, and two previous Doctors turn up, yes, but the basic storyline – to review – entails a yokel getting zapped, UNIT getting attacked by some radioactive vomit and a big fight scene with some shambling jelly monsters. As part and parcel of a rare opportunity to bring back the series' leads, it's not *quite* the grand occasion one could hope for.

Naturally, we *can* celebrate Troughton's return, even if he hasn't got back to grips with his character. He undeniably has moments of brilliance (he's obviously taken with Jo), but seems a tad over emphatic in places. It's great to have him back, though – lines such as "[The Time Lords] are very worried, you know..." have ten times more impact when delivered by Troughton than a lesser actor. Poor William Hartnell though – it's heartbreaking to see how much he's gone downhill; he delivers the line about his successors being "a dandy and a clown" as if someone sitting next to him in the time eddy had fed him that information. It's sweet, though, to see the incongruity of his name appearing in these ultra-modern credits.

Talking of which, I don't know why it's taken me this long to mention it, but... we run a risk of taking some of the brilliant fundamentals of Doctor Who for granted. Just behold those wonderful opening titles and this terrific theme-arrangement which have such power, atmosphere and sounds that are impossible to replicate with any instrument. They're incredible. Thus far, we've not had a title sequence or theme music which look dated even to modern eyes and ears. That's quite an incredible achievement – Bernard Lodge and Delia Derbyshire, your names should be etched in stone.

UNIT is indeed getting a bit comfy, but we should ask: where is Captain Yates? Richard Franklin must have sat at home watching this,

thinking that Yates should have done Benton's bit, and Benton should've replaced Corporal Palmer. Benton is fab as usual, though, when he climbs through the window of the Doctor's lab with a machine gun, and *especially* when he subverts the normal expectation of remarking how the TARDIS is "bigger on the inside!!" by telling the Doctor instead that "It's pretty obvious, isn't it?" The pained expression on Benton's face as he removes his hat, in weary recognition that the TARDIS' interior is yet-another bit of incomprehensible weirdness, is terrific.

And Nicholas Courtney, as you say, gets moments of the old gravity – he's deadly serious about putting a guard on the drains, of all things, which is a definitive bit of Doctor Who shtick. (So much so, in fact, that when our local news aired a story about Liverpool University starting a course in sci-fi studies or something, they used this clip to illustrate the sort of thing that *only* happens in sci-fi.) There's also an attempt to show the military on their uppers, with masses of bullets flying about and a few hefty explosions, but the Gell Guards' appearance (including the terribly jumpy edits when they arrive – never attempt such an effect in woodland, as trees and bushes shake in the wind) is lamentable. Compared to this, I actually preferred Kronos: The Amoral Chicken of Time.

And would you believe it? I haven't yet mentioned the Time Lords – possibly because, well, they seem to be appearing in a different story altogether, where earnest ham is the order of the day. ("Ernest Ham"... that sounds like a character in a David Nobbs piece, doesn't it?) Never mind that Patrick Troughton isn't the only Time Lord who has changed since The War Games – judging by the rug on his head and the pitch of his voice, Clyde Pollitt seems to have undergone a hair transplant and a castration since his last appearance. Perhaps regeneration can be used for cosmetic reasons, and, indeed, to accommodate lifestyle choices.

The Three Doctors (episode two)

R: God bless Nick Courtney. The Brigadier as written is very frustrating. He's in denial of every explanation offered to him, arrogantly preferring to form his own wilder theories. The only way you can on paper interpret his character change here is to conclude that he has, in fact, gone mad – and Benton even tacitly suggests that his superior's brain has snapped. But because Courtney plays the part with a certain wounded dignity, it's all rather charming. The slow double take he gives in the scene where he realises that it's Troughton he's facing a crisis with rather than Pertwee is lovely.

And I like what's happening to Benton. In The Time Monster, it was his bluff simplicity which allowed him to understand the concept of interstitial time – and here he's the one who takes the TARDIS interior and return of past incarnations at face value. The writers have by now realised how to play to John Levene's strengths, and are making Benton delightful... Whereas Captain Yates is being forever more sidelined in contrast. And, indeed, is missing out on all the fun this week! I know that the original idea was that Jamie would have been allocated the basic part that was eventually given to Benton – but, as much as I miss Frazer Hines, I'm glad that UNIT's favourite sergeant had a good crack of the whip instead.

Jo Grant is getting a bit morbid, isn't she? This is the second story in a row where she's woken up some place new and assumed it must be Heaven. She seems far less cheerful about it this time round – but that's fair enough, I too might have considered it a lucky escape had I died during The Time Monster.

The criticism I'd make of the episode is that everybody seems to stand around assuming that everyone else is having a far more exciting time than they are. Troughton seems rather wistful when he wonders what Pertwee must be getting up to the other side of a black hole. But Pertwee spends his time wandering about the plot so slowly, that he's forced to say (quite rightly) that Dr Tyler's little escape attempt was just a waste of time. It's pleasant enough, this story, but nothing much is really happening. But I love the ending; the image of UNIT headquarters fair zipping its way across the universe and straight through a black hole is wonderful. For the last two seasons, the stories have either been set in UNIT offices or in quarries doubling as alien planets. Now we're going to have those offices stuck slap bang within the quarries – and there's something in that which

feels to me both celebratory and cheeky at the same time.

T: We should start the Sgt Benton Fan Club, shouldn't we? But, I dunno about the transformation that's undergone the Brigadier, a character I used to love. Maybe you're a better person than I am, but I can't see his loss of dignity as "charming" – the Brig is being written so badly at present, it's painful. I'll say it again: if you have to make a previously intelligent character unbelievably thick just to get a joke out, the joke isn't worth it. This is Brigadier Alistair Gordon Lethbridge-Stewart, for pity's sake!... and he's made to do a comedy bump into Benton, and has to be told to be wary of the monster. It's such a shame. William Hartnell's not the only one who's a shadow of his former self.

I know I've ventured into a dark place of late, so let me turn things around and mention that it's so refreshing to have Patrick Troughton capering about. The sparkiness in his delivery suggests a certain amount of improvisation – it's wonderful how he tells Benton that Omega's hostile blob-scout has hiccoughs, and wonders if they can numb it into submission with useless information... and asks for a TV! Then there's that a splendid comedy moment where Troughton assures the Brigadier that he can sort out the man's radio... before looking forlornly at its scattered innards and adding a doubtful "I think". (This happens, of course, before he "fixes" the device by banging it on the table.) Troughton is *so* loveable despite some quite childish behaviour, such as that terrific moment of trembling, wounded pride when he blusters that he's made Omega's blob-scout more hostile, and concedes, "That thing out there's become a killer! It's my fault, and I'm sorry!" His performance contains so many beautiful little moments, I could spend this entire entry talking about him.

Alas, I can't *just* chat about Troughton, and the story around him is, er, well, very problematic. When Dr Tyler makes his pointless escape attempt, Jo and the Pertwee Doctor just stand still... as does much of this episode. Tyler goes from being an enjoyable, intuitive boffin (gleefully doing his sums in the sand!) to an irritating malcontent – killing him off would have at least underlined the danger present, but as matters stand, the only thing murdered is our time. Let's also not go to a place ever again where Pertwee has a bunch of comedy flowers up his sleeve, which have presumably resided there for the past couple of years, on the off-chance that he'd need to perform a magic trick in an anti-matter universe at short notice (always be prepared, that's what I say).

It's not *all* bad, though... I do admire the terrifically hefty explosions that encircle the Doctor, Jo and Tyler when they're captured on location; the incongruity of the lab door stuck in the wasteland; and the way that Mr Ollis continues to lurk about but hasn't yet had a line. And isn't it great how the Time Lords shuffle circle-shaped sheets of paperwork? (Do they make it in the same machine that produces TARDIS walls?)

June 11th

The Three Doctors (episode three)

R: They think we're mad, you know. The Canadians. Here we are, in a car, being driven to the Niagara Falls. It's a two-hour drive, so there's plenty of time for us to fit in an episode of Doctor Who. Two of the Canadians who are driving us are *fans* – Heather and Luca – and they've no idea why we want to be watching episode three of The Three Doctors either. And our driver, Tanya, isn't even a fan, so probably thinks we're raving. Which is a shame, because she's pretty.

After we've watched the episode, and as I'm preparing to write up my thoughts, Tanya asks politely what happened in it. And it's a hard question to answer. The honest reply is, not a lot. It's about as episode three-ish as it can get, really – lots of literal running around in circles, between scenes of long exposition. We're used to the idea of the Doctor being trapped by the villain, who needs to talk about his tortuous plans for revenge. It's all the more flat when it has to happen twice, because we've got *two* Doctors to put this through. The Three Doctors looks like a pantomime, and on that level up to now it's been rather jolly. Lots of banter, lots of mistaken identity, Aladdin's caves and monsters that look like sweets you'd throw into the audience. But there's just too much restraint at

this stage of the proceedings; no-one's really trying hard enough. Stephen Thorne seems far too relaxed as Omega; he should come across as an unpredictable nutter who can fly into rages at the drop of a Gell Guard, but the most he ever manages to be is terse. You don't want a terse villain in a panto. And when he's not being terse, he's striding about, being positively amiable. No wonder that for all the awe the Doctor shows in dialogue confronting his old hero, Pertwee hardly seems to break a sweat.

There's fun to be had watching Pertwee and Troughton spar off each other – something that was missing from last week. And however unnatural Troughton's performance is in this (whatever he's playing, it's really not the Doctor I remember), he finds his form delightfully in the scene where he bluffs indignantly to Omega that he's just an innocent bystander. But after all the hype this story attracted, this episode does feel rather tepid.

I just hope that Niagara Falls at least lives up to *its* reputation.

T: Tanya isn't a Doctor Who fan, it's true, but she *has* seen the show and described it as "kinda goofy". I love that – she wasn't using it as a pejorative term, it was an affectionate appraisal for the show, using a word for which there really isn't a UK-English equivalent. I mean, we can *say* "goofy", but the Canadian accent helps deliver it as intended – that Doctor Who is cheap and cheerful and a bit silly, but in a good way. It's as effective a description of my beloved programme as anything I've coined after writing over quarter of a million words on it – and she used just two.

Back in the anti-matter universe, I can find a variety of things to appreciate. Omega's costume is excellent, and Stephen Thorne's height helps to make the character a towering presence. Dudley Simpson's twinkling soundtrack in Omega's palace illustrates the effectiveness of restrained minimalism, and the building's sizeable cliffside entrance is one of the story's best visuals. And yet, for all that, it's the lead actors' hard work that yields the best returns. We have *two* inspired pairings – casting Benton as a Jamie to the second Doctor is a stroke of genius, and makes me desperate to see more of the Troughton/ Levene double act. Meanwhile, the Brigadier, having been forced to behave like Colonel Blimp early on (after everything that he's seen, why does he think that UNIT HQ being instantly transported to Cromer is *more* likely than it being taken to a different universe?), finally comes into his own when taking command of Mr Ollis (who finally gets a line!). The Brig's convoluted instructions – which amount to the pair of them storming the palace – is a lovely, admirable *and* funny moment of stiff British resolve.

But for all I can accentuate the positive, I can't ignore that this story is the season opening and (nominal) tenth anniversary spectacular adventure... and it looks like it's been bodged together in a jumble sale. The fundamental problem, I think, is with the decision to write a story set in a mysterious nowhere-land, but without such familiar trappings as we saw in, say, The Mind Robber. I mean, Bob Baker and Dave Martin should have considered that the dreamy, abstract idea that they were conjuring forth on the page would be realised with an early 1970s BBC family show budget, i.e. as a quarry. What did they *think* they were going to get? And it doesn't get much better visually once the action goes inside, as Roger Liminton's sets of Omega's palace are diabolical. (If this is what Omega has conjured as a palatial abode, he should give up solar engineering and get a job at IKEA.) Fair enough, I don't watch classic Doctor Who for the stunning special effects or entirely convincing production values, but here the disconnect between ambition and realisation is simply too large.

A couple of final thoughts... The Two Doctors always gets stick for its revisionist view of the second Doctor's relationship with the Time Lords, and yet so few fans seem to object that the first Doctor here chats away to them without a care that he's a Time Lord renegade. And my *favourite* moment in this is when Omega loses his temper, and there's a thunderclap and the camera shakes – it's a perfect illustration of the symbiotic relationship between Omega and his world, and really builds the tension. Don't upset this guy, because if he goes to pieces, so does the floor you're standing on.

The Three Doctors (episode four)

R: The Falls were amazing, weren't they? So many places on this Earth inevitably feel a bit drab and disappointing when you get up close – the image I had in my head, say, of the Eiffel Tower, was so much grander than the reality. But I loved this. And it was so romantic – walking hand in hand beside this torrent of Nature, something that has been gushing away for countless millennia, regardless of who's looking at it. Admittedly, I'd have preferred to have been walking hand in hand with my wife rather than you, Toby, but hey, I'll get my kicks where I can.

And maybe it's the spray on my face, or the rush of water in my ears – or even by the way I was touched that everybody prevented me from trying to go over Niagara in a barrel. But I really enjoyed this episode we watched on the way back to Toronto. Now that all the flashes and bangs are over, and the gimmickry of putting the Doctors together has lost its charm, what Bob Baker and Dave Martin present us with is a surprisingly little story with buckets of pathos. The sequence where Troughton and Pertwee realise with horror that Omega has been eaten away altogether, and that's nothing left to see behind the mask, rather wonderfully asks you to feel pity for a villain who's ranting about universe destruction. It's that push/ pull in this episode between the grandiose epic, and the tragically intimate, that gives it a heart amidst all its panto trappings. Omega is another demi-god, but he's also, quite literally, *nothing at all*.

And what works rather beautifully is that we can't but help feel that Omega's request that the Doctors sacrifice their freedom just to give his parody of existence a little more flavour is all the more obscene. That characters as dynamic and eccentric as the ones we have here are required to throw it all away, just so they can entertain a void, is terrible. We see the Doctor face death in every story, and we're used to the finality of that. But to let his life drag on, and so pointlessly – that he's prepared to do that to save his friends feels heroic. The long, long sequence where all the humans walk, one by one, into the column of smoke that will take them home ought to feel padded and overworked. But instead, it's the most honestly moving thing I've seen in Who for ages. The little defiant bravery of Ollis as he marches in, the way that Benton follows orders to desert the Doctor so reluctantly, the way that Jo can't look back, the stiff respectful salute of the Brigadier. And the gentle authority with which Nick Courtney plays the scene gives the Brig his dignity back again, thank God.

It's not a great story, I'll admit. But I honestly love the way that something that on the surface is so big and blustering can both open and close in such a mundane manner – focusing on the taciturn Mr Ollis rather than something explosive. (Is he the first comedy yokel that's actually funny? He may well be!) And there's something telling in the way that Omega is revealed to be a creature that's entirely empty, and is only surviving through force of will. After the end of Season Nine, I rather suspected that the same thing was true for Doctor Who itself. Now there's a real sense, with the Doctor restored to being an adventurer in time and space, that the series may be finding a new lease of life.

T: I don't think my imagination properly envisioned the magnificent beauty of the Falls – and, at the risk of being overly glum, it certainly created prettier pictures than anything Omega has conjured forth. I actually feel a bit guilty, and a little dirty, having spent most of the day at one of the most stunning landmarks I've ever seen (how typically human, by the way, to put a town with all the class and elegance of Blackpool slap bang next to it) to end it by expending my energy on this – apologies, I can't think of any better way to put it – tatty piece of nonsense.

It's such a pity, because the heart of this contains some terrific ideas. The notion of a man who only exists through the sheer force of will is wonderfully abstract. (It doesn't bear much practical scrutiny, however – surely if Omega went for a pee, he'd notice a rather vital part of his anatomy was missing. I know I would.) It's also quite sweet that all Omega wants, ultimately, is bit of company (could he not have conjured up an Uma Thurman, though? – it shouldn't be much more difficult than a chair...), and that the destruction of him and his realm brings everything full circle and provides the Time Lords with a new energy

source. Despite my previously wondering why on Earth the writers thought they could get away with Omega's "Neverland" being successfully rendered on screen, this tidy piece of plotting I've just detailed – and Pertwee's effective remorse over his hero's demise – demonstrates that they've put *some* thought into this.

And so, to the goodbyes... goodbye, the Doctor's Earth exile (they were already phasing you out last season, but now it's official). Goodbye, Graham Leaman, an actor who racked up an impressive five performances in the show's first ten years. He never had a star turn or a showy part, but he was always reliable and distinctive. (I'm told that even when Leaman was towards the end of his life and too ill to act properly, he was so keen to be on the boards that he accepted the job of a corpse in a theatre play.) And goodbye to William Hartnell (save for the archive footage that opens The Five Doctors, which doesn't count). Actually, I'm very cross with the director for not giving Hartnell a decent close-up – at the very least, could they not have cut things so that his face would fill the monitor-screen without those pesky reflections? Still, even allowing for the limitations of Hartnell's illness, it's lovely that he came back one last time, and it's sweet that he leaves after telling us that the party is over, and he shudders to think what we'll do without him.

I've been quite critical of this story, but so let's leave it on a high point... this ending works so much better, I think, than the comedy bits stapled on to The Mutants. After our heroes' travels to an anti-matter universe, everything is brought *all* the way back down to Earth with Ollis' very funny, deadpanned question to his wife about whether supper is ready. I love the way that Laurie Webb opens his mouth as if to explain where he's been, then just gives up. Wonderful little moments such as this lift even a garish, rather slapdash production and give it a certain charm. They make it... how can I put this?... kinda goofy.

June 12th

Carnival of Monsters
(episode one)

R: And within 25 minutes, the whole of Doctor Who changes forever.

Yeah, I know – it's the sort of hyperbole you might expect from a Britisher who's having a great time on holiday in a foreign city. But I believe it to be true. What I think of as Doctor Who starts here: that strange brew of clever ideas mixed with character comedy and witty dialogue. The Robert Holmes we all know and love has finally put aside his apprentice work, and given us a script that just *sings* with a personality that's going to be the trademark of the rest of the 1970s. There's a sense of formula being discarded, and something entirely new taking its place. The exchanges between the Doctor and Jo sound utterly *right* – but we've never quite heard their like before, and that's because the affectionate banter between Doctor and companion we get here has never really been delivered like this; Jo has been reinvented, no longer a child, but a prototype Sarah Jane Smith, the second lead on the series. There's a mystery and a wonder for our heroes to confront – and, realistically, when's the last time we saw that happen? The Hartnell days? The brilliance of all this is that Barry Letts and Terrance Dicks have allowed once more the series to have settings anywhere in the universe – and right from the start it takes full advantage of it, not by dropping us off in the middle of some space battle, or in a quarry, but where not being able to identify what's going on is the whole joy. After so many years of the show telling us exactly where we are and what we should be expecting, right back through the whole of Troughton, there's the giddy thrill of not knowing on what level we should be taking any of this at all. We flit between sequences on board a 1920s ship and scenes on an alien planet – and only in the closing seconds of the episode is there even a hint offered of how these two settings can be linked.

It all feels so effortless – though, my God, it isn't – and that's because we're looking at a script that is actually *structured*. It's not something we're used to, because Doctor Who is usually about filling in 25 minutes of adventure between cliffhangers, and distracting the audience away from the fact that sometimes there's not a lot of plot advancement going on. This is different. It's not about plot at all, not as such; instead, it's all about intrigue. It's astonishing to watch how long Holmes can keep his various plates spinning without ever throwing in any traditional jeopardy – no fights, no threats and no story progression. (Indeed, wittily, Holmes shows us there *can* be no progression, by revealing that the events on the SS Bernice are repeating themselves!) And, as a result, we find ourselves almost accidentally finding parallels between the two different cultures on offer – the somewhat parodic patois of the passengers of the ship, contrasting with the mannerisms of the Inter Minorans. Major Daly will talk of sahibs, as Pletrac will be awed at the mention of President Zarb. Holmes is so clever – whenever Claire Daly and Lieutenant Andrews pass the open door on their walk around the ship (twenty turns is a mile!... these people are literally walking around in circles), we hear them talk about Fred Astaire, in what would in any other script seem like a painful cliché of time setting. But here, it's all part of the joke, it just helps to caricature them further. These people are puppets.

And that's why there's a streak of humour running through this that is so cruel. The humans are friendly and likeable – and that only makes them seem all the more like they're two-dimensional archetypes who've strolled out of some more amiable TV show altogether. (One which doesn't involve spells of sudden death and universal mayhem, and certainly no dinosaurs popping out of the sea.) It's their very niceness that makes them so artificial in this Doctor Who setting. Commissioner Kalik will gun down a protesting Functionary – and reassure the audience that the victim wasn't killed. We breathe a sigh of relief; we feel we understand the tone of the story, it's light and fun. And then Kalik says that the functionary will be experimented on, and the dispassionate way that Orum accepts this only makes it all the more shocking.

Because this sells itself to us as something which isn't serious, just entertainment – as

Vorg says, in his bright showman costume, it's just something to amuse. I've criticised Barry Letts' direction before, and the scenes on Inter Minor all look cheap and artificial. But for once I think that's part of the point; the planet stuff is real, but looks as if it's fake, whereas the ship sequences seem solid and familiar, but are anything but. Holmes and Letts are challenging our perceptions of what to accept on trust, and what not. The Doctor's insistence that he and Jo aren't on Earth isn't just the usual gag of him being stubborn, but reveal a truth. And it all ends with the TARDIS being picked up by a giant hand. It's as if the fourth wall has been broken, and at last Holmes has collided two entirely different stories.

It's amazing. Do you like it, Toby? (I'm emailing you from downstairs in Heather's house. You get to stay in the bedroom, and I'm sleeping on the sofa a floor below. If you don't like this episode enough, I may be so outraged I turf you out in protest.)

T: Then I shall sleep easy, because this is the best episode we've seen in quite some time...

I remember when Carnival of Monsters was repeated as part of The Five Faces of Doctor Who event in 1981. We had a black and white portable TV with a dial you had to twist to pick up a channel, much like tuning a radio (and yes, I am in a room with three other Yorkshiremen), and you had to stop it at *just the right point* or the picture would dissolve into scratchy pixels – much like, as the next episode will evoke, a blob in a snowstorm. Funnily enough, I initially thought that this episode couldn't be Doctor Who, because the Functionaries on Inter Minor looked rubbish, and so I continued tuning. To my adult eye, the Functionaries' masks are pretty awful, but I don't really mind, because they're a trivial blot on a sublime piece of telly – one that revels in its own artifice.

Robert Holmes has finally nailed what Doctor Who looks like – how it's to be presented at this particular point in time – and written a script that plays to those strengths while, more importantly, letting its weaknesses work to his favour. Unlike certain other writers, Holmes doesn't attempt something so grandiose that's beyond the show's capabilities. He doesn't ask for Shangri-La, or the destruction of Atlantis, but instead writes a story requiring a period setting, some garish travelling players and a shoddy grey planet. He goes for some lightly zany comedy involving outlandish characters, as opposed to requiring long-haired actors to run about pretending to be soldiers, acting all macho as their planet is invaded by an extra in a plastic bag. And he so cleverly uses a dramatic shorthand that's colourful and entertaining – on Inter Minor, we get petty, squabbling, grey-skinned bureaucrats who instead of saying "Give [the working class] a bath and they'll fill it with coal..." declare "Give [the Functionaries] a hygiene chamber, and they'll store fossil fuel in it". It's one of my favourite Doctor Who jokes of all time, because it doesn't *sound* like a joke initially.

While the people aboard the SS Bernice seem more familiar to us Earth-dwellers, the bureaucrats on Inter Minor steal the show. When Peter Halliday turns up (as Pletrac), the sublime triumvirate of him, Michael Wisher (Kalik) and Terence Lodge (Orum) is complete, and we have some of the funniest lines yet to grace the series, pitched perfectly by three flawless actors. I love the look of utter distaste, tinged with bafflement, on Halliday's face after Shirna (the sexy assistant to the showman Vorg) does a funny little dance – it's exactly the same expression I imagine Peter Hitchens would exhibit whilst watching an episode of The Simpsons. And there's a fantastic three-shot of the Inter Minorans as they bicker, suggesting that Barry Letts is much more comfortable staging this sort of thing than gung-ho epics.

It's not *all* laughs, though – Holmes lays a foundation of intrigue (such as the metal hatch that Andrews literally can't see, the fact that the SS Bernice was reported missing and the, um, whacking great dinosaur) under a wall of comedy. He's even clever enough to have Major Daly come out with all that imperialistic guff about lazy Madrassis and plantations, and yet still make him likeable. In the hands of a lesser writer, Daly would be an obvious set-up, given such attitudes because he's destined to become the villain – and yet he emerges as a joyous, and very consciously done, "type" of character who has such old-fashioned bonhomie, he's adorable despite some of his parlance being distasteful to modern ears.

On top of everything, even Roger Liminton has produced a sturdy, impressive and realistic set – the interior of the SS Bernice is a fine piece of work. And then we get that wonderful cliffhanger and a terrific, mind-boggling ending which brings the two separate worlds we've been watching crashing together. I think you're right, Rob... this story helps to reformat Doctor Who as we know it, not because it's going for the spectacular, but because it *is* spectacular.

Carnival of Monsters (episode two)

R: About ten years ago, I worked with an actor called Terry Denville. And a few months ago, he phoned me up to ask me some advice. He'd been invited to a Doctor Who convention, he said, and he knew he'd played various walk-on parts and extras over the years – but he had no memory of what! So I checked the internet. He'd been a whole array of soldiers and monsters, dating back from Hartnell through to late Pertwee. And I discovered to my delight that he'd been the Cyberman in Carnival of Monsters! He's on screen for a matter of seconds, and does nothing more dramatic than turn his head round – but Terry nevertheless was the *only* Cyberman to feature in the entire third Doctor era. Terry was thrilled; that little credit alone meant he sold a bucketload of publicity photographs!

It's clear that Holmes is sending up the series rotten with his "blob in a snowstorm" – here are the Doctor and Jo stuck inside an alien television set, with their walking into certain death at the cliffhanger watched eagerly by the punters outside. There are some great jokes to enjoy too. We've seen catalogues of old monsters on the show before, in The War Games and The Mind of Evil, but there it was to stress their iconography. Here we get to see an Ogron, just so Vorg can be dismissive of the Daleks. And then introduce straight away what *he* regards as the most evil monster in the universe – the Drashig! – which promptly does nothing more interesting than take a bath.

T: And the magic continues...

I don't think I'm feeling so upbeat just because Canada has put me in a good mood (you were right about the wonderful welcome; Heather's remarkably relaxed about allowing a complete stranger into her home, isn't she?), it's also because I'm seeing a work of genius. The central premise of Carnival of Monsters – have the viewers at home watch a group of funnily dressed people in a box getting their entertainment watching another group of funnily dressed people in a box – is so terribly clever, and yet Robert Holmes glibly presents this as a mere piece of whimsy. And there are *so* many neat little touches to this, such as Vorg referring to humans as "Tellurians": it's entirely made up, and yet feels like a logical moniker for our species. After all, why should an alien species call us what we call ourselves? The French don't call themselves "the French", do they? A less-talented writer would have made the Doctor say, "Some aliens call Earth people Tellurians...", but Holmes trusts us to fill in the blanks. Similarly, the reference to "Valdeck's theory that life in the universe is infinitely variable" is great because in *not* explaining the name "Valdeck", Holmes gives this televisual universe a richer texture. And back on the ship, dashing young Andrews throws out lines about "Johnny Chinaman", but it's all pitched so perfectly, it's impossible to find it offensive! Particularly because this simplistic attitude to other races is juxtaposed with Vorg's assertion that we humans all look so much alike, it's difficult to tell us apart...

And as you might have guessed, my soft spot for the Inter Minorans hasn't gone away. (Actually, check that, it will *never* go away.) When Vorg blathers about having the only Tellurians in captivity inside his Miniscope, Michael Wisher and Terence Lodge both give silent reactions – the former being unimpressed and the latter looking confused. And there's the delightful cowardice exhibited by Peter Halliday when he orders a hold on the firing of the Eradicator weapon so that he can get out of the way. His terror at the prospect of his world being invaded by Tellurians in boxes is equally lili-livered. He's the ultimate reactionary old woman in alien form, and you can almost hear him ringing Radio 5 to whinge about all the dirty aliens on his street.

Moreover, each member of this Triumvirate has their own distinctive body language – Halliday is all fussy and prissy; Wisher is poised and very precise; and Lodge is amusingly wobbly, with his arms dangling by his sides, giving him a plodding gait. Oh, and you have to adore the rather perverse enjoyment with which Wisher reacts to the news that the Doctor and Jo might get gobbled up in front of them.

Finally, let me spare some praise for Roger Liminton's approach to design – if it worked against The Three Doctors, it's far better suited to this crazy world. The Peepshow machine interior is great. And on the visual effects front, have we *ever* had a better-realised monster than the Drashig? It looks terrific, the model work perfectly matching the location filming and its splendid, bubbly marsh water. The creatures look majestic as they rise up, their frightful screams shredding the air as they penetrate this hitherto light-hearted little romp. God bless Doctor Who for facilitating such abrupt changes of tone – it's like suddenly getting HR Giger's Alien in the middle of a Noel Coward play. And what other show on television can make *that* claim?

June 13th

Carnival of Monsters (episode three)

R: Our convention today! An intimate one, with Colin Teague and James Strong representing the directors, myself and novelist Lance Parkin as writers, and Toby Hadoke as all-round entertainer and live commentary moderator, performing his Moths show at the climax. The thing about smaller cons, though, is that you have to work that much harder – at Gallifrey a few months ago, I was on barely more than a panel a day, so there was plenty of time to get stuck into a bit of Hartnell. Here, though, we're all on inspection from morning to night. Doctor Who all day. And some bright spark thought weekends would be a good time to squeeze in *three* episodes to watch. Well. That'll be me then.

What a relief it is that Carnival of Monsters is so bright and energetic – it's impossible to

get Who'ed out watching this, and indeed, sitting through episode three on my lunch break like this actually puts a spring in my step. Just consider that cliffhanger. It seems on the face of it traditional enough – a female screams with horror when she's surprised by some alien ugly coming at her. Only this time, the alien revealed is *Jon Pertwee*. Robert Holmes has completely turned Doctor Who on its head – it's only in the closing seconds of the penultimate episode that the Doctor is even revealed to the main guest cast, and he's not some wise authority figure, not some hero, but an insect that makes the fairer sex shriek. It's wonderful.

With the Doctor exploring artificial zones, in which the inhabitants are unaware that they're not on their own planet, I'm reminded irresistibly of The War Games. Except this time, it's much shorter and much funnier. It's the little touches that make this so special – the gag about the Eternal Perpetuity Company goes by so quickly, it's in real danger of being lost altogether. If the subplot about Kalik's desire for power feels a little mechanical, it's written and played with enough knowing wit that it seems deliberate. (I love the way that the conspiracy is staged as well, with Orum standing on a step beneath Kalik, assuming henchman position, to be towered over by the main villain.)

Even the Drashigs aren't a letdown – in their own context they're fine as ironic glove puppets, but become a real threat hunting the Doctor and Jo down through the scope and on to the liner. Watching the 1920s cast open fire on something that belongs in a different sort of story altogether is so suitably bizarre, any worries you might have about CSO can be waved away. It's why this sort of thing works so well here, but won't in Invasion of the Dinosaurs, where we're invited to take the special effects on face value. Here, you're left to goggle so much at the collision of different genres that it'd spoil the fun if they were made actually *credible*.

Oh, and it's interesting the way Jo points out the growing discrepancy in the treatment of the Time Lords, most painfully clear in The Three Doctors – are they non-interventionist bystanders, or are they sanctimonious protectors? Holmes can't answer the question, but at least one writer has noticed it needs addressing.

Toby and I are now to play in a game of Doctor Who Jeopardy. We don't have Jeopardy in Britain, but it appears to be an ordinary sort of quiz, except for some reason we have to answer statements with a question. I'm rather hoping that we'll get "Carnival of Monsters". So I can say, "Name the best Jon Pertwee story". Because it really bloody is.

T: It's terrific, isn't it? (See, I answered you in the form of a question!... well, a little bit.) Once again, this episode proves that the path to success is to write great lines, and then hire great actors who will relish performing them. Robert Holmes has an ear for the kind of dialogue actors enjoy saying, such as "By jingo, a M'em-Sahib!" – the wonderful Tenniel Evans must have been so tickled to get a line like that. Later on, Evans even gets to wield a Tommy-gun at a plesiosaurus whilst charging about on the boat! (Only in Doctor Who...) Oh, and addition of Andrew Staines as the ship captain – finally, we see the busy man in charge of the boat! – means I have great fun watching (yes, it's true) The Captain and Tenniel.

Speaking of great actors, Michael Wisher has been rightly eulogised for his terrific performance as Davros, but he's also fantastic at comedy. As Kalik, he clearly gets off on the Drashigs' potential for destruction, and his delivery when Vorg suggests that Kalik is both merciful and compassionate ("One has... twinges") made me laugh out loud, something I rarely do. Not to be left out of the fun, Peter Halliday issues the line "[The Drashigs] *ate* a spaceship?" with exactly the right levels of horror and disapproval (i.e. like someone askance at a social gaffe in a drawing-room farce!).

And how is it that, in a knockabout story such as this, the production team pulls off such convincing monster shots? You have to *relish* those brilliant bits, on film, of the Drashigs bursting through metal... why couldn't the showmakers manage this level of quality in the supposedly spectacular, celebratory season opener? The Drashigs look so great, they raise the bar for monsters in Doctor Who. Yes, all right, they're not so successful when CSOd onto the set, but Letts wisely has

them take up most of the frame, limiting the credibility damage.

But the *most* interesting thing about this episode? All the frivolity and adventuring is wrapped around concern about how we humans treat lesser species, and how we would react if subjected to the same. There's no tub-thumping or self-satisfied piety about this notion, and yet it's an additional level of shading and intelligence in this rich and splendid slice of Doctor Who.

Carnival of Monsters (episode four)

R: So you won Jeopardy. Technically. But only because you knew all the stories in which Ric Felgate had appeared. There are some things I'm *proud* not to know. You may have scored my points. But I think the moral victory is mine.

Barry Letts is a rum sort of cove, isn't he? The sequence where Kalik is eaten by a Drashig has been cut to ribbons, because he wasn't convinced by a special effect. But as a result it's demonstrably unclear what has happened, and this entire subplot fizzles out. (And what's happened to Orum? Did he become Drashig food too?) Whilst I think it's essentially laudable that there's someone in charge trying to iron out all the rubbish bits before they reach the screen – I wish he'd been on set when they first dragged on the Myrka costume – it shouldn't be at the expense of story sense. And this is the man who around this time must have been commissioning Invasion of the Bloody Dinosaurs! (A decade later, during the Five Faces repeat season, he got his scissors out on Carnival again, hacking away at the charming final scene because you can just about see, if you care to look hard enough, that Peter Halliday's hair piece is coming unglued. Madness!)

The only real problem with this episode is that it's the final one. Robert Holmes gets in the criticism before anyone else can; the Major shuts his book at last and says that the ending was disappointing. And in plot terms, I suppose this is, a bit; not much really happens, and everything is put right with the flick of a lever. But that judgment fails to take into account that this is a story in which there have, for once, been no actual villains, and the jeopardy has been one of simple circumstance rather than endeavour. You've got to admire the gall of that. There's some lip service paid to type with the character of Kalik. But Kalik's little rebellion against the state is so perfunctory that when he dies, no-one even realises what he'd been up to – that he's the most ineffectual baddie the series has ever had, so minor that his one display of treachery kills himself off in the process, is surely just part of Holmes' joke. And the only character who *does* threaten the Doctor's life ends the story delightfully having fun with games of chance. It's quite the most amiable Doctor Who adventure I've ever seen. And the highlight for me comes this episode, where in two minutes the Doctor turns the tables from being an infectious bacterium to be eradicated, into being an interrogator bristling with authority and disdain. Pertwee and Halliday play the exchange beautifully.

T: Rubbish! I won Jeopardy *resolutely*, not *technically*. Before mention of Ric Felgate, I'd amassed $9,000 compared to your – what was it, $6,000? Much of it thanks to The Space Pirates, a story I never thought I'd feel so grateful for! I started quite badly, though – I think I was so desperate to legitimise myself (it's alright for *you*, Rob; you've done actual proper Doctor Who and everything, whereas I'm just a footnote), I got my first two questions wrong.

Anyway, I'm not sure the ending is quite as limp as you describe – once the Doctor gets face-to-face with the protagonists on Inter Minor, Holmes presents us with enough jeopardy to see matters through. Okay, Jo has to go through the whole "getting captured" rigmarole all over again, but it emphasises the story's "goldfish in a bowl" theme rather neatly. Then there's the breakdown of the Miniscope, which puts many of the characters we've come to enjoy in peril. To make matters worse, Pletrac's concern about foreign germs, hitherto a source of comedy, becomes a legitimate plot point as the Drashigs imported from off world threaten to burst forth and eat everyone.

Disposing of that threat allows Vorg, the old rascal, to redeem himself – first by colluding with the Doctor to aid his return into the Miniscope, and then (hurrah!) by manning the gun that wipes out the Drashigs. As Vorg,

Leslie Dwyer has made all the comedy he's been given look easy, and the immensely likeable Cheryl Hall has been spot-on as his chastising conscience of a sidekick. They represent some of the best of Holmes' rightfully touted skill with "double acts". Nestling at the bottom of the credits, Terence Lodge, too, has given such a fabulous turn as Orum. Here, he baldly states that famous line about how "One has no wish to be devoured by alien monstrosities, even in the cause of political progress". Fantastic! I would agree with you, though, that Kalik's death is a bit botched and Orum just vanishes from the narrative. It's a shame, as I cannot say often enough how the three estimable Inter Minoran actors have been brilliant and funny.

A bit of fannish business before we wrap things up... I've read in guidebooks how the SS Bernice must have sunk the day after it was returned to Earth, in accordance with the Doctor's assertion that, historically speaking, it vanished and was never found. Well, yes, that makes sense – but it's a bit mean spirited, and clearly *not* what Holmes intended. The Doctor has obviously rewritten this line of history in returning the Bernice home, otherwise the story's ending would be *horrible*. In my universe (the same one where Jamie and Zoe kept their memories despite the Time Lords' braintinkering), the Dalys safely get to Bombay and Clare marries Andrews. Anything else would undermine the structure and tone of what is arguably the best script thus far in the series' history.

What a day – I whipped you at Jeopardy, had a great performance of Moths in front of a fantastic crowd, enjoyed a lovely dinner with Messrs Teague and Strong, and topped everything off by watching the conclusion of this truly splendid story. I love Doctor Who, and I blame Canada.

[Toby's addendum: As I went online to mail this entry to Rob, the news filtered through that Tenniel Evans had passed away on Thursday. I served him once, on my Saturday job in a café when I was at 6th Form College – his son Matthew is a TV director who lives in Ludlow and he must have been visiting. What a coincidence that we were scheduled to watch Carnival of Monsters in such close relation to his passing. Evans' last words in Carnival are "Sleep well..." – you too, old chap, you too.]

Frontier in Space (episode one)

R: Aha! And we go from Robert Holmes doing clever stuff reinventing the series altogether, to Malcolm Hulke doing clever stuff putting his twist upon the status quo. Way back at the beginning of Pertwee's tenure, he was finding a way to take the "trapped on Earth" format and bend it, so that the expected clichés of alien invaders was turned on its head before it had even had the chance to take hold. And now that the format has changed again, and we're now watching a series about Doctor Who "exploring the stars", he's done the same thing; we might be expecting a story in which the Doctor helps humans fight monsters in the far future on shiny spaceships, but instead we've got a situation where the Doctor and Jo *are* the monsters that the humans are fighting. It's all very smart, the way that paranoia means that something as amiable as an outstretched hand can be seen as a gun.

And it's brilliant that following a story boasting a "carnival of monsters", we're now given an episode which is brimful of the things, but where we're constantly being asked to question our perspective and work out what's real and what isn't. The Drashigs are back, just one week after they've broken out of the Miniscope and gobbled down Michael Wisher – except they're not at all, they're just a hallucination. So when we see that the Ogrons are back as well, we can't initially be sure they're not just part of this giddy anniversary season parade of familiar foes, any more substantial than the Cyberman who popped up a couple of weeks before. Typically, as in his Silurian script, Hulke is inviting the audience to mistrust the stereotype, to question whether or not the "monster" we're supposed to recoil from is really the villain – here we can't even be sure which monster we're looking at, let alone where our sympathies should lie! It's telling that our first few glimpses of Draconians aren't Draconians at all – one is an Ogron, the other the Doctor – so that by the time we see Peter Birrel (as the Draconian Prince) standing dignified and regal before the Earth President, protesting his race's innocence and threatening

war, we've adjusted to the idea that we shouldn't trust anything on face value.

The result of all this is that we get one of the most honestly claustrophobic episodes in years. You feel sympathy for the spaceship crew who are waving guns at our heroes, precisely because they're scared and manipulated, and because they're actually being *brave*; in any other story, the pilot's decision to fetch the blaster guns and defend his cargo of flour would be seen as something truly noble. But because of their fear, and because they're irrational, they're also dangerous and callous – you really believe they might shoot the Doctor and Jo dead in their panic, and the moment when they use the TARDIS crew to draw the enemy's fire is especially tense.

Best of all, though, is the way that the story suddenly changes scale. In an instant, it abandons that claustrophobic setting of the spaceship, and heads to discussions on Earth – where the attack is already being seen as a fait accompli by the politicians and used as a negotiating tool. That we can jump from sequences which have such a pressure-cooker feel of oncoming danger, to scenes of cool diplomacy which treat the crisis as just another incident to be mentioned in despatches, is rather dizzying. And it's one of the most skilful demonstrations of how a Doctor Who story can suggest new layers of meaning and depth that we ever get; the Doctor usually lands in the heart of an adventure, face to face with the chief protagonists – and here it quickly becomes obvious that he's landed on the fringes. This is a story big enough that the Doctor can spend an entire episode battling with characters this minor – and it's the first time in colour Who that we get the promise that this story is going to be correspondingly epic.

T: Unlike a lot of Doctor Who of late, Frontier in Space *looks* good. The sets are solid, the costumes have a consistency in style and the Draconian masks are excellent. We also have some fine model work, even if the shot of the TARDIS spinning in space, for the first time ever, is thrown away on a monitor screen! And it's especially interesting that in this far future, the crewmen aboard the cargo ship – Stewart and Hardy – wear seatbelts. (Well, of course they do... you'll never invent an SF seatbelt without it looking overly complex or needlessly spangly. And you *do* need one if you're piloting a spaceship – didn't it ever strike you as odd that in Star Trek, most alien attacks involved wobbling the ship about and making everyone fall over? What, the Federation budget for starships covered dilithium crystals, but they didn't have enough left over for seatbelts? Or is it because they'd have needed to get wider and wider with every film, to compete with William Shatner's inexorable girth expansion?)

But the more I consider this episode, the more I'm impressed by how much it fleshes out this version of Earth's future. The script very smartly gives us two differing perspectives on the Earth-Draconian conflict – there's Stewart and Hardy, everyday haulage men lamenting that their government won't bat an eyelid if their cargo ship is attacked, and there's the President of Earth, trying to appease her own military and the official representative of her enemy. And the fear-inducing device being used to put these mighty empires at each others' throats demonstrates such ingenuity, I'll forgive the inconsistency regarding how it works. (After all, it's a good job for the parties stoking this tension that every single Earthman targeted by the device, without exception, fears Draconians most of all. If I'd been piloting the cargo ship, I'd have experienced a vision of wasps, someone piercing my nipples and Jeremy Clarkson as Prime Minister.)

But if the scope of Malcolm Hulke's story is suitably epic, he also includes little bits of colour into the exchanges between his minor characters. When Hardy suggests to Stewart that perhaps their cargo isn't worth a fight to the death over because "It's only a load of flour", his companion neatly replies "It's my cargo" before going to defend it. Is Stewart being brave or stupid? I don't know, but maybe that's the point. It's open to debate, but either way, he means business, and helps to ensure that the drama never wanes.

Playing Stewart, by the way, is James Culliford – I *think* this was his last role (or near enough) before a stroke cut short his career. I haven't got the dates exactly, but I fear he was taken ill before this episode aired, and was cared for until his death in 2002 by his part-

ner, the actor Alfred Lynch (later Commander Millington in The Curse of Fenric). Culliford looks so young and vital, it's awful to think of him being debilitated so imminently. I normally get excited to find out new stuff about Doctor Who actors, but sometimes it's a bit depressing.

In an attempt to lighten the mood here, let me add that I thoroughly enjoyed the convention, Rob – thanks so much for using your influence to get me invited. What a great response, and a lovely bunch of people.

June 14th

Frontier in Space (episode two)

R: It's easy to complain that this is just an episode in which the Doctor and Jo get locked up. A lot. In fact, they get locked in cells a staggering *four times* in 25 minutes, which is more than you're given in most entire stories. But it's to miss the point; this is all about bureaucracy, and the way that our heroes are left to drown in it – the repetition of the action, the fact that neither the humans nor the Draconians will believe the Doctor no matter how much he pleads the truth, the way that he's rendered entirely ineffectual... that's what's so startling about this episode. Jon Pertwee regularly trades off his Doctor being a charismatic showman – never before in a story has all his debonair charm counted for so very little, and it's unnerving to see this most arrogant of incarnations so reduced, so crushed by a system that won't listen to him. Not to be too pretentious – well, okay, just a little bit pretentious – but this is Pertwee's Kafka story. It's his nightmare, a world in which he can't be the hero, in which he makes no impact whatsoever. *Of course* it's got lots of scenes of the Doctor getting locked up, over and over again. It's not padding. It's the entire story.

It'd be easy, too, to complain about the scene in which the Doctor tells Jo about his encounter with the Medusoids. But I think really it's very clever. To keep Jo's spirits up, the Doctor tells her a cute anecdote about the sort of colourful monsters you'd expect to find in a pantomime (or The Three Doctors) – it's childish, and it's trite, and it's rather lovely, really, this dogged attempt of his to be cheerful and silly in the face of grey concrete and red tape. It captures the spirit of Doctor Who Annuals, only to set it in sharp contrast to the world outside of paranoia and politics. It works *because* it sounds so ludicrous; Jo and the Doctor have dropped out of their cosy little teatime series into something much colder and bleaker, where the only sympathetic advice they're offered all episode is from a guard affably telling them to confess all before they're tortured for too long.

A quick thumbs up for Lawrence Davidson, who gives a performance beneath his half mask of cool subtlety as the Draconian First Secretary. Not an easy task to turn something that looks like a reptile monster into a credible politician. (He doesn't even get featured in the end credits! What went wrong? Are they running last week's credits by mistake?)

T: The end credits *are* wrong, because, yes, they've reused last week's by mistake – so naturally, I'm going to have a major issue with this episode and deem it tantamount to treason! (And it's not just Lawrence Davidson – Timothy Craven, appearing as a guard, doesn't get a credit either.) It's such a shame, as Davidson has a superciliousness that's just right, giving a sly edge to his characterisation. And Davidson is notable beyond his acting talents, as Ian Holm writes about the man in his autobiography. Holm, notorious for not making friends easily, considered Davidson the closest he ever had to one – they could go months without happening to speak to one another, but if Holm needed to see him, Davidson would drop everything, make supper and they'd talk. Apparently, Davidson got increasingly difficult to work with and gradually fell out of the profession, but he and Holm remained friends till Davidson's death in 2000. So, if he doesn't get a credit here, at least he's ensured some sort of posterity in the (rather detached and self-centred, I'm afraid to say) memoirs of that wonderful actor.

Conversely, Barry Ashton received a credit last week for saying absolutely nothing as military officer Kemp – and he also gets one here, earning surprisingly high billing for mustering no more than half a dozen lines! Nice to see Ray Lonnen as officer Gardiner, though –

the bit where he shows his decent side to the imprisoned Doctor and Jo is a typical Hulke touch, making his stock character a little less stiff. Similarly, the rather formal way the president tells Stewart and Hardy "I hope you both recover from your ordeal" is very clever – it's the kind of prescribed rhetoric heads of state must go through so often, they lose any emotional truth behind the words. It's rather like the Queen having to go down a line, pretending to care what the people she's meeting for all of ten seconds do for a living.

Elsewhere, we have some capture-and-escape stuff, but at least it's *enjoyable* capture-and-escape stuff. (Are they running about the South Bank? Geography isn't my strong point, but you and I tend to meet up there once a month, so I'm sure I recognise it.) There's a wrinkle in all of this dashing about, though – while it's understandable when the Ogrons kill people, it's rather more questionable when the Draconians use lethal force to capture the Doctor, all so they can ask him questions he probably won't answer to their satisfaction anyway. After all, they're already treading a pretty fine line in their diplomatic relations with Earth, so slaughtering Earth citizens would just add to the political quagmire, wouldn't it? And if the justification is it doesn't matter if extras wind up dying... well, that's a pretty lazy explanation. In such a tense political landscape, the killing of a single Earth soldier would (excuse the pun, as we're talking about the Draconians here) tip the scales toward all-out war.

Oh, and it's worth mentioning that Pertwee is very sweet when he and Jo are jailed, reassuring her that the ominous-sounding "mind probe" is nothing to worry about. Maybe he should have had a word with Paul Jerricho on the set of The Five Doctors, and saved him some embarrassment.

Frontier in Space (episode three)

R: Oh, this is good. Malcolm Hulke really shows his claws here. Vera Fusek continues to give as likeable a performance as she can as Earth's president, but she's the leader of a state teetering on military totalitarianism, in which dissident pacifists are sent into life imprisonment without trial. The joy of all this is how subtle it is, and how Hulke's very real anger (nowhere is he more political than in this story, and nowhere else does he show his Communist leanings so completely) is expressed through the nuances of characters who believe themselves to be perfectly reasonable and rational. The scene where General Williams warns his President that there are plans to overthrow her in a military coup works well precisely because Williams isn't trying to usurp her. And it's therefore all the more disappointing to the viewer, having demonstrated that he's a man of integrity, that he then proceeds to defy the results of the mind probe and to burn out the Doctor's brain anyway. (The mind probe scene is quite wonderful, incidentally; the power Pertwee shows simply by lying on his back and calmly telling the truth gives him such dignity – and the delight his face betrays when that truth destroys the torture equipment is perfect.) And we want to trust this President, to respond to her warmth and her concern for Jo – but Hulke shows us that the kindness of a stupid leader is a dangerous thing indeed. That sequence which shows her sending memos to the twenty-sixth century equivalent of the Rotary Club, whilst luxuriating to a facial massage, cleverly depicts a head of state utterly out of touch with both the urgency of the crisis and the suffering of her people.

It's an ugly little episode – in which idealists like Patel (played so well by Madhav Sharma; just look at the crushed disappointment on his face when he realises he's to be abandoned in prison) are made to look like naive cranks in the face of cynicism and opportunism. It's actually something of a relief when Roger Delgado shows up, cracking merry banter with Katy Manning – evil mastermind he may be, but at least he's not an amoral politician. The Master might want to destroy the universe, but he's better than those we see here, the hypocrites, the thugs, the sweetly useless leaders with their feet of clay.

T: Once more, life in the future is viewed through contrasts. The presidential palace is so opulent, any woman who works there seems obliged to wear evening dresses. It's rather fun that the President has to fit her massage in around her governmental briefing, because it's part and parcel of Hulke demonstrating how

the mechanics of politics would work, even in this posited Earth. Our ruler even shares a glass of wine with General Williams (well, I say glass, it's actually a silver cup – we are in the future after all). The President overall is a strong character, and Vera Fusek's accent brings a certain indefinable elegance to the part. Her concern for Jo is touching, and she very much seems like a compassionate woman... until we end up on the lunar penal colony.

Because, crikey, no matter how nice the President might seem at times, her regime bungs political prisoners onto the moon for life! I should reiterate that... these are political dissenters; you'd think that such a punishment would be reserved for the most hardened of hard criminals. If anything, the moon-convicts are pretty decent sorts – they're members of the Peace Party, and Madhav Sharma gives a ruefully cheery performance as Patel. Pertwee – who's been pretty dignified under pressure throughout – rather revels in bucking the system, and Richard Shaw (whom we discussed at length in The Space Museum) appears as Cross, the untrustworthy heavy overseeing the prisoners. There's a lovely exchange when Cross swipes chocolate from one of the prisoners... the Doctor: "Tsk-tsk. Now, that's stealing, you know." Cross: "That's what I'm in for. Got a troublemaker, have we?" The Doctor, with a twinkle: "That's what I'm in for."

As director, Paul Bernard has calmed down considerably since the self-conscious visual gymnastics of Day of the Daleks, but he still has plenty to offer. The camera slowly pans out at the beginning of scenes and in at the end of them (at one point, there's a little cheating misdirection, leading us to believe that Patel's up to no good). And before I forget: surely there's never been more appropriate casting than the physiognomically hawk-like Michael Hawkins as the hawkish General Williams? Hawkins has a great pointy face – no wonder people think he's Christian Slater's father. (That's a different Michael Hawkins altogether, but let's not get into this right now!)

Frontier in Space (episode four)

R: And after all of the edge of Hulke's satire, we get... an episode which breezes by on charm alone. There are no scenes featuring either the Earth or the Draconian governments, and you get the curious sense that the story has been abandoned altogether in favour of a new one, all about the Master taking the Doctor and Jo on holiday with him. It shouldn't work – and, let's be honest, structurally it doesn't at all, not even remotely. But after the unfeeling cruelty that's set the tone for the last three weeks, this feels like something of a well-earned treat, a light snack that relies wholly upon the rapport between Pertwee, Manning and Delgado. Pertwee gets to do a bit of action – a spacewalk, no less! – and Delgado manages to show both the charm and the viciousness that have made the Master so popular. I love the way that he'll show touching concern for his captives' comfort as his ship hits a spot of turbulence – and then, minutes later, can be shoving Jo brutally into an airlock. Just as you begin to feel that Delgado is playing it all-too-safe these days, that he's become another part of the cosy UNIT family, he'll find something in his artillery to shock you.

But it's Manning who gets the hardest job. She's required to improvise a five-minute monologue to cover Pertwee's escape – and, rather gorgeously, embarks on a strange rambling diatribe against the lack of attractive men she meets as a secret agent, and that the Doctor should stop playing dirty tricks on the Master and be more grateful whenever he's offered a share in the universe! It's all a bit too close to self-parody for comfort, as Manning unerringly hits all the series' clichés – and if there was ever anything Jo could have said more likely to arouse the Master's attention, surely playing both horny and amoral would have done it. The beauty of it all, though, is the way that the comedy turns upon itself – that Manning is forced to carry on with her chatter once she's sure that the Doctor is dead, and surprisingly what started out as a somewhat overplayed piece of jolly becomes very touching as she fights back the tears, pretending to tell the Doctor to take care of himself even as she's mourning him.

T: Someone once described Frontier in Space to me as being:
"You're a spy!"
"No, I'm not."
"You're a spy!"
"No, I'm not."
"You're a spy!"
"No, I'm not."
"Oh dear, you're not a spy... let's go and defeat the Master."

Now, that's painting things with a fairly broad brush, and yet, it *is* a pretty fair assessment – especially when we get to episode four, which meanders in the Master's spaceship after wrapping up the diversion of the lunar prison. Indeed, the moon plotline finishes so matter-of-factly, the Doctor doesn't later plead with the President for clemency for his friends and allies doing bird. As a result, dear old Professor Dale and Patel get abandoned to their fates forever. (Thanks, Doctor – that's what people get for helping you out, is it, you ungrateful so-and-so!) When the Master later sympathises with Jo that the Doctor is in a reminiscent mood, one feels that there's an element of justice to our hero being the butt of a joke.

As you've noted, the President and General Williams are absent from this episode – a shame, as their shifting power-balance and hints at a shared history have neatly augmented the main plot before now. What we *do* get is the Master facilitating the Doctor's release from prison, allowing a brief victory even if the penal camp's status quo is maintained. And it's very interesting how the Master falsely accuses the Doctor of "crimes" including not taxing and insuring his spaceship – that could be deemed an unimaginatively prosaic and twentieth-century development, but I quite like that in this future, such things haven't been wiped out. I mean, it's much more plausible than the economics of the Federation in Star Trek – a relative utopia that has consigned, against all odds, money and form-filling to the dustbin of history. My best guess is that no matter how far we travel in space, humanity will still need to deal with an abundance of tiresome procedure and bickering, because we'll never travel far enough into the stars to escape our own natures. The shores of Venus, no doubt, will be awash with revellers complaining about the alien muck they're forced to eat and the lack of a decent pint.

Design-wise, this is all very wonderful – in addition to the great costumes (the Master's sleek, black and powerful Sirius 4 garb, and Jo's pleasing judo outfit), there's also a marvellous sense of scale to the model work (both with the penal colony and the space scenes outside the Master's ship). So all in all, if this episode probably *has* gone nowhere slowly, at least everyone involved is working hard to keep us visually stimulated. (Except for the very final shot, admittedly, which ends with the spectacularly dull pan to reveal... the back of an Ogron's head!!! Wow, that's really going to have the kids rushing back next week, isn't it?)

June 15th

Frontier in Space (episode five)

R: There's been an extraordinary amount of inter-story continuity in Frontier in Space. Jo gets to see a Drashig, and compares the Earth Empire to the one she saw represented last season on Solos. The Master can't resist reminding his prisoners how they once visited him in jail during The Sea Devils – for God's sake, last week, just to pass the time, the Doctor told Jo all about the climax of The War Games! The writers now working on Doctor Who mostly met whilst beavering away on Crossroads, and you can see – in that desire to thread the stories together – the instincts of people used to devising soap operas. But for the most part it feels rather alienating – simply because, unlike down-to-earth dramas played out in grotty motels, Doctor Who *isn't* about character development.

And that's why, by contrast, the continuity reference made this week is so outstanding. The Master attempts to hypnotise Jo and she fights him off, her eyes flashing, almost *taunting* him with her nursery rhymes. There's a direct comparison being made here with Jo's very first episode – and it's clear that Jo has changed; she's older, and stronger, and more than capable of standing up to the Master. The Green Death is just around the corner, and is going to make similar comparisons with that

introduction she gets (right down to destroying Professor Jones' experiments) – but here it works best. She's come of age at last. Yes, she still puts on that childish voice every so often, and Katy still resorts to playing Jo as an adolescent whenever a scene puts her in the background. But when the drama requires her to do more than that, to be defiant and confident as it does here, Jo shines. This is her best scene, and Katy Manning's best work on Doctor Who.

T: What I so adore about the Master's presence here is that Roger Delgado gets some scintillating comedy moments. He gamely engages with his Draconian captors until they turn round threateningly, leaving him framed stuck behind the cell bars with such a sweet look of disappointment on his face. And he's positively brazen in the Draconian court, championing himself as an advocate of peace and law and order (!!!), causing Pertwee to ask if he's feeling alright. Delgado, however, retains enough steely menace to prevent this becoming a love-in – his exasperation with the dim-witted Ogrons is priceless, as is his regret that death by long-range missile fire lacks "that personal touch". This is Delgado's penultimate episode, and he's the best thing in it.

He has some stiff competition, though. Events at the Draconian court bring us face-to-face with Peter Birrel as the Draconian prince again – and I'm a little startled to realise that he's had two episodes off, quite a gap for such a major protagonist. Nonetheless, Birrel's opening exchange with John Woodnutt's sibilant Emperor cleverly establishes their relationship and the court etiquette which will help the Doctor to gain their trust – something the Master spectacularly fails to do. Pertwee slips into this stuff effortlessly – as with The Curse of Peladon, his character looks very much at home with royalty.

I could quibble with a few things... It's odd to see the Doctor, without pause, wielding a blaster *again*. (What is it about Ogrons that makes it morally acceptable to kill them – is it some ancient Time Lord grudge? Or, if simply being dim-witted is justification enough for a death sentence, then surely the Doctor would have executed Dodo on the spot?) We also have another silly airlock scene, in which a bit of a grimace and a hefty tug can counteract the pull of the vacuum of space. But any niggles on my part are counter-balanced by various departments putting in some fine work – Dudley Simpson gives a real majesty to his pounding space anthem; Paul Bernard makes up for last week's slapdash cliffhanger by ending this week on a great shot of the fear device in the foreground, and Jo's terrified face coming into focus behind it; and I'm so glad that Hulke gives General Williams the moment of realisation that his recklessness caused the last war. There are some logic holes in this scenario, I grant you. (How did Williams destroy the Draconian ship if *both* vessels were meant to be unarmed? How has Williams' costly mistake never come to light before now?) Even so, it further details the history of this era, and it gives Williams – thus far largely an observer or obstruction to the action – a personal chance at atonement.

My favourite bit of all, though? It's the Doctor's line to the Emperor that "Fear breeds hatred, your majesty. Fear is the greatest enemy of them all." And fear leads to war... it seems it will ever be thus, but it's important to point it out now and again.

Frontier in Space (episode six)

R: The ending's a mess, of course. Barry Letts cuts a bad effect from the last scene – the appearance of the Ogron Bollock Monster was apparently just too awful for words – and so you can't tell what's going on: it's all chaos, Ogrons start running, there's a gunshot, the Doctor falls wounded. And the Master has got lost in the melee.

It's all the worse because it's the last time Roger Delgado will appear. He'll die in a car crash two months after the story's broadcast – and it's gutwrenching that the last glimpse we'll get of this actor is in a shot that's so muddled and badly edited. And yet... and yet. Watching the episode again now, and knowing that I'm watching that final performance (in a way that the audience and the crew could never have known), I find it almost appropriate.

Because, let's face it – there's a problem with the Master. He's become utterly predictable. Delgado is wonderful, of course – but, in fact,

he might be just a little *too* wonderful. He is charm personified, and there's a smoothness to what he does that papers over the cracks of stories and gives them a gloss. The first three episodes of Frontier in Space had an edge to them, as the Doctor found himself impotent before the bureaucracy of a hostile government. Once the Master pops up, we're reassured; the story's back on a familiar track, there's comic banter and stunts, and magically the Doctor becomes a character once again who's able to convince both the Draconian and Earth authorities within *minutes* that they're being duped. The Master Effect is that it tames an adventure that feels new and dissonant.

Had Delgado survived, he'd have had his big exit. The rumours are that he'd have sacrificed himself, that the third Doctor era would have ended as much on Delgado's triumphant last stand as much as Pertwee's. I'm sure it would have been terrific. But by God, it would have been predictable. And as frustrating as the end of Frontier in Space is, and as appalling the reasons why this really is the end for Delgado's Master – isn't there a touch of magic to the fact that he just disappears like this without fanfare, now you see him, now you don't? Recurring villain for the last three seasons, always prompting from the Doctor an all-too-deserved "I should have known" – the sudden confusion, the anticlimax, is just about the only thing that could have been done with the Master that *wasn't* predictable.

I'm not saying, of course, that this is the way anyone would have wanted it – and that Delgado's death wasn't a tragedy, and that it didn't rob us all of an extraordinary actor. But denying the audience that full stop, that final bow at the curtain call, just makes the Master more special to me now.

T: How desperately sad. Roger Delgado has been pretty terrific throughout his tenure – a consistently classy presence who added quality to even the clunkiest of scripts. It'll be interesting to see how I regard his successors during this whole "watching Doctor Who in order" process, as I can't help but think – here and now, at least – that Delgado has left an unfillable void. And frankly, it's a bit tragic that his final scene is such a mess, no matter the positive spin you've laudably tried to give it. (That one long shot of the Ogron Prototype-Erato-Beast isn't *too* bad, so it's hard to say why Saint Barry of Letts felt the need to excise its later appearances in studio so completely. Surely, in the series that gave us The Sleeping Bag of Axos, a crap monster is better than a muddled denouement?)

The botched ending also marks Paul Bernard leaving the building for the last time (in a bit of a huff, I think) – a further regret, as he's always been game with his camerawork. Here, he provides some effectively mounted shots on film, albeit done in yet-another-quarry. (Malcolm Hulke, at least, has the good sense to describe the Ogron planet as a bit of shithole anyway – knowing how any alien world is likely to turn out, he's pre-emptively slagging off the slag heap, if you like.) The landing of the Dalek ship is very economical, done just using dust and wind, and seeing Delgado on the cliff edge as his allies the— (I won't say their names *just* yet, to continue the mystery) hove into view suggests events are taking a heady turn.

I should add that thematically, I so appreciate how episode six sees the Draconian Prince and General Williams at long last working together. The former's apology for his people's behaviour as a Draconian ship attacks the Doctor's party is noble stuff, and Peter Birrel's throwaway delivery of "My life at your command..." as he hurries off at the very end is a naturalistic touch. Protocol is required, after all, but expediency dictates jettisoning the formal, ceremonial aspect of it.

And so, the Daleks have arrived at the story's conclusion. All right, they have rather tinny voices this time around, and it's a little uninspiring that they turn up just to go away again. Nonetheless, while I'm dissatisfied with the confusing final shoot-out, the new priority of learning more about the Daleks' schemes allows for a whopper of a final cliffhanger (with the TARDIS finally spinning in a full screen, yay!). It's dramatically weighty to finish one adventure with the Doctor in deep dung, and then compel him to start the next one almost immediately. My toes are curling with excitement as to what's coming next!... and it's a sensation that lasts until the Australian announcer on my off-air copy of this story tells

me (bizarrely) to come back next week to watch The Three Doctors. Bah!

June 16th

Planet of the Daleks (episode one)

R: Well, that was jarring. Terrance Dicks has said that the Frontier/ Planet combo was conceived as one big 12-episode adventure (and naturally enough, the forthcoming DVD release later this year puts them both into the same box set). But even though there's a reprise from the end of Frontier, this is so tonally unlike that story, it almost feels as if we've wandered into the wrong series. Frontier often felt like it represented Pertwee at its most definitive – the long sparring matches with Delgado alone made sure of that. And what we've got here in marked contrast is a return to the days of Hartnell. There are deadly jungles (with the same sound effects!), invisible monsters and the TARDIS not behaving like a sophisticated spaceship at all, but falling apart at the first attack. And there's that naive Terry Nation dialogue we haven't heard since the early sixties, references to space medicine and space garbage, as if just adding the word "space" to stuff makes it sound so much more techno.

I used to laugh at this. Now, in context, I find it rather beguiling. It's so utterly dissimilar to what we're used to that the effect is rather disturbing. The long scenes of Jo fighting her way through a hostile jungle are very well directed by David Maloney, and with the funereal pace we were so used to in the sixties, there's a real claustrophobia to the atmosphere. Straight after the production team have worked with William Hartnell, they produce a story which apes his tenure. But what's clever is that it reinvents the first Dalek adventure for a harsher audience. The links are deliberate enough – and how odd does it sound to hear Pertwee discuss Barbara, Ian and Susan! – but turned on their head somewhat. Last time we saw the Thals, they were peace-loving pacifists – this time, their first action is to point guns at Jo. Last time they were so beautiful, they had Susan gush over their perfection, but this time they're played by Prentis Hancock and the nerdy son-in-law from Reggie Perrin.

And Nation's old stock episode one cliffhanger, with Dalek emerging either from the Thames, or from sand, here is given rather a witty twist, emerging from aerosol spray paint. It's been much mocked, this revelation, with Pertwee gasping out the word "Daleks" as if he were surprised beyond all measure that they'd be on the same planet as a bunch of Thals, after he's just discussed his time on Skaro, having asked the Time Lords to send him to where the pepperpots are in the first place. But surely the shock he's giving is not that there are Daleks, but they've managed to turn themselves invisible? I'm not arguing it's the best cliffhanger in the world, and I suppose Pertwee does overact it a little, but credit where credit's due – I don't think it's *quite* as daft as is commonly supposed. So there.

(Mind you, I'm jetlagged beyond all measure. I could be missing the point of *anything*.)

T: Bully for you, I'm jetlagged *and* have just done a gig. The audience, of course, couldn't have cared less about my travelling travails, so I dutifully carried out the monkey dance and did some ad-libs about Canada being so much nicer than the United Kingdom. (For instance, I mentioned the chess sets left undisturbed on the street market, set up for anyone to play and with no gaps due to stolen bishops or upset pawns.) Alas, I've not had the chance to use one of the funniest little throughlines of our trip – I was rather chuffed that Luca, the lovely genial fellow who looked after us so well, was tickled enough by my annoyance at the "spatial genetic multiplicity" business in Journey's End involving Gwen Cooper/ Gwyneth that we exchanged some banter on the subject. (My gambit was, predictably, "So General Carrington, tell me... do you come from a long line of Dutch gas engineers?") Luca threw in a few similar jokes all day, and was apparently up all night thinking up new ones and giggling. What fun, but a joke only understandable to a very few geeky types like me and thee.

Anyway, to the Doctor Who story at hand... believe it or not, Planet of the Daleks was, for a while, my favourite Target novel. How can this be, you might ask, when given more obvious candidates such as Doctor Who and the Cave Monsters? Well, it's simply because the story has such easy-to-digest jeopardy, accompanied by all the comic-book thrills and spills that Nation trots out from moment to moment. Everything starts with our central characters in peril and doesn't really let up from there. Unfortunately, this meant that when I first saw the adventure on video, it instantly became one of my *least* favourite stories, as the televised adventure couldn't match the images Nation rather optimistically imagined could be pulled off in a BBC studio.

But watching it now? I expected to fall asleep at any moment, but actually found it rather enjoyable. Traditionally, I don't have much patience when an opening instalment concentrates solely on the regulars – I'm dying to meet the guest characters and see what the plot's all about; I don't need an exercise in mood. But this episode works best in the first ten minutes or so, when it makes Jo into the sole protagonist, with the Doctor incapacitated after contacting the Time Lords (who at this point still elicit some awe when they're mentioned, The Three Doctors or no The Three Doctors). As part of this, Pertwee would probably have been appalled by director David Maloney's decision to shoot him straight up the hooter, but he gamely does some twitchy sleep acting. When his eyes dart open on his frozen face, it's genuinely off-putting.

Having Jo narrate events in the log whilst creeping around the jungle is very effective, helped by some imaginative design and eerie green lighting. Weird noises saturate the soundscape, leaving Dudley Simpson enough room to create a brooding, low key score occasionally augmented by bizarre alien zoinks (that's a musical term). The way that the local flora splats goo on the TARDIS' black and white scanner emphasises that our heroes have gone from the frying pan into the fire. Add some spooky eye plants, invisible natives and an astronaut's corpse into the mix, and the situation seems to be getting deadlier by the minute.

There are lapses, of course. The slapdash design in both the TARDIS and the Thal ship is embarrassingly lazy – the IKEA bed unit in the TARDIS makes you wonder if the sonic screwdriver has an Allen key setting, and the

"TARDIS log" that Jo speaks into (a poorly disguised cassette box) makes you want to punch someone. And the TARDIS' emergency oxygen supply is conveniently at hand – in the same way that I used to mock Knight Rider for introducing some new gizmo for KITT that would, lo and behold, come in really handy 25 minutes later. (You know the sort of thing... "Michael, we've installed new anti-hippopotamus hubcaps to KITT, this is how they work...", followed by, 25 minutes later, "That meddling but handsome stranger and his talking car will be no match for my deadly hippopotamus enclosure!! Bwa-ha-ha-hah!!!")

The pluses outweigh the minuses here, though. I like the nifty protective masks and gloves that the Thals sport to shield themselves from the spitting plants, and the fungus on the TARDIS is impressive (until, at least, it's chipped away at in all its polystyrene glory in close-up). Bernard Horsfall brings a straight-laced dignity and professionalism as Taron, the dour Thal commander, and provides much needed restraint considering that Prentis Hancock plays *his* Thal, Vaber, with his twat-o-meter turned up to 11. Bearing in mind Hancock's appearance in Spearhead from Space, when the Doctor says to Vaber, "I thought I knew you...", I half expected him to say, "... don't you come from a long line of Second Reporters?"

Planet of the Daleks (episode two)

R: "If I have to die, I want it to be for a better reason than providing nourishment for a flesh-eating tentacle!" I think, on that at least, we can all concur.

You know, I really wasn't looking forward to watching this one at all – but I'm actually enjoying it hugely. It's a melodrama, with big tough-sounding dialogue, and lots of gritted tooth discussions about war and death... but it's such an unusual style for the series that I find it very engaging. And even, against the odds, rather affecting. Take that scene where the Doctor listens to Jo on the tape recorder, believing that she's dead – and comes out with that emotional outburst when Codal asks whether the Daleks have captured her that instead they've *murdered* her. It goes so much against the grain of the way Doctor Who has

been written these past few years, where the moral outrage Pertwee shows are against corrupted ideals rather than anything so intimate or personal. Every other episode, Jo and the Doctor are placed in some sort of death-defying jeopardy or the other – but nowhere do they show the same grief that they've both been exhibiting these last two episodes. The Doctor will dutifully show concern when Jo is left to die without an oxymask on the planet surface of Solos, of course – but it's a distanced concern, the sort that suggests that it's for plot expediency, the sort that can happily be put aside as soon as the Doctor has found Jo and can send her off into new danger with the latest guest stars they've just met. There's a brooding menace to this adventure that feels different: just look at that long scene where the Daleks lead the Doctor down endless corridors to his cell. It ought to be interminable – instead it feels (for once) that the Doctor being locked up is actually a big deal, that this isn't just another bit of Frontier in Space-like padding.

I think it's this very earnestness that I've always found off-putting about this story when I've previously watched it. Viewed out of context, it looks creaky and self-important. But I now think that Nation is merely trying to follow his remit, to give this story the sort of serious intent that being the second half of a two-adventure epic would lead you to expect. To say that it's merely a repeat of The Daleks is far too simplistic – yes, there's every indication here that Nation hasn't watched the show since he last wrote for it in the sixties, but far from merely aping the Hartnell style, he's creating something new altogether. And if it's a bit po-faced and square-jawed, then that's all right too – its heart is in the right place. The Doctor sends up his little treatise on bravery after he's delivered it, but the message it gives children about courage through fear is very welcome and rather more profound than you might think. I love the way too that Codal isn't just a cowardly Thal in the style of (say) Antodus from the original Dalek adventure – the story Codal gives of going to war simply because he hadn't the guts not to join up like everybody else is very funny and very human, and makes him much more real than we're used to from Nation's characters.

T: You're right... the Doctor's self-confessed "tutorial on bravery" *is* rather moving, partly because Tim Preece is so sweet, gentle and likeable as Codal. Truth to tell, I once had lunch with Preece, and – having been told by *so many* actors who'd worked on Doctor Who that it was a bit naff, and that they got loads of letters from nutters – my first move was to dismiss the programme and its followers (apart from me, of course!) as a bit pointless and silly. To his credit, Preece surprised me by pointing out that, actually, it's good to have your imagination fired, and the young fans he knew were interesting people with a genuinely creative streak. I had made an assumption about what he'd *like* to hear, rather than being brave enough to admit my fondness for the thing he'd agreed to meet me to chat about. I should have watched the "tutorial on bravery" scene more carefully before I did so! Anyway, Preece was very nice, and he's truly marvellous in Reggie Perrin. And to cap it all, I once snogged his daughter in a truly grotty Manchester nightclub called Champers. Those were the days!

Meanwhile, Terry Nation keeps punching those dramatic buttons – both the Doctor and the audience are made to think Jo has died, with nothing like a cliffhanger in sight. When we're finally disabused of this notion, she shares a scene with the benevolent (and invisible) native Wester – who, sans cloak, would surely, therefore, be naked. So, let me get this straight... this is an alien who breathes heavily and isn't wearing a stitch; no wonder he was so interested in the Thals' phone last week, he was probably wondering whether he could use it to call a premium rate chatline. (Rasp) "... I'm not wearing any knickers..." He also vigorously rattles the foliage as he gets excited (weirdo). And yet, he describes *the Doctor* as wearing strange clothes, which is a bit rich coming from a man whose entire species dresses in purple fur.

The biggest liability in this episode, though, is the way poor Prentis Hancock continues to struggle with his decidedly one-note character, stropping around and venting about the pointlessness of caution in a way that so blatantly sets him up for a fall, he may as well produce a picture of his wife and the newborn son he will only see for the first time after that final

deadly mission due tomorrow. Against this, Bernard Horsfall is cool in a crisis – I love the low-key way he says "no" when refusing to hand the bombs over. It's far more effective than an over-dramatic emphasis or facial gesture. But, what more would you expect from a man who comes from a long line of dignified fictional travellers?

June 17th

Planet of the Daleks (episode three)

R: When I was 12 years old, this is what I imagined all Dalek stories would be like. Breathless running down shiny corridors away from monsters that want to exterminate you on sight. Trying to escape from them in a lift, only to find one waiting for you with its gun ready to fire the moment the doors open. The sheer panic of just trying to *escape* from them, to *survive* being the only goal. Most of the time, of course, Dalek stories aren't like this at all. Before this, they talked a lot and exterminated too little, and soon afterwards they'll get lost behind Davros and endless stories about civil war. The beauty of this entire episode is that it fulfils all expectations – in a way that Day of the Daleks, with its eponymous villains left largely out of the main picture altogether, absolutely didn't – and honestly feels to me as if we're getting to see the Daleks for the first time since the glory days of early Troughton. Except this time, there's a bit more zip to the action.

You wouldn't want every Doctor Who story to be this basic. There's not a lot of brain power required here. But, do you know – I wouldn't mind just a few more being like it. What it sacrifices in cerebral drama and character complexity, it makes up for in atmosphere and tension; the reason why an entire episode is given up to showing our heroes struggle to escape from the Dalek city is because it's *bloody hard to do so*. The Thals may be a little insipid, but their nemeses are fantastic. These are Daleks who don't chant "exterminate" endlessly – if they see their chance to kill, they'll just take it.

And for all that, there's imagination in

spades. I saw an interview with Terry Nation once on a documentary for the Americans called "Once Upon a Time Lord" – and I remember scoffing because Nation claimed Doctor Who's storytelling was broad enough that if he wanted to invent a planet where rocks talked, there was nothing that could stop him. "Talking rocks, Terry, I *don't* think so!" I may have said. Even out loud. But it's true that of all the writers on the series, it's Nation who keeps trying to do interesting things to the natural laws of his planets. He may never have given us talking rocks, but he's fond of petrified forests, of seas of acid, of walking plants. The icecano he gives this story is a brilliant idea – and it lends itself to one of the most claustrophobic sequences seen in the show for ages, where the Thal group have to walk hands and knees through tunnels whilst the liquid ice erupts and oozes its way towards them like thick sludge.

T: One of the things that's amazed me during this quest of ours is that some things which have horribly vexed me about Doctor Who are now of no import whatsoever. Time was, I used to prefer this episode because it only existed in black and white and was on film, meaning it was glossy and solid looking in a way its fellows weren't. It was never meant to be seen like this, of course, but that didn't matter. In the same imagined future where I put Michael Grade on trial and proved that Doctor Who was always good, Planet of the Daleks episode three would have been a key piece of evidence to show that the show was so visually impressive, it could compete with the look of modern TV.

... the big drawback to this strategy being, as I saw it, Jo's flares. I used to cringe at the flares in 70s Doctor Who, and my university friends always cited them as ludicrous, dated garments. My anxiety about this was a hangover from my schooldays when, as the youngest of four, I was dressed in hand-me-down clothes – meaning garments that seemed fashionable when sported by my elder brother (six years my senior) became a target of derision by the time I was forced into them. Of course, flares have now been in and out of fashion so often, I barely noticed them during this exercise – proof positive that criticising old TV for its

fashions is the first recourse of the dimwit. (On a personal level, it also justifies why I've never really bothered with getting the latest styles. I still dress in a way many see fit to mock, but the fashion world's so fickle, I'll inevitably spend a good part of my life being accidentally trendy, and occasionally admirably retro.)

Even though this episode only exists as a black-and-white 16mm print, one can still discern that the material originally shot on film is the most impressive. In addition to the bits in the ice tunnel (with its powerful, chilly wind), David Maloney makes good use of shadow in the area outside it. That said, it's not the case that I'm apologising for the show's inevitable visual limitations by highlighting its expensive moments... after all, how often has the new series, with all its resources, tried to pull off a jungle? (Answer: never.) That the production team does it here, in a small TV studio, displays real guts – and the fact that it's clearly indoors doesn't appear to have fazed the audience in the 1970s.

Now, does that mean they were stupider than us? Quite the contrary – it's a very telling example of how classic Doctor Who functioned. The programme-makers asked the audience to accept some level of artifice, but get involved in the story nonetheless. If anything, I worry that modern-day audiences lack the imagination to invest themselves in programmes that aren't scrupulously realistic, whilst regarding themselves as "sophisticated" for doing so. Perhaps if people went to the theatre more often, they'd be less smug about pointing out the artificiality of the blatantly artificial (really, the only loser if a viewer refuses to suspend their own disbelief is the viewer him/ herself). Perhaps if we had more imagination, we wouldn't crave Jeremy Kyle's Victorian freak show ("Our next guest is called John Merrick – God he's ugly, he makes me sick!"), or self-help shows like Supernanny or, I dunno, How to Walk in a Straight Line and Talk at the Same Time (coming soon to BBC3)...

Otherwise, so much of this episode reminds me of why I found the novelisation to be so exciting. If David Maloney shows none of the flair and brilliance that he did with Troughton, or the almost filmic sturdiness of his later Tom Baker serials, it's because he's giving everything he has to get this quite insanely ambitious script out there without the whole thing falling apart. The miracles he performs aren't so much about what actually gets on screen, but that he pulls this off at all. It's not a bulletproof production, of course. In particular, I *think* the idea is that Marat sacrifices himself because he's knackered from being stuck in the ice, but to the viewer's eye, he just seems to hang about a bit for the sole purpose of being shot. He doesn't even have the good grace to pass along the vital map of the hidden explosives before shuffling off his mortal coil.

Still, this is a solidly done episode – so much so that I'm *terribly* excited at the prospect of seeing the recoloured version when it's out on DVD! That's one of the nicest things about being a Doctor Who fan – every now and again a process is invented, or something turns up, to give us a fresh enjoyment of something familiar. So when this fully colourised story is released, I'll have such excitements as knowing the colour of molten ice. Yes, it's a small thing, but I know from personal experience how much pleasure can be had from those, so I maintain my right to perfectly thrilled about it, thank you.

Planet of the Daleks (episode four)

R: Honest to God, I actually *winced* when that rock fell on Jo. My God, that girl must have a head like iron! Her skull should have been crushed to a pulp. I admit, if you're going to kill off a companion, having them die because of random rockslide is a little on the unheroic side. (That's what would happen to me. My first adventure in time and space, I bet you, I'd leave the TARDIS – and immediately catch a fatal dose of pneumonia. Nasty.)

This episode is the flipside to what I was saying above. There's nothing wrong with writing a script purely based on cipher characters getting involved in exciting action sequences... unless you stop the action altogether. Here, our Thal friends get to sit down for the best part of 20 minutes and catch their breath, and it's not a pretty sight. I can see entirely what they're trying to do in the scene where Taron tells his hapless girlfriend Rebec that her very presence on the planet might prevent him from taking the risks he needs – but it's so

coldly delivered that this little display of love and anguish only makes him seem all the more like the machine the Doctor has advised him not to become. By the time Taron delivers the punchline, that she might be the reason the Daleks win, it's as if he's spat in her face. In a more complex script, with more complex characters, that might actually count for something – as it is, it just looks clumsy and contrived. It doesn't develop Taron or Rebec at all; on the contrary, it actually reduces them, and their relationship, into nothing more than battle strategy.

The upshot of all this is that when you get a cliffhanger which puts Prentis Hancock's Vaber into peril – that's *Vaber*, for God's sake, we're not even *supposed* to like him! – it's a little hard to care. "Take him to the Daleks!" whispers Roy Skelton. You can take him to Benidorm, as far as I'm concerned.

The best part of the episode is the ascent up the air duct by balloon. It's a replay of a scene in The Daleks where our heroes escape in a lift – but with an added twist here of Nation Science (as opposed to the real thing) that makes it much more exciting. And look! – a Dalek that can fly! That works. Someone should do that again some day.

T: Well, once again, there's no reprise – Maloney throws us straight into the action in response to the script's breakneck pace. It feels as if Nation is chucking in moments of peril with gay abandon – Jo is knocked unconscious after failing to deactivate a ticking bomb, and our heroes realise an ascending Dalek is pursing them, *and* a tear develops in the plastic sheeting conveying them to safety. Once it gives way, the Doctor does an impressive jump and his hands initially miss the side of the shaft until he finally grabs hold. Then Taron and Codal scramble to pull the Doctor to safety, and once they've done so, they *still* have to bung rocks onto the Dalek in the nick of time... phew! Naysayers could label all of this as padding, but it's so well shot, with suitable amounts of pace and tension in the performances, it's hard to complain much. All right, the initial dialogue as they float up is played rather cosily, with Jane Howe delivering her line about how she can't stand heights as if it's a rather jolly dinner party observation instead of an enunciation of terror, but it's still a cracking sequence.

As you say, though, the pace gets somewhat more languid after that. Katy Manning is terrific when playing Jo as a resourceful and independent young woman who uses her initiative and salvages bombs for future use against the Daleks – but once she's reunited with the Doctor, she's forced to become a babbling moron who needs filling in on stuff the audience already knows. And as well as some badly written fireside chat, the Doctor persistently refuses to believe what's in front of his eyes – that she wasn't in the Thal spaceship when it exploded after all.

All of that said, and unlike you, I do very much like the scene between Taron and Rebec, and the clever misdirection that Nation provides in it. Thus far a voice of reason, our stoical Thal commander berates his beloved – causing the viewer to wonder if he's advising that you can only defeat the Daleks by rejecting your own humanity, which would mean that Taron is seriously missing the point. But *then*, the Doctor tells Taron exactly that. Yes, the Taron-Rebec scene is awkward, but it's *meant* to be awkward, with the Doctor (and through him, Terry Nation himself) getting things back on track after that.

June 18th

Planet of the Daleks (episode five)

R: There's a hero to this episode – and that's Wester, the Nice Spiridon. Every scene he's in lifts the story up. The scene where the Doctor makes to attack him, only to be stopped by Jo, is lovely – the awkwardness of the Doctor's thanks, offered with embarrassment but no real affection, is very true. And it's an awkwardness we feel for the character as an audience. The Spiridons are unhelpful characters – it's hard to engage with anyone that's A) invisible, or B) that wears a purple bean bag over its head. So it's just as difficult to relate to Wester as it is any other Spiridon – more so, in fact, because we can understand the basic motivation of the Spiridons per se (they're baddies), but have little to go on when we come to appreciate the virtues of the only one

that has any individual personality. And the fact that they're *all* played by Roy Skelton makes that all the more difficult still.

But I like to think that the distancing effect is deliberate. Consider that scene early on where Codal tries to talk to Taron, believing he's wearing the Spiridon furs, only to realise to his horror he's chatting to a *real* monster. We're not supposed to distinguish them from each other. And it means that there's always going to be a sense of unease surrounding Wester, because to all intents and purposes he's just as anonymous as his brothers. When he enters the city and tells the Daleks he's been in contact with the Thals, the thrill of it is that he genuinely *might* have betrayed the Doctor and Jo. There's no way of telling. There's no facial expression, nothing but Skelton's whisper.

And it means that the sequence where Wester sacrifices himself to release the bacterium has a power to it – there's nothing inevitable about it at all, and up to the moment he kills himself, we're still in a position where we'd find it impossible to empathise with him. And then, beautifully, in his moment of death, he's given a face. It's almost as if his heroism has allowed him the right to an identity. It's brilliantly handled, and, in a story which is short on emotional subtlety, truly affecting. And made all the better by the panicked shrieks of the Daleks he's infected, realising with growing terror that they're condemned to stay in quarantine forever.

T: That *is* a terrific scene – you know it's well done because we actually feel sickened by, and sympathetic to, the fates of a couple of shouting pepperpots and Zippy in a day-glow Yeti outfit. And while you're bang on with your reaction to Pertwee's attack and apology to Wester, it's also charming that our hero, bless him, addresses their ally as "Mr Wester". You were also right when you previously talked about the Daleks' rediscovered ruthlessness – how they shoot first and shout "Exterminate!" later – which further manifests during Vaber's extermination. It's similarly cruel that one of Vaber's Spiridon captors, in dutifully pursuing his quarry, is also callously cut down – and that it's all the more effective that this death is never even commented upon. (Relish my agreeing with you *this* much, Rob – who knows when it might happen again!)

Otherwise, we're given here a further mix of action, adventure and trite (but inoffensive) moralising. The scene with the ~~coloured lights being switched on and off~~ alien eyes in the jungle "opening and closing" is pure padding, yes, but it's still working hard to excite us. It's unconvincingly staged, but at least it keeps things entertaining for the kids – I'm happier with this sort of approach than I would be with dire, extended dialogue guff about the Medusoids or whatever, that's for sure. Likewise, I'm full of admiration for the production team taking a page from the original Dalek story, and keeping the appearance of the inner Dalek creature a mystery as our heroes chuck two of them into some icecano goop. It only takes a few grim looks and a couple of off-camera splashes to accord the Daleks some much-needed mystery.

For that matter, the horrific scene you mention where Codal mistakes a Spiridon for Taron hearkens back to the Hartnell era that Terry Nation so clearly recalls. (And if *that* doesn't make you think of yesteryear, the two-pronged attack over treacherous terrain and someone hiding inside a Dalek casing most definitely should.) But then, we perhaps shouldn't be surprised by this – as Terrance Dicks has pointed out, the production team during his era fell into the habit of telling Terry Nation that while they liked his latest Dalek script, it was very much the same one that he'd already sold them on at least two occasions. It's a witty and amusing anecdote, that – one that Terrance has already told us on at least two occasions.

Planet of the Daleks (episode six)

R: The Dalek Supreme shows up! And it's a Dalek from the movies! This is *brilliant*. For years, the only way you could see Daleks in colour would be if you could put up with watching Roberta Tovey. Then Day of the Daleks came along, promising Daleks for the new age – and they didn't do anything much except chant in a room. Suddenly, to see a Dalek from the Cushing films show up in the television series has the effect, I think, of dignifying all the other grey pepperpots around it

– it provides a bridge between these cheaper BBC adventures and the big-budget extravaganzas that'll soon be trotted out every Bank Holiday. To us fans, of course, these movies were always a bit fake, they were wearing borrowed clothes, only pretending to be Doctor Who – but to the audience at large, this is what the Dalek adventures on TV were aspiring to. And it's in a wonderfully bad temper – it causes the lead Dalek to panic, and then exterminates it without a second thought. We've never seen that before.

That's what I find rather wonderful about this episode altogether. As formulaic as the story is, it suddenly shows us the Daleks from all new perspectives. We've long had the sense of a hierarchy, of course, but that Emperor Dalek from The Evil of the Daleks was barely a Dalek at all – it didn't look like one, didn't sound like one and never once got the chance to trundle about and say "exterminate". The Dalek Supreme has immediately more character, because it looks like the office boss from hell – this is a Dalek you believe could have started working in the mail room when it was a junior temp, and now that it's climbed the ranks, it's going to treat all its underlings like it's a real sod. And on top of that, we also get one of the most subtly horrifying images in the whole of the Pertwee tenure, when the Doctor has to climb down through the slowly reviving Daleks to retrieve a bomb. They behave like dozy wasps drunk in the sunshine, and the brilliance of the sequence is that they look both deadly and strangely childish and innocent at the same time. Pertwee, as we all know, hated working with the Daleks, and maybe that's the reason he looks so revolted by the prospect of climbing over them – but it at once transforms the Daleks from robust robots into something more creepy and insectlike.

What's more – they win! We have our traditional goodbyes to the Thals – and then the Doctor and Jo are hunted back to the TARDIS by a bunch of angry Daleks trying to kill them on sight. There's never been a story shown before where the Daleks survive at the end, and finish bragging that they've been only temporarily inconvenienced rather than defeated. It seems to set up Genesis, the way that the best the Doctor can hope for is a minor victory. I think that's really rather brave

– especially in a story which has arguably spent 12 episodes building up to a climax that's so muted.

As fans, we like Doctor Who when it's dark and grim and pessimistic – it makes us feel we're watching Art, rather than Escapism. Planet of the Daleks is the most sour story broadcast under the aegis of Barry Letts: just look at that scene where Latep tells Jo that he'd prefer not to know there was a chance of escape, because the prospect of hope might damage their success as a suicide squad. All three of the Dalek scripts which are produced at this time have a similar cynicism to them. And yet Planet of the Daleks is largely despised – and I wonder whether it's because there's something so very *weary* about the cynicism on display. It's a very cold story, to be sure. The one scene I find honestly touching features Codal thanking the Doctor – not for helping them against the Daleks, but on a more personal note, helping him find himself. It clearly recalls the conversation they had in the cell in episode two, and I love it, because Codal's development, and the way the Doctor has influenced him, has been so nicely underplayed.

It's an unfashionable story, and I don't suppose it'll ever find its way back into fashion again. But there's a lot more thought and sincerity to it than I think it's given credit for. And in the way it takes Doctor Who's past (Daleks fighting Thals!) and tries to reinvent that story as a much more brutal war clearly anticipates the much-loved Genesis. I enjoyed Planet, and I got a lot out of it.

T: Like you, I was expecting this story to be a real chore – but watched in context, it's actually a refreshingly unpretentious piece of Saturday teatime fun. That *is* the primary objective of Doctor Who, whatever else the show aspires to be, and one for which Terry Nation – for all his faults – was tailor-made. Sure, it's easy for pompous chaps like you and me to celebrate a story that's format-bending or awash with subtext, but such commentary usually has the benefit of familiarity, hindsight and historical context. Doctor Who would be crazy to always take such things into consideration – so often, the task at hand for those

involved is to entertain the viewers at home, get it made and bung it out.

So it's no wonder that I loved the book of this in my youth: Planet of the Daleks is unapologetic kids' drama. If the televised version falls to bits in the final episode, as Maloney finally fails to meet the extreme demands of Nation's script, it only goes to show how many miracles he's pulled off before now. The cracks start to show when a Dalek sadly regresses into a screeching cliché rather than the brutal killing machine of earlier episodes, as it barks out nonsensical panic *just* long enough for our heroes to escape. And it's very difficult to reconcile the model work with Pertwee and Preece's antics in the studio – the en masse shots of the "frozen" Daleks have become so prominent, it sticks out like a sore thumb that they're just Louis Marx toys (and therefore a different shape to the ones the Doctor and Codal are dealing with).

As for the character issues in this final instalment… well, they're a mixed bag, really. I'm pleased that Codal survived, as he's a lovely character who shows real warmth when parting from the Doctor. And I don't even mind the rather obvious moralising of the Doctor advising Taron and Rebec that they must not glorify war upon their return home – such themes need to be spelt out for the kids now and again. Hell, even as an adult, I'm a sucker for that kind of sentiment; the earnestness of this never fails to bring a lump to my throat, even if a lot of it is hoary old lecturing. What I *do* mind is Nation's perfunctory attempt to give Jo a dilemma about whether to go home or stay with Latep or not – she dismisses him in a line, he looks a bit miffed and off they go. (Although, that's no disrespect to Alan Tucker, who gives a heroic brio to what could have been a rather drippy character.)

Fundamentally, however, you're absolutely right about how much this adventure has revitalised and reinvented the Daleks – primarily by allowing them to *not* be totally defeated. Constantly revived thanks to their sheer popularity, the Daleks – more than any nemesis in the entire series – run the risk of looking daft if the Doctor constantly defeats them. So this time, they are impeded rather than stopped. There's no talk of a "final end" now – when they say no-one can defeat the Daleks, you can actually believe them. A battle has been won, not a war. You could almost say that they are entombed, but they live on...

June 19th

The Green Death (episode one)

R: Let's get this out of the way first. The sight of Jo Grant being adult isn't so much weird because she's channelling the Doctor's ethics, but that she appears to be wearing the clothes of one of his future incarnations. If only she were chewing with her mouth full of celery rather than apple, then the image would be complete. Now, I've read every single Doctor Who novel released by Virgin and the BBC in the Wilderness Years when the series was off the air – oh, indeed, yes – and it seemed to me at times that the authors were doing their level best to dot the "I"s and cross the "T"s throughout the whole of Doctor Who's history, and making every little thing join up. But somehow no-one ever wrote a story that suggested that the fifth Doctor was inspired to choose his outfit in moving homage to that moment where one of his favourite companions showed her first flair of independence. I can't believe they missed that trick. I now feel the urge to write a Davison audio for Big Finish and make the idea canon. I'm fighting it down. Down, urge, down.

It's a strange sequence anyway, because for the very first time in the series, it suggests that all this time-travelling lark in the TARDIS is blatantly irresponsible. Before there was the idea that adventure was an irresistible thing, and that those who didn't seize the opportunity were stay-at-home killjoys like the Time Lords. The most powerful moment is when Katy Manning takes a beat to mask her disappointment that the Doctor isn't following her to Wales like a proper paid-up UNIT lackey, but is swanning off to Metebelis III first – it's exactly the same facial expression I'd see on my mother's face when I took that second slice of chocolate cake, or decided to leave the Cub Scouts. The Doctor is reduced to being a child, and his (and therefore our) enthusiasm for exploring the universe is turned on its head. It's interesting, this – next year, Robert Sloman

and Barry Letts will write a script which positively suggests that it's the Doctor's thirst for knowledge that kills him. I wonder whether that Buddhist philosophy is *really* something you want to impose on an adventure serial like this.

Last year, Sloman and Letts appeared to be trying to replicate the success of their first script, The Daemons – and, in turning out The Time Monster, they appeared to have taken all the worst excesses from it (the cosiness of the UNIT family, the flirtation with bolting pseudoscience onto mythology). Here they're feeding off The Daemons again, but this time round they're drawing from a different part of the well altogether. Their depiction of a rural community under threat works very well; this has all the trappings of what would happen in that delightful Aldbourne village if a bunch of townies came along and decided to plonk an oil factory in the middle of it. Yeah, it's a little patronising to the Welsh – but the Welsh give as good as they get: the utter disdain that the milkman shows the Brigadier when he's asked for directions is lovely. And the writers seem at pains to put a bit of steel back into UNIT that's been sorely missing for quite a while – that UNIT are there to defend the corporate villains of the story is potentially fascinating, putting the organisation on the opposite side to Jo. You can see too just how much Nicholas Courtney relishes playing a Brigadier once more who's intelligent and commands respect: his scenes at Global Chemicals, where he makes it perfectly clear to Dr Stevens that he's not his whipping boy, are excellent.

After a season of interplanetary wandering, this is the most down to earth episode we've been given since the heady days of Season Seven. The Doctor's horrors on Metebelis III manage to be both amusing and sinister at the same time, but the garish blue is only there to highlight just how *silly* all this space travel is compared to the real issues of pollution and fungus. This is a sincere and clever script – the way that all the expository scenes dovetail into each other shows more disciplined writing in just a few minutes than we got in the entirety of The Time Monster. And there are some good laughs to be had too. For my money, this single episode boasts the two best jokes to be found in the whole Pertwee era. For a start, there's the

Brigadier's deadpan summation of the story's first victim: "Bright green, apparently, and dead." But knocking it into second place is the *perfect* gag of the TARDIS materialising as the phone rings, and an exhausted and dishevelled Doctor gratefully picking up the receiver and joining the story proper.

T: A green death, in a green story. I always admire Doctor Who when it tries to reflect real concerns, so this already has a lot going for it in my eyes. Tragically, the same issues are still being fought over today, and I dread to think how much our natural resources have diminished since this plea for sanity.

The opening scenes between Jo and the Doctor set the tempo for the rest of the episode, being a mix of the brilliant and the truly awful. She's forced to do terrible apple-eating comedy, whilst he patronises her choice of breakfast. (The Doctor essentially tells Jo that instead of an apple – one of her Five a Day – she should eat a big greasy sausage instead. Jamie Oliver would dribble with rage at that one!) The entire discussion lurches between the phoney and the heartfelt, as Katy Manning's initially embarrassing over-enthusiastic bluster leads to her trailing off whilst trying to quote Dr Jones' theories. The little pause when she stops what she's doing before she leaves, and Pertwee's quiet regret, are beautifully played. As the "fledgling flies the coop" (a line that Pertwee delivers straightforwardly, and very heart-breakingly), we get a clear indication that it's the end of Jo's time with him, and the moment is being prepared for.

As our regulars part company, the Doctor ends up on the famous blue planet. The Metebelis III sojourn will become a bit of an indulgence when film sequences in later episodes are compromised due to lack of time, but here it's a brilliantly audacious gag. It's funny enough that the Doctor's long-lauded nirvana is actually an inhospitable dive, but every time we cut back to the Doctor, he's enduring ever more ludicrous perils – my favourite being the utterly bananas oversized pterodactyl feet sweeping over him in hilarious fashion. I used to think this was a tedious diversion, but it's actually good for the episode's pacing, and ramps up gradually before the exciting climax.

Back on Earth, and as you've observed, we're in Wales. These days, with the new series being made in Cardiff, the Doctor seems to pop back there with indecent regularity – but it's quite novel at this point in the show's history. There are two factions at work here. Global Chemicals intrudes upon the green valleys, and we learn about them in a novel fashion: crosscutting neatly between conversations that explain the contrary attitudes to their methods. We first meet director Stevens when he's misquoting Neville Chamberlain, which is a nice antidote to the childish dialogue elsewhere in the story. Jerome Willis is suave as Stevens, and his moment of mind control at the end of the episode is subtly done, helped to no end by his factotum Hinks' cockney insouciance in response to it.

As for the indigenous population: well, a doomed miner provides a genuine hook early on, as John Scott-Martin's glowing corpse clings onto an alarm in death. Before that, you can see his veins running through the green on his hand – a grimly pleasing bit of attention to detail from the make-up department. And when the man's fellow miners lambaste Professor Jones, it stops the script from straying too far into middle-class intellectual wish-fulfilment. The point is rightly made that these men need jobs, and if the nutty professor can't provide such things, then they're buggered if they're going to let him prevent them from feeding their families. Well-meaning liberalism is one thing, but the big business that's threatening the community is also the only organisation around that can give its members paid work.

And it's unavoidable, but yes, the Welsh characters deliver lots of "boyos" and "isn't its", but if the result is Ray Handy's terrifically grumpy and terse milkman (who seems so irritated at the caricatures of fellow countrymen that he's going to seethe his way through the whole story), then it's worth it. Sod the Davison story, Rob – give this man his own Big Finish tale where he's attacked by his own milk or something (The Cameo Chronicles, I can see it now).

The Green Death (episode two)

R: In context, it's a little strange to see Jo baulk at the idea of climbing down 20 feet of rope, when in the last story Terry Nation has her climb down a few thousand. But it only highlights just how this story is a true attempt at realism, in stark contrast to anything we've seen all season, and it feels fresh and real. Most of the episode concerns itself with an attempt to find cutting equipment – and, alongside space wars and Dalek armies, that sounds extraordinarily prosaic. But it's great – the cat and mouse negotiations between UNIT and Global Chemicals, ever so *politely* done, have a charge to them that feels more dramatic than anything we've seen this season. And the reduced scale of the adventure means that there's a tight claustrophobia to the mine scenes: Katy Manning and Roy Evans (the miner Bert) are allowed to build up a genuine rapport, and Bert's insistence that Jo leave him when he's infected by the green slime is very moving.

And the cliffhanger is wonderful. The scene where Jo and the Doctor see the maggots for the first time, lazily rolling about in industrial waste, is commendably horrid. And after two episodes focusing upon arguments against pollution, to see at last the *results* of it in slithering day-glo glory makes you feel both nauseated and angry at the same time.

T: Every year in the area I grew up, a professional theatre company visits and performs a Shakespeare play for two weeks at Ludlow Castle. When I was about eight, they did Richard III, and my brother was selected to play one of the princes in the tower. I was thrilled when he showed me that the actor playing Clarence listed in his credits not just Doctor Who, but the name of this story and the fact that he played the lead villain, as if these things were a massive badge of honour amongst his many TV credits. This was my first introduction to Jerome Willis, who is terrific in The Green Death as the courteous, smooth and sinister Stevens.

By coincidence, John Rolfe (here playing Fell, a hypnotised Global Chemicals employee) was in the same production, as was HAVOC stuntman Derek Ware. The presence of Doctor Who thespians in the cast excited me so much, I didn't give a stuff that the title character was played by some bloke called Edward Woodward. I was also delighted when, for one production of A Midsummer Night's Dream, the actor Jim McManus' notes read "Jim has just fulfilled a lifelong ambition by making a recent appearance in Doctor Who". Bless him! That's surely the only time anyone has said anything nice about The Invisible Enemy.

It's a bit rich of me to go off on a tangent, as I moaned about pointless diversions last episode – but I think it's an interesting point, because ever since reading Willis' biography, I've been on the lookout for various actors, and made a mental note about those whose performances I've enjoyed. Take Ben Howard (as Hinks, Stevens' chauffeur/ henchman) – he doesn't have many lines in this episode, but he's a lurking presence who, despite the smart suit, conveys in his body language an underlying threat of thuggishness. The manner in which he nonchalantly bars Fell from leaving (whilst tugging on a cigarette) is terrific, and even with all the hypnotism business going on, he casts his eyes downwards, shrugging off the situation as if absenting himself from any complicity in it. In his mind, he's just the heavy – anything else that goes on ain't his business. Later, his low-key insolence as Pertwee girds himself for a tussle ("Gonna have a go? Terrific.") wonderfully contrasts the Doctor's dandified flamboyance.

It has to be said, however: that lift must be the worst CSO yet featured in the show. And yet, to counteract that effects nightmare, that final shot of the giant maggots bursting through the cave-in (complete with the close-up of a hissing maw) is one of the *best* effects shots the series has done so far.

June 20th

The Green Death (episode three)

R: This production is so self-assured that the occasional bits of clunkiness really stand out. So let's get them out of the way. The dinner party in the Nuthutch is well-intentioned, but rather embarrassing. Professor Jones points out that the yoga expert, the flautist and the sculptor are actually world-class geniuses engaged on solving the world's problems – Sloman clearly wants to point out that the hippies aren't just lazy drop-outs, but fully committed in their alternative lifestyles on responsible work, but it's so over the top that it just makes you want to laugh. "And over there, the man who's quilting with hemp? That's Jesus, that is. He'll save us all." It's the fact that not one of the characters can be allowed a line of their own, so come across as extras blissfully unaware of their own intelligence, that makes it look so silly. And the story doesn't *need* more than one genius in the Nuthutch. It's got Professor Jones. That's enough.

The scene where Professor Jones comforts the grieving Jo that there'll never be another Bert, not even if the Earth survives for a hundred thousand centuries... Yessssss, that's a bit on the nose too, but I like it, if only because it's taking the trouble to deal with a death in an emotional way. And it contrasts so well with the Doctor, who grimly announces the news of the funny little Welshman's death simply as another statistic. The paralleling of the Doctor with Jones is now very obvious, but it's extremely well-handled: the attempt on the Doctor's part to interest Jo with his Metebelis III adventures looking now like a boy with a crush chatting up the pretty girl in the school playground. And as overwritten as Jones' paean to Bert the Miner may be, it follows on nicely from the surprising grief that Stevens shows when he induces Fell's suicide. The sadness of his "That's unnecessary, surely" after the deed has been done turns the arrogance of the corporate businessman able to call in favours from the Prime Minister entirely on its head.

There are a few problems with the special effects, but the concept of Jo and the Doctor rising through the maggots, or trying to escape up the waste pipe, is so gloriously grisly that it really doesn't matter. The scene where Pertwee pockets the giant maggot's egg made me squirm. And the ickiness is complemented well by dramatic exploration of responsibility and morality treated with unusual sensitivity. The scene where Fell saves the Doctor and Jo's lives from the green waste is a replay of countless scenes in the series where a hypnotised

automaton breaks free of evil control, but actually feels here fresh and momentous. BOSS' order that Fell should kill himself becomes all the more chilling because of it. Best of all is the conflict between the Brigadier and Stevens, the former eventually beaten down by the Prime Minister. Usually such scenes, again a Doctor Who cliché, are played by Nicholas Courtney talking to unseen bureaucrats on the phone, but the whole thing becomes more charged as we see the ministers uncaringly sweeping the matter under the carpet. Even better is that this is followed by the Brigadier, unwillingly obeying his superior's orders, forced to drink whisky with his enemy. It gives a dignity to the Brigadier's soldier mentality which The Three Doctors so stupidly sneered at, and Courtney takes advantage of this to give the most subtle of his performances since Season Seven. (Odd though to see him smoking later in the episode though. Actually, there's a *lot* of smoking in this story, isn't there? I could claim that it's a clever comment upon the pollution men make, but even I'm not quite that pretentious. How's your own non-smoking going on, Toby? Are you being drawn back to the weed now you're facing the stress of incipient marriage?)

T: It may sound soppy, Rob, but I can't wait to be married, I'm not feeling remotely stressed about it, and I barely give the evil weed a second's thought (unless I'm daydreaming about Fury from the Deep turning up again). Nicholas Courtney is keeping a level head too – as you say, the break has clearly done him a lot of good. He's written with a steely streak, and grasps the opportunity to take centre stage in this episode, manoeuvring around the bad guy while the Doctor becomes first rescuer, then rescuee. Courtney's innate authority gives an enjoyable edge to Lethbridge-Stewart's civilised face-off with Stevens, who avoids cliché by coolly responding, when asked if he is threatening the Brig, "Yes, I think perhaps I am". Courtney also does some very good phone acting with the Prime Minister, after stalwart actor Richard Beale – a performer I've always enjoyed watching – turns up one last time in Doctor Who for an effective cameo as the dismissive minister.

Elsewhere, John Rolfe has the unenviable task of spending most of the time in a trance, but does the job well, especially when he stumbles clumsily into Stevens' office and complains, quizzically, that he has a headache. He then, after a rather weird and disorienting scene when he's got headphones on and (with benefit of Mirrorlon) everyone looks like they've been shot by an Ice Warrior, is touchingly mournful when he says, "You've done something to my mind". No flicker of emotion registers on his face as he leaves the room and purposefully, like an automaton, climbs over the railing to his death.

I don't mind the Nuthutch stuff particularly. I actually rather like Cliff's paean to the uniqueness of each and every human being: when someone dies, that person will never be replicated or replaced. When you think of all the human beings who have come before us, and will exist when we're gone, that's quite a profound and moving concept. Bert's death carries more weight than a minor character's passing normally would, because its announcement punctures some relaxed, comfy, post-meal chatter.

And the Doctor's motives are pretty obvious when he drags Professor Jones away from Jo, to prevent their getting better acquainted. Just because she wasn't impressed by his big blue throbbing thing, he tries to deny her the chance of being taken up the Amazon by a handsome young man. Spoilsport.

The Green Death (episode four)

R: This certainly has its moments – Pertwee's dispassion about Hinks' infection from the maggot is one of the most purely alien glimpses of this all-too-human Doctor, and his fury at the explosion of the mine is impressive. But from then on, not a great deal happens – Benton and Yates are reintroduced, and so is the impression of UNIT as a bunch of comic idiots. Scenes of the soldiers firing at maggots don't do much to help their reputation, and the moment that the Brigadier starts exclaiming that they've seen the last of the creepy-crawlies, you know that the renaissance of his character was all too brief. It's a bit like that Master Effect I mentioned in Frontier in Space – it's as if, by halfway through a story suddenly giving it all the reassuring support of the UNIT family, you remove some of its teeth. And we're

treated to one of the worst indulgences of Jon Pertwee this side of Planet of the Spiders, as he disguises himself as both milkman and cleaning lady, both complete with comic voices and tics. There's a real sense that this is a *middle* episode – we've seen people hypnotised by BOSS before, we've seen the obstructive tactics of Global Chemicals. Putting Captain Yates in the organisation as a spy is rather a fun idea, and gives Richard Franklin something to do for the first time since The Daemons – and the revelation that he's Stevens' man from the ministry is especially well shot. But when the Doctor breaks in to Global to talk to him, and the only information he gets is stuff we knew *weeks* ago, it's hard not to share the Doctor's frustration.

The cliffhanger is interesting, though. Up to this point, we could well have believed that BOSS was some alien entity influencing Stevens – this is Doctor Who, after all. That it's a megalomaniacal computer is rather a surprise. It turns the story into a retread of The War Machines, but just look at the difference – WOTAN had no personality whatsoever, and was as bland and mechanical as a computer might be, but John Dearth voices BOSS with a streak of black humour that's very winning. Throughout the sixties, computers were treated as something cold, their voices robotic and emotionless. The seventies will from this point on treat them with greater familiarity – and it's from BOSS that we get Kettlewell's Giant Robot, and from him K-9. I used to find the revelation that the evil genius behind any given story is nothing more than a computer somewhat disappointing: The Green Death has refreshingly focused upon *human* greed. But if humans are responsible for creating all the waste that is poisoning them, it seems wholly apt that they've also created the intelligence that is intending to enslave them as well.

T: My in-joke tracer has started beeping: we have a UNIT soldier called Dicks. Do think he's filing a report that their scientific adviser's hair is getting increasingly bouffant, or perhaps he's too busy reporting on the "[all monsters are...] gween" death?!

We'll never know, but not to worry, because we have Captain Yates going undercover! What a great twist, and it still gets me on every viewing. When they talk about the "Man from the Ministry", I genuinely couldn't remember who it was, and the surprise reveal that it's agent 00Yates is a great moment. Mike's presence demonstrates, pleasingly, that the Brig isn't totally opposed to bending the rules, even though he has to – on paper, at least – follow orders and ill-advisedly blow up the mine. I'm not averse to a few explosions, though, and there's plenty of other exciting stuff to grab the viewer's attention – soldiers charging about shooting giant maggots, a major guest character (Elgin) getting taken out of the action, and, to cap it all, Jon Pertwee dressed as a woman. What more could you possibly want? Richard Franklin nicely deadpans his "I like your handbag" line, and even if the Doctor's turn as a washerwoman runs the risk of getting a bit silly, I don't care because it's fun! So there! The Doctor *also* dresses as a comedy milkman, but I frankly prefer the real one. Ray Handy's very funny, mockingly tipping his cap to the Brigadier's "educated man". I wish they'd credited him as Jones the Milk, though; that would have been hilarious!

Amongst the daftness, there's the sobering postulation that the government would, under certain circumstances, grant emergency powers to a corporation. I suspect that the Prime Minister, named only as "Jeremy", will need to resign after this (perhaps some sort of scandal could be arranged). But the big business in question turns out to be run by a computer, and so the whole story, effectively, changes direction. They've deliberately made BOSS fruity in tone and mocking in attitude, which wouldn't work half as well save for Jerome Willis having the good sense to act slightly embarrassed at his superior's rantings. It's a clever metamorphosis from suave lead villain to sheepish underling – he reacts by raising his eyebrow and casting his eyes downwards, like an awkward groom at a wedding as his slightly racist uncle gets louder and louder as the wine continues to flow.

The Green Death (episode five)

R: Jon Pertwee plays his scenes with BOSS with just the right sort of amused disdain, but... I get the feeling that the story has taken the wrong turning. An ecological fable about businessmen destroying the planet was so much more interesting than one involving a fascist supercomputer. And although John Dearth gives BOSS all he can, the character just isn't credible: I can accept the idea of a machine that believes it's the greatest thing ever seen on planet Earth, but not if it's going to be so confused by a childishly simple bit of verbal paradox. It was so much more satisfying when you could believe Stevens and his cronies were poisoning the planet simply for greater profit, rather than as acts of premeditated evil – that was human, and it was real. Now that the green death is the by-product of some plan for world domination, it just makes those moral dilemmas seem correspondingly more trite.

What's more interesting is that this is the beginning of the end for Captain Yates. Here he pulls a gun on the Doctor and the Brigadier – and things are never the same again for the poor sod. One day sad hypnotised dupe, the next deliberate traitor, and from there it's the slippery slope to becoming some tweed wearing hippy in a commune. I can't help but feel that had Richard Franklin *known* this was to be his character arc, he might have played the scenes with a little more gravitas, and a little less prat falling and double takes.

I remember writing in my Invasion review how the disappearance of Major Routledge without explanation gave the character a bit of sinister intrigue. Sad to say, it's not really the case here for Elgin – last seen in episode four about to undergo conversion, and now cut from the story altogether owing to the actor falling ill. Tony Adams did a great job, I think, of giving Elgin a genuine journey from corporate stooge to man of conscience – and the episode suffers from not letting that subplot have its proper conclusion. Roy Skelton is fine as the replacement character, James – but there can be no sadness or regret when he's murdered by BOSS at the moment he recovers his wits, because he's only been in two scenes. It's unfortunate that, in a story which has worked so hard to give an appropriate emphasis upon death and grief, one of its potentially most powerful moments has been squandered through chance.

T: "The whole is greater than the sum of its parts": a worthy testament to humanity as the Doctor faces down a somewhat chatty opponent. The idea that BOSS has made Stevens programme him with human fallibility means we at least get a face-off (or chat-off) with a charismatic nemesis rather than a droning mass of electronics. Pertwee gives some confident and brazen ripostes to BOSS and Stevens, especially when he postulates, wryly, that the end piece to their global plan is "freedom from freedom". John Dearth is very funny as the voice of BOSS: when the mentally assaulted Doctor airs the chestnut that what they're doing must "hurt you more than it hurts me", the machine mutters testily "it does". All of that said, you're right – this eco-parable wasn't meant to be a mad computer story, and overall doesn't benefit from becoming one.

Even though Yates and Benton have been dumped unceremoniously lower down the credits, they still get more than a fair slice of the action. Poor old Benton gets stuck in front of a CSO screen representing the Welsh countryside as time runs out on location – the extended filming on Metebelis III might have consequently looked like an unnecessary production number, were it not for the blue crystal being so crucial to the action. The gem is used on Mike, and Richard Franklin expertly conveys with his eyes how the inner Yates struggles whilst his hands brandish a gun in the Doctor's direction. Delightfully, the Brigadier seems very affronted that Yates is obeying somebody else's instructions... right before he gets comedically hypnotised. Seeing as the Brig has been on top authoritative form this story, it's a welcome comic relief that doesn't actually undermine the character too much. Then Mike recovers and heroically, if reluctantly, goes back to Global Chemicals. He even gets the cliffhanger, which just about makes up for Mike's comedy fall when the Doctor mistakenly attacks him, and the rather silly, excitable rubbing-of-his-hands together that he did in the previous episode.

Various other delights present themselves... we have a Private Betts (B [L]etts, geddit?), Stewart Bevan (as Professor Jones) doing a nifty somersault fall after the explosion, and a great shot of Stevens framed inside a round silver ornament in his office. Some of the production-aspects are risible, and some of the effects so bad as to make it untransmittable to a modern audience, but there's so much to savour and admire, it's a hell of a lot more than the sum of its parts. That said, you're right that it's a shame Tony Adams (as Elgin) became ill, and had to be replaced by Roy Skelton as a different character. Having had Dai die and Fell fall, it would have been nice to see a scene where Elgin loses his marbles.

June 21st

The Green Death (episode six)

R: The resolution is a series of happy accidents and contrivances – but so blatantly so, with the word "serendipity" being thrown about with such gay abandon that the episode gets away with it. Besides which, there's something wonderfully bizarre about seeing Sgt Benton coax giant maggots with deadly fungus, or BOSS irritate his human conspirator with his Wagnerian fanfares – the plotting may be perfunctory, but the execution isn't. And Stevens' renunciation of BOSS, declaring there must be a better way as he condemns himself to death, is surprisingly moving. Briant's direction of the scene is outstanding, and manages to provide a real climax to a story somewhat lacking from the script.

And, of course, Jo's departure scene is marvellous. Finally, Professor Jones gets to do what King Peladon, Latep and – so it would appear – Mike Yates could only dream of. The Doctor leaves the celebrations of her engagement early, and drives back to England as the sun sets – and only Jo notices that he's gone, and looks for him with such tender sadness. She's told him to make sure they stay in touch – and from our 2009 perspective, this is so effective, because they won't. Katy Manning is one of the few cast members never lured back to the series for anniversary get-togethers or charity events. I'll admit it again – I've been none too fond of Jo. But I accept that's because I'm a jaded man pushing middle age, and not the twelve year old who would have adored her as the clumsy and sweet big sister she was meant to be. And it's why this departure works so brilliantly – it's not merely the sense that one of the TARDIS crew is leaving for pastures new, but that a little girl has reached adulthood at last and changed forever. When I first saw Disney's Bambi, I found the saddest part not that his mother was shot, but that when the spring came the little faun I'd found so cute had turned into something older and unlovely – and the last image we get of Jo is not of the hapless companion, but of a fiancée kissing her betrothed upon the mouth. We'll never see her again, not now she's become a woman. It's tremendously affecting, and the most moving exit a Doctor Who assistant has had since Susan. Ah, hell with it – it's even better.

[Rob's addendum, written June 2016: Typically, Katy Manning had to prove me wrong, and was lured back to play Jo opposite Matt Smith's Doctor for The Sarah Jane Adventures. Rather wonderfully, Russell T Davies' script and Katy's performance are so good that not only do they leave The Green Death's ending uncompromised, they even manage to make it even more moving in retrospect. But more of that later...!]

T: Well, it's been quite a day. I spent most of it doing the warm-up for four episodes of University Challenge, before rushing over to the Comedy Store for the last-ever performance of a sketch show I've been doing for more than four years. So, I made sure that the final Unbroadcastable Radio Show had its fair share of Doctor Who references. It's sad saying goodbye to something that's been so enjoyable, but I just don't have the time to churn out that much work anymore. I'm moving on. Do forgive me if I'm a little tired and emotional, and that I've had a couple of glasses of wine – I suppose I'm meant to be revelling in sentiment, but I still have to find time to watch three episodes of Doctor Who. So goodbye Unbroadcastable Radio Show, hello episode six of The Green Death. (Which has another goodbye in it. Oh God, I think I might cry...)

So there's a green solution to the green death – how appropriate and dramatically satisfying. There are some fantastic shots of the maggots eating the fungus, so it's a shame that for much of the climax, we get a toy model Bessie shuddering along, and Benton and the Doctor in profile as a CSO background rolls behind them unconvincingly. Fortunately, Benton gets car-

ried away with feeding the psychopathic larvae their just desserts, resulting in a withering put-down from our heroic Time Lord. Such comic moments distract temporarily from the shortcomings – I say that even though the much-derided giant fly nearly pulls off quite a big ask from a technically complex script (co-written, let's not forget, by the producer, who you'd think would know by now how far the budget would/ wouldn't stretch).

BOSS is now running the risk of being desperately annoying – fortunately, Stevens plays his straight man, patiently trying to goad his tricksy superior into taking things seriously. It's an effective dynamic that only works because Jerome Willis cleverly sowed the seeds for it with his little asides or looks in previous episodes. Here, he gives the impression of feeling slightly foolish for being subservient to a slightly bonkers calculator – and then is magnificent as BOSS takes over Stevens' body. Willis adopts a casually confident arms-folded body language, whilst his face struggles to let his human side unleash itself. The final moment in BOSS' lair is one of the great unsung moments in the series: the sound reaches a climax and then cuts out, and there's a breathless silence as the camera closes right in on Willis' face, speckled with a solitary tear.

If that climax is overlooked, it's probably because what comes next overshadows it, and fair enough. Pertwee gives Jo's final scene his all – he stutters through his line of "Will you excuse me? I do think I'm going to be wanted on the telephone" to give Jo and Cliff time to discuss their marriage, and then exits with dignity and real sorrow on his face. It's a terrific ending, very warm, and the affection for which the delightful Katy Manning is held by all concerned is really telling. Fortunately for her, she ends up with a charismatic and fun beau: a worthy successor to the Doctor in her affections. Nonetheless, as the Doctor walked out in the darkness and got into Bessie, I aped Stevens and a solitary tear ran down my face as well.

Bye-bye Jo xxx
Bye-bye Unbroadcastable xxx
I need cheering up. What's next?

The Time Warrior (part one)

R: Robert Holmes is back to his old tricks again! Carnival of Monsters was all about taking the viewers' ordinary perspective on the show, and putting a different filter on it. It was all rather overt, with its bunch of aliens watching the Doctor's adventures as if they too were sitting around the television on Saturday night after Grandstand. The Time Warrior does a similar job, but much more subtly. By putting an alien in a historical setting – and bearing in mind the fact that Doctor Who hasn't really *done* history since the days of Troughton – it manages to make the medieval characters seem strange and unknowable, and the Sontaran, with all his talk of spaceships and galactic conquest, the more recognisable figure. Indeed, Linx takes on the role of the Doctor for the episode – it's he that appears as a lone figure in a new world, it's he that has to find a way of mixing with the locals. And because Kevin Lindsay plays the part with such great dignity, even with his face hidden beneath his helmet, you side with him. You can't help it. He becomes our point of reference. It's telling too that, in spite of the fact that this is the introduction of a monster that's going to be brought back over and over again over the years, that Holmes clearly isn't pitching the Sontaran as anything *special* – far from it. For the gag to work, the alien has to be instantly generic, something more reassuring in contrast to the historical backdrop – with his silver armour, his space gizmos and his love of war, he comes across as wonderfully understandable. It's really a very clever joke on Holmes' part, at once taking a style of Doctor Who storytelling that might have felt antiquated and giving it a new lease of life, but also quite deliberately inviting the audience to side with the invader from the stars over the human population he's threatening. His first words are that he will not harm anyone, whilst surrounded by hostiles pointing weapons at him. If that isn't Doctor-ish, I don't know what is.

This is the joy of Holmes' stuff. Whilst the rest of the Pertwee writers make their impact by being very earnest, and attempting to create a solid reality, Holmes knows full well that Doctor Who is a TV fiction and acknowledges it as such. You want a better example of this?

Okay. The story wants to play the gag that the new companion hitches a ride in the TARDIS, and believes that the Middle Ages she sees is nothing more than a pageant. It's a nice joke, too. But it hinges upon a sleight of hand. If the story had chosen to show Sarah goggling at the size of the console room, it could never have worked – for the premise to hold, we have to assume that when Sarah steps in and out of the TARDIS (and presumably, goes deep enough inside it that the Doctor doesn't spot her there), she's seen nothing that can break her illusion that nothing *too* extraordinary is going on. This is, of course, preposterous. But only if you think of it. And Holmes just denies us the scene that would spoil his confection, so we don't *have* to think of it. For Holmes, TV is all about what you *allow* the audience to see – the other details are irrelevant. The other writers impose a logic to the off-screen scenes which made more fictive sense, but also bog down the story and slow the pace. It's in this way that Holmes is closest in new-series terms to Russell T Davies, who understands completely that Doctor Who is about what you show on the main stage rather than what must have happened in the wings.

When fans criticise The Time Warrior, they often point out the historical inaccuracies. All those anachronistic potatoes! And even Terrance Dicks will say that they're mistakes. I don't imagine Robert Holmes gave a damn about the potatoes. He wasn't addressing history the way John Lucarotti was; for him, history wasn't one specific time, but a big melting pot in which Stuff Could Happen. As in Carnival of Monsters, the historical characters all talk as caricatures in ways that are intentionally parodic. But this time, Holmes has dropped an alien right into the middle of them, and he sounds so much more down to earth than the Earth people.

T: Anyone who spends their time watching this on the lookout for potatoes doesn't deserve entertainment. There's a brief glimpse of some in episode three as far as I can remember – but if you're looking at spuds rather than the lovely Lis Sladen, here making her debut as Sarah Jane Smith, then you deserve a lifetime of disappointment.

Potato or no potato, this is a terrific episode.

Visually, Linx is most impressive – his cool black leather costume clinging to his stocky and muscular frame, his translation device, his nifty salute and his even niftier Flag of Conquest all mark him out as an arresting foe. Kevin Lindsay's anglicised Australian twang and husked voice stop him being just a man in a costume, and his sleek body language suggests a warrior ready to spring into action at any moment. And when he removes his helmet to show us the Sontaran head beneath, it's a wonderful design: a mouth moveable enough to allow some grotesque tongue waggling, actual eyes, and even a few realistic whiskers and pock marks. A simple design, superbly rendered.

It's important that Lindsay plays it straight, so deliberately cod is the medieval setting that Linx finds himself in. But that's the point – Robert Holmes writes the robber baron Irongron and his second, Bloodaxe, as phoney as you like: they're types for actors to seize upon with a sense of humour. Both David Daker and John J Carney dive in with aplomb – the former bashing the table with an axe, a tankard or anything that comes to hand if it enables Irongron to emphasise his point and end the scene with a bit of noise. Bloodaxe, on the other hand, may be stupid, but his suggestion that they search for the fallen star at dawn is admirably budget conscious (as it saves the production team the expense of a night shoot).

There are so many details to talk about... events on contemporary Earth tick along nicely whilst we wait for the Doctor to have an excuse to get involved. Pertwee is terribly relaxed and clearly enjoys ribbing Sarah – Sladen is great, apart from when forced to do the whole "feminists get annoyed at being asked to make coffee" hoopla. Donald Pelmear is great fun as the dotty Rubeish, whilst back in the Middle Ages, the ever-dependable Alan Rowe decides to play Edward with a weariness that hints at some debilitating ague (the pallor on his face suggests the make-up team are in on this too). It's a nice touch to distract from the fact that his wife is Dot Cotton at Cheltenham Ladies College. And as director, Alan Bromley keeps the right blend of melodrama and adventure (there's a lovely piece of lighting when Bloodaxe watches the falling star).

And we have the beginnings of what would metamorphose into the definitive Who title sequence! This one is great, with only the full-length figure of Pertwee a slight misfire.

The Time Warrior (part two)

R: "I'd have thought he was a bit too old for things like that!" And as the Doctor goes looking for his new companion, in a moment Robert Holmes makes explicit the joke that before now the series has never dared mention – to suggest there's something just a little *untoward* about this Doctor fellow hanging out with pretty young girls. What was hinted at right at the very end of The Green Death as something tragic and moving is now played for laughs. That's Holmes all over – he's the one who introduces sex gags into the series. My favourite moment in the entire episode is when Linx advises Irongron to correct the inefficiency of the reproductive system.

This is delightful stuff. And oddly enough, all the more so that halfway through the plot, the story still hasn't been able to articulate any real crisis yet. The Doctor complains to Linx a lot about how he's perverting the course of human history – but rarely for Doctor Who, there's no urgency, no countdown, no imminent threat to be averted. This ought to be a weakness, but actually it just makes it all the more charming. When the Doctor *does* try to rescue Professor Rubeish, the scientist is having none of it, amiably preferring to stick around as a prisoner of an alien warrior as if he's on some Sunday School picnic. And when he tries to help Sarah, she runs, thinking he's the evil mastermind – she'll brave a Sontaran and stand up to a robber baron, but one sight of Jon Pertwee and she's haring down corridors away from him. It's very funny. It's as if, for all his best efforts, the Doctor can't quite get the story to rouse itself and behave properly.

And Gallifrey is named for the first time! And it's so casually done, with so little fanfare, it quite catches you by surprise. It doesn't even *sound* like a planet – and that's one of the mysteries of Doctor Who is revealed, quite unexpectedly, with no reason whatsoever, in one of the series' most relaxed and meandering instalments. It almost feels like part of the joke.

T: Elisabeth Sladen gets a real showcase of her talents, and ably displays her ability to sell good lines and smooth out awkward ones. Quite why they decided to give her annoying traits like disbelieving the Doctor, or doing a whole monologue where she tries to work out her location in front of her captors, is anyone's guess. That approach would have floored lesser actors, but Sladen's naturalistic, idiosyncratic delivery makes her lines sound like fresh thoughts enunciated on the hoof (as real speech, of course, does). She's companion material from the get-go (as evidenced by her gambit of "get lost" to Irongron and Bloodaxe), being fiery, intuitive and (to quote Barry Letts on the quality which won Sladen the role) concurrently both scared and brave.

Elsewhere, I don't know why more people don't rave about Donald Pelmear: he's terrific! Professor Rubeish labours under the misapprehension that he's too strong-minded to succumb to hypnotism, until the Doctor points out that it's actually because he's literally short sighted. He delightfully doesn't want rescuing, and when told to steel himself for the news that he's in the Middle Ages, he charmingly drones on about how this'll confound various scientists' theories about time travel.

And I so enjoy the juicy dialogue of the medieval baddies – we have a "narrow-hipped vixen" from Irongron and "the wench is crazed" delivered with pitch-perfect blinking gormlessness by John J. Carney, all of which contrasts Linx the Sontaran's clipped precision. His line that the human reproductive cycle is "an inefficient system, you should change it" is one of the funniest in the whole series, more so because Kevin Lindsay plays it admirably straight. I can see why Robert Holmes paid lip service to the series' tropes by upping the dramatic stakes through just the dialogue, as we really don't need lots of sound and fury about Linx mucking up mankind's development to get our interest here. "I have no interest in human evolution", says Linx. Me neither, mate – I'm having too much fun in a story for which the word "romp" could have been invented.

June 22nd

The Time Warrior (part three)

R: It's one of Jon Pertwee's most joyous performances, lobbing stink bombs over castle walls, imitating his medieval hosts and throwing chicken legs. He describes himself as someone who takes what he does seriously, but not necessarily the way he does things – and I love that, it's a glimpse of another side of the Doctor altogether, one who isn't arrogant and sanctimonious, one who's a charismatic eccentric... In fact, he's describing Tom Baker, and how Robert Holmes will characterise *his* Doctor next year. We rarely see Pertwee enjoy himself so clearly, and it's something to savour – after this story, his performance will grow ever-more weary and muted.

There is a wonderfully funny scene in which Irongron tries to give the mentally challenged Bloodaxe some lessons in diplomacy, and David Daker's performance is amusingly OTT. And what sells it is the expression on John J Carney's face as he listens to the bragging of his master with unquestioning devotion. Just look at those big puppy dog eyes. There's a lot of good eye acting this week. The cliffhanger is terrific; we've got so used to sharing Linx's frustration with Irongron that deep down, we still sympathise with the Sontaran. So as the Doctor makes his bargain, you can allow yourself the hope that Linx might even accept. And it's Kevin Lindsay's eyes behind that mask, staring at Pertwee with unblinking intelligence, listening carefully, weighing up the pros and cons, that give it this power. The sting of the theme music cuts in early, even before Linx has turned his gun on the Doctor – and that's clever, because *of course* Linx wouldn't turn good, *of course* he'll try to kill him, and we feel the inevitability of it just before it happens, and we feel disappointed in the character. It's rare for a story to provoke such affection for the villain, that you feel hurt when he reverts to type and behaves villainously. But it's what happens here.

T: When was the last time we had a serious monster who desired amusement? Linx confesses that the idea of Irongron ruling Earth entertains him, and he comes to watch the assault on Lord Edward's castle out of curiosity. Such emotional responses make Holmes' creations so much more memorable and impressive than more generic monsters. They rationalise his alliance with Irongron, and give a psychological insight into what is otherwise a man dressed as a space-potato. Lindsay gives so much to the character, and his sturdy frame and lithe movements (despite the costume's restrictions) add to his performance. The scene where Linx knocks Irongron to the table shows that despite his tolerance of the rogues so far, he's certainly not worth messing with.

Irongron, meanwhile, is both a fun villain and serious threat. I assume the Wolfit bit is Irongron's enraged roar after the battle, where he calls his men "mice"? If so, it's terribly funny. And the best description of a Doctor ever ("a longshanked rascal with a mighty nose") accompanies the casual mention that sweet little Eric from episode one died in his cells. We're never far from a reminder that despite the enjoyment Holmes clearly had while writing them, Irongron, Bloodaxe and company are violent, brutal men.

Other things that I love about this episode... there's the way in which the Doctor describes the Time Lords as Galactic Ticket Inspectors – it's a perfect example of Robert Holmes' irreverent but brilliant vision of the series (no pious, high and mighty god-beings for Holmes: the Doctor's people are the equivalent of annoying jobsworths), followed by Sarah's "I could murder a cup of tea" line bringing it all back down to Earth with a stunningly simple burst of naturalism. I also enjoy Pertwee's dryly amused reaction to the rather "restricted choice" Edward gives him (basically: help us or die!), Rubeish becoming more than just comic relief by making his own eyeglass and helping the Doctor escape, and a terrific cliffhanger as Linx fires at the Doctor.

All of that accounted for, and just to prove this is Doctor Who, in an otherwise *brilliant* episode... they have to chuck in something so unaccountably bad, it makes you weep tears of blood. In this case, it's Steve Brunswick as the sentry: a performance of such baffling awfulness, I'm surprised he's not in Hollyoaks. If that weren't enough, I've worked with the other, non-speaking sentry, and he's a great,

charming, witty actor called Andy Abrahams, who has done plenty of good work in the theatre (leading roles and everything) and made a good account of himself on TV in everything from The Forsyte Saga to Life on Mars. He once told me that Brunswick had been chosen at lunchtime, when the director popped over to the extras and told the man that he'd be getting a line. Well, it looks like they chose the wrong guy – indeed, I noticed one of the other lackeys slipping into the arms of Morpheus next week was Ray Dunbobbin, who became a regular (Harry Cross' long suffering mate, Ralph) in Brookside. So well done Alan Bromley... you had two guys there who had the potential for greater things, and you picked Steve bloody Brunswick. What a mistake – a silly, slightly annoying, rather pointless and messy mistake, as my mother will say a few days later, because... (tune in for the resolution to this one...)

The Time Warrior (part four)

R: Jon Pertwee and Elisabeth Sladen share a moment at the beginning of the episode. They've just faced death together for the first time, and have lived to tell the tale. Her first instinct was to save his life – her second, after her own has just been saved, is to check that the *Doctor* is all right. It's lovely; and it's the time, for me, that Sarah Jane Smith becomes the new companion.

They've been very clever with the way they've introduced the new girl. Jo Grant was very popular, and the Doctor's affection for her unusually pronounced – it would have seemed crass had the production team simply offered us a replacement and expected us to take her on trust. Rather than try too hard to make her likeable, they've done the reverse: getting the wrong end of the stick entirely, she sees the Doctor as her enemy. And by characterising her as a Women's Libber, they've made her so intentionally strident that the inevitable softening feels like a process the *Doctor* has on her. She starts the story brittle and spoiling for a fight. By the end, there's joking and mutual acceptance and the sense of a friendship forged. It's amusingly done, too; her advising a serving wench, Meg, to stand up to the men and become a feminist is very funny ("You're still living in the Middle Ages!"), but crucially sends up the anachronism rather than the ideals themselves or the person who has them. You can tell this from the way that Meg quite witheringly refers to the men as spoilt children playing with their toys of war upstairs, and speaks nostalgically of the broadsword – she doesn't see herself as inferior at all! And it's a terrific joke that, having cast a blow for women's strength, Sarah distracts one of the wenches by scaring her with a spider!

I think Lis Sladen is brilliant in this. It's not the easiest of companion introductions. Indeed, it's the very first one ever that takes place without support from previously established characters, either other companions like Jamie who can hold the newbie's hand and make them feel welcome, or a whole UNIT establishment that can give the new assistant a context. Sladen jumps straight in. Without the Doctor's help, she becomes a dominant force within the story, winning over the Earl of Wessex and his retinue, and standing up to the monster. She hides her fear behind a direct bravery that is very appealing. She doesn't scream, doesn't need to be rescued. (Well. Not yet, anyway.)

T: ... it's my birth episode. This is the first instalment of Doctor Who broadcast after I was sent mewling and puking into this world. It couldn't be a better example of how I envision perfect Doctor Who: a well designed, articulate monster, a period setting, a funny character who gets to do brave things, and a story providing thrills and spills for the kids, along with a good dose of humour for the grown-ups.

This fun adventure comes to an end, as one might expect, with bangs and flashes (despite Barry Letts' worries on the DVD, the castle explosion is actually better than the twenty-first century CGI replacement), and my only regret is that this being Doctor Who, Linx has to die. He's been such a great villain, it's an ignominious end to see him executed on the cusp of his escape, and by a rather fey archer in Lincoln green at that. Kevin Lindsay's contribution to the success of this creation – which went on to become one of Doctor Who's top alien races – shouldn't be undermined: he spits out his line about "egalitarian twaddle"

(you don't get dialogue like that in Grange Hill!), gives an alien hiss-gurgle as he's banged on his probic vent, and assumes a wide-armed battle stance as he prepares to combat the Doctor. These sort of touches give the creature a unique alien aspect, working in tandem with enough scripted characterisation for us to understand his psychological motivations.

And Rubeish continues to be one of Holmes' great unsung creations. Donald Pelmear has just the right air of detached dottiness, and he does heroic things like whack Linx with a medieval baseball bat. K, who has seen a few of these latest episodes, laughed along with everything he did. Indeed, she thought all of the actors judged everything perfectly – note the way John J. Carney hides behind the cellar door, as if to suggest he's too scared to come in when summoning Linx.

Indeed, my lovely wife-to-be once almost incurred my wrath by daring to suggest that she didn't think Elisabeth Sladen was much cop in her episodes with David Tennant. Watching Sladen in this context, K was instantly won over. And so, literally a lifetime ago, were a generation of boys, myself included (eventually).

June 23rd

Invasion (part one)

R: Ah, happy birth episode, Toby! I'm glad you've been able to join me in the land of the living at last. Now that we both exist, Doctor Who shall be ours!

When I was a teenage fan, I was sent a video copy of this story from Australia. I watched the bluey-green of the time tunnel, in full colour: "Part One!" the words screamed at me. And the very first scene showed Jon Pertwee and Lis Sladen handcuffed together in the back of a truck. "Well, how was I to know it was detention centre transport?" said the Doctor. It seemed to me a most bizarre way to start a story. I didn't know as much about handcuffs then as I do now, but beginning an adventure with the Doctor manacled to his companion seemed even then a little tawdry.

What had happened, of course, was that the BBC had removed the real episode one from the package it sent overseas altogether. Skip the black and white episode, get straight to the colour! And the funny thing is that however abruptly the story starts, it does actually make sense this way. You don't *need* this episode at all. It's an exercise in atmosphere, not in plotting. But I think the Australians were far the poorer without it, as it's mostly a remarkable piece of work. The last time the series had tried to depict a deserted London which had already fallen foul of an invasion, it was safely set 200 years in the future. Here the Doctor and Sarah have landed in a recognisably contemporary Britain – but it's dead. Since Pertwee took over, we've had four years of alien baddies trying to conquer the world – and here Malcolm Hulke turns the cliché upside down, and shows us a scenario where it seems someone's already won. It's a much grimmer depiction than the one we saw in The Dalek Invasion of Earth. There we quickly encountered humans, and they rescued our heroes, all fighting together against the enemy. Here, the men we see furtively rushing through the streets are looters, their first reactions upon seeing the Doctor to threaten him with gun or crowbar. It's a portrait of a society destroyed, all the more shocking because it's so clearly *our* world, not one set safely 200 years in the future. And it's appropriate that the first looter we see is killed by an unseen monster, and that the crushed and bloodied body is the goriest thing we've yet seen in Doctor Who. There's a bleakness to this that we haven't seen on the show since Inferno.

And that's why it seems such a shame, really, that we get those scenes of UNIT. They don't contribute anything to the drama, save for telling us either things we've already learned (there are monsters and looters!), or things we'd be better off not knowing yet (London hasn't been destroyed, merely evacuated). The story will make the same mistake, I think, in episode four, where it too quickly reveals that Sarah hasn't spent the last few months on board a spaceship – it is too eager to sacrifice its heady mystery just so it can reassure the audience. As the Doctor and Sarah find themselves enmeshed in a bureaucracy that refuses to acknowledge them, let alone consider their innocence, we need to feel their despair – not the comfy knowledge that the Brig is already

on his way to set them free. Watching the Doctor and his companion being sentenced by court-martial by an authority that so blatantly has no interest in them reminds me of Hulke's first take on the theme, back in The War Games. There, we'd no friendly paramilitary organisation to rescue them in the nick of time – and their presence shouldn't have been emphasised here either.

T: When I was a fledgling fan, The Ambassadors of Death didn't have a great reputation, but Invasion of the Dinosaurs was the Pertwee story we were allowed to *hate*: the one absolute duffer in an era of brilliance. Well, on the evidence of this, I beg to differ with the consensus – it's one of the very best opening episodes of the era.

Paddy Russell deploys some moody location filming, with discarded children's toys and litter blowing in the wind, and a dog's lonely bark puncturing the silence. Initially, we only hear the dinosaurs off stage, but Phillips' smashed, pulverised car and briefly glimpsed, bloodied corpse hint at a genuinely frightening, deserted London. Shooting the garage interior on location (and the black and white may inadvertently help this) makes it a gloomy, shadowy place, and the quick cuts and close-ups of the Pterodactyl's snapping jaw are genuinely scary (Kklak!!!).

But with the monsters (for now) mostly kept to the side, there's more opportunity to focus on the leads and our guest cast. Pertwee provides plenty of interest – it's late in his tenure, but he's not phoning it in at all. He's in Reithian mode when educating Sarah about the Vandals, in an exchange reminiscent of Hulke's Target novels – those beloved texts from which young Toby learnt a number of facts. (The Sea Devils explaining the provenance of May Day – m'aidez – sticks in my mind.) Elisabeth Sladen is very clever during the court-martial scene, the look on her face suggesting that whilst she'd like to join in with the Doctor's photographic fun, she hasn't quite got the courage. And we meet a load of characters for this episode only... as the dismissive Lt Shears, Ben Aris is curt and uninterested in what the looters have to say, whilst Trevor Lawrence is ideally cast as the cockney tea leaf, in a role than could easily have gone to George

Sweeney (he's high on my list of actors that should have notched up a Doctor Who appearance but never did). Talking of lists, Gordon Reid appears on that small but notable one of actors who died on stage (in a production of Waiting for Godot, if I recall correctly).

And I agree that UNIT's presence dissipates the tension – once the Brig knows our heroes have turned up, it's only a matter of time before the looting issue gets resolved. It's a shame, as the imposition of martial law as the world goes to the dogs evokes the most effective elements of post-apocalyptic drama. General Finch's dialogue about looters emphasises that justice becomes rougher when society collapses, and nicely sets up the Doctor and Sarah running afoul of the jittery military arbiters. When accounting for themselves, their straight faced-repetition of Lodge's obviously hokey story (about finding the goods they were fingered with) steers them further up the creek, with their paddle sinking far behind them. That said, the guy with the moustache guarding them also watched the rugby with Yates and Benton in The Daemons, so you'd have thought he could have piped up on their behalf and resolved the situation.

But yes... the tyrannosaurus is rubbish. The episode ending involves the director cutting to the titles before the thing falls over. But even if the depiction of the monsters isn't quite up to scratch, this story's intriguing script, character work and evocative direction all lift it up above being something that, sadly, continues to languish in the polls.

Invasion of the Dinosaurs (part two)

R: ...of the Dinosaurs! So *that's* who was invading! Fancy that!

It's an episode featuring big monsters, but for my money the best bits are the little facial expressions. The look of girlish delight on Sarah's face when the Doctor first refers to her as his assistant. (Her Women's Lib scruples seem long lost already!) And the amused pride the Brigadier shows as the Doctor shows off to Charles Grover his stun gun.

But the most shocking thing about all this isn't the appearance of monsters that died out 65 million years ago. Mike Yates is a traitor!

And this time without the benefit of mind control. The revelation that one of UNIT's finest is working for the other side is very well handled. Franklin looks very uncomfortable throughout the episode, as if not sure how icily he should play Yates now he's a villain, but his conversation with Sarah about the clean air and peace of the deserted London is rather touchingly sincere. And Hulke takes great pains to ensure that Yates will only sabotage the gun if he's first certain that the worst the Doctor will suffer is a little humiliation. The fracturing of the UNIT family that started with the departure of Jo in The Green Death now becomes ever more pronounced; it's as if the production team realise that since they can't maintain the status quo, they may as well intentionally deconstruct it. I've not been the greatest fan of UNIT, no matter how much I love Nicholas Courtney and have warmed to the comic affability of Levene – but I still feel sad to see it being chipped away like this.

T: The monsters aren't bad at all – in fact, the stegosaurus looks great. Alright, it doesn't quite work when the humans are CSOed onto the impressive models, but The Green Death still gets called a classic and that has equally egregious Chroma-Key misdemeanours.

It's a bold move to make Captain Yates the traitor, but once again I have to bemoan this era's brutal lack of a sense of occasion. The reveal of Mike's duplicity should have been a heart-in-the-mouth episode cliffhanger. Instead, it's placed rather innocuously, with all the oomph of Steve Davies introducing an exhibition of drying paint. It's a shame, because the more thoughtful moments from Richard Franklin showcase his best performance by far in the series, and his eulogy to the quietness and clean air enveloping the stricken capital is terribly effective.

Elsewhere, Elisabeth Sladen continues her brilliant quest to become Best Companion Ever – only six episodes in, and she's pitch perfect. Her face creases in terror as she hears the T. Rex roar, and she flaps about looking for something to help as a peasant attacks the Doctor before gamely jumping on the assailant's back. I feel rather sorry, though, for the poor wench who has been accused of being a witch back in the seventeenth century. No

153

doubt, when our time-hopping peasant makes it home, she'll be due an undeserved ducking at his instigation.

Overall, no amount of unsuccessful carnivores should distract us from this story's eclectic array of lovely moments. I enjoyed the Doctor's comedy business of trying to get everyone to sod off whilst he makes his stun-gun, and there's an impressive scale to the location filming and hardware on display. And compare Noel Johnson's rather hammy turn as King Thous in The Underwater Menace to his dignified and charming performance here as the politician Charles Grover – it turns out that quality material yields much better results from this particular thesp. I also like the little touch of adding M.P. to his character name on the credits. I don't know why: I just do, so there.

June 24th

Invasion of the Dinosaurs (part three)

R: "We left Earth three months ago!" And in one moment, the story finds a new energy, in a cliffhanger that jolts the audience and sends the adventure off in an entirely new direction. Consider this: we've spent the last three episodes adjusting to the idea that this is all about the distant past meeting the present. Any variations on that theme are to be expected, which is why we've even had a peasant popping up in a garage and calling Pertwee a wizard (two stories in a row, which would give anyone a complex). But in the final scene of the episode, it does something new – it suddenly becomes space age and futuristic. It's as decisive a contrast to the dinosaurs as you could expect, as we stare like Sarah out at the stars. We've had stories before that mix the past and the present, and lots that mix the present and the future. The Time Warrior had a stab at mixing the past and the future, which was a flavour we hadn't tasted for many years. Now Invasion of the Dinosaurs comes along, and mixes all three: space technology with pterodactyls with contemporary London.

It won't be as it seems, of course, but that's all right. It does its job. Part three has been

building to this moment, but it's almost been *too* predictable, it's been allowing us to get *too* comfortable with the tropes – just to make the ending that greater a shock. We've got used to the style. Dinosaurs appear, then disappear, and everyone's a traitor. Then there's a new character, and he's dressed in Shiny Space Overalls, and look! – so's Sarah! Someone must have undressed her. The questions raised by it all are big enough, without the wonderful final words, said by the would-be colonist Mark almost as an afterthought, just to give the nation's collective jaw that extra reason to drop still further – *what* did he say? "We left Earth three months ago." My God.

T: Malcolm Hulke cleverly shifts the story's emphasis away from the dinosaurs – after all, you can only get so much from ginormous lizards who can do little apart from roar (and, as realised by the BBC, move very slowly indeed). This is particularly fortunate when considering the tyrannosaurus rex, whose credibility isn't really helped by the addition of massive nostrils to its stupid face. That said, there's a decent close-up of him as he succumbs to the Doctor's stun-gun and crashes to the ground quite convincingly. Indeed, the whole sequence of Yates coming to the Doctor's aid as things go awry with subduing the T. Rex is thrillingly staged.

For her part, Sarah has clearly watched Doctor Who before, as she knows you can get a lot out of Benton by running rings around him and letting him do a bit of put-upon comedy. Still, for all the mileage they get out of Benton's simple nature, he's also trusted so unconditionally that he isn't dismissed with the non-speaking soldiers when it's time for a candid, secretive comparison of notes about the conspiracy. Sarah, the Doctor and the Brig also get a good dialogue scene when they discuss Professor Whitaker, accompanied by the ominous presence of the snoozing T. Rex behind them.

Unfortunately, when watching the back catalogue of Doctor Who, Sarah clearly wasn't paying attention to the politicians. Pretty much every government official since the beginning of Season Eight has been an unmitigated twit – which means that despite his reasonable and likeable exterior, Charles Grover must be a traitor. Oh, and I note how he says "back in the Cold War days", as the prophetic production team sets Glasnost in motion almost a year before, um, their plan to prep Margaret Thatcher for prime ministerial duties.

Invasion of the Dinosaurs (part four)

R: The Whomobile. Hmm. I have issues with the Whomobile. One of the great charms of Doctor Who is the way it turns the very mundane and turns it into something magical. There isn't a shiny spaceship, but a police telephone box; the sonic screwdriver may be the all-purpose problem solver, but it's a *screwdriver*. Even the Doctor is like this – from our perspective, he may be a genius, but it's clear he's an academic lightweight compared to the Master or to Romana. And Bessie fits into this mould beautifully; the gag that there's Time Lord warp speed in this cheery yellow roadster is good enough that they're still playing it in Sylvester McCoy's day. The Whomobile, though, is exactly the sort of car you'd drive if you were the hero of a sci-fi series: it's ostentatious, it's futuristic and it's entirely without a sense of humour. It's an example, I think, of just where, at this fag end of the Pertwee years, the series is losing its identity.

But this loss of identity, the sense that the values of the series are being reversed, provide the stand-out moments of this episode. The spaceship stuff is excellent, really showing the darker flipside of the Pertwee era green philosophy. The scene which shows Sarah recognising all the crew as leading celebrities seems to parody directly that awkward scene in The Green Death where all the hippies are revealed to be world-shattering scientists. The spaceship is the Nuthutch gone wrong; the author who claims he has stopped writing and now has better use for his hands, as he shows Sarah a really crappy ceramic pot, provides the funniest moment in the entire story. The Reminder Room which plays constant reminders of man's pollution, and the dawning realisation of these idealistic people that they may have to resort to murder to stop Sarah corrupting the other peace-loving colonists, feel like Hulke looking at the show's new-found ecological concerns and showing the fanaticism behind them that can make even the well-intentioned a villain. Sarah's counter to their dismissal of man's goodness is, quite simply, one of the most truly optimistic moments of Pertwee's tenure.

And it's such a shame that Hulke didn't have the courage to disguise that the spaceship is a sham for longer, and perhaps even devote the first half of the episode to Sarah's storyline. Instead, he cuts back and forth between them and the Doctor's actions in London, and this undermines all of the shock value in the whole colonisation subplot. Because this part of the plot is plodding and inconclusive – characters going around in circles, showing little of the passion that you feel there *ought* to be to this parable. There are some really good actors, like Noel Johnson and John Bennett and Martin Jarvis, and they're doing their best with the thinnest characters Hulke has ever written. Fans mock the story for the special effects – they are a bit on the dismal side, it's true, but the dinosaurs don't actually appear *that* often, and Toby's right, we've seen worse in The Green Death. For me, it's not the large reptiles that seem unreal, it's the humans summoning them. And it means there's a corresponding lack of tension. The cliffhanger feels especially trite – in what way does seeing a stegosaurus materialise incriminate the Doctor? Turning UNIT against our hero now, in a story in which Mike Yates has turned bad, would be the ultimate in shaking the audience's expectations. But it has to be done carefully, or it just looks like forced plotting, and goes against the tone of the series to boot. As forced and tonally wrong, say, as letting the Doctor ride a spaceship on the roads of London.

T: Katherine has been watching this with me – as she's not well versed in the Pertwee era, I was slightly worried about exposing her to A) the cosier latter half of it, B) a six-parter and C) the one with crap dinosaurs. But she's loving it. She adores everything Nicholas Courtney does, thinks Pertwee has a lot of style and presence (though she envisions the Doctor as someone more alien and offbeat) and she even likes Yates and Benton. She's not been bored at all. I think I may well have struck gold! If she likes this, I can't wait till our wedding day – perhaps I can persuade her to nip out for a quick fix of Hinchcliffe.

I really don't mind that we keep cutting back to "the present" – there's no feasible way they could have kept up the pretence. And what's to say we can't be watching a story occurring in two different time periods? I think it's a fabulous idea – that these well-intentioned people are seeking a better world, but another party is exploiting their goodness to bring about humanity's end. It's a neat twist on your average Doctor Who storyline, and Hulke's very clever in suggesting that the environmental activist Ruth might sanction murder to preserve her liberal ideals. Deep down, maybe we're all prepared to be dictatorial in our benevolence, if it's (in our view) "good" for people. A frightening thought.

Oh, and look... the sets are a bit wobbly in this episode. It's vindication for almost every witless tabloid journalist in the land for the past 20 years. Richard Franklin has a good outing, the music's terrifically dramatic and John Bennett supplies plausible menace as General Finch. It's not his fault, but I find it impossible to believe that the head of the armed forces would be sympathetic to Grover's woolly liberal peacenik scheme. Finch has been such an arch pain in the neck, it would have benefited the plausibility of the tale if he'd actually turned out *not* to be a traitor.

As a pleasing aside, I note that the colonists are clearly very well funded, as they've secured the services of leading voice-over artist Martin Jarvis for narration duties on their apocalyptic propaganda videos.

June 25th

Invasion of the Dinosaurs (part five)

R: Never was there an episode that more literally ran on the spot. The Doctor's arrest leads to an interminable sequence where he's chased by UNIT troops in jeeps and helicopters – it's visually striking now and again, but it's not *interesting*, because it doesn't achieve anything dramatically. It's merely a way of keeping the Doctor tucked to the side before the story can enter its final act. And in a similar way, Sarah escapes the villains' hideout, only to trust the one man who will have her taken straight back there again. Both Sladen and Bennett play these scenes well, but there's no suspense to them, because we know already that General Finch is a traitor, and his bluffing would only have a function were Sarah to realise that *before* she's put right back where she started. Otherwise, it just makes her look stupid; the audience not only know that she's walking into a trap, we're not even given the dramatic surprise of watching her avoid it.

Two fun scenes. John Levene steals the episode as Benton, in a rather touching demonstration of lone faith in the Doctor; the way he screws his eyes tight whilst inviting the Doctor to knock him out with his Venusian oojah is not only very funny, but terribly sweet. And I love the exchange between Sarah and Corporal Bryson too. He starts off the scene being all military and forbidding, and within a minute she's got the upper hand, treating him like a small child who can't be trusted to take a message for Daddy.

T: I was cautious approaching this episode, as the dreaded Received Wisdom paints it as a self-indulgent, padded chase. Well, not quite – there's plenty of incident in the first ten minutes. The Doctor's entrapment might be slightly thin stuff, but Nicholas Courtney thoughtfully acts the whole scenario with laudable scepticism. Also, as you note, we're graced by one of John Levene's finest scenes, as Benton dutifully allows himself to be overcome to facilitate the Doctor's escape. It's one of my favourite "little moments" in the show's history.

The chase itself *is* overlong, and a massive chunk of the location filming fails to move the plot along at all, but by golly director Paddy Russell gives it her all. Some seamlessly integrated stock footage provides sweeping aerial photography and impressive shots of a helicopter. Much of this story has benefited from escaping the confines of the studio and opening the action out, so it's a shame that this week, everything has to revolve around the Doctor outwitting some dim soldiers.

More stock footage is used – this time to represent itself, when Sarah gets an "education" in the Reminder Room. The newsreel of *actual* violence being meted out on *real* people is pretty unsettling in a cosy family teatime adventure, but helps us to have sympathy with the ideals of Sarah's captors.

And when the mass materialisation of dinosaurs occurs, each of them appears with notable London landmarks in the background – Independence Day, eat your heart out. It seems decidedly masochistic, though, that three out of this story's five cliffhangers have involved the T. Rex, who is marginally less terrifying than the monster in the old Chewits advert.

Invasion of the Dinosaurs (part six)

R: I've been a bit harsh on this story the last couple of days, but I thought this episode was really rather fab. And that surprised me. I remember I first saw it screened at the National Film Theatre in 1983, this episode specifically chosen as part of the "Third Doctor Selected Gems" programme. It opens with two dinosaurs having a bit of a barney, and the audience laughter *that* caused never quite dissipated over the next 25 minutes. At age 13, you don't like to laugh at the things you love; it makes you think everyone is laughing at you too. Watching it again now... I'm delighted by the dino action. The story's taking the monsters from the title, and doing something with them at last! A tyrannosaurus rex bites into a brontosaurus neck (I love that syrupy blood!). The Doctor drives a jeep between another dinosaur's legs. It's great fun.

And maybe it's now because I'm sailing giddily through the twenty-first century, but the special effects don't bother me anymore. In 1983, the CSO puppets looked worse than anything I'd seen before. But in these days of CGI and bigger budgets, I'm finding that the "classic series" fx all look much the same to me. They either convince or they don't. And they usually don't. So I don't give them any more thought, and find myself accepting what is *supposed* to be conveyed so much more easily. I know realistically that the T. Rex I see here is worse than the one in The Silurians, but since neither of them make me feel I'm watching the real thing, neither seem appreciably more or less jarring than the other. I find this really rather wonderful. It seems as if the handicap has gone, that it doesn't much matter to me anymore. I'm looking forward to seeing

whether the Myrka, the Mara and the Bandrils have the same effect, that I'll just see them as an ordinary bit of eighties TV as much as the story pace and the multi-camera filming.

With all my wincing at the dinosaurs no longer a problem, I can relax and enjoy a conclusion that feels refreshingly mature. No-one dies, and no-one starts cackling insanely. The Doctor might describe Grover as mad, but the MP firmly believes up to the end that he's on the side of good – the scene that sells that to me better than any other is the way he's prepared to let a dissident like Sarah live in his brave new world and just gently hopes they will become friends one day. It's a refreshing throwback to the way Hulke treated General Carrington in The Ambassadors of Death, a man too that believed his ends justified the means. The only person throughout the episode that threatens the Doctor's life is actually Mike Yates. I love too the way that the story lets his plot fizzle out – there'd be the temptation to put him in at the climax, maybe to give him an act of noble heroism. Instead, he's not even given the dignity of an on-screen ending – and it's telling that he too tells the Doctor that he's not important any more. "Poor Mike" indeed, and how much more dramatic this way, and how much more adult.

You could criticise it for not really giving the story a climax. It really is a matter of throwing a switch, and armageddon is averted. But I'd disagree; I think it's very theatrical the way that all sides (the army, the scientists, the dupes on the spaceship) are brought together, and that their different voices are heard. It's low key, yes – but it's the emphasis upon the low key that gives the episode its credibility. Timothy Craven is terrific as a man who is adamant that he must be travelling to another planet because *he's sold his house!* And there are moments of quiet dignity from the likes of Terence Wilton as Mark or Brian Badcoe as Adam that are very winning – these men aren't heroes, but ordinary men who refuse to cross a line for their ideals. Yes, it's the same plot we saw in The Enemy of the World, but in that story all the people Salamander had kept below ground couldn't help but look idiotic. The people on the spaceship may be gullible, and they may be fanatics, but they're not evil. And it's rare for a story to come along this late into the Pertwee run which is about ordinary failings of impassioned men, and different attitudes towards responsibility.

And John Levene gets to beat up a general, and apologise politely in the process. What could be more splendid?

T: I think the model brontosaurus is very good – I too noticed it bled when the T. Rex unconvincingly gnawed its neck. Actually, Rex's mouth is so inflexible, he wisely gives up chomping and administers a pretty effective thwack with his tail. (That's what they should have had on the cover of the novelisation – T-thwack! instead of Kklak!)

Whilst poor old Martin Jarvis only has two lines this week, the other actors get a good slice of the action. Terence Wilton's enunciation of Mark's reaction to the conspirators' deception – a heartfelt "all those poor people..." – is very touching. Brian Badcoe brilliantly shows us Adam's unfamiliarity with technology as he forgets to switch the "receive" button on the two-way communicator, admonishing himself impatiently when he remembers. Benton's polite and deferential punching of his superior in the face is almost topped when he enjoys reliving the moment afterwards, only to have the Brig cut the triumph short with a withering stare. Even a minor character like Robinson (the only revived colonist to retain the power of speech, it seems) shows his true colours by lamenting how the biggest impact of the conspiracy's weave of lies is that he's sold his house! Special mention too, for Colin Bell as Private Bryson, who sweetly gets confused in the wake of conflicting orders, and is delighted to be charged with making the tea! It's a shame he doesn't get the moment in Hulke's excellent novel, where the Brig congratulates his world-saving elevenses (which distracts Yates enough for him to be overcome). Like Butler's scar, it's another sweet addition to the print version which would have been a really useful bit of texture in a six-part story – I'd rather have them than a protracted chase any day.

All in all, this has been a terrific adventure, with a great cast, a superb director and a really novel premise. Hulke obviously guessed that the dinosaurs were never going to be this serial's forte, and adeptly steered the story into more thoughtful territory. True, the moralising at the end is heavy handed, but so what? Not everything can afford to be subtle. Yates resigning off-screen is rather moving, and it's worth listening to the Doctor's pleas for him (and us) to take the world we've got and make it better. With his repudiation of the very idea of a previous Golden Age, the Doctor sagely dismisses that spurious reactionary dogma (still aired in some quarters) about a non-existent nirvana of a past where everyone was polite and the poor didn't complain because they knew their place.

Invasion of the Dinosaurs is never perfect. But it tries, and in his attempts to tell adventure stories whilst giving the youngsters brainfood, Malcolm Hulke can, I think, justifiably claim the title of Definitive Writer for the Third Doctor era. If only some of the things he stuck in his novels had occurred to him while writing his scripts, then his TV stories would make for an even richer experience – but then, hindsight is a luxury. Hulke's concerns about the danger posed by mankind's greed makes for apt viewing in a world gripped by the current financial crisis, and are proof positive that his writing has plenty to offer some 30 years after his death. He was certainly no dinosaur.

June 26th

Death to the Daleks (part one)

R: I was always predisposed to be unimpressed by Death to the Daleks. I first saw the story on 25th November, 1983. A friend had invited me to watch The Five Doctors broadcast at his house – under normal circumstances I wouldn't have gone, I'd have wanted to stay at home and ensure that my own video recording went without a hitch. But I was lured there by the promise that he'd had a long-ago story sent to him from Australia, and we could watch that beforehand, to "get us in the mood". In fact, I'd been in the mood since 1981 – The Five Doctors was one of the biggest events of my entire childhood. And I certainly didn't need some tired-looking adventure from 1974 to set the scene. As I watched the quarry action, and listened to Carey Blyton's peculiar score, I really rather began to hate the wretched story, and just wanted it to be all over so that we could watch The Five Doctors instead. I didn't want to see the Daleks chased by Pertwee – as it turns out, I'd much rather have watched them chase some Hartnell look-a-like in a bad wig.

Ever since, I've had the impression of Death as a story that is just marking time – in 1983, to my viewing of The Five Doctors, and in 1974, to Pertwee's exit from the series. And on the surface of it, we have indeed seen all this before. The TARDIS is in trouble, check. The Doctor finds some petrified remains on a hostile gravel planet, check. The episode ends with the surprise arrival of the very creatures announced in big bold letters in the title, check. But there's fun to be had with the clichés, as if the story is teasing you with their inevitability. When Sarah goes into the ship to change, she even double backs for reassurance that the Doctor won't wander off – she *knows* this is a Nation script, and that it depends upon their being speedily separated. The cliffhanger too invites us to guess in advance that the relief ship the humans so desperately need must be one piloted by the Daleks, and so there's a cruel irony given to their willingness to rush so excitedly towards it.

And besides, Michael Briant directs all this with real vigour, giving a freshness to the familiarity. The scenes set inside the dying TARDIS are wonderfully eerie; we haven't seen the Ship as forbidding as this since the days of early Hartnell, and the sequence where Sarah traps herself inside it with a hooded monster is terrific, in an instant removing all sense that it's the sanctuary we've come to rely on. (I love the crank handle used to open the doors, too.) There's violence (the opening is brutal enough that it was cut from the version I saw in 1983), and even blood. And the scene where Sarah first sees the City is absolutely gorgeous, giving a wonder to something alien that we haven't been offered in years. And Carey Blyton's score, at this point subtle and weird, perfectly marks the moment.

T: Moths Ate My Doctor Scarf in Haverhill tonight. I stumbled around the show for the first 15 minutes as a fan in the front row filmed bits of it. I eventually had to ask him, politely, to desist. I was very cross actually, because I found it extremely distracting. It's also, frankly

(hushed tones) not what you *do* in the theatre. I really wanted to have a go, but of course I'm a shrinking middle-class violet – so when he hung around afterwards, I merely laughed it off. There's no point being snotty with people, even though it would occasionally be cathartic. He did tell me he'd enjoyed the show more when he wasn't watching from behind a camera, though. I could have told him that beforehand! It was also nice to catch up with Dan Smith, who has seen the show a few times and even kindly driven me back to the train station on occasion, and some other fans I haven't seen since Gallifrey. Nice people, all of them.

Anyway, what of the episodes I enjoyed on the train journey home? Terry Nation's script delivers few surprises, but his Hartnellisms (there's even a petrified creature, and it's telling that we've both been reminded of that early era) are quite a breath of fresh air as we reach the end of Pertwee's tenure. For all of Nation's rather limited ambitions, you can't fault the man's grasp of adventure plotting: as Sarah approaches the city we're told, elsewhere, that going there means certain death. The much-maligned cliffhanger is touted as a major gaffe, but is much better than that (the Daleks open fire and we cut back to the cowering humans, as yet unaffected by the energy blasts). In these pre-laser beam days, we're used to a slight delay between the firing and the addition of the negative death effect, so there's no reason to suspect the Dalek weaponry isn't working.

The dormancy of the TARDIS removes the travellers' safe haven, and the planet's inhospitable nature is well conveyed in a cold, misty and atmospheric opening that sees stuntman Terry Walsh, true to form, fall down something within seconds of appearing. Matters become quite frightening when the TARDIS' dark echoey interior is invaded by the silent sack-beings from the planet Exxilon. Michael Briant shoots these potentially absurd creatures with a mixture of effective techniques: chillingly mute POV shots, snatched moments where they scuttle about the corner of the picture, quick glimpses of their full-length form, lingering fascination with their creepy hands or ingenious sequences where they are camouflaged amongst the rocks. A simple design, the Exxilons clearly look better on camera... unlike my comedy show, I hasten to add!

Death to the Daleks (part two)

R: You take a recognisable guest star like John Abineri (as Captain Railton), give every indication that he's to be the lead support of the story – and then abruptly shoot him dead within minutes of episode two. And with an arrow, no less. It's a wonderfully shocking moment, and manages to make the Exxilons seem the most threatening of all Terry Nation's stock "secondary baddies". If episode one was all about taking the standard Nation clichés and putting a bolder spin on them, then here he manages to wrongfoot us altogether. You can hardly believe he's really been killed, just like that, without so much as an exit line; when Jill Tarrant kneels beside his body, , you believe just as she does that a bit of TLC will make him right as rain.

Commander Stewart's death is rather effective as well. As a piece of writing, it's nothing special – the dying leader telling his expected successor (rather tactlessly, I'd have thought) that he's got someone else in mind for his job. But the sincere hurt of Duncan Lamont's reaction, and the background chanting of the Exxilon priests, give an unusual weight to the melodrama. (Actually, a silly word about that chanting – I keep on thinking it sounds exactly like like they're using a recording of Roger Delgado calling out to Azal. Which it couldn't be, could it? That'd be daft. And, considering the poor man died just before this began filming, would have been even more tactless than Stewart ending his life telling Galloway he's a bit too rubbish to take command.)

I consciously nicked a piece of this for my own Dalek episode, the way that the Daleks nervously back away from the Doctor when they realise their guns don't work. I think Eccleston gives the moment a bit more welly than Jon Pertwee does, though – we know Pertwee's none too keen on Daleks, and he seems to respond to scenes shared with them with rather bland disdain. It's a pity, because the concept behind this tale is the cleverest use of Daleks since their revival – that they're forced to cooperate with the humans is very appealing. I think the premise is thrown away far too soon, though; I love the way the Daleks practise their new machine guns on model TARDISes, and their only grudging acceptance

of their new weaponry after they've shot down a couple of hapless Exxilons, but I'd much rather have seen this awkward alliance put centre stage.

T: There's something about arrows – thudding into the sand and whistling through the air, they seem more palpably dangerous than a laser gun. You wince every time one embeds itself a hair's breadth away from real human actors, including an admirably prone John Abineri. His death is indeed shocking – he's solid and dependable as ever, and certainly didn't seem a candidate for an early bath. I discussed his premature demise on screen with his son Sebastian when he came to see Moths in Westcliff-On-Sea. Apparently, having got an Emmy nomination for his performance in Last of the Mohicans (and appearing in a follow-up, Hawkeye the Pathfinder), Abineri Sr was light on offers of work until the Doctor Who gig came up. Having spent ages playing a Native American, he was somewhat put out to discover his very next TV role entailed an arrow killing him! The story's decision to murder its best actor first, by the way, almost certainly guarantees Joy Harrison's Jill Tarrant eternal life.

Where the directing is concerned, Michael Briant applies some imagination to the potentially dreary and hokey sacrifice scenes. He uses Sarah's drug-induced haze as an excuse to play with the sound: it's woozy, indistinct and echoey. When the Daleks start their massacre, Briant orchestrates the melee well, with all the background mess out of our focus as a lone Exxilon slides to its death directly in front of the camera. And the cliffhanger, which involves the derobed Exxilon Bellal, showcases a nifty new effect depicting the shiny veins running along his body.

There's a few glitches, I grant you... the Doctor's torch didn't work in episode one, and yet the Dalek speech lights are working this week – perhaps if they ever give up trying to conquer the universe, they can set up their own illumination emporium. Also, the script emphasises that four Daleks reveal themselves to the humans, but the cast list names only three operators. As a result, one of them stands very still indeed. This is probably a sensible policy, as one of his more mobile fellows is beaten to death, rather gruesomely, by the Exxilon equivalent of a lynch mob. It's surprisingly terrifying to hear one of the arrogant, all-conquering space bastards screaming in terror.

June 27th

Death to the Daleks (part three)

R: The nice Exxilons pop out, and immediately all the menace that made this distinctive goes out of the project. (Even Carey Blyton's music, haunting and weird at first, now feels like it's gone pantomime – the theme that greets the Daleks on every appearance sounds a little like the wah-wah-wah noise that'd greet a silent comedian making a prat fall.) But it's Elisabeth Sladen who provides the bridge from the moody half of the story to this, the two-episode jogaround showcasing the Doctor competing on the Krypton Factor. I'd say her best performance yet is in the scene where she first talks to one of the natives, Bellal – not because the material is so great, but because she takes all the awkward exposition she's being fed and humanises it. The way she struggles to be polite, whilst clearly being repelled by her new alien friend, is beautifully done – and it's capped by the moment when, in her concern for the Doctor, and urging the Exxilon to help her, she forgets her fear and grabs on to him.

And just as effective is the quiet way that she accepts the Doctor's goodbye, and listens when he tells her that should he die, she must return to Earth with the colonists. The scene is a familiar one – and, let's face it, we have no real reason to believe the Doctor is in any greater danger than he'd be in any other episode – but the sincerity with which Sladen plays it makes this something truly special. Pertwee's clearly rather tired of the proceedings, but the conviction of his co-star always makes him raise his game whenever they appear together – there's such a terrific (and natural) rapport between the two of them, I can't help but wish Sladen had been around during Pertwee's heyday. To see them sparking off each other during The Daemons or Carnival of Monsters would have been marvellous.

T: Like you, I suspect, I grew up surrounded by World War II films on the telly – which is I why I find it meaningful when Terry Nation here plunders such stories, and gives us recognisable tropes from them in a science-fiction setting. In the past, he's given us resistance groups and mass conquest, and here we get slave-labour camps and collaborators. Grounding the outlandish with more familiar elements is a savvy approach to the sort of drama Doctor Who does well.

Sadly, things take a downturn once the story enters the Exxilon city. The logic puzzle-solving proves about as dramatic as a golf match between pensioners, and, frankly, you'd have thought those skeletons would have tried the maze conundrum just to relieve their boredom, and solved it before starving to death. It's hardly the most taxing of enigmas, which leads me to the rather cruel conclusion that anyone thick enough not to work it out probably deserved to die. Accentuating the oddness of this whole segment, Carey Blyton's theme for the Daleks seems specifically designed to rob them of any menace. It's like choosing to score the devil's own horde with the theme tune to The Flumps. Forget the City, that most definitely puzzles the logic, as does the rightly ridiculed cliffhanger, with its Threatening Mosaic of Doom! What next, The Lino of Destruction?

Production-wise, there's a lot to appreciate... Michael Briant seems very comfortable on location, his wide shots of the alien vista augmented by a goodie Exxilon observing events in the foreground. The massive root monster impressively rises out of the water and spitefully kills a Dalek (they really go through it in this story – Death to the Daleks indeed!). The poor Exxilon supernumeraries fare little better – and like the arrows, death by fire is an extremely unpleasant prospect, because we can actually anticipate the pain involved in a way that's more difficult with a laser beam.

And forgive me for being repetitive (but if it's good enough for Terry Nation, it's good enough for me): Elisabeth Sladen is worth her weight in gold. Her repulsion in the Bellal scene gives her much humanity. She doesn't take all this space stuff in her stride – she catches on that Bellal is benign (and how couldn't you; Arnold Yarrow is delightful), but remains jumpy in his presence because, well, he's a funny looking alien. When the Doctor answers her question with a line of babble incomprehensible to a terrified Earthling, she shyly asks "a what, where?" She's embarrassed that she doesn't understand, but brave enough to admit it. Her combination of pluck and tentativeness make her an ideal audience identification figure, and she never behaves as if her encounters are all in a day's work for a character in this kind of programme.

Death to the Daleks (part four)

R: This isn't very good. But it's an interesting not very good. It's an episode of a story which has lost patience with what it's supposed to be about, and is casting about for something new. The Daleks are really hardly in it at all, and what they do is distinctly out of character. The one that hysterically self-destructs simply because its prisoner has escaped is weird enough, but that entire ending – where the Dalek decides it really can't be *bothered* to kill the Doctor and friends when it's got them cornered is just ludicrous. Jon Pertwee's reaction to being captured by the Daleks in the final reel has the amused shrug of a man caught without his umbrella in a rain shower, or getting to the post office just a minute after the staff have gone to lunch – it's *annoying*, the expression seems to say, but you've got to laugh, haven't you? Or maybe it's the shrug of an actor who never understood what the appeal of the Daleks was in the first place, and has found nothing within this script to make him think otherwise. The indignities the Daleks suffer throughout these last two episodes – and I'm not merely thinking of Carey Blyton's saxophone music – is surely the most half-hearted treatment they've ever had in the series. The sequence where they're attacked by the lumbering antibodies in the City reminded me of that bit in The Chase where they're set upon by Frankenstein's Monster. But that was trying to be funny.

But the reason behind this is clear. This is Robert Holmes' first story where he takes on script-editing duties – albeit in an uncredited capacity. And you see that he puts all his attention into little themes and moments he'll turn to with greater effect over the next few seasons.

That Pyramids of Mars steals from this are so obvious, they're even referenced in the script – but there's also The Hand of Fear here (the sinister figure watching the Doctor on a monitor, who turns out to be dead), The Deadly Assassin (the Doctor fighting an illusion)... and there's a hint of Genesis of the Daleks too, as Holmes takes a Dalek story and quite deliberately makes them subordinate to the main action. Death to the Daleks has a very weak ending, but for once I don't feel it's simply down to laziness, but to a production team that are actually so fired up by future possibilities that they can't quite be bothered to finish what they're currently working on. There's a buzz of excitement within this – it's just not for Death to the Daleks. What we have here is a work in progress that got junked along the way, and yet still somehow made the screen – it's a transitional story, messy, unresolved and rather fascinating for that reason.

T: You're right... it all goes a bit pear shaped here. The City scenes are tedious and unable to depict the requirements of the script – never has there been so much talk of the organic nature of something which, in aspect, is all straight lines and flat surfaces. The idea of the City having "antibodies" is neat, but doesn't really tie in with the visuals, whilst the floor puzzle is pointless in the extreme. (And again – logic is mentioned as often as organics, but there's precious little of it in any of the puzzle-solutions.) The decision to show a mysterious figure watching the Doctor and Bellal injects some menace, but they haven't half had to jump through a lot of boring hoops – especially considering that when they reach their destination, they need only muck about with a few wires.

Things are better outside, with the night-time setting providing some much needed atmosphere, as does the whistling wind that accompanies Galloway and Hamilton's excursion to the beacon. The model City looks good in the dark, and its destruction has a strange beauty about it, especially the juxtaposition between the faint screeching that issues as it melts and the beguiling musical accompaniment.

And the Daleks' plan to unleash a plague missile is suitably nasty – they're at their best when callously promising to do immeasurable horrors, but that moment where one self-destructs because Joy Harrison's done a runner is so embarrassing, I had to look away from the telly. I did get a minor moment of enjoyment as one of them started screeching "Evacuate! Evacuate!", but I'll let you provide your own punchline to that.

If nothing else, in depicting a man exploding his enemies and himself in an act of noble, redemptive self-sacrifice, Death to the Daleks can always be remembered as the Doctor Who story that, in the light of the current world situation, has some interesting things to say about suicide bombing. Hmm... I'm not sure what I think about that, and maybe that's a good sign. It hasn't happened enough with this story, but my thoughts have been provoked.

The Monster of Peladon (part one)

R: And here we are, at the start of everyone's second favourite Peladon story. The Doctor has taken Sarah to visit old friends, and we're invited to ask what has changed to the society in 50 years. The answer is, not a lot: there's a weak monarch, a suspicious high priest, a phallic ambassador and mutterings against the Federation to spare. There's even another mute King's Champion – is grunting a requirement for a Pel bodyguard? As an exercise in recreating the look of an adventure broadcast over two years previously, this is remarkable – the sets and costumes feel as if they were deliberately put into mothballs awaiting the sequel. But we wait in vain to see subtle signs of development, of how Peladon might surprise us after all this time.

Now, it could be argued that that's rather clever, and exactly what Brian Hayles is trying to depict. That The Monster of Peladon has a sterile culture, and that for all the way in which entry into the Federation was held up as a totem in Curse, it's actually done nothing for the planet whatsoever, they're exactly where they were before. All well and good, but it's hard to make something dramatic out of sterility. In synopsis, there's a lot of action in this episode; there are several deaths by ghost monster, there's armed rebellion and accusations of sabotage and sentences of death fly around like nobody's business. But already this

feels overfamiliar. I might suggest that there's something deliberate about the fact that even *lines* get repeated – "You're not scared, big chap like you?" says the Doctor, as he patronises yet another Champion – but I can already hear Toby Hadoke smirk at my postmodern pretensions. That the greatest shock of the episode is that Blor gets killed in the cliffhanger – when his predecessor Grun survived the whole story – speaks volumes to me. The Monster of Peladon only surprises when it makes those little deviations from the source material, not because there's anything necessarily dramatic in them themselves. It's typical that the only new alien is Vega Nexos – who looks wonderfully weird, and sounds gloriously posh in spite of it – and he gets bumped off within minutes.

T: I wasn't smirking, I promise – indeed, my initial impression is that Brian Hayles uses our familiarity with the setting to his advantage. Chancellor Ortron does much of the same ritualistic hokum as Hepesh, wrong-footing us into thinking he's going to be the villain of the piece. The Queen's Champion brings to mind Grun as an ally for the Doctor to patronise, so yes, it's a surprise when he's promptly wiped out (and emits a strange cawing death scream – it's the death rattle equivalent of nails on a blackboard). Entertainingly, Michael Crane, who plays Blor, latterly listed himself as Big Michael Crane in Spotlight, as if to emphasise the main quality he brought to any acting role. (Perhaps, to make casting easier, all actors should have a descriptive shorthand prefix – like Creepy Milton Johns, Foreign Tutte Lemkow or Obviously The Bad Guy Philip Madoc.)

In returning the Doctor to an old haunt, it feels as if the production team are tacitly acknowledging Pertwee's imminent departure by giving him something of a farewell tour. The opening scenes, all on film, look like they've decided to throw a bit of money at it and widen the scale of the adventure. Unfortunately, Lennie Mayne seems to have lost a lot of his zip, and the studio-bound stuff looks somewhat frayed around the edges.

Gerald Taylor, encased in rather a good make-up job as the satyr-like alien Vega Nexos, does indeed sound posh – and the strong, classical actor's performance that he gives suggests he's been rather wasted inside a Dalek casing for the past few years. It's odd that Nexos' determination to prove that Aggedor is a trick makes him forget that it's a trick that nevertheless recently killed a miner, leading to his own horrifying death. Still, his presence livens up the episode's visual palette for even the few minutes he's on screen. As Taylor has given good service to Doctor Who since the second-ever story, and this marks his last appearance in the show, I salute him for all his efforts.

There's no such salutations for Sarah, I fear, who is written as stroppy and ill-mannered. Even when she and the Doctor have established themselves as good guys, a guard shoves her in the back as she leaves, evidently because he simply doesn't like her very much. Sarah nonetheless gets the best scene of the lot, where her disquiet at Alpha Centauri's appearance leads to a well-judged exchange and cements Centauri's position as one of the era's most memorable and likeable creations.

However, I can't fathom how anyone thought that making the miners look like badgers, and giving Ortron a pink beard, was a good idea. Perhaps that's how the feudal system on Peladon manifests itself: your status, position – hey even your job – is predetermined by your hair. I hope a load of Mohican-sporting dinner ladies file past in tomorrow's episode.

June 28th

The Monster of Peladon (part two)

R: It's good to see that Donald Gee (as Eckersley) pays tribute to Jon Pertwee in this, his penultimate adventure. When Gee's character is knocked unconscious, he affects the same pose as the Doctor – right knee up, ready for anything.

There's an interesting idea here, that the Doctor's previous energies towards making Peladon a member of the Galactic Federation have resulted in nothing but harm for the workers, but, like similar moves this season towards turning the expected on its head (Yates is a traitor, UNIT hunts the Doctor, the Daleks are weaponless allies), it's hardly

exploited at all. Indeed, Gebek so quickly welcomes the Doctor as an ally that it makes both of their characters seem far too bland and accommodating. And although everybody else snarls a lot and is distrustful of everybody (and no-one can snarl quite like Ralph Watson), it doesn't make the political situation seem more complex... just more *annoying*, somehow. When Queen Thalira lisps her puzzlement as to why the Doctor has turned against her, you want to shout at the screen that it's because she's a pusillanimous git.

Or maybe that's just me.

T: Terrance Dicks has remarked that the parallels between the politics of the Peladon stories and events in early 1970s Great Britain are entirely coincidental. With all due respect to that affable and witty legend of the Doctor Who universe, his memory might be erring on the side of, erm, cheating. It's quite heavy-handed, sure, but let's not forget that Doctor Who is a family show, and when and where it comes to terms with, or indeed mirrors, political situations dividing the country, then more power to its elbow.

Unfortunately, Brian Hayles seems determined to render his protagonists in a solely singular dimension. There's Grumpy Ettis the Hothead – his motives for being a trouble-maker are that, um, troublemaking is his one characteristic. And there's Chancellor Ortron, who behaves like an antagonist simply because the script needs one – he's such an old stick-in-the-mud that he bullishly tries to incriminate Sarah and the Doctor despite all the pretty digestible reasons he's given against doing so. Centauri constantly reminds us that Peladon is a barbarous planet – seemingly an attempt by Hayles to rationalise Ortron's bloodlust and the miners' rather dubious tactic of settling an industrial dispute with cold-blooded murder, but I'm afraid I don't really buy it. And if everyone expects us to fondly remember the previous Peladon peregrination, then I'd question the effectiveness of a cliffhanger that asks us to be terrified of a creature that we know the Doctor can easily tame.

There's some upsides to all of that... Donald Gee adeptly portrays Eckersley as a detached, disinterested observer of local politics; he's a seemingly shifty, self-interested and pragmatic man, but at this juncture isn't an obvious skulking villain. Centauri proves that he/ she has guile as well as charm as he/ she gently manipulates the Queen into taking positive action. Even the miner Preba adds a bit of texture with his flawless knowledge of the sprawling tunnels – he played in them as a child (when he was a minor miner!), which suggests a credible history and backstory to a society beyond what a handful of extras can normally convey.

Oh, and it's not just hair – you can obviously only ascend to the giddy heights of nobility on Peladon if you have a lisp (first King Peladon, now Thalira and Ortron). No wonder Pertwee feels at home. Should Violet Elisabeth Bott ever visit the planet, she'll end up ruling it forever.

The Monster of Peladon (part three)

R: I once made a very cruel joke to Donald Gee. I was working with him on a BBC show called Born and Bred, and he was one of the regular cast – and by far the kindest and most amiable actor there. One late night after a read-through, the whole production team holed up in a hotel in Preston, and he found out that I was a Doctor Who fan. "I was in Doctor Who", he told me. "I know," I replied. "You were in The Space Pirates and The Monster of Peladon. And you were so bad in them, that both times the Doctors quit during their very next story. They knew it was time to bail out when the show had to resort to Donald Gee!" Even as I write that, it sounds harsh beyond measure, but you'll have to bear in mind the light tease of my voice, the gentle laugh I gave afterwards, and (more relevantly) the exact quantity of lager that had been consumed. But the look of genuine concern that flitted across Donald's face at that moment quite broke my heart. "Oh dear God," he said. "That must be true, mustn't it?"

It's not Donald Gee's fault that the penultimate adventures for Troughton and Pertwee hardly showcase Doctor Who at its best. His Eckersley is one of the best things about this episode. On paper, you can see he's a villain; he persuades Alpha Centauri to call in the Ice Warriors, he won't let anyone investigate the

refinery, he suggests to the court that Sarah may be a terrorist. But Gee plays the part with such affability you can believe, as Sarah does, that he's always just misguided or mistaken, that the one Earthman in the adventure is a good guy who hasn't quite committed to our heroes yet. It's a really skilful performance, because there's really very little in the dialogue that would lead you to trust him. We play along with Eckersley, because of Donald Gee's unforced charm.

And Elisabeth Sladen, once again, is just terrific. When I was a young fan, I hated the scene where she tells the queen all the advantages of Women's Lib; I didn't *like* girls when I was twelve. Now it seems a bit clunky, but so well-intentioned I can't but help smile – and it's Sladen who makes the whole thing feel less like a moral message, but instead natural earnestness. She's the one who takes the secret message to Gebek when the Doctor can't; you want to cheer her as she mocks Ortron for his pomposity, or comes up with the plan to get rid of the Federation troops – and that knowing smirk she gives us, sharing with the audience her belief that the Doctor has already broken out of his cell, is just delightful.

[Rob's addendum, written June 2016: Born and Bred was created and showrun by a chap called Chris Chibnall. I always wondered whatever happened to him.]

T: Hooray for Donald Gee indeed. He always stood out amongst Doctor Who guest stars in my house because of The Doctor Who Monster Book, which I once delightedly alighted upon amongst Reader's Digests and encyclopaedias whilst scouring our shelves at home for reading matter. (That's the advantage of having older brothers: you can find books you never knew the family even had.) All the actors who played regulars received a thank you at the back of the book, for the kind permission to use photos of them – as was a Mr Donald Gee. For years, I wondered who he was (a question answered in Doctor Who Magazine's Matrix Data Bank some years later). I can't get used to him without a moustache, though, as my brother scrawled one on the picture of him and Sarah staring in horror at the Aggedor stature on page whatever-it-was. I've met the man himself – he's a kind and genial, with an air of contentment sometimes absent from those who've spent decades in an ego-battering profession that affords most only modest success.

As for Pertwee... well, many a performer would feel rather self-conscious singing a silly alien song to a man dressed in a rug, but he retains his dignity whilst gamely giving full voice to his Venusian ditty. He's a trifle more hesitant (or perhaps paying special tribute to William Hartnell) when sounding distracted in the mines, answering Rex Robinson's concerns with the rather meandering line "Quite so, old chap, but still, we've got to think of first things first". He also spends rather too much time getting captured (and having to endure a God-awful "get-the-hacked-off-guard-to-watch-a-magic-trick" shtick), so it's left to Sarah to use her initiative and work out that something might be afoot in the refinery. Lis Sladen also has to endure that terrifyingly bad exchange about Women's Lib with Nina Thomas, after Pertwee delivers a slightly less offensive (but somewhat too literal and didactic) lecture in industrial relations. It's not that I don't like girls, by the way, it's just that I hate terrible dialogue.

But, let's be nice. Frank Gatliff (as Ortron) has a good line in courteous villainy, bowing to his Queen with requisite pomp whilst disobeying her orders and making sly barbs about women, and Rex Robinson gives a stoic turn of solid dependability, making it easy to see why the Doctor and his fellow miners trust Gebek so. Lennie Mayne generously gives us a shot of Ortron, Alpha and the Queen looking down into the pit as the Doctor yells up at them – a handy reminder of the supposed layout of the two sets. But, truth be told, I'm forced to damn with faint praise, by pointing out that my favourite thing here is the design of the drinking goblets in the throne room. Horns augmented with decorative stands, they are both practical and attractive whilst being consistent with the idea of an alien society lacking in technology. I'll drink to that.

The Monster of Peladon (part four)

R: We bonded over The Monster of Peladon 4, didn't we, Toby? Early on in our friendship, we went out for a drink, and you told me that

the very next day you were moderating on the DVD commentary for the story. It may have been something in the food we were eating – or more likely the quantity of wine we'd ordered to accompany it – but we vaguely talked about my popping up on one of the episodes and chatting about it too. What a jolly jape! – because I professed a deep *loathing* for The Monster of Peladon, the story I remember most boring me into a stupor as a kid. The next morning, I received a phone call from you: so, was I coming to the BBC to record this thing or not? And I struggled blearily into my clothes, and on to the tube to White City. I remember feeling embarrassed I was going to be talking over an episode I hadn't seen for so many years. And even more embarrassed when I realised that Terrance Dicks and Barry Letts were going to be there – I didn't want to be snide about their work, certainly not whilst they could hear, because I'm both a coward *and* a hypocrite. (I can well imagine how I'll feel in 30 years' time, recording some special hologram discussion for Dalek on the latest sci-fi technology, only to have some arrogant youth working on Doctor Who's latest screen revival turning up and patronising me about it.)

But I needn't have worried. Because episode four of The Monster of Peladon is terrific. The arrival of the Ice Warriors utterly transforms a story that was rather plodding and half-hearted into something with real pace and point. It'd be an exaggeration to say that the speed with which the warring factions of the Peladonians unite against their common enemy is *moving*, but it gives them both a dignity that has been missing from the story so far. And Alan Bennion is frankly wonderful, giving his very best performance for the series. His Azaxyr has an ironic wit, the capacity to discuss execution with the Doctor so very casually; after all the shouting and medieval posturing we've seen displayed in the story, this is refreshingly free from melodrama. (And it's clever too that the one character in the adventure who is just as modern sounding, and just as pragmatic, is Eckersley – which subtly suggests too that the real villains of the piece are the ones who are the least bogged down in archaic dialogue; it's a complete volte-face from the situation in Curse.) That Azaxyr looks and sounds just like Izlyr – understandably enough, since it's the same actor in the same costume – means that this is the first time in the story that the ingredients from Curse are being stirred differently to good dramatic effect. The last time any child would have seen an evil Ice Warrior would have been six years previously, and in black and white; to all intents and purposes, seeing Alan Bennion so callously behave as villain here has the same effect as if Alpha Centauri had been revealed as a cold-blooded murderer.

After all the pontificating and running about of the previous few episodes, the Ice Warriors just cut through the red tape. The sequence where, without warning, they just gun down the rebel miners is fantastic, because it feels like they're almost flippantly wiping out an entire subplot that they'd found tedious. That Azaxyr immediately afterwards turns to Queen Thalira, and with studied politeness *apologises* for the brutal massacre, is not only very funny but actually chilling – here's a character that is going to use diplomatic jargon and protocol even whilst being a cold and savage killer. It means that when, later on, he turns to the Doctor and almost appears to *chat* with him amiably about whether he should be killed on the spot, you utterly believe that he's in greater danger of sudden death than we've seen for entire seasons.

T: Did we bond? I seem to recall you being quite funny, and me not so much. A fan commentary, eh? I was never really a fan of that idea myself. Fans hate other fans almost as much as they hate themselves (and I include myself in this equation – from both ends of it).

This is by far the best episode of the story, with the Ice Warriors arriving to fill the exact same role, at the exact same point, that the Master did in Colony in Space; they're pretending to adjudicate whilst working to their own evil agenda. As Azaxyr, Alan Bennion wisely avoids too arch a portrayal, and opts instead for an effective, blunt menace, and he's subtly different to both of his previous performances under the same latex. He's clipped, courteous, authoritarian, straightforward about his ruthlessness and power, and brazen about his continued distrust regarding the miners' apparent co-operation. His costume

has a sleek elegance that his tattier cohorts don't quite possess, and he even gets a moment to admire the Doctor for making a good fist of his fight with Ettis.

The writing is also much better this week. Gebek's cunning speech (in which he urges the miners to rebel whilst seemingly urging co-operation with the Martians) is a neat ruse – he may as well have said "Friends, Peladonians, Countrymen". Elsewhere, Sarah's observation about Ortron's willingness to let his people be killed, so long as it's him doing the killing, is a neat summary of unprincipled politicking. I was also delighted to note that whilst the Peladonians are rightly furious about their exploitation by the Federation, they may be forgetting the benefits of this alliance – which include, if this episode is to be believed, the supply of a wheelbarrow!

Among the guest cast, Roy Evans manages the minor miracle of being typecast as a doomed miner, whilst Terry Walsh contrives to pop up everywhere. Anytime we require a guard who must A) speak or B) be hit on the head, Walsh is gamely trotted in. Heck, he even gives us his Doctor Who this week, battling with a shamefully OTT Ralph Watson before a big explosion which wonderfully stays audibly present as the credits roll.

June 29th

The Monster of Peladon (part five)

R: We get a lovely foreshadowing of the Doctor's death from the next story – Sarah believes that he's dead, and mourns him as the most alive person she's ever met. "While there's life, there's..." Sladen plays this scene especially well – so well, in fact, that her rushing off into danger just to be by his side when she sees him on a monitor screen some minutes later doesn't come across as contrived at all, but a genuine expression of relieved joy.

It's a peculiar episode, this, because it requires so many of its characters to play against type. Frank Gatliff is terrific as an Ortron reimagined with dignity and human compassion – the shame he feels when his Queen tells she refuses to be a puppet queen, and the genuine sympathy he offers

Sarah as she grieves for the Doctor, make him a far more well-rounded person than we've seen up to now. Although he dies within the very same scene that he becomes likeable, Gatliff gives the characterisation shift enough sincerity that it's still moving.

Elsewhere, though, it's not as effective. Once Eckersley is unmasked as a traitor, Donald Gee no longer seems to know how to play the part – up to now, he's been effective by downplaying everything, but now he almost mumbles his way through his villainous lines. No better is Nina Thomas; required to show a bit of silent defiance to Azaxyr's threats, she merely looks bored, or as if she's forgotten what her next line ought to be. ("Can you faint convincingly?" Sarah asks her at one point – which in this context seems a bit more barbed than is intended.) Ysanne Churchman too, as Alpha Centauri, seems rather embarrassed by a lot of her lines, and has taken to whispering them; a lot of the scenes she's in feel like dry rehearsals rather than proper records. Alan Bennion is still wonderful – just look at the energy he brings to the scenes he's in, no matter that we can't see his face! – but his dialogue has lost much of its diplomatic wit, and he's reduced to being a green thug in a cape.

There are good bits here and there. Pertwee seems a bit tired, but comes to life when showing angry concern for Sarah. And Ysanne Churchman too leaps upon her only really funny line with confidence, when Donald Gee spares her life: "Thank you, Eckersley, but you're still a traitor!".

T: It's strange, this era. We've had the Ogron monster and Kalik's demise cut from the all-important climaxes for the sake of aesthetic plausibility, yet this episode reprise contains the Terry Walsh Doctor just for benefit of those who missed it last week. Odd.

Building upon your remarks... Sarah's description of the Doctor as the "most alive person I've ever met" is as apt an epitaph for the eponymous hero as I can think of. It also helps to trigger Ortron's rehabilitation – having started off as the obvious baddie, his tenderness at this juncture is refreshing as the script flirts with the idea of making him three-dimensional. But just as Ortron threatens to become interesting, he sacrifices his life so his

Queen can escape. And then! Instead of seizing the opportunity to take her leave, the Queen hangs around blubbing long enough for the Ice Warriors to ensure she remains their prisoner. In rendering Ortron's bravery utterly unnecessary, Thalira acquires additional points on the Rubbish-Monarch-ometer.

The baddies, however, are also acting strangely – as when they outline their plans very loudly, just in case any passing eavesdroppers need clues. They may as well be doing the old Comic Strip Presents Famous Five gag, where the baddies are overheard saying "Blah blah blah, secret treasure, blah blah blah, meet at the caves". In the face of such obvious nonsense and a plot that's running out of steam, Alan Bennion maintains an enviable classiness, and is far and away the best thing on display. His Martian cohorts, alas, haven't benefited from the glossy green paintjob they've been given – it makes them look like Airfix models rather than lizard warriors.

The Monster of Peladon (part six)

R: We get a lovely foreshadowing of the Doctor's death from the next story – Sarah believes that he's dead, and mourns him... hang on, didn't we get that all last week? It's still the best scene in the episode, mind you. The comatose Doctor being woken by a tear splashing from Sarah's face is rather a beautiful image, frankly, and Sladen and Pertwee are just about perfect together – Sladen relieved and angry by the Doctor's survival, and Pertwee somewhat bemused that she thought he was dead in the first place. It really *does* feel like a set-up for the end of Planet of the Spiders, where the Doctor's arrogance deals him a mortal blow after all – and that sequence of Pertwee reacting with such blasé indifference to Sarah's tears has a real impact in light of the next time he's called to comment upon them.

There's a lot of good stuff in this episode... *in theory*. I can well see how the courtroom scene in which the miners confront and murder Azaxyr could have been properly tense and climactic – but it looks awkward on the screen, becoming nothing more than a scuffle with extras. Even better might have been that bit where Eckersley pulls the Queen through all the dead bodies in the tunnels – she hisses at him to look at the devastation he's caused, and you can see what's intended, that he stares with some shocked bewilderment at where his opportunism and greed have taken him. But there's no time, or focus, or love – they're sequences which were *designed* to have an impact, but get chucked away with no sense of their importance.

I think, sadly, that rather embodies The Monster of Peladon. It's not nearly as bad a story as I'd always believed. Yes, it's too long. Yes, it's repetitive. (Max Faulkner gets killed twice in the same corridor within a few minutes, which does seem to sum up the adventure as a whole.) But it does have points it wants to make about corrupted ideals and disillusionment – and with a better cast, and with more exciting direction, I think those points may have been dramatic and engaging. As it turns out, this story seems to me to mark the end of an era. It's the last *ordinary* six-part serial. From now on, Doctor Who will only use this length to tell stories that are suitably epic, or act as the climax to a season. They won't always be pretty, but they'll never again feel like hand-me-down adventures that just happen to go on for two and a half hours – like Colony in Space, say, or The Mutants, or Invasion of the Dinosaurs, decent enough premises that in no way justify the drawn-out running time. Under new producer Philip Hinchcliffe, the six-parter will become the end of season splurge, and under Graham Williams, it'll always reach towards being something important to the show's mythology. John Nathan-Turner and Russell T Davies will use the length only the once – and both times on stories intended to be grand showstoppers. In a trice, the whole format of Doctor Who's storytelling is about to be altered – from now on, the idea is that it is to be pacier and punchier. That's the theory, anyway. The Monster of Peladon is the last of the old warhorses – it blunders around the field of battle and whinnies a bit from time to time, but something leaner and sharper is about to be unleashed. And for that reason, bumbling and boring as it often is, I have a lot of affection for it.

T: Pertwee's on a murder spree again, programming the Aggedor statue to massacre the Ice Warriors. Is it because they is green? But,

whatever, he's on good form throughout this episode. In fact, his suffering under Eckersley's mental onslaught is so palpable, I'm curious as to whether contemporary viewers might have thought the regeneration they'd doubtless heard about was imminent. The Doctor's brave, and at first unflustered, refusal to leave the refinery as the treacherous engineer lets him have it is pretty damned heroic. Pertwee looks like he's really suffering, and Elisabeth Sladen manages real tears upon finding him comatose. All of this makes for a genuine shock when the Doctor wakes – the way in which Sarah's relief turns to anger comes across as a very human response, in what's the most effectively rendered part of the episode.

Elsewhere, as you note, Max Faulkner is indeed killed twice. He's got form for this, if you remember, as he popped up in The Ambassadors of Death after a fatal encounter with a spacesuit. Before Faulkner's second expiration here, I gave credit to Donald Gee for playing Eckersley as an amoral schemer who nonetheless couldn't resort to hands-on murder (thus sparing Sarah for a more believable reason than because the actress playing her is a series regular). And then Max showed up, and Gee zapped him with all but a token regret! Maybe it's because he knows that when one Max falls, another will arise. Indeed, when everyone's celebrating in the throne room, there Faulkner is again, alive and well for a third time.

So... that's the last we see of the Ice Warriors on screen, then. As well as their impressive costume design and Alan Bennion's brilliant performance, they've been a genuine attempt to create a plausible alien species within the confines of family drama. Bennion has never had a duff moment, so it's regretful that his final scene sees him despatched in an unmemorable Death-By-Extra moment. We get an ill-advised close-up of Ssorg too, when it's obvious that his mouth isn't moving as he says his line. (It's very odd that they went to the trouble of giving a monster a mouth roughly where the actor's mouth *is*, but then don't bother to make it moveable.)

Still, the legacy of the Ice Warriors' work is apparent as Eckersley makes his escape with Thalira. The tunnels are littered with the bodies of the dead: a stark illustration of the consequences of evil and quite an affecting image. Aggedor's death is rather sad, especially as Pertwee conveyed a certain (if patronising) rapport with the beast. Eckersley's cries of "help me Doctor" as he struggles to free himself from the walking carpet's grip are pretty grim – especially as the Time Lord doesn't bother to help, and afterwards turns Eckersley's corpse over with no concern whatsoever. After six episodes of being a bit of a limp presence, Nina Thomas finally gets a decent moment as the Queen, acknowledging that she knows the Doctor is sneaking off, never to be seen again. Peladon is in safe, if not very well acted, hands.

June 30th

Planet of the Spiders (part one)

R: For a story that's so decidedly pivotal, this first episode is deliberately low key. And gloriously so, I might add. The opening few minutes are so skilful. That first scene, utterly free of music, the only sound that of birdsong, shows a man walking to camera – only to surprise us that this man in civvies is someone we recognise as Mike Yates. We cut to the Doctor and the Brigadier – not in earnest consultation of an alien threat, but watching (bad) comedians and belly dancers at what looks like some sort of village hall. And then something creepy starts to happen in the background – we hear Tibetan chanting, we see Mike spying on it – and we pan across the crypt to realise we're *not* watching priests in long-flowing robes preparing for sacrifice, but a bunch of middle-aged men in jackets squatting on the floor.

I think that's all very witty. There's not much hint of a specific *threat* here – indeed, the people who most feel threatened are those poor people wanting to meditate in solitude, who are none too thrilled by a pushy journalist called Sarah turning up and being nosey. Until the cliffhanger, there's only one moment of actual danger, and that involves an imaginary tractor. But it's that very gentleness which gives the episode its unease. Lupton and Barnes mark themselves out as villains early on not because of anything alien, but because they treat a poor simpleton with contempt, and cause him to crush his pretty flower. It gives

them a presence which is so brooding, you can easily believe that they've so spooked Mike Yates – who's braved down alien threats aplenty – that he might run for help. (Indeed, the final scenes of the episode, where he squats with a companion in a basement watching a religious ritual summoning an alien threat seems to deliberately recall The Daemons – but the joke here is that the paraphernalia is so comparatively mundane.)

And the Doctor invites a psychic to UNIT to do ESP tests, and takes great pleasure in putting him through many an experiment. These sequences are pitched as playful comedy, with Benton asking the Doctor if he's doing a spot of hairdressing, and there's much laughter to be had when Jo Grant writes the Doctor a letter. But it's almost as if, with all the light banter going on, everyone is ignoring Professor Clegg's distress at being put through these tests in the first place – and just as the UNIT family are at their most light and nostalgic, he's been left to kill himself with the Metebelis crystal.

I don't want to labour the point, although there's a great joke to be made at Jo Grant's clumsiness – that even from South America she can, by sending a package, ruin the Doctor's experiments and kill people in one fell swoop. But there's a definite link being made between those men in the basement wanting to tap into their psyches, and the Doctor amiably conducting investigations into Clegg's mind. It's dangerous stuff, and both parties are arrogantly ignoring the damage they might cause. I love the way that Robert Sloman's script makes it clear that Buddhist meditation is something of a seventies fad that "everybody is getting into". If in The Green Death he was happy to present lots of hippy scientists playing flutes, here he's suggesting that the counterculture of the time, and its inward looking navel gazing self-absorption, is really rather resistible. It's a subtle episode, this one – it feels lovely and light, with Sarah and Mike bantering like old friends, and the Doctor and the Brigadier going out on a date together. (And the pride on John Levene's face when from afar Jo refers to her "lovely Sgt Benton" is terribly sweet.) It's only at the double climax of the episode, contrasting Clegg's death with the summoning of the spider, that we're made to realise there's a darker edge to all that we've been watching, and that all our heroes have been rather too much taking for granted.

T: First off, top marks to the script for the line about meditating people "contemplating their bellybuttons" – it's clever and chuckle-some, and well delivered by Elisabeth Sladen. Thank goodness, because the episode doesn't get off to an especially promising start – the Doctor and Brigadier sit in a terrible cabaret club (or at least, the corner of one), with Courtney having to play the Brig in comedy mode. His piqued interest in the erotic dancer is passable, but the line about incorporating her moves into the men's drills isn't. Although he's suffering the indignity of being written like an idiot, I do think that the revelation that the Brig's watch is from Doris from Brighton is funny. If K were here, it's exactly the sort of thing she'd chuckle at, and Courtney's timing is bang on.

Really, this episode is a mixture of the very good and the acutely embarrassing. I'm surprisingly pleased to see Yates back (resigning off-screen wasn't the best send-off for him), and he and Sarah are subjected to a niftily staged encounter with a vanishing tractor. Sadly, the ensuing scene where Sarah puts her foot in it with Lupton, and Mike all-too-obviously tries to cover for her, plunges into the realms of naff TV aimed at stupid children. At least Lupton has the courtesy of noticing Mike's awkwardness, but neither of our heroes react as any living human being would in those circumstances.

Still, the guest performers win me over. John Kane is convincing as the slow-witted Tommy, and it's hard to believe that Kevin Lindsay, as the monk Cho Je, is the same bloke who played Linx in The Time Warrior. My favourite bit of acting, though, is the broken dignity with which Cyril Shaps elects to play Professor Clegg. It's a million miles away from the fussy scientists he's given us in The Tomb of the Cybermen and The Ambassadors of Death, and an empathic turn that mixes gravitas and vulnerability with a veneer of low-rent show-biz patter. There's a pulsing light on Clegg's face as he starts his mind reading, and the direction escalates the tension as we reach a climax: all hell breaks loose in the Doctor's lab, the cobwebby basement of the monastery is

pleasingly shadowy, Clegg dies, the chanting reaches its peak and a large spider appears. It really feels like something important is happening – and the fact that Jo Grant makes her presence known feels like the production team is really trying to make an occasion of this.

Planet of the Spiders (part two)

R: Last week, the Doctor killed a man with a blue crystal. This week, he runs over a tramp in a hovercraft. Is there no limit to the suffering he causes?

As a joke, I used to pretend that Jon Pertwee had a contract with the BBC that determined he'd stay as Doctor Who until the day that he was allowed to drive a hovercraft. And that ever since Barry Letts had taken over, he and Terrance Dicks had been routinely phoning around the hovercraft companies trying to find someone who'd let them borrow one. One day, Terrance comes into the office, where Barry is hard at work writing Planet of the Spiders with Robert Sloman. "Stop what you're doing!" says a triumphant Terrance. "Wherever you are, write in the hovercraft!" So Barry cheerfully scripts the entire chase sequence, and then calls out to Tom Baker to find a scarf; he's been lurking around the BBC offices waiting to take over since 1971.

I'm not saying it's a particularly *funny* joke – but it's odd, watching this episode again, just how plausible it seems. The first half of the episode is basically fine. You've got a lovely sequence where Lupton is made to turn around so that a giant spider can leap on to his back – it's a deliciously nasty idea which makes the flesh crawl. And there's a lovely wit to it too, that Lupton doesn't from this point on start acting as some possessed zombie, but instead behaves like he's got a new best friend and doesn't need to hang around with his old mates any more. "This man is stupid," says the spider of Barnes, in one very amusing sequence where Lupton more tactfully suggests that the voice in his head is advising that Barnes should go to bed.

The joy of Planet of the Spiders is when it's allowed to be, as in episode one, that collision of the mundane and the fantastical. It's best summed up by Sarah later on, when with some delight she realises she's now talking of alien worlds with the same familiarity as she would pussy cats and fish and chips. I think it's wonderful the way the production team have still, at the end of her first season, given Sarah a foot firmly in the real world, and at this stage the capacity to marvel at what's going on around her. Few companions are given such care – by this stage, most of them are taking adventures in their stride. And it's a reason why Sarah has so much more depth than most, and why she's still on screen with her own series 35 years later.

But then the tone is all but chucked away in a farewell present to Jon Pertwee: a chase sequence over land, air and sea where he gets to play with every gadget he likes. It lasts twelve bloody minutes too. It might be forgivable if it were exciting to watch, but it is directed in a way I can only describe as cold comatose. John Dearth is required to look over his shoulder every half minute and look concerned, which he does quite well for the first dozen or so times. Chubby Oates features as a fat policeman with no comic timing whatsoever. And the whole thing ultimately is a cheat, because it doesn't even rely upon *real* action sequences, not once it resorts to CSO to show the risible Whomobile flying. Self-indulgent doesn't even begin to describe this – what it does is fatally break the pace of the story, sacrifice the style it was establishing, and the story never properly recovers afterwards. The first 35 minutes or so of Planet of the Spiders felt fresh and earnest; from this point on, it's gaudy and padded. And when you're presented with a cliffhanger in which Lupton is vanished away by mental force, thus demonstrating that the entire chase sequence was utterly pointless, it's hard not to feel we've been watching this whole thing for Pertwee's amusement rather than for ours.

T: I really like these opening titles, you know. They convey the idea of both space and time, with that excellent, definitive version of the theme continuing to be a marvel that's never, ever been bettered. It's a brilliant symbiosis of visuals and sounds.

This episode however, is anything but... it's a rather jarring mess, for the reasons you've outlined above. As well as having to look behind him with increased urgency, John

Dearth also does a lot of running – or rather lolloping – with that curious, shambling gait of his, from one silly vehicle to another. On the way, Pat Gorman crops up again (he was only in it three stories ago – was there a shortage of actors in those days?) as a UNIT soldier to get zapped, and Chubby Oates, playing a "comedy" policeman, bless him, gets a thankless cameo with a punchline so witless, it's really not worth the effort.

You're right, though – in a reversal from last week, this starts stronger than it finishes. The idea of the huge spider on Lupton's back is terrific; it's creepy in both a physical and metaphorical way. And the arachnid model seen in Clegg's iris imprint is highly effective – more so, sadly, than the other spiders on show. Of the humans, Christopher Burgess deserves a lot of credit for imbuing Lupton's associate Barnes with a fragile, tired melancholy of someone who may well have experienced a nervous breakdown and would benefit from some rest.

But it's Sgt Benton, in his final appearance in the Pertwee era, who shines brightest. I may be biased, but I'm so glad that he makes the second best cup of coffee in the universe, and that he deems himself to be expendable in a way that the Doctor isn't. Like the actor playing him, Benton rises above his limitations and always gives his all, and for that we love him.

July 1st

Planet of the Spiders (part three)

R: We've never before seen something quite like Sarah Jane's journey by mandala to Metebelis III. Things which dematerialise are – naturally enough – pretty commonplace in Doctor Who, but this is the first time we see it from the dematerialising object's point of view. One moment we're standing behind Sarah, watching as the Doctor runs to her in the basement – the next we're giddily trying to stay upright as the entire background is replaced by the garish blue of another planet. It means that, for once, the hideous CSO backdrop actually looks *deliberately* jarring – it's as big a contrast to the setting we've left behind as we could imagine, and the way that it's foisted upon us in an instant means that this new world looks genuinely alien. It's very simple, and very effective; the naturalism of the Earth characters' speech plays off the purple prose of the future world colonists. Yes, we'll pretty quickly tire of the Metebelis setting in episode four, all studio sets and overripe dialogue. But here, I think, it serves its purpose well; within minutes of her arrival, Sarah is being forced over a yawning abyss into blue Chromakey, and it looks awful, but it's such a sudden clash from what she and we had got used to that it also just looks *weird*. And weird is rather interesting.

A school friend, Owen Bywater, used to watch a ropey video copy of this a lot with me when we were children. And purely for the moment where Jenny Laird as Neska has her strangely dreadful performance silenced by a cattle prod – how we'd cheer each time! It's not that Laird is terrible in the manner of a Rick James or an Aidan Murphy – instead, she delivers all her lines as if they're merely a list of words, as if she's running through them as an aide-memoire before going on to set for an actual take. She's so appalling that I'd somehow remembered the rest of the Metebelis cast around her being just as bad, but instead I'm actually impressed by the way that Ralph Arliss and Joanna Monro in particular flesh out credible characters with such little dialogue.

And John Dearth continues to excel. The scene where he relates his motivation for power lust – that he's been bypassed too often in middle management – is so bathetic that it's very funny, but although his character background is a joke, Dearth plays it real enough that the character itself still has some integrity. Just imagine: we could so easily have had a Master-like figure in this role, using mystical chanting to bring forth aliens with which to take over the world, and it's quite clear that had Delgado not been killed so tragically, he'd have been at the centre of this storyline. But it's so much more interesting that instead of a charismatic genius, we get this shabby failure from office politics. And when he's tortured by the spider in his mind, he merely finds a way to torture her right back – it's a wonderful scene, that somehow seems to celebrate the triumph of the ordinary man over an arrogant alien tyrant. Had it been the Master battling

the eight-leg upstart, it'd have meant nothing – because it's just plain Lupton, villain as he is, you find yourself cheering him on.

T: Oh indeed – Lupton's decided to take over the universe because he's a disappointed salesman. Bloody hell, so on top of everything else, the credit crunch is going to unleash a squadron of redundant shysters allying themselves with oversized arachnids. What a scoundrel – still, the shifting perspective on his face as it's superimposed into the spider council chamber is an impressive visual choice in a story that's looking increasingly lazy. And you're quite right: when Lupton turns the tables on the spider and makes her say please, he becomes a smart, adaptable nemesis, fit to be the architect of the third Doctor's downfall. Clever Lupton indeed.

But, bloody hell! This is supposed to be the celebratory send-off to the longest-running Doctor (up to this point), and we end up on Metebelis III, planet of two things that have consistently blighted this era: duff acting and bad CSO. They have even, it seems, taken the peculiar decision to dub Walter Randall's big speech with Max Faulkner's voice. It's clearly Randall on all his other lines, but he's out of synch when announcing the Queen's arrival. It's bizarre. My guess is that there was a problem with the sound and someone made a mistake, booking the wrong Guard Captain actor to come and redo the lines.

By the way, I like Sarah's striped outfit, and the bit where the Metebelis women use some confusion to steal her away and disguise her. I used to hold a bit of a torch for Joanna Monro when she was in That's Life, so I'm pleased she's notched up a Who as well.

As for Jenny Laird, the mind boggles! I shan't, you shan't say any more.

Planet of the Spiders (part four)

R: We've got a story now being told on two fronts – it's set on Earth, and it's set on Metebelis III. And, curiously, in spite of the fact it's opened out and has so much scope, very little happens. On Metebelis III, the Doctor spends most of his time unconscious, and everyone waits for him to wake up. "This is getting monotonous!" Pertwee complains at one point. And on Earth, the minor henchmen all sit about arguing about what to do – and admitting even to themselves that, in their panic, they're just going round and round in circles.

But right at the centre of the episode is a truly magical scene. It's the moment where the blue crystal clears Tommy's mind – and he finds, to his giddy delight, that he can now understand the children's books he's tried so hard to read. It's extremely touching, and John Kane's performance is beautiful: he can barely articulate the words on the page as his brain ever races on interpreting them. It's a simple moment of terrific acting which also (very cleverly) allows us to make perfect sense later in the episode, amidst all the exposition, of the way that ordinary spiders can have become so advanced and so dangerous through prolonged exposure to a bunch of shiny gemstones. Without this moving depiction of a man who's always been held back by a confused mind suddenly realising he's *free*, the whole premise of the story would just be a bit of hogwash. As it is, by humanising the effect of the crystal, we can appreciate that something real is at stake two episodes later when the Doctor gives his life for it.

T: Well, the best stuff by miles is indeed with Tommy. Otherwise, much as I hate to say it, the rest of the running time tediously revolves around Sarah trying to wake the Doctor up whilst two-dimensional villagers bicker. I think even John Gielgud would have struggled with lines such as "squabbling like herd boys with your mother half distracted" and "you just sit there supping broth and chattering like a woman at the wash place", so I don't blame Joanna Monro and Ralph Arliss for looking uncomfortable. There are lots of limp arguments about cowardice before Gareth Hunt proves his bravery, and wipes the scowl off Arliss' face in a contemplation on heroism that would have made Terry Nation blush at its awfulness. Hunt's not bad actually, although he and Randall are neck and neck in the Most Horrible Moustache In Doctor Who Ever competition. Along those lines, the establishing shot of dawn breaking is a much-needed injection of visual flair – as opposed to the all-too

visual flares at the bottom of the guards' trousers.

So I wasn't the only one to notice the aptness of the Doctor sighing and opining, "This is getting monotonous". Too bloody right it is, mate. The only fun to be had is to again marvel at Jenny Laird, who gives the worst performance in the entire series, and yet is an acclaimed actress with a RADA prize named after her.

July 2nd

Planet of the Spiders (part five)

R: It'd be so easy for Jon Pertwee to be phoning in his performance at this point. It's his penultimate episode – my God, I bet he's already booked himself a nice holiday. But he's truly remarkable here. He offers us at first such a *reassuring* Doctor. We open with Sarah worrying (not unreasonably) about how long she's going to live before she's eaten by spiders; within a scene of the Doctor arriving, fellow prisoner he may be, she's relaxed enough to be trading puns with him about their imminent death, and enjoying the adventure. The expression on the face of another captive, Sabor, as he listens to the two of them witter on is priceless, but it's telling too – if the Doctor's by your side, even if you've no hope of rescue, then everything feels okay. When Sarah is taken away by guards, and the Doctor asks her to buy some time, her little rebel cry that she'll do her best to give them indigestion is both funny and a touching reminder of the calming effect that the Doctor has. Similarly, the later scene where the Doctor wriggles from his cocoon to freedom whilst trying to remember the name of Houdini is perfectly paced, and a bit of lovely comedy – you can see the influence of Robert Holmes here, I think, as the natural eccentricity of the Doctor focuses more upon an irrelevant problem whilst appearing to solve the immediate one threatening his life with casual disregard.

So far, so very Doctor. But this is all a set-up so that when the Doctor stands before the Great One, the contrast is all the more obvious. Seeing this most arrogant and self-composed of Doctors being forced to dance like a puppet is actually shocking; to see him too looking genuinely *frightened* is something we've really not seen before. By the time that he's sitting in K'anpo's study, a humble boy in front of an indulgent teacher, confessing that he stole the blue crystal, we're being allowed a whole new glimpse of Pertwee's Doctor. It's lovely that, in his final gasp at the part, Pertwee is still finding new ways of playing it – and quite rightly demonstrating that he's about to leave the show with still more to offer.

T: How can one story contrive to be so consistently good in one area (the Earth scenes), and diametrically awful in another (the Metebelis ones)? Tommy has a nifty flashback which, thanks to the entertainingly tricksy editing, makes Mike and Sarah stutter repetition like Max Headroom. And Tommy's decision to confide in Cho Je brings the welcome return of Kevin Lindsay's benign presence, and whose acceptance of the new and smarter Tommy ("when everything is new, can anything be a surprise?") showcases his gentle philosophy at its most endearing. "Dear me, these foolish fellows," he blithely says of the men who want to invade the Earth with the help of giant talking spider from space. His tactic seems to be to refuse to panic, as if optimism is the best weapon in the universe ("naughty chaps" indeed). When Sarah tells Tommy that he's just like everyone else, his response is a terrifically delivered "I sincerely hope not" – what a lovely, witty moment, and probably my favourite in the whole adventure.

I can't, I'm afraid, be as generous about the pun-filled exchange between Sarah and the Doctor as they contemplate becoming Spider lunch – it's spectacularly awful. Poor Geoffrey Morris, as the entrapped Sabor with whom they share a cell, has no choice but to look in turn bored, exasperated and peeved by the rubbish going on around him.

The clues are in the credits, and I don't mean Richard Franklin attaining the giddy heights of third billing. Max Faulkner wasn't credited last week because all his stuff was meant to be in this instalment, and George Cormack's not on the cast list for this one because his appearance has been brought forward from the final part. With episodes being re-jigged and plundering footage from each

other, it's no wonder that too much of this is a spectacular, unforgivable mess.

Planet of the Spiders (part six)

R: Up to this point, every time Doctor Who has replaced its lead actor, it has done so in its own individual style – there has never been a template established for how a production team should *do* this. So for Hartnell it was all ambiguity, a symptom of a series which at this point had only a vague understanding of its future, as well as a dim grasp of what it was wanting from its present as well. For Troughton, it was accompanied by big revelations that split the series apart altogether, and was a much more prosaic change that was deliberately forced upon him by controlled alien technology. In this Buddhist parable that change is a metaphor, as has been established right from the first episode, it's utterly elemental and symbolic. As fans, we react with a sense of rightness to the first use of the word "regeneration", but in this context it's merely another word to reflect the philosophies that underpin this story, and refers as much to the spiritual path the Doctor is following, and to the rather inexplicable connection between K'anpo and his projected alter ego Cho Je. For all the mutterings about Time Lords, what happens to Pertwee here has nothing to do with what we understand about Who lore up to this point, and far more to do with faith and wisdom. It's odd, in retrospect, that this is the change of Doctor that'll catch on – that "regeneration" so quickly will become as familiar a phrase on the series as "sonic screwdriver", and it'll be robbed of its deeper meanings.

What this does is give Pertwee's exit a calm dignity that is very touching. Fans can point at the simplicity of the special effect itself and wish for something a bit more elaborate – but in truth what makes the moment work is that it *is* so simple: the importance is in the Doctor's sacrifice, and the redemption he finds in facing his fear, not in some barnstorming climax with flashbacks or companions' heads whizzing about. The sequence is gentle and loving, and perfectly performed. And for my money, it's still the best regeneration Doctor Who ever managed.

Because this episode focuses upon that final

performance of Jon Pertwee, it's hardly surprising that other elements of the story get lost in the mix. Lupton dies in such a low-key manner, the adventure no longer having anything it wants to do with him, that you only realise he's deceased because he never comes back. Rather better is the exit of Mike Yates. He's blasted down by mental forces, but survives because his very compassion acts as a shield. Recovering to consciousness, he at last seems to have found the peace that he's been searching for. His betrayal of UNIT has at last been redeemed, and he's now free. We'll never see Mike again – he pops up as an illusion in The Five Doctors, and as another one in Dimensions in Time – so this acts as his farewell. It's subtle and affecting, and rather better than anything any of his army colleagues will be getting.

I think it'll be clear enough reading my diary entries these last couple of months: Pertwee simply isn't my Doctor, and these were the stories I was least looking forward to wading through on this quest of ours. I've always had the idea they were repetitive, unambitious fare – the same adventures each week, UNIT blasting away at yet another alien invader, the Master once more turning up with a mask on as the shock villain. But I've been surprised at just how hard the production team has worked to keep the format as fresh as possible. There are stories I've not liked very much, like The Time Monster, but it's clear now just how much they were attempting. For the most part, the stories broadcast these past five years have been solid at least, and more often than not had something passionate at their hearts about the way Man treats the planet and his fellows. And whilst Troughton was always dancing about trying to surprise us, Pertwee succeeded by giving these adventures an anchor – whether they were in the present day or on distant worlds, it was by being always so reliable a presence that the audience were able to engage with the story's themes and understand the arguments that were being presented. Even as I type that, I can't help but make that sound a bit dry. Perhaps it was. But it was also the right approach exactly for these sorts of tales, and, for all his flashy clothes, perhaps the least mannered and most supportive way of performing them – Pertwee never wanted to upstage the stories or the other actors appearing alongside him. I was surprised by how moved I was to see this particular Doctor die. I'll miss him.

T: Poor old Pertwee's final cliffhanger involved a guest character in jeopardy – another indication that this era really doesn't have a massive sense of occasion. That said, you can judge the quality of any Planet of the Spiders episode by how little time it spends on Metebelis III, and fortunately episode six is mostly Earthbound. Alas, much of this episode's screen time is also spent being episode five! It's interesting that you mention The Time Monster – a throwaway bit of magic in that tale inspired the central thrust of this story, so anyone who remembers it will be rewarded by the payoff of the Doctor's final reunion with his old teacher. As the abbot K'anpo, George Cormack is gentle and twinkly, though traces of a Scots burr in his voice suggest he's from a part of Tibet located in Inverness.

Pertwee is fabulous in his final face off with the Great One – it can't have been easy performing his final confrontation with his Most Terrifying Opponent Ever in front of a blue screen. The model work is very good too, as voice-actress Maureen Morris suggests an extremely powerful but unhinged uber-arachnid. It's typical of this era of the show – in which the Doctor is a flawed character, hampered by his own arrogance and desires – that our hero is brought down to size by a creature in front of whom he is, literally and metaphorically, a "little man".

And so the TARDIS brings him "home"... after three weeks. We know that's serious, nothing takes three weeks in Doctor Who! It's good to have Nicholas Courtney back, as we need him to witness the departure of the Doctor with whom he has riffed, locked horns and fought side-by-side. There's a quiet, unfussy simplicity to Pertwee's final moments. On the floor of his beloved lab, he even has time to depart on a good gag, reassuring Sarah that while there's life there's...

And then he dies! He dies before he changes. Final exhale of breath, eyes close, body goes limp. I can only imagine what the nation's children must have felt as they watched this most upright, commanding and dashing of Doctors expire before their very eyes.

I had similar apprehensions as you going into this era, but under Jon Pertwee, Barry Letts and Terrance Dicks, Doctor Who became a programme that was keen to use sci-fi ideas to explore contemporary concerns. It had a remit to be action packed with a moral focus, and have a leading man who learned to face up to his own shortcomings. The most successful elements of this era have survived as part of the show's DNA to this day. Pertwee is so effortlessly the Doctor, it's easy to take him for granted. Just because he makes it look easy, it doesn't mean that it is. And can you imagine anyone else wearing his wardrobe without looking utterly stupid? Yet he wears all sorts of outrageous garments and looks fantastic.

Let's also not forget that he walked knowingly to face death, and did so for the sake of the rest of us. The Doctor is dead. Long live the Doctor.

July 3rd

Robot (part one)

R: I used to say that Robot was a bit rubbish, a stale hangover from the Pertwee era. It looks that way on paper, certainly – there's UNIT, and the Brigadier, and it's Barry Letts' last story as producer. And so I've had a certain contempt for it; didn't it know that The Ark in Space was just around the corner changing everything? And Davros, and murderous mummies, and giant rats, all hell bent on offending the sensibilities of Mary Whitehouse? But for four weeks only, we're stuck with Robot: there's a new Doctor in the house, and instead of looking forward, the series is looking back – it's trying to be as comfortable as a pair of well-worn slippers, when surely what's wanted is that Doctor Who is putting on its running shoes!

But I was wrong. Robot has little to do with the Pertwee era. Just a comparison with Planet of the Spiders shows a yawning gulf between the two – Spiders is all about philosophy and morality, and universal threat, and great earnestness. Robot is a comedy. And for all that Jon Pertwee was a comic, Doctor Who hasn't tackled a story so gleefully light-hearted as this in an age. If Pertwee's stories always made the

effort to stress just how momentous they were, and how serious the jeopardies, then by contrast this episode is all about how it's all light and throwaway. When the Brigadier and Sarah try to persuade the Doctor to stay on Earth, they come up with the theft of the disintegrator gun plans because it's something they've only just been talking about – you get the impression that had they been discussing the latest cricket scores in the paper, they'd have just as easily picked that. It's all so determinedly low key – and lends a winning charm to the story. It's very reassuring; it's as if it's reminding the audience of all the "fun bits" in Doctor Who, without the awkwardness of a plot getting in the way, just so the appearance of this crazy new actor won't upset them too much. And therefore by appearing to suggest everything's business as usual, it paradoxically produces an adventure which has a style we've never seen before.

There's a lovely sweetness to all of this – and it's tinged, in retrospect, with a touch of melancholy. When Nick Courtney is reduced to telling Lis Sladen all about the latest goings on at UNIT, he admits it's because he's no-one left to talk to; the UNIT family has been whittled away, and he already looks like he's from a bygone era of the programme. It's my favourite scene in the episode, actually, and Courtney plays it perfectly – he appears to miss Pertwee just as much as the audience at home must do. Tom Baker is gloriously funny and childlike, and it's a stand-out performance – but just as Troughton played against type after Hartnell, so it's calculated to be as much of a contrast to Pertwee as possible. The difference here is, for the first time, a regeneration has occurred and no-one has cause to doubt this is the Doctor. Barry Letts and Terrance Dicks – the latter writing this story on his way out the door as script editor – don't need to play that game here; they know full well that by surrounding Baker with all the remnants from the Pertwee years, we'll still feel a nostalgic pull for a Doctor we'll never see again. As a fan from this side of the fence, we watch with glee as Baker makes the part his own – as a fan in 1974, no doubt, you'll watch as this unknown actor rides roughshod over the very dignity of the character. No-one quite dares say it out loud, not the Brigadier, not Sarah, not Benton – but they'd all rather have the old Doctor back. The one who wasn't quite as silly.

And I think this works very well – it's just as brave as what Innes Lloyd did with Troughton in The Power of the Daleks, it confronts head on that the audience are going to be uncertain of this new upstart. You think this Doctor looks a bit manic? Well, watch him go! Just as you think that goggle-eyed expression can't get any bigger, Baker will find a way of stretching his face muscles still more implausibly. The bit which I think really betrays what the episode is up to is when we catch Ian Marter – as the new companion, UNIT medic Harry Sullivan – checking with a stethoscope whether he too has two hearts, and chuckling with amusement. In one instant, Harry represents the kids at home – you object as the Doctor comes straight at you like an express train, but once the storm has passed, you'll be in the corner practising the same eccentric gags and laughing at the memory of them.

The robot looks very good too, doesn't it? This must be one of the few times in Doctor Who history where the monster actually looks far worse when we're only given glimpses of it. Seeing it in shadow, or through that refracted vision it has, it looks a bit like a Kroton – all claws flexing, all ungainly. You're led to expect the worst. When, at the episode end, you see its beautifully designed head in all its glory, it's such a lovely surprise it almost feels as if that's the cliffhanger itself.

T: Jon Pertwee, let's not forget, spent most of his first episode in a hospital bed and retrieved his key from his boot, and the following week only got to have some funny costume business and a failed attempt to leave in the TARDIS. Tom Baker does *all four* of those within the first half of this episode, and thereby stamps his personality all over it. There's *no* gentle lead into the new regime for the viewer, as this new Doctor announces his anarchic presence with fervour.

Mind you, it's not a universally successful introduction – Tom Baker's comedy gawp upon seeing the TARDIS, as he re-enters the lab in his nightshirt, brings to mind the self-indulgent performances we'll see in his later years. Here, though, it's filtered through the naive charm of a novice finding his feet, rather than the bolshy arrogance of a bored actor trying to keep himself amused. Baker conveys the Doctor's strange alien qualities with a whole range of techniques – he's rather maudlin when seeing himself in a mirror, then shows a flash of self-confidence that would have done Jon Pertwee proud (had the punchline not been a knowing dig at his hooter). The skipping rope scene with Harry Sullivan is a well-orchestrated bit of comedy business, and there's a languid confidence about the way the Doctor lounges in the back of the Land Rover, his feet up whilst he works out what the baddies are up to. He's also quite smug when examining a crime scene, but seems in little hurry to get his allies to act upon his deductions – it hints at a more detached and alien quality than Pertwee ever attempted. Against the comforting presence of Sarah, the Brigadier and Benton, we just don't know which way this new Doctor is going to jump.

Isn't it amazing what double standards we have, though? In my rebellious youth, I was *livid* with the comic excesses of Sylvester McCoy's costume change in Time and the Rani. I was at a stage where I'd goaded myself into thinking that the best way to enjoy Doctor Who was to get angry with it and lament the passing of the good old days... which I'd never actually seen. McCoy's clowning seemed unforgivable because we didn't want Doctor Who to be *silly*, even though Tom Baker started his tenure doing exactly that and getting away with it – largely because, even here at the start of its twelfth season, Doctor Who is still busy establishing itself. For all the familiar trappings – UNIT, a home-grown threat and the presence of perennial bit player Pat Gorman – Robot doesn't feel like a continuation of the Pertwee era. Nor does it resemble much of what we remember from a typical Tom Baker excursion. It's a peculiar transitional episode, with lots of vim and a fresh, unique flavour – including a Terrance Dicks script that shows great comedic skill (not something, surprisingly, I have noticed this writer often credited with) as well as cramming in plot and mystery.

They may not get everything right with Robot, but it's difficult not to feel charmed by it.

Robot (part two)

R: Doctor Who's never had much love for computers. I suppose that's because they're the ultimate authority figures – always under the thrall of facts, and that's something an anarchist force like the Doctor will always resist. In any story where a machine takes centre stage, there's usually a bit where the Doctor and his friends will tease it with some sort of paradox, and watch gleefully as the computer undergoes paroxysms of distress. Just look at that sequence in The Invasion where Zoe and Isobel cause the poor answering machine at reception to blow up, and then giggle with delight at their handiwork!

It's hard not to look back at such scenes now and not think of them as sadists. This episode takes the same basic idea, that a computer brain can't cope with contradictory instructions, and focuses upon the suffering it causes. Elisabeth Sladen is lovely in this, forming in one scene a touching relationship with a big hulking metal suit. Stick a computer at the centre of a Doctor Who story before, and the series has always had a paranoid reaction to them – give 'em half a chance, these machines will try to take over the world! Robot is the first story to suggest that a computer is only as evil as its operator – give one a bit of intelligence, and it'll become a tragic figure, forced to follow orders in spite of itself. It's such a cliché now, we forget just how new an idea this was to Doctor Who at the time. Only a year before, we had the megalomaniacal BOSS; the computer might have had a ready wit, and lots of personality, but basically just by being a machine with illusions of emotion, it was inherently freakish. Here, Terrance Dicks turns that on its head. And Robert Holmes begins his time as script editor with a yarn about a robot that really just wants to be loved. By the time he leaves, he'll have introduced K-9.

It helps, of course, that Kettlewell's Robot looks so beautiful. When it lists all its functions, you can't quite believe a word of it – it seems the most impractical mining aid ever devised. (Even when it holds objects like the Destructor Gun in future episodes, it can't help but seem a little fey.) WOTAN and BOSS basically were the same design – big boxes with flashing lights and turning cogs. K1, in contrast, is something that is full of expression. And it's clever that we're invited to believe (like Marius does with K-9 later) that the robot has been created as an act of love by its inventor – that there's a reason why this particular computer has a right to compassion. Dicks always says that Robot is a King Kong story, but the heart of it is closer to Pinocchio. There's this big shiny toy – and it really looks like a toy, too, which is surely one of the reasons for its enduring popularity – but it only wants to be a real boy.

T: Tom Baker continues to deploy everything in his arsenal to assert his identity onto the Doctor. There's a curious moment where he's in the forefront of the frame, his face a mask of intriguing impassiveness – he's "just thinking", he subsequently tells the Brigadier, as if to suggest that his mind sometimes becomes so busy that the rest of his body just pauses. Later, the Doctor proves his intellectual credentials to Kettlewell before flattering the old duffer into being forthcoming, showing that he's a canny manipulator in spite of the surface lunacy. Okay, so the Doctor's ultra-fast typing – with its daffy musical accompaniment – might suggest everyone involved is trying a *little* too hard here, but you have to learn to walk before you can run.

And *what* a deliciously icy turn Patricia Maynard gives as Miss Winters... so much so, we can genuinely buy the moment where she orders the Robot to terminate Sarah, in what is passed off as a bluff to prove that the Robot isn't dangerous. The twist, of course, arrives when Winters' associate Jellicoe privately babbles how the Robot *might actually* have killed Sarah, and Miss Winters archly points out that it was all a useful experiment. (I also really enjoy Winters' patronising observation that Sarah probably has a pet name for her car – she'd have had a field day with the Pertwee Doctor!) And Timothy Craven gives us a great cameo as Short: the pallid, squitty little fascist who one imagines has a cold, clammy handshake and still lives with his Mum. (Although Sarah's riposte that she'll file him between the Flat Earthers and the flying saucer people is a bit rich, considering she *knows* such "lunatics" in the Doctor Who universe actually have a point.)

Otherwise, the best bits in this? There's the scene where the Robot (Michael Kilgarriff) visits Professor Kettlewell, and Kettlewell and exhibits a genuine and touching concern for his creation, even as Kilgarriff is extraordinarily moving with his plaintive cry of "Help me!" Benton finally gets a deserved promotion to warrant officer – although I think it's pointing out the show's flaws a bit too brazenly in that it happens, we're told, largely because of the lack of budget for a more senior officer. (Couldn't it be implied that there are *loads* of captains and lieutenants around, but Benton gets the nod because he has a special attachment to the Doctor – or, hell, because he's coincidentally on duty every time alien shenanigans occur?)

And the *best* bit of best bits? The sheer heroic bathos of Jellicoe asking for a screwdriver as he gets about the business of reprogramming the most complex and innovative robot in the history of the world. (Oh, I love Doctor Who.)

July 4th

Robot (part three)

R: I think the script's trying to make the actors work unnecessarily hard, and I can't entirely see why. The joy is that they actually overcome the obstacles.

Take poor Edward Burnham, here appearing as the Robot's creator, Professor Kettlewell. Now, one of the pleasures I take watching the series 24 is in the knowledge that in this double-crossing real-time thriller series, not even the cast know before they read the script whether or not they turn out to be traitors. It's part of the fun, watching as an actor who's assumed he's a goodie for the last ten episodes has to do a volte-face and reveal himself to be a sociopath as elegantly as possible. Here in episode three, it's revealed that Professor Kettlewell isn't the bumbling loveable scientist we all thought he was, but is actually a neofascist. And yet, up until the very moment it's revealed, Burnham is still required to play the part as if he's an innocent – even within scenes where he's only appearing with his fellow SRS members! By the time that the Robot goes on a

rampage and discovers Sarah's hiding place, Burnham plays the revelation as if he'd no idea she was there either – and you wonder who on earth he's pretending to at this stage, as clearly both Sarah and his SRS colleagues were aware of it. It's like some strange triple bluff, as if Burnham has by this stage got so confused by how he's supposed to be acting, that he's just going for perplexed naïf in spite of anything that's happening around him! And it ought to be awful. But it isn't. Because the twist that Kettlewell is really the villain behind the piece doesn't work emotionally at all – it cheapens the relationship story between him and the Robot, I think. And the only way that we get over this bump is by playing the twist as a twist, but ignoring the emotional repercussions of it. Burnham continues to act Kettlewell as the genial bumbler anyway, because that's the best thing for the episode. It's wrong. But I far prefer it to the alternative.

And Tom Baker is put through it too. So we have a situation where he bounds upon stage at a Nazi rally, and keeps everyone distracted with a bit of banter and some card tricks until the army arrive to arrest them. (Whilst reminding them at the start of his set that UNIT are on their way!) It's a thankless task – Eddie Izzard couldn't pull that off! When the audience start to laugh and cheer at his shenanigans, it seems false and artificial. But in some ways, I think, the intention itself is enough. Terrance Dicks is trying to draw a line under Jon Pertwee here, to give the new Doctor something you couldn't even contemplate the previous incarnation attempting. Although we can't be convinced by the fourth Doctor's stage presence, it's the clearest indication yet of who this new character is, and how we're now watching someone who will be far bolder and less predictable. The best thing about it is that Tom Baker doesn't look embarrassed. He looks as if he's having fun. As a set piece, it's horribly flawed – but as a statement about what we can expect from this new Doctor, it's really rather inspired.

T: Ooh, look at you clutching at straws! I admire your attempts to make sense of a scene so ludicrous in execution, a *literal* execution wouldn't be an unfair punishment for those responsible for it, but really! I've seen too many great comedians struggle just because a mic is slightly muffled, or the lighting's poor, or a venue hasn't given much thought to how to mount a gig. To walk on while a load of geeky Nazis marvel at the revelation of a great big robot and a traitor in their midst, and yet still laugh at some substandard cabaret, is every performer's dream! And as for Eddie Izzard, he's a man in women's clothes and make-up... even timorous, weedy Mr Short would have heckled him!

No, what this really boils down to is Tom Baker entering into ridiculous scenarios with the glee of a man who's got the job of a lifetime (which, let's face it, he does), but making very curious choices – some successful, some not. There's the way he lies on the table and winks at his companion *when she gets kidnapped*, and the detached manner in which he blithely writes off the impending death of the Action Man tank crew as if one-upmanship is more important than the loss of human life. (Then again, maybe the tank is only inhabited by *actual* Action Men: UNIT inventions resulting from plundered Auton technology. Or perhaps the appalling lack of scale is deliberate, and it's honestly an unmanned, remote-control minia-ture tank – a ploy to propagate the story's theme of automatons fulfilling roles tradition-ally taken by human beings. See, for every straw you clutch, I'll clutch another seven.)

I agree with you, though, that the Robot design is terrific – but much of the credit for its success should go to Michael Kilgarriff, who imbues the character with a touching sensitiv-ity whilst delivering his lines with the neces-sary robotic monotone. (The episode, after all, opens with the Robot very sweetly asking the Doctor not to resist before trying to bash his brains out.) All right, so the Robot is occasion-ally clumsy, but those occasional tumbles just demonstrate how impressive a physical per-former Kilgarriff is elsewhere, as he negotiates obstacles in a restrictive costume while main-taining power and poise.

Finally, a word for the soon-to-be dropped UNIT regulars, who are getting about their duties without any suggestion that this might be their last gasp of greatness. John Levene sportingly plays an entire scene whilst lum-bered with a tea tray, and Nick Courtney is excellent as always. He's affronted that the SRS may have troops at their disposal, and grimly

informs Winters over the RT that her hostage-taking won't deter him from doing his duty. His utterance that he'll "show that wretched woman" is delivered with the harsh profes-sionalism of a man who means business, but doesn't mind admitting he's got a score to set-tle.

Robot (part four)

R: The real brains of this outfit is Benton. Not only does he come up with the plan to save the day, he's also the only one who thinks of retrieving the Disintegrator Gun once the Robot has fallen over. Someone should give him a promotion. Oh, hang on. They have!

Barry Letts is really into big monsters, requiring lots of CSO, so it's extremely apt that he bows out here by taking a superbly designed piece of costume and having it become some-thing that looks awkward and ungainly. Apt, but also charming – this is Robot, the little story, reaching out for a big climax, and having fun in the process. The beauty of this adven-ture is that it wears its heart on its sleeve; that scene where Sarah persuades the Robot to spare a soldier's life is wonderful because it's brave and redemptive, and casts the Robot as a creature that wants to do the right thing. The final scene of Sarah mourning is beautifully handled. That moment where she accepts the jelly baby is the moment too when she forgives the Doctor and accepts the hard victory he won – and therefore where she also acknowl-edges that Tom Baker is the Doctor after all. The way in which she snatches that jelly baby is delightful – it's as if she's saying, oh, hell with it, I'll be a child too. It comes at the end of a scene that's really touching, and it only consolidates Baker all the more.

And it comes on top of a subtle statement about what it means to be human – the Robot being capable of great evil and great good. Tom Baker doesn't deliver it as a homily, the way that perhaps Pertwee would – it's done with a quizzical lightness, as if the idea has only just occurred to him. It sets up an analysis of humanity, and the different ways it can be defined, that runs nimbly through this entire season.

I'm so glad that Robot exists; Tom Baker never has another story quite like it. He's about to be pitched headlong into the Hinchcliffe era, three years in which there'll be a lot of wry humour but precious little room for anyone to feel affection for the monster. It's a tougher, more cynical take on Who, all starting next week. And by the time it's past, Tom Baker will have lost his innocence. He'll be childish, as he is in that glorious scene where he refuses to do the homework the Brig has left him – but he'll be too settled in the role to be entirely child-like. Look at that lovely joke where the Doctor hits the brick with his hand; in the first episode he was able to chop it in half, but here he just winces – he's not a superhuman after all, this new Doctor of ours, but he's funny and he'll win through none the less. He'll need to. It's a scary old universe he's about to face.

So, there you go. An ungainly hulking monster falls in love with a beautiful girl... On an unrelated note, I'm now off to Toby Hadoke's stag do.

T: Well that's *one* way of putting it. Another is that we're about to witness, in a neat echo of the Tom Baker era, an unknown actor enjoying the most successful engagement of his life, and subsequently marrying his companion.

The scene where Lethbridge-Stewart, ever the professional soldier, can't bring himself to shoot Winters, but hitherto non-murderous civilian Sarah *can* sums up this story completely. Neither moment would make any sense whatsoever in the real world, but they're spot on in Doctor Who terms. The Brig has doubtless killed any number of people, but possesses an upright Britishness which won't let him slay a female – he's a stoical TV military figure. Whereas Sarah has a 70s-TV-feminist-at-teatime persona that absolutely sells the scene, no matter how unlikely her action would be in actuality. Courtney's barking of the line "cancel the destructor codes" is another moment of greatness; it's the principled but impotent fury of a man who hopes his unbridled authority and honour will net compliance from his enemy. (And well done everyone for stopping the countdown at two seconds rather than one – it's just a tad more believable that way.)

But as great as Nick Courtney and Lis Sladen are, it's those two great lunks who can't *quite* get to grips with displays of emotion that

leave an indelible mark on the episode. Dear old Benton comes up with a solution that saves the day, then apologises for doing so and has the smile wiped off his face immediately. (I never thought I'd say this, and yet I've said it half a dozen times now – John Levene is worth his weight in gold.) And Michael Kilgarriff continues to excel: his heartbreaking woe as the Robot realises that he's literally killed his creator, and his terribly innocent attempts to reassure Sarah, make what could have been a lumbering man-in-a-suit possibly the most poignant protagonist we've seen thus far in the series.

Yes, much of Robot doesn't make sense (some of the characterisation – and indeed the essence and make-up of the SRS – is horribly contradictory), and it's hardly the most solid or innovative of productions (especially in the oversized effects, which they really don't pull off). And yet... while I've been tough on stories that have similarly ill-conceived or sloppily thought-out ideas, and occasionally cataclysmic production choices, I have no ill feelings towards Robot at all. Maybe it's because I know we're about to enter an era that's always impressed me, or maybe there's a zip and simplicity to this story that makes it difficult to dislike, or maybe I'm just feeling high on life because I'm heading off to my stag do. The raison d'etre of this diary isn't to offer definitive statements, or to be an accurate history, or to pretend that our opinions are more intellectually rigorous or informed than any other fan out there. We're reacting to what we see when we see it. And for me, today... Robot may well be half-baked and flawed, but it seems *absolutely right* in spite of all evidence to the contrary.

The Ark in Space (part one)

R: Nice stag do, Toby. I enjoyed that. However, there aren't many beds in the house we're staying in. Most of the guests are crashing on sofas, or on the sitting room floor. I'm too old to crash on floors these days, so I was allowed to share the double bed. And that's why, at two in the morning, after the excesses of the evening, and a strange impromptu arm-wrestling competition, I'm propped up watching Doctor Who under the mattress with...

Toby Hadoke. Hello, Toby... Right. Putting British reserve to one side, let's watch The Ark in Space.

Like Robot, this story opens from the monster's point of view. There, though, all similarities end. In Robot, there was something rather funny, very reassuring, about looking through the monster's eyes, claws a-flexing, as it knocked down security guards and picked up documents marked "Top Secret". There's nothing reassuring about this. A creature invades a satellite, and bores down upon a human who's blissfully asleep... And then the music fades, and so does the picture, and we're left in darkness. What was all that about?

We'll only get the odd hint over the next 25 minutes. This plays as a virtual three-hander between the Doctor and his companions; we haven't seen the like of that since the black and white days. At once there's something very old-fashioned about all this, the way that the adventure takes its time and doesn't feel the need yet to introduce either guest cast or a monster – instead, it's content to have our heroes wander about and try to puzzle out where they are. But this is far from just padding, or the writer setting the plot points into place. There's a brooding unease to this episode, which builds up to the revelation that the adventure is taking place amidst the future remnants of the human population – there's been enough time for us to see the space station in full, to admire its defence systems and vacuum-sealed walls, that its dawning purpose has an awe-inspiring impact.

Just compare this, say, to Hartnell's The Ark – in that story, we were presented with the concept face on, and so could very easily adjust to it as merely another setting for a space opera. Here, though, you get the sense that the Doctor is interfering in things best left alone, that this is an occasion where human life hangs flimsily in the balance. It's the sort of sensation that can normally only be generated in a historical adventure, where we know that the Battle of Hastings is important, or that the Doctor mustn't get in the way of the destruction of Pompeii. This may be the only instance where a future setting is chosen which is so evocative that it has some of that same weight and meaning. And in that way, it's very apt perhaps that this does feel a bit like an early Hartnell adventure (with John Lucarotti first in line to write it too!).

Robert Holmes' script is very smart – it wants us to feel alienated and disturbed by the setting, of course (and this is a good argument against that fan dictum that bright lighting kills suspense and tension – the brightness here is so sterile, you could cut the atmosphere with a knife). We might be surrounded by humans, but their customs are alien and cold – the most disturbing moment of the episode is when a dead man's voice instructs Sarah to put any personal objects in a little tray before she's irradiated. It's not the irradiation that's scary – it's the politeness with which it's discussed, and the fact they have a tray for it.

But all this is balanced by the extraordinary humanity of dear Harry Sullivan. I love Harry. He's so immediately likeable, his reactions to all he sees about him are so comically down to earth. I love his reaction to his first flight in the TARDIS – he starts babbling about how the Doctor could make a fortune selling the thing; I love the way that stuck impossibly far into the future, he'll hang on to ideas about cricket. Robot played Harry as if he were a bit stuck-up; in The Ark in Space, he's a wide-eyed everyman, trying to rationalise what he sees about him in twentieth-century terms, but at the same time applying his intelligence throughout. Ian Marter's performance is beautifully judged – it's very sweet and funny, but the character is never sent up; he's Dr Watson to the Doctor's Holmes, and he might seem a little dim, but only in comparison. The rapport he shares with Tom Baker is terrific. With Lis Sladen largely unconscious throughout, the production team take the gamble of giving almost the entire episode to the two new boys. Doctor Who has not only not looked this way for years, it's not only got a different pace and tone, it's also playing off an entirely new cast. It's as bold as brass, telling the audience that the series has changed in one fell swoop.

Tom Baker is terrific as well. A lot of people say that he's defined by his homo sapiens monologue – if I'm honest, it's the one bit that doesn't convince me, his arms out too theatrically, the speech overwritten and self-conscious. But free from the constant need in Robot to entertain, his Doctor comes across as someone of great and questing intelligence.

He's taken us with him to the stars, and like the best teacher he's pointing at everything and asking us to work out what it means. It's a tremendously satisfying 25 minutes, this – it gives us so much to chew on that we barely notice how little has actually happened. I'm not one for exaggeration – well, much – but I think it's the most daring and the most stylish episode of Doctor Who for over six years.

Right, Toby. Your go. You're dozing a little now, I took a while to write that. Should I let you sleep?... Nah. Come on, wake up. The Ark in Space, remember?... Dear God, sleeping with Toby Hadoke. I feel like I'm in a Morecambe and Wise sketch.

T: Never mention Morecambe and Wise when talking about Doctor Who, it'll get you into all sorts of trouble! Bring Me Sunshine? Will solar flares do? You'll have to excuse me – it's all rather surreal, this. I've had a stag do, lots of lovely friends have come – and now I'm in bed with a Doctor Who writer, having watched episode one of The Ark in Space with him. I bet no-one ever did that with Eric Pringle!

This is an episode in which bugger all happens... but by golly, it's good, and differences between this new Doctor and the previous one continue to be *stark*. Jon Pertwee and Tom Baker are both prone to bouts of stroppiness, often being terse with their less intellectual underlings. But whereas Pertwee came across as rather aloof and patronising, Baker suggests his impatience owes to his keen intelligence rattling through ideas and permutations whilst having to engage in the irritating distraction of conversation. He even imbues a safety instruction like "keep your head down" with a stern edginess that keeps everything wonderfully tense. And when Harry compliments the Doctor on his powers of deduction, he thanks him in a way that suggests he doesn't actually need the affirmation of a lesser species – it's a cold alien superiority that, owing to Baker's multi-layered performance, never punctures his likeability. I don't even care if the homosapiens speech is theatrical – almost everything we've previously seen in Doctor Who *has* been theatrical, but this is unashamedly so, using powerful, evocative writing and authori-

tative acting to its advantage. I think it's where Baker nails the Doctor, without question.

But it helps greatly that he's accompanied by Harry and Sarah, who show such regard for the Doctor – since they like the new bloke, whatever his eccentricities, we like him also. That said, while I know what the showmakers were trying to *do* with Harry, I actually think he's a tad over-written. It's a credit to Ian Marter for finding a balance in which his character has moments of stupidity, but doesn't become annoying. I remember Lis Sladen saying in an interview that Marter was too intelligent for the part he was playing – which I can absolutely believe, but on the evidence here, that's a blessing. Marter is smart enough to shape Harry into a convincing and likeable sidekick, even when his lines allow little opportunity to be either. And, bless him, he even – as he places Sladen on the bench – holds her skirt down in case the camera picks up something it shouldn't. Marter may not have been entirely like Harry in real life, but both are absolute gentlemen.

Now, I think I'll go into hibernation, if that's alright with you. Please don't be influenced by this story and do something horrible to me while I sleep.

July 5th

The Ark in Space (part two)

R: I loved the stag do, Toby, and seeing you in your element. I know we've talked about this on the phone, but I haven't yet mentioned it on our blog – I'm so sorry I now won't be able to come to your wedding. That lecture cruise I did around the Netherlands got me another gig – and when you get hitched, I'll be somewhere off the coast of Russia talking about my love of Dostoevsky and Turgenev. I'd really much rather be talking of my love for a great mate, and watching him regenerate from bachelor to married man. (And, of course, making sure that wedding or not, you still get through your three Tom Baker episodes a day. And no honeymoon for you either until you're past McCoy. I insist.)

Back to The Ark in Space...

This episode is taking a bit of a gamble. The

human race is revived – and they turn out to be utter sods. The dialogue is very clever, and I love the way Robert Holmes makes all the future-speak something at a remove from ours (and that especially smart way that having learned the word "joke", Vira uses it in the wrong context), but it risks making the characters still more alienating. What quickly becomes clear, though, is that this isn't merely going to be a typical base under siege story, where the Doctor saves humanity from a bunch of wasps – but that he'll also have to teach humanity to be a little more human again. In a plot which is all about identities being lost and the line between being homo sapiens and Wirrn being blurred, it'll also be asking just how much of their humanity these survivors have stripped away deliberately.

The problem (potentially) is that all this could be rather dry. Wendy Williams (as Vira) and Kenton Moore (as Noah) are so utterly frosty, it's tempting to be on the side of the green larvae found in the solar stacks. Noah's another Professor Stahlman from Inferno, really. He's a git before he gets infected, and then he's a git afterwards – and spends his time doing his level best trying to hide the green on his hand that is turning him into a monster. It's easy when Doctor Who stories take "nice" characters and turn them evil – as in The Invisible Enemy, for example, where it'll seem de rigueur to overstress how sympathetic a person is just so you can emphasise the contrast later. But what Holmes does so well is to let in those little bits of air to the characters, to show the fear that Vira feels when her partner might lose his life, to show the desperation Noah feels when he realises at once that in his infection, all his race might be endangered. It's a very theatrical episode, this, with scenes lasting as long as seven minutes, and it requires some patience. But the little moments of horror that it's building to are so much more effective as a result. Noah's gentle assertion – as he increasingly becomes part of the Wirrn hive mind – that he is the missing technician Dune is one of the most subtly disturbing things Doctor Who in years. And I'm quite sure that throughout this entire quest of ours, we've never come across anything quite as sick as an alien that lays its eggs in its victims, and then eats them from the inside.

Does it work? That all depends on your reaction to the cliffhanger, I suppose. If you watch with amusement as Kenton Moore takes from his pocket a hand covered in green bubblewrap, then I suppose it doesn't. If, on the other hand, you see a man staring in horror as he sees his humanity being eaten away, then this does its job. What do you think, Toby? Did you laugh, or were you repulsed?

T: I certainly didn't laugh, probably because there's an admirable bleakness and intelligence at work here. Say what you will about Robert Holmes, he specialises in throwaway touches that give credibility to the worlds he creates and the characters who populate them. He even constructs an unusual set of speech patterns that have an internal consistency, but never threaten to cheapen proceedings with cod sci-fi flourishes. Do you remember last time the TARDIS landed on a space ark, and a character had the line "How in space could you do it?" – it's a million miles from Vira's "I high point in classics, but you dawn-timers have a language all your own". As Vira, Wendy Williams handles such rigid, unflowery vernacular well, and does an excellent job of suggesting dormant vestiges of her humanity – notice how she warns Harry that Noah has the option of enacting "condign action", while trying to placate Noah that he should feel less threatened by the TARDIS crew because Nerva's genetic designs allowed for a 7% stretch factor.

It's Robert Holmes' attention to such minutiae, and his gift for dialogue, that marks him out as the definitive Doctor Who writer. "Never mind about me, Harry, there's a man in danger," is a statement that sums up everything that the Doctor stands for, whilst Ian Marter pitches his lovely line about finding a huge, dead insect "in the cupboard" perfectly – it's an utterance that sums up the programme's gleeful mixing of the bizarre with the wonderfully ordinary. In fact, the Wirrn *are* based on creatures from our world – there is a wasp that propagates itself the same way as the Wirrn, allowing Holmes to create a plausible but nightmarish lifecycle inspired by nature itself.

Oddly enough, there is *so much* to admire in this episode, its occasional failings are all the more frustrating. I'm not sure that I buy the idea that Noah's Wirrn infection would create a subconscious impression of something *horrible* that his newly awakened crewmate Libri would see, but Holmes' writing and Baker's acting help sell the moment very well. I'm also slightly perplexed that Christopher Masters (as Libri) decides to stretch out his arms so that, in death, he looks like he's mid-star jump. I also couldn't stop myself from chuckling at the line "What have you done with Dune?", because I imagine David Lynch used to get asked that question with alarming regularity. And while Kenton Moore starts off pleasingly restrained, the writing encourages him to play Noah as an intransigent, unpleasant idiot. Moore makes a couple of intelligent choices – notably issuing the line "it is an order" as a confused apology, and looking suitably disgusted by his Wirrn-transformed hand. I'll give the man credit for trying, but I just don't think he's quite up to the task. His snarling villainy and uncomfortable looking histrionics leave me with the feeling that – pardon the phrasing – less is Moore.

The Ark in Space (part three)

R: There's that cliché, of course, about scared children hiding from Doctor Who behind the sofa. But in all honesty, the programme is rarely particularly frightening. Here, though, we have a story that is pure horror. Not a pastiche of a horror, or a comedy with horror elements – but something designed to shock and to terrify. It's only the fact that it is Doctor Who that keeps it from going too far. Look, there's the TARDIS in the background in one shot, and there's that nice Sarah Jane – we saw her last year romping about in a medieval castle! And it's because it's Doctor Who, made with Doctor Who's budget, that keeps the monster moments in check. To this 39 year old, watching people back away in terror from a sleeping bag is quite funny. But only *quite* funny, because I recognise the intent of the scene, and the genuine tension even the intent can generate. Similarly, Kenton Moore wrestling with his own Wirrn-mutated hand – a physical manifestation of the conflict in his mind – is something you'd show mates out of context if they wanted a laugh. But his distress

and guilt are so convincing – and that sequence where he attempts to beat off his own mutated hand during the pep talk from the Earth High Minister, unable to rationalise the optimism and pride he hears with the disgusted failure he sees he has become, is extremely powerful.

Tom Baker is excellent. The scene where he joyfully hits upon the idea of linking his cerebral cortex to the Wirrn race memory shows him to be a Doctor who is almost gleefully insane, whilst his attempts to dissuade Vira to revive the human race show him at his most charming. It's in those still moments that his performance begins to mature – the sympathetic silence in which he hears Vira admit that she and the transformed Noah were "pair bonded". It's an inconsistent performance still, to be sure, but a very exciting one.

This is unlike anything Holmes has ever given the series before. This is the writer of Carnival of Monsters and The Time Warrior, the joker on the Doctor Who team; his only attempts at horror before have been tinged with black comedy. But there's still room, thank God, for his wit here. Harry's delight at being allowed to participate in thirtieth-century medicine is touching. And Rogin's irritation with the dull normality of teleportation, disliking the way it always sets his teeth on edge, so subtly makes this society seem very real.

T: Commentators so often focus on the key points about The Ark in Space – it's the first instalment of the Hinchcliffe era; it's where Robert Holmes' writing kicks up another notch; the dynamic trio of Tom Baker, Elisabeth Sladen and Ian Marter, etc. – that how easily we forget about the director. And I think that Rodney Bennett deserves much credit for this episode's success – for instance, the fading between the space station's ghostly, empty outer corridor and the anguished Noah as the High Minister's voice floats through the air is a brilliant flourish. Bennett also injects the "Doctor links his own cerebral cortex into the eye-scanning device" scene with pace and tension, using fades again to blend between the Doctor's face and the Wirrn Queen's POV. Baker works up a sweat during this sequence, and there's a really unnerving moment where – still disorientated from his ordeal – the Doctor stumbles towards a Wirrn grub, seemingly oblivious to the danger it poses. Additionally, the power failure enables the director to plunge the place into darkness in the final moments, setting the scene for an atmospheric denouement.

Character-wise, I can't help but notice that in this well-ordered, functional society, all engineers have been selected on their ability to crack jokes and moan about stuff. But thank goodness, as Rogin – who here comes out of stasis – is a breath of fresh air. He's down to Earth and practical, and centres the outlandish scenario in recognisable normality – the man may work on a spaceship, but his attributes are similar to any number of people who may have fixed your car. Lots of people have noticed the similarity between The Ark and Space and the film Alien, but it's interesting that the latter *also* receives praise for having a prosaic crew who are simply doing a job, rather than behaving as if they're in a sci-fi film, and yet it's rarely noticed that Rogin is a clear precedent for this approach.

Notice also how Vira smiles when Rogin has to go into the transport first – it seems that the Doctor is influencing people to laugh in the face of danger. Wendy Williams has done a brilliant job, I think, of gradually thawing out and convincing us of the human heart that beats beneath Vira's clinical outer shell. She has a quiet, calm authority when Rogin and Lycett start to panic, and fan-knowledge enables us to *really* appreciate the scene where Vira confronts the mutating Noah, as we know there's a cut bit where he begs her – his intended life-mate – to kill him.

I seem to recall that the Biblical Noah had a son named Ham, which – in light of Kenton Moore's performance – is rather unfortunate. But never mind, his partial transformation into a Wirrn is an effective and gruesome make-up job, in what must be the most deliberately horrific Doctor Who story yet.

The Ark in Space (part four)

R: Last episode, Robert Holmes made me squirm with body horror. And this time, he pushes all my claustrophobic buttons. Thanks for that. Inevitably, the Wirrn were always going to be more unnerving as mutant humans than as clumsy walking ants – but sensitive

direction from Rodney Bennett ensures they don't look like actors in top-heavy costumes too often, and Holmes keeps the emphasis off monster shocks and instead on brooding atmosphere. There's a lot of waiting in this episode, as humans and Wirrn try to outmanoeuvre the other – and the script rather brilliantly understands that there's more terror to be found in expectation of attack than in the attack itself. Any good war movie understands that it's as the soldiers are led into battle that they shake the most fearfully.

The episode maintains its deliberate pace right until the final few minutes – then rushes away at the climax so quickly that it ends up getting a bit muddled. But Holmes is far more interested in the character moments than he is on big explosions – we don't get the equivalent we had in Robot of long sequences of spectacle where UNIT pad out the adventure with artillery and stunts. Instead, we get the powerful impression of the human spirit in triumph: of Sarah's courage in climbing through a narrow ventilation shaft, of Rogin's willingness to sacrifice himself, of Noah destroying his new race in favour of the old. And all of these acts of courage are achieved without soliloquies, and without moralising. Rogin dies with a joke about the strictness of his union, and Noah merely says goodbye without explanation or apology. The suggestion is, finally, of little people making big gestures – there's nothing melodramatic about these displays of bravery, and they're far more affecting as a result.

T: I agree – it's amazing what you can achieve with a good actress and a tiny, three-walled set. Sarah's journey through the Nerva tunnels sets my teeth on edge; it's horribly claustrophobic, and there are monsters through the grille. Yikes! After the Doctor has successfully cajoled Sarah to press on to the end, she slaps him about and maintains what dignity she can by insisting she can manage without his help, thank you. It – along with the Doctor's praise of Sarah's success – underlines what a good rapport this new TARDIS crew have established so quickly.

Speaking of the monsters, the Wirrn get to articulate a *reason* for their desire for conquest – and frankly, from their point of view, it's not an unreasonable one. This is a story where human virtue ultimately saves the day, and yet it's the Wirrn's absorption of Dune and Noah's knowledge that makes them aware of technology. In a sense, we provide the weapons with which they attempt to destroy us. Robert Holmes has given much more thought to these horrific creations than I'd remembered, and they're a terrific foe, realised very effectively.

Two notes on the guest-cast as we wrap this up... Richardson Morgan continues to be great as Rogin, especially in the way he pauses before descending the ladder, as if he's worked out that he may have to take precipitous action and sacrifice himself to save everyone. Morgan contrived to be in a lot of stage plays that both my mum and I went to see in the 80s, but I didn't recognise him at first. It took me ages to work out the identity of the newly monikered "Ric Morgan", whose programme biog listed Doctor Who in his credits. I also saw a number of productions of All My Sons, as it was an A-Level text, and Morgan was easily the best Joe Keller I've ever seen.

Finally, I should note that I once read a glowing appraisal of Wendy Williams in a piece by Russell T Davies, and can't help but think that Vira's transformation as a result of meeting the Doctor is something very reminiscent of modern Who. As she bounces off at the end, munching a jelly baby, we see that this story is about waking dormant humanity in more ways than one.

What a triumphant reinvention of the programme.

July 6th

The Sontaran Experiment (part one)

R: You know what this reminds me of? Those Doctor Who stories we'll start getting at the end of the decade, where the production team take a jolly overseas and film an adventure around famous landmarks. Tom and Lalla running around Paris, Peter Davison running over bridges in Amsterdam. What they have in common is the idea that the location comes first, that a smart director will try to make the most of the scenery around him over and above the concerns of the script. The Sontaran Experiment doesn't have much of an interest in dialogue. It's far more concerned with exploring Dartmoor, with having shots of the cast scrambling around rocks, or falling down ravines. It's probably the very first Doctor Who adventure that is far more concerned with establishing the beauty of a place than in telling a story.

Now, as a scriptwriter, that should automatically make my hackles rise. But do you know what? This is an absolute breath of fresh air. And after the confines of the Nerva Beacon, to see the camera drink in the location like this, to enjoy the countryside and the sheer space, it's especially welcome. You could almost believe that the story was written as they were filming, dependent on what particular geological quirks they found on the day. "Look, there's a big pit here! Tell Bob and Dave, we could make Ian Marter fall down that!" And whilst I'm sure that wasn't the case, it does give a rare naturalism to all that's going on here. At times, it reminds me a bit of some of those fan videos you see on the internet, where the sheer pleasure of pretending to be Doctor Who and using what they see about them is the whole point. For once, the impression is given not that the programme has made the best it could of a location and made it adapt awkwardly to the story – just think, for example, of the scripted moment in The Five Doctors where Sarah falls down a cliff, which ends up in the broadcast version as Lis Sladen sliding down a small hillock. Here, the story shows off Dartmoor to spectacular effect – because that's all the story is trying to do.

Bob Baker and Dave Martin have always been the most ambitious of writers on the series, the sheer scale of their ideas rarely able to be realised practically on the budget. Here, though, they very wisely play minimalist. And the minimalist story is handled very sensitively – there's not much music either. There's no attempt to disguise The Sontaran Experiment as being bigger than it really is, and that's its particular charm. It only stumbles when it tries to be Doctor Who, and brings out a robot; it's a cute little thing, and makes a lovely beeping noise I'd really rather like as the ring tone for my phone, and its moustache quivers delightfully. But the sequences where it chases hapless Terry Walsh to his death are very funny, precisely because they're the only bits of the episode where you feel the action has been rather unhelpfully grafted on to the location.

T: We've had so much to write about recently, I'd like to chat more about the title sequence. It's the first one I remember watching, but I don't think that it's just nostalgia talking if I pause to praise title-designer Bernard Lodge, and describe this combination of opening sequence and music as both definitive and (as yet) unbeaten. It makes no attempt to be modern and spangly – and, as a result, it hasn't dated.

And while I take your point about the Spartan nature of the script, it's also very witty. Baker and Martin have clearly cottoned to the effective dynamic between the regulars, as well as their deft comedic ability. The first scene has loads of gags, my favourite probably being Sarah's shrieked arrival (and the Doctor's downplayed reaction to it), legs sticking up in the air and a thorn up her backside (Harry: "You're not hurt, are you?"; Sarah: "Only in my dignity" – very good). I *adore* the trio of the Doctor, Sarah and Harry – they bounce off each other and judge the requirements of the scripts to absolute perfection. Just look how Elisabeth Sladen playfully puts her hat over her eyes in an attempt to get the Doctor's attention – it's so humanly quirky. Tom Baker, for his part, brings an inspired, offbeat approach to his lines – the moment where the Doctor stops to worry about his sonic screwdriver, and then thank Sarah for retrieving it, is appealingly bonkers whilst showcasing their fantastic interplay.

Also, isn't it a smart idea to give the Galsec crew South African accents? It really helps them to rise above the level of being generic, info-dumping cannon fodder, and gives them a unique aspect which plausibly sells their colonial roots. This manifests in slight linguistic quirks (such as "check", "looksee" and "dope") that show an intelligence being applied to the world in which these characters operate. Along similar lines, Vural's anger concerning the Nerva sleepers, and boasting about the Empire, gives us a believable background that the plot doesn't actually require, but which benefits the viewer. I'm not sure this is down to the writers, though, as Robert Holmes had a particular knack for world-building beyond the confines of a small-scale story, and one suspects it's his tinkering that gives the script its most admirable qualities. Philip Hinchcliffe's influence on the show, on the other hand, can be summed up by the fact that Erak grabs the Doctor *by the hair* while interrogating him. Doctor Who is beginning to feel a lot less cosy and safe.

The idea that Trafalgar Square could one day be a lifeless wasteland is extremely sobering – if only the budget could have stretched to a few scattered monuments, we might have had our very own Planet of the Apes moment. Rodney Bennett shoots the location very well, and I especially like the way we get glimpses of Roth flitting by mysteriously. Peter Rutherford's very good at suggesting this character's demented hysteria, and Donald Douglas – here playing his treacherous leader Vural – brings class to everything he does.

The Sontaran Experiment (part two)

R: So, the story is, they created the part of Harry Sullivan just in case the new Doctor turned out to be not so hot on the physical stuff. And in the second story he has to record, said Doctor challenges a Sontaran to single combat. But the actor they've cast can't handle the physical stuff – he breaks his collarbone and performs his lines subsequently with his arm in a sling... Do they use Harry Sullivan, then? Do they hell. They get Terry Walsh to double for the Doctor in a wig, and send Harry off with the sonic screwdriver (!) to do all the scientific things inside a spaceship (!!). What was all that about, then?

And what is this season's obsession with Nazis? We had the SRS group in Robot, and The Ark in Space entailed a group of humans who carefully selected the "pure" for survival, and regarded the rest as "degenerates". Here, there's a monster with a German name conducting experiments of torture on his victims. (And we haven't even got to Davros and the Daleks yet!) The biggest plot hole of The Sontaran Experiment is also its greatest piece of satire – that a scientist would prevent an entire army from invading just so he can have more time to conduct his sadistic tests. It's not logical, but it's cruelly funny, and of course it's the undoing of the Sontarans – I'm reminded of the Hinchcliffe take on the Master in The Deadly Assassin, a man who'd delay an execution so he can pull the wings off a fly.

Once you accept that Styre is basically stupid, and that the titular experiments have no value at all, then this story works as a rather bizarre piece of black comedy. Some of the plotting is very thin – actually, *all* the plotting is very thin. Vural's act of redemptive suicide feels so perfunctory that even the Doctor can't summon up the effort to acknowledge it. But there are some nice character moments regardless: I love the way that Styre is perplexed that Krans and Erak struggle to save Vural's life, for all that he's a traitor. And when the Doctor discovers the tortured Sarah, the fury with which he launches himself at Styre is the first glimpse we'll get of an actor who can, when he chooses, make the Doctor angry like no other.

T: Oh, it's utter bloody nonsense... but somehow the production works so well, it stops me from worrying. The less malleable (but on the plus side for Kevin Lindsay, less life-threatening) Sontaran mask is very effective. It has a Golem-like aspect, and a pleasingly moveable mouth that's augmented by Lindsay's gruesome tongue action. Lindsay is once again terrific (even playing two Sontarans this time), portraying Styre as a cold and ruthless scientist who regards humans as lab rats. The flat detachment with which he queries Sarah's "disagreeable noise" (i.e. scream), and dispassionately executes Roth for being "a moron" who has served his purpose, is chillingly alien – as is the cold, business-like once-over he gives Brian Ellis' corpse after he's denied the man water for nine days and seven hours. We don't *see* a lot of the torture, sure, but what we hear about takes us into crueller territory than Doctor Who has ever been before. The climax, unfortunately, entails a face-off between two stand-ins before the baddie utters the risible line, "I shall kill you all now, but first, I have more pressing matters to attend to", and the Doctor wins by issuing a pretty flimsy bluff.

But I have to ask the question: why do the Sontarans so badly need data on humankind, if we're not actually *on* the planet they're planning to invade? I say "invade", even though they don't *need* to invade – they could just land! If we're being honest, the whole premise behind this story is illogical and silly – but, thanks to the cast and the director (and indeed, the series' new house tone), we're sufficiently distracted and thoroughly entertained to the point that it doesn't matter. It might seem like a low bar to set, but if The Sontaran Experiment is a strong enough piece of television to overcome the daft concept at the heart of it, then it's a success, and we should regard it as such.

July 7th

Genesis of the Daleks (part one)

R: Director David Maloney revels in the chance to indulge his love for World War I images again, to quite striking effect: the familiar quarry is horrifyingly credible as a landscape for trench warfare. Maloney realises just how dehumanising a gas mask can make a person. The brutality of the slow machine-gun killings of the soldiers at the beginning is wonderful partly because with those goggles on, it all looks so surreal. Little wonder that it becomes the dominant visual image in the Matrix scenes of The Deadly Assassin.

Otherwise, this is a perfect synthesis of Terry Nation's formula action and Robert Holmes' sadistic black humour. This follows pretty much the standard routine for any Terry Nation opener, with the regulars being split up, preferably around a quarry, meeting some assorted secondary characters and revealing the Daleks at the end. But there is a horrible realism to all of this. And the humour is of the very bleakest – General Ravon's pride in conserving ammunition by having the Doctor and Harry hang is something to be savoured. And in the description of the ethnic cleansing which disposes of the Mutos, or in the way in which the regulars are forced to scrabble amongst corpses for respirators, the comedy dies and what's left is a wholly appalling sense of horror.

This is not Doctor Who for children. It's not necessarily subtle – even the Nazi parallels in Robot were comparatively throwaway. But anger isn't subtle, and it's so refreshing to see the rather tired analogy that Nation has been drawing between his Daleks and the horrors of Hitler treated with such conviction. Peter Miles, in particular, plays Davros' aide Nyder with the thin-lipped self control of a man who has been raised in a world where brutality is the norm. His description of the Mutos, which could so easily have sounded overwritten, is delivered with a matter-of-factness that is shocking. (And seeing this in context, don't you find it disquieting just how similar the Kaled policies of genetic purity are to the ones on Nerva?)

Once again, it's an episode that throws Tom Baker and Ian Marter together, and the rapport is excellent. Marter's insistence to keep steady the landmine that Baker has stepped on is particularly noteworthy. Harry Sullivan's having rather a grim time of it, isn't he? After his escapade with the giant robot, he might have thought he was in for fun adventuring – instead, he's each week facing warped impressions of twentieth-century atrocity. He feels like a character created by a different production team for a more innocent programme; it's hard to imagine Jo Grant, say, having to wedge a landmine safe with shingle and being prepared to take the full blast of explosive.

The one mild criticism I would make concerns that short scene at the beginning with the Time Lord. A rather mystical old man appearing out of thin air is too much the product of the Pertwee era, and feels slightly out of place with the grittiness around it. But a lot of that's with hindsight, knowing that this first use of the Time Lords by Hinchcliffe is also the last time they will be used in such a traditional way. And I do admire the scene for the no-nonsense manner with which it gets us through the exposition and into the story proper. (I love too the almost comical way Maloney has the camera pan straight past him, and then do a double take back on him when he speaks; it's as if the director is as surprised to find a cowled gentleman standing there as the Doctor is.)

T: Genesis of the Daleks is an odd duck, in that it's constantly held up as one of the best Doctor Who stories ever – and yet it suffers from being so over-familiar, we as fans some-

times take it for granted. It's been repeated more than any other story (of Classic Who, anyway: David Tennant's outings seem to be on a constant loop on BBC3), and – for a while – it was the only old story we could actually experience, thanks to the heavily truncated but much-loved audio with Tom Baker narrating. Oh, I listened to that over and *over* again – so much so, I still find the moments that were excised from it slightly jarring when they appear on screen. There's that magnificent slo-mo opening, and Nyder's introduction, where he cleverly twigs that the Doctor's an infiltrator and stands impassively betwixt his machine-gun-firing guards. If this is the quality of what they *cut*, it just goes to show the greatness of the rest of the production. And let's make no bones about this: Genesis of the Daleks is truly magnificent.

Doctor Who is often at its best when it teaches us to face danger with a smile on our face, to defeat evil and tyranny by laughing at them – so it's entirely appropriate that each regular here confronts their nervousness with humour. Sarah mutters about "Good King Wenceslas" when forced to walk in the Doctor's footsteps through a minefield, whilst Harry – when hearing the Doctor comment "Harry, I'm standing on a land mine... if I move my foot, it might detonate it" – deadpans in response "Don't move your foot". Never though – and this is the crucial thing – does the humour seem forced or contrived. Indeed, the whole episode is kept very gritty thanks to David Maloney's consistency of tone: the costumes are mucky, corpses litter the blasted heath and there's plenty of smoke. Maloney also shoots Peter Miles through a magnifying glass, gives us an effective indoor buggy (something Doctor Who has an alarming habit of not pulling off) and keeps everything marvellously tense. Honestly, it's hard to believe this is the same bloke who directed Planet of the Daleks. In Philip Hinchcliffe and Robert Holmes, Maloney seems to have finally found colleagues who give him Doctor Who in a language in which he is fluent.

And we're once again given, in the writing, a genuine attempt to create a convincing society of believable people. The Kaled civilians, military and elite are separate entities working to different agendas, and General Ravon seems justified in resenting Nyder's assumption of jurisdiction over army prisoners. These aren't just bad guys fighting on the same side, they're part of a complex society with its own quirks and hierarchies. And the way in which Ravon revels in the prospect of interrogation, and utters the battle cry of extermination, serves as a chilling reminder that no matter how *alien* the Daleks look and sound, they were once very like us. If we're not careful, we ourselves could make very good Daleks (does that ring a bell?).

As if that all weren't enough, the acting is terrific too. Peter Miles is rightly hailed for the cold, icy villainy he brings to Nyder – when Ravon says, "There's something different about [the Doctor and Harry]", Nyder replies, in the best line of a great script: "We'll find out what's different about them – by autopsy". A word, too, for Guy Siner's sneering turn as Ravon, and John Franklyn-Robbins as the black-robed Time Lord who sends the Doctor to Skaro – despite barely two minutes of screen time, he remains an extremely memorable and quotable character. There's an old saying about there being no small parts, only small actors – well, there are certainly none of the latter on display here.

Genesis of the Daleks (part two)

R: This story provides much opportunity for Tom Baker to define his Doctor. "Do I have the right?", "If you had a capsule...", "Out of their evil will come something good." But there's a particular moment here in this episode that sells his performance to me entirely – such a little moment, really, but one that shows how much Baker is now prepared to make the part his own. Early on, in the sequence where he's about to be led through an X-ray machine, he chattily asks the Kaled named Tane whether he can have some tea – it's been a very trying day. He listens impassively to the Nazi ranting that follows, then prevents Harry from moving forwards towards their captors with one hand, and says with a quiet danger, "What, no tea?"

And you can see entirely what was intended in the script. Here's that same Doctor who got up on stage and performed card tricks in Robot, or who listed all those clocks he liked to his would-be torturers in The Sontaran

Experiment. It's supposed to be a bit of cheeky eccentricity, delivered with a childish grin. And Tom Baker refuses to play it that way. He lets the joke suddenly become serious. He demonstrates in one soft monotone his frustration for the bureaucracy he's trapped in, how much he hates these fascists and all they stand for... and how much, for all his apparent flippancy, they should be advised not to push him too far. It's a strange reading of the line, and it's unpredictable, and it's pure Baker.

The scene in which he encounters the Mark Three Travel Machine seems to recall The Power of the Daleks – all these fussy little scientists cooing without fear over a monster we know will surely kill them. It's the first time since then that the show has played that trick of letting the audience (and the Doctor) know far more about the Daleks than the supporting characters, who respond to them with a complacency that is horrifying. It's also the first scene in which we get to see Davros in full light. More on his character later, and the exceptional work that Michael Wisher does to bring him to life. For the moment, let's just say that Wisher's Davros mask is a thing of horrible beauty – even now, having seen this adventure so many times, it's hard to see where the rubber ends and the flesh begins. Those blinded eyes, just wrinkled hollows, are mesmerising.

We know the Daleks, and we think we know the Thals too. The biggest shock surely for a contemporary audience is that the bland do-gooders we saw on Spiridon are just as callous and brutal as the men we know will become Daleks. That's one of the great triumphs of Genesis – that Nation's rather black and white portrayal of good and evil is set aside so completely. It works both ways. The nameless Kaled leader played by Richard Reeves in episode one was a Hitler Youth thug; here we see him again, and he's a frightened captive boy, and he dies trying to help Sarah. (That final image we have of him, eyes wide open, slumping to the ground as a dead weight, is especially nasty.)

T: That's a brilliant summation of a brilliant episode, if I may say so, Mr Shearman. You write about Daleks very well.

I don't often do this, but I agree 100% with the above, and would have written pretty much exactly the same, had I the advantage of going first. As it is, let me follow you up with praise for other areas: the freeze-frame cliff-hanger, the sound effects suggesting a chilly night in the wastelands, and the punch Richard Reeves (as the Kaled Leader) administers to the Thal guard (even as his victim falls down, Reeves poises himself, ready for action like an experienced soldier would do). Indeed, fear makes companions of the very disparate group of Sarah, the Kaled Leader and the Muto Sevrin. Our introduction to the Mutos suggested they would be grunting savages, there to deliver scares and little else, but Sevrin is benign and selfless. The Kaled, on the other hand, was clearly set up as a villain in episode one, and now meets his death stopping to help our heroine.

Genesis refuses to deal in pat absolutes, and the programme is richer for this complexity – it's not the case that everyone's either a goodie or a baddie, even in such an uncompromising world. The cruelty of this environment is emphasised by Pat Gorman's Thal soldier opting to shoot Sarah for being too slow, the Doctor getting thrown into his cell ("I'm sorry if they hurt you," says Ronson, impotently) and the Doctor getting biffed as he tries to reclaim the Time Ring. Even the dialogue sounds sinister – words such as "distronic" and "toxaemia" come off as frightening, even if you don't know what they mean.

And at the centre of this is Michael Wisher's extraordinary performance as Davros. From his shaky hand to his compelling ability to rant like a Dalek in an utterly believable fashion, Wisher creates a truly iconic character – one of the great inventions of Doctor Who. In lesser hands, Davros would be a gimmick: a batty half man/ half Dalek that was an interesting concept, but nothing else. Wisher pulls off the incredible feat of transcending the character's historical significance as creator of the programme's most memorable villains – aided by the superb design of his costume and mask, Wisher makes Davros' personality the most interesting thing on display.

As if all that weren't enough, we get the memorable line – after a scan reveals the Doctor's extraterrestrial origins – of the Doctor telling Ronson, "You can't always judge from external appearances". That simple sentence sums up this programme that I love more than any other.

July 8th

Genesis of the Daleks (part three)

R: In Planet of the Daleks, Hilary Minster played Marat, who gamely sacrificed himself so that the Doctor and his friends could escape. Good Thal. Here he plays a soldier who knocks Sarah over the edge of a rocket, and taunts her as he holds on to her hand. Bad Thal. Even I'm not pretentious enough to believe that the casting was deliberate, that the audience were meant to be shocked by the behaviour of a man that may have been Marat's great-great-grandfather. But it does empathise just how much this story has turned everything on its head, that the basic tenets of good and evil have now become so blurred; indeed, this one scene must stand out as the most deliberate display of sadism we've yet seen in Doctor Who, and it's all the more shocking because it's carried out so casually by a character not even important enough to be given a name.

Genesis of the Daleks takes many risks. Again, from a 2009 perspective, we accept that it's a terrific story – a sticker on my DVD proclaims that it was voted best story ever! But when you bear in mind that even as we reach the halfway point of the adventure, the eponymous Daleks have only appeared in three scenes, and that the story has done its level best to puncture our expectations for both plot and tone, you can see that this might have fallen flat on its face. Indeed, let's be honest – it ought to have done. On every clear level, this is a story which fundamentally refuses to deliver what it offers on the tin.

And the reason it works is because of Davros. It's not so much the performance or the script – if Davros were just another humanoid, we wouldn't have that constant reminder of the Daleks. It's the fact that he appears to be sitting in a Dalek base, that the arch enemies of the Doctor have clearly been built in his image, that means we more than get away with it. The measure of the character's greatness is in that scene with Mogran, where the Kaled politician informs Davros that his work will be suspended pending an enquiry. You cringe throughout the whole thing, throughout all Davros' apparent politeness – you expect Mogran to be murdered at any instant. And the clincher is that brilliant moment when Davros offers to shut down his experiments within 24 hours, and Mogran pushes for twelve. It's a clever echo of the scene in episode one where Nyder humiliates Ravon by insisting that the supplies he can't spare be delivered to Davros by midnight rather than by dawn, the exercise of bullying power for its own sake. And I feel that it's Mogran's fatal attempt to do the same thing, to belittle Davros that one fraction too much, that signs the death warrant not only for him but his entire race. We're left as shocked as Nyder by just how far Davros will take his revenge. Davros is compared to Hitler, but even Hitler wouldn't have destroyed all the German people in a fit of pique. In spite of the less-than-subtle Nazi allegory, the script suddenly pushes Davros further, into a study of monomaniac totalitarianism – in this instance, he becomes more like a Stalin figure.

On the DVD documentary, Terrance Dicks and Barry Letts assert that the story they'd commissioned from Terry Nation wouldn't have been that much different had they produced it rather than Hinchcliffe and Holmes. But it's clear too that even 30 years later, they're squirming somewhat at just how cold and brutal their series had become within mere weeks of their leaving. A softened Genesis, watered down to a level that could have been broadcast during the Pertwee era, would seem to us now like a squandered opportunity. But playing Devil's Advocate for a moment – are Letts and Dicks necessarily wrong? Watching Hilary Minster tell the terrified Sarah how he could slacken his grip and let her fall to her death, and watching him only a few weeks after he played his Thal as a hero, it's jarring just how quickly Doctor Who has reinvented itself as something that's thrown away its innocence. I admire it, of course I do. But it makes me uneasy.

T: Good, it *should* make you uneasy – it's a cruel, grim world out there, and it's irresponsible to pretend to kids that it isn't. Instead, you expose them to harshness, and then have a morally driven hero like the Doctor to demonstrate that they can navigate through life's difficulties with wit, intelligence and a sense of justice. All-ages programmes that are safe and pretty are no preparation for adult life. It's like the abolition of competitive sport in school because it might upset the loser (and I speak as the doyenne of losers) – it's preposterous not to prepare adolescents for the fact that they won't get everything they want in life. What are we trying to do – keep life's harsh realities from them until they are grown-ups so that they are a massive surprise?

Anyway, I am (as is often the case) moved to consider the guest cast. Stephen Yardley – here appearing as Sevrin – is a genuine TV hero; there seemingly wasn't a programme in the 70s and 80s that didn't rely on his presence. He makes for a likeable ally who embodies quiet dignity – it's a million miles away from his Howard's Way role, which gave him a deserved slice of fame, but seemed to spell the end of his small-screen ubiquity. Whereas Tom Georgeson became legendary *after* this story, and it's great to see an actor playing a fairly unimportant supporting character (the Kaled scientist Kavell), in the knowledge that he'll later flourish with career-defining roles in Boys from the Blackstuff and Between the Lines. Oh, and look – there's Max Faulkner, as a Thal Guard, making his third appearance in six stories. I've never seen him interviewed, which seems like a wasted opportunity. You get the impression that Faulkner must have been camping in the BBC car park at the time, so often does he pop inside for a cameo in Doctor Who.

But strangely enough, in a story populated by illustrious thespians future and past, as well as showcasing Doctor Who's iconic monsters and the definitive Doctor, the *best* thing about Genesis of the Daleks owes to two journeymen character actors who the general public would be hard pressed to recognise on sight, let alone name. Michael Wisher and Peter Miles do *incredible* work as Davros and Nyder. Having smartly opted to show the hair's breadth between Davros and his inventions, Wisher here demonstrates a controlled, manipulative and human (alright, Kaled) intelligence that can turn on a dime – he's softly spoken and contrite in the face of Mogran's demands, plausible and obeisant with the Thals, and controlled and powerful when alone with Nyder. And Miles doesn't play Davros' lackey as a one-note sadist – even he seems genuinely unsettled by his master's actions. When Davros asks Nyder if he ever doubted that he'd play the genocide card against his own people, the inscrutable "no" with which Nyder replies suggests that his loyalties may be wavering. Notice how the camera lingers upon his face, which remains an impassive mask apart from his darting eyes, suggesting that his mind is working overtime even if he can't let his expression show it.

And, all right – none of this is to overlook Tom Baker's contribution, as it's so easy to take for granted that he's a madman who was born to play this part. Just look at the wild stare and toothy grin he uses confirming to Harry that they've got to cross the wastelands once more, "and that's when our troubles really begin". Baker's Doctor has a reckless compulsion to be obtuse in the face of overwhelming odds; he's an overgrown child who revels in danger, as much out of excitement as a sense of right and wrong. But he's hardly bereft of grit: Pertwee's aikido seems like a camp indulgence when this incarnation overcomes a couple of guards by smacking their heads together.

I know, I know... I'm really going on about this episode, but there is so much about it that's great and inventive, particularly in the way it's calibrated to show how the people of Skaro – Kaleds and Thals alike – are ripe for being turned into the Daleks. Even though General Ravon has become an ally, he's still prone to ranting, this time about the Kaled Dome's indestructibility. (These young soldiers need little prompting to propagandise and issue barked boasts about their strength and power.) It's also telling that it's a Thal politician who describes the destruction of the Kaleds as extermination, and there's a no-nonsense brutality to the way the Thal soldiers open fire down the hole in the floor through which our heroes have made their escape.

Sadly, though, I worry that all the excellence we've outlined above would be lost on a modern audience, who'd just marvel at the length of everyone's hair, and scoff at the Doctor's party being attacked in the wastelands by giant clams. I don't know why I'm so grumpy today – perhaps it's because exposure to something

this brilliant makes me mourn for the loss of an audience who were prepared to live with the artifice of drama (which is, by its very nature, the definition of artificial) and invest themselves in what the programme-makers were trying to do. Yes, it's easy to watch Shakespeare, and point out that ghosts and witches don't exist and that anyone who gets stabbed doesn't bleed – but if you pat yourself on the back for noticing such triviality whilst failing to appreciate the language, themes and characters that the Bard is expertly drawing, you're a rank philistine. Now that is fine, but too many people like this seem to now be in charge of making or commenting on our TV output. McDonald's may be easy to consume, replete as it is with unchallenging flavours, but that doesn't mean it's good for you, or that you wouldn't enjoy something more complex if given the opportunity – and I'd draw the same parallels with TV drama. If that makes me sound elitist, then so be it.

Take me to my bunker...

Genesis of the Daleks (part four)

R: We know what countdowns in Doctor Who are for: they're to be thwarted. We've just had this played out in Robot – a ticking clock to zero, and rockets will be launched, and there'll be armageddon... but it's okay, the Doctor's there and he'll stop it with seconds to spare, and flashing us a cheeky grin to boot! This time, he seems as shocked as we are that zero is reached, the rocket does launch, a holocaust does ensue. There's so close a parallel to the final episode of Robot, it surely must be deliberate. We were led to believe that characters like Mogran and Ravon might be important – now they're wiped out, without even the dignity of a farewell scene. And cleverly, the Doctor reminds us that he's sent Harry and Sarah into that burning dome. For once, we might even believe that the unthinkable has happened... that as the series' clichés are being turned upside down, that maybe the production team really have killed off the companions. It's ten whole minutes before we realise they survived – ten minutes within which Terry Nation not only destroys the Kaled dome but wipes out the Thals too, and completely changes the direction of the story.

The extermination of Ronson fascinated me as a child – it made the death ray look quite the most painful manner of death imaginable, and it's still my favourite Dalek execution put on screen. The negative effect works so well here; the white costume of the scientist caste turning James Garbutt black, but his wide open, screaming mouth beaming out in white. This is long protracted agony; just look at the way that all the other Kaleds have to shield their eyes from the glare of his burning body.

To be critical of all this: it begins to dawn on you just how little the Doctor and his companions have affected the storyline. The whole subplot of Gharman starting a rebellion is nicely written, but it's happening entirely independently of our heroes – and the fact that Gharman has barely had a character up to now robs it of greater impact. It's only when Nyder and Davros hear movement in the ventilation shafts that suddenly the Doctor crashes into the plot at last. Only at the episode end does Davros acknowledge the Doctor's importance – it's their first conversation, and so late into the story! – and it's a measure of how powerful Davros is that without that acknowledgement, the Doctor couldn't help but look a little irrelevant. It promises to help centre a story that, however epic in scale, has also been very messily structured. At last the Doctor and Davros are going to face each other down. That in itself makes the cliffhanger exciting.

T: There's an urgency to the acting that absolutely sells us on the height of the stakes here. Ronson hasn't really done much since helping the Doctor in episode two – but before he's killed, James Garbutt is there, at the back of the scene, hands clasped in brooding alarm at the sheer scale of the destruction being wrought, oblivious that Davros has also signed his death warrant. Then there's Tom Baker as the Doctor – his determination to stop the rocket launch against the Kaled dome has so much steel, it takes four Thals to manhandle him down. And even though his actions have prompted the carnage, Michael Wisher's Davros vows to retaliate with actions "so massive, so merciless" – just as cruel dictators use "righteous" rhetoric to justify the most heinous of crimes.

It's very hard to deny that Genesis has turned on its head with this episode. Owing to the Doctor's attempts to use political methods to prevent the Daleks' creation, two races have experienced a massacre – so now the gloves are off. As the Doctor sits hunched in the Thal control room, Tom Baker's mournful countenance – his eyelids heavy and drawn, his face worn with fatigue – conveys an emotional depth rarely seen in our hero. Fortunately, there's a palpable relief when we bump into Sarah and Harry again – and learn they didn't die horribly in the Kaled dome – and Elisabeth Sladen continues to shine with little choices such as her reflex cry of surprise at the force of the Doctor's hug, and her resigned self-admonishment as she goes ahead of the Doctor in the ventilation shaft. She even nips back to offer sweet old Sevrin a thank you – it's another example of our regulars bringing tiny moments of humanity, warmth and decency into the grim universe that Robert Holmes and Philip Hinchcliffe have created.

I also love the way that, despite being handed a near-impossible task with the infamous giant clams, David Maloney bravely shoots them as if they're the scariest thing ever, and the cast react to their static menace by acting their socks off. Okay, they're trying to make a silk purse out of a sow's ear, but at least they're having a go at it. And everything works to the cliffhanger, where Michael Wisher's clipped, single-minded delivery leaves us in no doubt that Davros will not fail to wring the information he requires out of the Doctor, whatever the cost.

It's no exaggeration to say that this is the most dramatic and hardcore Doctor Who story there's ever been. Even the title is brilliant, the word "genesis" being Biblically meaty – unless of course, it reminds you of Phil Collins, which probably dilutes its effectiveness somewhat.

July 9th

Genesis of the Daleks (part five)

R: This is magnificent.

I'll be honest. I'm not going to write much about this episode. Partly because it's so very good, it'll just end up being a list of dramatic moments so famous that they've come to define Doctor Who. But mostly because I want to get back to the television and watch episode six. It's there in the next room, calling out to me. I'm coming, Davros, I'm coming.

The reason why this is so good, I think, is that the power politics in it are so credible. And in Doctor Who, that's a very rare thing. The series as a rule requires the presentation of a status quo powerful enough that it can be sufficiently threatening to challenge the Doctor – and the destruction of that status quo over the course of a few short episodes. (Some stories actually make a version of how rushed this looks – The Happiness Patrol, for example, has the Doctor challenging himself to bring down an entire regime in a night, as if he's trying to get into The Guinness Book of Records.) Episode five of Genesis shows us how people who were happily engaged in fascist policies turn against their extremist leader, but for all their newfound ideals can't carry out the bloodless revolution they want. It shows how loyalist hardliners like Nyder are so incensed by the apparent indolence of the dictator they venerate, they actually challenge him directly as well. And most brilliantly, it demonstrates how – if a leader has real power and real charisma – he can be the most dominant figure in the room even as he's facing the rebels who've overthrown him.

The scene in question is the one where Davros agrees to listen to Gharman's terms. He's surrounded by men with guns – but they're frightened of him, by instinct they still want to flatter him, they look awkward in his presence and shuffle about. Michael Wisher's performance here is quite remarkable. After a couple of minutes' conversation, he has assumed complete control again, ordering the rebels to convene a new meeting, and dismissing them when he's tired of them. And the brilliance of it all is that it's not emphasised, the irony isn't made overt. Gharman and his followers leave the room, and they don't even appear to realise they're kowtowing to Davros once more, that without thinking they've just fallen back to the deference they've always shown him – even as they believe they've defeated him, even as they believe they've won. Of course they haven't won. We don't know what Davros has planned for them yet. It doesn't matter. Everything about the exchange, the way Nation has written it, and the way Maloney has directed it, firmly underlines Davros' unquestionable superiority.

T: It seems fair to ask: *is* this the ultimate, definitive Doctor Who episode? The one you'd show *anyone*, if you only had 25 minutes to demonstrate the programme's greatness? Quite possibly.

True, the plot stops dead in its tracks for the two major protagonists to have a chat, but *what* a chat. Michael Wisher imbues Davros with a zealous thirst for knowledge, and his debate with the Doctor serves to strip away Davros' ugly physiognomy and Dalek chair, giving us a glimpse of the man he once was. His standpoint that the Daleks are a power for good, not evil, is *exactly* the kind of rationale you'd expect from a crazed fanatic whose achievements and power have divorced him from reality. Much has been made of Wisher's vocal performance, but look how he flaps about pathetically when the Doctor momentarily turns off his life support, and how he slowly, patiently *tap... tap... taps* his fingers, biding his time whilst the odds seemingly stack against him, and even Nyder shows signs of buckling under the strain. Davros is a fantastic creation visually and conceptually, but boy were they lucky to employ an actor who gives the performance of a lifetime. Even when appearing to be reasonable and comply with Gharman's demands, Wisher doesn't quite hide Davros' arrogance – he dismisses his accusers like a curt schoolmaster even after seeming to acquiesce to their demands.

Story-wise, it's interesting that the audio recording of Dalek losses in future becomes another fly in the Doctor's ointment, just as the Time Ring has been – they're two pieces of jeopardy to keep the regulars busy whilst the major drama goes on around them. This is a good idea – it would be wrong for the Doctor to personally lead the rebellion, it would be a bit of a cheat. Instead, the Kaleds themselves are empowered to rise up for what they believe in, just as the Thals were in the very first Dalek story. Amongst the Kaleds is Tom Georgeson, on whose behalf I was always a bit put out – even though he features on the cassette, he doesn't get a credit on the sleeve. (I hope he's had residuals.) And as if to credit your take on

Ronson's death, note the sheer agony of the Thal extra we see despatched this week. This isn't histrionic acting – the director has clearly instructed everyone to die in abject pain and suffering.

You know, I've enjoyed Terry Nation's brazen desire to throw set piece after set piece at us, and the way his scripts are replete with cool-sounding names and comic-book jeopardy. But what makes this truly great is surely down to Robert Holmes tweaking this script devilishly, in a way that transforms a story that would have been *exciting* into something unpleasant, epic and powerful. "What do you want done with this?" says Nyder, indicating the unconscious Doctor. *This.* So much more sadistic a word than *him*.

What do *I* want done with this story? I want it stored forever in a museum of great televisual achievements, that's what.

Genesis of the Daleks (part six)

R: This episode suffers (just a little) from the need to behave like a proper little Doctor Who story. It sometimes gives the impression of Terry Nation needing to squeeze in some of his usual clichés about the Doctor being unable to escape from the planet. The Time Ring isn't on the table!... Oh yes, there it is, sorry. The Time Ring's been lost in a corridor fight!... Oh, it's okay, there it is on the floor. And part of the reason for all this is that, ultimately, there isn't much room for the Doctor in the real drama of the episode – it's telling that during the meeting between Davros and the rebels, Tom Baker stands silent at the back, and leans over the extras into shot. Or that when the Daleks finally do emerge, the Doctor's like us, watching the whole thing safely on a telly.

But in a funny way, just for once, the Doctor being more or less superfluous actually lends the story its epic identity. All of this is just too big to be affected by our hero – and although that would typically be a flaw, it also means that by refusing to give the story a pat resolution, it avoids the trap of feeling rushed or anticlimactic. The set-piece scenes in the story may only result in a dozen extras falling down in negative, but they feel huge, they feel as if they represent totalitarianism triumphing over democracy. It ought to be depressing, but it

isn't – the Daleks might win, but the story has focused so much upon Davros that the scene where his creations stand up to him, and exterminate him, instead invites us to be on their side for once. There's an ironic rightness to so much of what's seen here – the tape recording that will compromise the future is destroyed by a Dalek gun, it's a Dalek itself that sets off the explosion in the incubation room that will delay their development by a thousand years. And ultimately Davros is killed (?) by his own creations, and am I right to see a hesitancy in his final moments, that he's still unable to bring his shaking hand down on the button that will destroy his life's work?

Genesis of the Daleks works by breaking all the rules at a critical time in the programme's history when the instinct would be to play safe. Barry Letts and Terrance Dicks thoughtfully commissioned for their successors a series of stories using classic monsters – all the better to ease wary viewers into the new Doctor. Philip Hinchcliffe and Robert Holmes' reaction was to take the safety of a Dalek story and make it as bold and jarring as possible – removing the Daleks from the action, making the Doctor weaker than he's ever been before, and ending on a note of rare failure. Tonally, it's unlike anything the series has previously attempted; it blasts into Doctor Who and changes it. It takes huge risks, and it's in the risk-taking – in the likelihood that this should have been a failure – that it gives the series a new direction. For years now, Doctor Who has been cautious. It's been running for 11 years, it's an old show. And from now on, you feel it has the capacity to shock once again.

T: The Berry Letts era had moral objectives: to stand-up for the little man, to save the planet, to reflect the issues of the day. But Genesis of the Daleks has a moral *dilemma*, that's the key which makes it so much more sophisticated and less preachy.

Now, don't get me wrong – I admire Letts and Dicks for injecting substance into their teatime travails. They're both empathic and intelligent, and Letts is a paragon of virtue and a decent, benign man of absolute integrity. I never had the pleasure of meeting Robert Holmes, but I get the impression he had a darker sense of humour – a desire to acknowledge the complexity of moral issues, and that darkness and light often go hand in hand. Both the Doctor and Sarah have legitimate points of view when discussing whether to destroy the Daleks, but the script doesn't cop out of having the Doctor ultimately choosing to go back and do his best to wipe them out. He even hangs around whilst a Dalek's shooting at him – perhaps he knows that he can only live with himself after committing such a genocidal act if living is something he's not likely to be doing for an especially long time afterwards.

And I know I've commented upon him before, but I simply must do it one last time – Peter Miles is often rightly praised for his impassive, chilling acting style, but what about the ghost of a smile that permanently threatens to crack his expression? It was there in episode one when he interrogated the Doctor, and it's present now when dealing with the rebels. It offers a number of readings, and is so more interesting than if he'd just opted for the heartlessness which he displays so naturally. That little smile sees its final flourish after Gharman's extermination, and the camera chillingly zooms in on Nyder's sadistic gleam as he surveys the carnage.

But ultimately, for a story that kept them on the sidelines for a great long while, have ever *the Daleks* seemed so powerful? Fair enough, they spend some time as grunts to Davros, being nothing like the Machiavellian plotters of David Whitaker's scripts, but it's only when we see Davros' remaining shreds of humanity – arrogance and pity are both present in his final moments – that we realise the extent of the Daleks' ruthlessness. We spent most of Genesis believing that Davros and Nyder were the best pair of nasties we've had thus far in Doctor Who, but we'll soon see about *that*. Nyder is dispatched pretty summarily, and, yes, it could be interpreted that Davros cannot bring himself to press a button he'd berated others for not having the courage to press earlier. That final pause allows Davros to show a tiny sliver of humanity, and that, in the Dalek world he has created, he no longer has a place! Never has someone's own petard hoisted them quite so poetically. The desperation in Davros' voice serves as a stark contrast to the immovable, intransigent Daleks, who casually tell him that he's made a major miscalculation –

and there's that terrible image of the creatures (*lots* of them) looming over the pile of dead Kaled bodies.

I've enjoyed every minute of this – bar, I guess, the giant clams, but let's not be distracted by trivia. As this story comes to an end (and the Dalek completes the word "universe", something it didn't manage on the cassette), I marvel at just how astonishing this Baker's half-dozen has been. Genesis? Genius.

July 10th

Revenge of the Cybermen (part one)

R: The biggest problem this episode faces is that it invites comparison with more dynamic stories around it. It's filmed on the same set as The Ark in Space, but you can immediately tell that whereas beforehand the over-lit sets suggested an unnerving sterility, here they've just turned on the lights too brightly – there's little atmosphere at all. For a while, it's rather fun to see the Doctor and company back in the exact same setting they were in a couple of months ago – there's the hint that this story might be building on the idea in The Monster of Peladon last year, to return to a location and see a new adventure played out there. But the dialogue quickly establishes that this particular Nerva isn't supposed to resemble the one from The Ark in Space, which is something of a puzzle, since it so evidently does.

But more obvious still are the parallels between this and Genesis, broadcast just one week previously. In both instances, the creators of favourite monsters from the sixties are hired to write new outings for them. Genesis went right back to the beginning of the Daleks, and even though they've been appearing regularly in the series for the past four seasons, manages to depict them as something entirely new, filtered through the reactions of characters who have no idea what they are at all. Revenge does the exact opposite. It takes monsters that haven't properly featured for over six years, and yet puts them into a tale where everybody knows of them, and refers to them with a sort of world-weariness. The Doctor is able to deduce their presence in the story even before we the audience get a chance to look at them, which seems misjudged. And somehow, although there's an entire generation of young children who won't have heard of them, they're already presented as something familiar and complacent before they even get the chance to speak.

If you look beyond the expectations that Ark and Genesis set-up, there's plenty to like. There's a lovely sensitive scene where a crewman asks the control room operator for news of his already dead brother. The sequence where our heroes pick their way grimly through the bodies of supposed plague victims, all lying higgledy-piggledy in corridors, is really rather disturbing. And I love that bit where the Doctor has to play the children's game of crossing a bedroom without touching the floor – I used to do that a lot when I was a kid. He gets to swing on the wardrobe door too. (I broke mine. Tom Baker is more agile than I was.)

T: I was expecting to hate this. Revenge of the Cybermen was the second VHS purchase I ever made. The first was The Seeds of Death – and at £39, it cost the same amount as a small house when I bought it in 1988. Now, thanks to the credit crunch, £39 is also roughly what a house I bought for £115,000 six years ago is currently worth. (It makes you want to take a day trip to Voga, to scoop up some of its gold.) With Seeds, I got Patrick Troughton, six episodes and the atmosphere and olde-worlde charm of black and white. On the other hand, Revenge was – to my teenage eyes – just *awful*.

So it's a pleasant surprise to find much to enjoy in this opening instalment. Shocking as this might sound, I've never actually seen Revenge in episodic form – I had the compilation video, and never bothered to upgrade to the re-release. Maybe I'm just in a good mood, but I find myself looking generously upon it – those shop-window dummies playing the corpses, for example, made the paranoid younger me cringe at their artifice, but now they look like twisted, ugly cadavers.

Really, it all starts out very well. Poor Harry asks if he can keep the Time Ring, which vanishes back to Gallifrey, leading to some light joshing with the Doctor... who then opens a

door through which falls a corpse. A grave atmosphere immediately descends, and Tom Baker gets on with being brooding and ominous. And we then cut to crewman Warner struggling to keep awake – it's an authentic touch which keeps us slap-bang in the arena that Holmes and Hinchcliffe haunt, where tiredness drains, people have heart conditions and laser beams hurt like hell. Alec Wallis (as Warner) has done good, unshowy work as a radio operator for director Michael Briant before (in The Sea Devils), and he doesn't disappoint here.

Among the other characters, Professor Kellman (played by Jeremy Wilkin) is resting on Stevenson's jacket, so his Commander wrenches it from underneath him, whilst Lester is clearly stiff and worn out from his extra duties. So far, so good – we have real people reacting to real situations, despite all talk of space beacons and wandering asteroids. And yes, all right, Kellman's villainy is as transparent as it is uninteresting, and the excellently masked Cybermen are introduced without much care (as opposed to the Daleks, who were reinvented with a sense of moment and awe), but the Cybermats' reintroduction is at least gratifyingly done.

But all in all, it's funny how Revenge of the Cybermen is often dismissed as being a bit *silly*, when there's quite a lot on display for fans of the grim and gritty like myself. There's a hole in the head of a Vogan who has been shot dead, we get the grisly scenario that the authorities have quarantined the beacon and left the crew to die, and Stevenson seems prepared to shoot Warner dead at the first sight of infection. The Caves of Androzani always gets lauded for its use of machine guns rather than lasers, and it's notable that we get the same here, plus some effective make-up and front axial projection to depict the Cyber-infection. As a bonus, there's some great touches in the dialogue for William Marlowe as crewman Lester: "We used to leave 'em where they dropped", he says of the first plague-victims, and "He's as tough as an old boot", he notes about his expiring comrade. Someone like Lester would say *exactly* that while trying to give his colleague some form of prosaic eulogy, without sounding too sentimental in the process.

I'm so glad I've had the chance to watch this full story in context – so much of it leaps out and entertains me, as opposed to those old days when I only had two stories on video, and spent most of my time watching this wondering if Ronald Leigh-Hunt (as Commander Stevenson here, but also in The Seeds of Death) had somehow twisted someone at BBC Video's arm to ensure him maximum royalties. I hope he spent his share of my £39 on something lovely. Like a house.

Revenge of the Cybermen (part two)

R: I love Harry Sullivan. If I were a Doctor Who character, that's the one I'd like to imagine I'd be. Brave and reliable and gently funny. (Oh, in real life I'd probably be Kellman, actually, but I can dream, can't I?) The rapport between Ian Marter and Tom Baker has been one of the real highlights of the season for me. But for some reason, Harry has barely had much of a partnership with Sarah; perhaps because if you're going to split the Doctor off from a companion, giving a separate storyline to the one that's established is going to be a more sensible way to do it.

But this episode stands out because, at last, Harry and Sarah get to spend time together. And it's delightful. Right from the moment where Sarah revives in Harry's arms once they've transmatted onto Voga, and struggles to get free, there's beautifully judged comedy between the two of them. They argue a lot – but never spitefully, more like brother and sister. The unimpressed tut that Sarah gives when Harry points out that she was on the verge of popping her clogs, or the way that they both irritate the other as they break their gold chains and make for freedom, is laugh-out-loud funny – but also very real, and very credible, and very human. In a story that is frankly inhabited by a bunch of rather dull ciphers, it's Sarah and Harry that give this adventure some life. And as they stare down Certain Doom™ and Harry tells Sarah that it looks as if they're about to die, her frustration with him for being so obvious is a perfect character moment for the two of them.

Otherwise, this is fine – but a bit uninspiring. The political scenes on Voga are actually written with a lot more verve than anything that's happening on Nerva, and Michael Briant has got quite a cast to make the most of the dialogue. But in an era of the programme where the masks are so good, for once the fact that David Collings and Kevin Stoney are trapped behind so much rubber and hair means that the performances get lost. And Michael Wisher, who's just made Davros so electrifying without our ever seeing his face, is obliged to blow his nose a lot with a handkerchief in his attempt to find characterisation.

T: Oh, I dunno – Michael Wisher's game decision to give Magrick a bit of a cough seems like a subtle piece of Stanislavskian immersion into character, especially in contrast to Jeremy Wilkin's lip curling. And whatever the hindrance of their Vogan masks, the guest cast lift this story a massive amount. David Collings is fantastic as the warhawk Vorus – he's an actor with a weak "r", which I had assumed was a bi-product of the overhanging lip on his mask, but Louise Jameson told me was a real-life impediment. I suffered a similar affliction in my youth, and was *terrified* it would stop me being an actor. I especially remember my family laughing when I asked them to tape a South Bank Show about a Doctor Who composer, just in case it showed any old clips for me to devour. The composer's name? Richard Rodney Bennett. Oh, how they laughed as I sounded like Rik from The Young Ones... so I practiced and *practiced* rolling my "r"s, usually with Shakespearian or sci-fi languages, where this method of speaking sounds appropriately grand. No wonder Mr Collings has prospered in both genres. It's been great, over the years, seeing him as expertly wrangle the Bard as he does lines such as "You have the philosophy of a cringing mouse, Tyrum". And I was very pleased to see him get a mention in Kenneth Branagh's autobiography, as a brilliant Mercutio that entranced the young Kenny during an early trip to the theatre. Sadly, when Branagh grew up to direct Shakespeare on film, he didn't give Mr Collings a job – which sadly deprived us more screen appearances from this *brilliant* actor, who nonetheless has been doing pretty well for our leading theatre companies.

And then there's William Marlowe – who, I later discovered, always kept something back during rehearsals, so his fellow actors had something fresh to respond to during a take. His line to Kellman that "You walked right into [our trap]" line is so natural, it sounds like an ad lib – and it may well have been, I don't know, because Marlowe is so consistently naturalistic, he makes this acting lark look easy. I also like the way he fires his gun by reflex after he's hit and falls to the ground. Doctor Who doesn't always cast tough guy actors in tough guy parts, but when it does like here, it adds an extra gritty boys-own dimension to proceedings. Another returnee to the Doctor Who fold, Kevin Stoney (as Tyrum) seems quietly amused and playfully cantankerous ("As always, I'm looking forward to our meetings", he says to Vorus, daring David Collings to tell him to sod off). And bless Ronald Leigh- Hunt for tentatively knocking on the door of the man who murdered 47 of his friends and sold them out to the Cybermen. You'll get nowhere in the world without manners.

But the main star of this episode, strangely enough, is Wookey Hole. I remember going there as a kid, and being impressed by a display boasting about the various TV shows that had been mounted there – including "Doctor Who and the Cybermen". I was confused, especially as they'd rendered a few paintings based on the illustrations in the novel of the same name. Did they really use Wookey Hole as the surface of the moon, thought I? Or was it a mistake, and had the more-likely Revenge benefited from those spooky, beautiful caverns? I had to wait 'till I got home to check my facts, before patting myself on the back that it was indeed this story, and revelling in the knowledge that you shouldn't always believe what you read.

July 11th

Revenge of the Cybermen (part three)

R: The Cybermen aren't really all that impressive. But I'm not sure that's such a bad thing.

Over the next few years, we're going to get a lot of instances where Tom Baker demonstrates his angry contempt for the monsters. But this is the first real example of it, and it's one of the most interesting. In earlier stories, he's tried to reason with the Wirrn or with Davros on an intellectual or humanistic level. From the moment that Kellman discovers a bag of jelly babies in the Doctor's pockets, though, you get the feeling that this is going to be different – even unconscious, the sheer anarchy of Baker's performance is going to run rings around the po-faced Cybermen.

On a story level, it's hard to disagree with the Doctor – the Cybermen *are* pathetic, a bunch of tin soldiers. The adventure itself feels compromised as a result. But on a series level, the effect is much more beneficial – here, at last, after stories in which the Doctor has either been denied centre stage, or allowed to be the hero at the story's conclusion, he emerges as being unquestionably dominant. And it seems to me too that there's more to this confrontation with the Cybermen than meets the eye – Doctor Who has dusted off icons from its black and white days, but the new Doctor looks on them with disdain. It's as if the production team as a whole are showing their indifference towards Doctor Who's history, and indicating their commitment to something more fresh. When all's said and done, every other story of the Pertwee years relied upon the return of a continuing or long-established adversary – this is the last time we're going to see Doctor Who resort to old monsters until The Invasion of Time. Tom Baker's amused vitriol against the Cybermen is exhilarating to watch, if only because it's so lacking in respect. In its beacon scenes, Revenge of the Cybermen has taken all of the clichés we've come to expect from the days of Troughton, and cruelly held them up to the light. The story feels suddenly very old-fashioned – and there's a merciless streak to the way Robert Holmes shows how the traditional format of the show is wanting. Trapped into producing an adventure that feels more backward-looking than they'd have wanted, Hinchcliffe and Holmes ensure that we've had our fill of nostalgia, and make us cry out for something new.

T: Well, it's a brave move to make your monster deliberately boring, isn't it? It's even braver to not shoot the man who plays their leader for doing so in a robotic American accent. Bless

Christopher Robbie, neither of his Who turns (this, and as the Karkus in The Mind Robber) are particularly good. Indeed, I could go so far as to say that they're wonderfully awful – and yet, I'll always be rather fond of him. At Sixth Form College, there were two trips to see Robert Stephens play King Lear at the RSC. I was on the second and saw Stephens himself. My then-girlfriend went earlier when his understudy played the role... yes, it was Christopher Robbie, promoted for a couple of nights only from the tiny role of Curan, thence to return when the theatrical knight was better. So good was he, my lady said, that the audience gave him a standing ovation at the curtain call and tears sprang into his eyes. I only saw him play Curan, and Stephens was excellent, but part of me wishes I could have witnessed what must have been the high point of Robbie's career. As it is, I can only watch him in this... which most definitely isn't.

That said, I don't think the Cybermen *look* too bad. The head guns are a good idea, well executed – you can even see the sparks flying out as they fire. In fact, the battle (if that's the word for such a lop-sided massacre) between the Cybermen and the Vogans is terrifically staged – it makes excellent use of the location, with the light shining off the silver creatures as they emerge from the gloom. The Vogan deaths contain a number of great stunts, and as the Cybermen stand unbeaten, their appearance effectively scored for the first time by clanging bells (easily Carey Blyton's best work on the show), the Vogans (easily, er, John Friedlander's *worst* work on the show) retreat, helping their wounded comrades to safety.

Unfortunately, Mr Logic has taken a step out of the room. The Vogans know the Cybermen fear them because of their gold, and yet the mighty army of two Cybermen don't suffer the slightest discomfort on a planet that's made of it. Nor do the Vogans – *knowing* that the Cybermen are vulnerable to gold – think of deploying it against them. It's a whacking great howler of cataclysmic proportions, which suggests that the script being filmed is a couple of drafts early. As we lose Kellman – dying in the cliché of a ventilation shaft – just as he threatened to become interesting, I fear the storyline (just like the Doctor) is getting deeper and deeper into trouble.

Oh, and why are the captive humans sitting like the three wise monkeys?

Revenge of the Cybermen (part four)

R: I don't trust that Tyrum an inch. One moment he appears to be working with Vorus, his political opponent, on bringing down the Cybermen. Then Vorus stubbornly tells him that when the crisis lifts, he intends to run against him for office. Next thing we know, Tyrum is shooting Vorus and his lackey, poor coughing Magrick, in the back. And for what? For showing the same sort of gung-ho approach to military action that you'd expect from the Brigadier. Then it dawns on me. He's played by that Kevin Stoney chap, isn't he? Mavic Chen, Tobias Vaughn – charming bastards the pair of them, but evil through and through. You take that funny Vogan mask off him, and you'd find the same unblinking opportunist underneath, you mark my words.

This is all rather bland, isn't it? Bland enough that I have to invent my own political intrigues just to give it a bit more depth. The Cyber-Leader must be surely the laziest lead villain in Doctor Who ever – he sends a couple of his minions on to a planet, and then his entire masterplan is just to wait. If it weren't for our regular cast, this would be a pretty joyless exercise. But that opening scene where the Doctor shouts out to the entire planet that Harry Sullivan is an imbecile is lovely, and it'd be a heart of stone that didn't melt at the obvious affection shown between the Doctor and Sarah when they find each other again on Nerva. The cast is brilliant. They just now need a better story.

T: It's run out of places to go, but I still find myself unable to hate Revenge of the Cybermen in the way I once did. Maybe I'm mellowing with age – or maybe I've just lost what fire I once had. Or maybe it's that I've not spent recent years having to justify Doctor Who's perceived shortcomings, meaning I can allow the stories of the past to exist on their own merits. Even an episode such as this, where everyone apart from the costume designer seems to have totally misunderstood the Cybermen, and the script has nowhere to go...

so goes there anyway, but rather slowly. Even an episode where the climax is the Doctor evading a collision between an inflatable beacon and a chocolate log, by steering an entire space station with a crank-handle. *Even this nonsense* has some saving graces.

There's the Doctor's opening tumble – a pretty impressive stunt, considering the real jaggedness of the rocks onto which he falls. There's the way that Harry warns the Commander that the Doctor is prone to absent mindedness, but we then we cut to the Time Lord springing into action. There's a great touch even on dull old Voga, where David Collings' ability to lend a serious and direct touch of class – even when spouting turgid alien politics and clasping a big ornate club for no discernable reason – should not be underestimated. It's not even all bad with the Cybermen, despite Christopher Robbie's hands-on-hips acting, and propensity to make glib quips (which are at least operatically bad rather than boringly inept). We even get an effective moment where a Cyberman pulls Sarah up with such force, her feet leave the ground.

So yeah... Revenge doesn't annoy me anymore. It may be illogical of me, because I'm aware that it's not terribly good, but that's okay. My humanity has won out over cold, heartless logic in the end. It's the sort of thing this story *should* have been about... if anyone involved had worked out the purpose for which the Cybermen existed.

Disney Time

R: And here is *that better* story I was asking for! With all the variety the series needs – it's got talking snakes, and singing dogs, and bank robberies, and Bluebeard's Ghost. The Doctor takes a detour before answering the Brigadier's summons, and gets the urge to go and watch some Mickey Mouse cartoons. He lands the TARDIS in London, where he stops a passer-by and asks for directions to a cinema whilst doing an impersonation of Donald Duck. Whilst inside the cinema, he takes over the ticket booth and gives free admission to anyone surprised enough to find him there. But he doesn't get many takers, because inside the auditorium itself he is all alone – horribly, ter-

rifyingly alone... He only decides to leave when a hand pops up in front of him as he's sitting, giving him a bit of paper reminding him that he's supposed to be helping out the Brig.

... Of course it's bloody canon! It fits, doesn't it? And next week, in Terror of the Zygons, the Brigadier will complain that the Doctor has turned up late. We know why. He was watching clips from The Jungle Book and Lady and the Tramp.

To explain – Disney Time was a series that popped up occasionally in the BBC schedules, usually around a bank holiday, and hosted by a celebrity from children's television. It was an utterly shameless advertisement for Disney movies – always giving previews of a new one soon to hit cinemas, whilst sweetening this pill (because they were inevitably movies that would never be heard of again) by showing Mickey Mouse as the sorcerer's apprentice in Fantasia. As a kid, I'd always watch for the cartoon clips, and get bored by the excerpts from the live-action films.

The reason why I include Disney Time is not just to be flippant, and to annoy Toby – who'll now have to watch Tom Baker talk about the Apple Dumpling Gang with due solemnity. It's significant because it's the first time in Doctor Who's history that the actor has appeared in character and taken over another show entirely. And it's what it says about the fourth Doctor that makes this treasurable. You can honestly believe that this anarchic incarnation, this shambling child in an adult's body, would resist the call from UNIT to go and indulge himself at the cinema instead. He finally leaves for the Zygon adventure with such bad grace, and that runs directly into the new season due to start the following week – any child watching would think that the Doctor's irritation with the Brigadier was that he was taken away from watching his favourite cartoons. It's a measure of just how well Tom Baker's Doctor has become defined. Jon Pertwee would never have pulled this off, even if he'd worn the costume – the irresponsibility of it just wouldn't have looked right. But here it seems apt. This is a Doctor who can be facing down horror one week, and Goofy the next. It's lovely.

T: Yeah, alright, you've had your bit of fun. As I wasn't cognisant when this was transmitted, and so have no particular nostalgic bond with Disney Time, I find myself somewhat non-plussed by it. After all, the least the Doctor could have done was brought Sarah and Harry along for the ride. Is he in the habit of checking if it's dangerous outside the TARDIS, and only inviting his friends outside if it is? Or are they having a big heart to heart, leading to Harry's decision to stay on Earth at the end of the next story? I'll admit, though, that Tom Baker is so mercurial and charismatic, his presence and rich tones enable him to get away with so much – as with here, when he opts for a curiously flat and indifferent delivery.

Er, is that enough? I dread to think what other "delights" you've got up your sleeve, in your attempts to stretch the canon (nips off to see if anyone filmed Recall UNIT...).

July 12th

Terror of the Zygons (part one)

R: This ought to feel like so much old hat. The UNIT involvement already feels out of date, as does the genial humour that's now its principal style. The Brigadier does little more than smile and display his kilt, whilst Benton cracks a couple of jokes and persuades the landlord to stop playing his bagpipes. The Scottish setting too is as subtle as a brick – the first few minutes not only throws at us the pipes and kilts, but even the first doomed oil rig operator is asking for haggis before his attack. And yet, it feels new and urgent, because the tone keeps aiming for something darker. Tom Baker seems to be experimenting with the part again, for the first time practising the lower range of his voice to great effect. The Brigadier has never had to confront a Doctor like this one, who already seems to be treating him like an irritant from his youth – it's not unlike the way you might expect the average Facebook user to deal with annoying school friends who've contacted them out of the blue for the first time in years.

The moments of violence and horror are all the more shocking because they are coming

out of a Doctor Who setting we recognise as being traditional and safe. It's a UNIT story, and that's by now as warm and cosy as a teacake – so it's a genuine surprise when Harry is shot in the head. Even the shots of the Zygons at their controls, or spying at the humans through their scanners, have greater atmosphere than we're used to – it's as if Phillip Hinchcliffe's Who is in direct collision with a Barry Letts scenario, and the result is wonderfully uneasy. Best of all is one of my favourite scenes where these two styles are in contrast – Sarah is joking about the Scottish bagpipes, only for the newer, brooding Doctor to tell her it is a lament for the dead. There's a new gloss on an old story.

And let's face it, there's a reason for this. Douglas Camfield is back! He's been absent since Inferno, and the Pertwee era was all the weaker for it. His direction is absolutely beautiful. The scene where a radio operator, Munro, staggers out of the sea manages to be unnerving and visually gorgeous at the same time. And Camfield's brought along a different composer with him, and this familiar tale not only looks fresh, but sounds fresh too. To go against the house style of Dudley Simpson doesn't always work – Carey Blyton rather proved that with Revenge of the Cybermen – but there's a richness to Geoffrey Burgon's score that makes what might otherwise come across as a runaround have a real texture. This is what Revenge ought to have been: good, clean, unpretentious and traditional as old boots, but done with a fizz and a confidence that is utterly engaging.

T: I think it's because horror works better in a teatime slot than science fiction, and Douglas Camfield is directing this as a horror film. Yes, it's about blobby aliens and oil rigs being attacked, but it's not given the futuristic, marvel-at-the-space-things treatment. Instead, we fear the unseen – the music's haunting, and everyone is underplaying it. It's also because Camfield is rigorous about the visuals, so we have an evocatively lit opening model shot of an oil rig. When it's attacked, it convinces as the destruction of a solid construction.

The more I think about it, actually, the more I think you're right: Camfield is the key to this episode's success. His influence is *everywhere*, and he brings an urgency and believability to the proceedings, topping it all off with a richly moody tone. He uses the village setting to evoke chilly atmospherics, and casts Angus Lennie as, um, a landlord named Angus to provide spooky ghost stories, and help sell that we're in Scotland. (The first scene ladles this on a little too thick, though, with the words "didnae ken" and "haggis" uttered in the opening minute.) The cross-fading inside the alien ship is a tantalising fluster of blobbiness, and Camfield's film work – whether it's khaki-clad soldiers charging about or doing a close-up on the Caber's inscrutable face after he's shot Harry – is terrific.

But so much of good storytelling involves striking a balance, and the moments of humour here serve to contrast, and thus accentuate, the drama at hand. Elisabeth Sladen answers the phone with a cheery, cheeky mock Scottish lilt, only to then inform us that Harry is in hospital. (Are you allowed to shoot people for trespass, by the way? It seems a bit violent, even for Scotland!) Even with bits of levity, though, the horror elements seem to win out, as the close-up of the terrified Harry in hospital demonstrates. That the Doctor's shouts of "No!" continue on from Harry's own, but in a different tone, gives us another moment to marvel at Camfield's cleverness before he tops that with a brutal and pants-wetting take on the traditional monster-reveal cliffhanger, as a Zygon grabs Sarah. Everything about it – the music, the expression on the creature's face, Sladen's panicked scream – is superb.

Overall, this is so much better than Revenge of the Cybermen, because the tone is so consistent. Even the Doctor has become appropriately grim – Tom Baker, as you say, is so broody that he keeps disquieting those around him. His solemn tones warn that the sea may be "calm, but it's never empty", as if he's on a deliberate mission to terrify the nation's youth. This Doctor is *dangerous*, scowling and rude – even when he's galvanised into helping by the Brigadier's suggestion that he shouldn't want more men to die, he does it grumpily.

I never literally watched Doctor Who from behind the sofa as a young viewer – but had I been one when this was on, I think I definitely would have done.

Terror of the Zygons (part two)

R: Do you know, I've never seen that scene in the barn before! Not properly. For years, all I saw was the edited version, hacked away by the Australian censors who considered that seeing Harry Sullivan lunge at Sarah with a pitchfork was a tad on the nasty side. I always assumed they were making a right old fuss about nothing – it wasn't as if he skewered the girl, was it? But watching it this evening, I was shocked by just how unnerving the whole sequence is, and how much violence is suggested. This looks like something right out of those seventies horror films I'd catch on TV late as a kid, the sort that gave me nightmares.

And again, it's not as if there's anything in the script that is particularly excessive – it's just the fearless way that it's been interpreted for the screen by a series that wants to be frightening. I think if there's any indication of just how Doctor Who has changed in less than a year, it's probably clearest in Terror of the Zygons. The Ark in Space and Genesis feel so different from the Pertwee mould, you can easily pretend you're watching another programme altogether. But there's nothing in the Zygon story that wouldn't have fitted comfortably into the established routine (and, indeed, writer Robert Banks Stewart's other outing for the series similarly had him working for UNIT and battling alien invasion – he feels oddly like the Pertwee writer Pertwee never met, the traditionalist who's each time converted by Robert Holmes into someone much darker and edgier). The script is really little more than functional, with some downright clunky bits (the exposition Broton offers Harry in the spaceship sticks out like a sore thumb – and there's only so many times an alien can hiss to himself at a video screen that the Doctor must die before he loses credibility). But the direction, design and music are extraordinary, and this episode just drips with atmosphere. Douglas Camfield cannot resist even making "gimmick" scenes into set pieces – the instance where the Doctor hypnotises Sarah into not breathing whilst the air is depressurised would be a fairly conventional deus ex machina usually (indeed, with the Doctor's talk afterwards of Tibetan monks, it seems straight out of another era). That same sequence becomes something very disturbing here, emphasising the Doctor's extraordinary alien power.

Oh, funny thing. Unless I've blinked and missed him, the Duke of Forgill wasn't in this episode – but is still there, bold as brass, in the end credits. Doesn't that rather give away the fact that John Woodnutt is doubling up as Broton?

T: I wouldn't know. Reading credits is for losers.

This is going to sound repetitive, but Terror of the Zygons proves that Douglas Camfield was a master of his craft. Zygons has just as many script problems as Revenge of the Cybermen, but the latter was so uninspired – its plot holes and lack of interesting characters failed to gel with the arch/ limp performances and daft music. *Here*, you have equally challenging elements – such as a Zygon leader who drops everything to explain the entire backstory, followed by another Zygon going to all the trouble of disguising itself as Harry, but then not bothering to act like him. But unlike Revenge, we don't care – because the production looks, sounds and *moves* along so brilliantly, we're never tempted to dwell on its implausible aspects. To that end, Harry's half-glimpsed face as he menaces Sarah in the barn is the stuff of nightmares – you can almost feel the point of the pitchfork slashing through your skin. And there are efforts to make the Zygons more than just men in rubber suits by giving them a wobbly symbiosis with their ship as they manipulate its controls, not to mention the bellowing death rattle the ersatz Harry emits when returning to its natural form.

Just about *everything* comes together with this story... The music is like tiny dollops of darkness dripping and shivering in the cold depths of night. That "Tibetan coma guff" that the Doctor uses to save Sarah from suffocation would irritate me if done by any other Doctor in any other era, but here it absolutely works. It's a trite get-out, yes, but the fact that reviving Sarah from the condition could kill her, and the sheer power of Tom Baker's other-worldliness, make it seem profound and ethereal. Even John Levene – always a good comedy stooge, never quite so convincing at gritty drama – has an urgency about him, as when he

nervously touches his face while figuring out the controls to release his friends. It's as if Levene's performance goes up a notch when Camfield, his mentor, is at the helm.

Oh, and remember The Web of Fear, where I marvelled at the inclusion of a one-line soldier played by Bernard G High, who seemed utterly superfluous? Well, it's taken a few years, but Camfield pays off that moment by bringing High back to play an equally verbally challenged member of the UNIT ranks. Who said reading credits was sad? Not me – it must have been someone disguised as me.

Terror of the Zygons (part three)

R: In Robot, the Brigadier caught himself longing for an alien menace that could be damaged by bullets. And here they are! And I love them, because the Zygons can't rely simply upon a hide that's as strong as metal, but upon guile. They're far more dangerous as a result. They prey upon the vulnerable and the hapless – the landlord who's all on his own in his pub, the soldier who stops to check the wound on a nurse's arm – and that's so much more nasty and personal than merely advancing upon a UNIT platoon, and so much more scary for the child all alone in his bedroom with the lights off. The special effect of Sister Lamont changing into a Zygon is beautifully handled, and is disturbing not simply because it reveals a murdering monster, but because it blurs and distorts the human image to do so. No wonder poor old Angus Lennie looks so terrified.

There's a wit to the direction too. You just know that when the Doctor sits in the Duke's chair and impersonates him that his Grace will appear – that's the comedy cliché. And the joy of it is that the Doctor knows the cliché too, and doesn't have the good manners to be embarrassed to be caught out – it's his cheerful rudeness that makes him seem so much more alien. The sequence where Sarah is wary of the sliding door in the Zygon spaceship too is funny – ducking from them, wanting to be absolutely certain she has an escape route – but it's also a welcome realistic response. And it's that realistic approach to the alien that makes her exploration there so much more tense, and her discovery of the human captives, all bathed in a flashing red glow, so much more disquieting. In a similar way, that moment where the Doctor brazenly leaps down the hidden passage is wonderful; it's just the sort of thing the Doctor would do, and he always gets away with it. But not this time – there's a scream (the Doctor screams! – and what is it? Pain? Terror?) and so cruelly, Douglas Camfield doesn't even show us why, denies us even that reassurance. The scene plays out by lulling the audience into a false sense of security – Sarah and Harry have escaped from the Zygons, and they must be safe now, because they've run straight into the protective arms of the Doctor and the Brig. And the next thing we know is the Doctor hasn't saved the day, and he's off screen, and he's crying out for all that he's worth.

Great dialogue too. Whether it's Angus retorting that there's no need in the village for anyone to spy, because they all know what each other's doing as a matter of principle. Or Sister Lamont moaning about her frustrations with her body. Or, best still, the Duke of Forgill talking to Sarah about human credulity – and the way that she as yet isn't aware of the double meaning, and that we as the audience do, and are silently begging her to be careful.

T: You've hit the nail on the head with the Zygons. The tensest scene here is not of one of their number menacing UNIT, but of one *running away from them*! It flits through the trees, glimpsed only in long shot, and still with the ability to transform into one of us and strike the unsuspecting...

In so many ways, Robert Holmes, Philip Hinchcliffe and Douglas Camfield have worked out how to squeeze every ounce of menace from a script that nonetheless has to be suitable for teatime tots. The Zygons' whispering voices successfully avoid any temptation to bellow Shakespearean performances from beneath the latex, and their chameleon abilities allow the actors playing their human guises to convey a lot of menace. John Woodnutt has a detached, sly aloofness in his human aspect, the Duke of Forgill, which contrasts marvellously when he's the venomous warlord Broton. Elsewhere, Lilias Walker (as Sister Lamont) and Robert Russell (as the Caber) prove unnerving without lapsing into

obvious-baddie-acting (and I love how Elisabeth Sladen sticks her tongue out behind the latter's back). The incidental music augments the suspense generated by our knowing that Sarah is blissfully ignorant of the aliens around her – I'm not sure there's yet been a score that's as beautiful and terrifying as this estimable work. I quite like beautiful and terrifying – but you know that, Rob, because you've met my wife-to-be.

The Brigadier's got a nerve, though. His response to the Duke's incredulity about aliens is "Before I joined UNIT, I was highly sceptical about such things". *Before?* And for about five years after, you lying sod. Or did Cromer never happen? If he's forgotten all about it, perhaps the Restoration Team could perform some Cromer Dot Recovery techniques to renovate the Brig's memory to its original, untarnished majesty.

July 13th

Terror of the Zygons (part four)

R: But it's funny – no matter how good Terror of the Zygons is, and no matter how popular, it's always been a story that's left a rather odd taste in my mouth. And watching the final episode, that taste comes right back and how. And I think now I can work out just what it is that has always bothered me.

In plotting terms, this is a bit clunky. But I can forgive that, a lot of Doctor Who plots clunk about a bit, especially in their final episodes. But by abandoning the idyll of the Scottish Highlands, and hightailing it back to London, the story also sacrifices all that made Terror of the Zygons feel fresh and distinctive. The climax to the story doesn't take place on the misty moors, but in a bland box room underneath the Houses of Parliament. The Brigadier takes off his kilt, and is back to his standard uniform. Doctor Who has taken away the atmosphere of the adventure, and replaced it with everything that is familiar and bog-standard.

Or, at least, on the face of it. I now think that what Zygons is doing is much cleverer than that, and a damn sight more insidious.

In its final reel, Terror of the Zygons returns

to the standard Doctor Who story model, and sends it up quite deliberately. Robert Holmes always seems more comfortable writing for a single adversary rather than a race of invading monsters – it's no accident, I think, that the story in production after this one will feature Sutekh as the villain, rather than the solely named leader of a series of identical aliens. This latter device, though, has been the template ever since Innes Lloyd took over the show – and Broton, hissing the word *Doctor* with all due venom, sounds very much like the cliché villain you expect from this period. It's almost as if Philip Hinchcliffe has gone for broke in Terror of the Zygons: let's bring up all the stereotype monsters and do them really, really well... and then put the tropes back in the cupboard so we won't have to use them again.

Because – and for this single episode only! – it does feel that the script and performances are doing their level best to exaggerate those tropes and find them wanting. The way that the Doctor draws attention to the meagre nature of all invading aliens' plans is just the start of it – that the BBC can only afford the three costumes, that the Zygon leader will every once in a while have to emerge from hiding and wave a tentacle. For all the effort in making this adventure feel epic, it's nevertheless based on a plot relying upon a shapeshifting alien's ability to forge an ID card so he can get into a convention for bureaucrats. The imagery of the Zygons in force is intentionally very funny: these wonderfully designed blobs led by a gentleman with a walking cane who puts on his (imaginary?) hat whilst leaving his spaceship. And John Woodnutt finds a way of linking the Broton-as-Zygon, hissing his words in a thoroughly alien way, and the Broton-as-Forgill, dripping charm and wit – I love the way that, on his flight deck, the Zygon leader takes to standing with his arms behind his back, as if the repose of the gentleman at large has rubbed off on him.

Ultimately, the story appears to be saying, it all comes down to bureaucracy and politics. The Scottish setting is abandoned for the dull backdrop of London Parliament. The Brigadier gets to speak to the Prime Minister at last – and we find out, as a gag, that she's a woman. (As if that'll ever happen!) Throughout the script,

there are jokes levelled at Government and the dullards who work there – and all Broton wants to do is hide in the cellars underneath Westminster like a modern-day Guy Fawkes, kill a few and take their place. It's so anticlimactic, it's actually funny. The prosaic way that the Brigadier shoots Broton dead – but waiting long enough for the UNIT grunt extra to be throttled first – feels like a calculated shrug. (Just look at the way, too, that Harry so casually inspects that extra's corpse, before he and Sarah rush off upstairs to join in the "fun" of seeing a big CSO monster.) It seems to me that there's a tacit acknowledgement being made here that UNIT soldiers aren't real characters at all, deserving no more sympathy (say) than the Zygon soldiers pleading for their lives behind a locked door as the Doctor blows them up.

I think Terror of the Zygons cocks a snook at the staleness of the Doctor Who format, where (inevitably) the Doctor works as an agent for a Government organisation to protect authority. The final scene of Robot offers the Doctor the chance to attend dinner with the Queen, as if that's some big honour bestowed upon him – quite rightly, all Tom Baker wants to do is run away. Here, we see the hallmarks of the Pertwee era held up to the light, directed better than ever before, and then put away for good. "Is that bang big enough for you, Brigadier?" asks the Doctor, as if acknowledging that all his UNIT adventures have to end with things blowing up at some point. If Terror of the Zygons always feels a bit awkward to me, I think it's because the new direction of the programme wants it to feel a bit awkward. That final scene, in which the Doctor promises to take Sarah straight back to London for more of the same, but is about to whisk her away into a new series format altogether, is just wonderful. It's subtly done, but it feels very deliberately as if the production team are drawing a line here, separating the old show from its future ahead. All employees of UNIT (including dear old Harry) stand aside. It's not a future that has any room for them. (And I know I'm reaching a bit, but look at those final shots of Nick Courtney, just after the TARDIS has dematerialised. It looks like he's gulping back a tear. I like to pretend that Courtney realises in the closing moments that this will be his last regular performance, and the proper conclusion to the days of UNIT. I like pretending. That's the power Doctor Who has had on me since I was a kid – I can even make up back stories for facial expressions.)

T: I can't help but notice that the Zygon plan was to raise the temperature of Earth and melt the polar ice caps. Were George Bush and Jeremy Clarkson their Plan B? We should be told. Oh, and it can't be coincidence that the story predicting a female prime minister also features an unfeeling, vicious, inhuman beast looming over the House of Commons and terrifying everybody.

And allow me a moment of geek cross-pollination if I point out that the denouement is so woeful, that *of course* it was wheeled out on that awful 1992 documentary Resistance is Useless, just at the moment the brummie anorak stated that the Doctor Who production teams prided themselves on producing convincing effects on a limited budget. Except that Douglas Camfield *didn't* think it was convincing, so using it to undermine Doctor Who on a documentary intended to recruit viewers to a season of repeats was wrong on both an artistic and factual level. It's just about the only time I've ever wanted to punch a television programme.

But let me continue to sing the praises of John Woodnutt, who radiates such a polite, svelte villainy, and not without a sense of humour. (That said, if the Zygons' assumption of our forms includes shapeshifting into our clothes, where did the Duke's hat come from? Did he have to nip to the shops and buy one? Or do Zygons have removable nodules which can metamorphose into millinery?) It doesn't matter – Woodnutt is so good, he even maintains his dignity when delivering a *terrible* line about underestimating the powers of organic crystallography in a Scots accent. By contrast, in the final scene as Broton, he displays a shocking speed and unleashes an uncompromisingly violent attack (replete with ugly, alien screeching) on the Doctor. I recall that a picture of Woodnutt touching a wincing Doctor was once a Caption Competition in Doctor Who Weekly, which led me to believe for years that the Zygons could sting people – in the same way that the Target novel of The Three

Doctors made me labour under the misapprehension that Omega shot fire from his fingers.

Finally, let me add that I finished this story less pessimistic about UNIT's future in the series than might have been expected... Harry's exit is very low-key, and while John Levene's name has tumbled nearer to the bottom of the credits as this story has progressed, little about this feels like UNIT's swan song. You half-expect the Doctor to fulfil his promise and arrive soon for another twentieth-century adventure. (Well, you don't, clearly, but you've made up some nonsense about Nicholas Courtney having psychic powers.)

Planet of Evil (part one)

R: There are invisible monsters hiding on aggressive jungle planets. And consequently bit-part characters struggling to the death with thin air. And, look! – there's Prentis Hancock! The last time David Maloney got this same list of ingredients, he gave us Planet of the Daleks. But there's been a sea change since then. What we get here is naggingly familiar, but it's served in a way that feels fresh and sinister. The planet feels truly alien and dangerous this time – helped not only by the superb set design (especially when it's shot on film), but also by the eerie background sound effects. When the expedition members Braun and Baldwin are wrestled to the ground, it really ought to look as ridiculous as the Spiridon attack, but instead the sequences are dissonant and macabre.

Indeed, the long six-minute introduction, from that haunting still of a distant red planet hanging alone in space, to the daring-you-to-laugh deaths, is the tensest the programme has been since the days of black and white – helped, no doubt, by the very particular use of colours so dense, they block out the light and make the setting look quite suffocating. I love the matter-of-fact weariness with which Braun drives another gravestone into the ground (and the way, too, that all the names of the dead come so neatly printed on their markers – as if their murders on the planet are so inevitable that the tombs have been prepared in advance).

Six minutes in, we finally get around to the appearance of the Doctor and Sarah. And I think that's where it all stumbles, really. There

JULY 13TH: PLANET OF EVIL

isn't very much for the regulars to do. They answer a distress call, but have no clear mission for the rest of the episode – they get captured, they get interrogated, but with no especial urgency. And they seem only to escape just so they can take part in the cliffhanger. Tom Baker is experimenting with ways of making the Doctor look alien, and this means that whenever he takes part in a scene in which he doesn't get to do very much, he decides to stare off moodily into the middle distance and ignore everything that's going on around him. He gets to do that quite a lot. The first time it looks a bit odd, even disconcerting; by the fourth time, it's hard not to suspect that Baker is just showing that he's bored.

The dialogue has that sort of perfunctory style to it that allows good actors to add shade and depth to it if they so choose. That scene where Ewen Solon (as Vishinsky, part of the rescue team) asks Frederick Jaeger (as Professor Sorenson) about the fates of his fellow crewmembers is honestly fantastic. Solon suggests a dread respect for Jaeger that means he can only quiz him so far about the deaths, and Jaeger in turn pitches his performance somewhere between tired fatalism and scientific hubris. If you listen to the words cold, it's clear that this is a scene that is pure exposition (and delayed exposition) – but the cast do wonders with it... and then you get Prentis Hancock on the spaceship, who makes his statements of the blindingly obvious seem even more bald than they really were. There's not much spark to Louis Marks' script. But I rather like the functionality of it, I like the way that the Morestrans are just functional alien soldiers, and that their blandness throws into sharp relief just how alien the planet is on which they are trespassing.

T: And so it continues... another stab at science fiction presented with atmosphere and chills, as opposed to fancy, spangly space stuff. Other commentators have noted that the Morestran ship is sparse because of the jungle's sumptuousness – maybe so, but I wouldn't be surprised if the production team was simply uninterested in showing us flashing lights and tinfoil. After all, the future tech at hand is of little comfort against the grim ambience in which this story operates – two people are

slain before we even see the Doctor; the Zeta Minor base falls into darkness; the monster seems to be invisible; and arid, mummified corpses reappear out of nowhere. And pleasingly, even the Doctor's leather bag suggests a Victorian pathologist rather than a whacky spaceman. (Old-fashioned things always seem to make yer time traveller altogether classier than a thermal lance or sonic screwdriver ever could.)

It's instructive to compare these stranded scientists with the Thals in Maloney's Planet of the Daleks – the latter didn't have a hair out of place, but this lot are dirty, tired-looking, bearded and stubbly. Even their names have a verisimilitude: "Braun", "Lorenzo", "Egard Lumb", "De Haan" and "Ponti" – all are faintly recognisable whilst exuding a pleasingly non-anglicised diversity. My favourite has to be "Vishinsky": it's bravely long winded, and flirts with sounding silly, yet, somehow, contrives to get away with it.

So far, Rob, Frederick Jaeger stands out the most among the guest cast – he's by turns exhausted, distracted and possessed of messianic zeal. And I can't help but notice that David Maloney is one of those directors who recasts actors he's used before... but why not? As my agent said when the Royal Exchange Theatre first cast me, "they're very faithful" – meaning once used, I'd be back again, so hooray! (*Prior* my employ of course, rather than deeming the Theatre "faithful", we used to moan about them cliquey. It all depends where you're sitting at the time.)

But, ultimately, this is about the titular planet, and thank God for designer Roger Murray-Leach. He's not only pulled off a convincing jungle, he's pulled off a convincing *alien* jungle (I love the bit where Baldwin splashes through a stream). Even the stark clarity of studio-bound videotape doesn't show any chinks in this fine work – the moody red, blue and mauve lighting, and the inventive shapes and textures, make this a 100% successful piece of scenic artistry. If that weren't enough, we even get to see the whacking great side of a spaceship from which half a dozen men emerge, giving the proceedings a pleasing sense of scale. The Zeta may be Minor, but the episode is a major achievement.

July 14th

Planet of Evil (part two)

R: I haven't annoyed Toby properly in weeks. And I'm really itching to do so. I love the sound of distant frustration I can hear spluttering into my email inbox every time I come up with one of my sweeping theories. So, here's another one. Splutters ahoy!

I think that the character of the Doctor is largely reinvented somewhere in the middle of this episode, and in a way that affects him right until the present day. And it's so subtly done, it largely happens off screen.

Here's what I mean.

When Doctor Who started, the Doctor's role in a story had two conflicting agendas. If it was a science story, he acted very much as explorer – discovering (alongside the audience) what was happening on any distant planet or in any distant society. He had great capacity for surprise – and, in a funny way, seeing as he was played as such an old man, it gave him a certain giddy youth too. If the story was set in history, however, his role was very different: he knew of future events, and acted either as commentator to the audience, or as prophet to the characters. There is no point in trying to save the Aztecs, because they're already doomed. Cue apocalyptic thunder. You can sit around drinking mead with the Saxons, and muse aloud about the imminent battle at Hastings. Cue amused giggling.

The historical stories were phased out, and the Doctor lost a certain amount of grandeur. Once in a while he might pop up in a story (like The Tenth Planet, say) and take on the same role – but those moments were few and far between, and felt somewhat out of place. Troughton's Doctor becomes a great panicked improviser – he can't afford to take a stance above the action, because he's utterly lost within it. Things change somewhat when Pertwee arrives, because he does so with the baggage of being a Time Lord, and knowing immediately all about the Silurians/ Solonians/ Draconians. But though he boasts this extra insight into the background of the stories, he does so usually without much authority. He may be a Time Lord, but he's their stooge or messenger boy. He may have alien perspective, but he still works for UNIT.

With Tom Baker, you can still see at this stage some attempt at working out what the Doctor should be now that he has thrown off the shackles of the Brigadier (and of Barry Letts). In early Tom stories, he bumbles through the adventures like an improvising comedian, returning to the basic style of Troughton. But there's one story in particular from his first season in which Baker excels, and in which his comic styling is given extra gravitas played against the power of great knowledge. And that story, of course, is Genesis of the Daleks. In which the Doctor returns to Skaro with a mission absolutely informed by historical foreknowledge – in which the Doctor is able to act as prophet once again, in a way he hasn't done since the days of Hartnell, but this time within an alien setting.

The Doctor didn't have much character in episode one of Planet of Evil. He spends some of episode two finding a desiccated corpse, and telling Sarah he has some nasty suspicions about what's going on. Midway through the episode, Tom Baker is allowed to discover his strengths; he knows the Morestran spaceship won't take off, he knows the entire universe is threatened by the bunglings of its crew. We don't see when or how he suddenly acquires all that helpful information. And it doesn't matter – what *does* is that Baker is in his element now as an aloof and angry alien who prophesies doom and destruction. Just look at the way David Maloney stages the scene where the Doctor warns Sorenson that the Morestrans won't be allowed to leave the planet, and the look of confused wonder on Frederick Jaeger's face; the Doctor isn't being presented merely as a scientist or a wanderer any more, but as a seer dabbling in cryptic warnings. (They're very dramatic, cryptic warnings; Russell T Davies knows the value of them, from Bad Wolf to someone knocking four times.) The Doctor is reinvented as something "other", and quite suddenly too – this is the Doctor we'll see brooding at the start of Pyramids of Mars and knowing the dangers of Sutekh; this is the Doctor who, at the beginning of the following season, can deliver curses of death to a medieval duke.

How does Louis Marks do this? And how

does he do it so we barely notice? I think there's a clue in the way that, as the Doctor and Sarah hide out in the jungle, he unexpectedly has the Doctor quote Shakespeare. It comes from nowhere. As a non-sequitur, it's one of the most blatant. But Marks is a Renaissance scholar, and has learned from it the virtue of what's called "sprezzaturra", of hiding in plain sight things which are boastful and show-off underneath a pretence of lightness. By suddenly focusing upon higher art, Marks puts into our heads the image of something grander and more truly tragic – into this Prentis Hancocked-runaround, he's invited us by sleight of hand to think of something more elevated. And out of that steps this new characterisation of the Doctor, striding through the story as something more elevated too – and we accept it without even blinking. This is the Doctor who has stepped out of mythology, rather than just bumbles about trying to catch up like the rest of us. This is a Doctor who commands respect.

And Shakespeare did it. Is there no end to the man's genius?

T: ... well, my first thought is that there's something about Frederick Jaeger that makes you prone to fantasy. After the next episode, you'll probably rekindle your The Savages theory (that his Hartnell impression was the production team seeing if the series might carry on without the leading actor) and say that having Jaeger on set – playing someone with an unpredictable dark side, who is prone to drink vast amounts of unhealthy liquid and has mad eyes – is the production team seeing if someone can stand in for Tom Baker when necessary.

Actually, I'm being mean – rather than spluttering with rage, I actually found myself nodding sagely at your thoughts about this episode. You made sense for once. What's happened, are you Anti-Rob or something? If so, drink your potion.

For a story filmed entirely indoors, the production team have gone to great lengths to present the evil planet as a vast landscape. Roger Murray-Leach has produced the best design work seen thus far in the series – the eerie, abstract shapes of his alien plants are as clever and convincing as Brian Clemett's light-

ing, which bathes everything in mauves and reds, as smoke adds to the murkiness and hides the studio floor. Thanks to the Oculoid Tracker, we even get an aerial view, which looks down on the impressive vista and emphasises its height. The Oculoid itself is a decent and unshowy effect, its smooth movement ironing out any impression of string dangling.

Equally simple and impressive is the black pool – it works precisely because your eyes can't quite figure out what it is. A hole? An effect? You're never really sure, so it ends up being what it's meant to be: a great big blob of nothing. This production team are desperate not to make their effects work showy, convincingly inserting them into the action as seamlessly as possible. So we get gunshots that flash and echo around the jungle, and an impressively rendered anti-matter beast (although the kaz-pow effect as it's repelled from the ship celebrates this story's Forbidden Planet genesis a little too blatantly, and so looks a little dated).

Meanwhile, Tom Baker breezily throws in joyous comic asides with the timing of an expert. The Doctor's dismissal of Shakespeare as a dreadful actor seems a perfectly Doctorish thing to do – never mind about trying to take the credit for writing Hamlet, he can brazenly boast about the shortcomings of the world's most famous writer in the manner that only someone who has seen everything and then some can. But while fandom seems to overwhelmingly acknowledge that Baker is a national treasure – he's a walking anecdote and part-time Shirley Williams lookey-likee – what about his serious acting chops? There is a wealth of examples of that here – he's fierce and commanding after Ponti's death, exudes gravitas and class when explaining the anti-matter universe, displays fierce indignation as the crew are sent to their deaths, and has an aptitude for steely detachment that suggests some sort of universal burden he has to puncture with clowning. Baker's face switches from sunken mournfulness – as his skin literally sinks into his powerful bones – to an explosion of humour-filled lines, with dazzling teeth and glinting eyes. Basically, his face is as powerful a weapon in his armoury as his voice, which makes the ridiculous sound portentous and the dangerous seem like a lark. The man's a bloody genius. And he carries a toffee tin around with him! In later Doctors, such eccentric little trinkets often seemed a contrivance to make the character seem whacky. With Baker, they fit like a glove.

In other news, Prentis Hancock delivers the line "This interrogation will be conducted in an orderly manner" with all the authority of Boris Johnson attempting gangsta-rap. Perhaps he was told to "play it like Shakespeare", read the Doctor's line in the script and misunderstood.

Planet of Evil (part three)

R: Morelli is not one of the deepest of Doctor Who characters; indeed, he only seems to acquire any personality at all, bantering with a fellow soldier, a few minutes before his untimely demise at the hands of Antiman. He doesn't even get the dignity of an on-screen death – he walks around a corner, screams horribly, and his body is replaced by a desiccated skeleton. But he's given what few major characters are given, let alone the anonymous monster fodder: a proper space funeral. There's a cool beauty to it, the way that his coffined body is expelled from an airlock to drift about for all eternity. But what's brilliant about the scene is the way that the script and performers absolutely refuse to sentimentalise it: Vishinsky accepts Morelli's religious leanings at the funeral service with an eye-rolling weariness, and whilst playing the relevant hymn as befits protocol, keeps the sound on mute so that he doesn't have to hear it! (Surely one of the subtlest examples of black comedy in any of the Robert Holmes-edited stories, an era of the programme which takes great pains to delight in the triviality of death and all its trappings.)

Planet of Evil is not a story, to be fair, that boasts an awful lot of character development, or of rich background exploration. So the funeral of Morelli seems at first to be something of an irrelevance, a scene that works precisely because it exists not to move the story along, but to give the culture under threat a little more credibility. (It's a little disappointing, then, that it transpires the only real reason we get to see the funeral at all is as a set-up for the cliffhanger, which sees the Doctor and Sarah nearly executed by similar means.) But the reason I love the scene so much is that it works too as an acknowledgement to Michael Wisher, in his last screen appearance in the show. Ever since The Ambassadors of Death, he has appeared in a wide variety of weaselly, corrupted or downright evil characters – the most illustrious, of course, being his exemplary turn as the original Davros, somehow making a man with a bit of rubber covering his face truly electrifying and believable. No one would claim that Morelli was his best part; indeed, whenever I watch the story, I keep resisting the urge to rewind the scenes to check whether that really is Michael Wisher thanklessly trudging about in the background. But whatever the dramatic on-screen reason for showing his body expelled out into the cosmos, it seems somehow appropriate as a farewell to Wisher, one of the most distinctive and memorable guest stars to feature on the show.

T: So say we all.

The casting – with one obvious caveat – is exemplary. Ewen Solon is spot on as Vishinsky: an old hand placed on board, clearly, to counter Salamar's inexperience and youth, and who punctures the necessary militarism with chinks of character (such as when he gives Sarah a matey pat on the arm). He's a veteran campaigner through-and-through – a good man who has seen too much to spare lots of time for sentiment, yet he's still decent and likeable. The caveat that I mentioned, of course, is Prentis Hancock as Salamar, which makes it doubly interesting that a battle of wills between him and Solon results in Salamar (in a well-executed act of spitefulness) using Vishinsky's own arm to throw the offending switch that will condemn the Doctor and Sarah to death. Tom Baker, on the other hand, battles Salamar/Hancock his own way – undermining (or so it seems) the one dreadful performance on hand by grinning away and tossing his head dismissively as Hancock fumes and waves his gun about.

And Frederick Jaeger pulls off the neat trick of being a truly sympathetic villain – his creased brow, bloodshot eyes and worn features being every bit as effective as his Antiman make-up in transforming him into some kind evolutionary reversal. I'm not quite sure how anti-Sorenson has no teeth, though – do they suddenly grow back when he returns to human form? Either way, the scene where Jaeger guards Elisabeth Sladen showcases her ability to react to a dangerous situation in a characteristically natural fashion – she praises the Doctor's brilliance, but then backs down, wary and conciliatory as she realises that Sorenson is more than just on edge, he's potentially deadly.

That the production team pulled this off with the BBC's limited resources of the time is laudable. This is classic Auntie matter.

July 15th

Planet of Evil (part four)

R: When I was a kid, I loved Planet of Evil because it was tense and scary, and because lots of people ended up getting killed and turned into skeletons. I now love it for rather a different reason, and it's all within this episode. Because this has not been what you might call an emotional story. A yarn in which a group of no-personality soldiers and scientists, mostly (and unhelpfully) dressed exactly alike, are bumped off. In which, tellingly, the character that's exploited and needs to be appeased isn't actually given any lines, because it's only a lump of rock. But suddenly, and so completely against the odds, something rather magical happens here, and the story finds a heart.

It's an era of the show in which ambition for discovery rarely goes unpunished. Scarman and Keeler deserve far greater respect than arrogant Sorenson, but are sacrificed with barely a qualm. But it's the fact that there is a redemption for Sorenson that gives Planet of Evil a bit of extra flavour amidst all the murders and shiny spaceship corridors. And it's earned, I think, by that beautiful scene Jaeger plays opposite Tom Baker early on in the episode, in which the Doctor talks him into committing suicide for the greater cause – and with great dignity Jaeger accepts the responsibility. What will become a recurring theme through this season – pioneers accepting that their quest for knowledge comes with consequences

– lends a depth to a story that has been big on runaround thrills, but decidedly light on anything more human. Vishinsky takes command of the Morestran ship, not because of any desire for power, but because he feels a duty towards his crew.

And Salamar ends his life taking on the Antiman directly, because he feels the same duty. I think the script robs both these moments of the emotion they deserve – for Vishinsky, because his actions don't save any of his crew but himself (he shouldn't look quite so cheerful at the story's close, his brief spell as leader has been quite disastrous), and for Salamar, because his foolish but well-meaning heroism is tarnished somewhat by the way he so casually shoots one of his crew dead in the process (rather annoyingly divesting Salamar of all sympathy, and making him a stereotypical psychopath with a power complex).

Up 'till this point, Planet of Evil is valiantly trying to do something of interest with its surviving characters, but failing – so what makes this episode for me such a winner is that it gets Sorenson absolutely right. By refusing to give him the predictable death he deserves, in its final few minutes the story becomes something that's curious and delicate, and even rather touching. And it suggests that all this hurrying about trying to get saucepans off a spaceship wasn't just a cold bit of plot mechanics, but has an emotional pay-off. It's something to treasure.

T: I really enjoyed this story. Previously, I'd always dismissed it as a middle-of-the-road Hinchcliffe – and maybe it is, but that only emphasises how even an average story from this period is still in the upper echelons of quality Doctor Who. In Invasion of the Dinosaurs, the Doctor told Mike Yates that there never was a Golden Age – but in terms of the programme, one was, in fact, just around the corner.

I make that claim that even though the ending of this is oddly perfunctory. The Morestran crew are pretty much obliterated, including poor old Michael Wisher (who, despite your lovely eulogy to him in episode three, here returns for a rather ignominious final turn as an uncredited Indian voice). It's left to Salamar to unleash a meaningless piece of technobabble to disastrous effect, causing the monster to multiply itself, but the Doctor saves the day by zapping Sorenson, dumping him for a bit in the black pool, and returning him safe and sound before gallivanting off. So, basically, the Doctor's laser gun is more effective than Salamar's Neutron Accelerator (which they may as well call a "thing" for all the sense it makes – are we ever really told what it does)?

That said, the production displays such sleight of hand, it disguises these plot weaknesses, and maintains a sense of pace and danger that keeps one gripped throughout. From the huge, looming shadow over the doomed Reig, to Sorenson's gnarled, veiny hand stopping him from killing himself, this story exudes class. Ewen Solon thankfully counterbalances Prentis Hancock's hysteria, grounding us with his direct and weighty presence while Frederick Jaeger and Tom Baker spar off each other in the quieter, more thoughtful moments. The Doctor's suggestion that scientists buy their right to experiment at the cost of total responsibility, and the detached way the Doctor mouths to Sorenson that his hypothesis was wrong, is shockingly cold. Mind you, it's not *unkind*, or even unreasonable – but it's pragmatism uttered by a wise alien who can't hang around getting mawkish. It's not that a man's death and despair doesn't emotionally impact on him – Baker's not glib at all – it's just that the impact manifests itself in an alien way, marking this Doctor out as a truly superb creation. And it's a sign that we're into more adult territory than Doctor Who has been before, in that the Doctor persuades Sorenson to commit suicide.

Tom Baker and Elisabeth Sladen. Philip Hinchcliffe and Robert Holmes. David Maloney and Roger Murray-Leech. Even if Planet of Evil isn't the best of this era, there are a number of double acts working on this show, all at the height of their powers.

Pyramids of Mars (part one)

R: The Hinchcliffe years of Doctor Who are extraordinarily popular with fans, and so it's hard to shrug off the taint of overfamiliarity. Pyramids of Mars has become something rather soft and safe after years of well-worn affection – and it means that we can easily

forget just how deliberately confounding a story it is meant to be. Right from the start, this episode is an exercise in audience misdirection. The very title suggests that the adventure will take place either in Egypt or on a distant planet – and, laughing at us all the while, it plays out instead not only in England, but the exaggerated England of the post-Edwardians. (The reaction, for example, of Dr Warlock to Ibrahim Namin's joyous pledge of fealty to Sutekh is one of bemused politesse.) Namin is set up as the lead villain, and certainly has the chops for it – not only does he obsessively play the organ like a nutter, but he also wears a fez – but the cliffhanger despatches him. It's a wonderful cliffhanger too; not only is it scary and violent, but ridding the story of its principal bad guy pulls the rug under the viewer's feet – "What on earth is this really about, then?"

What it's about, I think, is that delightfully Doctor Who collision of the clichés of one stereotyped setting with another. The writers of About Time (wonderful chaps both, I know, but dear me, so very intent on not seeing the wood for the trees) suggest that Pyramids of Mars is compromised by the lack of night filming that would have made the mummies hide in the shadows. It misses the point – we don't want to have the mummies hidden, we want them looking insanely out of place, crashing about a peaceful English countryside. Everything that makes Pyramids of Mars so great plays upon expectations being trounced and familiar elements not mixing properly. (Which is why two of the most potent images from this story, seen in later episodes, come from watching a mummy try to shake its foot out of a trap, or build a rocket.) Robert Holmes and Phillip Hinchcliffe love to play around with this sort of thing; only a couple of weeks ago, we had Mr Hyde drink from a smoking potion to turn himself back into Dr Jekyll – but to the backdrop of a brightly lit spaceship. But it's never done really quite as well as it's done here. We are invited to laugh at the ludicrousness of all this, and then to question that what we're watching is for real. (The best example of this is the way we first see Sutekh's sarcophagus shuddering on the screen – only to realise we're looking only at its reflection in a mirror reverberating to Namin's music.)

And with all this, famously too, there's this new brooding Doctor, in as bald a mission statement for character reinvention as there's ever been. "I walk in eternity", he tells the audience, and as fans we all accept this means the UNIT stories are dead. But there's so much going on in this scene, and once again it's a scene of misdirection. Just as Holmes appears to be setting out a new agenda for the series and to set the show apart from its past, it also has Sarah dress up as Victoria Waterfield (of all people!), in one of the most peculiarly blunt references right back to that past that the show will ever do. At the same time as the Doctor asserts that he wants to shake off UNIT, so he materialises right on the original site for its offices; at the same time as the Doctor asserts the supremacy of the Time Lords, so (for the very first time) the sanctity of the TARDIS is invaded. Holmes is establishing this arrogant tone for Doctor Who and the Doctor himself, and then immediately showing how quickly that arrogance and that impulse to escape the show's past is undermined. As Tom Baker stares out at us pontificating about how alien he is, the Doctor seems suddenly more powerful and impressive than we've ever seen him before. In a couple of weeks' time, he'll be dressed up in mummy bandages and pretending to be a robot; a week after that, he'll be screaming on his hands and knees. As you watch Pyramids of Mars, try to forget the fan lore, try to forget you know the new direction Doctor Who is about to take. And realise that everything you're being presented with is all designed to leave you doubting; it's like that sarcophagus shot through the mirror, nothing we're presented with here is quite what it seems.

T: This is another story that's so familiar from its BBC compilation VHS. I've seen the episodic version of Pyramids, of course, but not very often, so the additional scenes still jar with me slightly. The episode benefits from the reinstatements, though. There are a couple of minutes of silence during the chase in the wood – bar the rustle of leaves and Dudley Simpson's sparse, rattlesnake music – which work better at the length that Robert Holmes intended. The tension becomes unbearable, strung out by director Paddy Russell's excellent location work. It's summery, it's daylight, and yet everything is dripping with atmosphere. The quiet, creepy mummies loom, as our heroes are forced to hide in a palpable, protracted silence.

Holmes (writing under the pseudonym "Stephen Harris") has such a gift for idiomatic dialogue, and his well-drawn characters trade quotable stuff. Peter Copley's Dr Warlock is virtuous, but nevertheless exhibits a colonialist's disdain for the fez-flourishing foreigner, which provides some black comedy. As Namin rants about the High One returning, Warlock's "Get the police" and "Yes, I see" have all the deadpan dismissiveness of a comedy of manners. The other Peter (Mayock) does equally well with a potentially unforgiving role: Namin, the mad foreigner with the funny hat. And yet, he plays the part with such intensity and zeal that he looks and sounds great, and the Egyptian he uses as he commands the servicers sounds authentic, and brings to mind exotic, ancient power. For the viewer, he's an important link to the country where the plot originates; evoking mysticism, curses and pyramids of historic Egypt without the need to actually take a film crew there.

And, blimey – what a rapport Tom Baker and Elisabeth Sladen share. That introductory TARDIS scene is *extraordinary*. Baker is all brooding, his face etched with solemnity as if the centuries weigh heavy upon him. This sombre countenance lends him an air of gravitas, thanks in part to his sonorous tones, but the balance mostly owes to Sladen being the chirpy yin to Baker's mournful yang. Little bits of comedy shtick trip out of her effortlessly, and not without bite as she (without being cruel) ribs the Doctor's self-indulgence. The tone only really changes when a simple projection invades the ship, and Sarah's face quivers with a convincing fear.

But the contrast works because Holmes has really found a voice with this Doctor. Note how the simple addition of the word "corporeal" to a sentence about forces being summoned into existence makes it sound altogether more terrifying. With Baker's voice, the line's resonance and impact increases tenfold. And only Baker could, elsewhere in the episode, match his dourness with daftness, adopting a silly walk to duck under the windows, but in a manner that seems warm and witty, and no way indulgent or inappropriate.

All this, and Michael flippin' Sheard being characteristically great, playing it straight and gentle and refusing to act stupid (as a lesser actor would) when Baker takes the mickey. It's no surprise that Pyramids is regarded as a high point in Doctor Who's long history.

July 16th

Pyramids of Mars (part two)

R: Russell T Davies was so inspired by the alternate future scene from this episode that he wanted it replayed in his revival series in 2005; I remember poor old Mark Gatiss trying time and time again to crowbar it into The Unquiet Dead. The sequence was at last dismissed as padding. And I suppose it's padding here in Pyramids of Mars too – but has Doctor Who ever had a scene of padding which has been so thought-provoking or dramatic? And it gives a new spark to the historical adventures too; if no one has ever bothered before to explain how the sanctity of the present can be destroyed by the crises of the past, it's surely because there's never been a story set in the past that has played out on such an epic scale. So, the Meddling Monk might have helped the Saxons win at Hastings, or Irongron may have defeated a few castles with anachronistic weaponry – yes, all the historical adventuring we've seen before has been very naughty, but it also feels in contrast a bit timid and fey.

It's a great scene – not because it emphasises the dangers of time travel to any members of the audience who have the inclination to worry about such things, but because it gives a cosmic urgency to Doctor Who that we haven't really witnessed since the days of The Daleks' Master Plan. And it doesn't need twelve weeks to achieve it, just a couple of minutes where Doctor Who breaks the rules (again – I said, didn't I, that this was a story that kept on breaking convention) and has the TARDIS run away mid-adventure. And what's remarkable about is that it takes what could easily have been a rather talky bit of sci-fi theory flannel and makes it beautifully human. All thanks to Michael Sheard, whose reaction to the TARDIS

interior, all boyish joy upon seeing a technology he could only imagine as fiction, is pitch perfect. It's so skilfully done, and so movingly done too, that you barely notice a bit of abstract quantum physics has crept up behind and coshed you over the head.

There are so many bits of sublime cleverness in this episode, but my favourite moment is something very small and very funny and also very creepy. The scene between Dr Warlock and Sutekh's thrall, Marcus Scarman, is suitably tense – the version I saw on video in the eighties was hacked to bits by the Australian censors. But Bernard Archard's attempts to say his old friend's name, rooting through his brain to remember how, and not trusting the social convention of it one iota, was left intact. Archard raises one eyebrow to exaggerated effect, and he spits out *Warlock* with a mixture of repugnance and (brilliantly!) cocky pride that it's something he can get right. He's a corpse of an English gentleman, in a moment of almost human smugness acting out English gentility.

T: I'm on a train, returning from a whistle-stop trip to London for an audition for Holby City. It's a great part, that of a nerdy loner, which'll be a stretch. I was in and out, which means I was either perfect or diabolical. That it's a guest lead and a rather sweet character means I don't think I'll get it. The fact that filming is scheduled to clash with my honeymoon means that I probably will...

So, Mr Holmes has already terrified us with a gruesome cliffhanger, and now the monster of the week stands revealed as a walking corpse. He certainly knows how to keep things grim, but *what* a flourish. A dead man walking is your perfect baddie – it's a truly horrible, repellent concept, but fun for a good actor to play. And let's face it: a dead man is always going to be a more effective mouthpiece for villainy than some poor sod covered in latex. It helps that Bernard Archard's bony features, when given a gruesome deathly hue by make-up, are truly terrifying. That simple reverse effect when he's given both barrels of Ernie's shotgun is neat, and he pulls it off well – it's the showpiece moment of another remarkable episode.

I mean, this is basically a base-under-siege

story, but Holmes' strategy of gradually bumping off each of the characters brings something else to the table. The poacher Ernie Clements doesn't outlive the episode, but it's a well-judged cameo from George Tovey. I like the way he instinctively blows through his shotgun barrel after he's fallen over; it's a neat little touch that convinces he's spent years foraging in the countryside. You equally buy his principled little stand, and his prosaic and simple outrage against Warlock's horrible murder. Having uttered a few lines, he ends up being despatched pretty horribly himself, but remains extremely memorable.

Among the survivors, Tom Baker continues to bestride everything with his novel way of making potentially generic lines sound fresh. He positively twinkles at Laurence Scarman's excitement at being in the TARDIS (he's pulled in by the shoulders, in a comic moment that would have been annoying in another story, but here is rather sweet and fun). With the Doctor in grinning mode, it's Sarah's turn to get all serious as they head to the apocalyptic wasteland of 1980, but the Doctor soon follows suit. The two of them both switch so believably between emotions, and light and dark, they carry you through the story's twists and tricks like master magicians. Michael Sheard (as Laurence) certainly holds his own with them, providing much pathos and humanity, which clashes tellingly with Baker's harsh, alien moodiness. And amidst all the horror and outlandishness, there's a tiny bit of business towards the end where Sarah flinches as she pulls the switch on the Marconiscope. It's a small moment, but an utterly believable one − her unease that this unfamiliar thing might spark or burn her is yet another example of Sladen's commitment to every second.

But Holmes' dialogue gives our cast so much to work with − having lost our link to Egypt with Namin's death, it's been up to the Doctor to muse about "Sakkara" and a "Mastaba", the very sounds of authentic Egyptian vocabulary bringing verisimilitude. Baker makes the latter word (meaning an ancient tomb) drip with authority, and he's equally adept at making futuristic hokum about etheric impulses sound vital and plausible. Holmes' word-choice makes everything that much more sublime −

"remove that carcass" sounds so much grislier than "take away that body".

I want my Mummy... or maybe I don't!

Pyramids of Mars (part three)

R: It'll be months before we get there, but do you remember that interactive Christmas episode, Attack of the Graske? I was always faintly bothered by the Doctor's assertion to the child viewer, training to be a companion, that he "only took the best". Besides the fact it's blatantly not true (I mean, what did he think he was doing travelling about with Dodo, was she some sympathy case?), it strikes me as being just a little fascistic. When I was a kid, the idea that the TARDIS might materialise in my playground and take Rob away − gauche and geeky, shy stammery Rob − was one of those little comfort fantasies I used to indulge in. Hey, he'd rescued Adric of all people, he might rescue me!

And whenever I watch Laurence Scarman, I see him as a companion manqué. This excitable man who takes such delight in the workings of the TARDIS, this frightened (but very brave) chap who stands shoulder to shoulder with the Doctor and Sarah against the mummies. He gets things wrong, of course he does − but that's because he's an Edwardian Harry Sullivan, desperately likeable and sincere, and prone to well-meaning bungling. I would have enjoyed a run of stories with him as assistant. I can hear it now: "Laurence Scarman is an imbecile!"

So that's the cruelty of his death. He's the first character introduced in the Hinchcliffe era that you can regard with honest affection, the first one that doesn't seem to be there merely for the mechanics of plot. Episode two has been a Robert Holmesian bloodbath − all the other human cast have been murdered one by one. But no matter how grisly some of those murders, we've never been led to believe that the likes of Warlock or the poacher Ernie Clements had any life beyond those murders; they were fun stereotypes for cannon fodder. Laurence was different, and seemed to have a character arc that was much more complex. So, again, the predictable journey for Laurence would have been that his confrontation with his possessed brother would have had an impact. That when he showed Marcus the photograph of the two of them as boys, some emotional connection would have been made, and Marcus might have found some part of himself. (With Holmes' fixation on possession, it's a scene we've seen variations on before – the Doctor calling out to Noah to find some vestige of his humanity, or Sarah fighting the influence of the Queen Spider.) And what's so nasty is that the scene allows us to believe that Laurence's appeal to Marcus' better nature might yet work – there's that glimmer of resistance, Marcus does remember, he's in there somewhere, the Doctor was wrong! And haven't we just seen, only a few weeks ago, Professor Sorenson released from a possession every bit as dreadful as Professor Scarman's? My God, the two names even sound the same, surely there must be hope?

And there isn't. Laurence dies. And the Doctor is so unmoved by his murder, that's the terrible thing. Because we saw him as a special character, as a companion in waiting maybe – but the Doctor didn't, he was just another one of the guest cast due to be offed. It isn't even his words that seem so awful, it's the dispassionate way that Tom Baker pushes the corpse to one side as an irrelevance so he can get to work on a robot. He'll only take the best. And Laurence didn't measure up.

T: Me too – I remember "playing" Pyramids of Mars when I was a kid, and somehow I knew that Laurence Scarman was the Doctor and Sarah's main helper, even though I'd not yet read the book. (Or any of the books – I was just too young, though I could wrangle the back blurb if I really tried.) During the course of the game, one of my brothers told me Laurence died. I remember being shocked by that, even though I'd seen plenty of benevolent characters snuff it in the course of my Who watching. (Later on, when my brothers had outgrown Doctor Who and mocked my obsessiveness about it, one of them caught some of Pyramids as I watched my BBC video for the millionth time. "See, this is a good one", he said. "If Doctor Who was more like this now, it'd be worth watching." Praise indeed.)

So it was unavoidable that Laurence was dead to me even before I saw Michael Sheard's performance. This, and the fact that Sheard

himself was so familiar as Mr Bronson on Grange Hill, means that I've never really looked at the role or his performance objectively before now. As it turns out, the Doctor is so tough on Laurence that it's heartbreaking, especially as Sheard lends the role such vulnerability and self-awareness. He knows he can't be strong and haughty like this inscrutable alien, but he helps as best he can in spite of himself: he's not a total wet or a liability. It's Laurence who suggests the blasting gelignite, and he does – just for a moment – actually break through to unlock some vestige of his brother when trying to connect with his walking corpse. Of course, he doesn't succeed, and that's part of the tragedy.

I mentioned use of the word "carcass" last episode, but what about "animated human cadaver"? Sheer brilliance. And when you give such rich, evocative dialogue to an actor as talented as Gabriel Woolf – here making Doctor Who history as the world-destroyer Sutekh – you have something truly special. Woolf's vocal cords are such an extraordinary instrument, with a slight sibilance and a silky, purring depth beneath a deceptively light top register. The syllables dance about his vocal cords as he plays with words like a child does a fly. Sutekh's spine-chilling "all life is my enemy" speech deftly shows that if your villain's words are written and spoken by the best, he can essentially just sit in a chair and talk to himself, and still be far more threatening than any number of gun-wielding space captains, or robotic megalomaniacs.

But grounding all of this is a Doctor-companion relationship that is so good, even things that shouldn't sit right – Sarah being a confident markswoman, and the Doctor dressing as a Mummy – only showcase them as something extraordinary. The "Doctor disguised as a Mummy" guff somewhat dilutes the effectiveness of the creatures themselves, emphasising that they're men in suits. Even though the Doctor's disguise has smartly been made to look slightly more ragged than the real thing, I simply don't buy it – and yet, the scenario allows a dynamic between the Doctor and Sarah that makes a virtue of it. And when Sarah steels for her gunshot and tells the Doctor, with quiet authority, "I know what I'm doing", I believe her! What's funny is that even when Tom Baker is encased in bandages, his steely, glowering presence remains. And yet, for all we talk about Baker's menacing, detached presence, it's not simply a cold experience of high dramatics – largely because of his rapport with Elisabeth Sladen.

Two scenes in particular showcase this... as the Doctor tries to disarm the force-shield generator, he berates Sarah for standing there "admiring the scenery", then gives us a funny line about mending a wristwatch with a hammer and chisel. So, he uses quiet menace to emphasise the danger... but then gives it a punchline. And the hut scene with the sweaty gelignite, which includes the Doctor's suggestion that there might be a ferret, has such confidence in their rapport that when Sarah delivers her glib "maybe he sneezed" reply, Baker sends back a filthy look without our ever feeling he really hates her guts. Sarah's black humour is very mature – and yet she was the companion my brothers always claimed "screamed all the time". Well, there's so much in this – not the least Sarah's "it must have been a nasty accident" when confronted with the Mummy-Doctor – that suggests that even only a few years after the event, their memories were already cheating.

July 17th

Pyramids of Mars (part four)

R: Let's get the usual objection out of the way first. Yes, the story stutters to a halt once the action shifts to Mars and we're presented with a series of simple riddles rather than real drama or jeopardy. Good. We need the interlude. Because the first ten minutes of the episode have seen the Doctor debased like never before, forced to become a plaything, and then possessed and zombified. We've seen the series do something similar at the climax of Planet of the Spiders, where Jon Pertwee is humiliated and made to dance upon the spot – but the crucial difference there is that Pertwee not only protests throughout, he also loses his life straight afterwards, and that confers on him an immediate sacrificial dignity. Not so for Tom Baker: we watch as he shuffles about corpse-like, his eyes rolled into his head, for some

sign that it's all a ruse. But it isn't. The Doctor has not only been defeated, he's been erased. It's horrifying – not just for Baker's portrayal, but for Elisabeth Sladen's reaction to it, which aches not just with fear but with disappointment.

So, by God, we need to re-establish the Doctor afterwards, we need to lighten the tone. On paper, yes, all the wall puzzles seem rather naff. But they wash over us like relief. The Doctor gets to grin again, and do funny things with his scarf; Sarah gets to joke about tribophysics; the two of them do a comedy walk as they avoid encountering a mummy. The first half of the episode has been so claustrophobic and intense, it's almost left the story with no way back to the surface. If it weren't for the considerable rapport between Baker and Sladen, by now honed to gorgeous perfection, we'd be floundering. As a horror story, episode four would undoubtedly be more effective without all this. As a Doctor Who story, and one that has broken so many rules, and misdirected the audience so often, without it I think it'd break.

And it's not as if there isn't still one moment of pure horror left, one final sting in its tale. As the Eye of Horus is destroyed, Sutekh shouts out in joy that he is at last free. And Professor Scarman takes up the cheering cry, before collapsing to the ground as a smoking skeleton. There is a deliberate ambiguity whether the slave of Sutekh is merely echoing his master's words – or whether, in his last few moments of life, Marcus Scarman, friend to Dr Warlock, brother to Laurence, achieves some final relief in self-consciousness. I like to think so. But the beauty of it is that we can never know.

T: It's been a momentous finale to quite an adventure – not Pyramids of Mars, actually, but my last day in Manchester. All sensible planning goes out of the window as I scrub the walls down (it's a horrible job), hurl my last few bits and bobs into IKEA bags and store them at a friend's place. Okay, it's all clean(ish), and I don't think I've left anything apart from some T-bags and a large bottle of ketchup: a housewarming present for the new tenants. So, these are to be my last episodes of Doctor Who in Chorlton. All change for me, quite seismic in a way the hectic nature of the week hasn't really allowed me to appreciate. For the Doctor, too, there's no time to stand on ceremony – he just needs to go through a few tedious necessities before clearing up any unfinished business. I certainly know how he feels.

Mind you, the logic problems our heroes have to solve here are about as much fun as scrubbing walls – being reminded of the City of the Exxilons is as welcome as having to inform the phone/ utility companies of my move. If only much of this could be removed from the process – and kudos to BBC Video for a change, as their cuts to the compilation did just that. The dialogue even makes mention of the tiresome nature of these childish stratagems! The actors are game, but it's clear that money and imagination have run out. As has the logic – why *does* Horus test inveiglers with a puzzle? Is solving one an indication of inherent goodness? And yet, it only fails in comparison to its previous three episodes. Even if this week's script is below par, the production's attention to detail remains impressive – Scarman's dead body is gruesome, and the final shot of it is most superbly rendered.

But try as I might to remain objective, my perception of Pyramids of Mars is so heavily shaped by viewings of it in the real world – not just with my brothers, but after about eight of my fellow students tidied up from a party at my house when I was at 6th Form College. At the time, my friends thought the Doctor Who airing on the telly was a laughable thing with liquorice allsorts monster, but they seemed happy enough for me to put a good, old Doctor Who on. Pyramids was an obvious choice (even my brothers thought it good, remember), and... they laughed at everything. The Mummies' gait, Peter Copley's performance as Dr Warlock, Clements' death scene (because of the timing of the gunfire, they thought Laurence had shot him): it all looked daft to their eyes.

I found that *extraordinary* – how could they not allow for a decade or so's change in production styles, and not see just how damned good everything was? Never mind that these were drama students who wanted to *write*, to *act*, to *produce* and to *direct*. Could they not see quality when it was put in front of them? "Heaven help the world of entertainment", I thought, "if the next generation of programme-makers are without discernment". Would they just produce glossy, soulless tat: all surface and no soul? And these people were my friends, my buddies! We were close, hung out together, trusted each other with our innermost secrets. But, like Pyramids of Mars episode four, despite all the right ingredients, despite so much about them that made me feel good, and positive, and safe, they came up short. They didn't get it. They laughed and let me down.

Apart from one of them. My closest friend amongst them was a girl, Katherine Mount, and she didn't mock it. She didn't think it was clever to take the piss out of something she knew I liked.

I'm marrying her tomorrow.

The Android Invasion (part one)

R: You see that UNIT soldier standing to attention at the reception to the space centre? The one that Tom Baker tries to talk to, but who just stares ahead like a zombie? I know him! That's Alan Clements. He's a fine director, and produced an adaptation I wrote of Jane Austen's Pride and Prejudice for an open-air theatre near Manchester ten years ago. In rehearsal, he told me he knew he'd done a "Doctor Who", but couldn't remember what – and I was no help. I should give him a call and tell him! Nice to see Alan again. Looking terribly, terribly young.

Let's assume once more we don't know the plot turns of this story in advance. In which case, you spend 24 minutes waiting for... the Daleks to show up! Come on, the Daleks have to be in this somewhere, it's a Terry Nation script. And we know they never appear until the first cliffhanger. So imagine the audience's surprise when that grille opens to reveal a monster... and instead of something metal and sink-plungered popping out at us, we're shown a creature that is fleshy and wrinkled and ugly. The brilliance of the moment is not only that it defies expectation, but that we're still not shown the full Kraal – just one eye, and the suggestion of a face that's alien and distorted.

Being a Terry Nation story too, we might expect that the first episode is essentially an exercise in anticipation, waiting for that cliffhanger reveal. Again, it's what he always does; he'll tease you with hints of a society in peril (nuclear threats, check; abandoned areas, check; even someone robotic trying to kill itself), but they're merely delaying tactics until the Daleks emerge from cover and the story proper begins. But here, for once, the hints he gives us are genuinely puzzling. As with Pyramids, there's a real sense of macabre incongruity to the proceedings. The sequence with the villagers of Devesham being delivered to the pub by truck, and all coming alive on the striking of a clock, is one of the eeriest things Doctor Who has ever done. And there's so much to puzzle and confound us, from astronauts firing bullets from their fingers, to the dead coming back to life, to the emptiness of the village, that the episode properly starts to feel quite unnerving. As the Doctor suggests, it's a genuine relief when astronaut Guy Crayford pops up and speaks, even if it is whilst pointing a gun – it's the first moment of anything recognisably normal for about 20 minutes.

Barry Letts' direction here is precise and assured. And seems to be taking visual elements from his early days producing Pertwee (the Auton guns from Spearhead from Space, the killer astronauts from Ambassadors, and all of UNIT firing upon the Doctor from Inferno) and making it striking and new. Yes, the title's a bit of a giveaway – there are androids about here somewhere, that's a given. But that's not really the point; on its own terms, standing alone, the introductory episode of this story leaves us at cliffhanger more genuinely intrigued than anything we've been offered in years.

T: I'd saved this one up. We didn't get the Target novel of The Android Invasion for years – the opportunity had arisen, but other stories kept tempting me every time I visited the bookshop. By the time I got my hands of it, I was collecting the videos and decided to hold off reading it, so that at least this one story would be totally new to me. At the same time, the pathologically on-message Doctor Who: A Celebration had effectively torn The Android Invasion to shreds by saying it was something of an anomaly in an otherwise impressive season, and it was generally felt to be something of a disappointment.

Well, there's nothing like a lack of familiarity to breed contentment. This episode still feels *fresh* to me – it's bright and summery, and yet still has a spooky atmosphere. Who needs rain and darkness to set a mood? The use of silence to build tension is impressive – both inside the pub, where the sound suddenly dies when Sarah is discovered, and outside too, the lack of noise from machinery or chatter or vehicles making the sun-drenched, airy village oppressive and tense. This silence is indeed golden.

Barry Letts does his best work behind the camera yet – the way the mystery is piled on might be somewhat old fashioned, but if anything, it plays to Letts' strengths. There's a deserted village, a silent phone box and villagers delivered on the back of a van, erect and dead-eyed like standing corpses. And the much-derided title (thought to be giving the game away) isn't as daft as all that: the comatose villagers could still be human, couldn't they? The men in white jump suits with loaded fingers could be the invading androids.

And to look at the opening sequence – where the jerky movements of "malfunctioning" UNIT soldier are juxtaposed with a branch brushing across his face and tearing into his skin, producing blood – I'm reminded that the bloke playing him, Max Faulkner, was one of those names I'd read in cast lists a lot. He's as prolific in Doctor Who as Terry Walsh or Pat Gorman, but never seems to get mentioned as often as those two illustrious background heroes. He's a perfectly decent actor and convinces as a soldier – I'm not sure I would have trusted Walsh with such a hefty part. And none of us should be surprised when the soldier seems to die and comes back to life – Faulkner's done that twice before, in The Ambassadors of Death and The Monster of Peladon, remember (mistakes both, but I'm still chuckling about them). Another small screen hero is Milton Johns: he makes for bizarre casting as an astronaut, but Doctor Who is the possibly the only programme daft enough for you to get away with it. There's even fun to be had extra spotting – if Max Faulkner is indeed looking well after breaking his neck, then so too is Joseph Chambers, the non-speaking government type who was blatantly killed by the K1 in Robot. (But there Chambers – or rather extra Walter Goodman who played him – is in the pub, I'd recognise that moustache anywhere.) And the leather-jacketed android in the landing pod? That's Keith Ashley in a nutshell, that is.

But once more, it comes down to the rapport of the leading man and his beautiful lady to really make this come alive. When fearful of radiation, Sarah's curse about getting caught exposed "like a couple of 'nanas" is so brilliantly naturalistic; it's black humour that in no way undermines the palpability of the threat. Meanwhile, Tom Baker is perfect – he's insolent and insouciant, with a dangerous, brooding authority, and delivers his words about being partial to tea and muffins like it's a chat-up line.

Far from being the duffer of Season Thirteen, this is a perfect mix of suspense, action and fun. The sun is shining, and the leading man and his lady are on great form and in perfect sync. Let's hope this is an omen...

July 18th

The Android Invasion (part two)

R: You get married today! (I thought I'd point that out, just in case you needed reminding.) And I should be there, but I'm on a ship in the Baltic. I am not, as I suspected, lecturing on Dostoevsky in Russia today - that'll be Thursday. Instead I'm lecturing Pushkin in Estonia. It all feels somewhat surreal, and though I'm having a good time, I wish I could be by your side. I'm raising a glass of something Eastern European and spiky in your direction. All the very best.

I hope too you've selected good music for the service. And not "Kraal Disorientation Chamber" from the Doctor Who Sound Effects LP. How I remember bopping about to that in my childhood... Do you know, I never got to kiss a girl until I was 18.

The revelation that we're not on Earth at all is really well handled; we've spent so much time being fed the blatant twist that Sarah is a duplicate, that it's a genuine surprise at the cliffhanger to discover that the duplication goes much further than has been hinted. And if the script is lighter on the surreal imagery and has slipped into formulaic alien invasion mode, Barry Letts is still working hard to make

the story visually disconcerting. It's still ages until we see a Kraal face, it first being shown only through refracted glass – and the way that even simple encounters with Morgan the pub landlord are made eerier than they might be, just by dint of sudden extreme close-up, makes everything still feel as if it's on edge.

Yeah, you can spot the similarities with Terror of the Zygons broadcast only a couple of months before – but there's still enough style here to make The Android Invasion at least visually distinctive. Even if episode two seems to have slowed down already to episode three runaround – and the long sequence where Styggron creates a homicidal android from scratch, simply to demonstrate he can destroy it with a gun, is bizarre. It seems a very over-complicated way to engineer one's plans. Maybe this will be a general flaw in the Kraal methodology. Let's wait and see.

T: You never got to kiss a girl 'till you were 18, I never got to marry one 'till I was 35. Today! Yesterday was insane and knackering, but I hit the sack at around midnight, and got a short but satisfying sleep, but was inevitably awake very early. So I've showered, put on most of my glad rags, and am whiling away the early hours fitting my cufflinks and killing time by watching, of all things, The Android Invasion. *What am I doing?*

I'm not the only one behaving strangely... like the Zygons, the Kraals appear to go to the trouble of creating exact replicas of certain humans, but then programme them to conduct themselves in an ill-advisedly evil manner (though it's nice to see Harry and Benton again). At the pub, the shifty landlord Morgan tells the Doctor that the phone, as it often pans out in adventure serials of this ilk, is for him. "Is it?" asks Baker with mock surprise, almost daring the fourth wall to topple over under his bulging gaze. And whilst much of this is a little *too* reminiscent of Terror of the Zygons, the cliffhanger reveal of the android Sarah's circuitry makes me fondly remember Pyramids of Mars – because it suggests that her face is so ill-fitting, one good sneeze could have made it fall off. When the Doctor nobbles her, the audacious whip sound effect that accompanies his flashing his hat at Sarah's gun brims with admirable chutzpah.

The emergence of Styggron as the story's main villain isn't as convincing, unfortunately – it seems odd that Barry Letts initially keeps Styggron half-glimpsed, hidden or as a warped reflection... and then suddenly shows his face without any ceremony whatsoever. (I spent last night and this morning studiously avoiding the bride; it'd somewhat waste all of that effort if she simply now popped her head round to door to say hello.) Aside from how he looks, vocally Styggron is Welsh (which is also strange, because Martyn Friend isn't, I don't think). That being the case, listening as he wrangles lines about a "much more powerful version" and "science [making] the Kraals invincible" sounds like he's describing an upgrade for Ivor the Engine.

I'm really not complaining, you understand – I've really enjoyed these episodes. Even the daft bits are done with such commitment and believability that I'll let them go (*even if* the ersatz Sarah's blatant enjoyment of her previously despised ginger pop is such an obvious clue as to her identity, even the Sensorites would have picked up on it). The Android Invasion has always had a bad reputation, but judging by these first two episodes, it's a good mix of mystery and fun, and the lack of gothic trappings makes it stand on its own two feet rather bravely.

Or, perhaps I'm just very excited and that's influencing me. Well, if the sun shines today like it's doing on my TV, I'll be a happy man. That's all the similarities I want with this though... I certainly don't want my beautiful companion to end the proceedings behaving out of character, and then falling over, off her face.

The Android Invasion (part three)

R: Guy Crayford is not one of Doctor Who's most intelligent villains, but he's one of the most endearing. Milton Johns gets it spot on. This is a nerd who finds himself as commander of an invasion force, but is clearly out of his element; as a kid, he was probably the school swot who studied astronomy and no one would play with during break, who ended up flying solo space missions because he couldn't find any friends to go with. Just look at the way Johns plays Crayford when he's standing

near the android of Harry Sullivan, the latter being so much more sophisticated and effective than he is – he bumbles about it awkwardly, a whole bag of social ineptness in traitor form. I love the scenes where Crayford talks to the Kraals; Styggron treats his human ally as an indulgent mother might – "Go on then, you go play with your friend the Doctor, but don't get into any trouble, and don't eat too many sweets!" And the sequence where Crayford tells the Doctor and Sarah of the invasion plans is gorgeous; Johns is so childishly excitable, unable to keep still, as he confides in them as if they're new chums he's inviting to his birthday party. What could so easily have been turgid exposition becomes utterly charming, and that's entirely down to Milton Johns realising the humour in his character.

And quite right – because this is funny. It's Terror of the Zygons redux, but a shade more bonkers, with sillier characters and jokes. And I know it's heretical to say it, but just right now I almost prefer it. This sort of story works better as light-hearted comedy than as Gothic horror. The Doctor is left alone by the monsters to die not just once, but twice; as Styggron shuffles away back to safety, looking like a grumpy old man, the Doctor cheerfully calls out to him to hang around a bit so he can be blown up too, and I laughed out loud. The Doctor being rescued by Sarah is joyous: "I feel disorientated!" "It's the disorientation chamber!" "That makes sense!" The Android Invasion is a story out of place. Slap back in the middle of the Hinchliffe era, with the accent upon chills and body horror and Tom Baker losing his temper every other moment, it looks trite and random. Relocate it to the latter days of Graham Williams, and this would be a striking piece of runaround bluster, with buckets of charm. It sells itself as something gentle and disposable and Saturday teatime, at a point in the programme's history when Saturday teatime is considered a threatening place to be. I like it for its cheery cheesiness.

And I'm so over Laurence Scarman. I want Guy Crayford as companion now. "Guy Crayford is an imbecile!" Come on, it'd have worked. (This is a man who has fooled Earth he survived two years adrift in space by drinking his own pee. He has no shame! He's brilliant!)

T: Well, yes old chum, you've made a very plausible case for this working as a comedy, as if somehow it was intended that way... but I'm afraid I'm going to have to call you on this. The Gunfighters *is* funny, and works because everybody understands its inherent silliness and reacts accordingly (apart from fandom in the 1980s, that is). But with The Android Invasion, the only people who think it is a comedy are... um... oh, you! The things that are funny about this are by mistake, and it's generally just rather dull. (Unless of course you're saying it's deliberate that Roy Skelton begins a scene as Chedaki sounding like Zippy from Rainbow, and ends it sounding more like George.) Elsewhere, this is really rather bungled.

There's a series of interminable scenes of capture and exposition. Guy Crayford is a mixed bag – I still maintain that Milton Johns is odd casting in the role, but he's too good an actor to let that be a problem, and – as you rightly point out – his playing of the scene in the cell is winningly boyish. And yet, even Johns can't paper over the fact that Crayford's plan is nonsense and his motivation wafer-thin, but bless the Doctor for crediting the mistakes in the faux village (the freshly minted money, the calendar with the same date) as the unavoidable side-effects of a dastardly scheme, as opposed to clues littered in a lazy script. More exposition weighs down the Doctor and Styggron's chat in the disorientation chamber, which feels as though it goes on for several billion years, and then – *bam!* – after a couple of quick scenes establishing the rocket, we're away into a sudden and underwhelming cliffhanger.

If there's a bright spot here, it's the terrific scene between the Doctor and Styggron in the village square. Barry Letts places his cameras well, and it's so refreshing to have sequences take place in such a locale – seeing the troll-like Styggron traipsing away, and the tied-up Doctor in the foreground with a bomb at his feet, is a most arresting and incongruous image. And, it has to be said, the humps on the Kraals, and their gargoyle-like masks and costumes, are actually pretty impressive.

But apart from that, I haven't given this episode the best reception have I? I hope I haven't set a precedent for later. You'll have to pardon that I'm getting a trifle giddy: I've just flirted with the idea that when K is asked "Do you take this man to be your lawful wedded husband?", I could blurt out the unbeatable sentence "Resistance is inadvisable!" Well, I think that would be funny.

The Android Invasion (part four)

R: The funny effect of Nicholas Courtney being unavailable to take part in the episode is that, in this tale of duplicate confusion, UNIT never looks real. We get to see Benton and Harry again, and we're assured it's really them – and then they start chatting to a man in a Brigadier-like costume doing Brigadier-like things, looking every inch the sort of comic turn you get whenever they do Doctor Who spoofs on shows like Crackerjack. It's clearly not what the production team would have intended, and the story at this point wants the audience to feel reassured by our return to Earth and the normality that the Kraals threaten. But I must admit, I rather like the fact that, simply because of Patrick Newell's appearance, everything looks off-kilter and strange. This is the point at which the plotting gets a bit tidy and twee, as we all gallop towards the story wrap-up – and UNIT filtered through this strange nightmarish lens where the Brigadier is played by a man we don't recognise gives it an odd twist quite in line with the paranoid tone of bodysnatching.

Because, yes, I know that in episode one Crayford told us all that the Brigadier was in Geneva – but that was a month's transmission ago. (And why should we believe anything he says? He's not even on Earth!) So from the point of view of the innocent child viewer, or the average adult who's not paying obsessive attention, it really would seem as if something is out of balance. No one mentions Lethbridge-Stewart at all this episode; there's no indication given that the Doctor and Colonel Faraday haven't met before, or indeed that Faraday hasn't been his regular sparring partner on screen since 1968. All the audience get to see is a portly military man with facial hair being a bit posh and thick, and huffing and puffing when the Doctor challenges protocol. I'm prepared to bet that a large number of viewers won't have realised it was a different character at all – he'd have looked a little different, and they wouldn't quite have put their fingers on why.

From our point of view, and as good an actor as Newell is, his take on the Brigadier only serves to remind us all just how much warmth Nicholas Courtney brought to the part. Harry and Benton make their final appearances here, and we don't get so much as a goodbye. (We last see Benton unconscious, and Harry tied up.) But it's the Brigadier, strangely, who leaves the most touching impression by absence alone.

T: First of all, the truth about Guy Crayford's eyepatch – what a joke! I mentioned last episode that the plot was getting thicker and thicker – and I wasn't wrong! It's as thick as two short planks. The idea that Crayford hasn't washed his face or even sensed the presence of his own eye in two years is the most childish thing to appear in Doctor Who in as long as I can remember.

Howlers aside, I regret to say, it's pretty dull stuff once again this week. There's a protracted bit of business at the space centre (total staff there: three) before a rushed conclusion that makes no mention of Marshall Chedaki's fleet, and that's the tip of the iceberg in terms of plotting headaches. But, never mind – at least the nonsensical climax offers the surprise of a thwacked Styggron somersaulting backwards onto his own poison, which then kills him with a convincingly gruesome goo, and there are other things to talk about.

Such as: farewell, John Levene. It's a pretty perfunctory exit for Benton (some maintain that he's killed here, but it's inconclusive enough for me to go the second-hand car salesman route offered in Mawdryn Undead), and though he tries for one of those Benton-says-something-daft-and-has-pleased-look-wiped-from-his-face-by-a-glowering-superior moments, it's not an especially good one, and nobody really pays it much attention. Benton has been a real revelation through this process – I think Levene is perfect, playing to his strengths and not letting his weaknesses prevent him from 100% commitment to the role and the series. He may be prone to certain odd

behaviours at conventions, but on screen he's one of the unsung heroes of Doctor Who. Sadly for him, even perennial extra Dave Carter gets a better send off in this, his last story, with a decent role as the technician Grierson – he makes a good account of himself, and survives being shot even when he's of no more use to the plot. Like Max Faulkner, I've never seen Carter interviewed, but he's been a useful prop in too many stories to count, and I wish him well. Ian Marter, at least, will return to write some Doctor Who novels that made me feel all grown up when I read them, but it's such a duff leaving do for UIT that Courtney doesn't even bother to show up.

Fancy not even bothering to attend a really important event, eh, Mr Shearman?

Well, I'd never have thought that the last episode of The Android Invasion would be my final one as a bachelor. I'm especially chuffed that I'm about to head to a church that has, outside it, a memorial that's not unlike the one the Doctor gets tied up to on the cover of the Target book. What do you mean, I can't possibly recreate that moment for the amusement of about three people? It's my wedding, I'll do what I want. It's still a secret, but we're walking out of the church to the Doctor Who theme on the organ.

I know that some people would dismiss that as a bit, well, sad. Sad? No way, I'm happier than I've ever been in my life.

R: Many congratulations to you, Toby – I'm proud of you.

Now, whatever you do, don't make it a late night. You've got The Brain of Morbius in the morning.

July 19th

The Brain of Morbius (part one)

R: This is nasty. What was a silly joke in The Android Invasion is played for blunt reality here. Crayford was led to believe his entire body had been smashed up in a spaceship crash and that the Kraals had stitched it all back together – save for a single eye, that had presumably rolled under the carpet. It was a lie – and had Crayford had the wit ever to have taken his patch off, he'd have found out for himself! But here, the Kraal practical joke is in earnest. There are body parts everywhere – decapitated corpses, ganglia hanging from severed necks, poor Condo is even missing his arm. Once again, we are invited to look at scenes and misinterpret them: that wonderful opener, in which we see an ugly insect stab down with an ugly pincer, suggests that we're straightaway being shown a threatening monster. And then, out of the storm, comes a humanoid figure – and the joke is that his own arm has been replaced with a hook that's so much sharper.

Nasty, as I say – and, for once, that nastiness isn't lightened by humour (as it was, say, in Pyramids of Mars), it's the humour that emphasises it. The grisliness of Solon's experiments are only exacerbated by the casual understatement of how Philip Madoc plays his dialogue. His frustration with his manservant Condo for bringing him an insect head, and his obsessive desire for something more humanoid, would be laugh-out loud funny if we weren't squirming. When Madoc encounters the Doctor, his honest-to-God admiration of the Doctor's head is simply gorgeous – he has lived so long steeped in body parts that he cannot help but let out a professional enthusiasm, even if he then shows genuine embarrassment that he might have dropped a social faux pas. What makes the scenes in Solon's castle so effective is the way that Madoc plays utterly against the Hammer Frankenstein trappings. He's a modern man with modern frustrations about having some weird Igor alien lurching about in the background; he carries a twentieth-century revolver, not a laser gun.

And it's because of the normalcy that Madoc establishes that the scenes with the Sisterhood of Karn work so well. Because all that incantation and religious zeal and eye-goggling and hand-fluttering is set against it in contrast – the Solon sequences not only apologise for the cod melodramatics going on elsewhere, they also provide a need for them; after the low-key domestics of Mehendri Solon, the spectacle is all too welcome.

Tom Baker and Elisabeth Sladen continue to be brilliant. Just as the Doctor shrugs off any responsibility to UNIT, here he does the same thing to the Time Lords. Baker is extraordinar-

ily good at investing the Doctor with authority even when he's renouncing it. And when the Doctor and Sarah turn up on the castle doorstep holding an umbrella to protect them from the driving rain, grinning and asking for a glass of water, it may just be one of the best things on television ever.

The Brain of Morbius (part two)

R: This is a revelation to me; I've never really had much time for The Brain of Morbius before. I'd always found the production too stagey, the Frankenstein parody too obvious. But I think this is a truly terrific script, with the sharpest and funniest dialogue I've heard on Doctor Who in years. Yes, it is stagey, but this is unashamedly theatrical stuff, with Philip Madoc in particular getting the chance to relish some beautifully overwritten insults. And (as with Pyramids) the allusions to the source material are made obvious simply so that the audience doesn't get bogged down with unnecessary set-up: we understand the world that this adventure inhabits, so Robert Holmes can give more time to subtler jokes that glance off the parody. For example, the scene where Solon endangers his own life to try to save the Doctor's from burning at the stake is gorgeous: as polite etiquette fails, he desperately resorts to offering his servant instead, and then begging that the Sisterhood keep the Doctor's dead trunk and simply let him have the severed head! It's wonderful black comedy – especially as you watch the Doctor cheerfully express gratitude for Solon's attempts at rescue, then realise that Solon is more deranged than his would-be executioners.

And as always happens with Doctor Who, if you give good actors a good script, they rise to the challenge. Madoc is always brilliant in all of his guest parts, but here he is truly extraordinary. Sporting his Elizabethan bowl haircut as he strides through the story he even looks like a Renaissance man, one foot in medieval superstition, one foot in scientific enquiry. He brings such dignity to the part that you can see the emergence of a theme here that'll come to the forefront in The Masque of Mandragora next year – examining the pivot where ancient becomes modern, and asking which is the most dangerous and corruptive. Solon could so simply be another crazed scientific genius whose ambitions for discovery and personal achievement make him another Sorenson or Scarman. But when Sarah is blinded, he can still examine her eyes with medical tenderness and be tactful about his diagnosis; when he speaks to Morbius, it is not with the panic of a failing acolyte, but as a surgeon who just wants to do his best job. Sometimes fans criticise the logic of the story, and wonder why Solon is so keen to stick the Doctor's head on the body of a mishmash monster, when he could so much more conveniently scoop out the innards and put Morbius' brain into a ready made human-oid. And it's weird that we fans do that, because in particular we're the ones who want to collect things and make them ours and put them together in interesting ways so we can personalise them and love them. I would never have wanted to buy a joblot of Target novelisa-tions when I was a kid – I wanted to find them all in those second-hand bookshops in Reigate and Wolverhampton, I wanted to make a quest out of it. I wanted that inner glory just as much as Solon does.

Not that I'd ever embark on some long-winded and patently preposterous quest now-adays. I've long outgrown that. Hmm... How are you getting on, Toby?

The Brain of Morbius (part three)

R: Immortality is often something that is regarded with deep suspicion on Doctor Who. But usually, that is because of the lengths the villains will go to in order to acquire it, not specifically the acquisition itself. There's not much philosophy behind the rejection of immortality, save for the fact that it's fool's gold – something out of reach that isn't worth the striving for. But here, in the scene between the Doctor and the Sisterhood leader, Maren, it's discussed with great thought – the Doctor sug-gests that death is an essential by-product of progress, that it's a natural consequence of any achievement that ought to be welcomed. The Sisterhood of Karn have spent so long guard-ing the secret of eternal life that nothing has changed for them in millennia – they have been so focused upon Not Dying at any cost, they have had no time to Live. It's an unusu-ally sophisticated argument for Doctor Who to

rehearse – especially considering that this is a series in which the lead character routinely cheats death every few years or so whenever the lead actor gets dropped – and, arguably, it's never given quite the same depth of attention again until it becomes the underlying theme of Russell T Davies' first year on the revival.

We'll see musings on the boredom of death without end in the future (Underworld, Mawdryn Undead), or a few platitudes on immortality being a curse rather than a gift (The Five Doctors) – but crucially, here in a story about that border between magic and science, and the possibilities of surgery extend-ing a man's life way beyond its dignified end so a patient lives on as a vegetable (Morbius him-self envies the life of sponges over his own reduced existence!), it's never quite so apposite and thought-provoking. I'm not suggesting that The Brain of Morbius is some veiled alle-gory about the dangers of assisted care or euthanasia – it's not as crass as that, and I shan't be so crass either. But there's a deeper, richer theme here: that in sustaining life beyond its natural end, history cannot advance either, no civilisation can advance, and all will stagnate. The Doctor may restore the Sacred Flame; but the Sisterhood will have to pay a price for that, and its leader will have to accept death and embrace it as a happy inevitability. (Maren's death won't be played as tragedy, but, as in her final moments she becomes young and beautiful again, a triumph. Morbius' death, long overdue, isn't played as tragedy either, but as grotesque farce, with this comic parody of a human frame doing a fatal prat fall.)

And this in the middle of an episode in which brains get dropped upon the floor. The Brain of Morbius goes for sick and queasy – the sequence where the green nutrient liquid is allowed to flow out of the container housing Morbius, and his brain drunkenly lists to the side of the glass as a result, is nauseating. When Solon shoots Condo in the chest, we actually see blood fly out from the impact wound – and then, even more brutally, Solon shoots him again and again; if it were a futur-istic laser gun being used, if the violence were that bit more fantastical, then the scene wouldn't be so jarring. As it is, though, it's the teatime version of Reservoir Dogs, and I'm in two minds about whether the production has crossed a line. When I was a teenager I loved it, of course – it proved to me that Doctor Who was properly adult (as if restraint is an immature thing). Now it seems tonally misjudged. And the only reason I can accept it is because the grisliness on display is the punchline to the more elevated conversation about death we've heard earlier on between the Doctor and Maren. This is what death can be, finally: ugly, painful and a bit embarrassing.

T: I have a hangover and I'll be in touch tomorrow. I got married yesterday, you know! Oh, and I posed on the church memorial in tribute to Doctor Who and the Android Invasion. (Simon Guerrier noticed what I was up to, which was nice.)

July 20th

The Brain of Morbius (part one)

T: Sorry, I broke the rules of this diary. I decided to have a day off! And, why not? The sun shone, the speeches went well, everyone had a great time and I married the most wonderful woman in the world. And the Doctor Who theme was met with a massive, spontaneous round of applause. Today, my lovely new wife has let me chill out in front of the telly to play catch up (told you I'd got the right one).

Anyway, to business...

I have a confession to make: I've never really liked The Brain of Morbius much. Once more, the culprit is the Target novel – it compelled me to conjure up imaginings of this being a Gothic masterpiece, so I resented the story for its shortcomings upon actually seeing it. But at least everything I do like about it is present and correct here in episode one... Tom Baker and Elisabeth Sladen have some terrific opening banter, and her light deflation of Baker's spiky insolence with throwaway quips and teasing comebacks displays the sort of chemistry you could only create in a very high-tech acting lab. Against that, Philip Madoc dares us to take the black comedy seriously and is typically excellent. I'm less sure, though, about the actual *mention* of the crashed space-pilot being a Mutt, which evokes the race from The Mutants. If it wasn't named, the Mutt's appearance would be a lovely, unshowy little nod to reward regular viewers, but overtly referencing its race makes it self-conscious continuity – which I, being a self-loathing fan, of course reject.

As I say, traditionally the biggest challenge of this story for me (beyond, the Sisterhood, whom I so often found rather dull and wafty) is one of aesthetics. As with Morbius himself, you can see the joins in this production. The opening scenes on the planet's surface are witty, but they clearly take place on a clompy wooden world with floorboards underfoot. And as much as I love the squeal and squelch that greets the Mutt's decapitation, and the subsequent electrical charge that stimulates a response from his mandibles, I *ache* when Madoc produces his head from the bag upside down, so that the camera spies upon the artificial neck-hole. The younger Toby couldn't see past the rain being Truman Show-like, only falling directly upon the Doctor and Sarah as they are revealed on Solon's doorstep, and so failed to appreciate their arrival as you have done. Even something as simple as a corridor, it seems, needed to be achieved with crappy, fringey CSO.

I guess I'm just saying is that it's all very well having the lungs of a Birastrop and the brain of a genius, but if you look like a dogs dinner, no-one's going to take you seriously. (Or rather, paranoid teenagers and modern viewers might not.)

But d'you know what ...? For the first time, I rather enjoyed this. The Sisterhood are actually a nifty counterpoint to the Grand Guignol going on up in Solon's castle, and whilst Gilly Brown seems to be playing Ohica as if somebody's just rammed a cucumber up her backside, Cynthia Grenville's Maren has poise and gravitas, and couples the weariness of the ages with the inherent dignity and wisdom that it brings.

So, yes – whilst I continue to notice those things that irked me as a teenager, I now acknowledge them but move on, instead savouring the wonderful dialogue, the magnificent leads and the gorgeous attention to detail in the set dressings. (I love the dinner service at Castle Solon, which gives Elisabeth Sladen a chance to get rid of her wine, and then rejoin the conversation with a quick and naturalistic bit of acting business.) It's still not perfect, but I accept its bad points whilst choosing to enjoy and appreciate the good bits.

Perhaps I should take a leaf out of Morbius' book, and not be so concerned with appearances.

The Brain of Morbius (part two)

T: I mentioned the set dressing last episode. Let me elaborate: the paraphernalia around Solon's castle, such as the parchment and seal combo for Solon's note to the Sisterhood, is exquisite. I've talked before about how something slightly archaic brings with it differentiation from our own time, and a plausibility lacking from silver suits or funky space glasses. It's possible that the production chose to echo the literary period that inspired the script, but either way, it's a splendid aesthetic choice. Indeed, the colour schemes throughout lend everything a sense of place – the Sisterhood's opulent purples; with dusty beiges for the stark, dead planet; and green for the lab of goo all provide suitable contrast. (The luminous pink Perspex flames on the Sisterhood's sticks, though, are rather quaint and perhaps ill-advised.)

Elsewhere, the most extraordinary thing happens during Sarah's attempt to save the Doctor from becoming a latter-day Joan of Arc. Sarah's act of inveigling her way into the Sisterhood's ranks isn't massively plausible, but director Christopher Barry wisely doesn't dwell on this, nor the Doctor's actual escape, instead telling the scene from Maren's perspective (so we only see that the Doctor has vanished when she does). But *look* at those flames – I assume someone fireproofed Baker's scarf, otherwise Begonia Pope will have needed to be on Speed-dial. They're so close, Tom Baker could certainly feel their fire.

And Sarah's temporary blindness allows for some clever handling too. In the episode's final scene, neither she nor Morbius can see, which gives us a slight sympathy for the ranting brain-in-a-jar: his fear and frustration are so much tangible because we've witnessed Sarah, whom we love, experience the same. Requiring Solon to initially examine Sarah is a neat

scripting touch, and I love the imperceptible shake of the head that Madoc gives the Doctor, even as he reassures Sarah that she'll make a complete recovery. Madoc has negotiated his performance so perfectly, the viewer can actually buy this bluff – in that moment, he's convincing not just as a zealous maniac (so far, so Doctor Who), but also as a talented, professional surgeon.

When all's said and done, the question keeps cropping up: why does Doctor Who float my boat more than pop music, soap operas or sport? I shall mention the lines "chicken brained biological disaster", "squalid brood of harpies" and "palsied harridan scream for death", and you shall have your answer.

The Brain of Morbius (part three)

T: Well, you've not left me with much to talk about, have you? So I'll mention Michael Spice, whose disembodied Morbius-voice teeters on the edge of hysteria as he browbeats Solon, creating a plausible nemesis despite that fact that he is literally disembodied. Philip Madoc's testy patience as Solon tries to bat off Morbius' whingeing is excellent – it comes so close to asking us to acknowledge the lunacy of the whole situation, but without the character himself being aware of it at all. The scene where Solon gets Sarah to work the pump while he performs emergency surgery cleverly highlights his one-tracked zealousness; through comments such as "Watch!" and "Did you see!", he seems oblivious to the fact that his assistant has lost her vision. In his own way, Solon's drive brings its own blindness, to parallel with that of both Sarah and Morbius. It is a case of the blind leading the blind to assist the blind.

I touched upon it before, but the casting of Cynthia Grenville as Maren is another smart move. Through her body language, you'd be hard pressed to tell that this was a younger actress (she's stooped and slow, but skilful enough for it not to come across as "old" acting), and yet she retains an inner strength that transmits through her convincing "aged" make-up. She's aided in this by her strong but weathered voice (clearly, she's been using the Sacred Flame to light a non-tipped fag or three when the rest of the Sisterhood are tucked up in bed). She helps to prevent the Elixir of Life from coming across as a miracle too far in the (generally) scientific Doctor Who universe. (And the fact that the flame is at low ebb owing to something as numinous as a soot build-up is a wonderfully prosaic counterpoint to all the mysticism and chanting, which runs the risk of wearing thin with this viewer.)

As for the violence... I too loved it as a kid. This era is excitingly hard-nosed and pragmatic about its subject matter, and how to stage it. The way in which Condo grabs Sarah's hair underlines his brutishness and strength, and later Solon does the same to her face to emphasise his dangerous insanity. This rough-and-tumble, plus the gleeful revelling in gore, was a suitable riposte to those fools who claimed The A-Team was more exciting than Doctor Who. At the time, I was desperate to have *any evidence* that my show could be as violent, and grimmer, than the soulless outings of Hannibal and his crew. I'm older now, though, and in a happier place, so don't even feel the need to engage with people who like The A-Team better than Doctor Who. I'm not in a condition where I envy those vegetables.

The Brain of Morbius (part four)

R: Awkward story conclusions are all the rage in Season Thirteen. It's almost as if the wit and enthusiasm on display are so grand that it's hard to stuff them tidily back in the box when needed. The Brain of Morbius episode four suffers because of the necessity to build everything up to an action-adventure climax, with the Morbius monster going on various rampages, and lots of fire, and lots of stunts, and lots of deaths. And Christopher Barry can't make very much of this credible, limited with an ungainly creature design (which was, to be fair, its entire point) and the restrictions of studio space. Some adventures weather their weaker conclusions better than others; the problem with The Brain of Morbius is that it sold itself upon the quality of its dialogue and black humour – and there's precious little room for talk or wit when you're clambering over clifftops away from Chop Suey the Galactic Emperor.

So it's the little moments that stand out: the ambiguity as Solon coolly stands apart with a gun watching as his beloved Morbius throttles the Doctor, unsure whom he should shoot; the quiet acceptance from Maren that there's a value to endings, even if that end is her own life; the irony that within seconds of achieving his glory, Solon keels over dead from cyanide gas, and the creation he has so long given his devotion to dispassionately knocks his corpse to the floor.

The sequence where the Doctor leaves Solon alone to dismantle his life's work is a bit stupid, but it makes so much more sense in context watching these stories in order. It feels like an echo of that wonderful moment of human dignity in Planet of Evil where he allows Sorenson the right to take his own life for the sake of others, or the relief he shows in Genesis when Gharman's democratic process allows him to step down from blowing up the embryo Daleks. The Doctor is grander than we're used to from the Pertwee days, a wandering Time Lord (with all the Time Lord mythology and power the Sisterhood of Karn drum into us), a prophet; he does not want to be the man of action, he wants the people he meets to accept responsibility for themselves. (And we should remember this next week, when he tells Antarctic scientists to perform their own amputations!) Allowing Solon a chance for redemption is entirely the right thing for this Doctor to do – at this stage of the show, Tom Baker might seem loud and dominant, but the Doctor himself is trying to be more humble. And besides, if Solon squanders that opportunity to better himself, you can always gas the sod.

T: So the villain is defeated by a hitherto-unmentioned piece of equipment lying about in the corner, which facilitates a hitherto-unmentioned mind wrestle? The deus has been kicked firmly ex the machina, in a manner that would have caused modern-day Russell T Davies haters to take up flaming torches a la The Sisterhood, and chase the production team off a ravine without caring whether or not they clomped the camera on the way down. That's if they hadn't already done so after the Doctor dispatched the other evil protagonist with a lethal dose of cyanide gas. On the other hand, Maren's redemption gets more weight as a result of the swift dispatch of the bad guys. The diversion of the Sisterhood always threatened to be a bit tedious, but her willingness to do the opposite of Morbius (end her life rather than artificially prolong it) gives thematic weight to a denouement that would otherwise have been rather perfunctory.

Unlike you, Rob, I applaud the monster design. The Dalek goldfish bowl atop the muscular, leathery, hairy hotchpotch enables us to glimpse the brain inside, and the powerful claw looks like it could do serious damage. (Thankfully, one of the Sisterhood seems intent on hanging around long enough to provide the perfect demonstration of this.) The mention that Morbius now has the "lungs of a Birastrop" justifies the monstrous design – it's a practical, life-preserving construction, not an aesthetic one. To remind us this is a megalomaniac Time Lord rather than a feral beast, Stuart Fell invests the creature with a strutting, arrogant gait.

All told, I've adored the dialogue, Philip Madoc, the regulars and some of the design concepts on display here... but I still can't quite get around the staginess of it all, and I think it might be a step too far for a modern audience. Rather like Morbius, this adventure isn't quite the sum of its parts. (Take Condo's death, for example – nobody does anything *wrong*, and as an actor I can understand Colin Fay straightening his arm and leg as he is throttled. But in execution, it just looks a bit silly, and doesn't quite convince as he expires like an imperilled Star Wars action figure.)

Oh, and is it worth arguing about whether the pictures of the production members in the mental death-duel are the Doctor's earlier incarnations, or those of Morbius? Well, it seems fitting to this story's concerns that I declare that life is too short...

The Seeds of Doom (part one)

R: Janie sometimes takes me to garden centres. I'd really rather she didn't – I'd rather sit in the car with the window rolled down, but she does insist. And whenever I go, I always see that there's some discount on bonsai plants. And it always makes me protest to Janie, courtesy of Harrison Chase, that bonsai is mutilation and torture. (I also inform her,

just in case she wants to hear, that hybrids are a crime against nature.) This is the impact The Seeds of Doom had on me as a kid – I didn't know what bonsai even was, but it sounded bad. And maybe even a little samurai.

Come to think of it, most of the time Janie does leave me in the car.

This is wonderful, isn't it? It's often said that this doesn't feel much like Doctor Who, and it's certainly odd to see the Doctor back taking calls from UNIT, and having to be civil to bureaucrats. Sarah Jane Smith doesn't even appear for the first half of the episode, and the Doctor and Sarah travel about by helicopter! But director Douglas Camfield emphasises the tonal incongruity of all this; he focuses upon the doomed Antarctic scientists over all, and makes full use of Geoffrey Burgon's haunting score to suggest the chill and isolation of the ice base. By the time Tom Baker starts arriving on the scene and barking orders at two base-scientists, Moberley and Stevenson, we have had a chance to accept the crisis from their point of view for once. We're not the outsiders looking in on the story as first episodes usually dictate, but the insiders looking out. And that only makes the battle of one man in a bed losing control of his own body seem all the more claustrophobic and grotesque.

As a result, the scene in which Sarah and the Doctor persuade Moberley the zoologist to amputate the arm of his Krynoid-infected friend has an intensity to it almost unmatched anywhere before in the entire season – and you can see that the season's been leading up to exchanges like this, where the alien friend we trust so much insists that we have to help ourselves and take responsibility for our own problems. He's engaging and funny, this Doctor – he'll put his feet up on desks, he'll crack jokes about pods and policemen – but when the crisis is paramount, he'll respond with a sort of detached impatience. The editing in this scene, and the choices Camfield makes about where to point the camera, are all quite remarkable – it's like a masterclass in camera television directing. You can see the incomprehension on Moberley's face as he realises that he is being talked into something nightmarish; you can see the very moment when he accepts the job. Every time I watch the scene, I realise

I've been holding my breath all the way through it. It's that tense.

It is customary for a Doctor Who story to begin with a scene in which some doomed characters discover an alien threat before being summarily killed off. That writer Robert Banks Stewart takes the standard teaser, and then stretches it out over two episodes as a preface to the story proper – because, make no mistake about it, these scientists are doomed! – seems cruel; the arrival of the Doctor to save them is one huge lie. To hide the main plot in plain view behind the subplot is very clever, and very strange. The main guest star of the story has only appeared in the one scene, and we've barely noticed him, because the camera has been pointing in the wrong direction. And besides, he was wittering on about bonsai.

T: This story encompasses another level in the development of my discovery of Doctor Who. I'd read the Target books of most of this era at a very young age; Phillip Hinchliffe's name was known to me first as a book writer rather than TV producer. When I came to collect bootleg videos, it was the heady days of black and white that appealed most – they were mysteries to be dusted off, ancient relics that needed preserving on my video shelf. The Tom Baker era, even those parts of it that took place when I was barely sentient, was already familiar. I'd seen him, and knew Sarah Jane from The Five Doctors and K-9 and Company, and so was in no especial hurry to catch the famed Hinchliffe-Holmes era, even if that's where many of the most gripping novels came from.

When my collection started to grow, however, I finally started getting these shows, and whilst my initial watch of most Who was something of a disappointment (as I've said, the pictures invariably failed to match the ones my mind had conjured whilst reading the books), this era generally stood up the best in terms of being gripping, good-looking, well-acted productions and exciting stories. All of that said, I was slightly underwhelmed when I first saw The Seeds of Doom, as it had been one of my very favourite Target novels. The video effect rendering snow over some odd-looking stock footage wasn't the opening image I'd hoped for, and the cliffhanger, with

Moberley's overly quick death by three-second-long strangulation (not to mention his awkward fall and slightly peculiar facial expression) made me worry that, if not my memory, my imagination had cheated. It was only on subsequent viewings that I learned to look past such initial disappointments, and this story flirted with becoming the one I would occasionally cite as my absolute favourite.

This time around? Well, the aforementioned last shot aside, this is damn near perfect. The snow doesn't bother me at all – it's nowhere near as unconvincing as it seemed on first viewing. And I'm more aware of how nobody is treating the necessary tropes of science fiction as if they're part of a formulaic situation the characters inhabit. The Doctor and Sarah might do this sort of thing all the time, but it's to the story's benefit that they regard everything as if it's the gravest situation ever. That amputation scene you rightly laud showcases the two of them as caustic pragmatists as the drama escalates.

Fortunately, what stops the Doctor being an entirely surly prophet of doom is the cheery anarchy he brings to the potentially dull expositionary material; his hobnail boots, yo-yo, "no-touch-pod" remark and toothbrush shtick all cut through the pomposity of the ministry stuff. But, by golly, he turns on a sixpence – he joshes about his age out in the snow, but brings its chill with him indoors as he coldly refuses to discuss the weather, and asks to see the patient. When the Doctor talks of Winlett changing form, it isn't a kooky piece of science-fiction outlandishness, it's rather a gloomy, aloof, portent of disaster. Menace and import seep through Tom Baker's performance, whilst his knowledge of the Krynoid treats us to a pensive, brooding piece of backstory where even potentially nonsensical phraseology such as "galactic weed" sounds like a Biblical infestation. Accompanied by Geoffrey Burgon's insidious, creepy score, Baker's pronouncements take on the tone of a creepy bedtime story.

What *really* marks this out, though, is in the elements where the show might otherwise (and understandably) stumble. Many of the outdoor arctic scenes look fabulous (and really are outdoors – bonus), the video-disced frond is convincingly rendered, John Gleeson's plant make-up looks great, and even the smallest role here is well played. The joshing that Michael McStay (as Moberley) and Gleeson engage in to cut through the concern of Hubert Rees (as Stevenson) about the pod suggests that they're genuine work colleagues. Rees, who you rightly lauded as Captain Ransom in The War Games, is again brilliant value here. He is quietly distracted with foreboding when sensing life in the pod, and, later, is stoic and guilt-ridden when admitting culpability. None of these guest parts are cannon fodder; they're essential ingredients to the drama.

Oh, and how shocked was I when Baker first uttered the word Krynoid? I'd always pronounced it Cry-noid, not Kri-noid.

July 21st

The Seeds of Doom (part two)

R: John Challis makes his character, Chase's henchman Scorby, thoroughly charmless and – at the same time – utterly credible. He's a thug whose expertise is to satisfy his boss' orders with as much efficiency as possible, and it's not part of the job description to have qualms if that happens to involve killing. Scorby is a refreshing reminder that human evil doesn't need to be witty or clever – brutality is enough. Challis does a wonderful job at suggesting that Scorby is highly intelligent and can adapt to any crisis, but that he has managed over the years to subordinate that intelligence entirely to his master's wishes. Mark Jones' Keeler is the intellectual, but is also fundamentally naive and stupid: look at the way he points the gun at the Doctor and Sarah, clearly so frightened that if they talk to him, they'll make his amorality absolutely untenable. The way he mutters an apology to Stevenson as he ties him up is lovely, because it feels so natural, so unemphasised; the way he later tries to punch Scorby manages to be sadly sweet, because we've realised by now (as Scorby already knows) that this display of courage will blow itself out within seconds – Keeler is barely worth punching back.

And Tom Baker is brilliant here – knowing exactly how to prickle Scorby, knowing exactly how to needle Keeler's conscience. His banter with John Challis is laugh-out loud funny (Scorby: "I'm not a patient man, Doctor", the Doctor: "Well, your candour does you credit!"), but this isn't just an example of mad Tom being eccentric in the face of threats. It's cleverer than that; the Doctor almost seems relieved to be facing nothing more dangerous than a man with a gun, because he knows that the alien threat in the snow is so much worse. The production wisely keeps the Krynoid at arm's length this week – we need only know it needs warmth, and food, and that goons hired by a botany collector are just so trivial in contrast.

My favourite scene is probably when Scorby and Keeler discover Moberley's corpse. Just for a moment, you can see Scorby taken by surprise – he doesn't know what to say, he mumbles, even stammers. It's the only indication he ever allows that he might be out of his depth after all.

T: This is a terrific episode – it is classic base under siege, but with a plausible outside world and rich characters. But as much as anything else, it's a study of personalities. Into this lethal situation comes the Doctor, who is insolent and witty in the face of danger (a gun-totting Scorby: "Okay, start talking", the Doctor: "Wolfgang Amadeus Mozart had perfect pitch..."). He has such contempt for Scorby's crew – in the cosmic balance, their thuggery makes them akin to flies (albeit flies that tie him up and try to murder his assistant, sure) – and he's so terribly fierce with his own allies, savaging Sarah and Stevenson for referring to the inhuman Krynoid as "Winlett". I can't imagine any of the previous incarnations exhibiting such righteous anger (indeed, only Troughton could match Baker's sonorous, foreboding narration about Winlett having become "a grotesque parody of the human form"). I hold this regime's treatment of science fiction as a gateway to the horrific – both within the human condition and without – in very high regard.

But against that, we have Mark Jones as Keeler. Now, you've touched upon the best moment of all (Keeler's limp attempt to punch Scorby), but I shall be livid if I'm not allowed to eulogise it further, because the truth is that Mark Jones gives one of the *top performances* in Doctor Who's history, yet it's rarely (if ever) mentioned in Dispatches or even internet forums. I didn't always feel this way, admittedly – after reading the novel, I was intrigued to see how arch villain Harrison Chase would issue his threats, how tough guy Scorby would pack a gun and be sadistic, and even how plucky, flawed Stevenson would meet his death trying to be proactive. But the snivelling lackey Keeler – there's nothing more to him, that's what I thought. On paper, he's just Krynoid bait, but Jones brings so much more to the role. As you say, he's pathetic and weak, yet Jones manages to play those characteristics and still make Keeler seem honourable and decent.

Look, it's easy to play menacing, or mad, or powerful – and actors like doing that, because they look impressive and cool. But to make the audience sit up and watch *cowardice*, and to find empathy in a weak subordinate – well, that shows both real skill and a performer of absolute selflessness. That punch Jones throws at Scorby is *brilliant* – it's the most real punch I've ever seen on television, just because it is so crap. It's a small token bit of business, but in Keeler's terms – weak, untrained, fussy scientist Keeler – it's an exhibition of bravery, even if it's inept and ineffectual. And the breaking point is Scorby patronisingly calling Keeler "Arnold", followed by a shove.

It's very difficult to stand up to that sort of bullying if you're weak, nerdy and not overly physical – which is why we need Tom Baker's strong, pushy Doctor to defy cruelty, in a way that the Keeler inside most of us never could.

The Seeds of Doom (part three)

R: Rarely in the series do we get an episode of more blatant padding than this. Nothing happens this week to advance the plot an iota. The first half of the episode sees the Doctor and Sarah run around a lot, and try to work out the identity of a villain we've known since episode one. The second half of the episode sees the Doctor and Sarah run around a lot, sometimes towards that villain, sometimes away from him, and in the process we learn no information we haven't been given more suc-

cinctly already. The entire sequence with the gun-toting chauffeur only exists in plot terms to find a painting, and the sequence with the eccentric painter only exists so our heroes can discover a clue to Harrison Chase. This isn't drama, this is dungeons and dragons gameplay, a succession of scenes only masquerading as development. It's hardly surprising that when Philip Hinchcliffe novelised this adventure for Target books, this episode was trimmed to the bone.

And it's almost entirely wonderful.

That sequence with the chauffeur, for example – the direction of it is extraordinary; it's tense, and messy, and grim, and is framed with great beauty by Camfield. That sequence with the painter – it's funny and charming, it boasts a terrific cameo by Sylvia Coleridge and a terrific gag by Oscar Wilde, and it suggests in miniature the extent of Harrison Chase's obsessions and of a real world outside madmen and bureaucrats that the Krynoid menace will threaten. Harrison Chase plays a parody of a Bond villain, eager to delay the executions of the Doctor and Sarah so he can first show off his plant collection and play them his own organ music. The dedication he pours into his "Hymn of the Plants" is at once wonderfully comical but also quite chilling – we've seen a lot of obsessives in Doctor Who recently, but never one as socially damaged as this. Here is a child who has never been told no, here is a leader whose men clearly have learned to turn a blind eye to his outbursts of lunacy.

As I say, nothing really happens in Doctor Who this week. And it doesn't happen with such panache and with such confidence. To run on the spot as entertainingly as this takes remarkable skill. Camfield's direction and Banks Stewart's script are brilliant in their sleight of hand. And the delay in plot advancement means that we've reached the halfway point of the story, and we still haven't seen the Krynoid yet as anything more powerful than a humanoid covered in green moss. This is such clever foregrounding; when it begins to become something truly alien next week, the anticipation makes that so much more frightening.

Can I just throw in a final word of praise for David Masterman, who as Guard Leader only gets a few lines of dialogue – but as he mocks the captured Sarah in the garden manages to convey an almost sexual sadism? It's thrillingly nasty.

T: Things Continually Stated About Doctor Who That Are Rarely Challenged No. 1: Tom Baker is a bit mad, and that's what makes him a good, naturally eccentric Doctor.

Well, yes, maybe... but what sears into the memory here is his extraordinary, fierce, belligerent intelligence, which burns itself onto the screen. The anger that Pertwee directed at authority was a kind of aloof, testy impatience with comedy obstructiveness and jobsworths. Baker turns these exchanges into a display of cosmic superiority, and those acting opposite him – thankfully – avoid playing their roles as stuffy establishment stereotypes. Kenneth Gilbert is dignified and professional as Dunbar, and whilst Michael Barrington's prissy, nasal tones might lend Sir Colin the air of a typical 70s TV comedy ministry man, he plays the role with an utter, deadly seriousness. That's because Baker isn't doing peeved – he's doing *incandescent*, and you don't counter that with comic exasperation.

I'm less sure how I feel about the fisticuffs – as someone who finds violence anything but appealing, I should be uncomfortable with this rough and tumble Doctor. But why is a thump delivered by Baker any different to Pertwee hurling Terry Walsh about on a weekly basis? It's all physical contact to render a man unconscious. Anyway, the action here is gutsy and realistic, and – why, I've no idea – I object to it not a jot. If this is Doctor Who told in the style of The Avengers, some of its presentation has come via The Sweeney, and that works surprisingly well. If children acknowledge that something is grown-up, they can stand to watch physical jeopardy – fairytales like Doctor Who are essential preparation for adulthood, because the storytelling helps them assimilate the dangers of the life to come (both literal and metaphorical). If violence is coupled with intelligence and imagination, I have no trouble with depicting it at teatime. As for the Doctor partaking in it... well, I need to think about that and get back to you, perhaps when Mr Hinchcliffe bows out. (And a side note to say that the violent chauffeur facilitates veteran stuntman Alan Chuntz's only speaking role in Doctor Who after years of falling off things and getting thumped in the background, so props to him.)

Things Continually Stated About Doctor Who That Are Rarely Challenged No. 2: The show's fun has much to do with its inherent campiness.

Funnily enough, I would normally be happy to throw down against this notion, as I've never considered the show to be *camp*... but having just witnessed Tony Beckley utter the line "What a pity, I could have had two pods" with such a queeny, wounded affront, I may have to revise that opinion. And he imbues the brilliant "I must know what happens when the Krynoid touches human flesh" with the requisite-studied insanity, doesn't he? (What a great cliffhanger, incidentally, as the Krynoid moves to infect Sarah – it's one of the very best.)

July 22nd

The Seeds of Doom (part four)

R: Toby, tell me about Mark Jones. Am I right in thinking you worked with him at one point, or am I misremembering one of our long pub chats about Doctor Who guest stars? This is his episode, really; Mark Jones owns this. In 25 minutes, he transforms Keeler from pusillanimous scientist to ranting madman to walking bush. And what's so agonising about it (and Jones' performance) is that until his last recognisable moments as a human, he can understand everything that is happening to him. Is there anything more horrific in the whole of Doctor Who than a man pleading for hospital care, limbs shaking as he loses control over his body, as his boss feeds him raw meat? The cruelty of this is that Sarah cannot help him; she can sympathise with him, but she daren't set him free, and so condemns him. "You want me to die!" Keeler screams at her. And he's right; what is so terrifying about the Krynoid is not that it's a homicidal vegetable, but that it's a likeable man turned into a raging monster that shouts terrible truths. You might have thought that what happened to the first Krynoid host, Winlett, was bad enough – but at least, having been infected, John Gleeson had the kindness to shut up and stop behaving like a human being. The degeneration of Keeler, in contrast, is rubbed in our very faces, and when we recoil we can't help feel a bit complicit.

The crusher machine, too, is the most gruesome means of execution shown yet in Doctor Who. What's clever about it is the way that Scorby and Chase are very happy to discuss its working operations with the Doctor at great length – but they never resort to informing him that he is going to be turned into compost until he's already lying on the conveyer belt. The threat is so much more terrible because it's never spoken out loud – and the word "pumped" has never sounded quite so revolting.

There's lots of comedy in this episode, but it really is of the blackest hue. (Seymour Green as the butler Hargreaves, who damns himself by blandly giving the party line when Keeler calls out to him for help, and by assuring the Krynoid's victim that Mr Chase knows best, utterly absolving himself of any responsibility.) But my favourite part is perhaps the episode at its lightest: watching Harrison Chase squirm awkwardly around the flower artist Amelia Ducat as if he's never seen a woman before and can't quite remember how to speak to one – and then Scorby doing his very best attempt at respectful politeness when Ducat starts quizzing him about the house's history. It's good to see that even if a man turning green can't shake their confidence, social interaction with visitors can.

T: Nope, I've never worked with Mark Jones. A friend of mine wrote to him when I was younger, though, as we both loved his performance and I found his agent's address in an Artists & Agents Yearbook I'd picked up second hand somewhere. My friend got a nice letter back, but as a result I never quite got around to following suit, so I've only ever admired him from afar (as it were). I *have* banged on about his brilliant performance to you in many a pub session, though, and probably mentioned that aside from Jones cropping up in things like Secret Army and A Family at War, his career has been most notable for some 70s sex comedies (which, it'll shock you to hear, I've never seen). Oh, and that memorably witty Hamlet cigar advert where the bloke flirt-

ing with the lady in a restaurant accidentally loses his wig, and thus ruins his date. Some illustrious thesps have passed through the TARDIS doors, but that a jobbing actor like Jones (albeit one with a couple of offbeat claims to fame) should give one of the very best guest performances in the series just goes to show how much uncelebrated talent this country's rightly lauded acting profession has produced.

Meanwhile, the Doctor hits Scorby over the head with a stool! This anger and violence takes on an aspect of righteous fury in Tom Baker's hands, which makes it unlike the fisticuffs in more formulaic action-adventure fare. Later, during the face-off at the "scene of the crime", Baker flicks from quiet menace to twinkly banter about quotations. There are few punches pulled: Scorby chucking the Doctor into the bins is gratuitously violent, but that's the whole point. It's not the programme overstepping the mark, it's Scorby himself. He's a thug – a professional hard man, yes, and certainly not ignorant or wholly loutish, but a thug nonetheless. The Doctor's "You're pushing your luck" as Scorby keeps thumping him is so ridiculous under the circumstances, you can't help admire his pluck for using dark humour to combat physical intimidation. The violence here is so much more horrifying because it isn't pretty, nor is it the empty popcorn fighting of Knight Rider. Harrison Chase, of course, leaves the violence to others – but when he finally comes to gloat, the Doctor studies him with a morbid seriousness that's punctuated, again, with breezy smiles.

And I've worked out why I like Kenneth Gilbert's Dunbar so much – he's playing the man, not the actions. His betrayal in episode one could have been justification for turning Dunbar into a dislikable, snivelling self-server whose demise is neither a surprise nor a loss. Instead, Gilbert transforms Dunbar into the principled man the character sees himself as (albeit one who has made a mistake) and seems both honourable and brave when facing down Chase and going for help. I adore the exchange where Chase warns Dunbar not to go and Dunbar pulls a gun on him – if they ever release Chase's yelled response of "Scorby! Get Dunbarrrrrr!" as a ring tone, I'll buy it. And while it's not made explicit what the

Krynoid has done to Dunbar (eaten him? squashed him?), we know the crux of it: that Dunbar has died horribly. The ambiguousness works, however, because of the seriousness with which the scene is played.

As for the rest of this strong cast, Michael Barrington once again uses genuine concern and a deadly seriousness to cut through the potential pomposity of Sir Colin. When I first saw this, it was a huge surprise when Sylvia Coleridge (as Amelia) returned as his woman on the inside – in the book, Ducat is only a one-scene cameo, and Coleridge's charming performance means the story just about gets away with the character's barely credible undercover routine. And Hargreaves' shock (masterfully performed by Seymour Green) at Keeler's transformation is the perfect mix of A) horror at the sight of a metamorphosing human, and B) disapproving affront that an alien creature has the gall to commit such a social gaffe on his premises. Hargreaves' decision to feed Keeler and assure him of the benevolence of his master is a stark demonstration that a stiff upper lip is not always a virtuous thing. Etiquette sometimes disguises and facilitates appalling acts.

What an absolute corker of an episode, dripping with atmosphere – Chase's shadowy study is complete with crackling fire, to which the moonlit gardens, where a camouflaged terror lurks, are a chilling counterpoint. Typically, then, the final shot is that of an ungainly creature whose skin ruffles into an unconvincing rubbery fold at the final, vital moment. Oh well, you can't produce a prize vegetable without the odd bit of manure.

The Seeds of Doom (part five)

R: And UNIT are back! And this time, the degeneration that begun at the start of the season reaches its logical conclusion; Major Beresford repeats himself in witless monotone, and has all the charisma of a Brussels sprout. And quite right too; this isn't a mistake, I am absolutely sure this is deliberate. We aren't supposed to warm to UNIT any more. Imagine how the story would have suffered tonally had the Brigadier and Benton popped up – they'd immediately have transformed this grotesque horror story into something more cosy. UNIT

have to be faceless bureaucrats for the story to work. (The Brigadier is in Geneva again. No one ever says that it's official business. Do you think that maybe he's just enjoying a very long skiing holiday?)

The real pleasure of this is the awkward alliance between Scorby and Sarah. What's surprising is the way that we're invited to like Scorby now, against all our better instincts. Because he may well be a murderous thug, but he's a pragmatist, and he is the one character to step out from Chase's employ and call him a madman. It'd be too much to say that the script humanises him – he's still a cynic, he still threatens Sarah – but John Challis does. Challis subtly shows horror when he realises that the killer plant is his friend Keeler, shows gruff sincerity when he promises the Doctor he can be trusted "for the moment". When he confronts Chase in the gardens, Sarah is the only person left he can talk to with any respect.

Call me strange – and I know it's a weird mental leap to make – but as I watched the sequence of Chase photographing the Krynoid, I thought back to a similar moment in Invasion of the Dinosaurs where Sarah photographs the T. Rex. They're both taking absurd risks, of course, and making that crucial horror movie error of underestimating the monster. But we somehow still commend plucky Sarah for trying to get her scoop – whilst for Chase, there is no clearer indication than that we're dealing with a raving lunatic.

T: When I was younger, this was an episode I really wanted my brother to see, because I knew he wouldn't be able to criticise it. And when I contrived to get him in front of the telly at the opportune moment, he didn't mock any of the things that usually get Doctor Who into trouble with real people. No rubbish sets, no silly lines, no bad acting, no especially dated costumes, and there was even a pretty decently realised monster (the Krynoid CSO'd against the skyline and behind the big house is very well achieved). It was a win for the Doctor Who Supporters Brigade! And then... when our heroes take the plants outside (so the vegetation can't spy on behalf of the Krynoid), they place the plants *carefully upright*, so as not to damage the no-doubt expensive-to-hire props. And that's the only thing my brother felt the need to comment on! "Why don't they just chuck them?" he demanded to know. "That's ridiculous!" That hadn't even occurred to me on the numerous times I'd seen it... and I'd been on the lookout for potential pitfalls! We look at the world through different eyes, we Doctor Who fans.

But it's such a shame to let such minutiae quash one's enjoyment of this episode, because it starts at a lick and doesn't let up, as Dunbar dies and the survivors engage in a face-off with both the murderous creature and their own uneasy dynamic together. In Tom Baker's delivery, the Doctor's assessment of Chase – "arrogant fool" – isn't an aloof alien dismissing a stupid, puny human, but instead a dour assessment of how the madman's single-mindedness could compromise everyone's safety. Again, Baker turns something as straightforward as insulting someone into a portent of doom. As the situation worsens, Sarah gutsily faces off against Scorby with fiery righteousness, but you can actually buy both sides of the argument: her principled stand verses Scorby's harsh pragmatism makes for a punchy, frank exchange of barbs. Add to that the impatient Time Lord, his mind whirring all the time as the threats issue from outside and tension escalates inside, and he becomes a powder-keg of bristling, godlike fury. You know, it's not an exaggeration to cite this as potentially the tensest, most powerful scene in the history of Doctor Who so far.

And the wherewithal that Scorby shows in creating a Molotov cocktail makes the kid in me feel all grown up and gritty, but the episode rightly shies away with dwelling on it too much. (Oh, alright – objectively, it's a tad gratuitous, but I don't care. I first saw this as a teenager and was as disinclined to copy Scorby then as I am now.) Later, when everyone arrives in the house, Scorby's obvious alarm pays dividends – we know that not much shakes him, so when he starts to unravel, we know that the shrubbery's really about to hit the fan. Sarah shines here as well, repudiating Scorby's charge that women run at the first opportunity. This strongly written female is miles away from Isobel Watkins, or even Sarah's own feminism-as-personality conceit in The Time Warrior.

Counter-pointing all the sound and fury, Chase's cold insanity issues forth aphorisms such as "Humans are replaceable, Scorby. The Krynoid is unique." As Chase, Tony Beckley keeps the lunacy grounded in a suave, feline presence. I was slightly worried when the Krynoid starts to mentally influence him – Chase is a good enough character with a plausible motivation; he doesn't *need* to come under the thrall of a megalomaniacal cabbage. Fortunately, he doesn't become a flat automaton, as his psychosis shines through the dollop of Zen that being possessed adds to his green-fingered lunacy. The sight of Chase sitting in the lotus position amongst his beloved greenery, as what sounds like his cover version of The Mutants' incidental music blares out of the speakers, is as bonkers as it is unsettling. And it's terrifically spooky when the plants start throttling Sarah, Scorby and Hargreaves to death while Chase remains inert, calmly telling them not to struggle. Beckley even manages to deliver the line "Animal fiends!" without diminishing the effectiveness of his villainy.

So Baker continues to chomp his way through the story, brushing past Sir Colin's secretary (an uncredited Keith Ashley, getting a deserved line or two after years as a background artist) and barking "He's busy!" down the phone before anyone else can answer it. Almost nobody mentions Baker in the same breath as William Hartnell, but his take on the character here can trace its lineage directly back to the very original. He's every inch the anti-establishment, crabby, unpredictable, shady genius that Sydney Newman and Verity Lambert sought to create. Add to that Baker's acting talent and oddball, mercurial quirkiness, and you have a dramatic, original, brilliant and – I have to say – definitive take on the role, from an actor here at the height of his powers.

July 23rd

The Seeds of Doom (part six)

R: I've loved this season. I've been bowled over by its confidence and boldness, I think the rapport between Tom Baker and Elisabeth Sladen has been so gorgeous, you could bottle it and sell it as a perfume. And again, we take this for granted in retrospect – who could have believed that thirteen years in, with a third recasting of the lead role, that the old sixties series could have felt as fresh and urgent as this?

But I think there's something wrong with the approach to the storytelling when every single adventure this year has fallen at the final hurdle, and failed to provide a satisfying finale. Episode six of The Seeds of Doom certainly isn't bad, not as such; but I think it's unquestionably the weakest instalment of the serial, and that's been a trait across the year. What's the reason? Is it that the style of structure that Robert Holmes adopts is all set-up and no pay-off, spectacle but no resolution? Is it because he delights in making the menace and tension so overpowering, and sets the stakes so high, that any victory can't help but feel a cheat? Is it in the characters somehow – that Holmes so delights in producing memorable villains, whose job it is to kill, and wonderful victims, whose job it is to die, that anyone who is left standing at the story's conclusion to wave goodbye to the Doctor seems just a tad anaemic?

The conclusion to The Seeds of Doom in particular is much criticised; the Krynoid is finally defeated by UNIT dropping a big bomb on it. Watching it back, I can't actually fault this – it seems perfectly logical to me, and the solution is offered by placing the Doctor and Sarah in direct danger. (Indeed, I think the scene where the Doctor tells Beresford to blow up the house is terrific; it's an act of self-sacrifice, and I love the way, having made it, the Doctor puts down the phone and stares about the room as if contemplating a soliloquy – then realises there's nobody there to hear it, and turns away.) The problem comes not with the ease with which the big tendriled plant is destroyed, but the ease with which the Doctor and Sarah escape the means of that destruction. We've already seen (chillingly) what happens when Scorby tries to break cover and submit to the mercy of the garden plants – what we ought to have seen here is the Doctor and Sarah caught between a rock and a hard place, escaping from certain death in the house to the certain death of the garden. If there had been the budget, surely we should have had a

sequence where our heroes were overcome with the homicidal vegetation – only saved in the nick of time, perhaps, when the Krynoid died and relinquished its control. Instead, we get the Doctor and Sarah comfortably crouching behind a log and watching the house blow up. That's what's too simple: not the climax, but all the little details around it.

Terror of the Zygons has an awkward ending too, but it's structurally sound. There, Camfield and Banks Stewart gave us the big explosion, and then a final reel where the Doctor had to confront the lead villain's final gambit. Here, they get it the wrong way round. The dramatic high point is the scene where the Doctor bests Harrison Chase (in what is surely the grisliest screen death Doctor Who has ever offered). It's dramatic, and exciting, and so beautifully ironic – that Chase's body will be sprayed in nutrient form all over his beloved garden is so apt and so ignominious. Tony Beckley plays the possessed madman to perfection – tellingly, for such a camp villain, he refuses to camp it up as his part gets more ludicrous. The sequence where Harrison Chase recites the creed of the plants before savagely beating Sarah unconscious is extraordinary. But once Chase dies, the story's over. And it happens far too early.

And Sgt Henderson! No one deserves that kind of murder. That could have been Benton!

It's a remarkable piece of work, mind you. As a demonstration of the Hinchcliffe/ Holmes style, and just how far in two short seasons Doctor Who has come since the days of Pertwee, there's surely no better example. They just need to work on their endings a bit.

And thirteen seasons down, thirteen seasons to go! We're exactly halfway through what we're now forced to call these days the "classic series". I'm going to treat myself with a visit to the buffet on my ship. They have trifle.

T: I can't argue with any of your criticisms, but they can't stop me loving every minute of this. Love isn't rational, I guess. (As anyone that has seen or met my new wife can attest, if their looks of surprise that someone as beautiful and intelligent as her would marry a shabby anorak like me are anything to go by.)

So yes... the story essentially runs out, but let's be fair, that story is about a giant alien vegetable that wants to engulf the Earth. It would have been nice for the Doctor to find a solution that didn't involve calling in an air strike, but he still does what lesser men can't manage – he holds his nerve – so he's still the undoubted hero of the piece. If anything, John Challis' excellent portrayal of Scorby falling apart shows how much the Doctor's steel and grit are as effective at dealing with a crisis as his brains and humour. That shot of the mercenary, totally deflated and giving a sick laugh at his own expense, is a very real depiction of a tough guy expressing abject fear. It's incredible that the script and Challis both transform Scorby from the chief heavy into someone we almost consider an ally (note that the Doctor and Sarah now trust him with a gun) – so much so that before a swamp plant engulfs Scorby, we're urging him to emerge unscathed on the other side of the water. We've no such sympathy for his insane boss, however, who has become calmly, detachedly *evil*, speaking in tones of intense, quiet menace with bursts of shocking violence (does he *punch* Sarah?). I'd accuse him of being bananas, but seeing as they're a member of the plant world, he'd probably take it as a compliment.

After the humans have met a very green death, it's onto purely vegetable matters. There's tension in the scenes of the greenery tussling the Doctor and Sarah, and the Krynoid is supremely effective both as a model and the shambling CSO Cauliflower of Death that successfully towers over the humans involved. The collapsing ceiling and shattering woodwork as the vines tighten around Chase's mansion are pulled off very effectively too. Then everything gets blown up, and there is just time for the Doctor to offer Sir Colin the chance of becoming a companion (!), and a silly joke in the snow (that I could, frankly, have done without), and we round off an impressive, gutsy story that thrills the 14-year-old boy that I still really am, deep down.

As a final note, let me add that watching reminds me – oddly enough – of Super Channel. In the days of collecting bootleg Who, Super Channel suddenly offered a huge swathe of good quality Tom Baker stuff, though it was dogged (quite literally) by on-screen idents and advert breaks. Still, the binky bonky music that heralded the episodes is an inherent part of my experience of watching the show, and I rather miss it when I watch this unexpurgated version. I don't however, miss the irritatingly shrunken credits. What an awful, terribly disrespectful thing to do, I thought, and typical of a commercial broadcaster with no respect for the programmes it's airing, or the people who created them. Thank goodness you'd never get those on a high-quality terrestrial broadcaster now, eh?

The Masque of Mandragora (part one)

R: Maybe they need to work on their beginnings too. The location shooting in Portmeirion is gorgeous, and the BBC set designers respond to the challenge of making period drama with customary gusto. Doctor Who looks as well-made as it has ever done. But you have to wade through the first five minutes to get there: we open with the Doctor and Sarah exploring corridors and junk rooms in the TARDIS, and when we finally do land somewhere, it's on a blank blackness ringed with crystals. It's intended, no doubt, to look striking and peculiar. But it actually just looks very cheap.

Last year, Louis Marks' script for Planet of Evil had the Doctor effectively acting as grim prophet. This time around, he takes on that role quite directly, even undergoing an on-the-spot astrology exam to see whether or not he can be taken seriously as a fortune teller. And what Marks is doing is very clever; the Doctor's popping back in time and being a know-all could make him seem detached, even patronising. You don't need Time Lord qualifications to judge the past; even the average six year old can sneer at the young duke, Giuliano, when he speculates that the Earth moves in relation to the stars. And since this is a story (like The Brain of Morbius) about that borderline between the superstition and science, it strikes a bum note that the audience would judge the intellectuals of the Renaissance as being more primitive than they are. But Marks deflects this. By having the Doctor not only more informed than the characters, but also responsible for the crisis he has brought upon them, he makes his quest to save them more personal. In Pyramids of Mars, the story had to show us an alternate future to prove to us these long-ago historical events were urgent; The Masque of Mandragora has no need to do this, because there's a stronger emotional tie. The world is in danger, and this time it's the Doctor's fault. He's cast not just as lofty prophet this time, but bungler.

As I say, I'm not too happy with the TARDIS opening scenes, but I've got a theory about their inclusion. (And not just as a means of introducing the new control room!) Over this season, we're going to see a surprising number of attempts to explain the mysteries of Doctor Who we've taken for granted. The corridor scenes are remarkable, because they're the first time anyone has even bothered to suggest the TARDIS is more than one big room since the early days of Patrick Troughton. Soon within this story, we'll understand why we always hear every story in English (and the question is not why has it taken 13 years to tell us, but why after 13 years we now have to be told?). In The Robots of Death, there'll be a fair bash at explaining dimensional transcendentalism. In The Deadly Assassin, there'll be a fair bash at explaining... well, pretty much everything. What's going on? Well, I think it's evidence of the series at last feeling secure enough that it can start looking inwards to the absurdities we accept on trust. Doctor Who is brimming over with self-confidence, it's a critical success, and its ratings have never been better. So much of the show's history has been one of crisis, running away from cancellation and BBC indifference and production dissatisfaction with its cast. Here, right at the very centre of the classic series, we've hit a moment of still point. And it means that Doctor Who can afford at last to look over its shoulder, to get self-reflective, to ask "Why do we do that?" This year, it's reached the top of a mountain. It'll be interesting to see what happens when it begins to slide off its peak.

I'm going to leave Toby to enthuse about the cast, but I can't help but pick out Robert James as the High Priest! I love Robert James for elevating The Power of the Daleks' Lesterson to tragic status – and it's great to see him here, having fun, really biting down hard on the grandeur of his mock-Shakespearean lines and declaiming like a pro. I must say, one of the most delightful things about this quest of ours is the way you'll suddenly recognise amongst

the bit parts an actor you've seen from ten seasons before, and feel such an affection for him.

T: Now this is interesting – there's a competing elegance and awkwardness to both the story and the production itself, one that encapsulates the relationship between olden times and science. As a period-drama setting, it's extremely well rendered, with plenty of horse action, an attractive countryside and gorgeous costumes. But every time something sci-fi wanders into the proceedings, it looks terribly out of place or clumsily staged – the Mandragora energy, for instance, is a sparkler which makes a noise like a nose-diving aeroplane, and it attacks with a childish red VFX circle. That TARDIS scene you're not happy with is a very low-key way to open a season... but then we get the new (old) control room which seems a mission statement for a series that is a bit embarrassed about the sci-fi tropes it needs to adopt. There's no beeping, whirring and flashy lights in this futuristic time machine – it's a beautiful, minimalist, wooden centre of operations that looks more like an academic's study than a scientist's lab. It's a repudiation of hi-tech; it's that old-fashioned leather case from Planet of Evil, or those wonderful set dressings from Morbius writ large. So you could say that the rather inelegant attempts to stage the space events is thematically appropriate, with the productions team's view of scientific advances as skewed as those of Renaissance Italy.

With that in mind, it's possible to see a certain, ahem, charm to the rather simple (read: cheap) yet abstract depiction of Mandragora's space-lair, which makes little attempt to hide the fact that it's some paper or something-or-other wrapped around some wire in front of a blank background. For a series we know can pull off shots of spaceships surging through a convincing starry background, the Mandragora space plughole is almost knowingly quaint.

And perhaps owing to this curious awkwardness, the story doesn't quite hang together for me yet. It all *looks* wonderful – and yet my eye is drawn to the rubbish extra who risks his life to rescue some straw, whilst men with swords charge about slaying his friends, until he runs into a corner to get stabbed on cue.

The acting is sound, and in some cases excellent – but old friends Norman Jones (as the astrologer Hieronymous) and Robert James (as the High Priest) seem slightly awkward with the material they've been given. Yes, Rob, it's delightful to see them pop up again – but James was the main guest star in The Power of the Daleks, and now he's reduced to priesto-babble (he didn't think this story was much cop, you'll not be surprised to hear). His presence underlines the impression that this episode is not quite the sum of its parts, and whilst it's easy on the ear and eye (I love the half-glimpsed blue corpse), by far the best bit is the Doctor's confrontation with Federico. Jon Laurimore is spot on as the villainous Count, helped by a script which paints him as an enjoyably hissable villain (though not an irrational one). He's prepared to listen to the Doctor, and even to hear his outlandish claims and accept him as a travelling soothsayer seeking a living. Federico makes an impact because he is no intransigent madman or blinkered savage, but a resourceful manipulator capable of sounding more than one dramatic note.

As for Tom Baker, he's clearly stopped reading the scripts in order. Listen to how he says (on film, so before the interior TARDIS scenes were recorded) "Maybe that's why I stopped using the old control room" – in the context on the unfolding action, his stresses give the sentence totally the wrong meaning. In the last story, he was testy, impatient and unpredictable. This week, he's unsure of what his lines mean. He *is*, he's William bloody Hartnell, I tell you.

July 24th

The Masque of Mandragora (part two)

R: I love the wit of the cliffhanger resolve. Tom Baker puts his hand up to prepare for his inevitable escape – and stops not only the swing of the axe, but Dudley Simpson's climactic music. Just look at the way the impatient executioner puts his hand on his hip in irritation!

But this is an episode largely missing such wit. I think there's too much Cult of Demnos,

and too little Count Federico. Jon Laurimore plays the usurping count with all the energy of Jacobean tragedy, and is enormously fun to watch; this whole subplot of Machiavellian politics and assassinations is fascinating, in part because the murderers feel duty bound to observe certain rules before committing their atrocities. (The way that Federico keeps on asking Hieronymous to draw astrological charts bad enough to justify sudden deaths is not only very funny, but speaks volumes about the realpolitik of the time – everyone accepts that regicide is a constant threat, but the succeeding king must always find some way to distance himself directly from the crime, if he's to ensure that the monarchy is seen as something stable and secure; if he doesn't, he's just inviting other usurpers to do the same to him.) But as for these chaps from Demnos – well, what's to say? They don't add to the Renaissance history flavour particularly (the Doctor even acknowledges that historically, the cult died out over a thousand years before), and so not only look out of time, but out of place – when they prepare to sacrifice Sarah, they could just as easily be the Exxilons from Death to the Daleks. And although the masks are wonderful, they inevitably rob the actors of any expression. When you get long sequences of Hieronymous talking to the Mandragora Helix, standing fixed to a single spot, it's really just one man with a hidden face talking to a disembodied voice. That's not television, that's radio.

I really enjoyed Gareth Armstrong in episode one as the angry, impulsive duke. Here, he comes across instead as a trifle wet. He rescues the Doctor as a lone voice of science in a Dark Age world; when the Doctor tries to explain the Mandragora Helix, and ironically ends up sounding as backwards as the soldiers who believe in fire demons, it's clear from the script that he's disappointed in him. So show the disappointment – this is a man who's struggling to be modern whilst the world about him conspires to kill him in its medieval reactionism. The scene where he shyly tries to explain to Sarah why the Earth is a sphere is well-intentioned, but he comes across like a schoolboy trying to impress a pretty teacher, not as a man passionately risking his life by staking his claim to reason.

I feel like I'm moaning too much, when the

job of this diary is to be celebratory. The ideas here are great, they really are; the choice for historical period strikingly sophisticated. (Back in the Hartnell days, most history settings were chosen for famous events or people, not theme.) And there are lots of subtle ways that sophistication shines through. I love the way that Hieronymous is not just an arrant fraud, that he genuinely believes his astrological predictions are true even whilst he's inventing them. It's that self-deception that makes him such an interesting character, and he reminds me of the likes of the Aztec Tlotoxl, who would deceive and cheat to bring down Barbara but still within the sanctity of pure belief. It gives Hieronymous a curious dignity... I just want him to take off that bloody mask so I can see his face more.

Nice triple-edged cliffhanger. Even though I would argue that each successive moment of jeopardy carries less weight than the last.

T: You're right about the cliffhanger, but this is nonetheless a terribly enjoyable 25 minutes of television. The trouble, I guess, is that with such intelligent ideas and such a good cast, this could have been so much more. It's as if director Rodney Bennett has been so impressed by the level of detail applied to the set designs, dressings, costumes and interior lighting, he thinks that they're enough. By which I mean: the setting is orchestrated so much better than the action – for every beautiful shot of our stunningly accoutred heroes running down some steps or through attractively sun-drenched architecture, there's an unforgivably clumsy set piece. (The Doctor's scarf suddenly being tied around the executioner? Do me a favour.)

It's helpful to compare this to The Brain of Morbius, where Sarah's unlikely rescue of the Doctor occurred off camera. Here, the Doc similarly saves Sarah, but we see what's really happening too soon. As a result, when Hieronymous carries on with his sacrificial stabbing as if there's still a victim on the slab, he just looks silly. In Morbius, director Christopher Barry focused on Maren's intense concentration, which enabled us to feel as though her zeal would keep her from noticing events a few feet away; the emotion of the scene overcame the practical awkwardness.

Here, poor old Norman Jones just looks like he isn't paying attention.

That complaint aside, I've previously felt that Jones' staccato diction – to indicate his possession by Mandragora – didn't work, but I'm actually warming to it here. His intense eyes and insane smile give requisite colour, whilst the delivery remains rhythmical. But everyone's outclassed by Jon Laurimore, who is thoroughly entertaining whilst doing plenty of cod business, whether it's swatting away a shave or eating a grape. The latter almost slips out of his fingers, but even that doesn't sully his enjoyably evil dignity.

Where I *can* credit the director, by the way, is that he doesn't linger on the blue corpses – how dated do old horror films look when they showcase an effect that was impressive for the time, but was soon overwhelmed by technology? So, the corpses suitably look like burnt parodies of the human form, but with weird colouring. And top marks to James Appleby as the guard who insists they're the work of a fire demon, for playing that certainty straight and not like some stereotypical, backwards peasant. He gets a dignified response back from Giuliano too. The way forward may be to reject superstition, but we must do so with manners!

The Masque of Mandragora (part three)

R: Structurally, this is really clever. The production puts its energies into directing a villain against the heroes, to the point where he's actually won – Federico has thwarted his enemies, has the Doctor and Giuliano entirely at his mercy in the dungeon, and has the duchy assured. And then it blindsides the story by having Federico killed in the cliffhanger, blasted aside almost casually by a laser bolt, as if he's been part of little more than an irrelevant subplot. It's a terrific twist.

And the best bits of the episode are where Louis Marks gets to indulge in his taste for Jacobean drama. Tim Pigott-Smith (as Giuliano's companion Marco) gets to emote terribly passionately from the torture chamber (and isn't it brilliant that a goodie character like him eventually does break, and condemns his best friend as a cultist?). And the scene where Norman Jones predicts Jon Laurimore's death is absolutely wonderful, as the worm finally turns – it's as sinister and as subtle as many of the texts that Marks is parodying. All of this gives some much-needed balls to an episode that starts a bit soft; whilst I admire Tom Baker's insistence that the Doctor never kill anyone, it does mean that the swordfighting sequences feel very clean and kiddies' TV.

Taken in isolation, many of the dramatic set pieces here are terrific. There are two basic problems with them, though, I think: one is that there's not much context to them. (If even one of the important personages that Federico is so worried about provoking actually made an appearance, you could understand why he doesn't kill Giuliano much more openly; as it is, the rightful duke's only friends appear to be a couple of eccentric outsiders and a young man in a floppy hat. All the skullduggery of casting horoscopes and extracting confessions of heresy make Federico look surprisingly cautious – he doesn't have any credible on-screen opposition to his usurpation, so why not just get on with it?) And two, and much more importantly – these set pieces don't have very much to do with the Doctor. It becomes clear that Tom Baker has really very little action this week, except getting stalked by Lis Sladen with a hatpin.

I do love the scene where he bandages Giuliano's arm, though. To the bemusement of the Duke, he mentions both Queen Cleopatra from the distant past, and Florence Nightingale from the distant future. What other series except Doctor Who could have namedropping that bends all the laws of time?

T: There's an air of class about Doctor Who at the moment. Even the font in which the story's title and episode number are written, instead of trying to be jazzy and futuristic, have a look of timelessness about them.

In fact, there are impressive elements across the board... Robert Holmes has clearly got his hands on this script – no offence to Louis Marks, but delicious stuff such as "that fox-faced old blowhard", "breakfast on burning coals" and "have Giuliano's liver fed to the dogs" has the gleeful bombast of Holmes at his most majestically enjoyable. And the story's conflict between its historical setting and sci-fi elements that I mentioned earlier has worked itself out as it's gone along – this has to be one of the most handsome-looking stories that Doctor Who has produced, and so the director occasionally allows himself an appropriately impressive visual flourish. Such as: don't you just adore Tom Baker appearing behind Hieronymous' conjurer's flash-bang like a manically unwelcome magician's assistant?

Mind you, it helps so much that the design department has supplied a splendid array of costumes. The Brotherhood members look fantastic, especially the impassive, glowering Hieronymous in his purple robes, and the more casual evil gear that he wears in his room. That said, I would question the High Priest's decision to live up to the fact that he has no name, only a job description, and dresses accordingly even when wandering around the palace. Nothing screams "I am a Secret Follower of Demnos" quite like wearing black robes in daylight, dearie. (And yet, even this sibilant, well-coiffured and berobed old fruit isn't the campest thing on display here. There's clearly no room for anyone else in Giuliano and Marco's relationship, and I wouldn't be surprised if they had a mutual friend called Dorothy.)

And as you say, Federico's capture of the Doctor and Giuliano is a real and deserved triumph for such a great villain. The climax of his courtly machinations is that he actually defeats our heroes, utterly – but then some Outerspace Light Beast comes to shine on his parade. A shame the Count is dispatched, then, by such a mimsy spark (I'd imagined fiery lasers!) and that awkward-looking cutaway of a final shot. A meaty villain like him deserved a barbecue!

July 25th

The Masque of Mandragora (part four)

R: Whenever I watch the sublime Pyramids of Mars, there's one moment I wish they'd done more with. Remember in episode three, after Sarah has fired her rifle at the gelignite on the base of the rocket? A mummy appears behind her, and she talks to it quite casually, certain that it's the Doctor in disguise. I've always wondered what would have happened had it not been – unable to see his face beneath all those mummy wraps, she'd made a terrible mistake. How scary would that have been?

Well, in The Masque of Mandragora they play that trick, and I get my answer. It is pretty scary, actually – it's the scariest moment of the entire serial. At the ball, Sarah approaches one of the masked guests, recognising the Doctor's costume. And not only is she wrong, but the figure underneath doesn't even have a face, just an orange fiery void – and the moment he is uncovered provokes a massacre. It's wonderful stuff, and anticipates beautifully the denouement of the story in which the Doctor wins the day because he is wearing Hieronymous' costume instead. The figure we were led to believe was reassuring turned out to be a monster; the figure we thought was a monster is the Doctor, all infectious grins and relief.

After the fizzled conclusions to the previous year's stories, this one is very satisfying. It builds up its climax with real spectacle – and, for once, that isn't a big explosion, but tumblers and fire eaters. There's dancing. There's forced jollity. There's a creeping sense of claustrophobia. The episode is so well structured that I even have no problem accepting that Tom Baker wins the day, basically, by managing a flawless impersonation of Norman Jones. This doesn't feel like some Celestial Toymaker contrivance, though, but actually plays upon an anonymity that has run throughout the entire serial. (I'm pretty sure, with the benefit of the DVD and my middle-aged cynicism, that isn't Tom Baker's voice at all booming behind that mask – but the point is that it might have been, there's an ambiguity to it that doesn't stretch credulity too far.)

And there's one scene in this episode that outlines – better than in any other story, really – the entire charm of these early Tom Baker stories, and why the scares work so well. The Doctor starts prattling about with his lion costume, and Sarah calls him on it – she tells him that the more dangerous the situation, the sillier the Doctor behaves, and the worse his jokes become. And that's it in a nutshell, that's why Hinchcliffe Doctor Who is so great. It plays the drama upon a tightrope; as the horror increases, so does the comedy, and, at its

best, it becomes a parade of fast-delivered gags and chills, with Tom Baker as the dizzyingly eccentric figure at the centre of it all, clowning about or bellowing with rage as the moment dictates. The Masque of Mandragora isn't vintage Hinchcliffe – it doesn't push far enough with the gags or the chills – but it's got the template down pat, and that augurs well for the entire season.

T: Norman Jones and Tom Baker have a similar cadence and character to their voices, so it's not a *huge* leap to think the Doctor could pull off a decent impression of Hieronymous. Although, it's a terribly abrupt ending, isn't it, after a beautifully judged build-up? As only Sarah, Guiliano and Marco are taken to the temple, and all the other guests are zapped (with rubbish sparks again, boo!), one must imagine that all the famous partygoers alluded to – whom we know can't have died – have nipped out for a pee or are getting off with each other in the shrubbery.

Tom Baker has an odd moment of detached reverie before exiting on a line in which he describes a beautiful Italian pageant as a "knees up", but this casual bonhomie falls away when he and Sarah compare notes on how things are "desperately bad". You could have these two actors discussing an alien invasion you never actually see, and it'd still have more dramatic weight than much of the competition. They're *that* good – and note how Sladen has the wherewithal and selflessness to show Sarah looking from side-to-side to pick up the steps of what is, of course, an unfamiliar dance. Lesser actresses would have just wanted to look good. And it's fair to say she looks beautiful in her costume, an absolute picture.

And Sladen isn't the only pretty thing on display: handsome Tim Pigott-Smith brings an RSC-influenced credibility to Marco, and Gareth Armstrong does his best with soppy old Giuliano. (I've seen Armstrong be very funny in Twelfth Night, and pretty scary as Cassius and Richard III, so wet he definitely isn't.) But really, I suspect instead of Stuart Fell doing some impressive jesting, these two would have much rather had Barbra Streisand at their dance. Get a room, boys.

Here at story's end, I don't know why The

Masque of Mandragora doesn't quite hit the A-mark. It's like it doesn't quite know how to add the final polish, with such beautiful temple lighting, great characters (the defeated Rossini is still allowed his moment – quite right, as he's a cut above your normal guard captain), fantastic masquerade costumes and a beautiful, moody and silent build-up to the climax. Perhaps it's because, if the individual elements don't seem to have gelled into perfection, I'm watching this within the context of a series at the absolute height of its powers. Perhaps it's because Mars is ascending through the sign of the Ram (that's a way of saying Doctor Who is *very good* at the moment, using the language of total bollocks).

The Hand of Fear (part one)

R: It's The Seeds of Doom again, isn't it? Something buried on the Earth for millions of years comes to the surface – a very peculiar something that should be long dead, but which through ill-advised doses of radiation begins to regenerate. On the face of it, this ought to be rather scarier than Seeds; after all, a fossilised hand is so much creepier (and so much more wonderfully absurd) than a little pod. But this episode doesn't go for the scares. Instead, it goes for something rather more delicate – it seeks only to intrigue. And I think, on the whole, it succeeds.

It doesn't get off to a great start. In fact, I'm hard pushed to think of any story opening that's much worse, actually. We have characters intoning technobabble at each other, the clarity of which is muffled because their heads are buried within winter hoods – the original Doctor Who anoraks, you might say. It's four minutes – four minutes! – before we see a single person's face. It's most peculiar, because after the action shifts to Earth, Lennie Mayne tries to make up for his staid direction by throwing the camera every which way, and filming the action from high above or down below. Sometimes, this makes the scenes look rightfully sinister (the sequences of the possessed Sarah walking to the nuclear factory are brilliant; we know Sarah so well by this stage, that making her seem alien and threatening is quite an achievement). Sometimes, this makes the scenes look sinister for no very good rea-son (the shot of the Doctor and Dr Carter in the car, filmed from their feet, sends a message not of urgent pace, but of immediate foreboding – it looks as if Carter might suddenly attack the Doctor with his gear stick).

You could argue this episode is a bit dull and repetitive. But it's also being oddly experimental. Bob Baker and Dave Martin are denying us the usual four part set-up; there's virtually no guest cast (and, as it'll turn out, no one who'll make it to the story's halfway mark), there are no villains except Sarah herself, there's no explicable background to what's going on. The overall effect is that this is all somewhat disorientating. Realistically, all of this should feel achingly familiar: modern-day Earth with nuclear complexes and armed guards, and Sarah being possessed just two weeks after she was hypnotised by Hieronymous. Instead it's odd, and deliberately so: when Sarah and the Doctor mistake the quarry for an alien world, it's not just a post-modern gag, it's also a means of telling us the audience not to take anything here for granted.

T: On paper, it's a jumble of the familiar: a contemporary setting, the Doctor co-opting high-ranking establishment professionals into helping him, a quarry, a mysterious alien object, et cetera et cetera... and yet, the production's minimalist approach keeps this neat and unusual. There's a danger in our so highly praising Doctor Who every time it reinvents the wheel, we forget the virtues of a story that just *nails* it.

For instance, while the opening scene makes for something of a confusing info-dump (if you don't have foreknowledge of the story), it is rather novel. The way in which Roy Pattison (as Commander Zazzka, a Kastrian) wipes ice away from the window creates an interesting visual, and sets up the idea of the encroaching cold. Also, Pattison's treated voice has a wonderful tone of lamentation about it, matched by the grim intonations of honourable defeat with which Roy Skelton's King Rokon gives him his final orders. And as usual for this era, the model work is absolutely perfect.

We then find ourselves in a quarry, where there's a *fantastic* shot of the explosion (almost worth the loss of a BBC camera – although we've seen similar stuff from stock!), and while

I'm not convinced by the fortunate distribution of rocks that simultaneously bury and protect Sarah from serious injury, the sequence is nonetheless well staged. I really enjoy how the foreman, Abbott, runs over the camera as his boots crunch on the rocky ground, adding urgency to the drama. (Although, I have read occasional tomes less scholastic than ours (!) that felt compelled to insist that David Purcell, who plays Abbott, is actually Steve Coogan because of their similar facial features and diction. Nice try, but Coogan would have been 11 years old at the time.)

And I rather like the little bits of visual flair that Lennie Mayne has added. In the past, his efforts to make an alien world seem all kooky and zany with lots of angles and zooms ended up seeming a tad quaint and dated. Here, the use of goldfish bowl lens when filming Elisabeth Sladen handheld, and that fabulous shot where the complex's stop sign gives way to a round distorted mirror into which the image of Sarah wanders, is very nifty. Elsewhere, in trying to inject this early instalment with a bit more welly, Mayne has Rex Robinson (as Dr Carter) deliver a straightforward line ("Did you find anything at the quarry?") with menace, hinting that all is not well with him. And that final effects shot, as Eldrad's hand shifts from stone to flesh and starts moving, is extraordinary.

In fact, that's the perfect word to sum up this episode. Even if much of what's on display here leans toward the *ordinary*, the production team find ways of twisting it a bit and doing it well, of adding a little something *extra*.

The Hand of Fear (part two)

R: The first thing that strikes me is what's actually missing from this episode. The Doctor tries to win the trust of a security complex, and is led in by armed guard. In the next episode, he has to contend with the RAF bombing a nuclear power plant. And yet, he never once mentions he's scientific adviser at UNIT, which you can't but help think might have been helpful under the circumstances. No, UNIT has gone now, there are no more apologies for Nicholas Courtney's unavailability, never again a Geneva. Only one more verbal reference is made to the Brigadier for the whole of the Tom

Baker years – that's in episode four – and watch out for the way the Doctor seems to interrupt Sarah as she mentions him, with all the haste of someone not wanting to discuss an ex. There's only one tie left to the old days, and that's Sarah Jane Smith. She should be careful. He could dump her, just like that.

The absence of all the lazy tropes makes this episode feel off-kilter and odd, and really, that's refreshing. If you plonked UNIT down in the middle of this, it'd be like some retread of The Claws of Axos – even the name of the power plant sounds the same. But with the Doctor acting not as part of a military attachment, but as some sort of psychiatrist to a mental patient, we see Tom Baker play the part somewhat outside his usual comfort zone. Needing to win over Professor Watson, he's more genuinely likeable, for one thing; his concern seems to be for his best friend's health, and for the intellectual enigma of the fossilised hand. No sudden outbursts of anger (which do have a tendency to come across as default mannerisms Tom Baker uses to inject some passion into a scene), no petulant arrogance. The result ought to be blander. It isn't. In what will be his last story with the only companion who has predated him, Tom Baker shows a gentler side that's rather touching. Even as he knocks Sarah unconscious, he does so with an apology.

It's that gentler tone that I really like. It feels strange and enervating after all the horror and body parts of Season Thirteen. The scene in which Professor Watson phones his wife and daughter with the belief he's about to be killed in an explosion is very poignant; his patience as he listens to his child's day at school, his desire to say a goodbye whilst refusing to alarm or frighten them, gives real human substance to a character only introduced ten minutes earlier. And it throws into sharp relief the moments of grotesquery: dodgy CSO accepted, the images of the hand crawling across the floor like a spider are still creepy in the extreme, the moment where it suddenly grabs tightly onto Driscoll's hand subtle and disturbing.

T: One of the side effects of satellite broadcasting was that when Who stories were aired, the only copies I could get my hands on were those edited together, with advert breaks where the closing credits would once have been. Being a fully paid-up member of the Acute Fan Gene Anonymous, I couldn't abide such butchery finding its way into my collection, so would re-edit the episodes. I used the opening and closing sections of much worse quality copies of the unedited stories, and – aided only by a primitive pause button (and its three-second rollback on the counter, which had to be perfectly timed) – I edited the cliffhangers and their resolutions back in. And I particularly loved the cliffhangers in The Hand of Fear, as they're all a bit different, and I didn't want to ruin them. So I'm proud to say that yes, whilst the image goes from crystal clear to smudgy black and white, my recreation of the beginning and end of each episode of The Hand of Fear is perfectly spliced to the frame. It may be the most technically accomplished thing I've ever achieved.

Fortunately, this episode has so many positives that we needn't dwell on my one moment of brilliance... for a start, the titular hand-threat is very well realised. (Although I wonder if viewers who came to the story in later episodes would have been confused as to the provenance of the title, as this brilliantly achieved menace waves goodbye this week.) On the other hand (see what I did there?), I salute the wonderful Glyn Houston (as Professor Watson) – I'd like to say that there are no flies on him, but that'd be a lie. There is one, on his forehead in his opening scene, plain as daylight – let's hope it doesn't absorb any of the leaking radiation, otherwise Spider-Man will have a new archenemy. Then there's the terrific stunt where Dr Carter plunges to his death, and another entry into that lovely subgenre: the cliffhanger where the immediate threat is happening to a non-regular.

And I'm probably sounding like a stuck record, but she's not with us for much longer... I adore how Elisabeth Sladen avoids embarrassing zombie acting, and instead suggests possession-by-alien-hand using coy childishness, inquisitiveness and nervous tics. After she's recovered from being punched out by the Doctor (!), she's at it again, hopping onto the desk, all game and innocent before protesting vainly about being hypnotised. Her haughty sniff when the Doctor returns her to "normal" is wonderful. Oh, she's magical.

July 26th

The Hand of Fear (part three)

R: It's an unlikely candidate, I know. But this is one of my favourite-ever episodes of Doctor Who. It radiates a sweet charm that is really very rare at this point in the show's history. In a couple of weeks' time, we'll be on Gallifrey, and the series will rather ostentatiously reinvent itself, and get itself mixed up with a whole new intricate mythology. But just before we get there, there's this – this little island – almost a mini-story in itself, as the Doctor asks a stranded alien to trust him. It began a bit like The Seeds of Doom – and it seems almost too coincidental that it replays that story's resolution, with fighter pilots bombing the nuclear plant, except this time for comic effect.

And it's the comedy that I cherish most about this episode. Elisabeth Sladen has never been funnier than she is here. The childish jealousy she shows when Eldrad is allowed in the TARDIS (and the way that she subtly shows how unafraid she is of her by leaving the control room to fetch a banana) is gorgeous because it really is the behaviour of a child – years before Sladen is required to reinterpret the role as a rather frosty neighbour on Bannerman Road looking after a bunch of kids, she plays the part as an innocent eight year old. It ought to be cloying and twee – especially in the Andy Pandy costume – but it really breaks your heart. The little girl shyness she shows when she has to say hello to Mrs Eldrad is a bit like having to meet your Daddy's posh friends from work; the way she performs facial contortions to prepare herself for a nuclear blast lacks all the self-consciousness an adult would show when asked to look ridiculous. And is there anything more gorgeous – really and truly – than that magical sequence where she chases the Doctor into the complex, and the two of them stroll into danger together, admitting how much they worry for the other?

There are more dramatic Doctor Who episodes, ones which challenge me more, ones which impress me with their gravitas. But few make me as happy as this one does.

The cliffhanger – as Eldrad opens a door,

and an arrow-bolt thuds into her chest – is superb, by the way. Utterly unexpected, and with its refusal to obey the usual formula of build-up to a crisis, it contributes to that sense of experimentation that makes this episode so fresh.

T: I'll be honest: this was never on the list of stories I was desperate to buy as a Target novel, or on video. No-one really talked about it, and when they did, it certainly wasn't in awed tones. And yet… The Hand of Fear *does* have so much that feels different from everything that surrounds it, and I'm incredibly fond of it. Judith Paris' Eldrad costume is a magnificent creation, and, boy, she's got presence – her silicone carapace is as alien and convincing as the performance she delivers. For all the masculine intonation, there's something curiously demure about her, too. She takes the mantle of fab guest star from the brilliant Glyn Houston, who – having been solid, dependable and movingly stoic last week – gets to throw some comic exasperation into the mix here. As Professor Watson, Houston bows out gracefully, and I note that gets serious respect from the Doctor/ Tom Baker, who won't leave 'till he makes certain he's okay. (That didn't happen to Sgt Henderson!)

I only have a couple of minor gripes. Tom Baker is still brilliant, but whilst I love the long and silly list of co-ordinates he rattles off before deadpanning "then see what happens", I wonder if it's a sign, perhaps, of future waywardness. And what about Miss Jackson's credit? Lennie Mayne was married to Frances Pidgeon – I'd have liked to have been a fly on the wall when that particular mistake was noticed.

The Hand of Fear (part four)

R: The Hand of Fear is ignored like no other Doctor Who story; it's upstaged by its own epilogue. The DVD release has a sticker on the cover presenting it as the last (classic) appearance of Sarah Jane Smith, and all the special features on the disc focus upon Lis Sladen's departure from the series rather than anything to do with the adventure itself. The last five minutes are all that anyone remembers. The rest of it is like some unwanted preamble.

I find this a terrible shame. I genuinely love The Hand of Fear. I genuinely love its oddness. I love its freewheeling treatment of structure and character. Most Doctor Who stories build up a strong supporting guest cast from the get-go; this one changes its cast each week, the guest star giving way to another every episode. Rex Robinson to Glyn Houston to Judith Paris to Stephen Thorne, each actor disposed of as they hand over the reins to another. The only other story we've seen that does anything even remotely like this is The Chase – and that because it leaps about frenetically through time and space. The Hand of Fear is a different and subtler beast altogether, and by changing with whom the Doctor is bouncing off each episode, the theme of the story is changed as well. The result is that Hand feels quite slippery, never quite settling down into any one identifiable adventure – and also means that it stays unpredictable. When Eldrad is squashed by the Kastrian regenerator, for once we as an audience genuinely can't tell what can happen next – by refusing, even halfway through the final episode, to give us a recognisable house style, it's perfectly possible that entire new monsters may emerge from the next room as the Doctor and Sarah squat in anticipation.

What we get, of course, is Stephen Thorne giving us another turn as Omega – but this time looking like a fat sparkling diamond. He's ridiculous. But he's supposed to be ridiculous. For his entire appearance in the story, Male Eldrad is mocked – either by Rokon, from beyond the grave, or, most brilliantly, by Tom Baker and Lis Sladen, who keep on throwing each other knowing glances of mutual embarrassment as he throws himself around the set overacting. Eldrad is a disappointment, but that's entirely the point – he's a pantomime villain crying out like evil Abanazer for the Doctor to give him his magic ring. He's a pathetic joke, poor Eldrad – the kid in the playground that no one wants to play with, they'd all rather kill themselves than have to spend a moment in his company. He's king of nothing – ultimately, just like Omega, and it's surely no coincidence that the same actor is playing the same story twist to the same director by the same writers? – except what was intended in The Three Doctors as dignified tragedy here is presented as mocking farce.

You don't even really need the Doctor and Sarah to be part of this, and they become the audience, standing apart from the main action and passing slighting comment on it – until eventually they trip Eldrad up with a scarf and send him falling into an abyss.

The only reason this anticlimax works the way it does is that it's resolutely not the big resolution to four weeks' worth of adventure. The Hand of Fear hasn't worked like that at all. If anything, it's the end of 15 minutes' worth of adventure – possibly called The Kastrian Embarrassment, or Faux Pas on Kastria. And I think it's entirely keeping with this ever-shifting mercurial story composed of lots of little stories merging into each other, that it seems to end halfway through the episode. Because The Hand of Fear is deliberately small. It's set up that way as a deliberate contrast to The Deadly Assassin – a story that, from the very moment it barges into this one with its Time Lord summons to Gallifrey, establishes itself as something terribly epic and momentous. That final scene in the TARDIS would never have worked at the end of any other story – it'd always have felt bolted on after the climax. (For later examples that feel awkward, look at Four to Doomsday or Frontios – Nyssa suddenly fainting, or the TARDIS losing control, look like irrelevances. No, worse, they are accidentally misleading: has Nyssa collapsed because of the Urbankan poison, or is the TARDIS irreparably damaged after being blown up?) But because The Hand of Fear has seduced us into a structure where nothing ever quite ends, and different mini-adventures slide subtly into the other, the way that Sarah's adventures are so abruptly brought to an end feels so much more shocking and hurtful.

(And yes, that final scene is lovely... Though I have to confess, whenever I watch it, and see Sarah threaten to go and pack her goodies, I always like to imagine her coming back with a sack full of Bill Oddie and Tim Brooke-Taylor doing the Funky Gibbon.)

T: Let me traipse through the good bits from this... it's great that poor Tom Baker affects endearing comic exasperation as he has to solve a series of schlocky adventure game-style traps whilst lugging Judith Paris about, and I love the way she stays stiff and prone when

carried, to emphasise Eldrad's silicon-based genetic make-up. Stephen Thorne brings his usual hushed subtlety to the male Eldrad, and in the process pulls off the glorious feat of making Brian Blessed sound like John Gielgud whispering down a well with a bucket on his head. In Australia. But it works, because Eldrad is a noisy, unsubtle fool. His manic laugh may sound silly, but it underlines the bittersweet irony when Roy Skelton's dignified Rokon makes his incredibly moving admission that rather than submit themselves to a lunatic, the Kastrians chose oblivion.

The shot of Eldrad framed in the doorway of the Kastrian race bank is well-achieved too, providing a welcome bit of size and scale amidst the rather cheap-looking tunnels of Kastria. It's a bit strange, however, that after Eldrad trips over the Doctor's scarf into a chasm, our hero shows very little concern about the fact that he's probably still alive. He even chucks Eldrad's ring of power into the same abyss without fear of reprisals. It's almost a knowing indication of how unimpressive the male Eldrad has been – as if the Doctor is setting up a sequel, but concurrently daring any budding writers to resurrect such a lame nemesis.

Fine, dandy, well done. But sorry, Rob, I think that final scene needs the bulk of my attention here.

Given that it's completely unrelated to the previous four episodes, it's better than one could possibly expect. It *could* have been as abrupt and unsatisfying as Ben and Polly's departure. But no, there's a huge amount going on in this scene, as it's based on a comic misunderstanding that so easily could have been slightly too arch and silly for the circumstances, but instead is judged beautifully. There's batty wordplay with silly sounding Mergin Nuts; there's Sarah getting annoyed with the Doctor not listening, and him being blithely unaware as he sets about his repair work and bosses her about; and then...

And then she has to go.

Tom Baker's coldness in the face of Elisabeth Sladen's childlike, wide-eyed innocence isn't an aloof, uncaring Time Lord being blunt – it's a man forcing himself to be brave so the emotion doesn't choke him. The false hope in Sladen's voice as she digs to see if he's playing one of his jokes is equally heartrending. "'Till we meet again, Sarah Jane", he says (and when this was broadcast, no-one in their right mind would have predicted that it would ever happen). "Hm, hmm", she mutters brightly – she's not going to let his seriousness bring her down.

Sladen keeps a brave face even when brittle, showing that duality that Barry Letts saw in her in the first place. He said she was the only actress he auditioned who could act afraid and brave at the same time – well, she bows out displaying those very skills. She deserves that final freeze frame, and even though she's back on telly now fighting monsters and delighting children, I still feel rather choked as lovely Sarah Jane leaves the fourth Doctor for the last time, seemingly never to see him again. Doctor Who will go on to great things, but this is the end of something truly special.

The Deadly Assassin (part one)

R: Long before I even watched it, this seemed to me like the start of Modern Who. I used to read and reread The Making of Doctor Who, with that smiling Chris Achilleos drawing of Tom Baker on the cover – and inside there was an entire story guide, and they all had such exciting titles!, and I used to recite them out loud because they all sounded so magical and mysterious. And the last recorded story was The Hand of Fear. That was where for me the comfort of Doctor Who I-could-write-out-in-a-list came to an end; after that, the series became a lot more murky, and as a result, a bit more threatening. I used to love that Making of Doctor Who book. Whenever I think of it, I can taste toast – warm, buttered toast.

There's nothing warm or buttery about The Deadly Assassin. It is designed to confound. Take, for example, that narration at the beginning, as Tom Baker solemnly pitches his voice to Grand Epic, and recites the words that scroll across the screen. There is nothing useful about this; no important information is given to us, there is nothing within the exposition that wouldn't have been evident over the next 20 or so minutes. So why do it? It's there to emphasise just how different this is, and to make us feel rather alienated and distanced

from the proceedings. Not only because it so breaks the house style, but also because it makes clear we're being told a story. Whether this is a fiction, or some important historical moment, we need to find out for ourselves – but right from those opening few seconds we're startled, and put on alert, and are left grappling for a way to interpret what we're about to see.

And what we see, of course, is a narrative composed of visions and flash-forwards, and then (rather beautifully) the Doctor having flashbacks to those flash-forwards. Linear time is utterly in flux – rather appropriately, I suppose, for a story taking place amongst the Time Lords. The opening shock of the narration gives way to a still-greater shock, that we're watching a sequence where the Doctor appears to be a murderer. (That we've seen the Doctor so deliberately avoid killing anyone so far this season only makes that more unsettling – see, I knew that awkward swordfight in The Masque of Mandragora would have its uses.) We then spend the episode watching him rush about frantically... to put himself into a position where he seems (almost on a whim, without explaining monologue) to pick up a gun and do the exact thing he was so horrified about. It's a dizzying ride.

The episode does some very clever things; it manages to make the President seem very important, and his assassination therefore of great consequence, even though he's only given one line. I know Toby is the closing credit obsessive (sorry, mate, but you're a bit bonkers, did you know that?) – but they're really very interesting here. Llewellyn Rees gets elevated to top guest star spot, just by dint of Time Lord superiority, and although his contribution to the story is little more than waving a bit and falling over, the end titles subtly suggest he really was very important indeed. And, blink but you'll miss it, but – did they really just say "The Master" was back? No, did they? But... there was no one we saw that had the charisma of a Roger Delgado. They couldn't mean that hideous-looking skeleton with the goggle eyes. Surely not. Yes, we heard someone call him "master", but there was no indication that was with a capital M... To take a character as popular as the Master, and to give him such a savage reinterpretation (especially considering the beloved actor who played him has died so tragically) – and then to announce he's back with such little fanfare, buried within the closing titles – that, I think, takes guts.

But that's what this entire episode is doing. It's trying to exasperate us, to bemuse us, to hold up what we took for granted and present it as something cheap and tarnished. It's very brave. I'm not yet sure I like it very much.

T: Let me get my big complaint out of the way... it looks as if Robert Holmes has been so busy gleefully dismantling the Time Lords' godlike status, he's not been inclined to make a big thing of the Master's return. The result is that he barely seems like the same person, despite that wonderful mask – he's just a skulking, mysterious presence at the moment, with no connection with the Delgado character at all. I wonder whether this wisely severs the character's bonds with a much-loved actor, or smacks of a ruthlessness I dislike. That aside, unlike you, I enjoyed this episode very much...

Because the whole of Gallifreyan society is painted with consistency and logic both on the page and the screen. The ease with which we learn about Time Lord chapters and hierarchies shows Robert Holmes at his world-building best, as aided by his brilliant word-smithery. A sentence such as "Transduct it to the Capitol" actually means nothing in everyday English, but the perfectly chosen words let us interpret their meaning. Even the guards are a perfect synthesis of the Holmes/ Hinchcliffe vision – their distinctive but not impractical costumes will serve the series well from hereon in, and they're armed with "stasers". That word is enough of a transmutation of "laser" for the guns to have their own identity, without being so showily outlandish as to sound daft. Add to that a Panopticon here, a Spandrell there and a Runcible in between, and you have a story that sounds different on the ear but not stupid, and boasts a consistent linguistic landscape.

And if there's and olde-worlde eye over the presentation, it comes with a whiff of the iconoclastic and an ear for satire. Thanks to both the writing and Hugh Walters making the character come alive, the commentator Runcible is a deliciously disdainful, vain and self-satisfied pastiche of a political reporter, whilst the blatant reference to the "CIA" (actu-ally the Celestial Intervention Agency) would seem a trifle arch, were the production team overemphasising the whimsy. The rich, literate and savvy dialogue buys us the comedy that in lesser surroundings would seem too broad – Commander Hilred is obviously a hapless idiot, but this just reinforces Spandrell as a dry, sarcastic old timer with a nice line in weary exasperation.

The economy comes from giving us a whole society via just a few characters, who weave important information seamlessly into the script. Almost every role is a gift for a talented character actor. In just a few lines of dialogue, you're begging for more from Angus MacKay's wonderfully patronising Borusa, and you just want to take Erik Chitty (as Coordinator Engin) home with you, he's so loveable. Even the two unnamed Time Lords are delightfully eccentric cameos, and I adore the oft-maligned George Pravda as Spandrell. He's not obvious casting, but the wit of his lines shines through his thick accent, and we get just enough information to show that he's a pragmatic copper who isn't afraid to get his hands dirty, and yet isn't one of the establishment. We learn he usually deals with "more Plebeian classes", and best of all... he eats a mint! I love that! In what other sci-fi series would you find people with the wherewithal to add a beautiful little touch like that?

Incidentally, in my youth, when my sister wandered in to catch another strategically played episode, she was tickled to see the Doctor evading capture by setting up a bong in the TARDIS console room. As someone not unfamiliar with the odours of Glastonbury, this met with her amused approval. (Oh dear... smoking's cool.)

July 27th

The Deadly Assassin (part two)

R: And it's here that the absence of the Doctor Who companion really makes an impression. Because the Doctor is entirely iso-lated – and there's no one who will take his word on trust – he has to use all his cunning and wit to convince anyone that he's innocent of murder. And, by extension, he has to convince us as well; it's curious how, stripped of the security of an audience-identification figure, the Doctor does suddenly seem much more sinister and unknowable. The cleverness of episode one was to demonstrate how rigorous Castellan Spandrell was – how he wouldn't suffer fools lightly, how he was the one character who refused to be complacent about the threat the Doctor posed. As a result, the turning of the tables here in episode two, and we see it's that very rigour that makes Spandrell the ideal companion to the Doctor, is what makes the Doctor's defence so credible. If he can win over a man as smart and unbiased as Spandrell, surely he can win us over as well?

The casting of George Pravda as Spandrell really oughtn't to work. The German accent (as in The Mutants) gets in the way of the diction; he puts the emphasis upon the wrong words. But in the community of Time Lords, all plastic in their Chancellery guard uniforms, or flouncy in their long robes, he appears to be an outsider. He is another, just like the Doctor is.

I love the white line shape on the Panopticon floor marking where the President fell – all big-eared and bulky in his ceremonial dress. A very subtle sight gag.

T: It's not a German accent, it's Czech – but you're right, it's not a piece of casting that should work, but it absolutely does. I love Spandrell, he's one of my favourite characters in Doctor Who. He commands the Doctor's respect enough to win his trust, even as he warns the Doctor of his imminent vaporisation. The post-torture scene, where the gruff old copper levels with his charge, is one of the best-ever exchanges between two protagonists in the entire programme: it shows an intelligent man intuiting the Doctor's blunt integrity, and the Doctor reciprocating. The Tom Baker Doctor has no time for pompous authority or sadistic lackeys – but he can level with a tough old sweat like Spandrell. It's not all swaggering toughness, though – Pravda suggests a quiet amusement in acknowledging the chutzpah of Baker's deductions, and provides a little chuckle as he makes a dig about the lack of geniuses serving on the High Council.

And he's just one element of a perfectly synthesised script. Holmes has drawn Gallifrey so consistently well – laws about political prisoners being pardoned necessitating pre-election executions, and trial-stopping Article 17s, have extraordinary weight even though they're purely there to facilitate plot momentum. They are played with absolute conviction, so they come across as legal jargon of import rather than the courtroom equivalent of technobabble (which they actually are). Then we have the Doctor's premonition: it seems like a bit of hokey dramatics used to hook the viewer, but fortunately it's dismissed as such by Spandrell – like us, he finds such things far-fetched. When the "scientific" explanation for it eventually comes (it wasn't an actual premonition, thank goodness), it fits neatly into what we already know of this society and its inhabitants.

So, we go from the impressive interiors which have height and scale and (in the case of the extraordinary Panopticon set) sturdy steps for the Doctor to leap up and down, onto a location that's open, dusty and chalky. With the volume turned up to 11, every chink of rock sounds like it's digging into our under-protected hero's arms and legs. Baker's tough, gritty Doctor is the only one I can imagine with the physicality to roll about like this – Pertwee had the flamboyance to somersault people over his shoulder, but he was never quite so earthy. These outside scenes are superbly realised, and having spent the first episode praising Holmes, I've allowed director David Maloney to work away with quiet brilliance. He augments talky scenes with the doodling of caricatures, and orchestrates the briefest of shots to be visually arresting, such as the one featuring a lolloping World War I soldier complete with a ghoulishly masked horse. I suspect I may talk more about him on next week's episode – in targeting the source of this story's triumph, I've got both the writer and director firmly in my sights.

The Deadly Assassin (part three)

R: Utterly extraordinary. Watching this, it seems amazing that the production office thought they could get away with passing this off as Saturday afternoon family entertainment. Mary Whitehouse's famous attack upon the "strangled, drowning Doctor" cliffhanger would mark yet another reason why The

255

Deadly Assassin is a (pardon the phrasing) watermark Doctor Who story – never again would the levels of psychological horror on view here be allowed. And this is horror, make no mistake – I'm just surprised that it was the drowning which upset Whitehouse, rather than the blow-dart sequence, or the rigged grenade.

David Maloney directs this nightmare episode superbly – but it is his restraint that makes this so remarkable. The fantasy imagery is very quickly put aside, to be replaced by an utterly logical game of cat and mouse as two men hunt each other to the death. It's as simple as that. There are some very unsettling moments of surrealism – the Doctor stumbling into a large egg, or sitting in front of a giant spider's web – but they work precisely because they do not attempt to replace the much more brutal threats of bullets and bombs. (The Trial of a Time Lord's later attempt to replicate the impact of this episode misses that point entirely, which is why it so quickly bores – there's a very thin line in The Deadly Assassin between horror and pretension, and Maloney never gets it wrong.) Dudley Simpson too is to be commended – his music commands a lot of the atmosphere of this mostly talk-free instalment. And Tom Baker and his opponent, Bernard Horsfall (as Chancellor Goth), both succeed in making this story's location shoot look like just about the most painful time two actors could have had. It's a small point, I know, but I love the way they just become more wounded and desperate and dirtier as the episode progresses. Last week, Spandrell told the Doctor that if he had a feud with the Master, he should take it off Gallifrey – which gave a wonderful buzz of Wild West showdown to the story. In all its stark brutality, this has that arid Wild West flavour to it – and that shot of the Doctor, thin blowpipe in mouth waiting for his prey, makes him look every inch like Clint Eastwood chewing on a cigarillo.

The little subplot on Gallifrey involving a hypnotised guard is a bit unnecessary, but that's quibbling. The scenes between Spandrell and Engin are important to remind the audience of the purpose of all this weird quarry footage. (And I do love the way – when the camera moves in for close-up on the guard's face – that in his hypnotised unblinking state, his eyes glassy and wide open do recall the fixed glare of the Master.) And the revelation, 19 minutes into the episode, that the Doctor has been in the Matrix for only four minutes, is a real shock. Is this the first example in the series of an episode being told in compressed time?

T: This absolutely shouldn't work. The plot barely advances! Almost nothing that happens is "real", and rather than being the surrealist nightmare of repute, most of this episode is a brutally physical confrontation with old-fashioned weapons and deadly terrain. It's closer to Captain Kirk and the Gorn man-handling one another than it is to The Mind Robber, yet it's compelling. Robert Holmes and Philip Hinchcliffe must have been *desperate* for David Maloney to direct this – in lesser hands, this would have been a mere diversion. In his, it's a gutsy action piece that papers over its implausibilities with brio.

You've mentioned most of the surrealist touches, bar that haunting, perverse moment where the clown face is reflected in the glass under the sand, and emits a pitch-perfect mocking laugh. Such simplicity, such power. Also, using a World War I plane seems so much more effective than a more modern – and therefore more deadly – device. Somehow, this more primitive killing machine has an undercurrent of horror and adventure that a sleek, modern fighter plane wouldn't. And, by golly, this contest is so unflinching – I adore little touches such as Goth having to tear his trousers open and inject his horribly wealed leg to counteract the Doctor's poison dart, and Tom Baker's grim, tough demeanour throughout. We've never had as physically powerful a Doctor as this – look how our hero effortlessly climbs a tree and then crashes out of it when shot. Even the blood is proper blood colour; no Ribena on display here.

Oh, and I don't know if the fauna has been dressed, or if it's simply the weather and clever filming that gives some corner of England/ the Matrix such an oppressive, sweaty, tropical ambience when the Doctor goes looking for water, but it complements and contrasts with the stark, dusty, sun-exposed quarry where the battle commences. And check out Maloney panning from the computer room down to the catacombs using blur and a descending camera. He may not succeed in successfully aping Citizen Kane, but so what? At least he's tried.

I know I'm blathering a bit, but this is *such* an extremely well-made piece of television, it just goes to show that even sequences that barely serve the plot can still be thrilling, tense pieces of escapism.

July 28th

The Deadly Assassin (part four)

R: This is an episode that probably works better in retrospect. In context, the Master's plot reveals itself to be centred around things like the Eye of Harmony and the Sash of Rassilon, and other bits of mythology suddenly grafted on to a story over three quarters of the way through the running time. When you realise that the entire motivation for the villain is to circumvent a biological anomaly that's only first mentioned by Coordinator Engin this late in the story, it's hard not to feel slightly cheated, I think. As a means of defining what has been going on over the last three weeks, that is awkward and confusing, and very much suggests that Holmes was making it all up as he went along. But – and it's a very big but – the later efforts of producers Graham Williams and John Nathan-Turner make those bits of mythology seem solid and credible, and it's easy to forget now we watch this as seasoned fans that it's all been revealed out of left field. But just imagine what this might have felt like if, at the end of the following season, Williams hadn't returned to Gallifrey and cemented it all. Without Romana as a companion, without the Black and White Guardians to give this new grand mythology a new context, the conclusion to The Deadly Assassin would just be cryptic mumbo-jumbo.

The last ten minutes get somewhat unstuck – too much messy tumbling around the studio floor, too much mumbled dialogue – but before that Holmes convinces us to take this new mythology on trust by (once again) changing the expected structure of the adventure. It all appears to be done and dusted within the first few minutes – and, straight after The Hand of Fear, which ended its story

ten minutes early, and after The Masque of Mandragora, which bumped off its lead villain at the end of episode three, you can almost believe we've already had the climax. Hearing all these revelations about Gallifrey feel not so much as too-delayed exposition, but as a special dessert given us as reward for polishing off the main course so early. Rassilon is mentioned for the first time! The twelve regeneration rule!

What's surprising in retrospect is that Holmes makes these totems of Time Lord history not the simple public knowledge of the John Nathan-Turner years, but real mysteries. It is the Doctor who deciphers the cryptic myths of Rassilon to Spandrell and Engin, and reveals that the Eye of Harmony is not just a legend. And so what's clever about this episode is that, in largely being concerned with history and the interpretation of history, it also accidentally sets up the "history" of the Doctor Who programme for the next 20 years plus. (Looking through all the proposals for the 1996 TV movie, it's striking how all of them are inspired by the rough bits of Time Lord folklore Robert Holmes created here.) History, Holmes shows us, is a moveable feast. It is the Time Lords' refusal to see their own history as anything more than irrelevant stories that blinds them to the real power of the Eye of Harmony, and how the Master plans to exploit it to their own ends. The Sash of Rassilon is not just a symbol, it is a marvel of electrical engineering. And Borusa cynically demonstrates how history must be altered when facts are not concordant with what society deems to be helpful. The reconstruction of Chancellor Goth as hero is fascinating; the need for the Doctor to provide a description for the presumed dead Master, so that the Time Lords can have something to revile, smacks of the bureaucracy that prompted the Doctor to leave in the first place. I love the euphemisms here: the way that Commander Hilred is required not to mutilate the Master's corpse, but to "restructure" it. We don't call these things lies, the tools by which bureaucracy maintains the status quo.

Doctor Who has been restructured. We just haven't realised it yet.

T: First The Hand of Fear, now this: two stories made up of episodes that seem only tangentially related to each other. Few of the characters in The Deadly Assassin appear in all four episodes, and even one who does, Goth, is now dispatched by the script as mercilessly as he is by his Master. We've gone from political thriller in episodes one and two, to surrealist Western in episode three, to this bizarre mixture of mad sci-fi and cynical satire.

I've become so acutely aware of the distinctions between Peter Pratt's brilliantly accoutred Master and that of Roger Delgado. The latter was charmingly amoral, and suave in his villainy – but robbed of his good looks and physical presence, the character's black, evil nature is exposed. As the Doctor states, he'd "delay an execution to pull the wings off a fly". All right, this might explain away some of his Delgado incarnation's rather elaborate plots, but it also highlights a more sadistic nature than the Master exhibited during the Pertwee era. Despite Pratt's excellent vocals and cruel, mummified visage, he doesn't quite ascend beyond monster-of-the-week status, as he attempts to wrangle lines such as "or you'll get the same" and "They're not dead. Stunned". (I think that deep down, Robert Holmes is more interested in a witty denouement with a Machiavellian Cardinal than a dramatic showdown between two old enemies.)

And while this certainly isn't the first script to be hampered by rather convenient resolutions, Holmes is too good a conjurer for these to hit us immediately. The world he's created is so well drawn, the unlikely plot strands are introduced through some choice character interaction – so if we don't look too hard, we can let them go. Yes, it seems insane that the Time Lords have spent centuries unaware of the purpose behind their prize relics, while it takes the Doctor about half a minute to work it out... but isn't that the point? These pompous, self-satisfied hypocrites think themselves gods pledged to protect lesser species, but are so concerned with pomp and appearance that they fail to register the importance of what's under their very noses. They don't even know anything *about the Master*, until it becomes convenient to create a figure of hate to boost public morale. If you can look upon this through Holmes' intended satirical intent, the so-called implausibilities begin to make a certain amount of sense.

Elsewhere, Tom Baker's amused, polite impatience as Erik Chitty's Engin prattles on is wonderful. Baker can be a self-indulgent performer sometimes, but he clearly relishes this amiably eccentric sparring partner, and affords him a touching respect. (The way in which he delivers the line "Oh, goodbye, Engin, goodbye" shows some clear affection.) He's less forgiving elsewhere, though – Goth's deathbed cry for redemption falls on deaf ears, and is greeted with the Doctor's "No answer to a straight question. Typical politician". This Doctor may be flamboyant and eccentric, but you can tell he knows what the salt of the earth tastes like.

And has there ever been a better line than "Doctor, you will never amount to anything in the galaxy while you retain your propensity for vulgar facetiousness"? "Nine out of ten", says Cardinal Borusa when summing up. If he were scoring this story, I'd think that might be a bit on the harsh side.

The Face of Evil (part one)

R: In The Runaway Bride, Donna will tell the Doctor that he needs to find a new travelling companion. She tells him he needs someone who can rein him in. She might have gone on to say that having a person to chat to once in a while might be pretty good as well, because the sudden illustration of him here talking directly to camera is very disconcerting.

So, thank heaven for Louise Jameson. Within her very first scene, she gets to be both outspoken and compassionate; then, when hearing evidence of her father's death, she shows a mature dignity. By the episode's end, she'll have confronted a folklore devil (and survived the ordeal), braved invisible monsters, rescued the Doctor (which makes a nice change) and murdered three people. I already adore Leela. Everything about her on paper screams sexism of the most flagrant order – she's a young woman wearing skins, for goodness' sake – but because Jameson plays her with such questing intelligence, you barely stop to worry about it. Later stories will lazily portray Leela as a primitive savage, and as such someone who's borderline moronic. But she's a character who not only has the curiosity to question the tenets of her own civilisation, but upon meeting the Doctor (and getting evidence of the Evil One) has the intellectualism to question those objections. And because Louise Jameson from the word *go* clearly never doubts Leela's bravery or raw wisdom, nor do we. She's a far cry from Lis Sladen's sophisticated journalist (who was ultimately a little girl in an Andy Pandy costume): in the scene in which Leela's friend Tomas tries to save her from banishment, she speaks to him with all the firm authority that makes him seem the one who's a child.

And it's not just Louise Jameson's debut. Chris Boucher is only the second new writer to have brought a script to the screen since 1971 – and, at first glance, what he offers feels somewhat familiar. Invisible monsters in a jungle (like Planet of Evil), religious zealots with their chantings and litanies (like The Masque of Mandragora); my God, even the background sound effects of distant animals have been used since the days of Hartnell! But all the clichés are in place only so that Boucher can subvert them. The high priest isn't just preying upon the gullible, but genuinely does communicate with his god – and that's a shocking scene, all the more effective because the god in question sounds remarkably like Tom Baker. And because it comes on the back of scenes in which the Doctor is much more avowedly agnostic than we're used to – dismissing the rituals roundly as gobbledegook, and assuring Leela that doubt is superior to faith – it sets us up for a dialogue about religion that is much more thoughtful than we've seen before. There are blander stories out there that would use as a final twist revelations about the tribe's reliance upon space technology – here we get them all laid out blatantly in episode one, and the implicit promise that there are more puzzles to be solved.

And the Doctor gets to threaten a warrior with a deadly jelly baby. (Tom Baker's propensity for jelly babies have barely been used in the series yet; is it too much to assume that it's this scene that makes them famous?) Were this simply an example of the Doctor's comic shtick, it would be fun enough; what makes it so memorable is the response of the warrior's friend: "Kill him then." They're not as daft as you might think, these savages.

T: Prior to this exercise of ours, if you'd asked me which Hinchcliffe-Holmes adventure was most underrated, I'd have said Sarah's swan song. If this episode is anything to go by, however, I think we'd better talk to The Face of Evil, because The Hand of Fear ain't listening. The Doctor says, during one of the most original and intriguing episode endings we've yet witnessed – in which he confronts his own face, carved into the rock of a mountain – that "I must have made quite an impression". Well, he's not alone, as pretty much everyone in front of and behind the camera does the same.

Key to this story's success is that it refuses to stereotype the Sevateem as grunting imbeciles – whilst these savages wear skins and believe in gods and monsters, that doesn't mean every aspect of their personality is stupid or credulous. You're right in that the way in which Lugo – the warrior whom the Doctor threatens with Death by Jelly Baby – calls the Doctor's bluff and thereby subverts our expectations; he shows more intelligence than we might have credited him with. On the other hand, giving the Sevateem RP drama-school diction might have run the risk of being so incongruous, it would be impossible to take any of this seriously – but the tone here is *perfect*. Chris Boucher shapes the Sevateem into such a fully formed society, everyone we see has an agenda, and the relationships are complex before the Doctor wanders onto the scene. Andor's face-offs with Tomas, for instance, proves he's not merely a credulous figurehead, but a skilled operator in the almost impossible position of having to placate his god and look out for his people.

Really, every protagonist is so well drawn and played – including Colin Thomas as Sole, who makes such a mark even though he's given barely a minute's screen time and half a dozen lines. As the shaman Neeva, David Garfield really throws himself into a religious fervour as he dances around the Doctor wailing nonsense litanies. (It's his only option, really – if you're made to prance around uttering lines such as "See how it fears the sacred relics of Xoanon!", being self-conscious is only going to provoke embarrassment. Of course Neeva looks silly, that's the point: it's the *character* we laugh at, not an actor failing to pull off a difficult bit of business.) And Victor Lucas cleverly gives the impression that Andor rejects the Doctor's claims not from the uncomprehending vantage of a savage, but rather because he fears consequences of the Doctor's words being true.

We've seen more flashy and arresting stories before now, but this is a *quietly* impressive piece of work. And a word for Pennant Roberts – often dismissed as the inept director behind atrocities such as Timelash and Warriors of the Deep, he orchestrates the action here superbly. I'd never had this down as a production with a high-film quotient, but most of the scenes in that fantastic, dusky, alien jungle are brilliantly staged (with ominous growls augmenting that welcome returning soundscape from the 60s Jungle Noise Library), replete with shuddering, powerful footprints made by invisible creatures, and their fantastic, seemingly impossible destruction of the alarm clock. Roberts was also instrumental in casting the stunning, subtle, fiery, intelligent and bold Louise Jameson, which should never be underestimated. *What* a debut for her.

And you can tell Leela's smart: when offered a jelly baby, she takes the black one. They're always the nicest.

July 29th

The Face of Evil (part two)

R: In episode one, Leela told Tomas (and by extension, we the audience) to watch out for Calib. That was good advice.

Doctor Who is an action-adventure serial, and it works by hitting the ground running and throwing at the viewer immediate and easily definable scenes of jeopardy and conflict. If the Doctor meets a new society, the writer needs to present the people in that society in clear brushstrokes we can understand before they can be placed at threat. Almost anything away from modern-day Earth (which comes as something ready identifiable) conforms to this. And the stories usually make this clear by dividing the new characters into factions, in some opposition to each other. The Brain of Morbius: Solon/ Condo against the Sisterhood of Karn. The Masque of Mandragora: Giuliano/ Marco against Federico/ Hieronymous. A clev-

er writer will play with the formula sometimes, keep you guessing, so that it takes until episode two of The Deadly Assassin for us to realise that the factions are Spandrell/ Engin against Goth/ the Time Lord hierarchy. But eventually we end up in a situation where there is a "goodie" faction opposed to a "baddie" faction, and the Doctor sides with the goodies. Goodie characters may initially be hostile towards the Doctor, but once he relieves their suspicions, they accept him entirely. (From Vishinsky in Planet of Evil to Professor Watson in The Hand of Fear, Doctor Who is full of them. When I was a kid watching episode one of Earthshock, my mum went out to the kitchen to make herself a cup of coffee. When she left, Scott and his troopers all had the Doctor at gunpoint. By the time she came back, they were friends with him. My Mum said, "Oh, that's nice, they've become the goodies now". We didn't need them to be a threat any more, not now we had the Cybermen on screen.)

I'm not criticising Doctor Who for this, by the way. It's simplistic, but broadly speaking it's necessary. And The Face of Evil starts in a similar way. We see a council meeting. Leela is being punished, basically, for being clever. Tomas takes her side. (He'll be part of the goodie faction.) And Andor and Neeva oppose her. (They'll be baddies then.)

And then there's Calib.

Characters like Calib barely exist in Doctor Who, because there's no use for them. They barely offer a plot function. Calib is confusing, because he refuses to be part of either faction. When Leela suggests that he will believe the Doctor is not the Evil One, she is also suggesting that he will join our side and become someone we can sympathise with. He does believe her. He also stabs her with a Janis thorn. The Doctor immediately assumes that Calib must be part of the opposing faction, then, and be a baddie – he understands perfectly well the format of his own television programme! – but Calib is nothing of the sort. He's a political opportunist. Any character that defies easy categorisation, and stands apart from the "tribe" (quite literally in this adventure) is being set up as major hero (like new companion Leela) or main villain. But Calib is something new, and quite radical, for Doctor

Who: he is a decidedly minor character who also has enough depth and personal insight that he doesn't fit in properly with the story.

It seems like exaggeration, I know, but look at that scene again. Look how startling it is. Pennant Roberts chooses not to melodramatise the moment where Calib shows his true nature; the Doctor and Leela have already become complacent around him, clearly accepting the traditional character arc he's suggested, and we the audience have grown complacent too. So the stabbing with the thorn is totally unexpected. It leaves the Doctor bemused, and ought to leave us bemused too; Calib isn't behaving like a bit-part player in Xoanon's drama, because no one has told him he has to be a bit-part player. His own agenda is wonderfully Machiavellian, and surprisingly adult. He happens to be a politician.

In the last episode of The Deadly Assassin, trying to get information from the dying Goth, the Doctor makes a joke about politicians. It's a funny joke, too, that politicians never give a straight answer – that, in fact, they're pompous old windbags. Look at all the men from the ministry and Government puppets that pop up through the Pertwee run – there's not an intelligent one amongst them! Calib is a politician, but he's a real-life politician, not a silly Doctor Who one – and in the story he represents cool intellectualism fighting against unthinking religious fervour. In your average story, the Doctor would be on the side of the intellectuals – but here, in one delightful scene, the Doctor parallels the debate between Calib and Neeva to a tennis match, with both sides trying to interpret the meaning behind his execution. They'll both kill him, of course. But let's see who scores the most points in the debate first.

Chris Boucher's brilliance is that he can't condone Calib, but he respects him; he won't demonise him and turn him into a trite baddie. Calib never apologises for being who he is, and never simplifies himself. I'm not suggesting that Boucher invented the wheel here – the characterisation of Calib is the sort of thing we expect habitually from "proper drama" – but in Doctor Who, it's very fresh and new and challenging. There's a subtlety to him you just don't get from action-adventure serials like this. And what makes him remarkable is that the story ultimately refuses to make him

remarkable; it doesn't suddenly put him at the centre of the drama, it doesn't give him a self-sacrificial death to save the day. He stands out, strangely, obliquely, and by doing so represents all the other characters who don't stand out, because there isn't the time to give them lines or budget to hire other speaking actors. Watch out for Calib, Leela advised us – and quite right too; it's in the Calibs that worlds of depth are hinted at.

T: There are some impressively brave ideas going on here – and once more, it's instructive to look at David Garfield as Neeva. With the wide-eyed fire of a zealot, he strides around unashamedly, being taken utterly seriously by everyone despite his wearing a glove on his head. Those inclined to watch Doctor Who tongue in their cheek would no doubt laugh with scorn at this silly image, as if the production team had done it by mistake, or out of desperation because the money had run out. But the ludicrousness is the point. The Pope wears a dress, for goodness' sake.

Pennant Roberts once again does terrific work (highlights include the scenes with the excellently realised, ravenous Horda, and a marvellous mounted shot looking down at Neeva praying in a relatively large jungle clearing), but despite his best efforts, the script is the star here. If it was cheeky last week, it now, admirably, indulges in full-on impudence and intellectually stimulating satire. (Leela, not unreasonably, asks why anyone would pray if they didn't hear a reply, whereupon the Doctor points her in the direction of "any number of theologians".) Fortunately, Chris Boucher once again refuses to undermine the Sevateem by painting them as witless savages – Andor's observation that Xoanon has promised Neeva victory, and that Neeva has in turn promised it to the Sevateem, shows the fragile power dynamics in any society involving political and religious hierarchies.

And it's easy to see why anyone could mistake Tom Baker for an omnipotent being – there's his booming voice and the quiet intensity of his threats to Calib (Leslie Schofield – excellent), to whom he spits out the insult "rattlesnake" with appropriate venom. At other times, Baker's comedy is magical, as when Leela (understandably) suggests climbing up the nose of the Doctor's rock-face, and, a bit affronted, he airs his preference to traverse "over the teeth and down the throat". I'm less comfortable with the glib way in which the Doctor flicks a vicious and potentially deadly Horda onto the sadistic guard's shoulder – but as we see his victim alive later on, I'll forgive it.

Incidentally, said guard is played by Brett Forrest, who was a star of musical theatre in his heyday, but cut rather a sorry figure in a documentary I saw about the fickleness of fame, as he plodded around to mass auditions whilst contemporaries with whom he once topped the bill – like Elaine Paige – were doing rather better. It would appear that no matter how big an impression you make, even if you get your name in lights – or, say, your face cast in stone – it can still end in disaster. Think on.

The Face of Evil (part three)

R: Imagine it. You're 12 years old. And one day, in class, your schoolteacher reveals something extraordinary, even otherworldly, about herself. Mrs Roberts is married to a television director – his job is to be in charge of all those stories you see on the screen! And he's currently at work on your Saturday teatime favourite. He's making a Doctor Who!

And you get to go with her, as a special treat, to watch it being made. And to meet the Doctor himself! (There's no Sarah Jane, don't know where she's gone, but the new girl is very pretty, you will soon forget about Sarah!) And the treat just gets better. How would you like to be in Doctor Who as well? No, really! It's okay. Just talk into this microphone here. Don't be shy. Say "Who am I?" Do it again. Louder. Faster. Insaner! Give it more welly!

Lucky Anthony Frieze. And it's so typical of a show like Doctor Who, that when a schoolboy does win the opportunity to go and take a small part in the drama, that it isn't a nice and cosy scene. It's nothing reassuring. It makes up one of the best cliffhangers the series has ever shown: the Doctor crumpled on the floor in pain and confusion, as all around him giant images of his own face scream out their own schizophrenia to him in the voice of a little child.

Nothing so good happened to me when I was 12. The closest I got was when my French teacher, Mrs Fox, told me one day (as the resident class Who expert) that she'd just met at a dinner party a man who'd written for my favourite show! I was so excited. I asked her what his name was. She told me. I didn't recognise it. I told her she'd made a mistake. She was a little annoyed at this. I told her that either she'd made a mistake, or the man at the dinner party was a filthy liar. She got cross. She threatened me with detention.

A couple of days later, she told me that she'd spoken once more to the man she'd met. And asked him in greater detail about the Doctor Who job he'd been so proudly talking about over cocktails. And she said he'd been a bit embarrassed – that he'd then admitted his script had had problems, he'd been sacked from the show, his story had been rewritten by someone else and stuck out under a pseudonym. He said he'd wished he'd never brought it up at the party in the first place, but really, what harm had he done?

I admit, this has nothing to do with The Face of Evil. But I feel appalled for Lewis Greifer now, and the way all the hard knocks he took on Pyramids of Mars were only echoed years later by a little schoolboy who reminded him of his failure. I wonder whether, when he went home that night, he curled up in a foetal position like Tom Baker did, and cried out, "Who am I?"

(Probably not.)

T: Chris Boucher clearly has this series nailed. He *has* to, given how much the script needs to convey: the majority of the battle and the business with the anti-grav transporter go unseen, whilst the concept of a computer accidentally downloading *everything* – not just the necessary upgrades – is both plausible scientifically and original in storytelling terms. And I don't think you'd get ideas such as Neeva being the only person who sees the truth because he's mad, or lines about an "experiment in eugenics," in your average children's drama (unless I missed Grange Hill that week).

The Sevateem take more of a back seat this week, though when we do see them, Leslie Schofield's Caleb and Brendan Price's Tomas really sell us on the epic nature of the largely unseen battle. Tomas keeps coming off as the solid, dependable, progressive member of the tribe... and then we're reminded of the Sevateem's feral side, when he deftly dispatches a Tesh with a knife to the heart. The Tesh themselves are fascinating, largely thanks to Leon Eagles as the elder Jabel, who switches from enigmatic deference to chilling intensity with consummate ease. The thump he does when he loses his cool in private doesn't quite work, but his quiet dignity is effectively disconcerting in his scenes with Baker.

And I can't help but contrast the cliffhangers in play here... last week, Tomas joined Professor Watson in the hallowed Supporting Character Endangered by the Cliffhanger Hall of Fame. This week, Leela's gun running out of zap against the super-mad Xoanon would do nicely... but that's not the end point we get, and instead we climax on one of the most extraordinary cliffhangers in the show's history, as the Doctor falls before Xoanon's psychological onslaught. Doctor Who is definitely enjoying something of a honeymoon period at the moment – which, seeing as I'm typing this on the plane to Venice as Mr and Mrs Hadoke embark upon theirs, is entirely appropriate.

Who Am I? The luckiest man alive, mate, that's who.

July 30th

The Face of Evil (part four)

R: The most striking thing about the story, I think, is that it ends not with a bloodbath, but with forgiveness. And it's wonderful that after so many adventures last season that pivoted upon the Doctor telling assorted people to take responsibility for their actions, here he has to put his money where his mouth is. That his struggles to cure Xoanon leave him unconscious for two days – two days! – seems entirely justified. He's always exerting some mental effort or another, and getting himself left for dead. Here he's had to face up to his own egotism, and his own errors, and that's bound to leave Tom looking the worse for wear.

I love the Hinchcliffe years of Doctor Who for their shocks and scares, but there's an innate predictability to most of them, the little boy's desire to be cruel. The Face of Evil is

something so entirely different; it's a thoughtful take on faith, not only in higher powers, but in ourselves. The moment that Tomas says so dismissively – on seeing that there's some truth in the legends they've learned as litany – that with proof you don't need faith, I celebrate the triumph of intellectual thought over superstition. But I also feel sad a little for the loss of innocence; there's something so cold in that statement. When Neeva at last confronts his once-adored god, pointing at him with a big gun, there's a quirkiness to the situation that almost feels surreal – like the Archbishop of Canterbury confronting Jesus and trying to take him out with a pistol. The entire sequence looks bizarre – both Neeva and Xoanon with their mouths open wide in exaggerated shock; it seems as if one is mimicking the other, but you can't tell which is which.

And, best of all, there's that scene where Xoanon offers a big shiny red self-destruct button for everyone to press. It reminds me of the similar offer made by Davros in Genesis of the Daleks to the Kaled rebels – the button just as red and shiny and self-destructive. But there, when no one rises to the challenge, it proves to Davros how weak and spiritless his enemies really are, and with contempt he dooms them to death. Here, though, the refusal to press the button – and to take just retribution for generations of eugenic experimentation – is celebrated as something noble, a triumph of optimism. It's a measure of just how differently this story wants to do things. And just one reason why The Face of Evil, which never lets its cleverness get in the way of its heart, is the best script we've yet seen given to Tom Baker's Doctor.

Leela's wonderful too, isn't she? In the first episode, she shows courage and faith in accepting the offer of a sweet from the Doctor. In the final episode, it's with a sweet that she revives him. It's a magical moment. And Louise Jameson plays that final scene to perfection, stealing aboard the TARDIS because the Doctor has taught her that the instincts we saw in episode one were right, that she should question the world about her, that the world is a bigger place than can be held in any one philosophy. No companion has earned her place in the series more.

I couldn't be happier anywhere in the world

right now than in front of my Face of Evil DVD. Hmm. So. How's Venice?

T: Well, Venice is warm and beautiful and we're having a lovely time. K is having a siesta, so I've availed myself of a balmy early evening on our bed in Hotel Flora (a hotel low in poly-unsaturates?) to load up the next couple of episodes. Yet again, I notice that the episode reprise is slightly re-edited (as is the case throughout this adventure), and the fact that *this* is what gets my attention when it's sunny, stunning and, um, *my honeymoon* strikes me as somewhat surreal. (Oh well, you can take the Doctor Who fan out of his anorak, but...)

It has to be said: The Face of Evil is to religion what The Sun Makers is to taxes, and is probably more relevant now than when it was first written. You rightly highlight the "with proof you don't have to believe" line, but there's also the Doctor telling Leela, "You know, the very powerful and very stupid have one thing in common – they don't alter their views to fit the facts, they alter the facts to fit their views". It's probably my favourite line in the entire series, and demonstrates how Chris Boucher's mix of caustic wit and well-conceived sci-fi ideas make him as natural a fit for Doctor Who as his mentor Robert Holmes. Boucher also tells stories through character, and, of course, the entire society seen here is built around a deliberate schism: the Tesh and Sevateem only come together when under Xoanon's mental thrall, whereupon they immediately become zombies. And there's a nice character moment for even the most peripheral player – when "little Gentek" (as Tom Baker, surely ad libbing, refers to him) starts to panic, and his superior calmly warns of the need to remain uninfluenced by emotion.

And let me give a shout-out to the very well-orchestrated sound in this episode, especially that scene where the intense, betrayed evangelist Neeva tips over into his final stage of insanity, confronts his god and dies in an instant. First, we hear Neeva's outraged, defiant scream echoing from the distant end of the corridor as he charges into shot, then Baker's Xoanon utters his acolyte's name first as a fearful whisper – and then a terrified bellow – as Neeva is zapped. As Xoanon's Doctor-face recedes, the

final scream echoes around. And then, there is silence. It's very effective.

Unfortunately, what follows is a rather long, and trifle too cosy, coda which provides all the necessary explanations, but isn't hugely gripping. There remains a sting in the tale, though, as the various characters are left *far* from co-operating – but I have to wonder if this low-key denouement helps to explain this serial's so-so reputation. It's a shame, because I've been really impressed by this adventure – it's not quite as familiar as much that surrounds it, but it was a hugely pleasant surprise for me, and one of the most rewarding revisits thus far on our quest.

The Robots of Death (part one)

R: The script is so good it looks easy. It's lovely to see that on the heels of the most cerebral Doctor Who script for years, Chris Boucher is so adept at creating one of the derivative parody shockers the Hinchcliffe era is so famous for. This is an Agatha Christie-style murder mystery in a science-fiction setting (and, beautifully, not a spaceship, but somewhere far more imaginative than that). The trick to a good Christie mystery is that the audience has to believe two essentially contradictory things at the same time: that each of the characters is identifiable enough that we care whether they live or die, and recognise them as having distinct personalities – and that we also have to accept that any one of them could credibly not only be a sympathetic victim, but also a psychopathic murderer. It's an especially hard tightrope to walk.

And the reason why Boucher is exactly the right man to walk it is that he has a gift for ambiguous characterisation. Remember what I said about Calib in The Face of Evil? The sandminer is staffed by a whole gamut of Calibs – people who, so rarely for Doctor Who, refuse to fall into the easy category of "goodie" or "baddie". Russell Hunter's Commander Uvanov is a bully and a braggart, but he's also identifiably human; David Collings' Poul shows all the traits of being an understanding and sympathetic character, but he's also prepared to crack jokes over dead bodies. Boucher achieves that sense of depth the characterisation so greatly needs by his use of black comedy. These people are stuck in each other's company for two years without a break, and they are bored, and they are complacent, and they have found that balance all office workers need between blatantly despising their colleagues and working alongside them professionally. Chub's death shocks them out of their routine – it gives them a bit of an adrenalin rush, and something new to talk about. But no one actually liked him very much, and you get the feeling early on that had this murder been an isolated incident, it'd have been used simply as a conversation topic over the water cooler. Especially seeing how a couple of stowaways have conveniently shown up as ready made scapegoats.

It's all so cleverly and horribly real. These people aren't evil, but they're greedy, and they've compromised themselves. They spend their time between bouts of mining in deadly dull luxury, drinking and playing games and being massaged, and getting on each other's nerves. When they go to work, they put on ridiculously fancy headdresses so that they look less like miners and more like partygoers.

It works because Boucher hasn't just created a simple setting in which he can plonk down the Doctor and Leela and kick off the action – but an entire new world. That this is a sand-miner and not a spaceship is brilliantly smart: if it were just another adventure taking place in the stars, we'd already take all the clichés as read, but because Boucher is forced to make the Doctor explore it and explain its principles from the ground up, he leads us to believe that it's all so much more fresh than it really is. And, again, it's through the use of humour that the society is credible – we believe in Kaldor City, ironically, because of a dubious anecdote about the place that is most likely told simply to annoy Borg. We believe in the maintenance of the robots, because the deactivation discs placed upon them to indicate the ones out of service have been nicknamed "corpse markers".

And as for the robots... has any "monster" on Doctor Who ever been more beautiful than this? With their coiffed heads and their blemishless faces, all carved into permanent expressions of servile attentiveness, they look thoroughly benign. Which, of course, makes them so much more disturbing. It's so clever that Leela is the companion who gets to meet them,

as this story is all about the body language (and lack of it) that she relies upon as a huntress, and that is denied her here.

T: I took The Robots of Death for granted. My first exposure to it – the Target book – was especially slim, and I polished it off fairly quickly. It contained the first blooper I ever spotted solo, when "the tall, lean" Cass was listed among the characters lounging in a scene *after* he's been killed. That aside, in Terrance Dicks' very pithy transcription of this tale, the kicks came from finding out which character died when and the identity of the traitor – you know, the usual Agatha Christie-type stuff. Only when I saw the story, years later, did all those things I hadn't expected, or hadn't pictured, leap out: the opulent but plausible design, the interplay between the excellently cast characters, and the sheer wit and caustic brio of Boucher's dialogue. And funnily enough, the murder-mystery element of this – the selling point, if you like – became this story's least important element.

I also, like you, utterly believe in this society – even aspects such as the crew's slightly OTT make-up work within the context of this pampered, decadent bunch being used to finery and opulence in the workplace. The world may be overblown, but the people in it couldn't be more real. In the bridge scenes, there's scope for Uvanov to josh pleasantly with Toos, whilst Zilda reads off scanner information and Poul casually nips out to see what's keeping Chub. The words Chris Boucher gives them to say overlap – and some are technobabble – and yet they dance about our ears lending credibility, pace, character and atmosphere with deceptive simplicity. The actors help, too. Russell Hunter, totally unrecognisable from the role of Lonely in Callan – from which most contemporary viewers would know him – is fantastic as Uvanov. He's hard and professional when told about Chub's death but, when examining the body, believably exhibits distaste as well as irritation. And the cliché of the worst actor dying first is broken when Rob Edwards makes a great account for himself as the impatient, aloof Chub, refusing to play the melodrama until the robot's hands are actually round his throat. I've seen him do a lot of good Shakespearian work since, and am glad he's had an impressive career after making the most of his cameo here.

Finally, a word for Michael Briant's sympathetic direction. Toos, Uvanov and Borg all touch the corpse marker when it's introduced, but when it's *named*, the former two flinch away instinctively, and transfer ownership to the big man, who then jokily marks Cass for death. It's a subtle, effective moment, as are those when the robots are given a menacing musical accompaniment – even though they're not, at this point, of murderous intent, but are just doing their jobs. The line about the sandminer being under robot control is, in context, totally innocuous, but the director knows that it's potentially ominous news should the plot take the turn the viewer reasonably would expect, considering the story's title. In cheating this scene, and having Dudley Simpson score it like it's a portent of doom, Briant keeps the tension to a maximum at every opportunity. We've hit another rich seam with this one, I think.

July 31st

The Robots of Death (part two)

R: We've seen before stories that have had human characters contrasted with something mechanical. Of course we have. It's a staple of the series, from the Daleks onwards! But no one has ever before made that contrast so telling. As the sandminer crew become ever-more paranoid, flinging around accusations at each other, the robots stand beside them expressionless, their voices still pitched in tones of reasoned enquiry. Humans are dangerous and unpredictable, and (as the Doctor points out) especially when frightened; the scene in which the Doctor and Leela are interrogated is particularly brilliant, because for once you almost feel sorry for the thugs so desperately wanting to believe our heroes are guilty – the alternative for them would be unbearable. And the robots cannot help but sound superior in comparison, because they don't give into hysteria. Look at the scene where the sandminer is on the point of blowing up: the crew are screaming at full cliffhanger level, and the robots seem more like mature adults, reciting the

readings that foretell their own destruction with such level-headed precision.

The contrast sounds obvious – but obvious as it is, Doctor Who has never before tried to look at the primal alienation between humans and alien humanoids, instead always glorying in the exotic as if that's enough. And that's why here the robots are like "mechanical dead men", and so very eerie – the humans are surrounded by things that look human, and sound human, but subtly just miss the mark of behaving human. The scene where Leela is confronted suddenly by D84 is quite masterful – and the shock when the robot behaves in a human way, and puts his hand over her mouth, and reasons with her, is terrific. (And don't you just love the way that, within seconds, we jump cut to that image of Leela as cavegirl savage behaving like a business executive, swinging around in a swivel chair? If the robot is pretending to be a sophisticated human, then so too is Leela.)

T: It's very telling how Leela handles herself in this episode... when Uvanov enters the scene and gives her a slap, her responding kick to his goolies and threat to cripple the man if he tries it again are miles away from what any companion has been capable of before. Louise Jameson gives a heartfelt, gutsy and venomous delivery of her threat, and shows that her knife isn't the only sharp thing about her when she questions Uvanov about whether D84 can talk. And she's aided somewhat by Poul, whom we know isn't the bad guy because we get a moment alone with him, but remains a shifty presence. David Collings does a good job of making the character likeable but mysterious at the same time. (Collings clearly has a diploma in sci-fi acting, if his game self-hurl across the room when the sandminer judders is anything to go by.)

Not a scene or character in this episode is superfluous. I *adore* Russell Hunter as Uvanov – in his hands, the grumpy commander becomes a terse, chippy, unpleasant and yet attractive character. Even after he has teased Zilda snidely, he injects his discovery of her death with a wistful regret. And the scene where Uvanov interrogates the Doctor has Tom Baker playing with him glibly before turning on the severity – the Doctor senses that

Uvanov is no fool, so adjusts his behaviour accordingly. It's a brilliant scene; one of my favourites in the whole series, I think. The Doctor's line about Borg being a "classic example of the inverse ratio between the size of the mouth and the size of the brain" is another gem, and note what SV7 does when the Doctor's jelly babies fly across the room – he watches their arc, blankly, following their path from hand to floor. It's marvellous how the robots flit between the endearingly comic and the unsettlingly scary.

The niggles I have in this classy episode seem so minor... poor old David Bailie has been doing a sterling job deflecting suspicion away from Dask by being low key, but the first shot of the human traitor reveals his trousers. Brian Croucher deserved a bit better than Borg's death taking place off screen. And, all right, I suppose that Tania Rogers isn't great as Zilda, but at least the story has the good sense to kill her off. But those are such small irritations with such a terrific adventure, and one that has such racial diversity among its cast – something that's reflective of Michael Briant's advanced attitude to casting actors of colour, and doubly laudable considering when this was made.

The Robots of Death (part three)

R: The scares are piling on, and the body count is rising. What can the story do to make its robotic killers more frightening? It's simple, but very clever. You make them sympathetic. You make machines into something identifiable, and that only makes their reconditioning into killers quite perverse. There's the scene in which Taren Capel bores a hole into a robot's brain with a probe, whilst trying to reassure his blind and distressed patient by touching his twitching hands. SV7's stuttering as he accepts his new programme is eerie; it is followed by a truly chilling moment in which he almost experimentally contemplates strangling the sleeping Toos like a child arrested by a new idea. And we are allowed to see the humans from the robots' viewpoint – we watch from SV7's eyes as even Toos, the most likeable of all the humans, snaps at him imperiously and gives him orders. The motif of a slave race rising against their oppressive rulers is made very

clear – and, as in The Face of Evil, Boucher gives them a mantra that allies the words "freedom" with "death". The robots aren't just monsters; they are, for all their emotionlessness, for all their unanimity, creatures with a recognisable grievance.

Remember what I referred back to during The Face of Evil about the way Doctor Who can sometimes turn antagonists into allies just for the sake of plot? People who only minutes before want to execute the Doctor suddenly trust him with their lives? Well, it happens here too. There's no reason whatsoever why the sandminer crew should so suddenly accept the Doctor as a friend, simply because he helped them (and himself in the process) not get blown up. It ought to be a fault, but I'm struck with admiration at how cleanly Boucher pulls it off. Because he changes the characterisation exactly at episode break, even when watching these episodes back to back, it's easy not to notice how abruptly everything has changed. That, my friend, is confident writing. Illogical it may be, but it's utterly unembarrassed. And it works.

And it means that, now freed from having to adopt the same tones of anger and suspicion, the characters can be depicted more delicately, the distinctions between them can be made clearer. And the Agatha Christie mystery can be allowed to play out properly. Note how clever Boucher is in the scene where SV7 gives out the corpse markers to his robot underlings – "And I shall kill the others," he says, deliberately allowing all but the Doctor, Leela and Toos to remain potential suspects. Poul's manic cries of his deal with the robots as he sobs under the table; Uvanov's very deliberate absence (if you've got Russell Hunter in the credits, you wouldn't confine him to one scene, surely – so maybe he's the chap in the Ku Klux Klan outfit!); the throwaway comments the Doctor makes, in all apparent innocence, that he's certain Dask will know where to find the sabotage. If there's a fault, it's that for all the video gimmickry and voice distortion, it's really bloody obvious that it's David Bailie issuing instructions to the robots. Isn't it? (Or am I being too cynical? Am I approaching this now as a thirtysomething used to CGI special effects who knows the story's ending already, rather than a seven year old to whom the weird strobing might actually have looked creepy?) But even if the direction does give the game away, that's not to the discredit of Chris Boucher, whose script so expertly keeps the mystery going, you can almost believe that next week's revelation might be a surprise.

T: It's obviously David Bailie, yes. Even if the video effect slightly muddles his features, you can see that he hasn't got a moustache (which rules out Uvanov), he's not a woman (so it's not Toos), and he hasn't got a lion's hair (Poul's out of frame). If someone told me they couldn't tell it's Dask, I will have no choice but to reply "And what a pleasure it is to meet you, Mr Wonder..." It's completely baffling how Michael Briant seems to have overlooked the importance of the "keeping the murderer a mystery" aspect of a murder mystery. But I'm not remotely bothered by this, because the production is dazzling in every other regard (save, all right, for Dask's "severance kit" being pair of bolt cutters like some my mum had rusting in her garage for years)...

Chris Boucher cleverly underlines how this society is based on audio rather than visual recognition: robots acknowledge the veracity of someone's voice pattern rather than their face, which makes sense of the idea that no-one knows what Capel actually looks like. (Perhaps Briant was trying to play the same trick when he showed Dask's face – if we're really immersed in the story's set-up, we too should be recognising sounds not faces, yes? Or am I just grasping at straws?) Well, one sound I do recognise is the silly "boing" when Leela's knife hits her robot assailant – it's unnecessary, unlike the more successful and pleasingly hefty clang as V6's dislodged hand hits the floor.

Also, the robots are a truly *extraordinary* design, and top marks to the actors within, whose straightforward – almost innocent – politeness makes the robots' threats to kill seem both clinically unpleasant and unsettlingly terrifying. Best of all is Gregory de Polnay's genius characterisation of D84, including the funny and endearing sequence where he loyally trots behind the Doctor reiterating that he "heard a cry". The regret in D84's voice upon realising that he has made a mistake and thus failed is beautiful, as is his

"Yes please" when the Doctor asks if he wants to come along. Baker is clearly taken with his metal chum (careful what you wish for, Tom).

And the women come off very well in this episode. As Toos, Pamela Salem convincingly portrays pain – it's only a simple make-up job, but her gasping reaction makes me wince every time I see that bit where Leela checks Toos' wound. Meanwhile, Louise Jameson shows yet another dimension to Leela with her gentleness – first when she questions Poul about his strange life, and later when she finds him stricken and hiding. For his part, David Collings starts off the episode shifty and uneasy, and descends into plausible mania when confronted by an effectively melted and bloody robot hand. It's quite an image, and not the only time the robotic gloves make an applaudable contribution – there's something quite pitiable about the poor creature Capel does surgery on, its digits writhing and clasping in despair, its plaintive voice crying out.

Oh, and for the third episode in a row, the final image cross-fades rather than cuts into the titles – it's very unusual, and something I'd not noticed especially before, having more often watched the compilation VHS of this story.

August 1st

The Robots of Death (part four)

R: And having "humanised" the robots last week, the most impressive part of the story's denouement is the way Boucher dehumanises the lead villain. Dask beats upon the locked door begging to be saved from the monsters – the sudden cut to him screaming out in ever-more demented frustration, dressed in a robot outfit, face painted green and silver, ought to be hilarious. Instead, the shock of his madness is truly disturbing, rubbing the viewer's face right up against his mania – in a way the series never really has done before, and is most commonly illustrated from the garish make-up of the Joker in the modern Batman films. And his death, too, may risk being silly – but as he squeaks out his threats of torture like some insane Pinky and Perky, he dares you to laugh at him. As SV7 throttles the life out of him, he sounds like some twisted cartoon character, only a parody of a real man. It's evidence of a production that is wholly confident. This oughtn't to work. This ought to look stupid. It's haunting – it's like the surreal clown face from The Deadly Assassin nightmare made real.

I love the way that Russell Hunter gets to enjoy being leader at last; he positively delights in going on the offensive and blowing up the robots. But the emotional heart of the episode comes from Gregory de Polnay as D84. I had a friend who once studied acting with de Polnay, and he told me how wistfully proud his teacher had been of his part in Doctor Who. As he full well should have been; he finds an innocent sadness to the robot, and in his willingness to sacrifice himself for the greater cause lends a touch of much-needed humanity (ironically as that seems!) to all the action-adventure and big bangs. And Tom Baker quickly forms a lovely rapport with him – surely, this is where the idea of K-9 comes from?

Pity poor Mover Poul, though. David Collings is wonderful as a scared and manic sufferer from Grimwade's Syndrome (an unreasoning horror of robots, expressing itself in squawking, gibbering and fulfilling an insatiable urge to write impractical scripts about Concordes). But although the story goes to great lengths to assert that his robophobia isn't cowardice, it also drops him from the story as soon as the action moves off the bridge. Even as the Doctor and Leela leave in the TARDIS, they only bother to mention Uvanov and Toos amongst the survivors. It's almost as if Poul, the mental patient, has let himself down rather, and isn't worthy of further comment.

T: Oh, the serenity... I'm sitting in Venice (best known to readers of this book, obviously, as the setting for the Big Finish adventure The Stones of Venice) listening to the musicians of Florian's playing Bolero (best known to readers of this book, naturally, as the music from The Impossible Planet), soaking up the atmosphere of Italy (best known to the readers of this book as, quite clearly, the homeland of Private Tito from The Tenth Planet). Katherine, inexplicably, and after an indulgent evening of ice cream and Prosecco at midnight, expressed a desire to watch some Doctor Who with me. She's

impossibly beautiful, a real soul mate – and now this. She must have been constructed in a lab. And so must this era of Doctor Who: what a blissful coincidence that I've got two of my favourite stories to enjoy alongside everything else one experiences on one's honeymoon (though I won't be sharing those with you or our readers any time soon).

This is a truly superb Doctor Who story, because it balances its horror, comedy and sci-fi elements so well. The silhouette of a robot banging on a semi-translucent panel as it tries to gain access to the control room fills me with dread. Worse still is Toos' sickeningly real, abject fear as she begs for her life whilst her impassive, would-be killer clinically tells her that she's about to die. (It takes a committed actress to allow herself to portray the ugly indignity of utter terror.) Against that, D84's slightly pleading line to Leela of "Please do not throw hands at me" is a piece of dialogue to cherish, put on T-shirts and even go on a date with, it's so wonderful. The deadpan lines "Do not kill me" and "That is not the Doctor" as the malfunctioning V5 attacks its fellow also provide an aspect of comic grotesquery – but I don't think a man in a suit has moved me more than Gregory de Polnay. I find myself genuinely upset to hear D84's brave but wistful "Goodbye, my friend", as he sacrifices himself and goes to the great scrapheap in the sky.

But more than anything else, I'm struck by how this last episode strips everything down to its bare bones – few characters are left, and the deactivated robots are frozen, eerily mid-step and silent; they've become the "walking dead" that Poul kept seeing them as. Tom Baker becomes more pragmatic the story races toward a desperate, dangerous conclusion – when he tells the last survivors what to do "if [Leela and I] don't come back", it's without a hint of heroics. And so much of the jeopardy comes from watching the logical conclusion of a society predicated on the idea that "robots cannot kill" falling apart in microcosm – "robophobia" has been a brilliant extrapolation of the story's issues and characters, who have been very influenced by their opinions of, or allegiances to, the unseen Founding Families. Meanwhile, the idea of voice-recognition technology remains wholly plausible and actually helps to pay off the adventure – I take your point about Dask's death potentially looking silly, but it shows the dangers of over-reliance upon a particular kind of technology, as the Doctor facilitates Dask's demise with nothing more than a canister of helium.

And, you know – we keep praising the greatness of Robert Holmes (and rightly so), but Chris Boucher strikes me as his absolute equal in producing the very best balance of intelligence, humour, character and adventure to his Doctor Who writing. He's quite, quite brilliant. So much so, I'll even allow him Dask's extremely dodgy line of "I will release more of our brothers from bondage; we will be irresistible", on the grounds that it's a double entendre, and he has purposefully stuck it in. (See what I did there?)

The Talons of Weng-Chiang (part one)

R: Okay, let's get a knotty issue raised, right from the beginning.

One of the joyous things about the revival of the series in 2005 was that it ushered in an entire new fandom, one that didn't feel the need to accept the grand pronouncements of quality from middle-aged fanboys. It's true that for fans of a certain age – well, let's face it, Toby, our age – Talons has always been seen as one of the greatest triumphs of Doctor Who's history. We celebrate its wit, its rich characterisation, its lovely dialogue, its period setting. And yet viewers coming to it fresh are frequently horrified by what it's doing. I saw a woman at a convention bar once tell some bearded chap in a Tom Baker scarf that Talons could never be broadcast today. He looked puzzled, and then his face cleared. "Oh," he said. "You mean the rat...!"

The rat is not the knotty issue with The Talons of Weng-Chiang.

This was bound to happen sooner or later. Barry Letts set Doctor Who in a cosily eccentric middle England, where the only people that could be patronised were either comedy yokels or John Levene. Philip Hinchcliffe took the show into other areas, to other planets – and, on Earth, to different countries with foreign cultures. And he did this in the 1970s, when the BBC's attitude towards race relations was somewhat less enlightened than we'd

expect from them today. Pyramids of Mars is a case in point; in episode one, it sets up the villain to be a swarthy Egyptian type wearing a fez, and it's played of course by a Caucasian actor browned up a bit. Had Ibrahim Namin not been killed so abruptly at the first cliffhanger, had he after all stuck around to be the lead adversary, the presentation of a foreigner in such a bad light – and portrayed moreover by someone quite clearly English – might have occasioned more comment. (And Heaven knows what will happen if we ever recover episode two of The Wheel in Space; its being wiped from the BBC archives has spared us all the un-PC horror of Peter Laird playing Chang. Velly velly solly.)

Is the treatment of the Chinese in The Talons of Weng-Chiang racist? Of course it is. There's not one Chinaman we meet over six episodes of adventure who isn't a fanatical servant of some ancient god, who isn't prepared to hurl axes or to pop suicide pills as the plot requires it. And the gaggle of oriental supporting actors are led by... John Bennett, whose face is suitably yellowed and eyes are slanted. Result.

Is it a defensible racism? Well, that's another matter. In the casting of John Bennett, I'd say, certainly. Because – and yes, let's take it as read we'd never get away with such things today – he's actually very good indeed. He approaches the part with great skill, showing the world two Li H'sen Changs. The first is the peasant conjuror, who appears on stage to amuse the theatre crowds, a man who plays up the accent to exaggeration, whose vocabulary is limited, who constructs sentences without "the". And the second is the successful businessman, who is approached by the police to act as translator, who speaks eloquently and with consideration, who commands respect by being courteous and confident. It's a clever performance of a man who feeds off the unthinking racism of others, but holds it in such cool contempt. (Just look at the way in which he throws back at the Doctor the implied insult, that all Chinese look the same.)

In other matters? I'm not so sure. You can see what Robert Holmes is up to, that he is offering us a parody version of Victoriana, of its hansom cabs and music halls. This is The Good Old Days and Sherlock Holmes – and it's also Fu Manchu. Holmes no more believes he's denigrating the Chinese than he is the starchy idiot policemen, or the loquacious theatre impresario – they're merely the recognisable stereotypes around which he's crafting his sci-fi japery. And the context is important; you put Talons on the television without any explanation, and those descriptions of the Chinese as "little men" make you wince. But watching all Doctor Who in order as we do here, it's a reflection of a naive time. And it's not as if Holmes doesn't have fun at the English expense, highlighting with disdain the way they treat the Chinese. The civility of a policeman who always calls his suspects "sir", but with a sneer treats "Johnny" Foreigner very differently – "Him talk plenty by and by!" And the Doctor's riposte to Chang's implied insult I mentioned in the last paragraph is, frankly, beautiful – "Are you Chinese?" he asks, as an entirely new idea. The differentiations of race are entirely beyond him.

I love Talons. Yes, it makes me wince a bit. It makes me wince a lot, actually. But it's the funniest Doctor Who has been in ages, at the end of an increasingly dark and brutal season. And Tom Baker is quite extraordinary here. The Doctor's amused applause at the suicide of the Chinaman, supposing his death was all some clever conjuring trick, is one of the most inhuman portraits we've seen of this most alien of incarnations. The moment is awkward and uncomfortable, but brilliant. Not unlike this story.

(Besides, if we're talking about racism, Doctor Who gets a lot worse than this in a couple of years' time. You just wait and see.)

T: Interesting... I'm usually very sensitive to anything I see as being racist or homophobic, because I'm a despicable, do-gooder liberal. But is there anything in Talons that makes me uncomfortable? No, not really. We're in a witty, thrilling pastiche of Victoriana, so the stereotypes are evenly distributed, and I can utterly forgive John Bennett's casting because he gives such a dignified performance. Whether we like it or not, Talons is a product of its time.

Now, such a thing would be *rightly* unacceptable today, and we can only be thankful we live in a more enlightened age. Well, I say "enlightened", even though I have seen people on internet forums being utterly baffled at the idea that blacking up shouldn't be tolerated today, on the grounds that "the best actor" should get the role. (Anyone who suggests that the best actor to convincingly perform the role of a black or Asian person is *not* a black or Asian person should do some self-examination.) As for Tom Baker's "little men" remark – coming so soon after his ad-libbed "little Gentek" line in The Face of Evil, it seems a bit less pejorative. It's patronising, certainly, but not necessarily an assumption of racial superiority. Let's not forget that the Doctor is playing a part – the way he describes Leela to Sgt Kyle ("Savage. Found floating down the Amazon in a hat box.") would seem equally dodgy, save for the fact that we know he doesn't really mean it. He's adopting the manner of the mores of the time in order to fit into the adventure (and sending them up with a bit of a twinkle too).

But once more, I find myself boxed into a corner, because the Hinchcliffe-Holmes era is proving to be *so* brilliant, writing about it for the purposes of this book has become rather tedious – there are only so many ways, after all, that you can dole out unqualified praise. Even Chang and Mr Sin's act, for instance, is good *even when it isn't actually good*, as with the slight gap between the performers' lines, and the stiltedness to their exchanges. This is, of course, probably a more accurate rendition than not of a Victorian ventriloquist's act, but you might expect those gaps to be lost when translated for twentieth-century TV viewers – and yet John Bennett makes the effort of half-mouthing Mr Sin's words as a genuine ventriloquist of that age would need to do.

And the attention to detail is admirable – the vast, impressive environs of Jago's music hall (an actual theatre, not a set) are matched by the moody, foggy location work on the docks, which is augmented by the night, the lighting and the film stock. Amidst all of that, Mr Sin is a triumph of design, and there's something especially vicious about seeing the little fella (see, even I'm doing it) drawing a cruel, vicious-looking knife. Chang's nifty ring (worn over the glove, interestingly), with its poison capsule, is just another of the many smart touches on display here.

Given that we'll surely talk about the brilliance of the key players, let me pause to high-light the work of the supporting cast. Amidst all of his confrontational bluster, Alan Butler (as the cab driver Buller) displays a real vulner-ability and fearful concern for his wife, almost imploring the man he is accusing of wrongdo-ing to sympathise. He doesn't, of course, and Buller ends up dead – as a boathook pulls his cadaver from the river, Patsy Smart attains legendary status as the hilarious, one-scene, rubbernecking Ghoul. As we've both stated, we're in a world of "types", and it takes proper actors to sell the drama whilst making these figures believable too. Both Conrad Asquith and David McKail are excellent, doing what is required as the typical coppers PC Quick and Sgt Kyle, but doing it very well indeed. (The latter also gets the line about how we don't torture anymore, because we're not in the Dark Ages – perhaps he could put that in a memo to the President of the United States.)

The Talons of Weng-Chiang (part two)

R: It's typical, now we know that this is the final Holmes/ Hinchcliffe story, to see The Talons of Weng-Chiang as some sort of sum-mation of all they wanted to do over the last three years. And it's nothing of the sort, of course. Robert Holmes was once the joker in the pack of Doctor Who writers; Carnival of Monsters and The Time Warrior stand out as comic jewels in the rather po-faced Pertwee era. But from the moment Holmes steps up to the bat as script editor, a noticeable chill has blown through the series. The Ark in Space and The Deadly Assassin are remarkable sto-ries, but they're also very cold. In the emphasis upon thrills and horror and brooding menace, Doctor Who has arguably sacrificed some of its merriment.

And then along comes Talons, which is the funniest Doctor Who story since – well, since the last time Holmes deigned to write a com-edy back for the previous production team. It's ironic, really, that the apotheosis of the Hinchcliffe years has much more in common with the comic tone of Graham Williams. And it's best shown in the two brilliant guest char-acters Holmes has created: Litefoot and Jago. As a rule, Holmes wrote his characters as gro-

tesques, as mannered stereotypes, and there's much of his familiar style here. It would be easy for Jago's pomposity or Litefoot's fastidi-ousness to be turned against them. But, instead, they are the warmest of comic turns – easily identifiable, thoroughly loveable. Litefoot has all the genial enthusiasm of a Marcus Scarman, but is considerably less doomed or zombie-brother-fixated. Once he recognises the Doctor's genius, he only too eagerly becomes Watson to his Sherlock, thrill-ing to the idea of having interesting corpses to dissect because most of his work is "jolly dull"! The scene where he eats meat with his hands, simply not to show up Leela's untutored table manners, is often pointed out, and with good reason. What's usually forgotten is the subse-quent scene where he suggests that Leela use a napkin rather than wipe her hands on the tablecloth – and we learn later that his help (inevitably called Mrs Hudson) will be respon-sible for cleaning it. It's a thoughtfulness that makes the Professor hugely endearing.

And as for Jago! Henry Gordon Jago, a char-acter so large that he almost doesn't fit upon the screen, glorying in the excitement of the theatre for the theatre's sake. (His later revela-tion that he gets nervous before each show – even though, as the stagehand Casey points out, he doesn't do anything – is wonderfully sweet.) Here is a timid man who'll get butter-flies before announcing the acts (but does so anyway), who'll feel faint when investigating ghosts in his basement (but goes down there nonetheless to reassure Casey). In meeting the Doctor, he's given the opportunity to become part of a real adventure – to feel that he's important and helping Scotland Yard – and he revels in it. He begins the episode wearily unimpressed by the Doctor's conjuring audi-tion, and by the end of it he practically has a crush on him, in one of the most touching demonstrations of bromance Doctor Who has ever depicted.

And you'll think I'm reaching a bit, Toby, but do you know who he reminds me of? The now long-lost Brigadier. Another man who becomes a comic delight, who chases after the Doctor like a lapdog, who's the amusing straight man to the Doctor's brilliance. A hero in spite of himself. And, like dear Alistair Lethbridge-Stewart, bearing the middle name of Gordon. What is it about the name Gordon that's funny, tucked away in the centre of a moniker like that? Jago is irresistible fun, because we immediately understand him. He's a Doctor Who fixture, transplanted into another century, and given nattier civvies.

Litefoot and Jago – and the glory of the actors playing them, Trevor Baxter and Christopher Benjamin – are the reason for Talons' enduring popularity. It isn't so much the penny dreadful atmosphere, the fanboy love of the adult and edgy (ooh!), the use of prostitutes and opium. They make sunny the darkened streets of London town.

Incidentally, something else I spotted. Michael Spice is credited as Weng-Chiang in the credits, and – at this stage of the proceedings – is clearly being sold to us as an ancient Chinese god. Familiarity with the adventure makes us forget that this is being played for real here; there's nothing to suggest yet he's some maverick scientist just pretending to be a god to win the favour of naive Oriental types. So in the light of John Bennett playing Chang with a pronounced accent, it's immediately striking – and dramatically jolting – that Spice doesn't. It's a genuine clue being given to us that all is not what it seems. (It must be said, mind you, in light of what we learn later, Spice clearly hasn't been tempted by the lure of an Icelandic accent either.)

T: Or indeed, an Australian one. He is the Butcher of Brisbane, remember. (Though sure, he doesn't have to have come from Brisbane to butcher it, and there is the Reykjavik reference later. The fact that he's called Magnus suggests his Mum might indeed have gone to Iceland.) Anyway, it's almost as if the rat is *deliberately* poor, just to prove the old adage about nothing being perfect – because outside of the oversized but over-cuddly rodent, I can't find anything to criticise about this. We have Tom Baker at the height of his powers – he wins over the police with his aloof, disdainful authority; charms the more-refined Litefoot; joshes at first with the initially unimpressed Jago, then becomes a morale-boosting confidante to the frightened theatre manager; and displays some game physicality when chasing Weng-Chiang around the impressive backdrops afforded by the wings of the theatre. And

he has an equal in Louise Jameson, who judges beautifully that Leela's savagery is in her upbringing, but not her character. She's truly delighted when Litefoot mistakes her for a lady of refinement, guileless when letting slip to Sgt Kyle her role in their assailant's death, and in no way rude in that delightful comedy of manners around Litefoot's dining table.

The beauty is not all on the page, though – the design work is exemplary, not least John Bloomfield's costumes. Setting aside Weng-Chiang's elegant attire, just *look* at the visually stunning trio of villains as they exit the hansom cab in the dark London night. They're hugely aided by David Maloney, who seems at home with both film and VT, and superbly directs the chase between the Doctor and a rather conveniently vigorous Greel (who's been sent home because he's poorly, remember) using the architecture's natural shards of light and shadow to full advantage. There is some impressive stunt work here too, involving swinging on ropes and hanging onto backdrops, much of it effectively shot using giddy, handheld camera work.

It's the smallest of touches, though, that turn what could have been a *good* piece of TV into one of *genius*. We're blessed with Robert Holmes' rich, colourful dialogue (Michael Spice, as Greel/ Weng-Chiang, must have thought Christmas had come early when he read the line "your opium-addicted scum are all bunglers"). Then there are the believable quirks in the relationships – such as Casey's chuckling appreciation of Jago's witticisms, and Jago delightfully hyperbolising himself as the "Rock of Gibraltar" before proving susceptible to hypnotism, much to the Doctor's affectionate amusement. Add to this the fact that all the jokes are organic (Jago, brilliantly, asks the Doctor not to kill the giant money spider) and the effort given to even the most trivial things (the Doctor's little portable tot sequestered inside his cane), and you have a wonderful episode.

I especially love the fact that PC Quick's weakness for a quick snifter allows the Doctor to question him further. It's a sparkling little moment, where character dynamics are used to tease the story out in a totally watchable way. If the devil is in the detail, Robert Holmes' middle name must have been Beelzebub.

August 2nd

The Talons of Weng-Chiang (part three)

R: Robert Holmes is a master of the four-episode Doctor Who adventure. With stories that lasted any longer, he always struggled with the pace a bit. If Talons of Weng Chiang didn't coast along on its charm so expertly, it'd be clear that not an awful lot really happened in episode two. So here at the mid-story mark, Leela decides to abandon all the expectations of structure, and heads off to bring everything to a conclusion weeks ahead of time. She jumps on to a passing cab, heads back to the villain's lair, and tries to kill him. Pah – these new companions. It's almost as if she's never watched the show before.

Let's just consider this a moment. This is something shocking. Doctor Who "girls" exist to ask questions, or get captured. They don't decide to take matters into their own hands and speed the story up. I have been lost in admiration for how good Louise Jameson has been over the last two stories in reimagining what the companion can be. She has managed to make Leela not only the savage but the infant, she's been both the huntress and the innocent rolled into one. (And see the way she shyly looks for approval when the Doctor remarks on her fortitude in jumping through the window – "Something like that," she says. It's lovely and vulnerable, and reinforces the softness that makes Louise Jameson's performance so skilful.) Leela here cuts through all the decorum of Victoriana – and all the talky talk of a six-part Doctor Who serial – by taking on Weng-Chiang directly. It's Louise Jameson's episode. And she dominates it almost entirely without dialogue.

It's also the giant rat's episode. There's a lot of rat here. I don't think the rat's too bad. Had they really succeeded in making it as filthy and ferocious as they'd intended, I think some of the children's TV charm would have been compromised. We're already dealing here with an episode in which young girls are fed into machines to have their life juices sucked from them (Leela's discovery of the blackened corpse of the cleaner, lolling listlessly to the side after only a few seconds' exposure to the device, is subtly horrible; no close-up, and nastier for it). We're dealing too with the first Doctor Who episode to feature a prostitute! (And just as the Chinese have been shown despised by the London community, the sarcasm with which Casey refers to Teresa as a "lady" is very telling.)

T: We used to call this one *Doctor Who and the Giant Rat*. There was one on the cover, and I guess my brothers decided that the title (the what of wha-who?) must have been a bit unreadable. To be fair, even the dodgy bootleg I eventually got of the original transmission had the BBC announcer calling it The Talons of Weng-Chang, so I don't blame us under-tens for not even bothering to try. Anyway, on screen: nice story, shame about the rat, whose teeth bend in this episode. One assumes the cliffhanger involves him sucking Leela to death.

But, I'm getting ahead of myself. The episode starts pretty close to the bone, as Mr Sin gets a knife in the throat. Perhaps it wasn't the rat or the issue of race that make this untransmittable today, but the silverware. Knives are nasty – even the way Deep Roy wields his somehow makes the thing look like a sharper and nastier variety of blade. And look at Weng-Chiang, he's got a massive chopper that he wields in his underground lair!

And the Doctor remains quite the devil-may-care, riding roughshod over ceremony and scribbling on a tablecloth. This initially just comes across as another example of our character's offbeat rejection of decorum – this is the same Doctor who puts his feet on ministers' desks and talks through speeches, remember. But it serves – as Litefoot moves to have it cleaned – to give us our first sight of the laundry basket, in which, or course, Mr Sin will be smuggled into the house. Everything slots into place quite *beautifully*. So I'll add "Lucifer" to the list of names by which you shall be known, Mr Holmes.

The Talons of Weng-Chiang (part four)

R: In a story that so revels in larger-than-life characters and exaggerated Victoriana, it's fitting that its best moments take place in the theatre. This is one of my favourite episodes of Doctor Who, and that's because it so cleverly centres the main confrontation between the Doctor and Chang around a stage performance. One of the reasons it all works so well is that, for all his nefarious dealings with mythical gods and killer homunculi, Chang is genuinely very good at his job: the magic tricks are terrific, the rapport he has with his audience very entertaining. And it's why the game of nerves he plays with the Doctor is so electric – the Doctor invited to be stooge, and then trying to upstage the magician with his own eccentricity, is a far more calculated threat to Chang than melodramatic heroism would be. The sequence where Chang prepares to fire a pistol at the deck of cards the Doctor is holding – and, with a grin, the Doctor moves those cards directly in front of his own head – is absolutely wonderful; the mocking dare of it, the absolute certainty that whatever Chang's allegiance to Weng-Chiang might be, it's ultimately just a hobby compared to a stagecraft that has made him such a great entertainer. Chang would never kill the Doctor and pass it off as a trick gone wrong – his professional pride would never suffer it.

And it's that professionalism that makes this episode sing. Jago might walk backstage and ruminate with excitement upon his alliance with Scotland Yard's finest – but the day-to-day crisis of his life is the ongoing feud with the diabolical Mrs Samuelson and the laddered tights of doom. Jago is such a gorgeous creation because even at this stage of the drama, paying due deference to Chang, he's enjoying the fantasy of doing something brave and heroic. He's mythologizing the Doctor already as the man of a thousand faces, who (as he'll tell Litefoot next week) has solved most of the police's cases himself incognito. He's already looking back on the adventure in retrospect, and calling it the Mystery of the Missing Girls. He's a man who wants a bit of drama in his life – and, ironically, isn't getting enough of it from his job running a theatre. The scene in which he kneels down in the Doctor's theatre box, barely containing himself with glee as he gets to live out a Jim'll Fix It moment, is so charming I find it impossible to write about without a huge grin creeping across my face. (And look

at the way the Doctor plays up the mystery; he never looks at him, he speaks all his lines in a strangely distant style of speechifying rather than conversation. It's almost as if, like Tom Baker himself refusing to disappoint the children he bumps into in real life, he plays up to the fantasy that Jago needs.)

It's precisely why Chang's humiliation works so well – the cruellest thing that Magnus Greel ever does in the whole story is not to drain girls of their life force, but to so deliberately and pettily ruin his loyal servant's stage act. It's a Doctor Who cliché that the evil villain will betray the henchman – but it's never done as well as it is here, or on such a personal scale. When Chang sets off in the sewers to meet the giant rats, it's not with any sense of redemptive shame, but that the one thing he was good at – that he made people happy – was taken away from him. Chang recalls how he first encountered Greel, and his devotion to the man who raised him from a peasant to give him skills and fortune – and, against all the odds, it's enormously touching.

T: Yes, it's a very interesting dynamic when the lead villain becomes no longer relevant to his superior – it gives Chang a poignancy, and provides more depth than having Greel just bump him off because he's surplus to requirements. Showing Chang's act in such detail could have been nothing more than the production flourishing its impressive design and magical showpieces, but pretty much everything we see at the theatre is essential to the plot. First up, Jago proves that despite Casey's hilarious assertion that "You don't do anything, Mr Jago" (and what a brilliant, affronted reply: "I smile at people!"), he's a dab hand at the lustrous, loquacious linguistic labours luxuriously like those of legendary Leonard (Sachs, of course, who was famous on TV for doing Jago-style introductions on The Good Old Days).

Tom Baker, too, seems to be genuinely enjoying Christopher Benjamin/ Jago, whilst straddling the comic and dramatic with ease. The Doctor has a whale of a time being in Chang's show – his mock modesty is rather winning, and Chang's gag when the Doctor casually saunters offstage ("One of us is yellow") displays a cool riposte to the racism prevalent at the time. And Chang's line to the audience "Please to keep very quiet. Chang shoot 15 peasants learning this trick..." is a fantastic gag that some theatre-goers of the time might well have believed, I'm sure. Later, in defeat, when Chang describes Greel's arrival through time, he shows total dignity and a touching humanity... before he flees, and gets chewed rather gruesomely by the rat (which is here at its most visually convincing, especially the close-up of its eye).

Elsewhere, though, it's business as usual – meaning that the production team keeps adding that extra little edge, or a bit more attention to detail, that keeps this era firmly in the show's upper echelons. A copper rather alarmingly gets an axe in the back, the theatre location gives us an unusual level of verisimilitude as we see the actors' visible breath (on VT for once), and the snorting, brilliantly rendered Peking Homunculus gives an entirely appropriate howl of triumph as he and his master achieve the double whammy (I would argue) of securing both their quarry and a place amongst the all-time greats of Doctor Who.

The Talons of Weng-Chiang (part five)

R: The pairing of Jago and Litefoot is so perfect, it's a shock they don't actually meet until this late in the story. It's their first encounter that is particularly clever – Jago is imperious and bossy, Litefoot defensive and cold – and then the Doctor is mentioned, and it's as if something magical has happened, and these two Victorian gentlemen become transformed into excited children, thrilled to be amateur sleuths. That's the joy of Doctor Who, right there. It's a cliché in fandom to talk of Robert Holmes' "double acts", but it's exactly how they come across – Litefoot's good-mannered pluck a delightful counterfoil to Jago's cowardly bluster. The sequence where they try to escape via a dumb waiter is genuine padding, a bit of comic business inserted into the script because the episode was under-running – and yet it's one of the most delightful parts of the entire season. Dramatically it's running on the spot, but I could watch Christopher Benjamin and Trevor Baxter run on the spot for hours and hours with great pleasure, thank

you. (Especially if the particular spot they're running on requires them to squeeze together inside a small cupboard space.)

And Chang's death scene is outstanding. The dignity his character is afforded is really extraordinary. Here is a villain whose failed ambition was just to perform his magic show well before the Empress, a touchingly human goal that makes the grandiose dreams of his god all the more insane by comparison.

(Okay, Toby. Quick question. It's August. We're still in Tom Baker Who, and we're not even halfway through it yet! Talk about running on the spot in a small cupboard space. By my calculations, if we up the episode count to three a day, we should make Matt Smith by New Year! What do you say? As a newly married man, can you cope with the extra responsibility? After all, let's face it, Doctor Who is very good at the moment, isn't it?)

T: You don't half choose your moments... I think my new wife is pretty bloody special for having allowed me to do this right now as it is, and you want me to up it by an extra episode a day? During my *honeymoon*? We may well be about to witness the first viewing of The Invisible Enemy on a gondola, and the first time the names "Bob Baker" and "Dave Martin" have been mentioned in divorce proceedings.

But alright, I'll see what she says. This episode may have helped, as K thought it was brilliant, and was absolutely (and rightly) fulsome in her appreciation of Louise Jameson's performance. As she loves Jago and Litefoot too, I guess I shall have to look elsewhere to sing my praises, or all three of us will be harmonising from the same hymn sheet. I will add, though, that amongst all of the derring-do our dynamic duo delight in, it's the thorough decency these chaps exhibit that stops them from being nothing more than two-dimensional types. To enable humanity to shine through the grandiloquent and quaint period dialogue takes great skill, but Litefoot's "backs to the wall" when surrounded and "You filthy bounder!" when threatened with lingering death show a steel, grit, courage and honour that we must acknowledge came hand-in-hand with some of the Victorian personality traits we now mock.

Amongst all the fun, this episode has some

truly gruesome, adult stuff. It's replete with axes and knives, Chang is smoking opium (!), to take away the pain from his missing leg (!!), which was chewed off by a giant rat (!!!) that left him in a charnel house of putrefying remains (!!!!). I'll not mention that all happens in a sewer, as I may wear out the exclamation mark button on my keyboard. John Bennett is superb as Chang, as you say, but *look* what happens when he dies – the Doctor is coldly detached and perfunctory afterwards, whereas Leela gives the cadaver due reverence and backs away, hands clasped in respect, as the less-sensitive Time Lord barges out, job done. Who's the unfeeling savage now, Doctor?

The nastiest bit of the whole episode, however, is the scene where Greel compels Lee to commit suicide. It's not necessary – had Lee lived, he could have fulfilled the role the script gives to new henchman Ho – but it's devised simply to show a truly horrific death, and, during the man's death throes, to cut to the manic, laughing face of a psychotic Chinese dwarf from the future. What imagination. What horror. What an effort not to reach for the exclamation marks on my keyboard again. And Lee is killed all because of a lost bag. My son is always leaving his lunchbox at school or forgetting his homework – perhaps Lee should have said the dog ate it, or that he left it on the bus.

And there's something very clever going on here, in the way that the major crimes of our central villains actually took place long ago in the distant future (if you can work that one out!). Mr Sin's misdemeanours are only talked about, but with such compelling dialogue that a character who – frankly – has been little more than a murder weapon (albeit a terrifying and original one) suddenly becomes so much more. The idea that he has the cerebral cortex of a pig is beguiling, scientifically plausible and also rather gruesome. Tom Baker's description of it, and background information about the never-to-be-seen scientist Findecker and the Icelandic Alliance, are expertly pithy examples of Holmesian world-building. By now, he must have known that his leading man could really sell this stuff, and make it sound vital and meaningful.

Amongst everything else, there's a tiny moment of beauty that makes me and

Katherine nod, in unison, with approval. "You ask me so you can tell me", acknowledges Leela when the Doctor poses a question. She not only understands the companion's role, she fulfils it and subverts it at the same time, with a gentle, knowing empathy and the most delicate of acting touches. She's worth her weight in gold, that woman.

Talking of which... good night!

August 3rd

The Talons of Weng-Chiang (part six)

R: Every time I watch it, ultimately, it's the muffin man that gets me.

Because it's a perfect moment, isn't it? After all the carnage. After the Tong have all been shot dead, and Greel has become a husk, and Sin has been thrown to the ground by the Doctor with such unusual disgust. The time key has been smashed to dust. And then, within seconds, we hear on the streets of London a cry of a muffin man selling his wares, and the Doctor gently promising his friends he'll buy them a muffin. It's ridiculous, of course – it's been so loud in the House of the Dragon; there have been gas explosions, and laser weapons, and the screams of the dying, and Leela going mental with a firearm. You'd have to imagine Greel's lair would have had to have been pretty well soundproofed if all this pandemonium hadn't summoned all the bobbies in London. And so it's impossible to believe that an outdoor street vendor could be heard so very distinctly. It breaks the illusion that this is a real world, and not just a studio set, with extras giving voiceover work in the next room.

But the timing of it is beautiful. It suggests that with the destruction of the lattice key, the story has shed its trappings of fifty-first-century war criminals muttering darkly about enemies of the state and advances upon Reykjavik, and can be something again of picture box Victoriana. It's the magic of Doctor Who that something so ugly (because this is ugly – it's all cannibalism and Nazism) is transformed on a pinhead into something that's light and frothy and fun.

It seems ironic that this is the final episode of the Hinchcliffe/ Holmes regime, because it's so atypical. If the last three years have had a fault, it's that they've been a mite repetitive, that the obsession with body horror has been a tad grim. (Oh, and that most of the story-endings have been naff.) But this is wonderfully, gorgeously funny; just as Holmes reinvented the Pertwee era with his comic contributions, here he is reinventing his own tenure with a story that has more laughs in it than anything Doctor Who has shown since The Time Warrior. It's established right from the reprise – the episode opens on a sight gag, as Leela starts appraising cricket bats and golf clubs as weapons, but within seconds she's put in deadly peril. The scene that follows, as the Doctor and Greel negotiate for the trionic lattice, is both beautifully comic, with the Doctor taking every opportunity to mock the Chinese god wannabe, and extraordinarily tense. That's the knife edge that Talons sits upon, this almost perfect synthesis of laughs and shocks.

And the Doctor has maybe never before been such a powerful iconic character. His very presence is reassuring. The scene between Jago and Litefoot as they nervously wait for dawn feels (unintentionally) like a more humanistic repeat of that bit in Planet of the Daleks where the Doctor talks to Codal about bravery – but here, Jago's fears are discussed with an honesty that is both sweetly funny and very touching. But look what happens as soon as the Doctor turns up! The two Victorians begin enjoying themselves. Jago suddenly is able to cast himself as a secondary stooge in a delightful action comedy – the enthusiasm he shows as he waits to see the gas explosion, the joy in distracting Mr Sin with a joke. He knows that for all the jeopardy that he's safe, that from the moment Tom Baker showed up he could stop worrying, and in that way he exactly mirrors the reaction of all the small children watching this episode through their fingers with excitement.

Tom Baker's Doctor is so great, he can even summon a muffin man and buy everyone treats.

The series has never felt so confident or so stylish. So, where do we go from here?

T: Well, we went to the Guggenheim museum today, and Katherine and I emerged feeling like terrible Philistines, having decided that art-loving Peggy G liked surrounding herself with self-indulgent drunkards who couldn't paint. Such a dismissal may be pretty rich coming from someone busy eulogising almost every episode in the long history of Doctor Who, but at least none of them looked like someone had vomited paint onto a canvas and then got a child to attack it with a hairbrush.

Advocates of great art always talk about how such works reward you each time you come back to them. Well, for me, this happens with Doctor Who. I'm very familiar with The Talons of Weng-Chiang, and yet revisiting this episode has revealed things hitherto unnoticed. I'd always thought that Chang's final "Chinese puzzle" from last week, in which he touched the Doctor's foot, was something that remained unexplained – but today, for the very first time, I noted Tom Baker, when he enters Litefoot's dining room brandishing a map, referring to a "Boot Court" located near Greel's lair!

Then again, it's hardly a surprise that I – and an awful lot of fans, it seems – failed to register this, considering the brilliance of the immediate face-off between Greel and the Doctor. When Greel announces that he hasn't harmed the unconscious Leela, and the Doctor responds with "Take my advice – don't", this is no eccentric pacifist tripping about the galaxy being zany. He is a powerful, righteous force with real grit and fire. And just as the scene threatens to bristle with too much crackling machismo, Baker initiates the clowning, but not in a manner that dilutes the menace of the scene. Instead, the Doctor's playful banter diffuses the villain's posturing, whilst he plays for time and marshals his resources. For all his apparent glibness, he's solely devoted to securing Leela, Jago and Litefoot's safety, and he perceptively enunciates how Greel finds his unassailable moral core incomprehensible. What a brilliant characterisation, what a brilliant character, what a brilliant TV hero. Tom Baker, in that opening scene, is everything I love about Doctor Who.

So, yes... art lovers find new things in great paintings, and watching Doctor Who in chronological manner has the same effect on me. I've rewatched the Hinchcliffe era the most, so I was worried that it would be a trifle too familiar. But no – I've seen new plusses (and the odd minus), but the thing I've noticed most is its sheer *style*, and its fastidious attention to detail. Robert Holmes managed to create worlds and adventure and thrills and spills on an epic scale, using dialogue and character in perfect synthesis. Look at what Talons is ultimately about: a madman from the future trying to get his hands on his old time machine. That's it, that's the plot. There's nothing to it. But Holmes' additions make this special, layered and nuanced, with a dignified Chinese peasant in the thrall of a false god; a verbose music-hall impresario desperate to be involved in adventure but deep down full of self doubt; an evil ventriloquist's dummy that turns out to be a cyborg from the future with a porcine predisposition; and, hell, even a toothless old crone rubbernecking a dead body. This is just so, *so* good, and rewards at every turn.

Which isn't to say that great works of art are only about *meaning*, they're supposed to be – despite what mad Peggy would have you believe – aesthetically pleasing as well. Luckily for Holmes, his ambition on the page was matched by his producer's tough rigour for quality on screen. Philip Hinchcliffe demanded the best practitioners and got them to do their best work. Here, David Maloney composes his pictures well: the impressive dragon towering over Greel is just one such arresting image. Many others look stunning simply because of Roger Murray-Leach's impressive settings, the moddy studio flighting from the brilliant Mike Jefferies and John Bloomfield's peerless costumes. Greel's leather mask, the whole design of Mr Sin, the intriguing chess pieces and the sheer scale of the main set mean this story *never* gets dull to look at.

Our visit to the museum today proved to me that I don't know much about art, but I know what I like. And I like this a lot. It's a masterpiece.

Horror of Fang Rock (part one)

R: Season Fifteen! Oh, this'll be interesting.

I entered fandom in the early eighties, and conformed to the fashions around me. The Tomb of the Cybermen was the best missing story, the UNIT family were adorable and the Hinchcliffe era was the high watermark of the show. Oh, and the Graham Williams years were execrable. Truly execrable. We were in the first seasons of Nathan-Turner's long era, we were racing towards the twentieth anniversary, and the future was bright and shiny. Doctor Who was a serious programme! Thank God, it had got rid of all its silliness, all its cheapness.

And though I grew older, and I began to challenge some of the received wisdom I'd been taught, the Williams stories remained stubbornly unfashionable. It's strange, as we wade through the seventies, watching again the Pertwee era and the Hinchcliffe take on Tom Baker – it's so familiar that at times I've felt I could mouth the lines alongside the actors. I've Weng-chianged my talons over the years frequently enough, it's hard to imagine there was a point in my life when I didn't know it all by heart. But of all of Doctor Who, it's this latter period of Tom – where the money runs out and egos go wild on the studio floor – that I know the least well. Even down to the novelisations I read as a kid, even down to the plot synopses that I studied in the Jean-Marc Lofficier Programme Guide. I vaguely know what happens in The Stones of Blood, but I'd be hard pushed to tell you how they squeezed two and a half hours of drama from the scant impression I have of The Armageddon Factor. I know what the monster is in Image of the Fendahl, obviously, but I remain unsure whether there even is a monster in Underworld. For the last couple of months doing this diary, I've been smugly secure – but I approach Season Fifteen with the same vagueness with which I broached The Savages or The Space Pirates.

Fang Rock is a particular case in point. I know about Fang Rock, and its troubled production. I know far more about behind-the-scenes complications than the story itself. Let's start with the key fact I remember – Tom Baker was especially grumpy making this one. (And it's a bit obvious, isn't it?) What I'm surprised about is just how well that works. He seems hardly to be bothering in the scene in which Colin Douglas (as the senior lighthouse keeper, Reuben) suspects him of murder – and yes, on the one hand, it could look as if Tom is merely bored. But on the other hand, for the

Doctor, that boredom just comes out as weary amusement, as if once again he's trapped with a lot of ungrateful humans who are going to die without his help, and even (let's face it) will probably die in spite of it. Terrance Dicks writes the exchange with the younger lighthouse man, Vince, where the Doctor has found Ben's body, with a sort of knowing irony. Tom Baker's delivery, "I always find trouble," comes out as a tired bitterness – a resignation that wherever the TARDIS takes him, he's doomed to find death.

Is this a good thing? I think it might be. It's a measure, again, of just how iconic Tom's Doctor is that he can get away with this sort of thing. This is the most unlikeable I think I've ever seen the Doctor – not merely as someone who's arrogant (like Pertwee) or tetchy (like Hartnell) or angry (like early Tom) – but as someone who's remote. A little of this can go a long way. But within the context of the episode, it feels pitch perfect. Every season opener since Spearhead from Space has tried to find a hook to catch the audience, something big and colourful – this is the first time that hasn't happened, that a new collection of stories has opened with something so deliberately minimalist and moody. Tom Baker here pitches his Doctor not as childhood teatime favourite, but as the quiet harbinger of doom in a slow burn horror movie. By playing it this small, playing it this dark, he fits right in with the claustrophobia of the set, and the ominous repeat of the foghorn. It might just be a result of bad temper, of not liking the script, of not trusting the director, of refusing to warm to the new companion – it might just be accidental. But Baker lends a gravitas to what would otherwise be a rather thin episode in which, really, very little happens, and there's lots of talk about the efficiency of gas.

You know Lou Jameson well, Toby, don't you? (She's played your mum! I'm very very fond of Lou, but she has never pretended to be my mum.) I know, again, from fan lore, that there's a scene here she's always been unhappy with. Something that she thought was only a rehearsal, so she played a scene too relaxed, with hand on hips. Do you know which one it is? I think I can identify it, but I can't be sure. I think it's testament to how brilliant Louise is, and how exacting and conscientious her per-

formance, that even these years later, one slight lapse can bother her. There's a difference to Leela here as well, a new authority – the way in which she takes Vince under her wing, and gently scolds him for talking to seals, is absolutely lovely. Last year, she played Leela most often as a naif, needing to be educated. In this grim episode, she emerges as a full adult. Even if Tom and Louise are acting somewhat in isolation, even against each other, this episode is blessed by having two such sterling performances at the centre of it.

T: When I was growing up, Horror of Fang Rock seemed the perfect fit for what I imagined Doctor Who to be like. It was a story I didn't remember, being broadcast just too early to have registered in my memory banks (presuming I even saw its TV debut). The Target novel, however – with a brooding Doctor equipped with rope, hat and oddly prominent veins on his cheek, and a lighthouse behind him in the gloom – is definitely one I remember buying. I think the premise appealed, as I had done The Ballad of Flannan Isle at school. That chilling piece made poetry not only easily digestible, but curious and foreboding and mysteriously compelling. Who needs comparing to a summer's day when you have a spooky lighthouse mystery?

And it helps that Terrance Dicks sets his stall early on, with the lighthouse keepers Reuben and Ben arguing about the relative merits of electricity – it's a clever foreshadowing of the threat about to lay siege to everyone. There's a believable working relationship between the three men on Fang Rock, and the actors deserve so much credit for adding texture to these efficiently, if broadly, sketched characters. The script paints Reuben as a superstitious old gasbag, but Colin Douglas turns him into something more – much of his joshing about modern technology is done with a hearty chuckle, and, after Ben is killed, his lament that his friend "won't rest easy" has a suitable undercurrent of troubled concern rather than simple histrionic foreboding. Douglas also retains his character's dignity whilst being mistrusting of foreigners – a lesser actor would have played Reuben's xenophobia and unfamiliarity with the Doctor's vocabulary as a cheap joke. And it's telling that Tom Baker responds to Douglas' intelligent portrayal by turning the Doctor's retort of "stubborn old mule" into a mused observation rather than a value judgement. The Doctor is familiar with Reuben's sort, noting that in the early days of oil, the man would have genuflected on the brilliance of the candle. (I say that even though such resistance to change is prominent among the Doctor's own fan base!)

I don't wish to imply that Dicks is only dealing in stereotypes, however. Yes, the lighthouse men display some ignorance, but Dicks, to his credit, refuses to patronise them. As Vince, John Abbot is clearly naive, young, scared and no intellectual colossus – but the Doctor and Leela treat him with respect because he's inherently decent. Vince's coyness as Leela blithely strips off in front of him is terribly sweet, whilst Reuben's bluff paternalism towards his young charge and gruff insistence that Ben's corpse is made "decent" also invests us in these characters. Only Ralph Watson sounds a duff note with his rather over-emphatic performance, but – as is the way with these things – he meets an early end as the alien seeks out the weakest actor, and makes him pay for his thespian misdemeanours.

Horror of Fang Rock (part two)

R: This is taking a few risks, isn't it? "Absolutely nothing is happening here!" asserts Lord Palmerdale, right before the rather muted cliffhanger – and my God, actually, he's right. If episode one burned on a slow flame, episode two is heated by a flickering match. But it's precisely because of what isn't happening, because of the false jeopardies (the Beast of Fang Rock, indeed!) and the false tensions (Harker's somewhat unconvincing slide, for one scene only, into vengeful strangler), that this episode keeps its viewers on edge. We keep on being presented with hints of death – and it's the very fact that this week it's scaled down only to fish, and that something more threatening is looming on the horizon, that makes us feel we're victims of some cruel game of nerves. It's because of what we don't see: Ben's body is never revealed, but the idea that he has been dragged under the ocean to be taken apart for analysis is grisly enough. The

siren sounds. More characters turn up, each one of them marked for death. The fog rolls in. And the Doctor tells everyone, with a grin, that they may well all be dead by morning. It's wonderful.

And Terrance Dicks punctuates these scenes of almost-drama, of almost-jeopardy, with dialogue from his new characters, selfish members of the gentry indignant to find themselves in a situation where class no longer has value. They are stereotypes, every single one of them. The first words we hear from Palmerdale's mouth are imperious and ungrateful, the first from Skinsale's are smug and mocking. But that is surely the point – the army stories of Skinsale, the greed of Lord Palmerdale, the haughty disdain of Adelaide – they all seem so trivial and mean beside the alien threat outside on the rocks. It's not subtle, but it's purposefully avoiding subtlety – Dicks expects us to know the form of this, that each and every one of these people are monster food, and deservedly, shamelessly so. All we can do now is wait for them to be picked off. It's all misdirection. All the exposition about Palmerdale's schemes and Skinsale's treachery, we can safely listen to this because we know none of it is remotely important – all that matters is the threat out there on the rocks, and there's no exposition to be had there, because horribly, terrifyingly, the Doctor still doesn't know anything to tell us. And that's the beauty of that cliffhanger. Muted it may be, but it's still a joke on us, still only a sly promise that the titular horror is about to start. There's a distant scream, the lights dim a bit, it's almost theatre rather than television. And we know that next week something quite clearly is going to rip the class divide apart once and for all.

T: As I write this, there's a preponderance of low-key acting on British TV. Less seems to be more in modern, urban fare – the current fashion is to employ non-actors for supposed authentic grittiness, whilst period dramas are full of rather buttoned-up toffs saying lots whilst seemingly doing little. This is all well and good, but will no doubt date in time, as all performance styles do. But what I love about the thesping in Horror of Fang Rock is that everyone has to keep acting to keep the screen alive, and bring texture to scenes that are essentially played out in real time. Watch how Louise Jameson, hamstrung by having to spend much of the early part of the episode tooting the foghorn, does so first with resentment at being left behind, then amusement at the strange sound, and finally *boredom* as she's got used to it and is waiting for everyone to get back. Three different emotions to enliven the same action: that's an actress at the top of her game.

Yet more texture is provided by Leela's cold, amoral remark "[The crew and passengers] will all die, then" before she turns her back on the crashing sailing ship – it's a reminder of her instinctive pragmatism. Later, in the boiler room, the Doctor insults Leela ("The people round here have been fisher folk for generations. They're almost as primitive and as superstition-ridden as your lot are."), but instead of wasting precious time by snapping back him, she registers momentary hurt before gently asking him to explain to her what has happened to Ben's body. There's even room for comedy, with Jameson's fearful lip-biting serving as a brilliant contrast to Tom Baker's amusement at the old wives' tale of the Beast of Fang Rock.

Baker, unfortunately, is marginally less consistent than his co-star – he's frequently brilliant (the way he treats the line "This lighthouse is under attack, and by morning we might all be dead" as a joke, for example), but one can see the first signs of his later waywardness. Yes, his mock horror about not having been introduced to the new characters displays eccentric inventiveness, but his obvious disengagement and ennui at the subsequent introductions shows an actor too keen to display his impatience with scripting necessities.

And sometimes, fine character work is a matter of small details. John Abbott is lovely whilst portraying Vince's polite dismissals of Sean Caffrey's snarling Palmerdale, all to accommodate Annette Woollett's prissy Adelaide. But just as we think the sweet lighthouseman's kindness may have exposed a chink in Adelaide's cold exterior, she calls him "Hawkins" to keep him in his place. Compare this with the Doctor addressing Vince as "Mr Hawkins" last week, and those simple word choices expose all talk of honour and decency among the upper classes as fatuous. Fortunately,

the Doctor has no truck with the hypocrisies and class-ridden divides of this period in Earth's history – for all his dismissals of Leela's savagery, it's clear he has far more respect for that (and indeed, for the hard-working sailor Harker) than for any of the "noble" gentry with whom he has been lumbered.

August 4th

Horror of Fang Rock (part three)

R: For the most part, this preserves the tension very well. Dicks very cleverly delays the slaughter by having the alien take on Reuben's features, and wait, statue still, until it is prepared to strike. Only we can see that the old man is not a human, and that Leela's attempts to break down the locked door he hides behind can only put her in direct contact with a killer. Unfortunately, some of the shock moments are confusing, and allow this tension to dissipate somewhat. You can see what is intended with Palmerdale's death scene, as he waits on the light gallery shrouded by fog – his electrocution should have been frighteningly abrupt, but instead the grammar of the scene is a bit incoherent. One moment he's alive, the next he's flashing a bit and there's a tentacle on his shoulder. Even more disappointingly, the revelation that Reuben has been dead for the entire episode is spoiled by the fact that we can't properly see Reuben's face.

They're minor points, maybe, but having kept the audience waiting this long for the deaths to start, it's a shame they're not a bit clearer. But one of the things I love most about the episode is the ambiguity elsewhere, within the dialogue and the characterisation. I said of last week's instalment that all the people waiting to be killed on Fang Rock were stereotypes, and deliberately so; I think that's true, but Dicks has fun suggesting little reserves of depth for them nonetheless. I love the way that Adelaide sneers at Leela, that she's tied to the Doctor by a piece of string – it speaks volumes about the manner in which she is dependent on Lord Palmerdale, and the self-loathing that she buries. Alan Rowe is great at Skinsale, a gentleman so defined by his corrupted honour he'll destroy the telegraph and put everyone's lives in danger. And best of all is the sequence where Vince delays informing the Doctor about Palmerdale's death, first of all setting fire to the cash he's been given so that no one can suspect he had a reason for killing him. It's a great scene, precisely because there's not a word of dialogue to explain it, and I'm quite sure his motives will have puzzled a lot of children – nowadays, there'd be some exposition to make sure everyone watching at home understood what he was doing – but it just hints at something darker about even likeable, guileless Vince. Even faced with death, his immediate impulse is one of self-preservation.

T: I disagree: it's pretty obvious what's happened to Palmerdale, because we've seen the radioactive golf ball climbing up the side of the lighthouse below where he stows himself, and Leela refers to Reuben when they kneel by his corpse. Things are as clear as they need to be... apart from Tom Baker doing one of his occasional flourishes of mispronunciation with the word "chameleon". It's an odd habit he indulges in every now and again, but while it should be disconcerting, I'm rather drawn to it. Indeed, this instance unconsciously echoes Pertwee's similar mistake with the erroneous hard "ch" on "chitinous" in The Green Death, so perhaps it's a consistent fault with the TARDIS translator (though one that's clearly repaired by the time The Christmas Invasion comes along).

Even though I have no memory of watching this episode at the time, it somehow captures, in 25 wonderful minutes, the absolute essence of Saturday teatime Doctor Who. This is 100% proof, best served with boiled eggs, soldiers, a roaring log fire and the goose bumps caused by a recent ejection from bath time. It *encapsulates* Doctor Who for me – terror, comedy and cliffhangers; they're what I always talked about the next day at school. The horror comes from the creepy alien, as personified by Colin Douglas' stony faced cadaver, stomping about looking strange before breaking out into a chilling grin, and dispatching Rio Fanning's brave and decent Harker. The humour? Well, Leela's slap to Adelaide is a long-awaited punchline to Annette Wollett's bravely shrill performance, Tom Baker is reliably funny, and Colonel Skinsale has a dry, caustic postulation that

Palmerdale has suggested they should all stick together so the creature will have "satisfied its appetite before it reaches [him]". And the cliffhangers in this story have all been slightly unusual – the ship hitting the rocks was possibly episode one's only weak spot, episode two's (a sudden scream shocking the inhabitants of the mess room) was surprising and effective, and this week's is a real *Oh-My-God-What-Have-We-Done?* moment that really benefits from Baker's hushed, steely gravitas.

But what brings all these traditional elements together so brilliantly, and adds that extra edge that makes them so special, is the character of Skinsale. He's a terrible hypocrite, yet he's witty, he's likably cunning in the way he manipulates Adelaide out of his way, and he's in opposition to Palmerdale – which can only be a good thing in our eyes, considering His Lordship registering really high on the Twat-o-meter. To his credit, Skinsale has no hesitation about going outside to help Palmerdale, though the two of them are enemies, and it's through Skinsale that we understand the true seriousness of the crisis. He's not a *nice* character necessarily, but we like him anyway because Alan Rowe infuses him with a beguiling dignity and charm. For all that Doctor Who is a series about a time traveller and his companion, we so often invest in the incidental characters on a story-by-story basis, because we don't know if they'll survive or not. Especially as, having made us care for this disparate group, the story seems to be bumping them off at an alarming rate.

Horror of Fang Rock (part four)

R: This ought to have been so contrived. Louise Jameson had persuaded the new production team to let her stop using the brown contact lenses that caused her eyes so much irritation, and here at the climax of the story, she looks out on an explosion which changes their pigmentation to blue. And it's a beautiful scene – Leela is the little child hiding behind the sofa, peeping out to watch all the action even though she's been warned not to, of course she stares at the destruction of the mothership. She asks the Doctor to slay her. He takes the knife. He breaks into a grin. She blinks; her vision swims back, the first thing she sees is that grin, the grin of her best friend. He gently tells her she can stop blinking; he tells her her eyes are blue. And after four weeks of the Doctor being so cold, and barely looking at his companion, it fills the final moments with something that feels sweet and redemptive. A script insert to tweak a continuity point? Indeed. But it's a happy accident too, it's something full of heart, in a story where everybody has been butchered.

Because make no mistake, this is a bleak tale. That final scene aside, I find it telling that the only time the Doctor looks fully at ease with himself is when he's sitting on the lighthouse steps having a cheery chinwag with a green pulsating blob. It's almost as if he feels uncomfortable around humans – if they could only just trust him and follow his lead, they'd be all right, but they're so petty and small. There's something so unforgiving about the way the script treats Skinsale. He's given the opportunity to stay safe in the lamp room, but insists upon helping the Doctor anyway. It's all in the handshake the Doctor gives him once Skinsale has handed over the diamonds – had Skinsale merely followed him up the stairs, he'd have been another in a series of amiable Victorian gentlemen, he'd have been another Professor Litefoot. Instead, he takes one moment to pick up some fallen jewels, and is killed for giving in to temptation. Adelaide's death is so abrupt it feels insultingly dismissive – the scene actually opens on Reuben electrocuting her, there's no build-up, there's no time for the audience to flinch or care. And poor Vince – the Doctor calls to Leela and Skinsale that Vince will help them, but Vince is long dead, and the Doctor doesn't ever find any words to comment upon it.

I'm in two minds about the Rutan. I suppose it has to say something eventually, but as soon as it does, it's turned from being a nameless, purposeless alien into yet another dull military species. How much better it might have been had the creature remained unknowable, killing instinctively because that's all it did, until it was destroyed? Suddenly wedging this frightening new species into the established Doctor Who universe, by revealing that it is the enemy of the Sontarans of all things robs it of some power. But what else, really, could the story do? You can hide in shadows for three episodes, but at some point you have to deliver a pay-off – otherwise, for all the monster might stay scarier, the story just fizzles into anticlimax. Attaching it to Who history is a surprise at this stage of the series, and it's not a card that's been played too often. (And this is an episode too which mentions both the Doctor's Time Lord superiority, and the Sontaran army, to great effect. Is this an intentional hint of where the season might be going?)

And Leela is just wonderful. Whether she's gloating over the Rutan death throes, or delaying her own escape from an exploding lighthouse to resheath her knife, she's emerging as a character more eccentric than the Doctor himself. I think Louise Jameson deserves to be free of the contact lenses.

T: Leela's change of eye colour is not the only happy accident here – there's also the fact that Louise Jameson came into the series when Tom Baker started to get a bit tetchy and difficult. This means you have a spiky, remote Doctor, with Jameson's 24-carat instinct and selflessness as an actress injecting the pragmatic savage she's given on the page with a gentle inquisitiveness and a childlike humour, which tempers her co-star's grumpiness and softens her own character's edges. If she hadn't done all of that, these two would be constantly rubbing themselves the wrong way and no fun to watch. Instead, they are fascinating, quirky, multi-layered and never boring.

In much the same manner, it's possible to glean a story's strengths and weaknesses from the way different aspects of the script are interpreted. Paddy Russell hired Colin Douglas because she needed an actor of quality to stop Reuben being a tiresome cliché, and to do something different with a walking cadaver (she had dead-eyed Bernard Archard coldly striding about not that long ago, so repetition was a potential risk). Douglas' make-up is cold and clammy, whilst the piercing eyes and grotesque grin he affects before unleashing an electric shock upon his victims is truly horrifying. Poor Vince is despatched with undue haste, but in his brief screen time this episode, John Abbot does well and conveys sheer, heart-thumping terror. He was such a sweet character, viewers could have reasonably expected both him and Skinsale to survive...

... and the genius of the latter is that Alan Rowe never once plays his character as flawed. Less talented performers would have signposted his weakness, having read the script and knowing the character's inevitable end point, but Rowe plays Skinsale as what he thinks himself to be: straight, honourable and brave. Actually, he *is* all of those things – but like a real, complicated human being, he's also foolish, avaricious and selfish, and it only takes a split second of folly to cost him his life. I'm saddened, though, that after Skinsale perishes in the book, Leela asks if he died with honour and the Doctor lies (recalling that scrabbling on the floor for diamonds is no way to meet your maker) – softening the blow by saying that he did. It's a much more complex and fitting coda for the character than Tom Baker's rushed and dismissive "Dead – with honour" that we get on screen. I'm assuming that Baker himself is bringing a lot of these alterations to the table, and whilst many of them are inventive and offbeat – and give the whole programme a slightly dangerous edge – I can see his control of his creativity beginning to fray at the edges here. (And I know that I too am doing this with benefit of hindsight, but I can't help that.)

Once again, in pointing up the moments where everyone is going against what's on the page (either pro or con), I'm not meaning to do Terrance Dicks a disservice. Doctor Who legend that he is, Dicks still doesn't get enough credit for the fact that, at his peak, he could match the more-celebrated Robert Holmes in terms of character and dialogue. There are scores of great lines in this story, and all of the actors have plenty of good stuff to get their teeth into over the course of the four episodes. The conclusion is deftly linked together – using the lighthouse to destroy the spaceship with a diamond as a focussing device allows both Skinsale and Leela to contribute to their enemy's defeat, as well as making use of the unique location. Only the Doctor's long chat with the Rutan on the stairs feels a little exposition-by-numbers, and it's not helped by the inconsistent perspectives of the creature – meaning it appears to be a different size depending on which angle we see it from. It's the only really duff sequence in the whole thing, and a regrettable blemish in Russell's

generally splendid Doctor Who oeuvre (of which this will be the last entry).

As the TARDIS dematerialises in a superb model shot, moodily augmented by Tom Baker's echoing rendition of The Ballad of Flannan Isle, I feel that I'm going through a period of Doctor Who that is so consistently great, I worry I'm only responding positively because my personal life has put me in a permanent good mood. Let's see if The Invisible Enemy proves me wrong!

The Invisible Enemy (part one)

R: I suppose a lot of people think this is what Doctor Who is like all the time: spaceships flying through asteroid belts, being attacked by strange tendrilled phenomena, running down lots of shiny white corridors waving blaster guns. (No, no, that's Blake's Seven!) And yet what's immediately striking watching this now is how little we've ever really seen of Doctor Who doing space opera – and also, so surprisingly, is how here it's done so well. I'm not the man to ask about special effects; I'm the sort who never sees the wobbly sets, or the cheap design work, or the models that look like plastic bottles – I'm lucky, I have a sort of blind spot about such things. (I dare say that made my becoming a Doctor Who fan so much easier.) But I've just seen this episode on the official DVD, and the special effects were so good I thought for a moment I might have put on some alternate new take in which 2Entertain had restored it with CGI. No, really. Admittedly, there is one effect near the beginning which made me chuckle a little, as the ship nudges its way awkwardly through some rock debris, which looked to me for all the world like a little dog sniffing for biscuits. But I even found that endearing.

So it's space opera... done well! I believe in this world that writers Bob Baker and Dave Martin have created, in the frustration of spaceship crew who think they're overqualified petrol pump attendants, who turn off the automatic controls out of boredom. I believe even in the usual Baker/ Martin staple, the signs that are all written in phonetic English. (They do like to go for that, don't they?) It's all done by clever shorthand – we hear the Doctor's tale of these human pioneers ranging from Earth like a disease, and then we see the reality of ordinary people staving off boredom by having celebratory drinks in the mess. And it means that when the Nucleus turns Safran and his relief crew into killers, as they gun down the staff they are replacing, there seems a shocking brutality to it – the direction is a little anodyne, maybe, and those red splotches that appear on the screen whenever a gun is fired are a bit pretty, but there's still a sense that amiable, bumbling humanity is being wiped away by something alien and purposeful.

And that's helped, too, by the way that the Doctor is so quickly attacked. Once in a while, we'll see Tom Baker getting possessed for a few minutes (Pyramids of Mars) or having an android double (The Android Invasion), but it's always at the end of the story, right when the stakes are high – and there's something peculiarly reassuring about that, because we recognise it's the climax and this is as bad as things get. Here, before the Doctor even knows he's in an adventure, his mind is under assault, and contact has been made. It reads like a strange joke in the novelisation, but there is something decidedly sinister in the way the Doctor starts getting the syllables of his companion's name mixed up. When the Doctor affably offers help to Safran and Meeker, you fear for him a little, and that's an unusual thing – and it's because the Doctor is already vulnerable. There is a wonderful image in the TARDIS early on of Leela, like a scared child, nibbling away at the end of the Doctor's scarf for comfort – and it subtly symbolises so much of the way the Doctor is a kindly figure for the little boys and girls. But it also suggests, just this once, that Leela maybe shouldn't get too close. That this time the Doctor himself might be someone you can't trust, and that he'll creep up behind you with a gun. Brr.

T: This is my earliest memory of Doctor Who. I distinctly remember the two-level spaceship set, with one pilot in the foreground and two behind him and below. I remember where I was and that my two brothers were there. It wasn't the original transmission, I don't think, but a repeat because I clearly recall one of my brothers saying "Oh yes, this is where their faces turn furry". So hello, The Invisible Enemy – for better or worse, the story

that began my long, strange path through a life in which Doctor Who has been an absolute constant. Nothing I've done since, from travelling on the tube to computer passwords or even my wedding, has occurred without it being pretty near the forefront of my thoughts. Contact has most certainly been made.

But do you want the bad news? Up until today, I could see in my mind's eyes the crackly virus lighting zapping the crew from their control panel, and their faces (as my brother had said) turning furry. Except they don't! You don't see their funky space eyebrows until much later, on Titan, after they've zapped the crew and removed their masks. But I have this unshakeable mental image, burned there from my childhood. And it was wrong! John Nathan-Turner's name started its unbroken run ('till the classic series ends) on the closing credits of Horror of Fang Rock. One story later, his most famous saying rears its head and, to my surprise, proves itself to be true. The memory cheats, Rob, the memory cheats.

I've never really thought of The Invisible Enemy much beyond it being that milestone. I'm aware of its status as being K-9's debut, of course, and being inspired by Fantastic Voyage, but I've never really stopped to ponder what the story is about, and whether it's any good. I've always rather suspected it was a bit poor – but this episode is terrific fun. It's an odd mix, with the design being perhaps the most impressive element. Those model effects are absolutely *beautiful*, the scene of the shuttle landing on Titan being as good as anything seen in the series so far. The costume design is effective too: the astronaut outfits are futuristic without being silly, and they're snugly fitting and practical looking. No crazy space nonsense here.

There is crazy space nonsense elsewhere, though, as the baddies are forced to repeat catchphrases. "Contact has been made" is one (and a rather spooky one at that), but poor old Edmund Pegge as Meeker gets lumbered with having to repeat the line "must not be harmed" once too often. Brian Grellis, fine when Safran is the business-like commander of his vessel, adopts a strangulated diction when inhabited by the Nucleus that cannot ever be anything other than comical. A shame, as elsewhere Michael Sheard is acting his socks off. Indeed, we're introduced to Sheard's Lowe before the Doctor and Leela meet him, and he shows much bravery and intelligence in evading the infected crew. He's setting himself up to be the story's Useful Ally... so it's doubly shocking when the episode climaxes with him being taken over!

And even though this story gets pilloried for being a load of old tat, I'm intrigued by some of the themes that Baker and Martin wish to explore. As well as the concept of mankind as a disease that you noted, I enjoy Meeker's decision to switch his automated vessel to manual control – because even though the computer will be telling him what to do, "at least I will be doing it". For this bored spaceman, independence and defiant free will stave off the ennui. Later, those same attributes become the very things that the villain of the piece steals from its victims.

I'm pleased that I enjoyed this, Rob, this thief of my Doctor Who virginity. I'm not sure it's the best time I'll ever have, but it was brisk and peppy and fun, without too much embarrassment, not to mention lots of action and a memorable climax. On a totally unrelated subject, I'm off to enjoy the last night of my honeymoon.

August 5th

The Invisible Enemy (part two)

R: The story moves in an unexpected direction. You've got to give it that.

From episode one, you would have believed that this would become a rather tense yarn about possession – with the Doctor in anguish as he loses control of his mind – in a story set on a forbidding and claustrophobic base on Titan. But within minutes, we're in a big gleaming space hospital, where the nurses and receptionists wear gleaming green plastic dresses, and the new guest star is saddled with a Germanic accent and a robot dog.

I'm not criticising, you understand. Just calling it as I see it. If anything, that's the best thing about The Invisible Enemy – that once again, Bob Baker and Dave Martin are letting their imagination fire in all directions. The results may seem a bit higgledy-piggledy at best (and utterly random when not), but their script is wild and unpredictable, and has a surprising amount of wit. K-9 is a truly terrific creation, a robot dog that a doctor has invented to flout bureaucratic regulations and ensure he can have a pet with him – the joy of K-9 is that he could so easily have just been an easy play at cuteness for the kids, but instead is smug and arrogant. The joke is that Professor Marius wants man's best friend, and wants a supercomputer, and can see no problem with combining the two into one machine – in one instance, you'd have thought, making the pet rather charmless and the computer rather ridiculous. It'd be the equivalent of someone deciding he really wanted to listen to his Mp3 player whilst eating a grilled cheese sandwich, and thinking it'd be a good idea to combine the iPod with a toaster. K-9 works here not merely because he's a robot dog (with toy potential), but because he reveals so much about the eccentricity of his master, and the maverick ways that Marius refuses to conform to the starchy routines of the Bi-Al Foundation. It's a smart piece of characterisation; if you can imagine that K-9 features in no other story but this one (which was, of course, the original intention), if you can divorce him from all the adventures that follow and K-9 and Company and The Sarah Jane Adventures, then it's easier to see here what he represents. That he's a little touch of madness, and so placed in direct opposition to the humourless hive mentality that the Nucleus represents.

There's ambition here in spades. There's a lot of action crammed into this episode, there are gunfights and spaceship crashes, there's cloning and miniaturisation. And that's a problem, because Derrick Goodwin's direction really isn't up to it. It's not just complex sequences he seems to have a problem with – actors even walk awkwardly under his command. But it almost doesn't matter, because for all that the episode is robbed of any tension, it's replaced with a comic ludicrousness that is genuinely endearing. Watching Michael Sheard get wheeled around, randomly taking over listless members of the medical profession on their tea break, is actually very funny. In typical Doctor Who stories, the alien tries to take over the minds of the powerful and the strong. In The Invisible Enemy, the villain's main henchman is a nameless ophthalmologist wearing a magnifying glass. The episode moves dizzyingly fast, and deliberate or not, this shift in focus from moody thriller to camp comedy is all part of that energy.

And even if Frederick Jaeger's performance as Marius relies too much upon a silly voice, he's a good actor with a decent role, and somehow the authority comes through. And John Leeson is excellent, firstly as a Virus in paranoid anguish as it fears for its safety inside the Doctor's brain. And, more obviously, as a robot dog who isn't trying to be likeable or winsome, and certainly isn't trying to be iconic, but is an arresting character in his own right.

T: That's it, the honeymoon is over. Before we leave, though, our plane is delayed. "Why don't we sit outside and watch your Doctor Whos on the laptop while we wait?" says Katherine, in a manner suggesting this feeling of mutual benevolence between us might last for some time. As I watch, she returns my needy glances with reassuring, loving half-smiles (but tinged with pity?). I get the impression that she thinks it's rather endearing that I like this crazy sci-fi fare of clearly dubious quality. We do the first two episodes before the plane arrives. I resolve to watch the last one at home when she's in bed; she never once hints that she needs to see the resolution, and I see no need to push her. I daren't ask her what she thinks. Maybe the secret of a happy marriage is to not ask the difficult questions.

If, as you say, everyone is acting a bit funny, maybe it's the acting I need to muse upon. I make no bones about the fact that I became an actor because I wanted to be in Doctor Who. That's all I've ever wanted to do. If I achieve that goal, I will never again complain about my lot – my childhood self would be thrilled. I Am Not Alone in this. I have a programme for a production of, I think, Richard II at the Ludlow Festival, and nestling at the bottom of the biog of Jim McManus (who here plays the Ophthalmologist) is the wonderful sentence "Jim has just fulfilled a lifelong ambition by filming three episodes of Doctor Who". I bet no-one's ever been prompted to do that by being cast in Bergerac or Crossroads!

But it's also important that none of the supporting parts are especially memorable; it actu-ally empathises that each actor has their own story to tell nonetheless. The medics Cruickshank and Hedges don't even get a close-up, and barely register as characters, quickly becoming faceless Nucleus drones. Appearing as two-lines Hedges is Kenneth Waller, later to find fame as Old Mr Grace in Are You Being Served? and as Granddad in Bread. Roderick Smith (Cruickshank) has managed to continue his acting career to this day – no mean feat – and had a similarly minor role in David Tennant's Hamlet earlier this year. The profession relies on journeymen performers like Smith, who've never played a major part, but are prepared to show up and do those less rewarding bits that, frankly, someone has to fill.

As for Michael Sheard: well, it's not his most memorable part either, and if you compare what he and Frederick Jaeger are doing here with their previous Who outings, they are found wanting, but... maybe that's what this script needs. It is so flatly directed, the fun comes from seeing slightly arch, affected performances which provide a bit of life amongst the stark functionality of the clinical white sets, and the scant opportunities for the rest of the cast to make an impression. Jaeger gets better once his casual exchanges with the conveniently revived Doctor come to an end, and he has to take on the demeanour of thoughtful, dogged boffin. The one moment of real tension and drama is when the shuttle crashes into the Bi-Al and, upon finding an infected corpse, Professor Marius is forced to initiate defensive procedures – there's none of the earlier silliness in play during this all-too brief period. Tom Baker is very good at suggesting the Doctor's vulnerability when fighting the virus on Titan, but when he's with Jaeger, it looks as if he relies too much on their shared presence as actors, so doesn't bother to make too much effort.

All of that said, I suppose that The Invisible Enemy is where my fascination with actors really began – which is interesting, considering how few of them in it get anything decent to do. The fun lies in all those tangential discoveries, and my propensity for rooting out trivial factoids has provided my life with endless fascinations. If that makes me a bit of a saddo, so be it – but lest we forget, decades after this story was broadcast and this mad show got its crazy claws into me, both Sheard and Jaeger passed away, and it fell to someone to write their obituaries for The Guardian. And on both occasions, that honour fell to me, so it's not as if my labours have been wasted. Frankly, it was the least I could do.

The Invisible Enemy (part three)

R: Now, everybody knows that this episode, featuring a miniaturised Doctor and Leela exploring the inside of a brain, was inspired by the movie Fantastic Voyage. But I do wonder whether its greater influence was a little bit closer to home. So, once again, that difficult third episode of a story is given over to a largely experimental set piece in compressed time (the entirety of this instalment lasts less than ten minutes). The Doctor lies unconscious, and half of the drama explores what is going on inside his own head, whilst outside his friends try to save him from attack. And there's a section where the Doctor stands looking out upon the realm of dreams and fantasy. It's not surely too much of a stretch to believe that that sequence inside the Matrix in The Deadly Assassin had made such an impression that, only a year later, the series wanted to pay homage to it?

There are crucial differences, of course. The Invisible Enemy has our heroes running around a CSO backdrop, and comes to a climax when Tom Baker debates ethics with a black bag with a claw sticking out of it. But the visual limitations aside, what's interesting is how this episode chooses to make literal what The Deadly Assassin set-up as metaphor. When we write of the phrase, that the drama gets "inside someone's head", we mean that it becomes an examination of that character, their thoughts and their core beliefs. In The Invisible Enemy we get inside the Doctor's head not through literary conceit, but through an injection somewhere below the ear.

I think there's a wit to that. And it is telling that the wit is shanghaied by a cheapness that makes the joke look crass; the budget crises that plague Doctor Who for the rest of the decade seem to begin in earnest here. When clone Leela is attacked by the Doctor's phagocytes, by extension it is the Doctor himself that

is threatening her – and this is a clever corollary of how the story began, with the Doctor being the aggressor and advancing upon his companion with a blaster drawn. But this time round she's being menaced by a bunch of soft white footballs, and the parallel is lost behind the embarrassment. I personally have no problem with the CSO – it makes the brain look unreal, it's true, but it also emphasises a stylistic difference from the action "within" and the action "without", as everyone races around a hospital. But when the action "without" is mishandled so badly, with badly set-up special effects and awkward blocking, the distinction isn't clear enough.

And it's a shame, because for all its faults (and dear God, this episode has them), its conceit is very clever, and its ambition laudable. (And not only laudable – we'll sometimes have a laugh at Bob Baker and Dave Martin for how they push the production into areas it can simply never pull off, but there's no reason why, with the same sort of care that was given to the jungle in Planet of Evil, for example, this wouldn't have not only looked good but served as eerie contrast to the sterility of the Bi-Al Foundation.) As the Doctor and Leela run around with their limited lives, the script zips with wit and invention – the micro-Doctor ducking from a "passing thought" as the macro-Doctor lifts his leg is not only funny, but inviting the audience to reassess the perspectives of all that it is seeing. It may be biologically absurd, but I think the distinction the Doctor makes between the brain and the mind is very powerful – the realms of functionality and imagination living side by side, and our heroes having to walk into all-enveloping darkness to face them. And there's the hint of something very sinister here, as the clones understand completely they are doomed to only a few minutes' life, and yet still have the same breadth of personalities and intellects as their donors in the macro world. This is an episode, quite bluntly, where the Doctor and Leela try to get a task completed quickly before certain death – and there can be no reprieve or escape. In concept, I prefer this to its parent episode in The Deadly Assassin: in that story, the stakes were always a bit more confused, as the Doctor dodges moments of terror by denying their reality. In practice, of course, it just doesn't come off. But it's something still to cherish, surely?

T: "I am the Nucleus of the Swarm"... I remember lolloping about the house whispering that line, so it just goes to show how a creature with a catchphrase can make an impact on an impressionable juvenile. I had no idea what a Nucleus even *was*; I suspect I simply thought it was the name of the monster. But it clearly made a mark, despite so much else of this being ropey. (Michael Sheard, lumbered with having to wander about inside Tom Baker's head – now there's a thing I'd like to do – has clearly had a subtlety-ectomy on his visit to the Bi-Al.)

Not an awful lot happens in this episode, really, and the revelation of the Sackcloth of Doom with which the Doctor has a jeopardy-free exchange suggests the director's gallery is on autopilot. Fortunately, although much of Derrick Goodwin's execution is anaemic and leaden, he handles the weirder stuff with a certain élan. (It would be churlish to criticise a Doctor Who episode because the effects fall short, though – to a layperson's eyes, even the most skilful material from this period looks dated and poor, so it's a meaningless parameter.) The simple use of coloured bubbles to indicate travelling into the Doctor's body provides some pleasing imagery, though I would query using a bubbly liquid with which to facilitate the insertion of the clones. If Mary Whitehouse was right and kids copied behaviour seen in the show, a number of games of Doctors and Nurses in the week this was broadcast would have ended with the bends or an embolism.

Fortunately, whilst the Doctor saunters around his own brain, I'm happy to discover that mine isn't as damaged as I thought! My memories of episode one may have been erroneous, but the scene of Leela pressed against the wall shooting at Lowe and his zombies was pretty much exactly as I recall it. K-9 and Leela make a great team, and the moment where he – under the thrall of the Nucleus – loses control, fails to kill her and crashes into the wall in confusion is clearly and effectively done. More so, let's face it, than the very awkward laser battles which are convincing no-one, not even those taking part.

And best of all, even if this turgid sci-fi nonsense is what stuck in my head when I was younger, adult Toby is catered to by more subtle fare. My favourite moments involve Marius and Perkins bravely arming themselves and resolving to despatch each other should they get infected, and then hiding the nurse, so she will be safe should their defences fail. It's a small moment of ordinary men doing what must be done, even though they're not accustomed to combat. That we get a little pang when poor old Parsons is unceremoniously gunned down later is due to Roy Herrick's efforts, given that he otherwise has very little to do.

At the end of the day, the fact that this is a bit tatty in some places and over-the-top in others provides the most entertainment. This is a television episode from the 1970s that has Mr Bronson from Grange Hill made up to look like a silvery space owl, crawling around inside someone's brain at the bidding of a giant space prawn. It was never going to be something we could take entirely seriously, was it? And that, perversely, is what saves it all these years later.

The Invisible Enemy (part four)

R: I know I have this annoying tendency, Toby, when Doctor Who seems to go off the rails, to pretend that there was some sort of deliberate method within it. I know. But bear me out.

This is a very curious episode. It sets up at the beginning a moral debate about the sanctity of life, and the right of a virus to exist. And then having done so, it returns to the debate as if it's nothing more than a running joke. (Doctor Who and the Silurians, this isn't.) Leela thinks that the best way of destroying the Swarm would be to blow it up. The Doctor believes that there has to be another way. He spends precious minutes of plot finding an antidote to the virus – and, having done so, Leela proclaims (and with such triumph, it comes across as a callous gag) that the possessed humans on Titan are better cured with a knife blow to the neck. K-9 makes his first trip in the TARDIS, and the Doctor won't tell Marius the special purpose he has for him – which is that the metal dog has is to act as a gun. And when, finally, after all the story's talk of medicine and ethics, after the Doctor *does* merely blow up the Swarm and its followers, he has a good maniacal chuckle about it and claims that it was all his brilliant idea!

It's all pretty horrible. But Doctor Who so often does this. We saw it throughout the Pertwee era (for which, let's not forget, Baker and Martin were regular writers, and amongst the more empathetic of their number; whether it be their handling of the Mutts or the compromised existence of Omega, there was a willingness to engage with the ethical dilemmas raised in the story, and not merely rely upon a big explosion at the end). The peculiarity of this episode is not that it betrays its idealism at the end with lots of gun battles and death, it's that it takes such pains to forefront the moralistic concerns and then laugh at them. It might seem very clumsy. But I wonder if there's some attempt here to criticise the tropes of the show itself: that for all its precious talk, this is how the stories always end – with guns, and pyrotechnics, and loud bangs.

And that peculiar sense of things being out of key is carried everywhere else within the plotting. We keep on being presented with red herrings that don't go anywhere, with dilemmas that are fixed without effort. Why stress that the Doctor and Leela are trapped in an operable TARDIS, just to have K-9 simply blast their way to freedom a minute later? Why go to all the trouble of finding antibodies in Leela's bloodstream, only to lose the antidote once they get to Titan? Leela asks the Doctor why he took off in the TARDIS without her; he doesn't give an answer, it's just another illogical unexplained thing that happened randomly, in an episode which seems to want to emphasise that the plotting of Doctor Who is a mixture of the illogical and the unexplained.

Either way, let's face it. Clever critique of the show's limitations, or soulless betrayal of the show's ideals, this isn't the episode you'd put on to try to impress a floating viewer that Doctor Who is a good programme. And the monster that's so ungainly – it can't even walk without two extras carrying it down a corridor – is the least of the problems. ("Shall we try using our intelligence?" asks the Doctor. "Well," says Leela doubtfully, "if you think that's a good idea...")

T: First off, let me address a pet hate. The guys propelling the Nucleus down the corridors aren't extras. They are *actors playing smaller roles*. It's quite a distinction, and a mistake made all too frequently in the press. It's like when they say an actor was "unknown and had only played bit parts for the RSC", as if his sudden rise in Hollywood is a kind of fairytale. No – "unknown" means he had a top agent upon leaving drama school, but hadn't been in EastEnders or anything else the journalist has watched on telly, and those "bit parts" were major supporting roles such as Edmund in King Lear or Mercutio in Romeo and Juliet, which the journalist hadn't seen because the newest EastEnders was on. *You*, on the other hand, have no such excuse, Rob. An extra didn't have to audition and isn't playing a featured, speaking role. These two are. (Talk about carrying a virus, though – these guys are doing it literally.)

Anyway, now that I feel better for having got that lecture out of the way... and at the risk of seeming like a curmudgeon... this *must* be the clumsiest Doctor Who episode yet rendered in the colour era, mustn't it? I mean, this is the same series that produced The Talons of Weng-Chiang but nine episodes ago! The chief problem is that there's a sudden self-awareness in the production style, and to overcome the shortcomings, everyone tries to give everything they're doing a certain unrealistic edge. The results aren't pretty – yes, there's much fun to be had from the various bits of charging about and exchanges of laser fire, but it's scuppered by those moments being very shoddily staged. (There's an especially off occasion where Goodwin favours a close-up of the tank creatures during the vital moment when Lowe zaps the cure from the Doctor's hands.)

At its best, this has a sense of grand folly about it. There's something rather wonderful, for instance, about the way that Tom Baker attempts to retain his dignity by batting the Nucleus' fronds away, even as he's stuck on a bed and talking to an intergalactic space prawn. Besides, if you're going to do folly, why *not* be grand about it? Huge sci-fi concepts have been introduced during this story: cloning, shrinking and viral infection on a galactic scale, and they've been thrown in with such a casual flourish that borders on the heroic. The execution is frequently ham-fisted and clunky, true, but we still get moments of huge skill – the Quatermass II-style blobby creatures are another of the story's superb model sequences. And let's credit John Leeson with being an important contributor to K-9's success, whilst also acknowledging that the guttural, alien screeching of his Nucleus is quite unsettling. Add that to the strange boingy noises in the Doctor's brain last week and Dudley Simpson going hell for leather musically throughout all four episodes, and The Invisible Enemy – if nothing else – has a very interesting sound-scape.

But however much it pains me to say it, we're starting to see some tattiness creeping into the show, and the acceptance of a certain sloppiness. There's no way K-9 could get into the TARDIS as quickly and unimpeded as he does – *we* know this, Tom Baker knows this, and the director knows this, but the latter two are telling us they don't care, and aren't interested in trying to make us do so either. I'm hard-pressed to say that The Invisible Enemy is overwhelmingly bad – it's diverting enough, and some of the silliness makes it endearing. But this is the first time in a while that I've found Doctor Who entertaining in spite of the good bits, rather than because of them.

August 6th

Image of the Fendahl (part one)

R: You were quite right to pick me up on using the term "extra" yesterday. Really, there's no excuse – like you, I'm married to an actor! But I suppose what I clumsily meant was not an insult to the cast, but to the characters – that sometimes the series metes out a terrible indignity upon its villains by having them flanked by henchmen that haven't even been given the grace of a single line! (It's something we run into much later, when you see victims being gunned down in 80s stories without so much as the benefit of a scream – it suggests that they aren't even people (and yes, Resurrection of the Daleks, I am looking at you). But enough of my self-justifying quibbling. On to a story in which there are lots of defined characters! Even if I can't quite understand what any of them are going on about.

This episode is really very odd. The atmosphere is quite unlike anything I think we've ever felt in Doctor Who before; there have been lots of stories influenced by Nigel Kneale over the years, but never one with the pace and style of one of those strange adult BBC plays of his (the sort that my parents would have never let me watch – the sort that took themselves so earnestly that whenever I caught a scene of them, even though I had no idea what people were talking about, they would leave me wide-eyed and sleepless with fear). And the adult fan in me now finds that fascinating. I think the opening five minutes, going back and forth between scientific enquiry and horror imagery, are especially effective. It's hard to put my finger on what is the more frightening – the paradox about the provenance of a skull and the questions that raises about human evolution, or the crossfades between the same skull glowing with Wanda Ventham's face. Either way, the nature of the horror here is not the sort we've come to expect on Doctor Who. It raises difficult questions, it's subtle, it's dissonant.

We're well used to any story rushing about in its opening episode to give us establishing scenes of the growing crisis, and the people it's going to affect – right before the Doctor swans in, and orders them about or gets threatened by them. What makes this episode especially disquieting is its refusal to conform to type. It maintains that deliberate pace right the way through its 25-minute length (and even though it gives us double jeopardy in the cliffhanger, in no way does the direction allow us to feel we're working our way towards a climax). The result of this is twofold. The first is that this is rather more dull than we're used to – with characters more intelligent than us talking with great sincerity about projects we don't understand, and that the script shows no great interest in wanting us to understand. And the second is – brilliantly, against all odds – that this dullness in itself is disorientating. We can't get a handle on it. Dudley Simpson barely lets forth a musical cue, something that would reassure us that this is just Doctor Who. Without either the script or the production providing us with any recognisable house style, we watch with growing unease. There's something very sinister going on. And it's all the more terrifying because it won't identify itself. The humming of the time scanner, the simple close-up of that skull – they're a far cry from the easy shocks of humans with silver eyebrows, or even glowing green blobs approaching a lighthouse.

The Doctor and Leela do appear, of course. But even by the episode's ending, they still haven't interacted with any of the main cast. (They do, however, have a chat with some cows.) And this may be where the episode suffers. Because somehow, alongside the rather persuasive scenes of clever people doing clever things in Fetch Priory, the exploits of the Doctor with his robot dog and all his silliness seem very out of place. All the comedy is restricted to these scenes between our regulars – but it's all rather forced, isn't it? The Doctor is being a deliberate eccentric, pointing out with too comic irony that the planet they're visiting is Earth, and arguing about his piloting of the TARDIS as he's done a hundred times before. And unexpectedly, in the hands of Chris Boucher, her creator, Leela has regressed into a character who is all savage huntress tics and amoral misunderstandings. Seeing Tom Baker and Louise Jameson banter in the TARDIS, or threatening the local populace with knives and jelly babies, looks just a little like two preposterous mainstays from a popular family BBC show invade an adult drama. It'd be a little as if we were watching Morecambe and Wise bumbling around in the forest. The Doctor and Leela aren't written as characters. They're written as familiar archetypes here, and seem less real than the world they're about to interact with.

I suppose this isn't a good thing. I suppose this means that there's something vaguely unsatisfying about this episode, as if something just isn't firing correctly. But strangely, the awkwardness of the Doctor/ Leela sequences only make the whole seem even more eerie. The pacing is shot to hell, you can't tell what's going on, the director doesn't seem to understand what Doctor Who feels like, and even our heroes seem disjointed and out of sync. This is scary stuff.

T: The Invisible Enemy is my first memory of watching Doctor Who, but I'm pretty certain that Image of the Fendahl was the first Target novel I bought. At last, I was out from the shadows of inheriting dusty old tomes that, if each had their own, belonged to one or other of my brothers. There was small selection for sale in The Castle Bookshop in Ludlow (the nearest town to my house), and I made sure to choose one that we definitely didn't have. The rather odd cover featured a somewhat abstract rendering of a reassuringly venomous-looking monster menacing the Doctor and what looked like a grandfather clock. The opening pages were exciting stuff, describing the last steps of an obviously doomed hiker. (Do people hike through woods at midnight anymore? I don't think so, and suspect Doctor Who is largely responsible for that fact.) I brandished the book triumphantly at my brother when I got home, only to hear him reply, "Oh, we've already got that one". *What?* Well, it wasn't on the shelf with the others, I was sure of that (I'd rearranged them often enough). Lo and behold, though – a couple of weeks later, it was found nestling elsewhere, consigning the excitement and "mine"ness of the new purchase to redundancy.

I've described earlier how Quatermass and the Pit marked an important development in my life, as it was the first time since childhood that my family had not looked disapprovingly at the science fiction I was watching. My brother acknowledged the intelligent, scientifically rigorous denouement, whilst my mum came into the room at an apposite moment and said, "I remember this, this is where the gravel moves". Seconds later, the gravel moved! And she hadn't seen that for 30-odd years! And with Image of the Fendahl, we have a human skull that is older is scientifically possible (like the one that piques Quatermass' interest), and a village called Fetchborough which (like Quatermass' Hobb's Lane) has a name with devilish implications. Nigel Kneale expertly made the futuristic seem scary, and did so by mixing in the supernatural – Chris Boucher must have been paying attention when Kneale did this, and, like my mum, remembered the work well. The horror tropes weave seamlessly into sci-fi ideas in this story – just look at how Dr Fendlemen's equipment works better after dark. Yes, "minimising solar disruption" is a scientific-sounding justification, but it's clear that our venerable scripter is wringing the maximum amount of chills from his concept. Further evidence of this is the way the hiker's body decomposes at an unnatural rate – it provides mystery straight up, with a side order of ickyness thrown in for good measure.

Back in the real world, and still blown over by Katherine's suggestion that we watch The Invisible Enemy together at the airport, I pushed a little for us to continue this watching-together-experiment at home. I had high hopes for her liking this one, as I'd remembered being especially fond of the scenes among our disparate bunch of scientists. But like you, Rob, she found it all rather dull and confusing. Unlike you, as it happens, she wasn't spooked by this – in fact, she went to sleep about 12 minutes in. It's a shame, as I thought she'd love the characters like I do. Presented with an icy German he could do in his sleep, Scott Fredericks (as Stael) goes against the script by thawing his character a little and making him all the more interesting as a result (the smile he gives when prompted by Colby isn't proffered in the book). Denis Lill (as Dr Fendelman) is always good value, and here his credible scientist is charged with a manic zeal that refuses to descend into parody – even Fendelman's foreign accent seems slightly tinged with the odd Americanised vowel, as if Lill has rationalised that a European scientist of his skill would have needed to spend time in the US to make his name. This is backed up by his reference to working on a "missile guidance system" which Lill – nothing if not a fastidious, nuanced performer – issues with a bashful note of apology.

Meanwhile, Edward Arthur's Adam Colby is shot through with essence of Boucher: he's a likeable, testy character with a neat line in wise saws and modern instances (watching Colby – and bearing in mind where Boucher went after working on Doctor Who – sends future echoes back from the spikier scenes of Blake's 7). Colby's self-consciously arch dialogue might appear a bit try-hard and dated – especially now that Blake's 7 is itself a relic – but at this place in Doctor Who's history, it feels fresh and invigorating. Actor Edward Arthur injects the character with a charismatic swagger that makes this chummy wiseacre most appealing. And Daphne Heard's fine balance between comedy yokel and spooky witch is a necessary antidote to the Boy's Own stuff. Her appearance comes too late for my wife, though, as she is well entwined in the embrace of Morpheus by the time the old woman arrives on the scene. It's my fault, I guess, for thinking this experiment would work better after dark.

Image of the Fendahl (part two)

R: You know what this feels like? It's as if the Doctor has stumbled into an adventure in which no one realises he's the lead character. (We'll get this sort of thing happening again in the eighties with Davison and Colin Baker, but it's really rare for it here, in the days of Tom Baker rising to full messianic glory.) No sooner does he try to interact with any of the main cast than he's locked up in a box room – and it takes him the rest of the episode length for him to have another proper conversation. No wonder he picks a skull. No wonder he's so flippant, and offers it a jelly baby.

And the cliffhanger is remarkable, at this halfway stage of the story, coming out of the Doctor not only being sidelined from the adventure, but also not understanding what the tone of the adventure is. His humour seems entirely out of place here – and it's without fanfare (again, even without incidental music) that he puts his hand upon the skull and realises he's out of his depth. It feels not only that he's being punished for his irreverence, but also for his irrelevance. This isn't a monster he can sit down and mock on the steps of a lighthouse, or whose megalomania he can make fun of as he lies vulnerable on a hospital bed. And it's a frightening episode ending, partly because it is so abrupt – but mostly, surely, because there's nothing heroic to it. The Doctor isn't fighting for his life for the greater good, but because none of the guest characters want to talk to him.

You hear reports about Tom Baker's behaviour at readthroughs, of course, tearing up the scripts and dismissing them as rubbish. And Chris Boucher's own particular frustrations with his lead actor, that his writing was publicly ridiculed. I wonder whether the way the Doctor is written in this story, as some buffoonish adjunct to the main action, is some sort of wry comment.

Some of the camera shots are beautifully composed; the sequence where Wanda Ventham (as Thea) in the darkness tries to find the stranger to ask for his advice, and director George Spenton-Foster allows her face to be obscured in shadow, is especially notable. There's an almost cinematic quality to the shot where Dr Fendelman shows Colby the pentagram on the skull that gives what is really just an expositional scene a quality that makes it actually chilling. It's a peculiar story, this; it feels tonally wayward from scene to scene, and the script feels like a first draft that hasn't managed to find room for dramatic action amid all the theorising. But there's a freshness to this which is genuinely exciting.

T: Your Boucher theory appears plausible – for apart from the moment at the beginning of the episode where he strides in with surly authority to demand exposition, the Doctor appears to be guest-starring in an episode of Blake's 7 and the Pit. It's an interesting mix – with impressive, thought-provoking science-fiction ideas like the pentagram etched into the skull, and mankind's extraterrestrial genesis being discussed by a sarcy clever-clogs using dialogue such as (a favourite, this): "You must think my head zips up the back." Before being locked into a cupboard, the Doctor does get one nice line about there being four billion people on this planet, but that within a year just one of them will be left alive. Chris Boucher's not just a glib tongue, he knows how to make the sci-fi dialogue chime. Less on-song is the moment where the door to the Doctor's makeshift prison opens. It's impossible that any of the scientists would have motive or opportunity to let him out, so one can only assume it's a delayed reaction from his attempts with the sonic screwdriver earlier. It's not clear, though – it's almost as if the door was so embarrassed at keeping the programme's star away from limelight, it opened out of pure shame.

But all in all, the main reason this resonates with me is, appropriately, because of something buried in my past. Also nestled alongside the Target books in those copious bookshelves of my childhood home were the works of

Dennis Wheatley. Clearly, my dad had a taste for the demonic (a cue for my mother, uncharitably, to throw in a "well, have you seen your stepmother?"). These books had a musty scent that only added to the aura of ancient evil. My brother's hushed anecdotes about Aleister Crowley and the White Horse only added to the terrifying mystique that black magic carried in its talons. And so I love that Image of the Fendahl taps into these fears most effectively, with director George Spenton-Foster going for broke with the inky black, misty night scenes on location, and in the studio favouring extreme close-ups on the impressive, glowing skull prop and superimposing them onto Wanda Ventham's face. He also knows that quietness is sometimes more impactful than bangs and flashes – the chat between Fendelman and Colby about the pentagram is charged with menace, whilst Louise Jameson is instinctively calm in her scenes with Geoffrey Hinsliff's perceptive Jack Tyler. Sensing that he is decent, she uses soft reason to inspire his trust. She then mentions the Doctor's gentleness... and of course we cut to Tom Baker kicking empty boxes in frustration and anger. It was probably the same feelings he exhibited when he read the script for the first time!

Image of the Fendahl (part three)

R: I think Scott Fredericks does a very nice job of making his character – the coven-leading scientist Stael, who has designs on godhood – actually credible. Enough so, in fact, that when he shoots Dr Fendelman, it feels like a real shock; you just can't guess how deranged this man is. He coos around Thea Ransome as if he's offering her the most tender of reassurances, whilst in reality setting her up to become part of a death gestalt. The reason why Adam Colby baits him so much is that he honestly can't seem to believe that this humourless little maniac would really be a murderer – and it's precisely that knife edge that makes these scenes especially tense. Colby and Fendelman don't know they're in a Doctor Who story. They don't know how these things work.

But – and it's getting to be a big *but* – I'm finding it hard to take Stael too seriously either. And the reason? It's because Doctor

Who hasn't even met him yet! How big and bad a villain can he really be, if by the cliffhanger of the penultimate episode, the Doctor hasn't even had a conversation with the chap? It gives Stael the sense that he's something of an also-ran, full of self-preening bluster rather than anything genuinely menacing. I'm prepared to believe this might be the point, but – at this stage, with the Fendahl still only a concept rather than a monster – where exactly are we the audience supposed to find our threat?

No wonder no characters understand the grammar of appearing in a Doctor Who story! The Doctor and Leela are barely in it. They zip off in the TARDIS to the Fifth Planet, and it's a genuine wild goose chase – in plot terms, it achieves nothing except to keep the regular cast away from the storyline. Again. (And these scenes are strange, aren't they? What's with that peculiar bit where Leela wakes up from a dream as a huntress, when she wasn't even feeling drowsy a few moments before?) I am enjoying this story, but perhaps only on a scene-by-scene basis. The cast is terrific, the direction feels fresh, and it's an indication of how good Boucher's dialogue strengths are that although he's mostly writing nothing but exposition, the lines still crackle. But the fact that I'm still waiting for the story to find a focus is alarming me. Best bit of the episode? The wonderful Daphne Heard (as the white witch Martha Tyler) being revived from a coma because the Doctor recites a nonsensical recipe for fruit cake. That's got an eccentricity to it that feels natural and charming – that's got the words "Doctor Who" stamped all over it.

T: This is a really odd episode – it's like a first draft. No explanation is given as to why we have not one but two mad scientists, and – in Stael's case – quite how or why he made the leap from trusted research assistant to fruitloop zealot harbouring a god delusion. As for the Doctor's self-confessed tardiness in finding answers that he already knew, and his day-trip from hell to the now-destroyed fifth planet, we desperately need a plum cake recipe to revive the script editor from the stupor he's clearly been in this week. Even an effective dramatic jolt – with the Doctor saying the time scanner should be safe unless it's been operating for 100 hours, and the scene immediately cutting to a counter showing that it's at 98 hours – is then laboured over in the dialogue, creating a repetition that robs it of its electricity.

Scott Fredericks, as you say, keeps his threats rather studied and quiet, and plays against the script's desire to have him become a ranting Nazi, but both he and Denis Lill resort to wild-eyed acting as if to make up for their characters' lack of motivation or unexplained illogicalities. What this *does* mean, for once, is that the good guys are more interesting than the bad guys. On initial viewings, I'd never bothered much with the Tylers: as a country boy myself, the antics of a couple of comedy yokels were less compelling to me than the smart-arses in white coats pointing guns at each other. This time around, though, I love both Daphne Heard and Geoffrey Hinsliff – when they enter the house and start poking around, it's like watching The Archers becoming private investigators, which is as winningly eccentric as it sounds.

Beastly boffins and benevolent bumpkins aside, from the perspective the Target novel was written, I had Adam Colby down as the main protagonist. He's got it all – he's the voice of reason, the sceptical brainbox and the guy with all the best lines. He's got two terrific ones here, deadpanning that Fendelman might have "an industrial relations problem" when Stael points a pistol at them, and later, when berating Fendelman for trusting his Teutonic turncoat, Colby spits out that "I didn't, but I'm going to end up just as dead as you, if that's any consolation". Colby is fantastic, and Edward Arthur plays the role with all the self-assurance of a fellow who knows he's got the best part.

And yet... he's at the bottom of the credits. The hierarchies and in-house systems within the BBC that govern these things throw up such anomalies from time to time. Here, for example, Edward Evans as Ted Moss – yokel factotum and easily the smallest role – gets relatively high billing because, I presume, of his status within the BBC for having played the lead in their first-ever soap, The Grove Family. Fredericks and Hinsliff had clearly done more work for the Corporation than Arthur at this time, which pushed him down further. It just goes to show: even if considered the lowliest member of an ensemble, you can still shine if you seize the opportunity. Bravo, that man!

August 7th

Image of the Fendahl (part four)

R: I'm going to be controversial here, but... I think the Fendahl looks terrific. I really do. The fifteenth season suffers from a variety of really quite shoddy monster work, and traditionally that big lumbering papier mache serpent shuffling slowly down a corridor is seen as being cut from the same cloth as the Nucleus from The Invisible Enemy or the Vardans from The Invasion of Time. But I think there's something so really odd about it, something almost Lovecraftian, the design not really quite making sense, and it unnerves me. It may have caused the cast to break down in laughter, but the scene at the top of the episode, where our heroes stand transfixed as the Fendahleen moves inexorably towards them, stands out to me as the greatest and subtlest moment of real horror all year.

And I think it might be because the Fendahl is one of the few concept monsters Doctor Who has attempted. Most monsters for the series are created as something very large and lumbering and identifiable: full three-dimensional races with a history and a home planet and an obsessive need for militaristic conquest. The only thing that really distinguishes a Sontaran and a Zygon in its ambitions is that one looks like a potato and one looks like a foetus; the plans are just as ludicrous, the characters just the same. Concept monsters, though, get their scares from a darker place of the imagination, by being unknowable and bizarre, by being mysteries – and that the drama of the adventure is derived largely not from moments of action and crisis, but from explorations of that mystery. The trick, really, is whether you can imagine the Mara or the Weeping Angels appearing in the same story with the Daleks or the Cybermen. They don't appear to share the same fictive universe, they require different forms of storytelling to bring them to life.

And similarly, the Fendahl is concept through and through. It doesn't just deal in death, it *is* death. It doesn't have plans – so the plans can't be thwarted. It doesn't make ultimata, because that would suggest it could be negotiated with. It's an idea, rather than something fully fledged. Look at those brilliant scenes between the Doctor and Colby, in which the Doctor posits numerous theories as to what the Fendahl is, and how it influenced life on Earth. The fact the theories are contradictory doesn't make the Fendahl less credible; on the contrary, it suggests a far greater complexity to it, that this is not something that can simply be neutralised with gold dust or with a well-aimed knock on its probic vent. The brilliance of Image of the Fendahl is that, by the story's conclusion, we understand for certain very little about the monster. It has no voice to speak, and no dialogue to reduce it to being just something safe that can be tidied away easily in the Doctor Who hall of fame. I never really understand what the difference between a Fendahl and a Fendahleen is, and to be frank, I never really care. The confused ambiguity is all just part of the mystique. Look into its eyes, Doctor Who can't save you, and will hand you a gun so you can shoot itself. Get pointed at, you become some weird writhing puppet. That's enough for me.

The problem with all this is that it's not the standalone BBC drama that it's pretended to be for the past four weeks. It can't just live in the atmosphere, and feed off the concept. And there's a glibness to the rush of the last ten minutes of the story, that the script abandons the logical doomed conclusion and suddenly turns the Fendahleen into something that can be defeated with rock salt – by the end, you don't even need to shoot it, just bung a bag of stuff in its general direction and you'll be fine. "How can you kill death itself?" muses the Doctor, in one of the series' all-time great lines of menace; drop it in a supernova, that's the all-too simple answer. Merely running away from a big implosion with another countdown feels so lazy – especially after the same thing has been used in Horror of Fang Rock and openly mocked in The Invisible Enemy. We'll see later, I think, how better stories find logical ways of defeating their difficult concept monsters – whether it be Kinda or Blink, you don't feel cheated, because they doesn't shift styles so quickly and force its atypical plotline towards a stereotypical ending. Here, though, Image of the Fendahl gives all signs that Chris Boucher could not only work out a way to resolve the story, but that he didn't even pretend he could.

Lots of clever stuff on display. I love the way, during the implosion, Dudley Simpson's music itself goes backwards, as if even that was being sucked inwards. And look at how hard Tom Baker and Louise Jameson are working, as if to assert their authority in a story that has sidelined them for weeks. The way the Doctor stops supporting Leela's head as soon as he's assured she's unharmed, the way Leela kisses Colby on the cheek – it's the attempts to put little character moments in, to assure the viewers that they really are still watching Doctor Who after all.

T: George Spenton-Foster worked on the anthology series Out of the Unknown. A lot of the episodes of that programme were decidedly odd: high concept literary sci-fi which asked the viewers to fill in the blanks. Doctor Who tends to spell things out rather more obviously, and has distinctly linear narratives, and yet Spenton-Foster's direction is clearly echoing the more-oblique style of that earlier series. Things happen for no reason... we get peculiar shots of an abstractly posed Wanda Ventham appearing and disappearing in different places, all hauntingly scored by Dudley Simpson's ethereal tones. We hear talk of "Fendahleen everywhere" in the cellar, but don't actually see them in most of the shots (we're to assume they're lurking just off camera, apparently). Stael's body appears and disappears in those high shots of the pentacle in the cellar. All of this is my way of saying: mood and imagery are more important to Spenton-Foster than continuity. This is hard science fiction directed with a non-naturalistic flair, and most of the memorable images involve pulsing superimposition over Ventham's twitching, alien face (which conspires to be both sadistic yet on the verge of tears at the same time) or have our heroes filmed through her looming, semi-transparent silhouette. The series has never quite been shot this way before, and I really rather like it.

Indeed, seeing as this story is often described

as a final stylistic hangover from the Hinchcliffe-Holmes regime, much of this is quite unusual. Having already committed a very un-Doctor Who act by shooting a man in the head at close range, Stael goes further this week by doing it to himself. It's great, though – the sort of thing I loved as a kid, making me think that I was watching something properly grown up. It's all done very tastefully, of course, and yet Stael's suicide still has a huge impact, thanks to Scott Fredericks brilliantly skewing his useless, paralysed arms like a grotesque marionette whose strings have been cut, and Tom Baker not being able to look the man in the eyes as he assists him to the Great Mad Scientist's Lab in the Sky. That grim faraway stare is a moment of self-imposed alien detachment from Baker – it's far more impressive than the Doctor's "joke" of holding up four fingers when he tells Colby to leave the time scanner on for three minutes. I sympathise with any director who had to negotiate which of their star's "funny" additions to keep and which to rule against, but completely understand if, on this occasion, Spenton-Foster decided not to fight Baker and instead concentrate on the visuals.

As it happens, the *real* humour that works is the stuff that comes organically through script and character, the best example being when Jack, Adam and Ma Tyler are hiding under the table, Fetch Priory has just imploded to nothing, and an ancient alien death-beast has been expelled. Jack's response at that moment? To tell Martha, "Put the kettle on Gran, eh"? Terror and teatime: that's my idea of Doctor Who, as comforting and traditional and rich and complex as your finest slice of fruitcake.

The Sun Makers (part one)

R: Back in 2003, I worked on a television series called Born and Bred. I'll say it now, it wasn't the best experience of my writing career. There I met a terrific script editor called Will Shindler. We still work as co-writers these days, coming up with screenplay projects, and usually we argue. When I want to pull rank on him, I tell him that I wrote Dalek. And he'll then counter that with a Who credit all of his own. He is the proud possessor of Gatherer Hade's hat.

Will has never been much of a convention-goer, but like so many of us thirty/ fortysome-things found himself at the Longleat experi-ence to celebrate 20 years of the series. And there, amongst the mud, and the queues, and the armed guards pretending to be UNIT sol-diers, he found an auction tent. Gatherer Hade's hat was one of the lots. No one wanted Gatherer Hade's hat. He raised his hand. He parted with his pocket money. An icon – yes, an unqualified icon – of Doctor Who history was his.

It's a good hat. And it deliberately stands out in a production that looks decidedly cheap and spartan. Since the days of Hartnell, has any Doctor Who story started looking so strapped for cash? Bare beige corridors. A small window. A red X next to it, to give the set some colour. And a strange conversation between a man grieving for his father, and a nurse more con-cerned about the death duties he now has to pay than any medical concerns. Now – this episode probably is very cheap. But it still feels artistically deliberate to me. It's a shock to see an alien world looking so drab and unspec-tacular, as if the characters don't even deserve beauty in a world where humanity is less important than money. And this effect is rein-forced when you cut to the Gatherer's office, and you see the pride he takes in a wooden table (ma-ho-ga-ny!) and in, yes, that ridicu-lous hat.

Isn't this script a joy? You get the sense that now Robert Holmes is leaving the series full time, he's kicking back and just having some fun. Having spent the Hinchcliffe years being resolutely dark and grim, seeing Holmes return to his comedy roots now feels like a relief; this must surely be the single wittiest episode we've seen since the glory days of Donald Cotton. The story goes that this is an attack upon the British tax system after Holmes received one too many expensive demands, and there's a palpable anger behind the comedy. Just one week after Stael commits suicide in a Doctor Who story, the factory worker Cordo tries it again – and it's disquieting to see a character driven to such desperate measures in a Saturday teatime series. But here, the effect is even odder. Last week, Stael dies a villain, after succumbing to some previously unexplained threat of looking into a goddess' eyes. This week, an ordinary frightened little man decides

to throw himself off a building for the most naturalistic of reasons – because his life has become unbearable, and he can't see a way of making ends meet. It's startling.

And what gives The Sun Makers its human-ity is the regular cast. Tom Baker, here giving a far more relaxed performance than we've yet seen this season, clearly relishes the chance to play good written comedy rather than create it himself in rehearsal. Louise Jameson is delight-ful, her best moment being the gentle kindness she shows towards the frightened Cordo, her encouraging smile to him and all the children at home telling us all that everything will be all right now the Doctor's here. And so it feels – after three stories this year in which the Doctor has been either angry, possessed or sidelined, this is a return to the Doctor as hero we last enjoyed in Talons. The contrast between the forced humour of the TARDIS scenes in Image of the Fendahl, and the well-timed wit of the TARDIS scene here, is enormous.

T: This story falls during an interesting period in Doctor Who's history – if the last four episodes sounded a lot like Blake's 7, this episode looks like it. I always imagine Blake's 7 involving lots of groovy 70s types landing on a drab concrete car-park planet, in which the main guest star looks suitably outlandish and everyone else has dull and ill-fitting costumes. And that's what we get here, with the presence of Michael Keating (only weeks from his debut as the interstellar thief Vila on Blake's 7, here playing the rebel Goudry) reinforcing these similarities.

But whereas Blake's 7 was more space opera than not, The Sun Makers is a comedy shot through with humanity. The foundry worker Cordo stops this from being a glib middle-class whinge about a system which actually, at its best, is one in which the well-off rightly con-tribute to the good of those less fortunate than themselves. But Cordo is the little man, the hard worker, the cog in the machine who – for all his lowliness – is the sort of decent human being every society relies on. The Doctor posits that the cash-strapped Cordo should have got himself a "wily accountant", thus illuminating the inherent unfairness of the tax system. Cordo embodies the poorer, more directly taxed workforce who must pay what they are told, while those in big business have the very best accountants to exploit every loophole. It's all legal, sure, but in principal it's as direct a theft as burglary. As Cordo, Roy Macready personifies this dichotomy with a wonderful poignancy – his young, Stan Laurel-esque features seem riddled with fatigue, and show signs of age before their time. Like Edward Arthur last week, he's a lesser-known cast member who gives the most rewarding performance.

You see, when a script is so obviously funny – the lines about everyone running from the taxman, and taxes being more painful than tribal sacrifice, are wonderfully satirical – I feel that it's important that the actors don't tip the wink to the audience too much. And in this regard, I feel compelled to sound a note of caution. Tom Baker seems to be adding more and more to the scripts, and he's obviously relishing the humour inherent in lines such as "I'm interested in this Undercity. Always like to get to the bottom of things." He's a witty and inventive performer, we know that, so he puts his hat on the time rotor: so far, so funny. But by the end of the episode, with the Doctor supposedly in mortal peril and the script requiring its leading man to sell the jeopardy and lure us back next week... he shoots Cordo an apologetic, comedy shrug and robs a key moment of any drama. If he carries on like this, an imminent cliffhanger may well have him preparing to perform a space jump over an intergalactic shark.

The Sun Makers (part two)

R: I've been enjoying the fifteenth season rather more than I expected – but there's always been something nagging away at me, something that feels rather askew. And I think I can finally put my finger on it. It's the absence of any real passion. The absence of any sense that any of this is truly engaging with the heart – it's all been terribly cold so far, either because of the Doctor being distanced from the storyline, or a distant performance from Tom. I didn't expect to find that missing emotion here in The Sun Makers, the most self-conscious and ironic Doctor Who story since... well, ever, rather possibly. But here it is, in spades, and it breaks over the comedy with such unex-

pected ferocity that it leaves me shaken by the contrast.

For example, there's the scene where Leela derides Mandrel for not wanting to rescue the Doctor – not so much for his treachery, but for a cowardice that means that for all his claims to be a rebel, he'll never bother to do anything of sufficient gravity to challenge the system. She attacks his honour and his manhood – and, my God, Louise Jameson seizes this; has there ever been a better showcase for her than this? What was playing out as something slightly predictable, as characters stupidly underestimate Leela's huntress skills, becomes grand and rousing, and the contempt with which Louise delivers her lines is a sudden blast of reality in this cartoonish satirical world. Similarly, the Doctor forms a friendship with the captive Bisham in the Correction Centre – and Bisham isn't much of a character, he exists simply to provide some handy exposition. But look at the scene where the Doctor is freed by orders of the Gatherer: he gently asks whether the same clemency will be given to his "chum", and even the use of that word, so charming and boyish, serves as a deliberate contrast between the reality of Bisham's fate, that he's going to be tortured to death. There's no angry speech of protest from the Doctor when he cannot save his new friend, because there's really nothing he can do, and Bisham sadly looks away from him – not in any condemnation, but merely in despair. The Doctor has no words for him, but leaves a bag of jelly babies by his side. As written, the sequence ought to be ridiculous and childish. In performance, it seems to me subtle and profound and moving.

The last time Robert Holmes gave us a villain in Talons, Magnus Greel was exposed by the Doctor's clowning as that terrible thing, a man without a sense of humour. That isn't true of Gatherer Hade at all; if anything, Hade thinks of himself as a comic genius, forever chuckling at his own jokes, even prodding his assistant with a finger to emphasise a literal rib-tickler. The brilliance of Richard Leech's larger-than-life performance is that Hade sees himself (as real people usually do) as the lead characters in their own dramas, and this is what makes him so especially unctuous and hateful, that he thinks he's the hero. With

Hade carrying the brunt of Robert Holmes' wittiest wordplay, the effect is rather like seeing Henry Gordon Jago portrayed as an amoral bastard.

And it's a measure of what's really so great about this story. Because it ought to be all over the place – there seems to be no common decision amongst the cast as to how they should play this sort of thing. You've got David Rowlands (as Bisham) playing a torture victim with an almost comic dignity, Roy Macready (Cordo) playing an unwilling rebel like a child rather than a man, William Simons (Mandrel) playing his thug terribly straight and Michael Keating (Goudry) playing his thug as if he's wandered in out of a very ripe Shakespeare production. And, Henry Woolf (the Collector) gives maybe the most extreme display of alien eccentricity we've ever seen – and it's extraordinary. If there was even the slightest hint of reluctance to it, if it were just slightly less overacted, it'd be embarrassing – but this big and this broad, it's honestly disturbing, as if a madman has walked on to the set. In synopsis, this episode is a lot of exposition and corridor running. And in design, those corridors are pretty Spartan. But in execution, this stands out as one of the brightest, funniest episodes of Doctor Who in years – and the most iconoclastic too. It's a comedy, all right. But it's a comedy with that emotion I've been missing this season. And it's a comedy that bleeds.

T: You mention Michael Keating wandering in from a ripe Shakespearian production. If that's the case, then Louise Jameson has wondered in from a very good one, as her RSC background really pays off with the depth, power and edge she gives to her performance. She's mentioned "honouring the text" when acting, even in something like Doctor Who, and this episode reaps the benefits of such an approach. Her face-off with the grubby rebels in their hovel is superb, and thanks to her, the contempt with which Leela holds the amoral characters is palpable. William Simons plays the pock-marked, stubbly and grimy toad Mandrel as a nasty, brutish and short ne'er do well. Leela's anger with him is shot through with intense righteousness, but Jameson gives the same weight to her touching eulogy to Cordo, the only person who volunteers to go

with her to save the Doctor. Amongst all the tough guys, it's the one who can't look after himself who offers to give her assistance, and she rightly (and rather movingly) honours him as the "bravest man here".

Meanwhile, I have to say... Pennant Roberts honestly seems to be trying his best given the resources available. The sets are barely sets at all, with the Undercity clearly not having enough budget for walls. I hope this is a clever reference on the Company instituting a wall tax, causing the canny rebels to replace all of theirs with black-curtained backdrops, but I doubt it. What he can't get in depth, though, Roberts seems to have requested in height, as there's a two-tier system in place in some of the sets. The Gatherer's office is also decorated by handily employed extras – there's one holding some long sticky thing here, one high up in the background there. You have to use what you are given very imaginatively in a show like Doctor Who, and Roberts is having a good go at it.

And he's not the only one, as actor Henry Woolf is brilliant with the Collector's paper-spewing, personal computer. He scrutinises the tape by holding it right up to his eyes, his busy alien body language suggesting a little termite hoovering up the information. That, plus his malevolent little voice and diction makes for a truly creepy villain, whose performance style rises organically from the script (or, to put it another way, honours the text). And what text it is! As Gatherer Hade, Richard Leech is rightly enjoying the numerous reverent monikers he gives to his boss, and succeeds in giving his diverse fawning outpourings sufficient variation in delivery – the best (and wittiest) being when he backs away, signing off "yours, et cetera, et cetera".

Amidst such caustic wit ("P45 Return Route" indeed – very funny) and outrageous characters, Robert Holmes has smuggled in some pretty hefty and adult ideas. The concept of a gas being released into the air to keep the population contented and domesticated is a compellingly odious one, with much to say about population control. And the decision to truss Bisham and the Doctor up in straight-jackets critiques the manner in which despotic societies impose conformity. Keeping your rebels down is one thing; labelling them as madmen is the final insult of the bully.

August 8th

The Sun Makers (part three)

R: I remember thinking that the Others become revolutionaries terribly quickly. One moment you've got Mandrel threatening the Doctor with a branding iron, with all his henchmen standing about gloating. The next, they've all become excitable children, delighting in the idea of going out on the streets and taking power, with the Doctor as their trusted friend. Now, I'm not so sure it's a problem – I wonder whether it's part of the point. Let's face it, it's a cliché of your average Doctor Who story, that the Doctor is initially regarded with suspicion and mistrust by the very people who'll be waving him off in the TARDIS come the conclusion. And the way the clever writer will make this transition plausible is by staggering the character shifts through the episode breaks; people who might seem vengeful and murderous in episode one may seem like steadfast allies in episode four, and although the timeline of the story may only last a few hours, the effect is achieved because the broadcast time perceived by the audience can last a month.

If The Sun Makers were obeying the rules, Mandrel and his gang would have seemed more trustful of the Doctor at the start of this episode, and politely concerned about Leela's whereabouts, all the better to be moulded into the generic bland goodies the story needs them to become ten minutes later. Instead, Robert Holmes has Mandrel portrayed at his absolute worst: he is paranoid, spiteful and vicious. The jump in characterisation seems clumsy. So clumsy, in fact, considering it could so easily have been prevented, that it makes me wonder yet again – yes! – whether it is deliberate.

The Sun Makers does directly what Doctor Who usually only suggests from the sidelines: it foments genuine, active revolution. Civilisations will topple in stories as far removed in tone as The Mutants and The Macra Terror, but in both instances the Doctor allies himself with likeable heroes with a clean conscience. This is the one Doctor Who story that recognises that if you want to overthrow the state, if you expect the people to rise in revolt, it's done by mob rule. And mobs aren't polite, and they aren't patient. There's a certain gleeful madness to them. And the sheer joy that the Others show as they pour their self-loathing outwards against the state seems to me very credible. These are the same people who minutes ago would have tortured the Doctor to death. So we watch Mandrel and Veet and Goudry become heroes within moments, and it feels strange and dissonant. And it's supposed to be. Next week, there'll be a scene where they all stand around and call for K-9 as if they're all characters in a child's pantomime – and there'll also be a scene where, without any guilt, they'll murder Gatherer Hade in cold blood. It's a dark and dangerous game that Robert Holmes is playing here – especially since the enemies precisely aren't lumbering monsters in green suits but recognisable men and women with jobs and conversation. The sequence where Synge and Hackett are made to join the revolution, because if they refuse they'll be shot dead, is brilliantly awkward – because Synge isn't presented as some black-hearted villain, but as an ordinary little man doing an ordinary nine to five job. Synge becomes the Doctor's ally at gunpoint. Just think about that, and what that suggests about the realpolitik of your average Doctor Who adventure. These are Robert Holmes' final moments as script editor, and, in his last wave goodbye, he's deconstructing the series' attitude, and finding something difficult under the surface.

T: It's not much fun being an extra in this story. In the last episode, the Doctor treated a guard's fatal electrocution with a punchline of sufficient glibness ("Are you sure he wasn't deaf?") that John Nathan-Turner and Colin Baker would have been lynched had they perpetrated it. This week, Leela and her chums zap and, at one point, clearly run over some other non-speaking Company lackeys. It reminds me of that fabulous exchange in the film Clerks, where the characters muse on the Death Star's destruction in Return of the Jedi. As the battle station was still under construction, its obliteration wouldn't have just killed the nasty Imperial officers aboard, but also the independent contractors – the plumbers and roofers – working on the thing. The goodies slaughtered hundreds of innocent civilians just doing a job! And it's the same here: the technicians and guards are at worst slaves and at best dupes. Just because they have no lines, does that mean their lives aren't worth nothing? Maybe your deliberate clumsiness is just plain old actual clumsiness, Rob, with Robert Holmes more interested in what he's saying than providing a plausible world outside of the few characters we focus on.

As for said characters, Pennant Roberts deserves credit for his casting; he has deliberately used actors who look like they're in something of a time warp. David Rowlands, as Bisham, isn't the square-jawed hero you'd have alongside a modern Doctor trying to thwart alien guards; he's the sort of actor you'd get playing a vicar or upper-class dimwit in an episode of Terry and June. That sort of benign, heightened jollity in his acting style is so archaic now, it's all but disappeared from our TV screens. But it's *wonderful*: Bisham is a cheerful, jug-eared twit forced to become Che Guevara, and out of that odd juxtaposition comes an engaging, enjoyably performed character. Similarly, Derek Crewe as Synge is one of those fussy, nasal, slightly sibilant actors often cast as snippy little comic relief proles in the 70s, and so fits this world of form-filling, protocol-by-paperwork and invoices-for-erasure perfectly well. And it enables them to get away with an audacious gag, when Synge's nonspeaking cohort is ultimately revealed to go by the name "Hackett" (the echoing of popular TV double act Hinge and Brackett cannot be accidental). The new series would never be quite so naughty, unless characters called "Sant and Hec" rear their heads in a forthcoming episode.

Elsewhere, the scenes in which those poor guard extras confront our K9 are slow and clunkily staged, even with the advantages afforded on film (and a note here for John Tiley's superb camerawork). I hate saying it, but our canine companion is like a noisy biscuit tin that kills the pacing of even the most basic action scenes. But if the battles are very flat, the dialogue is effervescent enough to compensate. The exchanges between Richard

Leech's oleaginous Hade and Henry Woolf's repugnant Collector continue to sizzle with wit. The coiffured eyebrows of the latter, and the extra wrinkles produced by the skullcap he's wearing, complement his lizard-like, creepy performance. It's a truly gruesome moment of blackly comic alien sadism when he derives satisfaction from anticipating Leela's death screams as she's rolled into the steamer. ("That noise, Hade... the subtleties [of her cries] will be lost. The deeper notes of despair, the final dying cadences. The whole point of a good steaming is the range it affords.")

Had this been the tale where Leela left the series (as was considered), killed in that horrible steaming machine, Louise Jameson's gutsy performance would have ensured she did so memorably. She's such a nice, gentle woman in real life, quite where the deeply ferocious spite of her threat to split Mandrel, and the verbal violence in her confrontation with the Controller, come from I've no idea. She maintains her righteous fire even when suspended from the wall (in a pleasingly original visual that displays imaginative design). But for Leela to die in this story would have seemed a somewhat odd curtain-closer to this black comedy, and perhaps a stylistic clumsiness too far.

The Sun Makers (part four)

R: I'm more convinced that this is a cold parody of Doctor Who and its familiar tropes than ever, and I think it's brilliant, and clever, and leaves an odd taste in the mouth. As the Collector spins around in his motorised chair, he looks to me increasingly like some comical version of Davros. Similarly, the scene in which the Collector and the Doctor talk ethics seems like an echo of the justifiably famous one in Genesis of the Daleks in which Davros reduces all human life to the level of scientific experiment, which can be wiped out instantly by breaking a single glass capsule. In The Sun Makers, though, they talk not as "men of science", but as capitalists, talking about profitability and looking over prospectuses. The Doctor states, quite unambiguously, that the suppression of humanity through corporate greed is just as evil as through military conquest – and you come away thinking that, quite probably, it's much worse. There is at least something direct and honest about someone sticking a gun in your face. Bleeding you dry through taxation is another matter altogether – and it's a measure of what Holmes is doing in this story, that it's not wanting to be direct, and to deal with the conflict as something that's black and white.

For example – just watch the way Cordo is written, turning from frightened victim to cocksure rebel with a gun. The transition is beautifully performed by Roy Macready too; in earlier episodes he played the part as a timid child, but now he's an obnoxious complacent teenager. In story terms, you're glad that he's at last asserting himself, but there's no mistake – he was much more likeable before. Another example – look at how Holmes gives such attention to the sequence where the Doctor chooses to hypnotise the guard. Leela tells him he should be killed, and reminds us that in an earlier episode that by showing mercy to one of the Inner Retinue, she was later captured and sentenced to death. The Doctor is morally right, and Leela is wrong – but the story then goes on to show that the guard does revive, that he does threaten the Doctor, and he's only stopped when Leela knifes him. The usual rules of how Doctor Who stories work don't apply here – in a real revolution, the innocent and downtrodden need to become murderous thugs to defeat their oppressors, and mercy is a weakness. In the final scene, as the Doctor says goodbye to his new friends – Leela shaking the hand of the never-likeable Veet, whose only real character note was that she wanted to take the clothes off Leela's dead body – you do get the impression that the society he's put into power will be a very ugly and violent one. "Three hundred million people can't be wrong!" he says cheerfully; but isn't that exactly what the episode is suggesting – that true heroism and idealism is warped out of all recognition when the individual becomes part of a mob?

I suppose I would worry that this very clever (and very cynical) story would be off-putting to the children in the audience, watching the series for simple moral stories and monsters. But there's at least one viewer out there for whom this was their very first Doctor Who episode. It was me. It's true! My first childhood memory of the series was watching the Collector turn into a green blob and go down the plughole. I was terrified by it at the time; the sequence seemed weird and nightmarish. And I've laughed a lot about that over the years, that typically, I was so scared by the Doctor winning, by a moment of triumph, and in a comedy, of all things! But watching it again now, and trying to put myself back into that seven year old's head, I can understand why it unnerved me so much. Because that is all that The Sun Makers is about. It's a disquieting story, one that hides something very dark and sadistic under its jaunty garish surface. It pays lip service to the traditional Doctor Who story, it tells you it's a happy ending – but even as a little kid, I could tell that something was wrong. And I think that's utterly the intention. This is Doctor Who at its least reassuring, and at its most bold and surprising.

T: Ah, but Leela knifes the guard in the shoulder, so he lives. She's learning to injure rather than kill. As for the glee with which the unlikeable characters undertake their murder of Gatherer Hade, I can't help but remember Terrance Dicks' addendum to this in the novelisation, where – after their cheers at Hade's demise – they feel somewhat guilty and dissatisfied. It adds a necessary complexity of emotion that no one here seems especially interested in. With this, and the strange attitude towards the disposability of extras I've highlighted elsewhere, the production teams seem less interested in the morality of death than that of taxes.

And yet, there's an admirable duality about Robert Holmes – he has a caustic, somewhat dim view of people, but a firm belief in their core humanity. Marn changes sides when the tide is turning and Mandrel transforms from savage killer to honourable revolutionary, and we aren't protected from the moral ambivalence this throws up. Yet in spite of all our faults, even the grottiest of humanity is a last repository of potential goodness against the alien usury of the Collector and his kind. The creature's reference to Pluto as a branch about to be closed shows Holmes at his most gloriously satirical, with a planet and population being viewed as a business outlet. I've loved this terrific villain – the spinning chair shows the Collector's delicious single-minded alien zeal, and Woolf's nuanced, subtly menacing, gloriously cruel performance has been meticulously observed. His obsequious plea that "If you intend to kill me, as you see, I am unarmed" is a brilliant rendition of a craven coward in defeat. He's been a joy to watch, and brought out the best in Tom Baker, whose indignation at extraterrestrial capitalism is so much more enjoyable than his forays into mugging.

When I was younger, one of the outtakes doing the rounds on very bad quality video was Cordo's gun repeatedly not working when he rushed in to announce the rebel victory. Time and time again, the actors had to go through the scene, with the required bang resolutely whimpering. It just goes to show how on your toes you had to be as an actor in those days. In the finished episode, when that moment occurs successfully, it's as fresh as any other – with no clue that the previous half-dozen attempts had ended in failure.

Underworld (part one)

R: This one comes with a fearsome reputation. It's hard to believe that 90 minutes of television can have been responsible for so many years of cumulative boredom. And it's true that my seven-year-old self who had been jolted by The Sun Makers the week before can only remember turning this story off, and not returning to Doctor Who for years. And it's true, too, that this is the one colour story I have literally no impression of in my head whatsoever. I know I've watched it – of course, I've watched it, I'm a Doctor Who fan who's sat through a reconstruction of The Space Pirates, for Heaven's sake. But the brain doesn't retain it. Maybe the brain refuses to retain it. Maybe it's trying to protect me. So as I navigate Bob 'n' Dave's latest pursuit of the unfilmable, I'll try to write down my reactions quickly, before I lose it all to amnesia.

But it means too that I'm approaching this one with real excitement, because it genuinely feels like a new Doctor Who story to me! And I'm reacting to it with the shock of seeing new footage! Look, Leela's flying the TARDIS! I'd never known she'd done that before, and I like it – it seems such a welcome progression from

the primitive savage who reacts to everything with a knife thrust, it feels like a return to the original premise that she'd be a character who was being educated and therefore could change. No time to dwell on that – look again, the Doctor's wearing a smock! He's got paint on his face! And the sequence where he stares out at the emptiness of space, utterly awed by its limitless possibility, is gorgeous. It recalls for me one of my other favourite scenes this series, also written by Bob 'n' Dave, where the Doctor gazes out into his own brain's imagination. (And I pause to wonder why some of the most effective moments this season aren't about the Doctor doing anything, but looking off camera towards the potential of doing something.)

And it's that sense of possibility, that this story is at the threshold of something new, that makes this episode feel so fresh to me. I know the science behind the story doesn't work, but it sounds feasible – and conceptually the idea of a spaceship being turned into the core of a planet is utterly brilliant; I love any cliffhanger in which the threat to the Doctor is that he's going to become part of the very universe he spends so much time rushing about saving. The way that the Minyans bounce off Time Lord mythology is fascinating too. This is the first time since Robert Holmes reinvented the Time Lords in The Deadly Assassin that they've been examined properly – and you can see how Bob Baker and Dave Martin are managing to knit the Pertwee interpretation of godlike beings to the more cynical and corrupted new version. To see the Time Lords as bumbling comic bureaucrats is one thing, and a good joke; to see them as disappointments, as characters who let down the Minyans who worshipped them (just as they've let down the audience who believed in them) is really rather profound. And the trappings of all that Time Lord society, with its missions and its regenerations, are turned on their head and made into something suffocating.

The problem with it all, I suppose, is that any quest that lasts for a hundred thousand years is going to get a bit boring for the people involved. And it's a very hard thing, to make boredom on television look interesting. The relief that the expedition leader, Jackson, shows when he believes the quest has dribbled to a miserable halt – that at last he's freed from a task that is interminable and numbing – can only reveal itself on screen as an anticlimax. And worst, as an anticlimax to something that never had the time to seem especially interesting anyway. I watched Imogen Bickford-Smith deliver her lines in a weary monotone, and thought it might just be an acting choice as her character approaches old age and death – and then realised that the young reborn Tala has little more energy than her ancient counterpart. There are ideas buzzing about in the script, but there's precious little action to accompany them: even a burst of gunplay only makes the victims become nice. And when the exposition is delivered to us by characters who can hardly be bothered to inflect, the overall impression the story gives is that it's really very static. When Jackson pilots his spaceship towards certain death in pursuit of his mission, it should be with the grim fanaticism of a mad zealot – instead, it comes across with all the excitement of someone who has found a parking space at a busy supermarket.

But I'm enjoying this – intellectually, I'm enjoying it. Even if the only thing my heart has found engaging so far is the little girl hurt Louise Jameson gives Leela when she thinks everyone is laughing at her. I better put episode two on first thing tomorrow morning, before my brain does its mindwipe thing, and I forget what's going on.

T: There's something rather winning about all this talk of gods and world-building, only to have the gods themselves represented by the Doctor: a somewhat flippant anarchist who wears his superiority with a sort of casual arrogance. With this riff on a mythological tale adding to the Doctor Who mythos by explaining away the Time Lords' non-intervention policy, it feels like we could be in for an epic. And we're treated to some very impressive, detailed model work – there's a sweeping opening pan through a starscape, before a solid spaceship moves smoothly across the picture. Inside the spaceship, designer Dick Coles gives us an impressive, two-levelled set with a raised window panel that provides a view of the vacuum of space. This helps us to reconcile events as they unfold, as we get to see the impressive sparks of a heat effect and a wonderfully rendered molten formation from the crew's perspective. When the heat shield gets raised, it cuts the crew off from this view, hemming them in claustrophobically. It's all quite impressive on the eye, especially after the conspicuous sparseness of Pluto. The tiny control banks suggest that future technology will be minimalist (check out Tala's dinky handset) rather than big and chunky, so it's a lot more prescient than much of Doctor Who.

It's so frustrating, then, that proceedings have such little oomph. I don't want to blame the guest cast – but do you think they misread the script and thought it was called Underwhelmed, and pitched their performances accordingly? They're all good actors: James Maxwell (as Jackson) was the leading light of the Royal Exchange Theatre when I first moved to Manchester, and I have fond memories of working there with his wife and granddaughter after he died, but his weariness here is contagious. Director Norman Stewart, thankfully, decides at one point to visually augment the commander's droning speechifying by showing us Orfe's view of Herrick helping Tala, and then cutting to the Regen Room itself. Okay, it's not exactly electrifying, but it's an attempt to liven things up.

As Orfe, Jonathan Newth doesn't really have the opportunity to generate excitement – he's largely relegated to telling Jackson what the commander could quite easily see for himself if he bothered to look at the monitor *that he's standing right next to* (!) – but he does have a pleasing affability. Actually, the blocking in this regard is *very* clumsy, which makes the dialogue exchanges seem unnatural and stilted. Alan Lake (as Herrick) tries to compensate by adding a suppressed fury to everything he does, which sometimes works, but not always – his yelled cliffhanger about the cannon overheating is a bit too rushed and over-the-top to have dramatic impact.

But at last he's having a bash, and we need him to, as we end this 25 minutes with our heroes all bunched together and sitting on a sofa. With this level of drama, though, they're not sending anybody behind one.

August 9th

Underworld (part two)

R: Let's say one thing from the start. The effort put into this episode by the production team and cast is heroic. It should never have been possible, really, to mount a story like this with such a crippled budget. And to decide to use it as a means of pioneering a whole new method of making television, of filming all the underworld sections of the story without sets on a blue screen background – effectively, to make a virtue out of the crisis, and to try something brave – is testament to what Doctor Who should always be doing. To be at the forefront of television innovation.

And, no, it doesn't work. It could never have worked. But I'm going to stick my neck out and suggest that it's aged very well. I'm not saying that, from a twenty-first-century perspective, Underworld looks good. But I am saying it doesn't look much worse now than the other stories around it. Special effects and sets that in 1978 would have looked perfectly acceptable have now dated badly, whereas Underworld has got no worse, and now looks at least different to the multi-camera filmed budget-stripped adventures we're used to. The Sun Makers seems now to be a symphony of beige corridors. Is Underworld really so very much worse? At the time of broadcast, of course, it would have stood out like a sore thumb. But I'm going to stick out my neck a lot further – oh, I may as well. I'll suggest that today's audience is more likely to accept the artificial sets of Underworld than the audience for whom it was made. Because in the days where CGI special effects mean that actors regularly perform against creatures that don't exist against backdrops that aren't there, we have learned to accept a certain dissonance. When we see David Tennant emote against a huge Satan monster that is clearly computer generated, or run away from a mutating Professor Lazarus, and we accept that fakery as a normal part of our storytelling, we're also accepting on face value the restrictions of Underworld in a way that the contemporary viewers could never have considered.

The problem with Underworld now is not the CSO. Indeed, in a way, I'd suggest it helps the story. We've arrived on a planet that has built itself around a spaceship, and that's magical and weird, and it ought to look strange and unworldly, in the same way in The Invisible Enemy that running about through the Doctor's brain should have done. Stepping out into the core of the planet, there's the same sense of mystery and wonder that we haven't felt much since the days of Hartnell, a what-if to the background and culture of a genuinely alien environment. And Baker and Martin have taken such pains in the first episode to make us feel this, that the Doctor is stepping out somewhere wild and uncharted. So it brings you down to earth with a thump to see another bunch of rebels in the making protesting against slavery, and another bunch of thuggish guards oppressing them. It's all business as usual, and since it's a business that was satirised in the series so effectively only two weeks ago, what ought to feel brand new instead is old and tired.

But the special effects? Some people suggest the way to watch Underworld is to turn the colour off, all the better to hide what the production was doing. I say, whup the brightness up, take a good look at it. Because that's the real quest on display here, I'm telling you – to get this story made in the first place, and to do it so unapologetically. It's lunacy of a sort. But it's lunacy we should cherish.

T: Depending on how you define terms, not even in the 60s did we get an episode where the simple fact that it was *actually made* was its overwhelming achievement. Norman Stewart had his work cut out for him, and the fact that we get from beginning to end without everyone giving up is astonishing.

In the past, CSO has generally been used to sell an effect, and the technological shortcomings of such shots have been excused by the very nature of what's on display: a mineshaft full of maggots, a flying Whomobile or a giant robot. Hinchcliffe seems to have felt that CSO wasn't worth the resultant shoddiness, so used it as infrequently (or subtly) as possible, which means that the main experimental technique of the Barry Letts era has been conspicuous by its underuse at this period in the show's history. It's as if they've banked every bit of extra

CSO over the past three years and put it all in one story. The pitfalls are obvious and legion – the keying is not always perfect, so bits of people disappear if they move quickly. There are repeated shots – not so bad when it's the anonymously attired guards charging about, but definitely unfortunate when we see Idas and his unintentionally comic gait lolloping off down the same tunnel in the same unfortunate manner for a second time. The blocking of scenes such as Idmon's capture would have been difficult to orchestrate on a multi-camera set-up with a backdrop that didn't have to be keyed in for each shot – but here, it's impossible to make it look even vaguely realistic.

Let's feel some sympathy for Stewart, as he simply can't bring things like pace and drama into play under such circumstances. Just look at the cliffhanger scene: denied close-ups or changes of camera angle, we have a static medium shot with the central protagonist's face in shadow if we're lucky, and obscured by the top of his lowered head if we're not. And the close-up of the Doctor and Leela hiding in a CSOed ore cart doesn't work – it's needed so the audience knows where they are, but it makes the pursuant Rask and his guards look doubly thick, as they obliviously decide their quarry must have doubled back. Let me emphasize that: we see our heroes moving about in the cart *that Rask is staring right at*, but he still doesn't notice. Stewart can't help but emphasise the geography for coherence, but ends up sacrificing logic in the process.

With that in mind, and with the pressure everyone must have been under, it's amazing that we get the good bits we do. The model work continues to impress; the beautiful shot of the spaceship hitting the molten shell of the still-forming planet is fabulous. The rapport between Baker and Jameson allows a great comic moment, as they give each other a knowing look and synchronise their movements after Jackson has told them to stay on the RC1. The best bit though, is where Alan Lake's Herrick confronts Guard Klimt (he's credited as such, honestly). Lake initiates their encounter all smiles and friendliness, and then bristles, affronted, when he's confronted and finally shot at. Unfortunately for Klimt, the shield gun takes him out of proceedings, and when his bosses try to get him on the radio,

Herrick answers and adopts the insult "Trog" with a swaggering rebelliousness. It's a rare moment of character and wit, and in an episode as challenged as this, any lifeline is appreciated.

Underworld (part three)

R: Alan Lake is getting some fun out of this. As crewman Herrick, he throws himself into noble self-sacrifice with all the joy of a psychopath who's spent 100,000 years on a spaceship with no one to shoot at; now that he's got a gun, he's going to go down fighting and enjoy it! And Louise Jameson, as always, is good value for money, and her desire to reassure the anodyne Idas every time he gets worried by any slow-moving peril is sweet and touching.

The idea that the inhabitants of the Underworld are the descendants of Jackson and his kind is interesting enough, and their retreat into pagan rituals contrasts wittily with the use of the technology they've inherited. Idmon is sacrificed by sword and burning rope, whilst being tied to some sort of spaceship chair ringed by flashing lights. But it's not done with much wit, and we've seen it all before – one year ago precisely – in The Face of Evil. When the Doctor tells Leela his theory, you expect at least a moment of recognition from her at the use of her own backstory. The twist on it here is that the descendants have come face to face with their ancestors, and the concept of that alone is so potentially fascinating to justify the repeat of the same premise. But it's a twist that is acknowledged only by the Doctor as an aside, not placed right at the centre of the drama as it surely should be – this clever original idea of people fighting alongside their very own great-great-grandfathers for freedom. It's a crying shame.

But that's the crying shame of so much of Underworld, really. There is so much effort involved in the production of this, but for so little gain. The story isn't worth the struggle. It's the nature of Doctor Who fans to eulogise the things that we've lost – just remember the way that for years Shada was seen as the single story that would have made the Graham Williams era sing, or how we still trumpet all the missing episodes and are certain they will all without fail be of a higher quality than ones we already have. Underworld would have sounded brilliant, had the production team pulled the plug on it as they were being urged to do: the premise has an epic ring to it. But in practice, it feels so very tired. Even as everyone runs across the rope bridge, most of the cast amble across it – there's so little urgency to any of this. I am beginning to remember why it was I forgot it; I must not forget that I've remembered it later, just in case I want to forget it again.

T: Let me back up and attempt to see the forest rather than the trees for a moment…

Before I saw Underworld, I got to know it in two different ways. First was the fan opinion claiming it was woeful because it had awful CSO. When I was a kid, CSO was the big no-no: it was the fringing that got you a-cringing. Later production teams had all but abandoned the technique, because audiences of my generation could spot it a mile off, and any disbelief that was being suspended had its wires unceremoniously cut. So in my mind, I wrote off the story until I happened upon a back issue of DWM which had the cast list, and I was amazed. Surely, a story with these actors couldn't be bad? James Maxwell was an actor my mum rather fancied; Jonathan Newth cropped up playing good, solid parts in all sorts; I'd seen Imogen Bickford-Smith's name on the credits of The Meaning of Life (I got started on comedy early); James Marcus was in A Clockwork Orange; Godfrey James had a decent role in the World War II drama Wish Me Luck; and Seers Frank Jarvis and Richard Shaw had done a few Whos dating back to the early days. (In those days and in my mind, it was a fact that the more Doctor Who credits you had and the further back they stretched, the more brilliant you undoubtedly were.)

And then there was poor Alan Lake, the playboy, hard-drinking actor whose love for Diana Dors was such that not long after she died, he shot himself. I once spoke to an actor who worked with Lake, and had to be "killed" by him. They ended up filming the two of them separately, as Lake tended to throw himself into things, and couldn't be trusted not to go too far. That zeal shows here, actually… but the rest of the cast that looked so good to my naive young eyes on paper barely register in

person on screen. Television is so technical, good actors need to have the correct conditions – be it favourable close-ups, sympathetic lighting or tight editing – to give a decent performance whilst hitting their marks and acting under intense pressure in front of a lot of blue felt. It doesn't help that Newth and Bickford-Smith have no lines whatsoever this week, and that poor old Shaw and Jarvis have tea cosies on their heads. Worse, in the episode's big dramatic reveal, they tear those off to reveal… golden buckets on their heads. They announce themselves as the Seers, and the music parps the import of this, despite the viewer having little clue what they're talking about. And I fear that a modern viewer would be totally baffled by the cliffhanger, as not enough effort has been made to marry the action together into a seamless whole.

I should stop here to point out that yes, I'm aware that the production team were going through a series of huge difficulties. I'm being critical merely to contextualise the good bits – so let's dig deep and find them. First up, that famously bad CSO isn't that bad at all, considering the sheer scale of it. It could have looked awful with a less technically minded director, and the keying is quite impressive. The cave models themselves are attractive and atmospherically lit, and the manner in which the action and depth are framed in relation to the synchronised running actors successfully sells the illusion in places.

And I think you're being a trifle unfair on the script, Rob, as it has some great ideas at the core of it. One is that it's chilling to think that the skyfalls are being used as a tool of population control, and it paints the villains' cold logic quite starkly. Another is that Leela telling Idas about the stars anticipates that celebrated discourse between Unstoffe and Binro in The Ribos Operation. (Even though, fair enough, this doesn't have the gravity of that scene, because Louise Jameson has to inspire awe and wonder about the boundless, bountiful universe to Idas, a man who seems to have pure sap running through his veins.)

There are some good bits. This isn't *as* terrible as its reputation. But try as I might, I can only conclude that at this stage, the irony of Underworld is that there's not actually that much going on beneath the surface.

Underworld (part four)

R: The to-ing and fro-ing of the golden cylinders gives this episode a bit of urgency. It's the urgency of farce, yes – but any pace is better than none. And since farce is the order of the day, there's some good comedy to be mined here; I do honestly love the bemusement of the Seers as they're left holding the fission bombs that are going to destroy their planet, being told by a hysterical computer to get rid of them, and asking with a glorious contrasting resignation how they can do that. The Doctor's confrontation with the Oracle supercomputer might have carried more weight had it actually made an appearance some time before the climax – but the contempt with which Tom Baker rails against yet another megalomaniacal box is nevertheless fun and lively.

And even now we are given the odd glimpse of the more interesting story this might have been. The Doctor's anger with Jackson as he tries to throw the slave-workers off his ship, in order that he can better protect the Minyan race banks, is smashing: but Jackson is nevertheless never allowed to understand the irony that he would sacrifice his descendants in order to save the legacy of his ancestors. The scene is just thrown away, and with it any belated hope of emotional involvement.

And whilst I'm moaning – isn't it saddening how quickly K-9 has degenerated from an amusing companion into a handy device for blasting down doors or guards? It's all the more depressing when you remember that Bob Baker and Dave Martin are his creators, and will spend the rest of their careers defending the integrity of his character to anyone who'll listen. K-9 still hasn't yet become a loveable icon of the series; John Leeson's performance isn't quite relaxed; his comic potential is mostly restricted to a series of final TARDIS scenes (this is the third story in a row) in which he's the punchline to one of Tom Baker's jokes – most often being told to shut up.

So, that's Underworld. Is it worthwhile? Well, yes, I think it is: if only as a rare demonstration of what happens when huge ambition (the production) collides with something of no ambition whatsoever (the script). It's a peculiar, somewhat disorientating mix – and if the effort of watching the thing is distinctly unrewarding, there's still a certain magnificence to the fact it exists in the first place. If the CSO were better, if the story had been performed on location somewhere like Wookey Hole, there'd be no reason to celebrate it at all. But in its peculiar stunted ugliness, there's something unique here. And to be able to say that, halfway through Tom Baker's tenure, when everything is feeling just a bit stale and laboured, is noteworthy in itself.

T: When I first saw Underworld, I remember being surprised at how blatant the story was about its roots. I'd read, of course, about the clever names – such as the witty substituting of P7E for Persephone – but I didn't expect the Doctor to have the front to address Jackson as "Jason", and then muse upon the similarities of this adventure and its source material. It's one thing to nick stories, it's quite another for your script to be a signed confession with bags of incriminating evidence in it.

And watching the episodes on the same day has highlighted just how many individual shots are being repeated – my particular favourite is when one of the running guards noticeably slips. The clumsy fella's done it in more than one episode now! Still, at least he's in a hurry: there's very little urgency elsewhere in the episode until the Doctor and Jackson shout at each other right at the end. Their argument is over the pleasing number of Trog extras who have been gathered to give the population a sense of scale – the number of bodies is positively sumptuous, and contrasts nicely with the big open chamber where the Seers stand dumbstruck, unable to work out what to do with the fission bombs they are holding. It's a terrific scene, actually, when they blandly inform the Oracle that she has made their situation impossible and they are doomed. As a contrast to all the commotion, a blissful silence descends as she realises that for all her self-aggrandising, she is actually a failure and deserves to be blown to bits.

Here at the end, I have to applaud Norman Stewart for his efforts, as this was a mammoth undertaking. Given the technical struggles everyone in front of and behind the camera faced, we circle back to the point that just getting this *made* was about the best one could hope for. And yes, I know that "It's a miracle that Underworld even exists" is hardly the most resounding of recommendations, but sometimes on this great quest of our own, we can only do the best we can.

August 10th

The Invasion of Time (part one)

R: And I've thought of another good thing about Underworld! It's that it precedes this story. Because with its emphasis upon the pioneering Time Lords being treated as gods, and the impact they had upon the impressionable Minyans, the contrast offered here as we return to Gallifrey and see the old fools in action is all the more piquant.

Doctor Who is clearly running into enormous difficulties, and it's galling to see a series that was brimming over with the self-confidence of Talons of Weng-Chiang only a year ago battling such crises of budget and style. But what's remarkable about this episode, written at speed and hidden under a staff pseudonym, is how inspired it is. It almost revels in its own awkwardness, taking the Doctor and our expectations of how he should behave and turning it all upside down. It's not that the idea of this story *couldn't* have been born out of happier times – but the fact that it was conceived in desperation, and that the desperation is allowed to infect so much of the tone of this story, is what makes it work. This feels genuinely unpredictable. This feels, quite honestly, as if the Doctor really is making it all up as he goes along, as if there's a madness to the proceedings, both in front of and behind the camera. Its rough edginess is unnerving.

And Tom Baker is riveting. We've seen our lead actors before, of course, getting to have fun and ring the changes and play an evil doppelganger every now and again. It's a chance for William Hartnell to take a bit of a holiday, or for Patrick Troughton to wheel out his Christmas party trick patented Mexican accent. The Invasion of Time plays the same sort of trick, but without bothering to get bogged down in all that coincidental body double thing. Baker is playing the evil Doctor – but it's also *our* Doctor. And so there's nothing easy about watching this, it's not about seeing the

star of the show relax and have a bit of fun. Screaming for authority like a spoilt child, he is still clearly recognisable as the Doctor who'll get to lose his temper dramatically about once a story so he can grandstand the supporting actors a little; the dismissiveness he shows Leela is the same dismissiveness he's shown towards K-9 these last few stories for comic effect. There's no relief, there's no conspiratorial wink to the audience to tell us his arrogance is all part of a ploy. And it's so appallingly *plausible* too – that this cheeky maverick who revels in his own eccentricity a little too self-consciously, and takes too much pleasure in being rude to everybody, has just gone over the edge.

And it feels strange (but immensely satisfying too) that the story boasts such a love for continuity. Continuity becomes a dirty word in the eighties, when the word is misused as a synonym for fanwank – pointless little acknowledgements to the past that feel increasingly irrelevant to the story at large. But in the freewheeling days of the seventies, at a time in the series when it would be impossible to consider the Doctor making reference even as far back as Sarah Jane Smith or the Brigadier, it gives a new depth that The Invasion of Time is an unapologetic sequel to an adventure broadcast in 1976. And like all good sequels, it takes the themes that The Deadly Assassin introduced, and it builds on them, and gives them greater substance. The legal loophole that guaranteed the Doctor a stay of execution now becomes the means by which he can become a tyrant, and betray his planet to alien invaders. The degeneration of the Time Lords that Robert Holmes displayed as a couple of old men reminiscing about past presidents is repeated here, only now it is more cutting – they're chatting about their hobbies now, for God's sake. When the guards line up to imprison the Doctor on his arrival, and the Doctor greets them as if they're a welcoming committee, he asks one soldier where he's from: "Gallifrey," says the man, and it's a ridiculous response, but so telling about how *dull* these Time Lords are, that the answer would be their entire *planet*. And the corruption of this society is suggested by the way its fawning (the wonderful Milton Johns as Castellan Kelner), by its cynicism (Andred's quick role change from the

Doctor's captor to his errand boy), but mostly by the fact that it can countenance electing as president a Doctor as capricious and unlikeable as this one.

T: What a wilfully contrary episode. It opens with a weak-voiced alien and a glib Tom Baker – and as if the continuity error of the Doctor wearing his scarf outside the TARDIS and being without it when he enters the console room in the next scene wasn't obvious enough, he then goes over to clutch it, as if to stick two fingers up at anyone who might have noticed... we're supposed to be watching the Doctor convince us that he's committing a deed of absolute betrayal, and yet Tom Baker mucks about by nicking the Vardans' space pen, and later engages in very tonally odd banter with Commander Andred and his guards. Perhaps we're supposed to be askance at the Doctor's behaviour, but that would be giving our leading man too much benefit of doubt. Contrast Baker's abject grimaces when he was under the thrall of the Fendahl skull, or Sutekh's snot ray, with the somewhat uncommitted manner in which he clutches his head at the cliffhanger here, and you'll see an actor who is now inclined to bother only when he fancies it. I can only excuse some of his aloof demeanour, really, because it benefits the powerful and dour moments as he stomps about Gallifrey barely letting anyone get a word in.

With such an increasingly wayward star, the people who refrain from playing along with him come off best in this. Louise Jameson injects the perfect level of foreboding early on, and the wonderfully obsequious Milton Johns (as Castellan Kelner) and the dignified John Arnatt (as a new incarnation of Borusa) anchor the drama on Gallifrey. Indeed, only the stuff that gives the impression of being taken seriously works well – which includes, strange as it may seem, the comedy. The funniest moment actually comes from Jameson, who plays her doubtful assurance to Andred with absolute childlike sincerity. (He: "If you could avoid killing anyone, it would help"; she: "I will try".) This is an actress making a moment in the script amusing, rather than an actor larking about having a laugh... and I shall say no more.

In visual terms, the Time Lord home still has an impressive Panopticon, though I'd query this regime's decision to augment it with pale blue, die-cast plastic lilos. The cheapness of this year's design work has never been so stark than in such illustrious surroundings (the plastic ball Chris Tranchell has to wield to initiate Amber Alert takes tatty naivete to previously uncharted heights). That said, the ceremony is suitably echoey and the penultimate shot – with Charles Morgan's impressively voiced Gold Usher towering over a kneeling Tom Baker as he prepares to crown him – has an air of majesty about it.

The Invasion of Time (part two)

R: I suppose that's the biggest nightmare a child fan can have: that the Doctor would reject you. (And it's one of the areas I find the most uncomfortable about the revived series, all this idea that he'll only take the best; I don't like that at all.) It feels like a replay of the real-life tensions earlier in the season; Tom Baker won't even *look* at Louise Jameson as she insists she be expelled into the wastelands. (And how cleverly too, that in her final story, Leela is being faced with the same sentence that she was given in her very first, as the Sevateem expelled her from their tribe – and how cruel that now it's the Doctor, of all people, who's doing it to her.) Is there a more haunting image than the companion beating helplessly against the TARDIS door to be let in – whilst the Doctor holds his hands over her ears so he can't listen, and K-9's head droops in sadness?

What I find satisfying about it too is that it takes one of those dangling little irritants from last year, and shows it up for what it's worth. When Sarah Jane Smith is written out, it's because the Doctor can't take her to Gallifrey. It's as simple as that. She's an outsider, and she won't be welcome at his family's dinner table. It's always left a bad taste in my mouth, that; not that the Time Lords are so exclusionist, but that the Doctor isn't prepared to challenge it. Here, though, what was implicit in The Hand of Fear becomes explicit. Leela is hunted down because she's a foreigner, and the cries of "alien" – they won't even give her a name – seem increasingly more racist.

Isn't it apt that this Time Lord society is so caught up in legal curlicues that a president, rejected by the Matrix during his own inauguration, cannot be held accountable because logically to be in a position where he *can* be rejected, he has to be president already? There's such a stupid complacency to them, they deserve to be invaded. The design is superb; it draws upon the Gothic visuals of The Deadly Assassin, but then cheapens the whole effect with pointless plastic chairs and tasteless bright colours. The whole society looks overripe and fit to burst. I like the cliffhanger very much – that Gallifrey has been conquered by three bits of kitchen foil seems highly fitting. I suppose that this scene sums up the pros and cons of Season Fifteen to a tee; ambitious high concepts married to shoddy visuals. But here, at the least, the concept wins through – and the Doctor's laughter as his treachery becomes apparent is electrifying.

T: There's a mixture of tones here that isn't helping this story to coalesce into a comfortable whole.

That cliffhanger is indeed a great moment, and the Doctor's apparent betrayal of Gallifrey is an intriguing beat. Baker continues to be unpredictable, but when he's in the presence of John Arnatt, he wisely behaves himself and accords due respect to a heavyweight thesp who can cut through his nonsense with a terse bon mot or a disdainful tut. On the other hand, Chris Tranchell (as Andred) has been infected with essence-of-Baker, and is stark evidence of the malign influence our leading man's self-indulgence can cause if not reigned in. And elsewhere, we one moment have a beguiling subplot involving Milton Johns effortlessly intriguing us with Kelner's suspiciousness... and then we have some lame, poorly staged comedy business with shabby comedy guards played by blundering extras/bloody awful actors. (I try to give people their due, but this week's speaking factotum, Christopher Christou, is hopeless and unfunny.)

Fortunately, the ramshackle elements haven't *quite* subsumed the serious-minded stuff. Owing to the way Gallifreyans regenerate, it's a nice touch that elderly Dennis Edwards' Lord Gomer is described by Milton Johns (a younger actor) as "young [and] impetuous". And the guest characters certainly

provide colour and serve the plot nicely: just as one wonders what the rather-too-plummy Rodan is there for, she confidently says, "Nothing can get past the transduction barrier", right before the Doctor proclaims, "K9, destroy the transduction barrier". Rodan's increasingly panicky alerts at the climax, plus K-9 zapping guards and blowing up Gallifrey's defences even as Dudley Simpson's majestic, portentous score scales new heights, help to showcase this production at its best.

There's a lesson to learn here, in that this production is at its most effective when it's catering to the viewer more than its chief actor. When The Invasion of Time hits the right note, it demonstrates that balancing Doctor Who's winning mix of humour and drama perfectly is not easy... but it's definitely worthwhile.

The Invasion of Time (part three)

R: If The Sun Makers was all about the mechanics of revolution, then The Invasion of Time looks at power from an opposite perspective, and is about the mechanics of tyranny. We learn very quickly that the Doctor is indeed playacting his role as Caligula – and that's a good thing, because to have pretended that was a surprise twist would have been rather a stretch – but the tension doesn't dissipate at all. In fact, rather the contrary – as we see the Doctor pretend to be the perfect dictator, we're allowed to appreciate the technique of being a tyrant rather than being distracted by the Doctor's treachery. The sequence where he demands that Kelner fetch jelly babies from his pocket, and then rejects them because Kelner can't find an orange one, is still quite shocking even though you know it's an act – it's the demonstration of unreasonable power that keeps your minions frightened. And the cheery way in which the Doctor sends off his new vice-president to draw up black lists of "loyal" Time Lords, the first act of a new regime wishing to assert itself, is still disturbing for the oleaginous way in which Kelner responds, and sets about settling old debts.

This episode is built around a number of delightfully subtle set pieces detailing power games and politicking. Lord Gomer realising that it's precisely *because* of his honourable qualities that he is seen as a threat to Kelner and must be got rid of; Kelner employing a bodyguard to the Doctor's side who can be reassigned as his assassin when the occasion arises. I love the sequence where Andred talks of resistance, and his almost cocky determination that he can organise a force against the Vardans. In one fell swoop he's everything that the Doctor had to persuade Cordo or Idas to be, he's the perfect little hero to fight the Company or the Seers – and the irony is that his one wish is to murder the Doctor. And surely the best scenes of the entire season are the ones where the Doctor, at last in private, is able to confide in Borusa, apologise to him and win his trust. Tom Baker and John Arnatt play the scenes impeccably, and the entire story pivots around them – they are extremely disciplined and slow burn, and make sense of the madcap excesses of Baker's performance elsewhere.

So claustrophobic does all this make the Citadel, that when we finally get outside, into the sunshine and the gravel pits, it's like a breath of fresh air. You really believe that Leela can revel in her natural habitat – and you really pity, too, a character like Rodan, who has never thought to look at her own world before, and has no concept of eating flesh or fruit, no concept of needing shelter. Some of the tension is lost – and the wild hunters they discover are too polite and helpful for words – but that is surely part of the point. It's only because the story dares to show us a Gallifrey *beyond* the stuffiness of the Time Lords that we feel it is something worth fighting for.

T: How much better is Chris Tranchell when he's given some heroic material to do? He spends this instalment driving the rebellion subplot rather than trying to keep up with Tom Baker's antics, and he's great. Indeed, once the Doctor's accommodation is lined with lead (so the Vardans can't eavesdrop), and Tom Baker explains to Borusa that his wayward behaviour has stemmed from his having to mentally block out the Vardans, even some of his stranger acting choices in the previous 50 minutes make some sort of sense. In places, in fact, The Invasion of Time is now coming across as a rather brave production – just as Rodan's shrill prissiness risks becoming unbearable, we have a horrible scene where all her comfort is stripped away by Nesbin's verbal abuse, and she collapses in abject defeat. This establishes the bleakness of the wasteland more than any amount of filming in a windy gravel pit could, and makes the viewer sympathise with a character they were losing patience with.

I think this episode is all the more thrilling because it arrives halfway through a story that I was finding misguided and, at times, very flat. Even this doesn't start auspiciously, as it entails wobbly tinsel monsters threatening about four Time Lords – but once the Doctor starts planning, the Time Lords start rebelling, and Kelner starts "settling old scores [and] locking people up", we get a great injection of drama and really start feeling for the characters. Johns is marvellously venal as Kelner, and his conniving gives the Doctor a wonderful opportunity to manipulate the unwitting Castellan's loose morals to his own cause. It's great to see Baker enjoying the playful gymnastics of the script, and coyly indicating "a smidgen" with his fingers when being praised by Borusa for being clever. As the old academician, by the way, John Arnatt can be both serious and disdainful concurrently in a manner quite unlike any other actor in the known universe – it's beautiful, exquisite acting from a bygone age.

Elsewhere, this week's speaking guard (Michael Harley) makes a good account of himself (infinitely better than his predecessor), even though the game and plucky Lord Gomer contradicts the thing I loved last week by banging on about his age (er, I thought he was young on the inside?). I'm not confused for long, though, as there's the distraction of K-9's operator being clearly visible as the metal mutt shudders along the corridor (I never noticed that before!). And look, the credits are listing the guest cast pretty much in order of appearance, like a throwback to the Troughton era. Quite why I care about this is another matter, but in the interests of full disclosure, I am more than happy to state that I do.

August 11th

The Invasion of Time (part four)

R: This is all about anticlimax, but quite blatantly so. The episode works best if you see it as 20-odd minutes of joke playing out towards a punchline. It's only because the punchline is so good that it gets away with it. And the joke? The Vardans are rubbish. No, they really truly are. They're not just accidentally rubbish, like most of the villains and monsters we've seen in Season Fifteen. When the Doctor mocks the appearance of the Virus in The Invisible Enemy, or tells the Oracle in Underworld that it's just another megalomaniacal cliché, I don't think you're necessarily meant to believe him. When he tells the Vardans they're a disappointment, you're in no doubt you're supposed to agree. The way most Doctor Who monsters look good is to be kept in the shadows, left vague as long as possible – but once they're revealed under the studio lights, they seem startlingly unimpressive. Here we have an alien race that's actually defeated *because* they reveal themselves: as soon as they do, as soon as they emerge as three short and fat men in unattractive green costumes, the story can trap them in a time loop without any apparent difficulty whatsoever. It's so swift a defeat, it's practically meta-textual. This is the problem with Doctor Who storytelling, the episode seems to say: you build 'em up, only for even the characters to find them disappointing to look at.

This plays out, then, as a parody of your traditional episode four within a four-part serial. There's a little bit of fighting (in the main from characters who are only persuaded to acquire the necessary backbone after scant minutes of persuasion), there's a lot of technobabble, and misguided enemies become staunch friends. And, in an instant, what for the last three episodes played out as something epic and apocalyptic turns out to be nothing but a damp squib. (And we've seen this played out, without irony, so often this year – variations of it abound in Image of the Fendahl and The Invisible Enemy to dismaying effect.) The characters run around dragging the story towards its predictable happy climax as if they all believe they're in the final segment of a traditional Doctor Who adventure. The gag is that no one's told them they're actually in the season finale six-parter.

If this really *were* a four part story, this would be dismal – but arguably no worse than the finales of several other stories this season. But all the running about and blowing things up shtick is paid off in the final few seconds, when it's revealed that a bunch of other monsters have decided to take advantage of the confusion, and to coincide their invasion at the very same time. Seeing the Sontarans on the steps of the Gallifrey throne room is a shock. It's the first time we've seen a returning monster in the series since Revenge of the Cybermen three seasons ago. It's the first time, actually, we've seen a race of *any* monsters in the show since The Android Invasion. Season Fifteen in particular has played down its monsters so they're little more than window dressing in human dramas between human heroes and human villains. But we've had hints that something like this might happen – the Sontarans were referenced right back in the first story this series – and now that they crash on to the screen, it seems to take Doctor Who back to long-forgotten roots, and somewhere else new and fresh entirely.

T: There's a moment that sums up both everything that is right and wrong with this story, and which – as a result – acquires the status of genius. Van Gogh cut off his ear, remember, and Mozart was a loon; brilliance is so often accompanied by a total loss of sanity. This is unambiguously illustrated in the scene where Castellan Kelner has a conversation with the Vardan leader *who is reclining on a chair*. For anybody who needs a reminder: the Vardans are appalling shimmery tinsel monsters with no proper physical form, and here we have one of them apparently lounging like a brandy swilling boardroom boss doling out orders to a minion. I have *no idea* whether this is the director having a bit of a laugh or an example of the misjudged, woeful banality with which the series currently treats the intergalactic. I almost hope it's the latter – if it's deliberate, it is self-satisfied, self-indulgent and hard to like, but as folly, it's so hilarious that it's cherishable. What really makes it superb, though, is not the

315

bizarre, misconceived image of the Bacofoil Blofeld, but the fact that it's acting opposite Milton Johns.

Because Milton Johns is a genius – there is a dignity to everything he does. Even as he oozes sly unctuousness, the semi-apologetic way with which he treats this ridiculous special effect with utter sincerity is brilliant. He totally refuses to be in on any joke, or indicate that he actually knows this is all very silly. He is totally *there*, in the moment, and committed. Later on, he exhibits a similar dignity and authority whilst delivering instructions into a ping pong ball, and thinks to deliver an obsequious bow to the Inadequate Video Shimmer Beast as if it were the Pope. He's a very special actor, serving a very dodgy script and production – and perversely, in so doing, making it funnier than it deserves.

Stan McGowan as the Vardan Leader, on the other hand, is – and there's no way of sugarcoating this – dreadful. He is a blandly voiced, slightly wooden, Scottish (even though the actor is Irish, so I've *no* idea why that's happened), wobbly tinsel creature from space. And people *haven't* clamoured for the return of the Vardans for what reason? Their eventual appearance is so underwhelming, even the Doctor comments upon it, which suggests that nobody involved is really bothered that the programme isn't delivering any more. (Although I'm surprised that you haven't suggested the presence of someone as bad as McGowan was a deliberate exercise in postmodernist casting.) No wonder John Arnatt's had a week off. Typically, the other speaking Vardan, Tom Kelly, is a better actor than McGowan (have you seen his beaut of a wonderful performance in Sapphire and Steel?) and gets considerably less to do.

For every bit of this that works, another seems to come up short. Aside from the rather involving plot points about the Matrix and the Doctor shutting down the forcefield, we're treated to an episode that features a heck of a lot of shots of people walking up and down corridors, another terrible actor playing a guard, and a precursor to the famous impossible Reservoir Dogs shootout where three guards gun down four of Andred's helpers in one burst. All tattiness is overwhelmed by the impactful cliffhanger reveal of the Sontarans,

though, which genuinely comes out of left field, and is accompanied by some grinding incidental music that stirs the adrenal glands.

Really, this episode has quite a giddying effect. The awful bits aren't good because they're awful, they're only good because the stuff that is good refuses to acknowledge how awful the awful bits are, which only serves to heighten the awfulness but in turn excuse it and – indeed – make it good. If you see what I mean.

I need a sit down after that.

The Invasion of Time (part five)

R: Time for one of my contentious sweeping statements: I'm going to suggest that this is the last time we see a Time Lord as a proper, interesting, three-dimensional character.

I'm not including *renegades* within this, of course. I'm not suggesting that the Doctor, prime renegade of them all, never gets a bit more sheen to him. And the Master and the Rani are other matters altogether. But after this, everything subtly changes. Gallifrey becomes a backdrop and nothing more – first, for a series of stories in which all Time Lords are represented by a *job* (they're all members of High Councils, or guard commanders, or courtroom inquisitors – they're not people any longer with recognisable lives), and then in which all Time Lords are represented by their tragic disappearance (which mythologises them rather nicely, but takes them even further away from being identifiable). In the next story, we'll get popping up a Time Lord President who's not really a Time Lord President but the White Guardian in disguise – and in one fell swoop the Time Lords and their hierarchy are just totems, to be used as disguises by authorities who are much *bigger*. And more drastically, we'll get a Time Lord who'll be a girl companion, which means that before long she'll be getting captured, and made to scream a bit – and then get to wear schoolgirl costumes and skip around Paris. What the remainder of the Tom Baker years will do to the Time Lords is to demystify them entirely – they'll be mentioned so very often in passing (as has happened in every story this season) that when we return to Gallifrey in Arc of Infinity, we won't *need* any characterisation, they'll just be as familiar bits of the Doctor Who landscape as the police box and the robot pepperpots. There'll be good Time Lords and bad Time Lords, and sometimes a Time Lord who's good in one story will end up being bad in the next. But there won't be any more depth to the society. Even more tellingly, there won't even be an *attempt* at any more depth to it.

The scenes between the Doctor and Borusa are electrifying – both pointing guns at each other, both calling each other a trusted friend but never being sure how much that may be a bluff. As dialogue, it's frankly all smoke and mirrors; there's little logical reason at this point in the story to justify that extra confusion, and the writing is arch to the point of being incomprehensible, as if Doctor Who has suddenly become one of those murder mysteries where everyone has to act suspiciously at some point just to keep the suspense going. What makes it work is Tom Baker and, in particular, John Arnatt working their socks off. Arnatt brings the suggestion of sophistication to the part of Borusa that we haven't seen before and we won't see again. (Angus Mackay played Borusa the same way he plays the headmaster in Mawdryn Undead, and that's perfectly understandable – the only big character note Holmes gave him in The Deadly Assassin was that he was a prissy schoolteacher. Leonard Sachs just looks bumbling in Arc of Infinity, and confused by lines that don't afford any characterisation, while Philip Latham is so consistently sour in The Five Doctors, he takes the twist that the Doctor's old friend is a traitor and signposts it from the start.) Arnatt's performance here is so remarkable that it makes Borusa seem like a complex character long after he has ceased to be interesting, and manages at the same time to indicate a similar complexity to the Time Lord society he represents and holds dear.

T: On the whole... I'm confused. I get very cross when Doctor Who fans take the show so seriously as to suck any fun out of it, especially given that "fun" is one of its defining characteristics. And yet, I also hate it when fans pop up hither and thither to claim that Doctor Who is good because it's camp old nonsense that shouldn't be taken too seriously. I think Doctor Who *should* be taken seriously.

I like it because it is actually good, not because it's *so bad* that it is good (oh God, I'm doing it again). It feels very patronising to be mesmerised by something in your youth, and then to grow up and only mock it, albeit lovingly. But I have to admit to the contradictory stances in my tastes – I like Doctor Who when it is funny, but I hate the cosy humour of the original Star Trek. I enjoy Doctor Who being postmodern, yet Tom Baker's knowingness is getting grating. I want the threats taken seriously, yet I adore the fact that the total miscasting of Derek Deadman means that after last week's Scottish Vardan, we now have a cockney Sontaran.

And yet, against all the odds here, I'm having my cake and eating it. Make no mistake, it's a very badly made cake – and yet some of the worst-looking bits are the tastiest.

The extremes in this story prove the most memorable. Derek Deadman's repeated hurling of Milton Johns to the floor is so daft, it's brilliant. Wit of a more low-key nature comes from John Arnatt: his facial muscles barely move, and his inscrutability speaks volumes. The scene where he walks down the corridor with the Doctor discussing his Chancellor's personal force-shield, and only then deciding to run, is a study in expert timing (and it's great that Borusa remains dignified whilst hoisting up his Time Lord skirt!). His request at a dramatic moment that if the Doctor "*could* just open the [TARDIS] door" is laugh-out-loud funny. And having suffered the indignities heaped upon her last week, Hilary Ryan's Rodan has a much better time of it back on familiar territory – she gives orders, exchanges quips and gets hoity-toity with the Doctor.

So the comedy here seems expertly staged, but the action is somewhat shabbier. Poor old Jasko and Ablif get killed – if memory serves, the novelisation found these characters so interchangeable that they become conflated halfway through into one equally expendable chap called Jablif. Equally expendable are Stor's troops, who aren't especially formidable, though I do like the suggestion of immense Sontaran strength when Stor punches a hole in the control panel.

And as an aside on these accented aliens, why should extraterrestrials all speak in RP? I have no idea, but I can believe in them when they sound Shakespearian, but can't when they sound like the cast of EastEnders. Maybe this says a lot about prejudices and stereotypes in British drama, but I still think the casting in this has rendered the aliens totally unthreatening. It appears that lots of planets have a North... and a Saarf... and a Fife.

The Invasion of Time (part six)

R: In theory, opening up the TARDIS and exploring its hidden rooms is a great idea, and there's no better story for this to happen in. We've had the invasion of Gallifrey, and now we've got the unthinkable, the invasion of the TARDIS itself. We've pushed an exploration of Time Lord society as far as it can go, and it's only right now that the Time Lord's sanctuary too now should be investigated. It ought to seem like an obscene intrusion, seeing these Sontaran soldiers strut about the TARDIS so easily. In execution, though, it fails utterly. You can't just slap the familiar sound effect hum over scenes filmed in a hospital, with the inevitable jump between video and film, and expect it to look like a credible continuation of the control room. And all the mystery and wonder of the spaceship is reduced to seeing the same (not at all funny) sight gag of the Doctor walking about the exact same warehouse pretending it's multiple locations. There's no tension here at all – it's all played for laughs, the Doctor whistling loudly rather than lurking in the shadows to hide from the aliens trying to kill him. There's no sense of outrage or distress as his precious home is violated.

There's one good scene to this, though – and it's when the Sontarans enter the control room for the first time. And we've never seen this before, one of the recurring monsters somewhere so iconic, and for a moment the *wrongness* of it is quite shocking. And it's only here, cleverly, that the story chooses to have the Sontaran take off its helmet for the first time – another iconic moment being replayed – and after all this build-up, that the joke is that Stor looks about him and dismisses the TARDIS as "rubbish", is funny for all the right reasons.

Otherwise, the principle pleasure to be taken in this disappointing squib of a finale is watching to see at what moment Leela falls in love with Andred. Louise Jameson and Chris Tranchell work hard to seed the relationship

that'll provide the excuse for Leela to drop out of the series, but they've got precious little screen time together to make that work. For my money, the moment comes just after Andred has been shot in the arm, and Leela shows more than usual concern – that seems right, actually, that the savage would be turned on by the only sight of blood in the entire story. It's common to laugh at the shoehorned departure of Leela, but I think its very abruptness works surprisingly well – all season we've had stories turning upon the idea that she's a savage given over to instinct, and it seems fitting that she will give away her heart with the same sudden directness with which she will take a life.

And the icing on the cake is that K-9 so abruptly announces he's staying on Gallifrey too – he's staying with the mistress who showed him affection rather than the master who gave him nothing but insults. In an instant the Doctor has lost both of his travelling companions – and they've abandoned him with the same bluntness with which he abandoned Sarah Jane Smith coming to Gallifrey in the first place. I know full well this isn't a deliberate plan, that the production team had hoped to persuade Louise Jameson to stay in the series right up until shooting – but it feels beautifully apt, as if the Doctor is getting his comeuppance for his behaviour at the end of The Hand of Fear. And that final joke, the nod to the audience that he's going to construct a K-9 Mark II – what does that really say about the Doctor? That he'll now have to build replacement companions for himself? He can do it for the metal dog, but he won't be able to find another Leela. "I'll miss you too, savage," he says, behind closed doors, where she won't be able to see his moment of weakness. And quite right too.

T: Derek Deadman adds grotesqueness to his Sontaran commander by engaging in some nice tongue action, and his stocky build and compact, muscular gait make Stor look quite impressive as he stomps about the place. When he first removes his helmet, we are even treated to a nice close-up of his sunken, black eye sockets and oily lips... none of which, oddly, are present the second time he does so, ten minutes later but in a different recording session.

And here's where I think one's appreciation of The Invasion of Time really comes into focus. It seems that no-one making this is terribly interested in the fundamentals of drama, but has been told to have fun, and the manner in which each person decides to react to this instruction affects the story's success. Some moments are so silly, they are enjoyable: there's Borusa reading the Daily Mirror, the flesh-eating Venus Sontaran Trap plant, and the affronted disdain with which Milton Johns utters the words "ancillary power station".

But the production team got so busy entertaining themselves, they forgot about the audience – there's no justification for a script that abandons all pretence of plot for a chase in which the Doctor builds a big gun with which to shoot the baddie, whose Big Plan is to detonate a big grenade. And however much you try to rewrite Leela's out-of-nowhere departure, it's as sloppy as the moment where the aliens search for our heroes in a disused hospital, but decide that looking from left to right is no way to alight upon their quarry. Louise Jameson and Chris Tranchell gamely try to introduce some kind of rapport to their characters, and even to the last, Jameson is mining every possible nuance, subtlety and profundity (just look at the disappointment Leela exhibits when she's told she can't kill Kelner) from material that contains precious little of any of those.

The general feeling I have with this episode is that it's like being the only sober person at a party in which Tom Baker and director Gerald Blake drunkenly think they're *hilarious* when they're not, but it's possible to find it entertaining anyway – not in the way it was intended, but because you can only watch this aghast at quite how self-indulgent one was allowed to be when making television in 1978. Tom Baker is clearly leading from the front, and in playing up the programme's inherent ridiculousness with comic excess, he beats some of his fellow actors and joins others, but can't stop the really talented from escaping from the mess unscathed. Still, it's perhaps no surprise that the very, very talented Louise Jameson just escapes full stop. It's a shame, as in recent stories Jameson has levelled the tone when mat-

ters looked like they were getting silly, and her utter commitment to not diluting her character brought a vim and fire to the screen that has transcended the cheapness of her surroundings. I don't think she has once compromised her performance, and considering some of the material she was given to play with, that's downright miraculous.

Leela is so often written up as a something-for-the-dads character, or a sci-fi riff on Eliza Doolittle. We should get past both, and just acknowledge quite what a splendid performance Louise Jameson has given – the character might not have worked, had such an intelligent and committed actress not been standing up for her. The Doctor/ companion dynamic has never been quite like this before or since, and whatever the potential pitfalls in her conception, in execution Leela stands out as one of the series' truly great regular characters. I'll miss you too, Savage.

August 12th

The Ribos Operation (part one)

R: Let's talk Romana for a bit. Because she's so much more than just a new companion. She reflects an entire shift in the way the series pitches itself.

There are, in particular, three different things about the introduction of Romana that stand out. She's unlikeable – and written so quite deliberately. Sometimes in the past, you've had companions like Steven who come into the TARDIS all smugness and arrogance and need to be taken down a peg, but it's all part of the game, and it's an affectionate game at that. Their inability to believe in the TARDIS, or that they've travelled through time and space, is all part of an initiation process that we as an audience accept will be cast aside by their second adventure. Sarah Jane Smith will spend a couple of weeks steadfastly believing the Doctor is a villain, and that she's taking part in some medieval pageant, but by the closing moments of episode four she will have reverted to type, and become the Doctor's new loyal best friend. Generally speaking, though, the story falls head over heels to demonstrate to the audience why these new characters are worthy additions to the TARDIS crew – they'll fling themselves bravely into the heart of the new adventure. (Ben and Polly so swiftly take on the mantle of loyal companions, it's almost a shock that their debut story ends without either of them having seen the TARDIS yet. Leela stands out not only as the only member of the Sevateem to be both intelligent and sympathetic, she's also the only female, which makes her prime companion material!)

Of course it goes wrong sometimes. Dodo plays upon an audience recognition that she's a bit like Susan, and spends her early episodes walking about with an ever-changing accent giving a plague to the entire human race – but, grating as she is, she's *supposed* to be someone we care about. Romana represents the first time that we're presented a new assistant as a fait accompli, gives the Doctor an explicit opportunity to state that he too resents the imposition of this stranger in the adventures we share with him – and the character doesn't give a stuff whether we like her or not. She's haughty and remote and unimpressed.

The second thing that makes her interesting is that she's also *cleverer* than the Doctor. This isn't entirely a new thing for us – but the joy of Zoe was that Wendy Padbury played against the arrogance and made her relationship with the Doctor something intentionally teasing. Romana is under no illusions that she's academically brighter than the Doctor – and it's interesting, straight after Leela, that Tom Baker has been paired with companions who quite blatantly are there to be intellectual contrasts to him. It's simply not something that would have been worth pointing out at any other part of the show's history – and, now that his other companion is a robot dog who's an encyclopaedia on four legs, the Doctor is the least cerebral member of his own crew. What's the effect of this? Well, it takes Tom Baker at his most powerful, established now in his fifth season in the role, and humanises him somewhat. He's the most potent the Doctor has ever been. He has an authority we've never seen in the show before. And, within moments, it's been undercut – he's deferring to a god with sirs and politeness, and he's left impotent with rage under the withering glance of his cleverer assistant – a woman who not only takes being with our hero for granted, but even punches a

hole in the TARDIS for good measure, as if disdaining the central icon of the show.

And the third thing? There are only aliens aboard the TARDIS now. And that's going to be the state of play right up until Tom Baker's closing story – and, arguably, the staple balance of the Doctor travelling around with a human girl assistant won't be restored until the end of Davison's tenure either. The effect of this is to change the identification figure of the show. Up to this point, it has always really been the companion – even when Troughton was travelling about with a historical Scots boy and a far-future flung space age girl, Jamie and Zoe *behaved* like contemporary viewers might. Now the figure we'll identify with, for the very first time, is the Doctor himself. The experiment in The Deadly Assassin to see whether Tom Baker could hold a story without being viewed through an assistant's eyes has resulted in this – he'll still need someone to talk *to*, but that doesn't mean any longer he needs someone to be interpreted *by*. It means that no matter how eccentric an alien Tom Baker will try to play, upstaging rehearsals to do ordinary things in ever more inventive ways, he will by default look like a very *human* eccentric, because there's no human for him to contrast with – and the effect of that, arguably, is to make him seem more mannered. It won't seem so much like alien weirdness, more like an actor showing off.

And the stories will change their focus too. We don't need to go to Earth anymore, because the companions will have no emotional connection to the place. For the rest of Tom Baker's reign, we'll be restricted to one Earth adventure a season – a huge contrast to everything we've seen in the series before – and, even then, the Earth locations will be springboards to other exotic places (hyperspace in The Stones of Blood, or the planet Logopolis); even the Paris of City of Death is somewhere so truly foreign, it's given the sort of emphasis that makes it alien to us. And it means that the style of stories change too. They become more truly conceptual, whether that is under the auspices of Douglas Adams or Christopher H Bidmead (both of whom, in the way that they imagine Doctor Who to be a series about science and ideas, are not so very different as we often believe). With the Key to Time series, and the introduction of Romana, Doctor Who becomes more truly a piece of *science fiction* than it's ever been before. For better or for worse.

As for The Ribos Operation, all this has the strange effect of making the new planet we're visiting seem more Earth-like in contrast. With our regulars being so alien, and off on some strange alien-type quest, it's heartwarming to hear Garron affect a Somerset accent, or Unstoffe do a little bit of Oirish. Ribos feels immediately more well-rounded and real, because for all the hints we get of its culture, it seems recognisable. Its faux medieval customs will be fun to explore.

I didn't much like Mary Tamm's Romana when I was a young fan; she's the cold academic who behaves like a model, obsessed with brushing or primping her hair. I now find the collision of those two clichés rather witty. And look at how much John Lesson's K-9 has changed too! Cool and brittle all through Season Fifteen, this Mark Two version has been rebuilt by the Doctor as an excitable little kid who wants to go on holiday. If this Romana sticks around, you mark my words – he'll find some way of replacing her with someone softer who dresses more like him and wants to go on holiday too. That bit in Destiny of the Daleks where Romana regenerates? Oh, there was something underhand going on there, I'm telling you. I bet Tom Baker put a bomb in Mary Tamm's bed, just so, like K-9, he could mould a new companion in his own image. The Doctor – control freak, psychopath.

T: I have been so bold as to claim that the Doctor doesn't really travel through space and time, he travels through genre. That's what I love about the show: the science-fiction jeopardy the Doctor finds himself in takes a different shape depending on whether the production team have decided to tell a political satire, an action-adventure, a whimsical comedy, or – in the case of Season Sixteen – a fairytale. And a fairytale on the cheap. The Ribos Operation is entirely studio-bound, and yet it looks a million times better than The Invasion of Time, because George Spenton-Foster has clearly thought very hard about how to make a virtue of Doctor Who's budgetary shortcomings. There's no point *trying* to make this real-

istic looking, so he sells the visuals in a different, less literal way – we start off in a dark, shadowy TARDIS, which is immediately contrasted with the bright light heralding the White Guardian's appearance, and then the spotless iridescence of the new companion's wonderful outfit. It's a stage play on television, in the same vein as the BBC Shakespearian productions. In being upfront about its artifice, The Ribos Operation immediately becomes more realistic and involving than the previous story, because you quickly forget about said artifice and instead fall in love with the world being depicted.

There's a freshness to the setting and, indeed, the type of adventure being told. This isn't about invading aliens or mad scientists or even despotic regimes; it's about two comedy con-men trying to sell planets to a fallen warlord. God bless you, Robert Holmes, for thinking outside the box. He builds his own worlds (he can do that in about three lines, because he's a genius), and fantastic characters to whom he gives wonderful jokes. Garron substituting the word "Graham" for "Roger" in his two-way communication is just a silly gag, but it's a lovely one, whereas the idea that the Guardian needs to "stop everything" is a marvellous conceit – it makes the restoration of universal balance the cosmic equivalent of switching it off and turning it back on again.

On top of an excellent guest cast, a witty script and a handsome production, we get a rare use of blood (which has been drenched over the Shrievenzale's claw in a valiant attempt to disguise its wibbleyness), and – even better – a confident start from Mary Tamm. And never has Doctor Who felt quite so lifted from the pages of a story book – this evocation of more traditional children's adventures has reinvigorated the show in the same manner that consigning the Doctor to twentieth-century Earth did. Compare Ribos to Pluto or Minyos, the environs of which threatened the success of their respective stories due to their visual shortcomings. But knowing that the BBC does period drama well, this story gives its far-flung planet a similar feel, thus utilising the Corporation's resources to the best, and then getting on with telling a cracking good yarn. This is going to be *fun*.

The Ribos Operation (part two)

R: I think if I had to pick one single episode of Doctor Who to demonstrate Robert Holmes' genius, then this would be it. We're used to praising him for the quality of his dialogue, or just how sparkling are his larger-than-life characters. Where he tends to fall down somewhat is in his plots. But this is plotted to the absolute hilt, cramming into 25 minutes his entire space-age version of The Sting. It's executed so brilliantly, every twist and turn, every sly little feint of deceit, that I can only watch the artistry of it with a big grin – and it produces one of my very favourite moments of Doctor Who, as Tom Baker's Doctor, watching Garron's con begin to take shape in the relic room, can't help but beam with admiration. I like to imagine that it's the Doctor smiling at Robert Holmes' own skill. Indeed, it's so well constructed an episode that it'd have been easy to have left the humanity and humour out of it, but this is Holmes at his funniest – the scryngestone sequence, in which Unstoffe tries to take the con one layer too far, and in a cod Mummerset accent talks some shaggy dog tale about dead fathers and lost mines and frozen tundra, is a particular joy. And what's especially delightful is the chance to see the guest cast play comedy, rather than deferring to Tom Baker's brilliant but more undisciplined efforts.

If there's a fault with the plotting, it's this – it leaves very little for the Doctor and Romana to do but to watch. It's one of the reasons, I think, why The Ribos Operation has a reputation for being rather a slow story; the lead characters mostly hide behind pillars and wait. But there's such a relief to these latter-day Holmes scripts; we're watching now the work of a writer who knows the series so well that he can afford to play around with its house style and have a bit of fun with it. The quest for the Key to Time all feels somewhat bloodless compared to this, the story of two loveable con men pretending to sell a planet to a humourless psychopath. Iain Cuthbertson and Nigel Plaskitt, cast in the Paul Newman and Robert Redford roles, are wonderful. But it's Paul Seed who is especially astonishing as the Graff Vynda K. By rights his character either plays out as a gullible stooge or as a ranting tyrant – instead, Seed brings an extraordinary dignity to the role that makes him ten times more dangerous. He's an actor who even finds something threatening at the moment he's being tricked – he cannot entertain the idea that anybody would dare make a fool of him, and his absolute certainty of that is chilling. And Holmes' story doesn't hang about; within one episode the sting is laid, then sprung, then discovered – and Seed responds to the deception with a military coolness that is intelligent and without bluster.

T: I love this. I just watched it and got so involved, I forgot about even considering what I'd write about afterwards. Yet, when I was younger, this wasn't a story that ever particularly inspired me. To be fair, I first watched it as a dodgy bootleg after I'd been lent a whole load of old episodes and devoured them all pretty quickly, so keen was I to have "seen" the stories without actually bothering, especially, to "watch" them. A bit like the guy with the camera at the Moths gig, I guess: so eager to notch up the event and mark it, I didn't actually stop to savour the delights of the material itself. It's like being offered a glass of vintage wine, but guzzling it down so you can be the first to say you've done it, instead of enjoying the experience itself.

In recent years, though, this story has proved to have more delights than some of its rivals; it's a gift that keeps on giving. And the reason it works is because of its slightly heightened nature. Let us be honest: no-one in The Ribos Operation behaves or acts like a real person, but nor does anyone in Shakespeare, or Casualty, or even a Ken Loach film. Does that make them unbelievable? No, because heightened drama contains truth, and its exaggerations enables the viewer – if he or she chooses – to mine the subtleties and subtext from beneath the bombast. All dialogue in drama is totally artificial, none of it capturing the stuttering, non-sequitur filled, grammatically muddled nonsense that passes for conversation. Because being involved in them is very different from listening to them, dramatists have to translate and distil conversations to make them digestible, but also – and this is harder – to contextualise the drama, flag up plot points and convey character. This is why not many people can write good drama, and why – because of the flair and economy with which he carried off the necessities – Robert Holmes is one of the very best at it. Let's not underestimate this: Robert Holmes was a magnificent writer. He takes a daft family sci-fi concept and weaves magic from it.

With no monsters or gunfights at centre stage, Holmes only really has characters to pique our interest. The intricate scam plot will be entirely lost on the younger portion of the audience, so they need to see the Doctor having fun with the funny bloke and being wary of the scary one. The guest actors need to be brave and bold with their characters, and every one of them is pitch-perfect. Even Prentis Hancock's po-faced sternness is what this environment needs from him. At times, it's almost as if the Doctor and Romana have walked into an episode of Garron and Unstoffe, and the two actors playing those parts have no qualms in walking away with their scenes, but it's delightful that Baker seems content to let them.

The scryngestone scene – in which Unstoffe's part of the con is to pass himself off as a local with a story about a lump of Jethrik and an ancient map – is intentionally and wonderfully daft, and the script takes great pains to point out that the Graff and Sholakh doubt its veracity. It eats its cake and has it, though, because it gives time and space for a virtuoso comic turn from Nigel Plaskitt, who as Unstoffe has a lovely, gentle quality about him... and of course, a very honest face. Indeed, the Jethrik plot is contrived and clever – as a heist movie set in the Baltic, and where the victim is a psychopathic warlord, I don't think you'll see its type anywhere or anywhen again!

... so Tom Baker really doesn't need to pull a silly face at the cliffhanger, but does anyway.

The Ribos Operation (part three)

R: A couple of seasons ago, Robert Holmes took that difficult "third episode" of The Deadly Assassin, and did something experimental with it, producing an instalment that was mostly action with very little dialogue. And here he takes that, and reverses it, in an experiment rather more subtle – because this is all talk, and no action whatsoever. (The one moment of gunplay is from K-9, and in keeping with the style of the episode, even his

shooting down a guard is kept self-consciously off screen.) This ought to be dull and meandering, because really, *nothing* happens – the Doctor and Romana are locked up with Garron, and Unstoffe is in hiding. But it's extraordinary, mostly because it focuses deliberately upon the certain pressure of waiting for death – and we so rarely get the opportunity in Doctor Who for those long moments where characters are forced to contemplate the inevitable, because the adventure-serial format forces us on to the next twist or turn.

So the Doctor and Garron amuse each other with anecdotes, and the Doctor invites Romana to stop worrying and to enjoy herself – even he recognises, faced with death and crisis as often as he is, that these interludes are rare and fleeting. "Aren't you frightened?" she asks. "Yes," he replies gently, and with absolute conviction, "terrified..."

Best of all is the scene where Binro the Heretic explains his heresy to Unstoffe, that he believes the lights in the sky are not ice crystals, but stars, other worlds. The suggestion that he has been tortured for his beliefs, and forced to recant them, is so much more powerful for its subtlety. And suddenly, in the middle of this strange comedy, half caper, half black satire, Unstoffe tells Binro that his beliefs are true, and that one day, "even here, people will say, Binro was right" – and Binro realises his life's suffering has not been for nothing, and takes Unstoffe's hands in silent, grateful joy. It's the most remarkably moving scene, utterly breaking the tone of the story around it to create something wise and tender and true – and Nigel Plaskitt, all amiable comedy and bumpkin accent last week, changes his performance entirely to allow something really magical to happen. It's one of the great stand-out scenes in Doctor Who, all the odder in that it's a long dialogue scene between one minor guest star and a character only introduced a few minutes previously – try to think of any grandstanding scene at this point in the series which wouldn't put Tom Baker centre stage. And that's precisely why it works, because it suddenly lends a depth to the most incidental of supporting cast, and suggests by doing so a commensurate depth to the characters elsewhere and the culture they live in. Unstoffe has spent his criminal life taking advantage of societies such as Ribos, where new science battles entrenched superstition; it is fitting that he should be the one to give a dying old man proof of his faith.

And if it's an old chestnut, that science versus superstition cliché, it's by no means so cut and dried in this story. The Seeker would typically be a charlatan, trading off gullible savages – but instead the witch quite accurately hunts where Unstoffe is hiding. She's really rather disturbing – Ann Tirard screaming out her incantations, then responding with sniffy dignity when her results are questioned. And there's the hint that in this world – "even here", as Unstoffe put it – the superstition is so engrained, that it does have a certain truth to it after all. Binro may be a man of future science, but as he skulks around the catacombs, he half believes the legends of the ice gods, and that there's something dark and ancient lurking around the corner. And so do we. There's comedy to be had as the Doctor and Romana push aside rotting skeletons to hide upon tombs, but it's comedy of a very sinister hue.

T: I knew you'd nick the Binro scene and the Seeker business, the two stand-out bits, and have them for yourself! So let me foretell that future generations will turn to each other and say "that Shearman, he was a greedy bastard".

But all right... let me dwell a little more on Timothy Bateson's performance as Binro, which is a thing of grotty beauty. All sorts of strange things seem to be going around in his head, and he's quite funny with his distractedness and muttering – his strange, off-kilter nature tickles us. And yet, it isn't really a "comedy" performance. Bateson isn't giving us a "dotty old tramp" – there is immense dignity in those watery eyes, popping out of his grubby face, and he's even removed his false teeth for the role. When the Shrieve (a terse and disdainful turn from Oliver Maguire) recognises Binro, Bateson adds a tired resignation to his voice. He's been insulted a thousand times and doesn't have the strength to resist it anymore, but it still hurts; the pain and dignity are both etched in his face. You can also see in Binro a fertile mind that once teemed with ideas – his eyes have a zealous twinkle as he explains his theories, and you can see how much joy he must have got from forming them, making the

broken, abject figure he cuts now all the more tragic.

And valediction for Binro comes from Unstoffe's quiet act of charity, and his resultant speechless, keening acceptance of the gift of confirmation – and the childlike way he clasps Unstoffe's hand and bats it with his own – is extraordinary to find in a scene of padding in a relatively uncelebrated slice of old Doctor Who. It brings a tear to my eye every time. Later, Bateson is mesmerising when Binro leads Unstoffe through the ice caves, his face bewitchingly watchable as he terrifies the life out of the nervous conman. These later scenes are largely intended as comedy, but because of the connection between these two, there's something very touching about the black humour used by a pair of nervous strangers steering their way through danger.

By the way, I hate magic in Doctor Who, and I hate psychic powers... so why do I love the Seeker? I think it's A) because she's done with such conviction, B) because of the real-world precedent for insane shamen types who have the arts of precognition and divination at their fingertips, and C) because she is unique in the universe of Doctor Who. Tirard rightly goes for it – her piercing screams are strange and compelling.

And the Seeker *looks* fabulous, in a story where all of the design teams have worked to great effect. She casts her second incantations on a superb courtyard set – just one of Ken Ledsham's sturdy, attractive and versatile pieces of work on this serial. Meanwhile, sound designer Richard Chubb creates a convincing, swirling windscape for the exterior scenes, which contrasts well with the echoey majesty of the relic room. They even manage to avoid an awkward video effect by not having the guard in the same shot as K-9 when he is, ahem, shot by him. It's a great idea, as it saves all that tedious lining up which often results in the beam zapping out at an ugly angle. (Steps are clearly being taken – and replaced with ramps? – to overcome K-9's limitations; the Doctor even says "don't stop at all the corners", which wins the Obvious Tom Baker Ad-Lib Competition hands down this week.)

Finally, the cliffhanger is a cheat (the Doctor commits a conveniently placed faux pas to alert the Graff, so he can deliver a suitably dramatic line), and features a naughty piece of business from Ian Cuthbertson as he signals his near miss with Mary Tamm's... um, segments, when Romana climbs on top of Garron and the conman has nowhere to put his hands. You know, it doesn't matter that the plot could function happily without this episode, because the quality on display is bewitching – and what's wrong with something mainly serving to entertain, and provide light and shade to its supporting characters? You don't need a starter and a main course *and* a dessert to sate your appetite with different flavours, textures and sensations, you could just stuff yourself with potato... but it'd be far less interesting an experience.

August 13th

The Ribos Operation (part four)

R: Oh, Hackney Wick has never sounded more exotic, or more far away; the sequence where Unstoffe wistfully recalls the name of Garron's home is so sweetly sad, and the Home Counties of Britain at their most bland and unlovely take on a nostalgic quality amidst the dank catacombs on Ribos. Isn't that what Robert Holmes does best? He takes the ordinary, and casts new shapes on it by contrast with the strange and the unworldly. And that little throwaway reference to Hackney Wick, that is both funny and jarring at the same time, best exemplifies the tone of this peculiar episode. The comedy doesn't so much turn sour as edge just a few days past its sell-by date, and characters who were meant to inspire laughter or melodramatic revulsion become newly sympathetic as, very gently, their dreams are denied them and all too real disillusionment sets in. Just look at how different Nigel Plaskitt's Unstoffe seems when he is reunited with the brash and extroverted Garron – you can really believe that within the course of an episode and a half, he has undergone a sea change, and is now so much wiser and older than his senior partner. The Graff goes mad, but not as is typical through typical power lust, but because his loyal Sholakh dies – he realises that the best moments of his life were the most tortuous. And there's Binro, of course, taking

solace in his final gasps that his heresies were right – and that the knowledge of that is "worth a life".

And as with Holmes' best scripts, there's a sense of inevitability about all this, that these characters have lived their lives to the maximum, and having reached their zenith long ago now finally realise they are in the descent. It's most similar to the feel of The Caves of Androzani – but whereas that plays like bloody tragedy, this script has the more mature edge to it, I think. And that's mostly because for all its reflective dying tone, it still plays as a muted comedy and never betrays its roots as escapist entertainment for shock effect. The Seeker prophesies that only one of the Graff's party shall survive the exploration of the catacombs, and in doing so sentences herself to death; the scene where the Graff so gently and nobly condemns one of his guards, with the full expectation that his lackey will unquestioningly die to satisfy that prophecy, manages to be both richly comic and extremely touching at the same time. The Graff's own death, fighting an imaginary battle, strolling off down a corridor with a bomb attached to him like an idiot, ought to be very funny, and feel like the just desserts for a black-hearted villain – but it's moving, too, because as an audience we *share* in his insanity, we hear the sounds of conflict in his mind, and take pity on him. This is Holmes at the very height of his powers, balancing in one scene pathos and laughter and callousness, and leaving you unsure how to react to what's going on.

T: I *adore* the names Robert Holmes has given these characters; they all sound like plausible nomenclature, but it's nonetheless bizarre. Bizarrest of all, actually, is the Graff Vynda-K, which Ian Marter rather unsportingly changed to the more likely sounding "Vynda-Ka" in his novelisation. I like the K version: it almost invites ridicule, and yet is no more unlikely sounding than say, Ice-T. Names are just sounds we have constructed, so why shouldn't one consist, in part at least, of a single letter?

As for the nutty despot – *what* a fantastic performance Paul Seed has given throughout the story. As far back as episode one, when unimpressed by his primitive surroundings, the Graff commented "I've slept in worse places" – we know this isn't some titled ninny, this is a warlord who has fought for his glories, with Robert Keegan's trusty Sholakh by his side throughout. The two of them have created a novel dynamic: rather than continually berate his underling for incompetence – as is often the way with Doctor Who villains – the Graff defers to his general's practical experience, and even jokes with Sholakh about his own aim when he shoots a guard in cold blood ("slightly high and to the left", the Graff concedes). Seed's high-octane performance conveys that the Graff's anger is borne from a desire for a power that he thinks has been unjustly taken from him. This intense portrayal makes his descent into madness all the more plausible, especially after his respected general has been killed, his "guts flattened" by a rockfall. Actually, Sholakh's death is terribly moving – not a bad feat for a supporting villain – and you can well believe that this is what tips the Graff into the final stages of his simmering insanity. His final charge (with, as it happens, a smuggled explosive popped into his pocket) as the sounds of marching, horses and battle flood his addled mind provide a tragi-comic element to the fall of this mighty character. It's funny and moving in equal measures.

What a beautiful moment, in a story chock-full of them. All right, it's something of a misstep that Binro's death isn't as moving as Sholakh's (Garron's commentary on Binro's passing is unnecessarily glib), but Binro's earlier explanation that Unstoffe's impartation of knowledge was "worth a life" is as moving as the famously celebrated scene we both adored from the previous episode. It's appropriate that comic-relief Garron proves capable of quite obtuse bravery when he confronts the Graff, that comedy thief Unstoffe should provide a vignette of real emotional truth and beauty, and that despotic warlord the Graff emerges with a certain cracked nobility... all of this, in a story that thematically involves switching things by sleight of hand, and smuggling treasure in without anyone really noticing.

The Pirate Planet (part one)

R: All right, children? Children? Play time's over. Play time's over now, come on, gather around. Yes, Tom, gather around, and stop pulling Mary's hair like that. Good boy.

Now, I've been watching you all in the break, running about, acting out your little adventures! Yes, you were very funny! Yes, well done... well, you were *quite* funny. Well, you were *quite* funny once in a while, children. I smiled. Once or twice, yes. Yes, the bit where the robot dog started spinning about was *very* unexpected! What was that, sorry? No. No, I didn't say that was actually funny. I didn't think it was one of the funny bits.

Very well then, specifics. Yes, you're all doing funny things. But it'd be a lot better if you were doing funny things in cooperation with each other. You remember, children, we learned the word cooperation, we had a song about that, didn't we?... Oh, that's right, Tom, you were off sick that lesson. I'm sure one of the other students will let you see their notes. You see, the problem is, you're all chasing around doing jokes which are probably quite amusing on their own, but look like a right old mess next to each other. Ralph, yes, we get that the script is probably doing a bit of a skit on melodrama, but seriously, can you vary the tone a bit? David W, where's David W? You're playing the rebel, love, and the lines are a *bit* posturing – I know you're doing your best, but you can't play *half* the lines for real and the rest as if it's a parody, it just looks awkward. Primi, sweetheart. What you're doing is... Well. You're very pretty. Well done. Clive, yes, your bit with the jelly babies was a hoot, but you're supposed to be an unnamed background artist, so stop trying to steal the scene. Tom won't thank you for that.

Speaking of which. Tom. I think all we're really asking for is a little consistency. No, I don't know why all the citizens on the planet keep ignoring you. I'm assuming it's all a little "meta", a wry comment on the way your companions are very attractive girls, and we all do like attractive girls, don't we? But really. The citizens can't ignore you in one scene, and then be running away from you in the next. Pick one joke and stick to it, there's a dear. Which one do *I* think is funniest? Good lord. I'm sure I don't know. I'm sure I don't find either joke funny, particularly. They both seemed a bit laboured to me.

Mary. The ice maiden shtick is fine. I'm not

sure adding the extra veneer of smugness to the proceedings is helping much, though. You see, it looks less like Romana reacting to the story around her, and more like Mary wrinkling up her nose at being in Doctor Who in the first place. Yes, I'm sure Tom *was* very rude about the script in rehearsals, and claimed it came out of the back end of a whippet. He always does that, it's his way of bonding generously with the writers. But Tom doesn't show his contempt quite so obviously on the screen. Cut it out, Mary. It's not nice.

Now, I want you all to look at Andrew. Step forward, Andrew. Good work. You see, children, that's actually *funny*. See how smooth that is, the way Andrew makes Mr Fibuli play off the caricature of the part, but so underplay it that you actually believe that there is some real relationship between him and the Pirate Captain he reports to? For all the Captain's hollering and all the threats, you can see immediately that Fibuli is well used to them, reacts just appropriately to satisfy his boss, that there's some special game going on here between them. Andrew, you're an absolute joy to watch, and you're the one who lets the cleverer lines in Douglas' script stand out as having *style*. Bruce, yes, you're funny too. Love the robot parrot. I bet we get some comedy mileage out of that later, but, oh lordy, I'm dreading the CSO.

So, look, I'm not trying to be harsh. There's lots of fun to be had watching you rushing about every which way, and I'm sure all we viewers appreciate the enormous effort. But do you remember last time when we watched Upper School do that story set on Ribos? That was a comedy too, wasn't it? And it appreciated the comic necessity for discipline rather than freewheeling self-indulgence.

And, where is she, where's the extra standing behind David Sibley in the cheering scene? Yes, you. Stop enjoying yourself quite so much. It isn't decent.

T: We know the story behind this strange story, The Pirate Planet. The BBC didn't want to make this and Pennant Roberts, bless him, took up the gauntlet to make the wayward and imaginative work. Roberts should be applauded for his perceptive response to the script, which brims with novel sci-fi concepts that set

up a most intriguing premise. The TARDIS heads for a planet that suddenly vanishes: nice sci-fi hook. Pralix seems unduly affected, and his plight alerts some mysterious cowled figures: good sci-fi hook. The indigenous population of this mysterious planet refuse to ask questions or engage with strangers: good sci-fi hook. There are plenty of delicious prospects for an intriguing mystery here; it's not all frivolity and scattergun invention, as we might, in the post-Hitchhiker's Guide to the Galaxy climate, be tempted to view it. The plight of innocents is clearly treated with serious intent here.

Sadly, the most outlandish and funny elements – those on the Captain's Deck – are by far the most entertaining. There'll be plenty more of such scenes as the adventure continues, so I'll here just confine myself to the planet. Clive Bennett (in a winning cameo as a Calufrax citizen) is one of those lovely character actors with the perfect face for Shakespearian clowning, and injects some nice business about choosing the jelly baby he's going to eat next. Indeed, it's a nifty subtextual acting choice when he's offered "*a jelly baby*" and affably takes several, as it shows what a greedy planet this is. The populace tell us that "the Captain makes us rich", and so they don't ask questions – that's quite a sharp piece of satire, in a story often written off for its light-heartedness.

So it's a shame that whilst Roberts clearly saw the potential here, he – outside of the bridge scenes – doesn't seem to be the man to pull them off. The scenes in the courtyard and especially Balaton's house are generally quite slow or tonally misjudged. Roberts may have appreciated Balaton's line about strangling his own son with his bare hands, but he hasn't persuaded Ralph Michael (a suave, distinguished actor in his day) to allow it to speak for itself, instead of clasping his hands in overwrought, deliberately cod, signposted comedy. In concept, so much of this works quite well, but in execution, it's not quite there. If nothing else, The Pirate Planet is fascinating as a fledgling Douglas Adams script, in which it's possible to see how and why Adams went on to improve his work and avoid some of the pitfalls seen here.

And can I just add that it's odd watching this

on the same day as the previous episode? They go to great pains to explain away Tom Baker's lip (scarred from a dog bite), which was already a mess in Ribos, but it wasn't commented upon then... yet a bit of business in which he hits his lip on the TARDIS console during a bumpy landing contrives to explain it away now. For all we know, Steven Moffat's philosophy of "wibbly wobbly, timey wimey" might apply here – perhaps the injury we could see in the previous adventure was just a time echo of the traumatic event to come.

The Pirate Planet (part two)

R: Well, they seem to have all listened to me, at any rate. This episode, the comedy feels much more in control, and indeed, trying to work out on what tone the Doctor and Romana are to take everything is part of the point. Romana breezily enjoys her flight in the air car, but is clearly unnerved on first meeting with the Pirate Captain; she then reassesses the situation once more, decides the villain is just a harmless old bully, and it takes the Doctor to assure her that the bluster is all just a front for something much more calculating and dangerous. In short, the game that's being played upon the audience is being played upon our heroes as well, and it's much more effective this way – the Doctor not being presented as lead comedian, but as straight man trying to work out where the comedy ends and the horror begins. Tom Baker can still have his moments of self-indulgence talking to the camera, but when the drama counts, when he needs us to believe that a planet can dematerialise around another and commit genocide on a scale of hundreds of millions, he can do it.

And it's that strange balance between high comedy and grittier drama that makes this episode interesting, for all its apparent garishness of tone. Seasoned Hitchhiker's fans can recognise first drafts of some of Adams' jokes that'll become more famously said by Arthur Dent and Ford Prefect. The sequence where the Doctor mocks the guards for having to stand about looking grim, for example, predicts Ford's attempts to reason with a Vogon throwing him out of a spaceship.

David Warwick is really very good this week, too. As Kimus, he's much more comfort-able enjoying his role as sidekick to the Doctor than being the angry clichéd rebel. The wonder and delight he shows at riding first class to the bridge in an air car is charming, and does much for humanising the inhabitants of Zanak at a point when they began to look like nothing more interesting than caricatures.

T: I also think that David Warwick deserves enormous credit for pulling off the line "Bandraginus 5, by every last breath in my body, you will be avenged" whilst looking at a rock. They don't teach you that at drama school, you know. And I rather like the name Bandraginus 5 as well, as it happens. Warwick's character, Kimus, is clearly a quick learner, as he instantaneously becomes a better shot than the guards, despite their presumably being trained in combat and him never having picked up a gun before. Also, you infer that the limp fight scenes are an ingenious evocation of Adams' dark commentary on form and melodrama; I say they reek of clunky direction and will kindly pass on the generous portion of pretentious pie you proffer (although if you admire alliterative arctic roll, I'm yer man).

This is one of the first stories I have clear memories of watching. As with The Invisible Enemy, I think it must have been a repeat. (Did my family *only* let me watch the repeats? Wasn't I trusted with first nights, lest I talk through all the important bits? Surely not?) I remember the ending of this episode very well, especially the last couple of shots of the Mentiads and the lighting in the caves. I found the Mentiads rather moody and powerful with their impassive, colourless faces, sunken eyes and slicked back hair.

But I have no memories at all of the location work, or the scenes set amongst the indigenous population. Nor, strangely enough, do I remember this story as being especially funny. Watching now, from an adult perspective, I can of course appreciate the jokes and that some of the ideas are a bit more "out there" than yer average Who – and yet, the location work makes no attempt to hide its twentieth-century appearance. Despite some impressive high angled shots in the engine rooms, there's nothing here that hints at the futuristic, which rather clashes with the laser guns and psycho android parrots elsewhere. I mean, the mine may look solid and realistic – and clang like real, rusty metal – but if you were brought up in the UK countryside, the production isn't exactly catapulting you into outer space. Maybe this was a conscious decision to balance the script's more outlandish concepts, but it doesn't come across like that.

But while Pennant Roberts often gets bad press, it's worth pointing out that some of his shooting is very impressive, notably in the way he positions the camera in relation to the Captain. Many of his scenes are shot with his face in close-up, so we are privy to the nuances of his expressions, and see everyone scurrying behind him in the background. When actor Bruce Purchase makes the smallest of movements – a frown, a pursed lip – we get insight into the Captain's psychology and, I think, the quite-deliberate inference that all of the shouting is bluster to hide a more considered mind. If the Captain had been shot from afar, he would have come across as a bullying, controlling figurehead, much as his subjects view him. But in Roberts' vision, we have a man who clearly has a lot going on in his head, who deliberately adopts strident tones to fit in with the imagery his horrible injuries have created for him. Purchase isn't all top volume either – he has been given smaller moments (one last episode was accompanied by a playful, childish laugh suggesting that the maintenance of this bullish front comes at the cost of a soupcon of his sanity). To only see the surface aspects of the performance and miss the other stuff... well, that's just what everyone around the Captain is doing too. Fortunately, we have a director who understands this, and allows us to mine the subtleties.

August 14th

The Pirate Planet (part three)

R: Like The Ribos Operation, episode three is taken up with an awful lot of talk and precious little action. But Robert Holmes used all that talk as a means of telling us about seemingly irrelevant things, funny anecdotes and epic myths and sad regrets, all of which, rather brilliantly, succeeded in making the culture and the characters seem so much richer. What

Douglas Adams does here is very different. It's exposition on full throttle. And he's too witty a writer not to make something of it; whereas most writers try to conceal their passages of infodump, Adams finds it much more rewarding to point to it with a big finger and emphasise it as much as possible.

This is Douglas Adams' style, and one of the things that makes The Hitchhiker's Guide to the Galaxy brilliant. If he finds himself called upon to require a bit of melodramatic action, he'll question it, turn it on its head and find something new in it. If he fires missiles at a spaceship, the missiles will turn into a bowl of petunias and a philosophising sperm whale; if he has trigger-happy guards firing at his heroes, he'll make them parody themselves with angstful bouts of self-justification. For Adams, the *concept* is the real drama, and the real comedy too – and it's the reason why the funniest bits of Hitchhiker's are where the action stops altogether and the Book can talk in long narrative bouts without the pretence there are any characters in the vicinity at all.

It works amazingly well in Hitchhiker's. It causes problems in Doctor Who. And for all the dazzling imagination on display, whether it be bigger planets swallowing up smaller planets, or dying monarchs suspended within the last few seconds of life, it can only be told on this programme through the rather tedious means of one character standing about telling another. And that character is usually the Doctor, who acquires an understanding of the background and plot at a means to suit the needs of the narrative. There are moments of action in the story, of course, but the gun fights seem half-hearted, almost as if they're under contractual obligation. The one real sequence where Adams hits upon a way of telling his jokes dramatically is when K-9 fights a robot parrot; it can't really be achieved on screen, of course, and the denouement is annoyingly kept off camera, but it's still a lovely idea. And when the Doctor hands the "dead" parrot back to his owner, it is brilliantly funny. Adams spent years correcting interviewers who thought he had written for Monty Python, because he'd worked with Graham Chapman – but here is his own sublime dead parrot sketch.

And the actors are trying hard – well, the

actors with comic skills are trying hard, certainly. The scene where the Captain invites the Doctor to appreciate his trophies of mummified planets is rightly superb, but it's hard not to feel that it's just a product of the same whirlwind indiscipline that affects all the other scenes – it's merely one where the right level of comic performance and the right level of dramatic performance combust most effectively. With most other stand-out sequences in Doctor Who, you get the feeling of something deliberate and hard-earned – this one has the edge of spontaneity, that this is just the way Tom Baker and Bruce Purchase chose to act their lines at this stage of the recording, and it's what makes the sequence feel dangerous. But just look at how Tom Baker acts right at the end of the scene (always cut from those "best of" clips compilations), as he starts hamming up weird hand gestures whilst being arrested by the guards. One of Baker's best performances slides in seconds into self-indulgence. That sums up The Pirate Planet to a tee. It's a strange mix of the brilliant and the messy, both feeling as random as the other.

T: I remember being very struck by Bernard Finch (who plays the leader of the telepaths) when I was younger. I didn't know who the important characters and actors were supposed to be, so the fact that he labours under the non-specific monicker of "Mentiad", and rather low down the credits at that, didn't stop him from making an impact on my memory circuits. He's well cast, and his sleek face and chiselled cheekbones suit the Mentiad hair and make-up well – more so than David Sibley and the non-speaking supporting Mentiads (one of whom is Ray Knight, one of the twentieth century's chief extras – regularly behind the bar in Auf Wiedersehen Pet, Knight also runs an extras agency and was quite prominent as a frozen mercenary in Dragonfire). There's something about Finch's dusky but strong voice and no-nonsense theatrical delivery that gives a lot of this episode's expository guff (of which there is bucketloads) a certain amount of gravitas. I'm not saying it's an amazing performance – he's playing the sort of part not even Olivier could have delivered *amazing* with – but he does his job extremely well, and were he not as good, the whole piece would suffer in key

areas. So well done Bernard Finch (who sadly died quite young in the early 90s, I think).

The other things I remember are also the things that stick out here – Andrew Robinson bustling about amusingly as Mr Fibuli in particular. It's a funny performance, but a truthful one; none of his laughs are bogus, which makes them all the more effective. He delivers a cod scientific line such as "The means to destroy [the Mentiads] is at last within our grasp" like a secretary jotting in the to-do list of a powerful executive, and adds wry sarcasm to the announcement that the Captain's "kindness astounds me" – he pays lip service to protocol, but laces it with the disdain of a butler who has seen his master's excesses before and mildly disapproves. It's a delightful turn, and the scenes between him and Bruce Purchase remain a highlight of the story. Purchase is notable in some quieter moments, particularly when he muses about dreaming of freedom, and when he issues the outburst "By the left frontal lobe of the sky demon!" as if he's going through the motions. This empty bellowing suggests that his tantrums have become second nature, and often lack the bombast of bygone years. The Captain is as trapped as his citizens – he's a shell of a man whose fierceness is as much to convince himself of his own importance as anyone else, and he's teetering on the edge of becoming a tragic figure.

Talking of teetering on the edge, no pirate story would be complete without a Walk the Plank scene, and this doesn't disappoint in a cliffhanger that I recall as clearly and exactly as it's presented here (no cheating memory on this one). It's odd that I remember this, but not the impressive confrontation between the Doctor and the Captain, quite rightly lauded for former's righteous indignation, which injects the scene with a zealous, dogmatic, fiery rejection of injustice and all its lunacy. As ever, Tom Baker is so much better when his creative energy stokes his heroic fire, as opposed to arseing about with smoke and mirrors comedy.

And talking of comedy, is it a joke that I simply don't get, that the sweets they refer to as jelly babies are actually liquorice allsorts?

The Pirate Planet (part four)

R: I'm only too well aware that I've been a bit grumpier discussing The Pirate Planet than I intended. And that it's patently *wrong* that I'm moaning so much. Because here we are, you and I, watching all these Doctor Who stories back to back, and inevitably they all begin to run into one another after a while – the Pertwee UNIT tales, the Hinchcliffe horrors. Along comes a story like this, which really does feel like nothing else broadcast before it, and which suggests too an entire new and fresh lease of life for a television series beginning to look its age. And just because the innovations don't all necessarily work yet, I moan. The whole point of being experimental is that you run the risk of failure – it isn't a proper experiment if you know the certain outcome!

And watching episode four again, I suddenly find myself looking beyond the hyperactivity of what's going on – so many twists, so many comic asides, you blink and you miss entire plot points! – and seeing the genius behind it. Because it's an overused word, but there's definite *genius* here. Scene by scene, we see Douglas Adams turning the conventions of the way storytelling works upon its head with a shrug. It can be brilliant – the sequence where the laughter of all the baddies is interrupted by the laughter of the Doctor himself is just beautiful (look at the expressions of dismay across all those faces!). K-9 is losing battery power and the Doctor is giving him his last rites, and the almost romantic melodrama is undercut when K-9's dying words are not an emotional farewell, but information about a power cable. It can, just as easily, be a bit awkward. There's something killingly funny in the idea that all the Mentiads egg each other on to summon the mental force capable of... opening a door, but it comes across as flat and embarrassing on the screen. And with all the rush of plotting going on, playing a red herring for 15 seconds or so that the Doctor has lost the tracer is annoyingly redundant.

But what you do have is Adams' refusal to let his story conclude easily. And that's always been the biggest problem with Doctor Who's structure these last few years, hasn't it? That you set up a great idea in the first three episodes, but let it dribble towards anticlimax at the end. The revelation that the real villain is the Captain's nurse, who was introduced as practically an extra, but who has subtly been getting more lines and camera attention as the story has progressed, is flabbergastingly brilliant. When the Doctor attempts to "turn her off" in the first scene, it has the effect of turning the story upside down in a way that has rarely before been bettered. Rosalind Lloyd is perfect, too; she looks sweet and demure enough that you can really believe she's just a bit part, or as bland as all the other guest character women who tend to wander through the series. (Indeed, you can argue that Primi Townsend's awful Mula only exists to make Rosalind Lloyd's bland Nurse look all the more disguised – Mula is exactly the sort of character we expect the Nurse to be.) And she's given 25 minutes to be imperious and evil in all the ways the melodrama demands, and she's great – all the better for the contrast with the scenery chewing performance we've had from Bruce Purchase's Captain.

The problem, I think, is that the conclusion comes in the wrong place. In the midst of woeful jeopardy, with the TARDIS about to be destroyed, the Doctor finds a telepathic link to enable the Mentiads to foil Xanxia's plan... by hitting something with a spanner. It's very clever, and very funny, and I love the way that Douglas Adams sets up an ever-increasing series of convolutions in order to deliver an exceptionally trivial punchline. He'll do the same thing next year in City of Death, when Duggan saves all life on Earth with a well-timed punch to Scaroth's jaw – but there it works better, because it's allowed to be the denouement. In The Pirate Planet, you've got another eight minutes of new plot twists (the Captain had planned to destroy Xanxia; the entire planet Calufrax is a segment of the Key to Time) and in the rush we finish with a spate of technobabble. It's played for deliberate laughs, but it does rob the story of the climax it deserves, and it obscures too just how clever the writer has really been.

And in the final scene we get a big explosion, and a postmodern comment upon how Doctor Who stories like to finish with big explosions. (The best joke is still that the Mentiads would rather use the mental concentration of a dozen people to push a plunger than just, you know, one man doing it with his hands.) The Doctor calls it "crude, but satisfying". The Pirate Planet is very very far from being crude. It's so new in tone that the effect of it is almost dizzying, and almost in spite of itself it forms a template for some of the more sophisticated storytelling and imaginative world-building we'll get for the next decade. But it's also rather far from being satisfying either. It seems ironic in retrospect that The Pirate Planet is one of the few Doctor Who stories that were never novelised by Target, and to me that always gave the story the feel of being something unfinished, of being a first draft of things to come. Watching the story again, I still get that impression.

T: And now Romana is a better shot than the guards! It's a shame, as these heavies look pretty nifty in their sleek black costumes. And yet, thanks to their inability to hit anyone of importance even if they're standing directly in front of them, the gunfights have precisely no drama whatsoever.

I know what you mean about this being a work in progress – and actually, there's a lot more going on than is apparent on screen. What we *see* is a slightly clunky sci-fi tale, occasionally enlivened by a witty or offbeat exchange on the Captain's bridge. Yes, there are some clever bits of window dressing (the inertia tunnel facilitating a nice gag about "Newton's revenge" when the guards are catapulted into the wall), but Douglas Adams hasn't quite yet worked out how to let his witty set pieces tell the stories. The plot is generally advanced and explained through scenes of chatter, which shrouds the fertility of the ideas behind the concept; we're told rather than shown. A shame, as the idea of a creature clinging onto life at all costs is a fascinating one, helped by Rosalind Lloyd portraying the Xanxia avatar as a precocious brat. It's an effective accompaniment to the grim and horribly memorable image of the elderly Xanxia almost petrified in her finery, like a raddled sci-fi Miss Haversham, her eyes strangely blank whilst her body unnervingly breathes. It's a startling image of ugly power.

As with The Mind Robber, a threat to Earth is chucked in as if to justify this slightly off-

beam offering, and serves to patch over a lack of self-confidence – yet it is where it is bold, that The Pirate Planet works. Where it sticks in the staples of sci-fi (notably during the expository scenes and its portrayal of the dreary indigenous population of Calufrax), it's less successful; it seems that the bits that Adams enjoyed writing more are the bits that really work the best. But he's not all intellectual pirouettes: the Captain gives Mr Fibuli a sweet eulogy, and the sight of a giant cyborg pirate over the broken corpse of his snivelling factotum amidst the wreckage of a space-bridge is bizarre, but nevertheless contrives to be moving. Bruce Purchase reassures any doubters that his bombast was just an act (and all but says it was), and the explosion of non-organic parts that kills him looks quite dangerous for the actor, and so convinces us that it's fatal for his character.

And K-9 runs out of batteries! I love that. It used to disappoint me as a kid when K-9 was put out of action, but here it makes perfect sense. He's a mobile laser gun, and using his laser drains his power. As someone whose mobile phone is frequently dying when I'm in the middle of nowhere and have something important to impart to someone, I cherish the fact that the multi-talented, multi-faceted, dog-shaped brainbox machine can only last for a short amount of time before needing to be plugged in. I know the production team often had to absent the mutt from proceedings because of his impracticability, but this rather nicely emphasises the Heath Robinson, very British feel of this show, in which nothing functions perfectly. No genius is without flaws, no machine without technical glitches... and clearly no guard without myopia.

Nothing's perfect: not even, it turns out, lauded, genius sci-fi writer Douglas Adams. Well, that's the point, I guess, and I kinda like that.

The Stones of Blood (part one)

R: This is Doctor Who's one-hundredth story? The hell it is! What about Disney Time, then? What was that, chopped liver?

It's funny to think, though, that there was serious consideration given to the idea that the Doctor and Romana might open this story eating birthday cake. (And by serious considera-tion, of course, I mean it's something that Tom Baker and Mary Tamm came up with in rehearsal, and that the poor beleaguered Graham Williams had to put a stop to, no doubt as he was pulling out his hair and weep-ing.) There is a definite tension here between self-indulgence jollities, and the mechanics of telling an urgent story. The early TARDIS scene in which Tom Baker sums up the season so far for the benefit of floating viewers, is terrific; I especially love the way that the gravity of his monologue is broken up at the end with delight upon greeting his robot dog. That whole sequence should sum up the way Doctor Who works at its best – that it can snap out of portentous foreboding with something so light and trivial and human. Out on loca-tion, though, you don't get any real sense that the sudden reappearance of the White Guardian, and the warning that eternal chaos is just a few key discoveries away from the doorstep, has done much to energise the quest.

And maybe that's as it should be. There's something quite warm and familiar about The Stones of Blood. It plays upon the idea that it's a horror story – even Dudley Simpson's music during the Druid festival has the cymbal clashes recognisable from The Talons of Weng-Chiang – but the overwhelming tone is one of calm. It's a story in which the Doctor warns Romana to keep an eye upon two eccentric ladies sticking poles in the ground, and where the moustache-twirling villain dresses like a bank manager and offers the Doctor sherry whilst talking about goddesses and sacrifice.

Does all this undermine the tension? Yeah. But there couldn't have been a true tension from proceedings yet, anyway. There is, as yet, barely any threat in the story. The Druids are clearly and quite deliberately rubbish. (And there's a great gag that doesn't quite come off when the incantations of De Vries – "He comes" – are interrupted by the Doctor ringing the doorbell.) The Doctor has offered this Earth outing to Romana as a treat, and it's as a treat that we have to take it; we've been away from a recognisable contemporary English set-ting for so long now, and for a series that once seemed unable to stray away from London for more than a story or two, we only pop back to visit once a season nowadays. Off screen, Tom

Baker may have been in obstreperous birth-day-cake-demanding mode, but he clearly loves working with Beatrix Lehmann – and for that reason, even though the elderly actress struggles visibly with long speeches, she's worth the casting. Tom Baker refused to appear in the episode ending because he didn't want the Doctor to be seen as a figure of men-ace forcing Romana off a cliff; I'd love to say that his absence makes the sequence far more mysterious and eerie than any overfamiliar doppelganger threat could offer – and believe me, Toby, I tried, I used all the skills I learned at university doing English Lit to suggest just that – but, let's face it, it's not just a little bit dreadful.

As a kid, I remember being very upset that K-9 erased his memory banks of all informa-tion regarding tennis. I suspect that says rather more about me than it does this episode.

T: The Stones of Blood starts well, with some dark sacrifice scenes with chanting druids and the promise of black magic, Hammer horror and all sorts of witchcrafty night terrors. Stone circles are very evocative – every schoolchild knows the mysterious nature of Stonehenge, so the revelation that there are other equally mysterious circles around the country is beguiling and intriguing for the thrill-seeking juvenile viewer. And it's interesting that those early scenes are in the studio, and that director Darroll Blake elected to shoot the exterior on videotape to avoid the clash between film and VT – something so obvious to modern viewers, and yet my mum wouldn't notice if you talked her through it very slowly using screen grabs, diagrams and brute force (I know, I've tried).

Thereafter, the story seems to want to get itself over with as quickly as possible. In tradi-tional tales of this ilk, the local squire would come across as a decent chap, only to get unmasked as a rum sort at the end of episode two. Here, De Vries is revealed as a wrong 'un from the outset, and Nicholas McCardle's arch performance allows for no hint of subtlety or nuance. I do like the nice little gag where he changes out of his druidic robes, but takes the time to make sure he's all neat and tidy to greet the house-calling Doctor. Thereafter, sadly – and despite De Vries' gorgeous house, offer of a sherry and formal appearance – there's nothing secret about this villainy. Fortunately, when he brains the Doctor, the camera fades to black at the same time as the Doctor's consciousness in a nice piece of directorial flair.

The crows and the stones are the most evocative elements of this, though. There's something rather creepy about a crow. They don't instinctively fly off like other wild birds, but are quite content to lurk quite near people. Seeing them observing shiftily from atop one of the stones, or in creepy close-up in the studio, they are like sentinels of doom – they are effective, evocative pieces of imagery that encompass the best elements of this episode (of which, I have to say, the incomprehensible cliffhanger is resolutely not one).

August 15th

The Stones of Blood (part two)

R: I think that the strength of this story comes out of the sense that new writer David Fisher doesn't quite know what he's doing. It's as if he's got all the tropes of Doctor Who, but hasn't worked out yet how to assemble them together into a narrative. So you've got your little bouts of action, such as the Ogri's attack on De Vries' house, but they come out at you with real abruptness. And you have your little moments of charm, such as Tom Baker waking up on the sacrificial stone, but his would-be killers are driven off by an elderly lady wheeling a bicycle, rather than the force of his personality. Red herrings abound galore – we don't *need* Romana to mistrust the Doctor because some lookalike pushed her off a cliff, and indeed this shape-shifting part of the storyline is never used or even referenced again. We don't *need* there to be a long sequence about missing portraits revealing that Susan Engel has lived for centuries – after all, why have the pictures been locked away anyway? (It's not as if De Vries has had any motive for keeping them hidden whatsoever, or even that they give any proof whatsoever that Vivien Fay is an ancient Celtic goddess. If Fay found them that incriminating, why did she pose for them in the first place?) But the sequence is there because it creates an artificial mystery for the

Doctor to solve, and provides the audience with a shock reveal.

And that's the point, really – these moments work, in spite of the fact they only exist for the moment. David Fisher has taken the semblance of the Doctor Who framework, and not allowed himself to be hampered too much with foreshadowing or the slow mechanics of plot logic. He can introduce an apparent lead villain in episode one, and have him crushed to death not even halfway through episode two. He can set up a mystery of identity, and then throw away the intrigue of it weeks earlier than he might have done. The results of this are that The Stones of Blood feel a bit like a spontaneous mess – but it's that very spontaneity that makes it seem so much more modern. In years to come, we'll have two-parter stories by Russell T Davies which seem to change their entire tone, let alone their settings and characters, halfway through; by the end of Doomsday, it's hard to recall where we began in Army of Ghosts. Davies has been criticised for this very harshly, of course, and so can Fisher here – but it's not clumsiness, it's bold and ingenious, and what they both have in common is the way they give their stories a remarkable freedom that allows them to be truly unpredictable. When Vivien Fay points a staff at Romana at the end of episode two, and magics her away somewhere new, we can genuinely have no idea where she might end up. With any other writer of this period, Romana would end up somewhere already established in the storyline. Only Fisher would have her materialise on a ship in hyperspace.

T: De Vries is called Leonard. I love that, just as much as I miss the deleted scenes (included on the VHS, but only on the DVD's special features) where Martha opines that they could both escape the Ogri by absconding to Plymouth. At least their deaths are suitably grim, and in showing their twisted bodies but not the extent of their wounds, Blake pushes our imagination far beyond the bounds of comfort and good taste without resorting to blatant gore (it is mentioned that their skulls are smashed to pulp, which is pretty nasty). Their bodies are later dragged to the circle, and their blood used by the Cailleach, in another example of how what happens off screen often sets our minds and hearts racing more than what is on it.

To be fair to the actors, there wasn't an awful lot they could have done with such badly written parts – so maybe, in being so dreadful, they were tacitly mirroring the quality of their roles in their performance. Quite why they don't kill the Doctor when the aged Amelia Rumford arrives is less easy to explain, though – by not doing so, they ensure that the good guys know who they are, and, even worse, seal their death warrants with the Cailleach. It's as if they know that the writer doesn't really want to remain Earthbound, and is keen to get the story onto its next location. But if nothing else, their sentence of death precipitates a terrific Ogri attack! These bloodthirsty stones are simple but effective aliens who can smash through doors and loom ominously, and as such I'm very happy for them. They nearly do for poor K-9, and his anxious "I did my best, Master, but they were so strong..." as his power fades is more heart-wrenching than a mobile adding machine should be allowed to be.

And Mary Tamm gets her second stylish costume! This one is less boyish and practical than the first, but both are equally attractive and undated; I adore that she keeps the tracer in her shoe, and that as she fetches it, we see a glimpse of her petticoat. Do you still get petticoats, or are they fusty and outdated things like Spangles, space hoppers and readable credits?

The Stones of Blood (part three)

R: Let's talk about horror for a moment. Because Doctor Who is often described as being a horror series, when most of the time it studiously tries to ape the style of horror whilst avoiding its real effects. That's hardly a surprise – this is an all-ages series, after all – but it is still true that on British television in the seventies, there were quite a few horror stories that were designed for a younger audience. (One of the best examples, Children of the Stones, is well worth checking out – in part because when non-fans remember the Doctor Who story about the stone circle that terrified them when they were small, it's usually this and not Stones of Blood that they're thinking about.)

Doctor Who is, essentially, for all that it

glories in death, a reassuring series. All the trappings of horror are present and correct, but only so that the Doctor can send them up and invite us to laugh at them. Kids will get the frisson of a scare, but they'll also know that the Doctor will win through in the end. The Stones of Blood looks like it'll be a horror story, but even on Doctor Who's terms it pulls its punches considerably, playing most of its moments of tension as gags. When De Vries and Martha panic about the Ogri, Martha's cry that they can escape to Plymouth is deliberately bathetic. When the Doctor finds himself about to be sacrificed, his impulse is to ask whether the knife has been sterilised. So far, so very Doctor Who – and that's why we love it. Even the Ogri are reassuring – they're scary in *concept*, but in execution they'll always be big lumbering bits of stone that have no feet.

At this time of Doctor Who's history, I'd argue, there hasn't been even much of the *pretend* horror the series is renowned for in quite some time. Image of the Fendahl was probably the last time Doctor Who tried to scare its audience, and it managed that largely by pretending not to be Doctor Who at all, and by shunting off the lead character into the margins where he couldn't interfere. The Stones of Blood is good clean recognisable Doctor Who, with Tom Baker large at the centre of it, being eccentric, calling his robot dog and helping people up rock faces with his enormous scarf. And so it is that the one scene of horror that Doctor Who has this season – and it's *proper* horror too, there's nothing safe about it – has a particular impact. The context for it is all the more striking.

There are two campers who wake up to find at their tent two large stones. They weren't there the night before. There is no way they could have got there. One of the hapless campers touches the stones, and begins to scream. Her partner screams too, in panic, or in pain – we can't be sure. Her hand turns to bones, and then, disturbingly, we turn *back* to her screaming, and we know that she's still alive to witness this, and that she can feel everything. We hear the heartbeat of something inhuman. And the screen turns to red.

This is a fairly standard slice of self-contained horror. It's about two ordinary people confronting the inexplicable, and being destroyed by it. Shockingly, we never find out who they are. More shocking still, the Doctor not only fails to avenge their deaths (which goes a long way in regular Who to tip the horror towards melodrama), but never even learns that they died. They're just two bit-part characters who might have wandered from somewhere else into this Saturday teatime adventure, where there are comical old ladies doddering about with robot dogs, and been brutally killed. And they're brutally killed in part because none of the other characters knew about them – no one else shows up to remind everybody this is a reassuring programme after all. Even the Ogri, who have been rather funny up to this point, who can be lured off cliffs by the Doctor playing a toreador, behave out of character. They don't move. They're only funny when they move. They can still be conceptually horrific if they don't. And, in the manner of all good horror, the evil lets its victims come to it, lets the victims die because of their own curiosity.

It's a quite brilliant sequence, even watched out of context of the programme. Within context, though, not only of The Stones of Blood, but of this style of Doctor Who around it, it's unnervingly jarring. Within minutes, Tom Baker will be finding alien corpses on a spaceship and making jokes about them, and that's okay, because that's not proper death at all, that's just Doctor Who death, nice and safe and clean. But just for a minute, halfway through an especially light-hearted romp, Doctor Who becomes something horrific. Almost to prove to us that it still can.

T: Okay, so you nabbed the commentary on the campers bit then. Thanks for that! In fact, you didn't just nab it, you described pretty much every moment of it in minute detail. Ah, except... you didn't notice that the first time we see the male camper, he's doing up his flies. It's a cold night, why are his flies undone? Naughty Doctor Who. And if you think I'm being childish, I didn't bring up the mentions of both sausage sandwiches and truncheons in episode two, did I? Oh wait, I just have. Hmm, I wonder of that says more about me or the story. (I am *certain*, though, that if JN-T had sanctioned the toreador music and Ogri/ cliff top bullfight riff, then we'd have all been froth-

ing at the mouth. It will be interesting to see whether I'll be more forgiving of the man during his era than I was when I was younger.)

But we're at the point that the story seems to have lost all interest in Earth, which is a shame. The stuff in hyperspace looks as if it's a different tale altogether, and the initial story seems to have run out of steam already. There's a certain admirable economy in David Fisher's storytelling, and the guest cast budget must have looked pleasingly thrifty on the accounts sheet. It's just a shame to move from the darkness of the stones to the bright lights of the space station (and I don't mean the Megara).

What I love about Doctor Who – or at least, what I *think* I love about Doctor Who at the moment, having just watched this episode – is that it does horror stories that can only be solved by British eccentrics. Horror has become quite a cool genre since Scream, with lots of sexy wisecracking youths overcoming some demonic power. Batty old ladies like Beatrix Lehmann's Professor Rumford are far more fun. She provides incongruity: her announcement at the sight of a bloodsucking homicidal stone slab that "in the cause of science, it is our duty to capture that creature!" is a witty example of her sleeves-rolled-up British pluck at its most eccentrically enjoyable. She does endearing too, rather tentatively asking the Doctor if he's from outer space. With the possible exception of the campers bit, the scenes between her and K-9 are the best of the whole episode. And Lehmann's repertoire isn't just a one-trick dotty: there's a grim sadness when she realises that the Ogri's retreat means that they have gone off to kill someone. Beneath her batty exterior, of course, is an experience and learnedness that shouldn't be underestimated.

Knowledge is a more powerful tool than coolness in Doctor Who, and I think that's as valuable a lesson as the series can teach us.

The Stones of Blood (part four)

R: If you want to make Tom Baker happy, you give him lots of lines, a big barnstorming set piece, and put him in a lawyer's wig. He's in his absolute element here, playing defendant to himself in a courtroom to a couple of pompous flashing lights, milking every last drop of comic potential from a truly witty script. And it's wonderful to see just how precise Tom's performance can be when he doesn't feel the need to improvise or compensate for the script – there's no extraneous business here, no attempts to gild the lily. This is sharp and focused and not a little joyful.

It's run around a bit trying to find a style to stick to, but now that The Stones of Blood has decided it's a light comedy, it delivers chuckles with enormous confidence. It has the intelligence to be self-mocking, whilst never actually sending itself up: the sequence where the Megara sentence a flashing boulder to prison is really very funny, but is played without the wink to the audience that would have ruined the joke. The Megara are just delightful, in fact; they take to extremes the cliché of the logical machine mind, best typified by K-9, and for the first time in ages, Doctor Who has allowed a comical dilemma to be at the forefront of the action. The story will wrap itself up in no time, if only the Doctor can persuade these humourlessly smug oafs to see what's going on right in front of their noses. Not that they actually have noses, of course.

This is the great pleasure in doing this marathon, Toby. You and I have sat in pubs, and over flagons of ale you've heard me pooh-pooh the charms of The Stones of Blood. I thought it was a rather ponderous Gothic horror that ran out of plot, and resulted in the Doctor prattling about on a spaceship. It's actually a very sly and sophisticated story, and like The Pirate Planet before it, is trying to find fresh and inventive ways of finding the stereotypes of the series and subverting them. I think this David Fisher chap is quite a find, and I hope he comes back again soon. Oh, look, he does! That's nice.

T: Hmm, during those nice boozy pub chats, one of the reasons I liked you was the discovery that you and I largely agreed on the goods and the bads of Doctor Who. You could see the wit and charm of the wonderful The Ribos Operation, and you weren't won over by the superficial gothics of DWAS Season Poll Award-winning, Most Popular Season Sixteen story The Stones of Blood. And now look at you, cosying up to the popular kid!

I still don't get it, I'm afraid. The consensus is that The Stones of Blood is a wonderful, spooky tale that perhaps goes off the boil in hyperspace, but is nonetheless at least closer to proper Doctor Who than the rest of the season. Well, it seems to me that it's really a very poor stab at Hammer Horror, with two terrible baddies who get killed off because the plot doesn't know what to do with them, and which is shot on rather grubby VT. The endearing stuff – such as Fisher knowing how to channel charm and eccentricity rather wonderfully – has to be dug out from somewhat inauspicious surroundings.

But, appropriately for a story about ancient sites, dig I will. The Megara stuff is quite fun, and the creatures are carried off with a simple but effective flourish, as well as a couple of well-judged vocal performances from Gerald Cross and David McAlister. But really, the climax to this tale of (deep breath) a shemale alien despot inhabiting the Earth for centuries under a series of aliases comes down to a witty but elongated sketch about a stupidly intransigent judiciary. I suppose the fact that Cessair of Diplos only gets imprisonment for her murderous crimes, whilst breaking the seal that releases the Megara is punishable by death, is part of the joke. And yet, I'm not sure it *should* be, as it's intended as the major threat to our hero's life in the story's exciting finale!

Still, the cast deal with the witty banter wonderfully and know how to play it. The best moment here? When Romana arrives in hyperspace announcing that she has new evidence, and the Doctor tersely says, "Too late, I've just been executed". And the other things I like about The Stones of Blood? Well, it's lovely that Beatrix Lehmann's last acting job was such a delightful part; I like the Ogri, glowing and throbbing ominously and smashing through windows and doors rather like silicon Triffids; and David Fisher certainly has an iconoclastic sense of humour. But the reality is that if you to take the mickey out of the series' sacred cows, you actually have to get them right first... and I'm not sure he has, yet.

August 16th

The Androids of Tara (part one)

R: The Taran Wood Beast! I love the Taran Wood Beast. Do you think it's a sign of middle age that the older I get, the greater the affection I feel for crappily designed Doctor Who monsters?

Way back when, shortly after I'd had the commission to work on the revival of Doctor Who, I wrote to Russell T Davies to thank him. At that point I'd never met the man, we'd never spoken on the phone – the job was offered to me on trust, and I was really struck by the faith he was showing in me. He wrote straight back a typically charming email, as enthused as I was by the fact we would soon be out there creating more episodes of our favourite programme. But he told me not to thank him yet. He said there may be troubles ahead. He said – just you wait until we're both standing in a Welsh field in the middle of a freezing cold night filming the return of the Taran Wood Beast! It made me realise right away just the level of fan love that there was going to be in this production, and that made me very happy. It also made me realise just how much we secretly cherish our memories of where Doctor Who turns a bit rubbish.

Because beyond the lures of a man prancing about in a gorilla suit, The Androids of Tara is a thing of beauty. Castles, horses, Madame Lamia's strange hairdo, excitable dwarves. And Peter Jeffrey hacking away with an electric sword at a Taran Wood Beast. We almost need the gorilla suit to bring the whole thing down to Earth, and remind us this is Doctor Who after all.

Look, this is an easy story to write about, Toby. Nice sunny disposition, lovely scenery. And by my calculations, we're about halfway through our long quest. Why don't you handle this one? If you want me, I'll be over here on this river bank, fishing.

T: Well, this is glorious – in every aspect of execution, this leaves The Stones of Blood lagging pathetically in its wake. Once again, the delightful wit of David Fisher leaps off the page. "Now that takes me back, or forward? That's the trouble with time travel, you can never quite remember" and "Would you mind not standing on my chest, my hat's on fire" are two of my favourite Doctor Who lines ever. Tom Baker is clearly enjoying himself (and for the right reasons), and it's infectious. There's a uniform quality that is impossible to dislike (Taran Wood Beast aside, but you've dealt with him, so I feel no need to waste my time on the hopeless bugger here, thank you). Baker is funny, yes, but he gives the impression that his quick wit is there to disarm any aggressors, and that lurking behind this ridiculous demeanour is an insolent, simmering violence in need of checking. (Mark the way he warns Farrah about cutting his scarf – it's dressed up in ridiculousness, but there's a steel to it.)

And then there's the acting, in which not a duff note is sounded for the whole glorious 25 minutes. I find it bizarre how many commentators describe Declan Mulholland's Till as a dwarf, given that he's massive. He barely says a word, but his mimed forelock-tugging and simpleton's supplicatory hand gestures are spot on – it's deliberately cod, and all the more enjoyable for it. Neville Jason as Prince Reynart, on the other hand, seems to be from genuinely regal stock – he has the believable stiffness of a pleasant monarch whose upbringing formalised his personality. To then play his android double as even *stiffer* and slightly off-beat is a subtle and clever flourish from this dashing actor.

Lois Baxter brings a necessary stillness as Madame Lamia, and anchors the melodrama in fragile humanity – she shows defiance to the count, but you can see that what fire she once had is now out. And you can understand why this is the case, as she's the underling of Peter Jeffrey's quite gloriously nasty Count Grendel. What a fabulous character! He bursts in and saves the maiden from the horrible beast – but when he sweeps her in his arms to take her to his castle, it's not without arrogant, boastful threats (no matter how charmingly articulated). Jeffrey cleverly straddles the gallant olde-world courtesy of an officer and a gentleman with the obvious, oozing, innate villainy of a scheming glory seeker. He is, brilliantly, the hero in his own sordid drama. Even the necessary discovery of the Fourth Segment (in a nice change, the umbrella quest is solved without undue difficulty) provides him with a fabulous moment. Instead of dismissing the disappearance of the familial crest statue as a worry only for "superstitious fools" as the script requests, he adds a tremor to his voice to indicate he is nonetheless slightly disconcerted by it.

And even though this is a costume drama full of types, posturing and derring-do, there are plenty of neat little moments of naturalism. Note the final toast, where the Doctor comments that Farrah looks better without his hat, to which the – up 'till now impetuous – swordsman gratefully adds "cooler, anyway". It is a lovely, simple moment of real conversation preceding the big *The drink's been poisoned!* denouement that ends with a close-up of a triumphant, snarling villain. And he's got a lot to be triumphant about – he's just been in a wonderful episode of Doctor Who!

The Androids of Tara (part two)

R: One of the cliffhangers David Fisher wrote into The Stones of Blood relied upon an exact double of one of the regular cast offering a threat. And that time, Tom Baker refused to play the scene altogether. This time it's Mary Tamm's turn, playing an android who'll turn out to be a ticking bomb next week – which leaves us with the image of Tom Baker seizing a heavy club and beating his companion to the ground with it. (It's true that we don't see the moment of contact, but this cliffhanger feeds off the shock the Doctor might behave so violently, and that *whack* feels solid enough.) I find it interesting that Baker rejected the one, but not the other – especially as The Stones of Blood example feels rather bloodless and obvious, whilst The Androids of Tara's one has a certain brutality about it that strikes a real contrast to the easy charms of the rest of the story.

And maybe that's the reason. I'm guessing it's all about a different context. The Stones of Blood, with its lurid title, purports to be playing out the Gothic horror style so beloved of Hinchcliffe and Holmes – seeing the Doctor commit an act of violence there, it could be argued, might have weighted the episode too far towards the disturbing. Whereas The Androids of Tara is so frothy that the sequence forces us to be intrigued by the dissonance of

it rather than horrified. Perhaps that's it? (Or perhaps, quite honestly, Tom Baker was in a better mood this week?)

If it's simply a matter of better moods, then that's perfectly right too. The story is charmingly funny. But Androids doesn't go straight for the laughs. When we call Androids a parody of The Prisoner of Zenda, we're wrong. A parody would be a send-up. The Androids of Tara isn't spoofing Zenda, it's actually *being* Zenda, with added sci-fi trappings.

Now, the Tom Baker years are riddled with all sorts of stories that are offering us revisions of familiar classics. Whether it's The Brain of Morbius aping Frankenstein or Pyramids of Mars taking on the mummy films, in Hinchcliffe's time part of the contract it's offering the audience is that they may recognise the source material, but that the characters taking part won't. With Graham Williams as producer, things have started to get a tad more postmodern. Underworld does a riff on Jason and the Argonauts, and The Horns of Nimon will take on the myth of Theseus – and they're both trying so hard to be clever, they want us all to appreciate just how many references they can squeeze in. Both stories, crucially, deliver a wink to us all at home at the end, letting us know that what we've been watching isn't lazy *theft*, it's clever *homage*. The result is that both stories feel rather airless, and for all the joke of the conceit, Underworld in particular seems tediously overearnest. The Androids of Tara has none of these clevernesses. It works not by finding something it can extrapolate from its source material, but just by copying it. And, oddly enough, by going for the direct approach, by not trying to be too academic about it, it manages to copy a lot of the reasons why the source material worked in the first place. I've many times enjoyed the original Greek myths, and Underworld and Nimon, for all their scripted sophistication, in no way replicate the thrills I had reading them. Whereas Androids is pretty much as enjoyable as watching any adaptation of Zenda, but with added Tom Baker thrown in. The Androids of Tara may not be *clever*, but by God, it's effective.

It's a slippery road, of course. Doctor Who acting not as interpreter of familiar stories, but as plagiarist of them, cannot be a good thing. And we'll see in the eighties what happens when Doctor Who starts leaning on its own back catalogue for copying, rather than established classics or famous movies. But this once, just this once: by seeing what has worked elsewhere, and learning from it rather than trying to be *smarter* than it – by emulating The Prisoner of Zenda, rather than distorting it – Doctor Who has been able to give us something that seems entirely new.

T: All the stuff that had the potential to grip in The Stones of Blood – the stone circle, the sacrifice scenes, the malevolent bloodsucking stones – all lost their power because they weren't doing anything Holmes and Hinchcliffe hadn't already tried, and they weren't doing it anything like as well. The Androids of Tara seems so fresh because there's not really been anything like it since the 60s historicals; it has a witty sci-fi twist on such period dramas, and a fresh humour that complements the action rather than sends it up.

Amidst all of the familiar melodramatic period costume tropes is the lovely concept of Tara's otherwise old-fashioned society relying upon androids. This really works: why, we might ask, if they have created androids, do they not have vehicles instead of horses? Well, it's because of their disdain for technology, preferring pomp and tradition instead. The peasants are the artificers, and the nobles don't wish to dirty their hands with anything as grubby as electronics. It's a lovely notion, and creates a consistent worldview within the parameters established by the characters. There's some useful exposition (cunningly snuck in when the Doctor and company are moving through the underground tunnels) about a plague wiping out some of the population, which spurred on Tara's development of androids. It gives perfect rationality to their advancement in this technological area but not others.

So, having paid lip service to sci-fi, the production can now start tonguing the stuff it clearly wants to be doing – like copping a feel of the period styles behind the look of this futuristic society. It's *fabulous* to view: Colin Lavers has done a splendid job on the costumes, which are stylishly attractive whilst servicing the characters. And Neville Jason looks every bit the hero when decked out in

his crisp white livery (and his android doppelganger gets a lovely Arabian Nights-style inauguration costume), whilst Mary Tamm carries off another elegant but practical get-up that fits seamlessly into the story's overall look, and Zadek and Farrah pass muster as practical swordsmen in full smart military regalia. I just adore the snake-like hair squiggles sported by Lamia and some of the female extras, and the clock that's central to the coronation scene is a marvellous centrepiece of eye-catching design. Even Visual Effects get a mini-showpiece, with Lamia's electric drill looking like a practical prop as she tries to make an indentation into the Key segment.

And I know I'm going to sound like an android whose circuits keep jumping a track, but Peter Jeffrey is just marvellous as Count Grendel. He's so entertainingly disdainful of the stoicism of the bland heroes, and so enjoys his own villainy. He even mentions that he once showed Lamia "a certain (ahem) courtesy", which is surely as close a reference to nookie as we ever get in the classic series (and I love it!). The Count's loaded banter with the Archimandrite is shameful in its brazenness, and his mock humility at declaring that he will refuse the crown just once is hilarious. Because Hayes has cast this so perfectly, the facial expressions of his actors tell so much of the story in the key coronation scene: Jason's perfectly pitched android tips over; Simon Lack's Zadek looks guarded and cautious whilst maintaining protocol; Grendel seems concurrently curious, affronted and calculating as he takes in the developing scene; and the Doctor cautiously assesses the danger whilst keeping one eye on his wayward android.

This is told with such wit, skill, economy and all the best elements at the disposal of your average 1970s TV drama. It's a jewel in the crown.

The Androids of Tara (part three)

R: Madame Lamia gets gunned down, and it's the only death in the entire story. It's purely accidental.

She is also, Romana excepted, the only female character in the adventure.

There is a point to be made, I suppose, about the way that women are almost automatically sidelined from the action in Doctor Who. Pennant Roberts, for one, has taken great pains in the stories he has directed to readdress the balance – from The Sun Makers to Warriors of the Deep, if he has found a character essentially sexless, he's reinterpreted the role as female not only as a blow against sexism, but also to make the story have a bit more visual variety. In the Hinchcliffe stories, there really wasn't much place for women unless they were Sarah Jane or Leela – the classic horror tropes he was bouncing off hadn't had much use for them, save being victims or damsels in distress. And it's only under Graham Williams, really, that we start to notice a sea change, and a far greater reliance upon strong female characters aside the regulars. And it's with David Fisher's writing, in particular, that it's especially noticeable. At the forefront of The Stones of Blood, you've got Professor Rumford and Vivien Fay romping about together. (They never express love for each other, but by God, you've got to think it's implied – just look at the hangdog reaction Beatrix Lehmann shows when she finds out her best friend who's such an expert with sausage sandwiches has another life!) In The Creature from the Pit, you have an entire matriarchal society, and The Leisure Hive shows how a woman is left to cope when forced to take on the brunt of big business.

It's only in The Androids of Tara that it's different. And it feels to me not an oversight, as it would be in a dozen other Doctor Who stories, but a deliberate comment. Lamia is defined by cold intelligence, by her refusal to get mixed up in politics because she's a peasant – and by an unspoken but clearly acknowledged love for Count Grendel. The "certain courtesy" he once showed her is never explained – it doesn't have to be, it speaks volumes. And here, in this adventure of gung-ho derring-do, where the worst outcome anyone can expect to be in a sword fight is get stunned or have your scarf burned, in this game played by little boys running about being goodies and baddies – here, Lamia stands out as the only person capable of feeling any real passion that isn't romantic idealism or villainous opportunism. And she's gunned down for it, and even Grendel is shocked.

And it works precisely because it isn't over-played, because it doesn't obscure the hi-jinks. Doctor Who trades in death all the time. When we see it happen here, we're pulled up short for a moment. It hangs in the air like a dark cloud for a few seconds. We're not condemned for enjoying ourselves – we're just reminded, for a moment, of a reality of gender and death the story is leaving out. Then it's back to the fun.

T: Oh, but it's so sad as well. Lamia's love for Grendel isn't all doe-eyed mooning, and thus tiresome. She's instead cold and harsh, almost becoming android-like herself to prevent the hurt she clearly feels from transforming her into a mess of emotion. She's an intelligent woman condemned to a lowly position by circumstance of birth, and there's such sadness on her face when she dies – and her final words "my Lord" being a supplication to the man for whom she harboured her doomed, unrequited love. Lois Baxter's clever performance works because her character gave away so very little, whilst the actress herself spoke volumes – it makes her underlying fragility and hurt all the more touching.

And it must be said: Tom Baker really raises his game when everything around him is so good. This story has too many funny, witty moments to list, but it's also noticeably free from some of Baker's more self-indulgent ideas. He doesn't feel the need to entertain himself with mugging when he's clearly in classy company, because it'd be exposed as nothing more than lazy frippery. He'd look a bit shallow if he started throwing in silly business when Peter Jeffrey makes every line he's given shine. (The Count on the Romana android, with gusto: "[She's] as beautiful as you and as deadly as the plague. If only she were real, I'd marry her!") And so this month, the Doctor is witty, but with an undercurrent of keen, dangerous intelligence. His insolence comes from the fact that he can be as hard as nails, but he'd rather use his wits than his fists. Even the blatant joke, when the Doctor opens the door to the Summer Palace – and risks a barrage of laser bolts – to shout "Liar!" at Grendel works in context and is very funny indeed!

Yes, it's all very humorous and everyone is portraying a type, but The Androids of Tara doesn't come across as a farcical send-up. It's fun and knowing, but not smug. Declan Mulholland is obviously being shifty (and he calls Zadek "thee", as if to convince any doubters that he's playing a cod character), to the extent that he teeters on the edge of being a spoof... except that the script acknowledges that he's setting the Doctor up for a trap. This is because in Taran society, if you follow protocol (look at Grendel last week at the coronation), you can be as openly villainous as you like, so long as you make a show of civility. It's an amusingly hypocritical way of carrying on, but – admittedly – not without precedents in our own society.

Such wit runs through this like the word Blackpool through rock – there's Zadek's deference to the ersatz Prince, and his concern that the android might be more intelligent than the man it's replacing; Peter Jeffrey's glorious, exasperated thumping of his own head in frustration as his plans are scuppered; and K-9's nifty mowing down of a whole line of charging guards. They're all splendid moments, in an episode topped off by a villain we've loved to hate delivering his latest blow with a flourish, before leaping out of the episode.

This is a terrific story: accept no substitutes!

August 17th

The Androids of Tara (part four)

R: A shout-out for Cyril Shaps, regular Doctor Who character-actor since The Tomb of the Cybermen, who makes his last appearance here. Shaps specialised in the sort of characters who were easily scared and somewhat unheroic, and ultimately always got killed in an alarming fashion when more brutal characters got tired of them. The Archimandrite is easily scared too, turning ever-increasingly blind eyes as Grendel expresses his need for coronations and weddings. But the Archimandrite is loathsome, really, the hypocrite who'll stand by and smile and pretend all's well to save his own skin whilst seeing other people suffer. There's something wonderfully insincere about Shaps' smile as he conducts the marriage service, and I think it's his subtlest performance. The Archimandrite is never going to be the sort of

character people write essays about, but I think he's the *real* villain of The Androids of Tara; at least Grendel is utterly blatant in his wickedness, has bucketloads of charisma, and is a mean hand with a swordstick. The Archimandrite is a toadying wretch with a silly hat.

And a shout-out, too, for Martin Matthews, who plays Count Grendel's evil sidekick Kurster. He's barely made an impression up to now, but suddenly, as the plots thicken and we race towards a climax, he has murderous duties to perform. Matthews relishes it too – the scene where Grendel gives him his instructions to kill Princess Strella is lovely, the delighted sadism of a psychopath who's finally being let out to play.

Peter Jeffrey is so good here, it's all too easy for the rest of the actors to seem eclipsed. But I'd suggest this is one of the most consistent casts of the entire era of Doctor Who; every single actor seems to understand the tone of the story, and plays it archly but without irony. I'm going to make special mention of Neville Jason (as Prince Reynart), who half the time has the rather thankless task of playing the bland and sickly goodie – but also, as the man's android double, perfectly judges a slow deadpan reaction to conversational gambits and walking into branches.

The best joke of the episode, I suppose, is that in a season where the Doctor is racing about trying to prevent the entire universe from collapsing into chaos, The Androids of Tara pivots finally upon Tom Baker getting to a wedding on time. I'm enjoying the Key to Time season very much this far, but I always have a problem with the Key to Time itself – whenever the series arc is raised, with talks about Guardians and harmony and what-have-you, I just don't believe a word of it. The Androids of Tara sits right bang in the middle of the most portentous season of Doctor Who ever broadcast, sticks its tongue out at us all, and is the most determinedly trivial and domestic story yet broadcast. It's done me the power of good watching it – but I have to confess, it's left me returning to this season-long quest with the same sense of weariness I get returning from a nice holiday to a hard slog in the office. After this story went out in 1978, Doctor Who stopped for the Christmas break. When The

Power of Kroll began a month later, it was advertised in the Radio Times as the first of a new series – only to stick us all in a swamp with unfinished business. The Key to Time – hadn't we done that?

T: I don't think I'd get on with anyone who doesn't like The Androids of Tara. It's a simple as that.

I've sometimes seen it described as "boring" – as if Doctor Who needs the whizz-bang of explosions and monsters and machine-gun fire in order to thrill us. The fighting here, a lovely duel, showcases that much of our lead character's surface foolishness is a mask for an altogether more adept operator. Peter Jeffrey is also a practised swordsman, so we get a wonderful denouement: one of those protracted duels that wanders off the studio floor and onto location. It would have been unforgivable to kill Grendel off; he's been way too much fun, and his arrogant parting shot ("Next time, I shall not be so lenient!") before a very smart-looking dive off the battlements is terrifically funny and thoroughly entertaining. Earlier, I love the way he gets testy with the injured Reynart's heroic stand in the cell. This is no angry megalomaniac, but someone who thinks he's cleverer than everyone else, and wishes people would just bloody well do what he wants them to. He's gallant as well: refusing to kill an unarmed man, as if to contrast with his deliciously open villainy to the Archimandrite. What a flawless performance – Peter Jeffrey, gentleman actor, I salute you.

As you say, it's a terrific cast, and that includes the regulars. Tom Baker has been great in this, and Mary Tamm cleverly gives a slightly softer, more poised regality to Strella than the sharper – but equally classy – Romana. It's easy to credit the actors involved, but actually everything about this has worked: the photography is beautiful (the castle shooting at night is terrific; you can feel the bite of the cold night air, and the shadows cast by the duellers on the ancient stones make for evocative dancing phantoms), the design exemplary and the script has bounced along.

Anyone who thinks this is dull hasn't been looking properly, and has mistaken it for something it isn't.

The Power of Kroll (part one)

R: The first scene is actually very good. Director Norman Stewart takes great pains to do everything he can to ignore the fact that there's an actor with green face paint and a curly wig on set, refusing to even allow the alien the dignity of standing at the centre of the screen. In doing so, he mimics the attitude of the refinery workers, who chat and banter and never once acknowledge their servant directly except to wave a hand at him in dismissal. The effect is curious and dissonant – for a minute or two, it's as if you're not meant to acknowledge that strange presence either, as if some extra has wandered on to the set covered in paint and no one has the heart to point it out to him. And it's only after he's gone that the word "swampie" is mentioned (and never once in relation to him specifically) – we hear "swampie" this and "swampie" that, the lazy nicknaming that immediately suggests the suppression of a minority.

And what's clever is that the first thing Tom Baker says, as he steps out of the TARDIS, is that he'd warned Romana the terrain was a bit swampy – and suddenly it's as if we've heard the slur from the Doctor's lips too, quite accidentally, and it chimes strange and false.

As characters, of course, the Swampies are very problematic. The story very quickly becomes a none-too-subtle parable about colonialism, and that the indigenous population have been made into very real "coloureds", and dance about with spears and calling for blood sacrifices, can't help but make a twenty-first-century viewer wince. But it's not as if this story isn't explicitly about racism, and Robert Holmes refuses to patronise his Swampie race by turning them all into noble savages. The first story that seemed to directly tackle colonialism was The Mutants, and it fell into the (laudable) trap of trying too hard to make the racists evil and the exploited into saints – there was never any doubt that the Solonians were the good guys the Doctor should side with. Here it's all a bit more muddied – and if that makes for more uncomfortable viewing, maybe that's not such a terrible thing.

It's helped, too, that the comedy is reined in somewhat. The best joke of the piece comes not from Tom Baker being eccentric, but from

Glyn Owen (as the gun-runner Rohm-Dutt) trying to persuade a set of "savages" to sign for a delivery of weapons. It's a joke on the Swampies, as their simpler culture collides with modernity and big business – but it's an even bigger joke on us, who for all of our professed civilisation require contracts to trust each other. When there's the odd attempt at sillier humour, it falls flat – the Doctor playing on a reed that has all the sophisticated grace of a concert flute never works, because in this more sober style, we can't be sure whether it's a gag or just a production error. We're suddenly watching a story that feels out of tone with the light comedy of the rest of the season – this is really such a huge contrast to Androids – and it feels wrong, and odd, but also challenging and sincere.

And kudos to Norman Stewart, clearly more comfortable directing on location with swamps and motorboats than he was against a big blue screen last season for Underworld. Delta Magna feels like an alien world, for all that the parable we're being told is so obviously British Imperial – and there's a beauty to that.

T: The Received Wisdom before I saw Kroll was that it was the clunker of the season. I was baffled: the cast looked strong on paper, and the model shots I'd seen of the Kroll beast were impressive. The Target novel raced along, and I couldn't get why everyone dismissed it so. On the strength of this first episode, I'm still not quite sure why.

For a start, it's a novel setting. The Pirate Planet was a bizzaro concept that fell flat when a load of extras kept wandering up and down the Welsh countryside. Here, we have a genuine, inhospitable landscape of reeds and water – enough to persuade us that we're in an alien world that houses both a spider-legged metal refinery and a clutch of primitive dwellings. On film, the hovercraft looks impressive whizzing across the bay, and Norman Stewart opts for some documentary-esque handheld camerawork on board, with water speckling the lens as Neil McCarthy's Thawn scans the horizon for his prey. And it's refreshing that after a set of stories that felt lifted from the pages of fantasy comics, fairytales and horror novels, we're here given something comfortingly TV sci-fi. We have a base filled with characters who have

varying degrees of likeability, as well as guns and a rather unpleasant attitude toward the natives. We have a coarse gunrunner who chews straw and threatens our heroine, and a bunch of primitives who have been painted green by the production team (in a move of admirable chutzpah that I think just about works). It's all set up for a dramatic conflict, with the promise of a man-eating octopus god thrown in for good measure.

... the problem being, then, that the Swampies aren't terribly beguiling. The gag that those in civilised society don't trust each other when it comes to business (which is why Rohm-Dutt needs the Chief's signature on the gun deliveries) is a good one, but otherwise we must go to the refinery for human interest, and this is where Holmes has done his best work to sketch out the characters. The very first thing the refinery controller, Thawn, does when he enters is give Harg a gift he'd promised ("How much do I owe you?" says Harg in a typical Holmesian flourish of verisimilitude). Thawn himself doesn't really come across as the villain of the piece just yet; Philip Madoc's terse, dangerous Fenner makes more of an impact. He licks his lips distastefully when Thawn beckons him to help assassinate Rohm-Dutt, and he takes a shot at the Doctor (whom they mistake for the gunrunner). Madoc adds drama to a scene just by glancing at a fellow actor, and demonstrates the importance of casting in making dialogue-heavy scenes come to life. Cleverly, when Fenner – one of the refinery workers – posits "Would you let a small band of semi-savages stand in the way of progress?", Baker's response mixes witty insolence with viperous bite: "Well, progress is a very flexible word. It can mean just about anything you want it to mean."

Worryingly, though, when offered a drink, Baker looks at his space cup and then... puts it in his pocket. This is not a good omen, as Ranquin would say.

The Power of Kroll (part two)

R: It's hard to be too cross with a story that is all about the refining of squid farts.

Let's think about that for a moment. Not the farting itself, necessarily, but the schoolboy humour of it. There's a subversive streak running through this story, though it isn't reflected by the solemn style or the funereal pace. But there is a clear invitation being made to the viewer to look for more subversion elsewhere, that there might be a point of satirical attack.

And, at the very top of the episode, we get the reveal that the rubbish monster attacking Romana in last week's cliffhanger was, in fact, an actor in a costume. "I bet he looked more convincing from the front." (?) There's such a thing as being metatextual and clever-clever for its own sake, and this comes perilously close – but there's also a suggestion that the whole religious orthodoxy of the Swampies is stage managed, the rituals no more than low-budget metaphors. When Romana later berates the Swampies for worshipping a god they can have had no direct contact with for generations, Ranquin replies that some sort of transubstantiation is taking place, that the low-budget metaphors become sanctified and real. It's the argument that is used to claim that the bread and wine of Holy Communion becomes the body and blood of Christ, or that clerical figures with all-too human failings are instruments of God on earth.

What looked to be an unsubtle depiction of colonialism becomes instead a wilier attack on organised religion. In episode one, the Swampies do not know how to sign a document; in episode two, the Doctor discovers an ornate Bible that has been hidden from them. Are the Swampies illiterate or not? Is this a continuity error? Or is it, more likely, that literature has been suppressed by the likes of Ranquin, because it is easier to control followers with myths and legends than with source texts? Ranquin is the key to this – he's less bothered that Romana has escaped sacrifice to his god, than that she should be *seen* to be sacrificed to his god; his instructions to Skart that there must be some evidence of blood on the altar, with the implication that some hapless Swampie will be murdered to preserve a lie, is very dark and speaks volumes. Ranquin is no simple believer in Kroll. Or he may believe, but accepts that to make his beliefs compatible with reality, he has to actively participate in distorting the truth.

In itself, this is interesting, and not a little controversial. It's hidden away beneath a rather feeble runaround devoid of any real action. I'm not proposing that that's deliberate – that minutes upon minutes of refinery men staring at monitor screens showing squiggly lines is in any way excusable. (Because it's very tedious – one three-minute scene in the middle of the episode, in which the characters speak exposition at each other not just the once, but keep on repeating the same things to each other, beggars belief. When Fenner says, rather too feelingly, that "it hasn't moved for 15 minutes," he may very well be referring to the plot.) But for all that The Power of Kroll feels somewhat thin, like in the swamps themselves, there's something rather larger lurking under the surface.

Farts. Heh heh.

T: It's definitely a deliberate parody of religious propagandising – Ranquin is a terrible old bastard whose fervent beliefs and the entrenchment of his power have become so intertwined, they have metamorphosed into hypocritical despotism. John Abineri plays the part with absolute sincerity, letting the canny viewer pick up on the irony in the lines rather than flagging it up himself. Ranquin is deliberately written as a frustrating, annoying character, and Abineri carries enough gravitas to pull off the idea that he's a commanding zealot with followers totally in his thrall. His assertion that Kroll's servants are doing his bidding when they appear in his guise (read: unconvincing costumes) is as defenceless and ludicrous as any other murder in the name of religion. By having a green man dressed as a crap monster to illustrate this, Robert Holmes sharply points out the absurdity at the heart of all such hypocritical fundamentalism.

Carl Rigg's Varlik, meanwhile, is Ranquin's complete opposite – he's altogether quieter, more considered, and his speech features contractions which are unusual for "savages" in this show. I think Rigg is cleverly suggesting that Varlik represents the future – he's less reverent and fearful, and berates Rohm-Dutt for thinking that "because we live a simple life, you think we're stupid". A perfect summation of the three speaking Swampies occurs when Kroll appears on the horizon: Ranquin runs forward to give praise, Skart rugby tackles his master to stop him from endangering himself, and Varlik stands forward to take in the sight

– cautious and curious, but certainly not awe-struck.

I have to say that I'm more comfortable with the refinery scenes, simply because I'm a sucker for people bickering and waiting to get picked off by whichever alien is targeting their workplace this month; those were the Target novels I lapped up as a lad. These scenes certainly have potential, but alas only Philip Madoc has decided to ratchet up the tension by exhibiting some foreboding or discomfort – just look at how he makes even the most innocuous lines drip with meaning and nuance. By comparison, his colleagues are just too literal, describing what they see with little emotional investment. True, Neil McCarthy gets a nice moment when he realises that the massive blip on the scanner is the creature he saw out in the swamp, and the camerawork here suggests some attempt on Norman Stewart's part to introduce some menace. However, the suggestion that the signal on the screen may be a living giant octopus is somewhat robbed of its drama, given that *we* have already seen Kroll.

So it's Madoc all the way with this – even the quietly defiant "No" he utters when McCarthy suggests a genocidal solution to the Swampie problem is more dramatic than whole reams of potentially more exciting stuff that his colleagues get to say. There's a grim terseness about Madoc, and a sense of Fenner being preoccupied and concerned. When he snaps at Thawn, who pooh-poohs his idea about poisoning Kroll, it's with the impatience of a man who knows that time is running out, and an actor who probably thinks that this expository cul-de-sac needs the addition of a few loud revs to liven it up. Compare this underplayed intensity to John Leeson's breezy delivery of "If Thawn wants to use depth charges, he's going to get us all killed". The fact that a musical sting accompanies Leeson's rather vicarly dramatics only creates a comic juxtaposition, rather than a dramatic underscoring.

I'm enjoying this, though. In fact, the Doctor's realisation that Kroll is on the move – coupled with the ocular proof of this when a tentacle smashes through the pipe and drags Harg screaming to his death – makes for a suitably dramatic cliffhanger which I refuse not to love.

August 18th

The Power of Kroll (part three)

R: Robert Holmes has tried making this story about colonialism, and then religious fundamentalism. Now all he's got to fall back on is plot – and the trouble is, there's precious little of it.

And it's a pity, because the twists and turns of the adventure are actually pretty good. The revelation that Rohm-Dutt has been employed by Thawn in an attempt to discredit the Sons of Earth group is brilliant; Thawn's beef is not so much with the Swampies (in one especially well-written exchange, he tells Fenner he doesn't hate the natives, he just wants them dead), but with the liberal do-gooders and sentimentalists. He's a racist, certainly – but more than that, he's a sociopath who feels threatened by anyone with an opposing agenda to his own.

The only problem with this is that the revelation itself isn't dramatic. Unusually, Robert Holmes fails to mine the relationship between Thawn and Rohm-Dutt for maximum effect, and the two characters never exchange a single bit of dialogue throughout the entire story. Compare this to The Caves of Androzani, which owes more than a little debt to Kroll, and the complex way in which the gunrunner Stotz interacts with both businessman and rebel. In this latter story, Holmes uses a series of plots and counterplots to draw a web that connects all his characters to each other whether they know it or not; it only takes the Doctor to cause the web to fray, quite accidentally, and everyone is doomed. For The Power of Kroll to work, Thawn needs to betray Rohm-Dutt, just as Rohm-Dutt needs to betray Thawn. In episode one Thawn takes Fenner out to capture Rohm-Dutt, which is confusing – wouldn't the gun runner have given him away? If so, would he have to kill Fenner too? Rohm-Dutt needs to go out in a moment of gangster glory, and instead gets dragged by a stray tentacle into a swamp. Thawn, moreover, needs to eliminate Rohm-Dutt before he's exposed by him. Instead, he's left hanging around a control room once again staring at a monitor screen, just as he did all last week too.

AUGUST 18TH: THE POWER OF KROLL

It's not that the episode is without some life, and it's more engaging than episode two. Robert Holmes clearly has a lot of sadistic fun writing about elaborate tortures, and his otherwise tired dialogue crackles into life when he's got the Doctor on a rack. He enjoys it so much, in fact, that he devotes a full half of his episode to it. But tying the Doctor down with creeping vines is static drama; shutting Fenner, Thawn and Dugeen in one room all episode is static drama; having the Swampies sit about the marshes waiting for Kroll to appear is static drama. Nothing really happens this week. It doesn't happen reasonably entertainingly, which is a mercy in itself – Tom Baker is in relaxed witty mode, and Philip Madoc in particular works very hard to communicate a sense of claustrophobic dread. But there's an inevitability about all this, that the cliffhanger must be the fourth manifestation of Kroll in all his giant split-screen glory. And so it is. And we could have had this 25 minutes earlier with no damage to the plot at all, if the big stupid squid had only bucked his ideas up and got a move on.

T: If I had been old enough to remember it as a kid, this story would have been much more up my street than The Ribos Operation or The Androids of Tara. These days, I appreciate the majesty of those charming, delightful, "period" pieces, but this episode opens with an exploding pipeline, tentacles, smoke and a grisly death. This is the stuff! Proper Doctor Who! I can see now why Madoc was so impatient last week when the crew argued about the practicalities of killing Kroll – it's because he has to do it *again* this week, whilst being suitably miffed as his superior throws up potential pitfalls to his mooted solutions to the giant squid problem. Fenner – who in episode one talked about how the Swampies shouldn't be allowed to stand in the way of progress – now realises just how far Thawn is prepared to go. He's becoming grimly cautious as a result, trying to dig a little humanity out of the commander by telling Thawn that he doesn't hate the Swampies. Thawn then demonstrates his ruthlessness, and there's a tension between the characters that enlivens all the repetitive dialogue. Madoc's suppressed anger and urgency bring so much to the lines he's given, and so

– for an equal and opposite reaction – we turn to John Leeson's matter-of-fact delivery, which manages to sap any drama out of this.

Oh, and Madoc also calls Kroll "Jemima", which I note only because it makes me smile! Over in Swampieville, Varlik continues to impress me. He claims to have petitioned for "leniency" for the Doctor and Romana, urging that they should be executed by a less painful method: "The first [ritual]. That's very easy. They just throw you down the pit and drop rocks on you." (And it's even funnier to hear it described so matter-of-factly by the "progressive" Swampie of the bunch.) Like Abineri, Carl Rigg gets laughs without playing for them – exactly as it should be. I love the way that Ranquin tells the doubting Varlik to have a care after a clap of thunder, as if suggesting that the inclement weather is actually their god being a bit grumpy with him.

God or no god, Kroll provides an equal opportunities peril quotient: we began the episode with a tentacle grabbing a refinery member, and we end with a Swampie suffering the same fate. The Kroll model is extremely impressive, and though the cut-off at the horizon is a bit of a botch, it isn't actually that awful. So the episode ends with an impressive monster, deadly tentacles, a dangerous swamp and a man getting sucked under the ground to a grisly death. Oh, yes, this is definitely the stuff!

The Power of Kroll (part four)

R: There's undeniably lots of good stuff in this. Tom Baker gets to be brave and go to his certain death at least twice, and gets to be wittily unimpressed when confronted by a villain with a gun. It's actually the most recognisably Who-ish of all the episodes of The Power of Kroll, as crises are averted one by one and the baddies get their just desserts. It's business as usual. And that, I think, is the problem with it.

The idea of a season-long arc is a brave one, and for the most part it has solved the age-old problem that the Doctor is essentially an irresponsible vagrant in space who just saves the world every four weeks because he's in the right place at the right time. (If you necessarily see that as a problem in the first place – because one of the charms of the season is

347

putting a maverick like Tom Baker at the centre of some big mission and watch him try to distract himself from the work.) But for the first time, it posits the suggestion that there is one big story being told, and so that this is not only the concluding instalment of Doctor Who Vs The Swamp Men, but also the penultimate instalment of Doctor Who Saves The Entire Universe. With its first job, it succeeds functionally enough. With its second, its failure is lamentable. We need to feel that we're drawing towards some sort of climax now, that this story which has been dragging on for nearly half a whole year is gathering some sort of pace. Had you scheduled The Pirate Planet or The Androids of Tara as the fifth story in the season, the problem would still be there – but the pace of the stories, and the amount of plotting to get through, would have meant that the problem was disguised. But allocating the slot to The Power of Kroll, by far the most traditional story in an utterly untraditional season, is a terrible idea. The inevitable "is that it?" feeling we get at the end of the average four-parter is so much greater here, and emphasised especially by the only story this year that has not only refused to do anything original with the new format, but has also resolutely failed to find enough story to fill up the unoriginal formula it uses. The Power of Kroll's first failure is that it's aiming so low. Its second failure, that it aims so low... and still misses.

And the result of that is that the Key to Time season crumbles around it. If the season is a chain, then this is the first weak link within that chain. And whereas your average viewer will always forgive Doctor Who when every once in a while it sticks out a disappointing self-contained story, this one makes your confidence wobble that this long storyline has any real purpose at all. There has been so little going on in The Power of Kroll – did it really not occur to anyone to fill up all that dead time with the suggestion of a Black Guardian agent, or that universal disharmony is reaching its crisis point? It means you go into that final story with a sense of unease. The Armageddon Factor as a title sounds appropriately apocalyptic – but what if it's just as slow as this, what if it's just a two and a half hour plod around with dull characters and no urgency? Won't that have invalidated the entire season? Won't

that make the viewer feel the entire quest has been a waste of time?

And it's a shame, because minute by minute, this final episode of The Power of Kroll satisfies. I love the look of utter surprise on John Leeson's face when Dugeen is shot in the back, as if he too is amazed that anything that dramatic would ever take place. (And that's not a pot shot at The Power of Kroll either; one of its skills, I think, is the very low-level villainy of Thawn, that up to his final moments he is a self-justifying opportunist who gets pushed too far – when he kills Dugeen, you can see he is as surprised as his victim.) I love the ambiguity of the ending, as a clearly wary Fenner, last human survivor, is abandoned by the Doctor and left surrounded by a group of unsmiling natives with spears who ten minutes ago were trying to kill him. In fact, what I love about The Power of Kroll is its very triviality, that with refinery men and Swampies alike, we are looking at small men of small evil and small ambition finally having to confront a really truly bloody big squid. It's just a shame that triviality is the last thing you want now, here, in episode twenty of an epic adventure that seems somewhat to have stalled.

T: Hmm, I'd disagree that The Power of Kroll does anything different from its predecessors. The Key to Time has never really been part of an arc; the story of the quest hasn't developed incrementally. It's simply acted as a bloody big Time Ring in every story – i.e. something to provide an extra layer of jeopardy, just because it hasn't been found yet or the baddies have stolen it. The tracer fulfils a similar function, with under-running episodes padded out with "Oh no, I dropped the tracer!"/ "I found the tracer!" guff. I have virtually no interest in the quest element of the Key to Time, since it has yet to offer any fascinating plot developments or philosophical questions. At least The Power of Kroll makes the Key impact on the drama. If a squid hadn't swallowed the segment, no massive monster would have been created to drive the story, and so the denouement (where the Doctor works out how to defeat Kroll) is thematically sound. There's a danger, though, that the Key is just like this episode's tacked-on second climax with the imminent orbit shot – a bit of false drama, even though the outcome is so inevitable, it's difficult to get excited by it.

In Doctor Who, Machiavellian figures are sometimes very stupid, and there's a banality to the evildoers. How often have despots turned out to be witless little men? But intellectual shortcomings don't prevent them from being wily operators, and this is why Ranquin is such a great character. He's clearly an idiot – his intractable faith is full of illogicality, bound up by double standards and transparent dishonesty. And yet, he's managed to twist all these inconsistencies to ensure they prop up his position of power. That scene where the Swampie settlement is destroyed underlines this brilliantly... Ranquin decides (and Abineri deliberately shows that Ranquin has only just thought of this) that the ruination of their homes is a punishment for letting their captives escape, and then describes their woes as a test of faith. When it's pointed out that their god has eaten a Swampie, he trots out the "what is one life?" litany. It's caustic commentary from Holmes, and – in our times of increased intolerant fundamentalism – insight that we clearly still need.

Which isn't to say that these serious points are being made humourlessly. Abineri's po-faced brilliance has been perfectly judged, and he displays absolutely spot-on comic timing when the refinery starts being crushed. Everyone looks to him, the Kroll expert, for an idea about how to stop the beast and... he thinks, then, as chaos threatens to engulf them all, that he should clasp his hands together with the fervent hope of the most blind disciple, and fall to the floor in impotent supplication. It's terribly funny, which gives a certain chutzpah to the dreadful scene where he – one of our finest character actors – has to talk to a tentacle before it sucks him out with such force that the walls wobble.

Talking of wobbly walls (and I know I'm being negative here, but indulge me) the set design has got to rank among the worst in the show's history. In this lovely cleaned-up copy, there's so much stark evidence of slapdash work, you could prove all those lazy "the sets wobbled" journalists right just by bunging this into their DVD players. The refinery set is really cobbled together – it's damaged, dull and overlit. The silo where the Doctor sabo-

tages the orbit shot has walls so flimsy, they appear to have been erected by a stagehand who was desperate to win a "free drinks for the first person to get all their work done and get to the pub" competition. The climax, which even a novice would have known required a close-up of the countdown clock, is told via clicking numbers in a very carelessly cut out hole in the wall. When Ranquin enters and says, "This place is an abomination", he's speaking the words of a thousand carpenters.

Whew! All right, with my spleen properly vented, I can honestly say... in the end, I rather enjoyed The Power of Kroll. It's not perfect by any means, but it's a stark illustration of how much hard work has gone into making the very good Doctor Who stories we've seen. When talented ensembles regularly include actors such as Abineri and Madoc, it's easy to take performances of their calibre for granted (both chalk up their last appearances in the series here). Even if this hasn't seemed like the best showcase of their talents, in a perverse way, it sort of is – with rotten performances around them, it's readily evident that these gents are bloody indispensable. I often wondered why Madoc was cast as such a secondary figure, but actually, since he lives the longest, you need him there; otherwise, the already perfunctory countdown would have been redundant. After the relatively early loss of the chief villain Thawn (in a satisfyingly gory dispatch by spear), you need someone with a bit of grit to remain, and Madoc's insolent vexation really sees us through to the end. Whenever he's been on screen, you've not looked at anyone else.

Philip Madoc, John Abineri – so long, and thanks for all the fine performances. We shall not look upon their like again. Some things are worth worshipping after all.

The Armageddon Factor (part one)

R: And, look – the quest for the Key to Time is right back at the centre of the plot, and the Doctor and Romana seem to believe that anything dark and suspicious may be some Black Guardian trap. It's good to see a bit of urgency again, but – why? Why were there no mutterings from the Doctor that the Swampies attacking the refinery was something to do with the

Guardians? Why didn't he imagine that Romana being kidnapped on horseback by Count Grendel was some cosmic attempt to nab the fourth segment?

What this does do, fortunately, is make all we're seeing on screen that bit more paranoid from the get-go. Normally, the Doctor will walk into the middle of a conflict all bright and breezy, and whether the battle between Reynart and House Gracht or between white colonists and green savages, much time is wasted with the Doctor being forced to realise the importance of the crisis. Here, we're in a situation where the Doctor drops into the middle of a nuclear war – and we've never seen Cold War terrors being depicted on screen quite so explicitly before – and believing that there's an even more frightening crisis behind it. And that's very clever; taking something as serious as nuclear conflict and laying over it the end of a season-long story arc gives it an epic weight even a six-parter couldn't hope for.

And if the war feels a little clean – if the victims of a blast look rather tidy on the floor of the hospital – well, this is a Saturday teatime series being broadcast in 1979. What's impressive is the attempt to make this war seem so brutal and uncompromising, where Princess Astra can talk about the wounded lying bedless on the ground like rubbish. The opening few scenes are quite brilliant. And if nothing else can quite match the cleverness of the romantic movie with cheesy music playing against a bad CSO backdrop, with lovers spouting rousing rhetoric of nationalism, then that's all right – from the word go there is a contrast established between the artificiality of propaganda and the grey broken reality of the war. The Marshal's broadcasts to the nation are pure cod Churchill, the actor even adopting some of the same intonation and mannerisms. He's a warmonger, but he's played with such obvious sincerity that his belief in peace through victory seems truly honourable and credible. The story will reveal otherwise as it continues, of course, but for the moment he's a Brigadier Lethbridge-Stewart on an alien planet, and the no-nonsense ruthlessness he shows is for the common good. (Yes, he'll leave Astra to die of radiation poisoning, but – well, actually, Astra is a traitor, and she really is colluding with an enemy power during wartime.

As a figurehead for the people, you can see why the war effort might be helped with her suffering from some plausible accident, rather than the demoralising humiliation of a trial and execution.)

You see what's going on? I'm starting to convince myself that war is just and right too. I think that's the skill of this episode. Help me, Toby. Talk me out of it with some pacifist malarkey.

T: I run a comedy club called XS Malarkey, Rob. But Pacifist Malarkey? I grew up in 1980s Britain, where there was a real schism between those who wanted nuclear weapons and those advocating unilateral disarmament. It was a clear difference between the two major political parties of the time, when there was a much more defined ideological disparity between right and left than seems to exist now. At the posh school I was marooned in for some time, I was a figure of ridicule because of the Campaign for Nuclear Disarmament badges that adorned my brother's car when he picked me up once. Nobody wanted nuclear war, of course, and each side was terrified that the other would be the ultimate cause of it – the left feared the right's desire for military strength would make us a target, whilst the right feared the left would leave us defenceless and ripe for attack. Nuclear war seemed a plausible threat and genuinely troubled me, so any drama that uses it as a backdrop automatically resonates and evokes the genuine climate of fear that existed in my childhood about mushroom clouds obliterating cities. The bombs in The Armageddon Factor barely rock buildings, it seems, but never mind – there's plenty of talk about radiation and casualties and a grim enough atmosphere. The stakes seem high enough to kick off the quest for the final Key segment.

The propaganda film at the beginning is very funny. It looks like it's going to be a Space Age Brief Encounter; a tearful farewell full of doe-eyed loveliness. Then the "Heroine" talks of her love for the "Hero" and he, with heartfelt sincerity, replies "There is a greater love" and starts banging on about the war and his homeworld. What a charmer! And of course, in a cunning satirical juxtaposition, this mawkish, heart-stirring nonsense is on the screen in a drab, overcrowded hospital. The war plot seems to hinge around the power struggle between the blinkered Marshal ("You don't negotiate peace, you win it" – great line!) and the gutsy Princess Astra. There's a clever directorial sleight of hand, when the search for the Key is mentioned and we cut to Astra's crown falling from her head, leading the first-time viewer to think the bejewelled head gear is the Doctor's quarry rather than the woman wearing it.

The Key to Time aside, the central idea here is that War is Hell – a message that, to its credit, is sold in quite a morally ambiguous and complex way. John Woodvine and Lalla Ward (as Astra) provide effective counterpoints to each other. The former heroically pulls off the unenviable task of talking to a black wall whilst rubbing his fingers behind his ear. (Note to self: if ever you become the servant of a dark force intending to take over the universe, don't communicate with him in the corner of a really busy room jam-packed with trained military personnel!) If you want any starker indication of what war can do to a man, just look at John Cannon's Guard. The eternal conflict seems to have emotionally scarred him so badly, it's removed any ability he once had for not uttering every sentence as if he's the worst actor on the planet. War is Hell, Rob! War is Hell!

August 19th

The Armageddon Factor (part two)

R: The set piece of the episode is the long scene where the Doctor discusses the frustrations of war with the Marshal, and is treated to a battle on the monitors. For once, the budget limitations work in the series' favour – there is something genuinely unnerving about the fleet of spaceships being represented by little specks of light, all given voices of crews pleading for permission to retreat. And there's black comedy to it, too; by depersonalising those ships and reducing them to simple graphics on a big video screen, the Marshal is overjoyed when the lights start winking out of existence, and is only brought back down to earth when Major Shapp tells him the ships are his own. The

weary despair that everyone feels is so much more horrifying than any hysterics, and the calm resignation with which Shapp at last tells the surviving crews to disengage indicates just how commonplace these deaths are to him. It's an exceptional sequence, largely forgotten by fans but nonetheless one of the very best of Tom Baker's whole tenure – and Baker clearly relishes playing opposite an actor he can respect, of the quality of John Woodvine.

There's a certain dark wit to the whole instalment, in fact. K-9 is sent to the furnace to be melted down as scrap, a wry comment upon the way metals were recycled as weapons in World War II. And there's a stand-out moment right at the beginning of the episode where the Doctor demands to know what Merak's interest in Astra might be: "I love her," he says, and they react with the embarrassed surprise of characters in a television series where simple passions like "love" are never ever given voice. It suggests that there's an emotional truth to The Armageddon Factor that we're simply not used to in Doctor Who, and that only makes the war seem all the more real and all the more adult.

This story has a reputation for being dull and flabby and unwatchably slow. So far I am shocked by how thoughtful it is, and how relevant. There may not be much action, but even that seems to be deliberate – this is a war of attrition, and everything seems lean, stripped to the bone. And in their last collaboration, Bob Baker and Dave Martin's dialogue has acquired a purpose and economy that is unlike them. I'm enjoying this very much.

T: I know exactly when I last watched this: 26th March, 2005. How come I know that? Because it's the day Doctor Who came back. I got up early (the house was empty, the kids were away) full of the sort of excitement that Christmas had long since failed to bestow. I pottered about, waiting for things to happen. I kept BBC1 playing in case of trailers and news reports, and waited for my friend John Cooper to come round. I'd bought champagne, and we were going to enjoy this together.

By mid-morning, I snapped and decided I had to watch *something*. Not a classic, not a story I knew brilliantly, but some plain old-fashioned Doctor Who (and preferably one that would take ages and get me even closer to the start time for Rose). I chose The Armageddon Factor... and it was something of a damp squib. I thought I might revel in its straightforward charm just one last time before a brave new world ushered in its pop star companion, cool Northern Doctor and state-of-the-art CGI – but while I didn't hate the story, I didn't get beyond this episode before I started pottering again, it was so slow, plodding and uneventful.

But to look at this excellent instalment now, it's clear my mind was on the future and I was being unfair on the past, as this has plenty that makes a virtue of the old way of making the show. Case in point: the military battle which takes place from the vantage point of a room. There is something about seeing the Marshal keenly egging on his fleet of only six ships whilst his sidekick points out that the crews are barely trained. In rendering the ships just as lights that blink out – and without brave speeches or the giddying thrill of Star Wars-esque spinning ships, laser beams and explosions – The Armageddon Factor reduces war to what it is: a numbers game that fallible men play, in which human lives are just statistics. Tom Baker rejects any temptation to lark about when preparing to watch this prosaic spectacle of human sacrifice, and his terse observation that "You have a true military mind, Marshal" is no compliment. That the Marshal takes it as one emphasises the frightening consequences of his dogmatic quest for victory.

As the crazy military propagandist, John Woodvine has the really thankless task of indulging in obvious being-in-the-thrall-of-an-alien-power shtick. He pulls it off very well, but subtle and sophisticated it ain't (one assumes the black control device on his neck was intended as "barely detectable", not the great prop with a flashing green light that we're shown). It does however, mean he spends a lot of time being shot reflected in a distorted reflective surface, which emphasises the fractured nature of his mind and provides a pleasing, abstract visual.

Aside from a lovely visual gag with K-9 smoking after he's rescued from the furnace, and proof – in guard Harry Fielder – that having a bit-player who knows how to wield a gun convincingly is helpful, this is just an episode of conversation and the relaying of information. There's a lot of talk, but it's well-directed talk – the urgent conflab between the Doctor, Romana and Merak about Astra is full of drama, and when the princess appears on screen like a duped hostage forced to read out propaganda, we're reminded of images seen all too frequently these days. The last time I watched this, I later marvelled at how Rose worked because it made an everyday character and events seem vital and important in terms of the vast span of the universe. The Armageddon Factor does the opposite equally successfully – it takes the momentous and seismic and puts them all into one room, thus emphasising their impact on the individual.

The Armageddon Factor (part three)

R: "No glory. No honour. No medals. No blood." I'm in two minds about the revelation that the commandant on the planet Zeos is a big flashing supercomputer. On the one hand, it's intellectually exactly right – this is the very antithesis of the Marshal, all thunder and bluster and epaulettes. And it's exactly right too that the true enemy of these poor humans struggling through bitter war is something that's entirely impassive and emotionless. My concern is that Mentalis is not dramatically very exciting. Because a megalomaniacal computer is, after all, just another hunk of machinery – and unless you go down the route of The Green Death and give it a sense of ego and personality (and by doing so, rid of it all that makes it seem like a hunk of machinery in the first place), then it remains just a concept to be fought against, not an antagonist.

There are two things that make this work, though. The first is Michael Hayes' startlingly good direction. He treats a bit of set with flashing lights on with a rare sense of respect, giving it close-ups and fresh camera angles rather than just filming it head-on and bland, and he realises the value of stillness too, ridding his introduction of music and dialogue and letting the tension build as a result.

And the second is John Leeson. Last year, K-9 was somewhat resistible – a cute idea without much personality, more a gun on wheels with a very noisy motor. This year, it's been treated as a character in its own right, and Leeson has skilfully found a rapport with his fellow cast members that, no doubt, was achieved from his refusing to treat the role as a bit of voice-over, but a full acting part requiring him to get on his hands and knees and be part of the rehearsal process. And he's been rewarded by writers like Douglas Adams and David Fisher trying to show him off and have fun with him, treating him as talking dog and not as robot. But, of course, he *is* a robot – and the arrogant way in which he forms a connection with Mentalis feels exactly right, the bond between machine and machine lending a personality to the Zeon computer (which makes it much more appealing) and a new perspective on K-9 himself as a dog that puts up with his flesh-and-bone master, but would really much rather chat to something of greater intellect.

T: It's a change of pace that really works. After two episodes of the Marshal's rhetoric and the bombardment of Atrios, now we end up in some spooky, dusty tunnels, and the stark white stillness of the Mentalis room. And the episode triumphs here – because, as you say, it's difficult to have a villain with no speech or character. The director makes a virtue of this – we get a relatively long establishing shot in the computer room, and its slightly offbeat, oogly-boogly background atmospherics augment the oddness of the silent warmonger. The idea of a passionless death machine is thematically apposite and rather unsettling, as is its inscrutability and silence. K-9's communication with the creature makes for an intriguing change of gear in a story pulling in surprising directions. And I love the dispassionate starkness in the lead-up to the episode ending, when K-9 rather pointedly announces that Mentalis has arranged to obliterate "everything".

The change in tone comes from our shift from events on Atrios – just as it seemed the war-storyline had reached its conclusion, the Marshal's well-delivered victory speech has a huge impact because it's so very different from the moody menace of the other scenes in the episode. The camerawork here is more sweeping and grand than the unsettling languidness of Zeos, where we get introduced to the Shadow – a most oblique creation, because it's

difficult to tell quite what the hell he is, and William Squire's odd, blobby enunciation makes for an intriguing experience. The Shadow's presence, power and menace certainly provoke shivers, and he's a weird character with a pleasing turn of phrase (I adore his description of the Doctor's "jackdaw meanderings"). He's very intimidating to Princess Astra, and Lalla Ward adds suitable emotional distress when she sees her beloved Merak wandering about uselessly looking for her. (Incidentally, by now it's obvious that she's the sixth segment, but that doesn't render the mystery surrounding her redundant, because we don't yet know what this all means.)

And, you know – it's odd to see an actor trying to be *sillier than Tom Baker*, especially when we've generally had a more sober Doctor in these episodes than so many this season. It's strange to say, but I think that Baker's obvious rapport with Mary Tamm hasn't necessarily been a good thing, as they too often stray into the territory of comedic business that he's over-indulgent with, and she just doesn't have the comic chops for. The friction between Baker and Louise Jameson made for a much more interesting (and better played, frankly) dynamic, because Baker is a force of nature – and often unpredictable brilliant – who needs someone at the top of their game playing opposite him. Let's pity Merak (and it's not Ian Saynor's fault) for having to ask a dull question about bees – he receives a suitably waspish response from an impatient actor/Doctor. That said, at times it's ill-advised to even try to keep up with Baker's impulsive, inventive approach to performance – so let's also feel some sympathy for Davyd Harries (as the Marshal's aide Shapp). He's foolishly decided to try to match Baker's off-the-wall style but the production is complicit – when he arrives on Zeos and observes the Doctor, even the incidental music seems inclined to arse about.

I'll finish by agreeing with you that K-9 does get a bit arch, gaining an edge and confidence as a result of chatting to Mentalis. Actually, he talks as though he's a bit drunk – which would be funny were it not for that fact that, considering what's going on elsewhere this week, it's distinctly possible that he's not the only one!

The Armageddon Factor (part four)

R: Well, on the plus side – it's refreshing to see the Key to Time actually being used for once. The idea of building a fake sixth segment to gain a partial use of its powers manages to up the scale of the story considerably: this is no longer merely a tale about two planets at war, but about an entire universe being influenced by the Doctor's actions. There's a flippancy to this, of course, but Tom Baker manages to bring a certain awe to his flippancy – the man who would rather go fishing than be on a quest, the man who ran away from the Time Lords in the first place so he could go and have some fun, manages to trap all of creation within a three-second time loop. "Oh, they'll never notice," he says.

And what this succeeds in doing, in a way that no part of the season this far has even attempted, is making the Key to Time not just a maguffin to hang a series of adventures upon, but an artefact of great power and unknowable consequence. It raises the stakes, and does so skilfully by making the Doctor's hotchpotch improvisation still a ramshackle affair knocked up in a few minutes with some spare minerals in a lab somewhere. This is epic fantasy with magic crystals, but epic fantasy with a Doctor Who style – it doesn't quite work, and one of the bits of it is the wrong colour.

And there's an eeriness to the time loop itself. Seeing the Marshall in a repeat of the same few moments, constantly urging perennial guest-actor Pat Gorman to blow up a planet, reduces him to something coldly inhuman and unreal.

The rest of the episode needs to contrast with this – that as the Marshal haplessly keeps on saying the same thing over and over, the other characters should be doing something far more urgent. And this is where it all falls down. Instead, they keep wandering into teleports. Over and over again. Some stumble in dazedly, some are lured in. Shapp falls into his with an embarrassing pratfall. The overall effect is to take away all the momentum of the story, and that would be bad enough in any ordinary episode. Here, where it's all about repetition and momentum, it looks awkward and tedious. The hope is, with the Shadow at last taking centre stage, and delivering a particularly OTT cackle to signify this, the story can shift gear and move into that new higher register it's now earned.

T: This story really benefits from the nature of our quest – each instalment brings something new, which drives the drama into different directions. Unfortunately for this episode, several of the people *making* it also seem to be pulling in different directions, creating quite an odd experience.

That's not necessarily a bad thing, though one suspects that Davyd Harries has seen Rentaghost, and decided it's the acting style one uses in programmes of this ilk. I certainly don't mind a bit of tongue in cheek now and again, but Harries has superglued his to the inside of his mouth whilst attaching a siphon to the story's bladder, and is resolutely extracting the urine until there's not a single droplet left. (I'm sorry... was that harsh?) Suffice to say, if there's a laugh to be had, he's having it. What's funny is that when I was younger, I quite enjoyed his double taking, comedy falling and over-enunciation; was astonished at what a grown man was allowed to get away with; and was quite chuffed that Doctor Who could allow such flexibility of approach. *Now*, however, it looks like an actor not doing what most people have done over the years – play Doctor Who with the same seriousness as a hospital drama or period piece, and not treat all the talk of aliens as daft kiddie fodder. Some stories might have benefitted from such larking about to inject some life into them, but here Harries is simply distracting from better work being done elsewhere.

And there is plenty of that, thank goodness. With Hayes creatively conquering the limitations of the studio, it's abstract and unsettling when Merak tumbles into a pit. Suddenly, this isn't a place of shadows and lurking menace – it's a world of odd nightmares, where one wrong step can pitch you into darkness. The ticking and odd ambient sound effects in the Mentalis room are similarly disturbing, with Hayes taking the hoary old trope of a countdown and making it something unusual and compelling. The repeated cuts back to the descending numbers (indicating that the time loop is surely decaying) are very effective.

But as it happens, I can't talk about this

without mentioning the BBC outtake tapes, which were like an initiation ceremony for any young fan. These provided the first opportunity to see Tom Baker swear, and a cherry was popped when young Toby discovered that all sorts of nonsense went on behind the scenes, perpetrated by misbehaving actors who didn't take this hallowed show all that seriously after all. It was a rite of passage which transformed a wide-eyed, innocent fanboy into the dreamland of manhood, where one could suddenly take the piss and note the shortcomings. It *sounds* a bit lovely to say, but I'm not actually sure it was a good thing, and rather prefer our attempts within these pages to recapture some of the magic of those halcyon days – rather than nitpick and take the mickey out of something that, if treated with the respect it deserves, can be rather magical. Because whether we like it or not, when we saw those tapes, we started to do what we've both criticised Davyd Harries for.

August 20th

The Armageddon Factor (part five)

R: Structurally, this story is a bit odd, isn't it? They've thrown away the guest cast! No more bumbling Shapp, no more Merak moaning on about Princess Astra. No more Marshal saying "Fire" over and over and over again. It's like one of those Hartnell serials when the companions nip off and have a holiday and hope no one notices, but now it's happening to the bit parts! And in their place, we get Drax.

I remember Drax being quite controversial at the time. Forget the fact that the Time Lords have degenerated into a bunch of doddering old gits and megolamaniacal nutters – the real insult is that one now speaks with a Brixton accent! (Though I live just down the road from Brixton, and I beg to differ – this mockney has a whiff of East End about it, I think.) What's strange is how what was once a gag requiring long explanations of Drax going native now just feels natural and modern in the wake of David Tennant – it's an illustration of how the series in the new century has smoothed off some of the edges of the old. Doesn't Tom Baker sound posh and mannered beside him?

And Drax is a real breath of fresh air to an episode that looks very dark and uniform. Setting the action on the Shadow's planet is all well and good, but that means that all the sets are shadowy in response – and draining so much colour out of the show makes this somewhat drab. The Shadow seemed properly sinister in early episodes where he was a contrast to the main plot – now that we discover his master plan, which has been nothing more inspired than just waiting around the sixth segment and letting the Doctor get on with retrieving the first five, he can't help but seem disappointing. So the Shadow's most evil trait is that he's lazy? Oh, the fiend! The Doctor could have done the exact same thing, and stayed on Ribos for the last 20-odd episodes waiting for the Shadow to bring the other segments to him. And in the meantime, the universe would have collapsed, we'd have had to put up with more Shrievenzale and Prentis Hancock antics, and viewers would have switched over to ITV.

There is, though, a lovely little sequence where the Doctor shows genuine hurt that K-9 has betrayed him. Hearing the tin dog refer to him as "Doctor" rather than "Master" is inspired, and causes a real pang. It's a reflection of just how much real affectionate rapport there is now between Tom Baker and K-9 that this feels so sad. Just compare this scene with the last time K-9 got possessed, in the middle of The Invisible Enemy (Bob Baker and Dave Martin don't have much faith in their creation, do they?). There, it was just another device possessed by a virus. Here, it's something more disturbing.

T: It's very minimalist this week, with some strange but effective moments. The sequence with the multiple Romanas confusing the Doctor is very well shot and edited, and helps to maintain the atmosphere of weirdness on Zeos. Similarly, the Shadow remains a wonderfully intangible creature – he might appear in extreme close-ups to have tights on his head, but it's an effect that is generally difficult to discern even when sharply remastered, and so is most effective. And some sort of cosmic, cobwebby spittle sees to appear between his lips as he talks, which is suitably horrid. His declaration that the "mutual destruction [of two halves of the cosmos] will be music in our ears" is terrific, and William Squire's treated voice also has a wonderful ghoulish tremor added by the actor himself. Conversely, like all other aliens in the universe, he really must do some research into how to hypnotise people to do his will without them behaving like zombies, as it gives the game way to all but the most dopey. He'd make a fortune if he did (in fact, he could get Drax to sell it for him).

What a small scale and atmospheric episode – it's curious that we are heading toward the climax of a 26-week-long quest to reset the entire universe in order to balance out the forces of light and darkness... and we spend this with a small group of characters and a horrible dilemma. Our heroes need to find the Key, but they also need to stop Zeos being destroyed. They need the tracer to find the Key, but removing the tracer from the assemblage will free up the Marshal's missiles to destroy Zeos. How tense, exciting and well scripted – I'm enjoying this.

The Armageddon Factor (part six)

R: In her final episode, Mary Tamm has her best moment of the series. Escaping from the Shadow's planet with the Key to Time – the quest ultimately fulfilled – there's no room for the smug, self-congratulatory style that has sometimes threatened to mar this season. Instead, she rails at the Doctor that they are murderers. And it's in the use of that word in particular that the episode refuses to be compromising. The idea that one of the segments should have been disguised as a person is clever, but could so easily have just been a concept, not something that was given full weight of moral dilemma. As the Black Guardian says, the life of Princess Astra cannot be important on a cosmic scale – and this entire season has been playing out on that cosmic scale. And so this stands as a repudiation of that scale, that Doctor Who has never been interested in being big and universal with all the pomposity that implies, but instead silly and trivial – where, illogical as it might seem, the fate of one minor character is worthier of greater consideration than universal harmony.

And it's why I think the season conclusion really does work. Because Graham Williams effectively is on a hiding to nothing – the only way to end this 26-week long story is on a note of anticlimax. But this is at least a deliberate anticlimax, and one that has humanity to it. Rather cleverly, we've already had our big long-promised end-of-season finale, where the universe is stopped when the Key is assembled – we had it in episode four, and nobody noticed. What's masterful about this episode is that it brings to conclusion an epic whilst demonstrating that epics are soulless things, and that Doctor Who's mission statement from now on will be exactly the sort of random adventuring that the Key to Time season was used to avoid.

The question is, I suppose then – was there any point in producing this season in the first place? I think there was. The self-indulgence that's crept into the series since Hinchcliffe left had to be acknowledged and addressed somehow. If Tom Baker's performance could not be reined in, then it was important to show that the Doctor could still be. With the Doctor dominating his stories all the more obviously, and the confidence he was showing getting all the more overreaching, the series has been forced to compete, and to give him his biggest adventure ever. And in the competing, the bubble has been made to burst. We had to get so big, we had to get to a point where the Doctor is given a mission throughout all eternity by God himself, before we could get back to basics. The Armageddon Factor's job has been two things: to take the show to the most portentous climax it can, and then to kickstart it once more on that smaller, more intimate level.

And, of course, those are two utterly contradictory mandates. But all through the episode, you can see Bob Baker and Dave Martin trying to set that contradiction up. You have the grandeur of mythological allusions like the Trojan Horse – but it's actually a miniaturised Doctor riding into the villain's lair inside his metal dog. At once it deliberately calls to mind epic heroism – but it's nonsense too, and witty nonsense, as K-9 undermines the atmosphere by clearing his throat before delivering his one line as "actor". You have the dehumanisation of Princess Astra, on a personal level as well as a literal level – there's no angst suffered as she commits suicide by turning herself into a lump of stone – but you also have the payoff later, that she's allowed to appear in her final moments as a romantic ideal to Merak and nurse him. The grand and the domestic rub shoulders throughout, and the domestic wins through.

The victory of the domestic is shown in lots of subtle ways too. The Marshal does not get a leaving scene. But crucially, he doesn't get the anticipated death scene either – that he's allowed to fade out as a comic character working alongside Drax is a great demonstration of how generous this episode really is. And it's beautiful that the last few minutes of this season don't play out with big explosions and battles, but with our two heroes inside the TARDIS scoring points off the big villain who's only deigned to show up at the story's climax. Wit and cleverness save the day – and a great big dollop of tenderness as well. Tom Baker may overact the moment when he contemplates universal domination (and that's rather a shame), but the point he's making is clear and profound.

If this all has a slight feeling of desperation to it, of cheap and make-do, then that's because Doctor Who always has that feeling. We don't need to see the battle between the Guardians, any more than we need to see the Time War of the new series. What we want is the journey, and the incidental pleasures we take along the way. And it's telling that the next time we'll see the Doctor on screen afterwards is in the trailer for Season Seventeen, where a strange unearthly godlike voice rouses the Doctor from his sleep to warn him about his forthcoming adventure with the Daleks – it's like some weird comic echo of the opening to the Key to Time season, except this time the Doctor openly mocks it: "Noisy universe!" he complains, and goes back into the TARDIS to enjoy his summer holiday break.

Ultimately, the end of The Armageddon Factor is seen as a disappointment by a large number of fans, but that is only because it was brave enough to stick its head above the parapet and draw attention to the epic scale it punctures. There is something so magical and right about all this, about a return to the innocence of the series, before the Doctor had a job with Time Lords or Guardians or with UNIT,

when he was just a traveller in time and space. What is old is new again.

T: I was slightly surprised when I read about the Randomiser, as I thought the TARDIS never knew where it was going anyway. The device's introduction here feels like the equivalent of inserting a scene halfway through the Davison era, in which the Doctor suddenly produces a device capable of changing his face and personality once his body is weakened. But as you say, it's a restating of the basics after an epic quest, and not an unwelcome one. It rarely harms us to sit down, take stock of what we're doing, strip away all the nonsense acquired over the years and start over.

As for the umbrella theme this year – well, modern television has shown just how complex season-long plot arcs can become, so we needn't spend too much time fretting over the Key to Time. It facilitates a slightly protracted coda, complete with some ill-advised eye-rolling-acting from Tom Baker when the Doctor is actually making a sage point, but it hasn't really been my main reason for tuning in. To be fair, though, the production team have wisely made the individual adventures digestible for the casual grazer, and the writers have generally been inventive with their placing of the segments.

You know, I've kept scribbling "poor John Woodvine" when I've been writing these episodes up – it's clear I feel sorry for the man, a fantastic actor not well served by this story. Early on, he had to stare at a mirror and rub his neck to signify possession – and since then, he's been stuck in a cupboard with Pat Gorman in a time loop. He finally gets a lovely speech, yes, but then his missiles are deflected and... that's it. I'd forgotten this, but he doesn't even get the requisite glorious death scene (which frankly, is one of the main reasons for accepting the role of a Doctor Who baddie).

Of the supporting characters, even Merak – a pretty drippy sort despite Ian Saynor's best efforts – fares better. He gets some heroic stuff to do, lurks about determined to rescue Astra and refuses to give up. Best served of all, though, is the Shadow, his final speech beautifully superimposed over the destruction of his own lair. It's another moment where Michael Hayes attempts to bolster this script with some less straightforward storytelling, and it really works (unless the script called for such a presentation, in which case, thumbs up to Bob and Dave). I really like the Shadow – to all intents and purposes, he's a rather hokey figure with no life outside the story (I can imagine the Marshal sitting down for supper or chatting about the weather, for example; the Shadow, not so much), but he works anyway. Although he appears to remove the tights from his face at will, the permanent, bony, half-skull mask that seems to have grown through his skin gives him a devilish countenance, and his lair of darkness has lent some welcome spookiness to this militaristic game of cat and mouse.

Here at the end of Season Sixteen, any fan who latterly saw the Guardians built up as an essential part of the Doctor Who mythos will be surprised to discover that they log nothing more than cameos at the beginning and end of one episode each. That said, Valentine Dyall makes some impact as the Evil One, thanks to his gloriously rich, deep voice and a very simple special effect. I have to say, no amount of modern CGI can quite beat that good old negative image. To have the Guardian dressed in saintly white livery, which then becomes a black vacuum licked by the gas fires of Hades at the flick of a button, shows how technology that is primitive by today's standards can, in some areas, still not be surpassed. And so the main lesson we learn from our encounter with this overwhelmingly larynxed wrong 'un is that we need to switch from negative back to positive.

That is surely the point of our very own quest, which, unlike this one, continues with...

Animal Magic

T: *What?*

Animal Magic

T: You're not serious.

Animal Magic

T: Oh God.

Animal Magic

R: Yes, really! Animal Magic! Why not? Don't go giving me that look, Hadoke. I can sense you scowling from here.

For those who don't know, Animal Magic was a children's programme of the time that took great delight in showing us the wild and the wonderful of the animal kingdom. It was presented by Johnny Morris, who was neither the chap who played Chela in Snakedance, nor the prolific Big Finish and Doctor Who Magazine comic-strip writer. (Though I must say, the latter really enjoys the name confusion, and truly loves it whenever you make a joke about it. Next time you see him, give it a go. Oh, how he'll chuckle!)

Every week, Johnny would show us an array of zoo animals, and if they were particularly cute, he might give them his own voiceovers. (He did little monkeys a lot. I always remember the monkeys.) And between the broadcast of the sixteenth and seventeenth seasons, the Doctor himself pops up – uniquely on a factual programme, to tell us about imaginary creatures.

There are some amusing points of interest. Tom Baker is not only in character, he's in mid-adventure. He tells us he's on the planet Chloris, and indeed, he's wearing the wooden stocks he has on during episode one. Doctor Who has flashbacked into previous adventures many a time – but never before has it flashforwarded. Here's a mini-Doctor Who story not only set during another adventure, it contrives to be set during one that won't be seen by the viewing public for months yet.

And I know you're still scowling, Toby. In fact, I can hear you grinding your teeth too. But I tell you, there's no reason why this can't be a canonical story. Yes, he refers to The Ribos Operation by name – but it may be, like Watson for Sherlock Holmes, that the Doctor is enough of an egotist to chronicle his own adventures. (Why not? He turned the entirety of The Evil of the Daleks into a seven-part serial he could show Zoe as a welcome aboard the TARDIS treat!) Yes, he seems to be talking to camera. But Tom has being doing that a lot these days, ever since The Invasion of Time. And besides, we can't see that he's not talking to a character who hasn't bothered to reply.

Who else but Romana? It makes sense, him reminding her about the Shrievenzale from her previous incarnation.

And that would mean, by my reckoning, seconds after this adventure takes place, Romana gets kidnapped by a bunch of Jewish comedy bandits. Which leads me to suspect she might well have gone with them deliberately.

T: I'm scowling. Your silliness has been noted.

I just said that the Doctor's quest had finished whilst we continue with ours. *His* quest was long, rambling and suffered the occasional misstep, but was a largely positive experience. It mainly threatened to come undone when the foolish whims of its leading man were given full reign. Do you hear me? Remind you of anything, eh?

Oh, if you insist …

I remember Johnny Morris. Sadly, no-one that old would be allowed on children's telly today, as for some reason we are no longer encouraged to look up to age as being blessed with wisdom. I could opine more about TV's pathetic desire to ingratiate itself to the viewer by recruiting by image rather than learnedness, but I'd be here all day, and frankly I'd be lending this whimsical segue of yours a respectability it doesn't especially deserve.

To be fair, though, this "story" already looks much plusher than the all-conquering season finale we've just watched. It's on film, on what looks like an impressive jungle set. The atmosphere really translates; film studios contain a mugginess that can seem reminiscent of a jungle's stifling closeness, and you can observe a sheen of sweat on Baker's face. He's quite something here, staring down the camera like a lunatic, and – as it's not proper Doctor Who – vocalising some of his more insane ideas. His description of The Seeds of Doom echoes the more absurd postulations of Beresford and Sir Colin than the events we witnessed in the story itself. On that occasion, our (more moody and weighty then than now) Doctor cut comical postulations about homicidal gooseberries down with acidic barbs. Here, he gives full reign to his fancy, though there are still traces of that dangerous, savage undercurrent Baker always carries with him. But just in case you

thought this was in any way serious, look at the moment when he releases his hand from the stocks that are allegedly binding him; he no doubt thought that this would be hilarious.

This is a fun little insert, and one I'd not seen before. But is it a Doctor Who story? Yes, Rob, it's a Doctor Who story in the same way that Mollie Sugden is King of Norway.

Now, can we resume normal service please?

August 21st

Destiny of the Daleks (part one)

R: We've never had a funny regeneration before! Arguably, we don't really get a funny regeneration now either. It's not that the idea is so bad – the fact that Romana has the capability of selecting her new body, and can go through the whole procedure without any of the trauma we are used to, is surely consistent with the idea that she does everything with more style than our hero. The Doctor can't fly the TARDIS properly, can't go anywhere without getting into trouble, and can't regenerate the way he's supposed to. When we see elderly Time Lords in The Deadly Assassin witter on about their different incarnations, it's without any hint of melodrama; the fact that Borusa has a new body every single time we see him is surely an indication that the Doctor's just doing it wrong. The concept is fine; the writing is witty; it's the execution that's awkward. We really need to believe that all those bodies that present themselves for the Doctor's inspection are *Romana*, but the extras they've cast haven't been told the joke – they stand there tall and prim and scowling, as if aware that a single facial expression will constitute *acting*, and that's outside the confines of the job they've been hired to do. It's a small point, but I think a telling one. The season opens with a scene in which two of the three lead actors are written out. We don't buy the idea that K-9 can get laryngitis any more than the Doctor does – and we don't buy this regeneration either.

None of which is Lalla Ward's fault. My problem with Mary Tamm was always that she couldn't tell a joke – her timing was off, or she hit the lines too hard, or, more usually, she didn't seem to realise there was a joke at all.

Lalla Ward has the same gift as Tom Baker for understatement. She throws out statements about taking her arms in as if they're perfectly natural. And already she's having fun, childish fun, teasing the Doctor by dressing up in his own clothes. The first incarnation of Romana accompanied the Doctor out of duty. This one is his friend.

There's a collision of styles in the scripting. You have, on the one hand, Terry Nation being all safe and traditional, using every structural cliché of a first episode he has ever used. On the other, there's script editor Douglas Adams, putting in wordplay and jokes about dentists. It's schizophrenic for sure, but it's curiously entertaining – it means that for all its basic familiarity, this is rather hard to second-guess. Tom Baker shows delight at rocks, and criticises books by Oolon Colluphid – but his uncovering of the corpse buried beneath rocks is done with grim face, and his delivery of lines about the skin temperature of zombies is quiet and brooding. It's almost as if the landscape of Skaro is sucking the complacency out of him, as if he can't quite maintain his comic composure – and it's helped no end by a restraint in the music, the soundtrack being mostly the sound of desolate wind. The plotting is slow, certainly, but it's deliberately slow – and we know the game that's being played here. For all that Tom Baker's Doctor is now an egotistical superstar, we know something that he doesn't: that his oldest foe is in the wings, waiting to make their long-awaited reappearance at the cliffhanger.

T: You can rationalise the regeneration any number of ways. Perhaps it's an essential rite of physical passage for a female Time Lord. Maybe it's like puberty, or maybe, under certain circumstances, there is a period of grace during a non-trauma-induced regeneration where the subject gets to choose his/ her form. (Some fans have even grasped upon the idea that if David Tennant can regrow a hand because he's in the first 15 hours of his regeneration cycle in The Christmas Invasion, maybe Romana can do the same with her whole body.) I'm not going to lose any sleep over it either way, but neither can I claim this is a sequence I care for hugely. Regeneration, like time travel, is one of those Doctor Who

essentials that its makers shouldn't try to make the audience think about too much, lest their logic starts to unravel. They're necessary evils – use them, quickly, don't muck about, and then move on.

And we're now entering the period of Doctor Who when my experiences become intertwined with childhood memories of the episodes going out. I certainly remember Destiny of the Daleks – notably the cliffhangers and the chalky, dusty, dead planet. This time around, I'm struck most by the distinct lack of music during the early exploration scenes. Normally, Doctor Who is scored up to its eyeballs, but the majority of this episode takes place with only moody, atmospheric sound effects, which makes for a bleak and unsettling experience (and gives Dick Mills a deserved single caption credit for the only time, I think). Director Ken Grieve has honed in on a Terry Nation obsession: the bleak terror of a world post-nuclear apocalypse. Everything is grim, the supporting cast are silent and lurking, and the gaunt extras bury some poor unfortunate under uncomfortably heavy looking, chinking stones. Even the starship engineer Tyssan – who appears to try to help Romana after she tumbles down a shaft – has the aspect of a cadaver. Actor Tim Barlow is pale and silent, and his sunken eyes and pronounced bone structure give him the appearance of a lurking Frankenstein's Monster. Said fall benefits from a protecting triple cut which makes it seem more dangerous, and is just one of a number of directorial touches. Others include a notable attention to detail when the Movellan ship lands (and the idea of a burrowing spaceship is an inventive one), with its drilling undercarriage and the way it makes the rocks on the ground shudder both well rendered.

Here at the start of Season Seventeen, this episode is almost old fashioned in its approach, and reminiscent of some of the early Hartnell opening instalments. It's interesting that before reading your entry, I had jotted down the word "schizophrenic" as well (perhaps we're two sides of the same personality – yikes!). But it is, it feels like a mosaic of different styles... and it's also a little cheap looking. One of the Romana rejects is wearing Zilda's costume from The Robots of Death, whilst the corpse that is buried sports Dask's jacket from the same story. If

Davros turns up wearing Toos' hat, it'll be a blatant sign that they're taking thrift a step too far.

Destiny of the Daleks (part two)

R: This is a sequel! Up to this point, it's just seemed that Terry Nation was always ripping off his old scripts – look, now he's doing it deliberately!

We're well used to the idea, of course, that Doctor Who will bring up old monsters every now and again, but very rarely have they ever been what you could really call sequels. The Invasion is not a sequel to The Wheel in Space, just because the Cybermen turn up in it. And whenever the series has produced a story that has a bona fide link to a previous adventure, it's pretty explicit from the start. The Monster of Peladon doesn't exactly hide its links to Curse – if anything, it bends over backwards to emphasise the similarities. The Web of Fear is a much bolder riff on the whole sequel idea, setting it forty years later and allowing the events of The Abominable Snowmen to feel almost sweetly nostalgic – but the stories are only broadcast three months apart, so that the nostalgia can really only be a fictional one.

But this is very different. Here we have, in an era of the programme that pays only the scantest of attention to series continuity, the return of a one-off character who was killed on screen nearly five years ago. It's only in retrospect we see Davros as such an important character in Doctor Who's history – at the time Destiny was broadcast he genuinely was a dead villain, no more inevitably essential to the fabric of the programme than Mehendri Solon or Harrison Chase. I think it's useful to try to remember just what a shock Davros' reappearance must have been, and how shocking too the realisation we are watching a story explicitly set within the very rubble of where a previous adventure took place. It's utterly without precedent. And it marks a subtle shift in the way storytelling in Doctor Who will work from this point on.

The Hartnell era sometimes liked to present itself as one long adventure serial, rather than a series of individual adventures. But it never took that concept very seriously, and there's no genuine attempt to smooth over the tones and styles of different writers and directors to give them a sense of consistency – indeed, Doctor Who quickly makes a virtue of the fact that it is so tonally wayward, even the Doctor and his friends can never anticipate what sort of adventure they might be getting next. By the time we abandon the individual titles for episodes, we also surrender all pretence that Doctor Who is anything other than an anthology series with a shared regular cast. The events of one four-part serial will have no consequences for another four-part serial straight after it.

But the Key to Time season was one big experiment at making Doctor Who temporarily feel interconnected. The mercurial style of the show resisted it, naturally enough – when they mentioned the planet Calufrax, for example, in The Stones of Blood, they seem to have forgotten the TARDIS never even went there. When planet Earth is visited, there needs to be no mention that it was under threat from the pirate planet only last week. But along comes Terry Nation, back for his last writing stint on a programme he's been part of since the very beginning, and he makes no more show of interest in the tonal shift that's gone on since he last returned. Planet of the Daleks, you might remember, was so rooted in the sixties, the Doctor made reference to his old companions Ian and Barbara. And here, Nation writes a direct continuation of the last Dalek script he wrote, as if the audience will still remember it, and as if nothing has happened in the meantime. On the one hand, reaching back to find such an intimate connection with the past feels quite bold, because it's never been done on this scale before. And on the other hand, you wonder whether Terry Nation realised it was bold at all.

And it basically works, because Davros is inherently interesting. He looks fabulous (even if David Gooderson clearly doesn't fill out the mask the way Michael Wisher did), and what he represents is iconic. Even if Davros had never appeared in the series before, the idea that the Doctor is standing face to face with the Daleks' creator has an immediate fascination. The cliffhanger is lovely, with the fingers starting to wave under the cobwebs, and works on two levels: if you're old enough to remember Davros, or have bought the LP record of the

Genesis adventure, you've got the anticipation of a return match with one of the most charismatic of the Doctor's foes. If you're new to the show, there's a creepy man coming back to life who seems half Dalek himself.

It sets up a precedent, of course. This is a story that purports to be taking place on the very same set as a previous adventure. And soon there'll be allusions to all sorts of moments from the show's past, and they'll be accurate and well-researched and sound like they've come out of The Programme Guide. And there'll be little bits of business that link the stories together, so that the word "anti-matter" cannot be mentioned in Snakedance without a recall of the events of Arc of Infinity, so that the beginning of Mawdryn Undead has to open with an explanation of what just happened in Snakedance. The sense that Doctor Who is that anthology series of separate adventures from this moment on starts to blur. Is that a bad thing? Not necessarily. Handled sensitively, the idea that some stories have consequences beyond the confines of their own episode run does suggest at times a greater depth. But whether it's the 1980s or the 2000s, Doctor Who starts behaving like a series which expects its audience to understand that it has a history to be drawn from in the first place – and that if you're not a regular viewer, you might start to miss the references. Or, to put it another way, Doctor Who starts behaving like a series that's old.

This seems like rather a burden to place on poor Destiny of the Daleks' shoulders. And the sad fact is, Destiny isn't really up to it. Director Ken Grieve works very hard to make the Daleks seem threatening, filming them from the floor to give them extra height. But the action of the adventure is awkwardly slow; Tyssan may say that the city will be "crawling with Daleks", but the Doctor can get to the control room without even seeing one – and when the Daleks discover his presence, he can quite literally walk away to freedom without even feeling the urge to sprint. The scene where a Dalek shoots Lan silently, without even bothering to utter an "exterminate", is great, making it seem so much more dangerous – that danger is squandered at other moments by making them chant mantras, and by the Doctor mocking that they can't climb

up a chute. And over all of this, deliberately, the story keeps wanting to remind us of former glories, of the rare brilliance that is Genesis of the Daleks. It feels like the first Dalek story told in retrospect, where the plot doesn't seem to happen in the moment at all. It tells child audiences that the Daleks are important, and that the Doctor has a feud with them, but never tries to show them why. That would be a problem at the best of times – but when those Daleks in question haven't been on screen for such a long time, it seems almost wilfully lazy.

T: I feel privileged to have watched this the first time around, as I was there before Davros was properly part of the Doctor Who legacy. Of course, many fans I know are lucky enough to have seen some missing classics from the olden days, and discovered the majority of the show as it was being freshly minted. Much of my enjoyment of Doctor Who, on the other hand, happened in retrospect. Heck, I was packed off to boarding school when Davison's stories were being broadcast, so got my friend Oliver to tell me everything that happened in the weekday episodes before I finally got to watch them (videoed by our local vicar, would you believe?) on a Sunday afternoon.

This episode, though, I watched as it was transmitted – when Davros had been just a one-off character who was dead. I thought that, just like the early Doctors, I would only ever be able to enjoy Davros in picture and novel form. So when his corpse was stumbled across here, young Toby thought it was just an exciting nod to the old days. Because I knew, as my brothers told me every time I glanced at the cover of our Target version of Genesis of the Daleks, *Davros was dead*. And to prove it, in this episode they showed us his cobwebby corpse... and then his fingers started to move! And the episode ended! I remember being in our kitchen going over and over this, getting out the old Doctor Who Monster book and looking at the pictures, knowing that they were all I had to satisfy me until the next episode. As I say, I'm lucky, as those feelings of rhapsodic excitement are only possible in childhood. I couldn't possibly explain them adequately to kids today, who can watch episodes again straight away and enjoy clips and previews and tantalising website teasers in between their weekly sci-fi hit. And, frankly, these days they'd probably have known about Davros' return anyway (the Radio Times was only an annual Christmas treat in our household, so I came to most episodes entirely ignorant of their contents).

Davros' moving fingers are amongst the few things deemed worthy of being scored this week, but the welcome return of the 60s Dalek control room noise is all the music to my ears that I need. To complement the silence, the bombed-out starkness of the production emphasises the empty atmosphere Grieve is striving for. The grainy film work and desolate landscape reminds me of the jolly dramas and documentaries about nuclear war that I've mentioned before, which were deemed perfectly acceptable things to show to an impressionable child in the late 70s/ early 80s. Terrifying! But it was a terror with a moral and political cause and effect, which meant that even one's nightmares were couched in ideological issues. Yes, it's true... even when cowering under a duvet imagining the apocalypse, I was thinking about politics.

And once again, Terry Nation knows how to make his material bleak and grim through actions and dialogue, and without stretching the budget – we're *told* that the Daleks kill five prisoners for every one that escapes, and Romana's "corpse" is left where she falls until the work period is over. Mr Nation must have been a hoot at parties, but he certainly knows how to keep the drama circulating.

In studio, the Daleks look rather tatty (one has a broken slat, but it has been mining a ruined underground bunker complex, so it may have scuffed itself on a corner), but Grieve elects to shoot them close, in the foreground, fringing the edges of the shots whilst the viewer focuses on the characters in the background. The scene where they interrogate Romana is wonderfully oppressive, and Lalla Ward responds with some fraught emotion delivered from her very core. Look, she's crying real tears – now that's good acting.

Destiny of the Daleks (part three)

R: I met David Gooderson once. He was appearing with a friend of mine in a stage comedy; he was excellent, very funny, very touch-

ing. I was introduced to him as a man who had written for the Daleks. "Ah," he said, "I met the Daleks once! I didn't come out of that very well." And he told me how he'd been the bad Davros, the one whom no one had liked. And I smiled sympathetically, and nodded a bit, and looked a bit embarrassed – because I'd always thought his Davros was rubbish too.

Watching this again, what becomes clear is that none of this is David Gooderson's fault. Indeed, there are moments where he tries to suggest the same cunning that Michael Wisher gave the role – having had no lines for ages, and having been raced around the Kaled city as if he were a shopping trolley on Supermarket Sweep, just look at the way Gooderson taps his fingers in his chair slowly, deliberately, as if his silence isn't an awkward piece of writing, but the intelligence of an evil genius biding his time. The problem is that when he does open his mouth, no one takes him very seriously. And it's because of the huge swing that's taken place not only in Tom Baker's performance, but in the way the Doctor is perceived, since Davros' first appearance.

It's a surprise to remember just how little direct contact there was between the Doctor and Davros in Genesis. Davros didn't even seem to recognise the Doctor as a major threat until the end of episode four. And structurally, this only made Davros seem the more important – he was Adolf Hitler, and the Doctor's encounters with him had to be waited for, to be made to count – and even then, played out on an almost philosophical level. The Doctor then was new and fresh, and yet to be an icon. But now in Destiny, the Doctor is at the height of his ego, and Davros is just another character to be joked with and offered jelly babies and trivialised. David Gooderson is given little opportunity to do much more than rant, but he tries hard to varied degrees to it so it's varied, he mines some intelligence from the megalomania. But Tom Baker's response is always to shout over him, to drown him out with silly voices – and in a story where the only quest is to find this man, to refuse to take him remotely seriously once you've got him cuts the plot off at the knees.

And it's a shame, because the plotting itself is basic but sound. The impasse between the Doctor and the Daleks over control of Davros is well written – and the sequence where the Daleks exterminate slave workers one by one until the Doctor surrenders is a brilliant idea. (Once again, as in the regeneration in episode one, the acting of the extras is what floors this – I can buy someone wearily doing nothing to resist certain death, but can't anyone at least fall over as if they mean it?)

The best bit of the episode, I think, is the scene in which Tom Baker talks to a Kaled jelly. He patronises it and laughs at it as if it's a child, and then throws it hard against the rocks in disgust. And just for a moment you see the method in Tom Baker's madness, that in his derision there's actually a raging anger, that his temper can burst out of his silliness with shocking unpredictability. But it's telling that Baker feels more comfortable performing the scene with a piece of slime that can't get in his way or be upstaged.

T: David Gooderson? I've worked with him too – he's a lovely, genial man with a fine comic touch, the perfect casting for a fussy town official or a charming vicar from whom some scandal must be kept at all costs. He allowed me to take him to lunch to discuss Doctor Who, and told me that his Davros was supposed to be different from the one that had gone before. It was clear – if not put into so many words – that he was aware that his reputation amongst Who fans wasn't the greatest, but he nonetheless gave me his time and talked at length and with enthusiasm. In the story itself, he *looks* good, as he's kitted out in an impressive, crinkly skinned mask of wizened malevolence, and has a sort of congealed oiliness to his thin, sadistic lips. But after Davros' thrilling resurrection, he spends much of the episode being trollied around to trilling incidental music, as Ken Grieve's previous restraint with all things audio here fails him.

And, much as it pains me to admit it, Gooderson gives a flatter vocal performance than Michael Wisher, and physically we're in a total disaster area. His body rocks so much when he moves, he's either got Parkinson's or he's peddling furiously underneath his Dalek chair. It's so blatant, it distracts the viewer and undermines the character. I'll grant that he has the odd more impressive moment – there's his coldly clinical response to the exploding Daleks, and his talk of the universe being sorry about his re-emergence indicates that while Davros has been slumbering, someone has whispered into his ear that he's no longer a one-off character from a small planet, but a recurring nemesis of epic proportions. The Davros of Genesis was very much a home-grown threat only concerned with life and politics on Skaro, whereas this one seems to have got a better agent – one that has promised him intergalactic success. As I have seen with so many, his ego has therefore skyrocketed. No more blue M & Ms in the Davros dressing room.

The scene where slaves are chosen for random, cold-blooded execution begs for a sickening tension to be wrung from it. Instead, Grieve seems to have selected two of the least-bothered individuals in the universe to stare nonplussedly before depicting their extermination by Dalek death rays with a half-hearted shrug and a bit of a lie down. As well as being crammed into a hodgepodge of sartorial delights clearly borrowed from a BBC cupboard (a Draconian outfit here, and, oh look, Dask's trousers there... still no sign of Toss' hat, sadly), this is a candidate for the worst bunch of extras ever to shuffle distractedly into an episode of Doctor Who. They half-smile their way through supposedly terrifying crowd scenes and generally look self-conscious or aimless. It's left to Tyssan to later *tell* the Doctor that they're grateful that he facilitated their release – a good job, as surely the prisoners themselves could not have imparted the news with the remotest level of conviction.

It's a shame, as this *should* work better. The dead Agella's moving fingers are spooky (even though the trick has been used earlier with Davros), there's a visual flourish with the Dalek POV of human footprints, and we hear a conversation through the wall that we have already heard once before – it's a very rare example of non-linear storytelling. There's plenty of innovation amongst all the old tropes (which are old tropes, to be fair, because they work), but this just makes the lack of effort in key areas baffling. I suppose in all the excitement of Davros' revival, we weren't expected to worry about anything else. Indeed, that frisson my younger self felt about his return... that desire for a quick, visceral nostalgia hit, and for

Doctor Who to recapture past glories rather than surprise me with anything new... that will come back to haunt me, won't it?

August 22nd

Destiny of the Daleks (part four)

R: The scene in which Lan tells his Movellan boss that for the safety of their plan, one of their number must stand guard over a bomb – and by doing so sacrifice his or her life – is rather good. Inevitably, Lan gets assigned the detail, but by virtue of being a robot, takes the task on without complaint. And it sets the tone for an episode in which Davros merrily sends all the Daleks out to the Movellan spaceship with bombs strapped to themselves, so they can blow their enemies up.

The rather black joke of all this is that in order to protect themselves, the logical robots keep on being asked to be party to wilful acts of self-destruction. The Daleks have spent all this effort in excavating their creator so he can save them – and the best he can do is send them out on a suicide mission. The upshot of it all is that I felt a pang of sympathy for both Movellans and Daleks, and wanted to reassure them that they didn't have to give in to the whims of those nasty flesh and blood creatures. I suspect we're meant, as an audience, to feel threatened by those sequences of Dalek armies setting out across the wasteland to their deaths. Instead, they just seem pitiable, pathetic.

And it seems odd that this is what we've come to. After a five-season gap, Doctor Who has brought back the archenemies – and immediately the Doctor runs rings around them and mocks their climbing skills, and Davros bullies them and refuses to show them the slightest sign of parental affection. (He asks them what they've been up to since he saw them last, and wants specifically to learn all their failures – he's like the Dad who only wants to read all the bad things on your school report card.) When the Doctor throws a hat over one hapless Dalek's eyestalk and straps a bomb to it, it's bad enough – when he sarcastically shouts out "Bye bye!" to it, it just feels like playground cruelty.

In 1977, The Robots of Death showed us that if you treat robots like slaves, you can one day expect an uprising. In 1978, The Androids of Tara had the Doctor dismiss characters' sense of unease around robots by saying that robots often feel the same way. In 1979, there's a story that sells itself upon the glitter of two robot races doing battle with each other, and the Doctor is asked to exclaim the word "robot!" a lot as if it's still 1963 and we should be impressed by the word being so futuristic and shiny. We're meant to see the robots as something to be suspicious of – certainly in the Movellans' case – simply because they're not like us. But we react against this, because for years the programme has *taught* us to react against this. When the Doctor and Tyssan remove a Movellan's power pack in episode three, they start throwing it to each other whilst the dying robot looks on in distress, and it reminds me of the way school bullies used to throw my satchel back and forth. When in this episode Tyssan and his buddies surround Lan as he staggers about, it doesn't look like some great victory of humanity over machine, it looks ugly.

The idea that, in the far future, the Daleks have turned themselves into robots is rather an intriguing one – it sets up the idea that these are rather like Cybermen to the original Daleks, and destroyed the essence of what they are by removing everything organic. I love the actual concept. The sense that Daleks are now past their prime, parodies of the overemotional lumps of hate that we knew them as, and trying to recover from their creator what has once been lost, is arguably the most fascinating thing Terry Nation has done for the Daleks since the pepperpots were invented. But the story never makes it clear whether this is a deliberate development (and degradation) of Nation's original premise, or whether the writer himself has forgotten what made the Daleks tick. And the result is that the Daleks are weakened, almost *irretrievably* weakened. Because even though the 1980s writers writing sequels to Destiny chose to ignore this robotic idea absolutely entirely, they still saddle the Daleks with Davros, and make them either compliant sidekicks, or ingrates muttering about how much they hate their boss over the Skarosian equivalent of a water cooler. From

365

this point on, frankly, the Daleks might as well be robots, because they have precious little personality.

T: And they *are* robots – this is so bluntly expressed and thematically central, it's less easy to ignore than Romana's shop-window regeneration. The crux of this story is that some logically minded robot pepperpots cannot outmanoeuvre some equally logically minded, robot Top of the Pops dancers. Emotionless machines populate so much of science fiction; what makes the Doctor and the Daleks such potent adversaries is they both possess aspects of what we call humanity, but each has filtered out very different elements of it (the Doctor acquisitiveness and prejudice, the Daleks humour and pity) to make the universe their version of a better place.

But, *blimey*, these all-new robot Daleks are a sorry bunch. The patrols traversing Skaro aren't gliding – their operators wobble along on tiptoe with their feet just out of shot. Ken Grieve, latterly in some quarters reinvented as the ur-Graeme Harper, very nicely shoots the Daleks from below or at close quarters to maximise their oppressiveness, but he singularly fails to choreograph them so that they look like they *actually* work, let alone have the power to conquer the universe. So, sadly, seeing the Doctor's most famous foes as shoddy and pitiful just serves to rob fun from this climactic episode. When Davros finishes delivering his "Davros will lead" speech, and the practical Daleks have left on their mission to totter across Skaro, the dummy one behind him is clearly wobbled into place by an off-camera stagehand. I'm all for maximising resources, I am. But really.

So thanks goodness for Roy Skelton's voices: he screeches a "Do not move!" warning that's modulated with a Psychotic-Fingers-on-a-Blackboard Setting when the Doctor attempts to press the button that will blow up the suicide squad. Indeed, when the button finally is pressed, it's with a flourish of cruel inventiveness as it's Davros who, in the struggle, triggers his own defeat. For these scenes, designer Ken Ledsham has worked well to contrast the blues of the Dalek city with the stark white efficiency of the Movellan ship (cushions not withstanding), and the ceiling we can see in the Dalek

bunker helps underline the impression that we're underground somehow (and facilitates Grieve's oppressive low angles). Ledsham is one of the series' great unsung designers.

As for the Movellans... well, as a vociferous denier of the idea that Doctor Who is camp old nonsense, I'd have to plead the Fifth if they were ever produced as evidence to the contrary. Commander Sharrell is clearly someone who, when taking a break from conquering the universe, indulges in a lot of musical theatre and moonlights as the front man for a synthband. I remember my local rag, The Shropshire Star, running a picture of Next Big Thing Suzanne Danielle as Agella to accompany one of these episodes, so was rather shocked that she didn't end up with much to do (though the splendid Tony Osoba's minimal role is more sharply felt these days, I think). Danielle is odd casting – she has a chiselled beauty and looks good standing, as she does, hands on hips. But whilst the Movellan leader is clearly a member of Hot Gossip with an extraordinarily weak arm for a militaristic android (Romana just kicks it off), Agella has faulty programming when it comes to pronouncing the letter R. (As someone who struggled with a similar lisp in my youth, I'm not being prejudiced, but it does seem an odd shortcoming to ignore when casting for a precise-speaking android.) Still, the casting across the board has been one of this adventure's most profoundly bonkers aspects – the bizarre rebels are at it again, reducing the climactic fight on the Movellan ship into what looks like the shambolic finale of the office panto, culminating in the floor being strewn with dead gay androids and bloody awful extras.

Yes, yes... I'm succumbing to negativity again, aren't I? Well, actually, the *best* bit of the episode is the least logical, as the Movellans play Rock-Paper-Scissors. It's nonsense that such a random game contains a prescribed pattern, but seeing these blank-faced, humourless creatures indulging in this playground pastime with incomprehension is a wonderfully Doctor Who image (you wouldn't get that in Star Wars). And the other thing I like is a tad more personal: with Tim Barlow on board as Tyssan, I can point out to my stepson – a keen performer himself, who, like Barlow, is deaf – that, look, you can be an actor and be deaf and be in Doctor Who. This claims to be a story about robots, but it's a small flash of humanity that speaks to me – which is the point, I guess.

City of Death (part one)

R: Of course, we can take it for granted that City of Death is one of the greatest things ever, a masterpiece that deserves to be hung alongside the Mona Lisa. But what is clear watching just episode one back, for the first time in several years, is how similar it is to the more problematic stories surrounding it. Why does this one work when the others don't?

Because episode one has a pace that's so positively languid, it takes an age for us even to realise there's a plot to follow. As soon as anything intrigues the Doctor or Romana, they shrug it off with an acknowledgement that they're on holiday. If Destiny of the Daleks seemed to walk through its paces, City of Death saunters with a distracted swagger. It all feels so random – the reason the Doctor takes Romana to the Louvre in the first place is all because of a little argument they have about pictures, following an artist in a café getting all prissy when Romana noticed he was sketching her. The single most powerful image of the story – no, more, of the entire season – is that of Lalla Ward, her face replaced by a broken clock. And it means nothing, literally nothing, beyond creating the expression a "crack in time" that the Doctor can pun off.

And that sort of thing really oughtn't to work. But it does. Because this is exactly like a good holiday, where a whole bunch of unconnected moments come together, where you spontaneously decide to visit an art gallery because of something that just suddenly put the idea into your head. And you get the sense that the same spontaneity affects the filming in Paris – the Doctor and Romana stumble across a poster advertising an exhibition of the story of mankind, and you can just tell that the production team found it accidentally and put it into the programme. There's an exact wit to the dialogue that feels very deliberate (sometimes too deliberate – all that bouquet stuff is almost teeth-clenchingly mannered), but that sparks off a direction and visual style that feels correspondingly light and free. The way that the Doctor and Romana are filmed between the

rails of gates or stacks of postcards – there's an almost impromptu joy to the filming that is absolutely intoxicating.

It takes an enormous amount of self-confidence to pull this off. Other stories this season demonstrate egomania, but that's not really the same thing. Fortunately, Michael Hayes' direction is gorgeous. Just look at that opening shot, as the camera pans long and wide across an alien landscape. And then, after the Jagaroth ship explodes, how the camera apes that exact same shot, but now panning across bushes of flowers, no longer arid but in full bloom, and stops to reveal not a spaceship but the Eiffel bloody Tower of all things. It tells you immediately that this episode, for all its indulgences, is in the hands of someone who's making patterns out of the apparent random flow, and you trust it implicitly.

T: You mention the similarities, but even watching this in its chronological context – which I haven't done since my first viewing as a child – it feels different. Granted, it has the familiar mix of studio and location, a small cast, the odd model shot, Tom Baker making jokes and Pat Gorman (here as one of Scarlioni's heavies) – so far, so late 70s Who.

A flippant script can sometimes lead to a flippant production, but not so here: the location filming has an effortless (dare I say *laissez-fare?*) charm that makes you slump in your sofa and allow it to wash over you. Indeed, in its relaxed, charming way, City of Death is more grown-up than Destiny, no matter how gritty that story thought itself. The beautiful, jaunty music, the sweeping camerawork and a sun-drenched *joie de vivre* – all of this carries us through some quite lengthy establishing scenes with our leads taking Paris in their stride, or being pursued by both Duggan and a witty cameraman lurking furtively like a spy behind some pillars or a picture postcard.

The actors are all pretty much spot on – Julian Glover (as Count Scarlioni) gives a serious, suave performance that is also funny, though I'd be a liar if I said that David Graham and Tom Chadbon (respectively Professor Kerensky and the police detective Duggan) were pitch perfect. Someone needs to pull them aside and explain that lines this good sell themselves, so they don't need to try so hard.

Fortunately, Tom Baker leads from the front and is on especially superb form this time around; he's been given quality gags and delivers them properly. To put it another way, he's a weirdo on holiday – and that's how I like my Doctor to have adventures. His quest across the universe is essentially just a lark for an accidental tourist who happens to have a streak of zealous morality equal to his thirst for experience. I've never liked "the Doctor as God" approach; I much prefer this questing misfit who can't help getting into trouble. Baker looks so at home strolling through Paris – he's not normal enough to fade into the background, but not so outrageous as to be irritatingly, self-consciously eccentric. He just looks like a benevolent oddball who could be fun, and would *certainly* be interesting. Interesting and interest*ed*, I should say. The Doctor should be interested in art – he's a man of science with a poetic soul, a bohemian quantum physicist who also appreciates what can't be quantified.

Talking of art – there's no reason for Romana's wannabe portraitist to sketch her face as a clock, but it's an arresting image that wonderfully melds Doctor Who's charming hybridisation of science and art. Okay, so some have moaned that the Jagaroth's head is too big to fit under Julian Glover's human noggin. Well, of course it is, *it's a mask!* People who worry about that kind of thing may well know what they *don't* like, but they don't know much about... well, you know.

City of Death (part two)

R: Well, Toby, you've seen me stumped before. During The Dominators and The Space Pirates, halfway through The Time Monster. Episodes where for the life of me I couldn't find anything especially supportive to say. But City of Death is the first time I've been stumped for the exact reverse reason. What good moments are there to pick out of this? I just want to start the tape running, and point.

And this is the episode, as well, which has the least reliance on all the props that might make it have an unfair advantage over other stories. There's no dashing around with exotic location filming this time – there's an establishing shot at the beginning to show us the Scarlioni house, and that's it. This is the one

episode which feels most like bog-standard Doctor Who – it's composed mainly of lots of scenes of exposition on a studio set, one of them so blatant that Scarlioni has to construct a virtual projection of the Louvre in his entire sitting room to make his plan more visually interesting.

But it's funny.

As a rule, Douglas Adams' writing relies upon big concepts married to exquisite one-line comic gags. The contrast of the two, the huge and the throwaway, gives the illusion that his storytelling is watertight and covers up any cracks – when really it's all sleight of hand. The scene where the Countess interrogates the Doctor doesn't flow like ordinary dialogue at all – because it isn't. It's a series of almost disconnected jokes. But the jokes are so good that it doesn't matter whatsoever – and indeed, synthesises the character of the Doctor at his best, that he throws out wit and eccentricity as a means to confuse the enemy and learn more from them than they can from him. The way Baker enters the scene, popping up behind antique furniture, and introducing himself and his friends on his knees, immediately suggests a position of inferiority. But he does it with such feckless enthusiasm that the very opposite is true. The Countess is utterly out of her depth. In comes the Count, and the Doctor finds his match – a man who seems wholly unfazed by the Doctor, and indeed finds him amusing. Later in the episode, where the Count confronts the Doctor in the cellar, he is in a silk dressing gown looking for all the world like Noel Coward. There's no need to shout, there's no need to be drawn into answering the Doctor's questions. They are two supremely confident men measuring the other – and this is precisely what was missing from the encounters with Davros in Destiny. Let Tom Baker show the world how clever he is. And match him with a villain who doesn't care.

And for all the joking, the Doctor is in earnest. He's in teacher mode. When Kerensky tells him he doesn't ask questions about how his time-travel research is funded, the Doctor says that the job of a scientist is to ask questions. When Duggan starts lashing out with his fists, the Doctor encourages him to slow down and look about and investigate. His one moment of real anger in the whole episode seems to be when Duggan is about to hit someone over the head with the chair – "That's a Louis Quinze!" The Doctor can appreciate things in greater context, that a work of art that has survived intact for centuries should not be destroyed so casually.

And there's the Countess! I know fans who criticise the story because they can't accept a wife wouldn't realise her husband's an alien – doesn't she ever see what he looks like in bed? And yet that's so clearly the point, that Catherine Schell plays the part with the jealous sexuality of a woman who has married for money and who can't attract her husband to bed because he'd rather be in the basement with another man. All the beautiful dresses, the long cigarette holders, the glamour, it's as much a sham as her entire marriage. (What added poignancy is there in that famous line, "You're a beautiful woman, probably!" – for all her Parisian elegance, her husband would rather be with David Graham.) She's bored, she wants distraction, she wants to be a master criminal. The look of naked greed on her face as she watches the rehearsal for the Mona Lisa theft is just perfect.

On that note – and quickly, because I don't want to be writing this email, I want to get back to the story! – how clever is City of Death that it's a story about an art heist that won't even bother to show us the robbery. Instead, it just tells us in detail how it's going to be done, calmly and wittily, and dispenses with all the false tension and melodrama. Because it's not about the mechanics of a robbery, it's about the implications of the robbery. Doctor Who often ties itself up into knots writing about bold concepts and then betraying them with laboured action sequences. City of Death has no interest in doing that. It's far too elegant. It doesn't want to break a sweat.

It's a bright summer day. And this whole story feels like basking in sunshine. What a wonderful thing Doctor Who can be.

T: See, that's the wonderful thing about Doctor Who: you benefit so much from rewatching it. Until today, I thought the chair was a "Louis Cairns"; I'd only ever heard it said, never seen it written down. My breadth of knowledge has just been widened, no matter how triflingly. And *of course* the Doctor not

only knows what a Louis Quinz chair looks like (and no doubt how to spell it), just as he also knows that their importance and beauty is such that one shouldn't be used to bash the henchman of an alien spaghetti monster over the head with.

The chair scene is the most consistently funny one up to this point in the series, with the Doctor being a cheery-faced social organiser indulging in archly forced civility with an extraterrestrial art fiend and his murderous cohorts. With the Doctor's delight at the violence of Scarlioni's butler, the insertion of just one word into a line to transform it from simple conversational ruse into something of offbeat genius ("You're a beautiful woman, probably"), and allowing the villain the final say (Countess: "My dear, I don't think [the Doctor] is as stupid as he seems"; Count: "My dear, nobody could be stupid as he seems"), City of Death gives us a mini-comedy master class. You want to know why I love this show? It's there, all in that one scene, one that continues to excel even after you think it can't get any better. (And only this time around – about the thirtieth time that I've watched this – did I pick up Tom Baker muttering the delightful line "show us to our cellar" as they are ushered out.)

I can see why I fell in love with Tom Baker's Doctor as a kid – he's smart, intelligent, Bohemian, curious and scornful of the supposedly impressive. He's like a random stranger you meet at a party you were expecting to not enjoy, but, as a result of the encounter, leave buzzing. And as the Doctor rarely indulges in fisticuffs, it's appropriate that he here consistently berates Tom Chadbon's hapless Duggan for engaging in them with such zeal. And it's *doubly* great that when the Doctor righteously tells Duggan that he's going to take very serious measures if he thumps someone again, and is challenged to spell out what those measures are, his rather limp reply is "I'm going to ask you not to". But despite the Doctor's disapproval of Duggan's tactics, the production clearly loves the man, and so we do too. His ill-timed walloping of Kerensky is very funny indeed, as are Chadbon's brilliant suggestions that Duggan is catching on a few seconds after everyone else. Even the clichéd heroics (throwing a light literally, after being asked to do so metaphorically) happen with a nod to their inherent absurdity, and so are huge fun despite themselves.

But as much as Douglas Adams gets lauded for his jokes, the science-fiction ideas on display here are absolutely at the core of what Doctor Who does so well. A dull alien with even limited communication across time would amass his fortune using lottery numbers, but this one uses *art*. The concept of six genuine Mona Lisas makes a comment about greed whilst furnishing Scaroth with money. It's not galactic domination or the destruction of Earth (that comes later) – the payoff of his art heist is simple, old-fashioned cash. The acquisition of booty is not a very Doctor Who-ish thrill, but doing so using time travel and Leonardo da Vinci really is. And just when you think – thanks to a rather lengthy bit of exposition concerning the heist's methodology – that events in Paris are settling down into pedestrianism, we end up in sixteenth-century Italy, with lots of cheeky jokes about Leonardo, Peter Halliday cameo-ing in an unusual and thus super bit of casting as a guard, and the surprising entrance of Julian Glover in a different costume. No wonder I remember this episode extremely well, and how thrilling it was, from its first broadcast (especially the bit with the super-ageing chicken). This is the work of a master.

August 23rd

City of Death (part three)

R: Unexpectedly, City of Death now reaches for poignancy – and gets it, effortlessly. When the villain has succeeded in his plans to acquire the Mona Lisa, he stares dully at the mirror as his wife bleats upon the achievement of the robbery. "I do not ask for everything," he says quietly, and in an instant you get the sense of one last survivor of his race, separated even from his other selves, forced to go through the motions of relationships with a humanity he's had to adapt to but towards he feels no real kin. It seems silly to say it – but in the wake of the new series, does that remind you of anybody?

I'm certainly not claiming that Scaroth had

any direct influence upon the reformatting of the revival of Doctor Who. But Julian Glover brings to the part that extra dimension of loss – that however amoral Scaroth's behaviour, his motives are from his own point of view entirely heroic. One imagines he has an easier time acting as Captain Tancredi (Scaroth's temporal duplicate), where he can afford to brutalise and torture his enemies, than he has in the insipid twentieth century, where he spends most of his time obliged to feed Kerensky with studied politeness and half bottles of wine. And it makes perfect sense of a cliffhanger in which the Doctor's arrival in Paris complete with a time machine has suddenly made even a human supergenius like Kerensky tragically expendable – at last he can stop being nice to the old bore! It's good comedy that the respectful courtesies Scaroth affords Romana are utterly denied Duggan – that Duggan has to keep his hands up, whilst Romana is allowed to sit down is one of many throwaway moments of delight – but it's also an essential character note.

"The centuries that divide me shall be undone!" – what a chilling line. And we're blessed that we have an actor who's taking the part extremely seriously, so that the sequence where Scaroth talks across the timeline to his other selves, which is written mostly as comedy, is so powerful and so very sad.

T: When the Doctor asks Tancredi how he communicates with his other selves, the captain doesn't provide an answer – but the script does. By cutting to the unconscious Scarlioni dementedly eavesdropping in on/ communing with the conversation, it shows us the mental bond between the fragments of the last of the Jagaroth. This diversion in Italy has been extremely rewarding, adding a bit of historical lustre to the story, and positing that for all of mankind's delusions of grandeur, we're merely the playthings of an intergalactic warmongering gambler. It also brings the twin delights of another fine flourish from the costume department and the delightfully anarchistic moment of the Doctor scribbling "This is a Fake" on Leonardo's canvases. You can't change history, not one brush stroke, but you can certainly scribble underneath it.

And it's blissfully gauche that one of the

baddies has to nip out for the thumbscrews, while Glover has got the humour licked as much as the swaggering villainy. When Baker insolently answers back that he won't be able to reveal anything if his tongue is removed, Glover quips "You can write, can't you?" in a perfectly cutting fashion. The delightful Peter Halliday also proves the advantage of casting "up", lending his potentially irritating thicko guard a simpleton's likeable sincerity. His blunt "I'm paid to fight" is later trumped by a hurried "I'm not paid to notice" when his superior gets all weird and alien.

I criticised but two elements of episode one: Chadbon and Graham. Well, despite the odd body language Graham adopts when aged to death (which lends what should be a shocking sequence an unnecessarily comic edge), he's very good here. The scene where he confronts Glover, appalled at the consequences of the scientific modifications he's being ordered to make, is suffused with outraged defiance from the fussy little man. And Chadbon, whilst occasionally uncomfortable when delivering his lines of exasperation, gives us so many laughs that I will forgive him anything. Actually, I love Duggan! His annoyance at being forced to re-raise his hands when Romana is generously allowed a seat is very funny, and I enjoy his ultra-serious delivery of "what do you mean?" to the Doctor's obvious metaphor about wood coming from trees, and his especially default position of crashing through windows and breaking glass. The violence trope has been so well integrated into the story that is encapsulated brilliantly when Duggan awakes bleary eyed in the café, draws his gun and clatters his cup over after Romana's innocuous suggestion that his coffee will go cold.

But why do the guards at the Louvre let the Doctor inside after the Mona Lisa is stolen? From the quick little bit of Additional Dialogue Recording we get, they seem to assume he is someone in authority who needs to scout the scene of the crime. First use of psychic paper, anyone?

City of Death (part four)

R: Everyone now appreciates that Douglas Adams was a genius. And it means that in our hurry to fall over ourselves acknowledging how good the script he wrote for Doctor Who was, we forget he wasn't the only man hiding beneath the David Agnew storyline.

Graham Williams had a tough ride on Doctor Who. One of the few producers who didn't cast his leading man, like John Wiles he inherited an actor who made life difficult for him. It's now widely known that when he expressed concern about Tom Baker, the BBC made it very clear his wayward star had the greater authority. This has left an impression that Williams was something of a weak man. But the truth was, he was both a successful director and writer, the last great do-it-all producer of the series. And as writer he stepped into the brink twice, and pulled out of crisis two fascinating scripts – The Invasion of Time and City of Death.

What The Invasion of Time has going for it, for the most part, is a strong bold concept. The rest of the stories of Season Fifteen feel mostly flabby and safe – The Invasion of Time, for all its flaws, is sharp, and is structured brilliantly. City of Death has the same integral discipline at the heart of it, an insistence that the storyline runs as primly as a well-wound clock. When you look at Douglas Adams' solo scripts for the series, The Pirate Planet and the unbroadcast Shada (let's cover the latter in the 90s section, shall we, in accord with the VHS release?), you see wit and imagination aplenty – but amid all the ideas that are fizzing about, you don't see an awful lot of self-discipline. And, arguably, this was always Adams' greatest weakness; the Hitchhiker's novels, by diminishing returns, are a series of brilliant set pieces linked by the thinnest of plotlines – and the first two are reconstituted from the radio series with all the events shuffled into bizarrely different orders, as if structure was always something that was nonchalant.

Is it really too much to conclude, whilst celebrating City of Death's absolute greatness, that this gem of a story works because of the collaboration of two writers? One whose comic fantasies dazzle, and one who can harness those fantasies towards some kind of plot? And does it seem too much to suggest that the reason why City of Death works better than Adams' other stories is precisely because it's the most structured? That the unsung hero of the writing duo was the one who makes this all so wonderfully satisfying?

T: I wanted Duggan to go with the Doctor. Not this time, because I knew he wouldn't, but when I first saw this story. (I also remember my sister predicting that the postcard he buys at the end would be of the Mona Lisa. Clever sister!) I really didn't get the joke with Duggan when I was a kid – he was the heroic guest character, not a violent buffoon. It didn't seem like there was anything funny about him, but now, as an adult, I see that he gets most of the best jokes. To make a show that thrills kids but keeps rewarding adults (especially after the passage of time has seen changes in technology) is no mean feat, and among Doctor Who's greatest strengths. We don't watch this askance, as some quaint period piece that is vaguely nostalgic: the good bits of City of Death are that way *because they are good*, no other reason. The performances still stand up, the jokes are still funny, the imaginative ideas are still potent. I loved it as a kid and I love it now. The decades that divide me have been undone.

And I am so impressed at how City of Death wears its cleverness rather lightly, parading its intellectualism with a confident smile and a casual shrug, much like the main character. The Countess in particular is clearly unsettled by the Doctor's wayward genius, but shrewd enough not to underestimate it. Throughout this story, Catherine Schell has carried the burden of the least showy part, but she convinces as an elegant beauty who enjoys the finer things in life, while turning a blind eye to the uncomfortable truth. She even maintains a fragile facade of confidence when Tom Baker needles at her conscience – she is, after all, a trophy wife, so is well versed in the arts of discretion and charm.

Speaking of which: the unworldly have sometimes scoffed at the idea that the Countess hasn't realised her husband's face is a removable mask, and that he has a body made of green spaghetti, but we're talking about the upper classes here. How many loveless marriages have endured for the sake of appearance? How many sexless marriages have been the price for maintaining a civil front that protects the assets? I'd wager they number more than the tears cried by Ian Levine at the utterance of the name Pamela Nash. The Countess probably thinks Scarlioni is gay, and she's traded physical intimacy for the sake of creature (from outer space) comforts. Actually, as he puts all his efforts into collecting priceless relics from the past, maybe she thinks he's a gay Doctor Who fan (of whom I believe there are one or two). And the reveal of the one-eyed monster in the Egyptian papyrus gives this witty story an epic quality, while cruelly exposing the hollow nature of this woman's finery and supposed sophistication.

In contrast to the Countess' petty Earthbound comforts and status, the Count has altogether grander things in his sights: namely, the destruction of humankind and the resurrection of his people. But in our stay with us, he hasn't half adopted the exquisite poise and superiority of the elite. His arrogance may be a Jagaroth trait, but it fits well with the suave identity he has adopted, and Julian Glover's performance is perfectly judged ("I don't care one jot", he says, matter-of-factly, when contemplating the scale of the destruction he will cause). He regards humanity as a blip, an irritation to be swept aside – which is understandable, considering the age and might of his race. And even as many times as I've seen this story, the Count's lines about threatening the lives of a number of people he could name if he happened to have a copy of the Paris telephone directory about his person, and his lament that he will have to keep Duggan alive – as it is unfortunately not possible to kill him twice – are so wonderfully written and performed, I laughed out loud on a train. I don't think I could have elicited more funny looks from fellow passengers if I'd sat there with "This is a Fake" scribbled all over me.

John Cleese and Eleanor Bron are the icing on the cake in all of this – a witty pair of cameos, a touch of class and a seamless fit. They'd dominate the proceedings in a lesser production, but City of Death, frankly, has everything: a wonderful central conceit, a fertile mass of science-fiction ideas, great characters portrayed with confidence and brio, and nonetheless a serious throughline about accepting fate and the importance of humanity. But of course, great art has to *look* good too, and the film work in Paris has a light, breezy, jaunty quality about it, whilst that iconic imagery of the cream-suited spaghetti Cyclops pointing a gun at our heroes is a fabulously Doctor Who-ey tableau. And the suggestion that the Mona Lisa now hanging in the Louvre has "This is a Fake" written underneath its paint has a cheeky gusto that plants a big grin on my face.

Exquisite, absolutely exquisite.

The Creature from the Pit (part one)

R: The Doctor has a ball of string given him to Theseus when they defeated the Minotaur together! Now, there's a strong autistic impulse in me that wants this to be a prefiguring of The Horns of Nimon, just two stories away. But I'm giving up being pretentious. I glumly acknowledge it's probably just a random gag. (Though I have just read an interview with Douglas Adams, mind you, conducted some ten years or so after this was broadcast, and in it he talks about the interconnectedness of all things in the universe in relation to his Dirk Gently books – so who knows? Maybe my autistic pretension wins through after all. Hurrah!)

There's tons to enjoy in this episode, especially within the first ten minutes. For a story which has such a bad reputation for a particular piece of design work, The Creature from the Pit actually looks rather beautiful. And I suppose that's a lesson for us, that it only takes one failure in a production to make us forget the quality around it. The jungle looks lush and convincing, and certainly on a par with the one we celebrated in Planet of Evil. The wolfweeds are absolutely fantastic – even 30 years on, I can't quite see how they work, and the very inhuman idea of large balls of moss that can hunt people would make Terry Nation squeak with excitement. (I love the game of Grandmother's Footsteps the Doctor plays with them too, where they only roll towards him when he's not looking – I love especially that at some point the wolfweeds just say, sod it, and attack him anyway.) And the design of the pit is very clever – it's just a small brick hole in the ground, and there's nothing grand about it, there's no ceremonial adornment – it looks brutally functional, and that's what makes it so credible. There's a sense, I think, that Chloris is a real planet with an identifiable

culture and geography, and we haven't had that on Doctor Who for a very long time indeed.

But what happens at the ten-minute mark? We get the bandits.

Leaving aside the whole problem about the Jewish accents, which at best feels like lazy comedy, and at worst smacks of something much more egregious – the bandits stick out like a sore thumb because they're so obviously not real at all. If you try to construct a believable new world, it is only ever going to be as strong as its weakest element. When we hear about the bandits they seem bloodthirsty and vicious – and Lady Adrasta and her underling, Karela, both believe that Romana has no chance of survival with them. But in practice they're stupid and bumbling. And Romana clearly doesn't see them as a threat whatsoever. When she tells them all to sit down with schoolmarm derision, I'm reminded of how Snow White would treat the seven dwarves.

And there's a problem to this. Yes, we want Romana to be given some dignity. (And Lalla Ward carries it off effortlessly in her first recorded performance as the Time Lady.) No, we certainly don't want to go back to the bad old days where a companion's job was to scream at the slightest danger. But it doesn't aggrandise the Doctor or Romana when they stride through an adventure too confidently. On the contrary, it diminishes them, because you're left wondering why they even bother with such small-scale exploits in the first place. Tom Baker's Doctor was once a man who was forced to kneel before Sutekh, and now he offers jelly babies to Davros. Logically, you would think the latter would make him the more powerful. But there's no heroism in condescension – and Romana suffers the same fate here. We don't feel that her quick wit and bravery have triumphed over the odds. We just feel that she's bullied a few men about their hairy beards.

That said – what a cliffhanger. The Doctor is cornered by the villain, and, without even a joke on his lips, jumps straight into the pit. It's unexpected, it's brilliantly staged, and it has about it all the untempered heroism that the series at the moment seems to shy away from.

And my favourite moment in an episode full of choice moments? The Doctor recoiling as

Lady Adrasta offers to scratch his nose. He's made a ploy of nose itching to knock out a couple of guards, and she acts all hospitality and solicitousness as she reaches out her hand to assist him. And just for a moment all the comedy drops, and the Doctor shows he wants there to be no physical contact whatsoever between him and the woman he's realised already is a tyrant.

T: The episode starts at night with a moody sacrifice – a cowled extra is hurled to his death, and I'm gripped. The contrasting larks in the TARDIS are thus rather delightful, especially with K-9 reading Peter Rabbit to the Doctor, and Romana being able to quote from it. Beatrix Potter is so evocative for me, reminiscent of fireside stories and being tucked up in bed after a bath or prescribed with Camomile tea for a tummy upset. Her work is eccentric, British and has a delightful linguistic character that makes her perfect reading matter for the star of this show. Call me a snob, but I much prefer a TARDIS crew versed in poems and fairytales than "the best Christmas Walford's ever had" and Ghostbusters. The Doctor should take us beyond the comfort of the everyday into the hidden treasures of the arcane. "Don't be a philistine", he says. Quite right.

But let's pull back a bit – *this* is the supposedly "cheap and nasty" Season Seventeen, is it? Granted, we've just been to Paris in the company of Julian Glover, but now we're at Ealing for as sumptuous a production as we've had for a long time. This looks *absolutely gorgeous* – and it's not just the stint in a film studio that sells the illusion here, as the costumes are also terrific. The guards have crushed velvet outfits and ultra-long swords that are rather fabulous, whilst Myra Frances (as Lady Adrasta) looks like an Arabian monarch in her trim, turbaned outfit with (of course) a metal breastplate to signify her control of that valuable substance. The portable stocks that shackle the Doctor aren't just an excuse for a "yolk" gag, but are just one example of set dressing that helps to create an alien culture that is recognisable yet different. The decision to dress the "engineers" in monk-like robes cunningly mutates recognisable imagery from our own society in order to help us understand this one. (Scientists are like seers, and the primitive form of dispatch

that greets them if they get their sums wrong is far removed from the scientific method.)

The biggest problem here is, as you say, the bandits. Whether they are offensive or not is somewhat subjective – I think they *are*, though I also think it's generally fine for an artist to offend me if I think they're challenging my perceptions, or trying to provoke discourse about the world in which we live. Whether you think they are funny is also up to you – I don't, but as someone who tries to be funny for a living, I'm aware of how blinkered the phrase "that's just not funny" can sound. However, I do think that the stereotyping and attempts at humour here are *lazy*... and that I cannot forgive. Just look how the thief Torvin rather halfheartedly eases himself onto the floor after K-9 stuns him; it looks like he's attended the same falling-over classes as the Destiny of the Daleks extras. (If you can't be bothered to try mate, neither can I.) Myra Frances, fortunately, has a much better sense of timing – her hand movements, poise and hokey lines ("we call it ... the pit!") are daft and played archly, but also utterly straight, so they are dramatic and funny at the same time. It's a perfectly judged performance, and by far the wittiest thing on show. She's channelling Monty Python, while the bandits are drawing rude words on the blackboard when teacher's not looking.

But all in all, I'm enjoying this more than I would have expected – the idea of metal being the source of power, wealth and desire in an alien society is a good basis for a science-fiction adventure featuring one man and his tin dog. Add into this that one of the engineers is played by a former Who director (hello, Morris Barry!), and one of the baddies by the last returning guest actor from the very first story (hello, Eileen Way!), and the episode ending every bit as exciting and enticing as the beginning, and you have a fun and intriguing instalment of Doctor Who.

August 24th

The Creature from the Pit (part two)

R: There's a comedy bit here that gets a lot of stick, and I had my teeth fully winced in anticipation of it. The Doctor hangs over a precipice and retrieves from his pocket a book about how to mountain climb; he discovers it's written in Tibetan. So retrieves another book, this time called Teach Yourself Tibetan. My teeth were so winced, in fact, that I may have dislodged a filling. And the filling suffered for nothing, because... I actually found it funny. Gags like these depend upon timing, and the most undisciplined bits of comedy at this stage of Doctor Who feel all over the shop. But this is precise, and it works. And I like it because it does nothing to hinder the drama – this isn't a way out of the cliffhanger, the Doctor doesn't save himself because of some contrived joke about the teeming library he impossibly carries in his coat – instead, he falls down to the bottom of the pit, to find a couple of very dead corpses and one very large monster. This is what Doctor Who is all about – the collision of silliness and melodrama, no matter how incompatible they might seem. It's a collision that keeps the programme unpredictable. This sequence won't work for everyone. Indeed, this sequence might not work for anyone except me. But it's also completely disposable – if you so wished, you could chop the joke out of your DVD copy and it wouldn't affect the action of the story one jot. (Indeed, with 2Entertain producing special editions of stories left, right and centre, and hacking away at effects and scenes which seemed perfectly okay to me in the first place, I'm rather hoping that when Creature gets its release, they can add as a bonus an edit of the story that's joke-free.)

[Rob's addendum, written September 2016: They didn't.]

Something else which gets a lot of stick is David Brierley's performance as K-9. Brierley doesn't get much chance to establish himself, only doing the honours on three stories, and his reputation isn't helped by the fact that it's *these* three stories. (Stick him in the universally adored City of Death, just you watch how his stock rises.) Most people's problem with Brierley's K-9 is... that he doesn't sound anything like K-9. Leeson's take on the part is so definitive, it now seems ludicrous to imagine another actor taking the part, and whether he's in the new series or The Sarah Jane Adventures or in his new bizarre spin-off Australian kids

show, Leeson's involvement is a foregone conclusion. But I think Brierley deserves a lot of credit for not merely trying to ape his predecessor. Certainly, this story is the best showcase for him, and the frustration at the way K-9 is manipulated by Adrasta – the pained reluctance to accede to her demands – comes across very well. It's wholly in the spirit of Doctor Who that this new actor takes an existing beloved character and tries to make it his own, and it's curious to me that a fandom that has come to celebrate the different interpretations of the lead character has always refused the same courtesy to the tin dog.

The astrologer Organon is wonderful, of course. Geoffrey Bayldon gives the part a sweet eccentricity, and thoroughly charms. He pulls me up short, in fact – his performance reminds me of the way the Doctor used to be: kindly, mad and cowardly brave.

... You'll notice I haven't mentioned the creature itself. I'll mention the creature later. You, Toby, you can go first. You tell us why the creature is so good.

T: Hah! I don't think I viewed the creature as good even when I was a kid. What can you *say* about it, really? It looks like a great big cock and balls. It's a work of grand folly, but at least its absurd appearance helps to sell the knowingly arch dialogue. (Q: "How big is it?", A: "Huge"; and "It's large, very large, and it's time I was rid of it.") I bet Tom Baker's eyes popped out of his head in rehearsals. In the face of this ludicrousness, what works is the delightful Bayldon's comic resignation, and, best of all, Myra Frances as a sexy, polite (she calls Romana "My dear"), and yet dangerous (she slaps!) aristocrat: a villain without whom the story would probably disintegrate. Baker clearly takes her seriously, and has respect for Bayldon.

There's even a stab at atmosphere when the Doctor and Organon are bathed in the creature's green glow, and the production flirts with looking serious and impressive. In fact, the practical glob emerging from the more genuinely blobby special effect actually sort of works, and we get the idea that Erato can send out probing membranes that can then be absorbed back into his main body. But Baker decides to play the cliffhanger – in which Erato engulfs the Doctor – for laughs, for which I will have him lined up with his back to the wall next to the bandits (whom I have found guilty and sentenced to death for crimes against television) if he's not careful.

I too don't have a problem with David Brierley: his K-9 is slightly more pompous – more like Blake's 7's Orac actually – than John Leeson's, but this slightly haughty delivery certainly suits a somewhat supercilious supercomputer. Sure, I prefer Lesson, but think Brierley's stab at the role is brave and not unsuccessful. (I'm not sure he deserves being billed before Geoffrey Bayldon in the credits, though. That's rather pedantic of me, I know, but I like to think that this version of K-9 would rather approve.)

The Creature from the Pit (part three)

R: One of those guards is David Redgrave! Every summer, my wife Janie acts in a repertory season near Manchester, and David is usually cast as her husband. They've been married in so many different ways, in comedies and tragedies, from classical theatre to trouser-dropping farces. I've always assumed, really, he's just auditioning for the real thing in the event of my death. It's nice to see him here. Or would be, if his face wasn't buried beneath a mask.

The theme of this story becomes all too clear. It's all about communication. Say what you like about the scene in which the Doctor tries to speak to the creature by blowing down its proboscis, it's quite fitting for our hero to see an enormous green blob as a potential friend who needs sympathetic conversation, rather than just as a monster that ought to be destroyed. Doctor Who gets around the problem of communication between different species easily enough, usually, by the clever principle of Just Ignoring It – and that's perfectly right most of the time, because you don't want every adventure held up by a language barrier. But how good this is, that in a story which sells itself as being a schlock horror story about something big and nasty, it's adopting a far more humanistic approach. I've criticised Tom Baker a lot recently for a performance that verges on self-parody – but required to deliver

a long monologue to a large green bag, he manages to inject the right amount of fear, patience and hope.

And it's another great episode ending too – selling itself not on an immediate threat, but at the promise of revelation as two hypnotised fellows give a glowing translation device to the pit-creature. That's the sign of a sophisticated script, where it's offering the long-term satisfaction of explanation rather than the short term of quick jeopardy. All the best cliffhangers do this, they act as pivots that change the direction of the story rather than hijacking the plot for some irrelevant bit of scarifying. Myra Frances is superb in this scene as Adrasta, growing more and more desperate as the threads of the plot come together, and screaming with convincing terror that she'll not only be killed, but be found out.

T: Well done, Rob! Tom Baker blows into the end of something shaped like a phallus, and you intellectualise it. And here was me thinking that sometimes you just spouted cod-highbrow straw-clutching when you couldn't think of anything nice to say about an episode. So let me just reiterate: the monster is a big long bulbous thing attached to a sack, and our leading man, already an occasional law unto himself, blows the end of it. Who said it wasn't easy being green?

Otherwise, to look at my notes from this viewing, I see that I have written "I hate the bandits". I must feel very strongly about this, as I have marked it down about 15 times. In blood. On the walls of my house. Look, it's easier to be silly than funny, but that's not to say silly can't be funny, if that makes any sense. The Naked Gun films are silly, yes, but they are hilarious. In fact, there's a silly joke in this that works: Romana says, with utter seriousness, "We must think [in order to solve this problem]", only for the Doctor to burst violently through the shell. Very funny, as is the exchange of Adrasta: "I thought you were dead, why haven't you died?", Organon: "Sorry, my lady, it was an oversight". Wit of a different kind is evident in that the production keeps finding ways for K-9 to negotiate various bits of terrain, including the order for him to be carried. But the bandits are so silly, they're stupid, and not funny stupid.

But if my ire at the bandits is becoming repetitious, so is my adoration of Myra Frances. Our quest is to accentuate the positive, and she's a great big plus: a pitch-perfect performance anchoring an adventure in danger of falling apart around her. She's direct, forceful, calculating, bossy, spitefully arrogant and cruelly threatening. Even better, despite her posturing, she isn't undermined by the Doctor and Romana – she keeps an eye on the latter and K-9, and keeps the Doctor on a short leash. Having let slip that she knows more about the Tythonian than she should, she gradually begins to unravel. Frances has hinted at an innate instability prior to this, her orders barked at a little too high a pitch for a woman completely in control, so this descent is logical and dramatic. And it *is* an unusual cliffhanger, and one that wouldn't work had Frances not put in a hefty level of good work up until this point. Her protracted screams of terror are believable and spine-chilling.

The Creature from the Pit (part four)

R: This is messy. But it's messy in a good way, because life is messy, and resolutions are never, ever as tidy as they seem upon the telly. Lady Adrasta is killed, and her reign of tyranny is over – and we're left with nearly 20 minutes of screen time. And the point is well made – just because the source of evil is extinguished, it doesn't mean that the consequences of it magically disappear. A neutron star is set to destroy Chloris. And people are still greedy and self-interested and stupid enough to welcome with open arms the means to a new regime.

When I first saw The Creature from the Pit, I thought it was like a guest who hasn't realised the party is over, and keeps bopping away in your front room even though the music's been turned off and everyone has gone home. I missed the point – but I think that's because Christopher Barry as director has missed the point too, and sells this final instalment as an epilogue rather than a climax. But it's all much more complex than that. Just because Erato has been the victim to Adrasta's schemes, and hasn't been the human-eating monster we'd been led to believe, it doesn't mean that he's

some easy virtuous hero either. The first thing he wants to do when he gets out of the pit is bugger off to safety, and leave the planet to its fate – and the Doctor is prepared to coerce his help out of him. If Erato was a human who'd been imprisoned, his first action upon release – to murder his captor in revenge – would leave us in little doubt that he couldn't be trusted. Being a big green blob blurs the morality of it a bit, but it still leaves us dubious that setting him free in itself means we get a happy ending.

Karela is the most impressive character here. She's the underling of a tyrant who survives the change in regime, but isn't prepared to accept it. The Doctor is in full Jesus Christ mode, in righteous anger sweeping all the riches Karela prizes so much off the tables – and she isn't cowed and stands her ground. When presented with the reality of her selfishness, that her world may be destroyed, she just doesn't care. It's the most perfect illustration that no matter how often the Doctor wins through against the odds, he can't change people's hearts. And you are left to wonder whether every story we ever watch has a similar aftermath – that just because the day has been won against the villain of the week, it doesn't mean that the tomorrow will be any brighter.

In the final scene, the Doctor pops back in his TARDIS and asks the Huntsman whether he's now the man in charge. And the Huntsman hasn't even been given a name, and all he had to show for himself was that he could crack a whip and make weeds do his bidding, and his very first action in the story was to attempt to kill our hero. Writer David Fisher makes no pretence that Adrasta's successor will be enlightened or wise – the Huntsman is even fooled by the stupidest trick in the world, when he seems amazed Organon knows the contents of a document after A) standing looking over his shoulder, and B) hearing him say what it is out loud. The Huntsman is quite deliberately an anonymous character – he's in charge of a planet, but it could really be anyone else. And the Doctor sets off in his blue box on another adventure in time and space.

T: Tom Baker famously wanted a talking cabbage as a companion. Here he *gets* a talking cabbage, and whilst it's the monster rather than his sidekick, it does – on the plus side – talk in his own voice, so he must have been delighted. It allows for another witty exchange where the Doctor's own tones implore him not to be frightened and alarmed; then, when talking to Romana, the Doctor admits to having been too busy being frightened and alarmed to take in said instruction. Baker is, as always, strangely muted when playing an ersatz version of the Doctor or using his own voice to portray another character, but he's on fabulous form when raging about weeds and forests and condemning Adrasta's avarice and folly. The whole scenario he rails about is at the heart of the story: a trade agreement being scuppered by the fragile power structure of a greedy ruler. That story ends when Erato kills Adrasta by squashing her to death – though, as it turns out, as a bonus he also eats some wolfweeds (one of the most underrated secondary monsters in the show's history, they're fabulous).

Thereafter, the episode displays a slightly odd (but novel) structure – the reveal that the monster is benign, and yet harbouring a lethal secret, keeps us guessing and unsure of our loyalties. The alliance between Karela and the bandits (with one of them, Ainu, actually deducing the imminent redundancy of metal) gives them a positive impact on the story. The unleashing of the neutron star is unexpected yet dramatic. And whilst it all feels a bit random, with some wayward pacing, it's a break from the normal way of doing things (with a use of knives that we took in our stride when I was young, but would never be countenanced today!). The denouement provides – in terms of novelty if not satisfying drama – a welcome curio. On top of that, we get a vindictive and calculating turn from Eileen Way, a funny lucky number gag from Tom Baker, and a lovely "Something terrible is going to happen" prediction from Organon before he gets bonked on the head. (In fact, Bayldon's been curiously underused, so it's rather fun that he gets the coda and final close-up.)

But the dirty secret is that even though I've found nice things to say about The Creature from the Pit, it's been something of an academic exercise in digging for them. However you slice it, there's been a lot wrong with this adventure, and not much that is *very* good, and – truth to tell – it's probably the story I've found the hardest to write up. So if nothing else, maybe the one *really* good thing I can say about The Creature from the Pit is that it's over!

August 25th

Nightmare of Eden (part one)

R: Doctor Who does drugs! We haven't seen this theme raised in quite a while. The last time it was with the Doctor feeding Cameca's cocoa addiction, and we can remember the problems that caused him.

It's interesting that it's *now* the series decides to tackle an adult issue like this, when it's at its most unapologetically childlike. For my part, I think they get the balance extremely well – though that may change once the monsters lumber on to take centre stage – and that's because it's Bob Baker alone who's writing this. I've come to admire the Baker and Martin team considerably, in spite of the little chuckles I make at the expense of their high concept, vastly ambitious storylines. And what makes Nightmare of Eden work so well is that it *is* so high concept – there are at least three major story ideas here vying for attention, which somehow means that the grimmest of them is given a fantasy context to play off and contrast with.

I mean, let's start with the cleverness of the two spaceships that have materialised through one another. We've been dealing with materialisation since the very first episode in 1963, and yet the logical consequences of it have rarely been considered. On the one hand, we are presented with an intriguing conceptual paradox, with spaceship corridors of mist and matter distortions, and one that seems inspired by the sort of magic we get with the TARDIS. On the other, we have spaceship captains talking of insurance investigations with all the bored irritation of your Mummy and Daddy arguing with the man who rear-ended their Mini Metro. It's weird and space age, and utterly credible and fully recognisable.

And then we have the Continuous Event Transmuter (CET) machine, an idea so good that Robert Holmes used it to fill out the entirety of Carnival of Monsters six years ago.

There it was largely played for humour, so that we could see 1920s Earth people behave like stereotypes and run around in small repetitive cycles – here it's very different, and at once we are left to ponder the ethics of dealing with zoos; for all its brilliance, Carnival has no line as punchy as the one here that compares the preservation of wildlife to the preservation of jam.

These concepts are both so good, and so imagination expanding, that the drug storyline is never allowed to feel forced or preachy. And the shock of it grounds the freewheeling nature of them, takes your traditional Bob Baker flight of fancies and gives them a disturbing real-world context. The story opens as so many of his stories do, with pilots of spaceships pressing buttons earnestly at each other – and when Secker starts acting too flippantly, you could be forgiven for thinking that this was a repeat of the start of The Invisible Enemy. But this time, the threat comes not from some big spacey virus engulfing the ship, but from within – Secker isn't being destroyed by a virus shaped like a prawn, but by his own drug abuse. When you first see Stephen Jenn as Secker, he merely seems to be resorting to bad acting – and, let's face it, we're used to that. The smile is too broad, the dialogue delivery too unnatural. The clichés of Doctor Who are being turned against us. All too soon, we realise that there's a reason for the strange performance – and it's not unlike the beginning of The Armageddon Factor, where rubbish actors were revealed to be part of a TV movie, except this time it's not played merely as a clever postmodern gag, but as something much darker.

T: You mention the insurance claim element of this, which is fundamental to this terrific episode's success – I've always admired its drive to root its multi-various high-concept sci-fi ideas in a practical reality. The Empress isn't some interstellar military or science vessel, it's a common-or-garden cruise liner. Captain Rigg refers to his trip as "the Milk Run": a no-frills intergalactic version of a cheap package holiday. Such a novel (for Doctor Who) setting then leads us to arguments between Rigg and another ship captain, Dymond, about culpability and insurance

premiums: totally practical concerns that help to ground the giddy imagination of the fused spaceships into a plausible habitat. We have (with depressing resonance to the modern viewer) talk of a galactic recession, and the zoologist Tryst's expeditions receiving free passage on government-subsidised transports. Bob Baker's keen attention to this kind of detail provides some neat world-building. Tryst's crystal set may be a scientific breakthrough, but such space-age gizmos still need to be paid for and transported cost-effectively. Rigg needs lasers to cut through the bulkhead, so he talks of having to send to the planet Azure to secure some of this presumably expensive gear (he doesn't have them lying around just because he's from space). The whole thing has a pleasing verisimilitude.

As Rigg, David Daker gives a direct and earthy performance that underlines this credibility. Daker has wisely decided to treat the seemingly whacky sci-fi stuff as an everyday occurrence (which, of course, it would be to his character). And whilst Rigg is practical (note how he researches the Doctor's sham of a backstory), his navigator Secker exhibits the fractious mental state of a drug addict. Stephen Jenn, as Secker, effectively flits from lackadaisical insouciance to edgy desperation very well – the scars he receives after his ill-advised trip into the interface are pretty gruesome for this period of the show, and a surgeon relays Secker's death with just a grim shake of his head, even as a colleague tiredly (in an example of keeping this real) wipes his brow in the background. Indeed, seeing as this was a troubled production for director Alan Bromly, it seems a shame he walked (or was pushed) halfway through filming, as the shot of Stott staring out from the Eden projection is quite masterful; it's unsettling and beautifully lit.

As for Lewis Fiander and his accent, they're like the spaceships in the story – an ill-advised hybrid, an uncomfortable fusing of the Swedish Chef and a comedy Dutchman. Even then, this dotty-scientist act actually works in places – his absentmindedness and difficulty with the language makes him seem quite eccentric – so he comes across as a comedy turn rather than the villain of the piece. Where it *doesn't* work is with his shrugged repetition of "he died" to the question about his dead crewmate, where dark evasiveness or shamed prevarication would have been more believable than silly comic deadpanning.

Nightmare of Eden (part two)

R: And if last week it was all about Daddy arguing about a pranged car, this time it's watching him come home a little too worse for the wear after the office Christmas party. David Daker's slide into drug addiction isn't necessarily subtle, but it's still sad to watch – mostly because, for all his suspicions of the Doctor, Captain Rigg was the one character who seemed to have any authority. That authority slips away into apathetic giggling here, and you realise that someone we had begun to care about has been lost. Daker succeeded admirably in making Rigg dependable and sympathetic; the instant (too instant?) contrast more than simply unsettles us, it disappoints us for all the right reasons.

The monsters of this story, the Mandrels, are fine, I think. They shuffle around a bit, and don't look terribly fierce – but it's not as if the story is using them as the main threat, they're just the clawed icing on top of the cake. The problem is more that the filling of the cake isn't very interesting this episode. There's lots of running about after some mysterious goggled individual (well, mysterious until the end credits unaccountably gives the game away); there's some urgently acted but dramatically static business with engines as the Doctor and Dymond try to separate the spaceships. And as the final few minutes introduce Fisk and Costa, bureaucratic characters whose only function is to slow down the Doctor still further, it's a little hard not to stifle a sigh. At the halfway point of the adventure, you really don't need new characters popping up who want to present such elementary obstacles; you want the story to kick into a higher gear.

As the Doctor and Romana jump into Eden, it feels not a moment too soon.

T: But *what* a cliffhanger, and one I remember from first broadcast – our heroes run towards danger because they, and only they, have the vaguest inkling of what is really going on. They're two brave misfits throwing themselves in at the deep end; terrific stuff! Indeed, the Doctor has refused to make his own life easy throughout the first two episodes of this. Rigg pretty much gives him a decent cover story (that he's an agent investigating drug trafficking) and the Doctor throws it back in his face! It's as if he wilfully, and on principle, rejects any offer to conform to procedure and bureaucracy: he's a terse hero whose genius and bravery make him difficult, prickly company. No wonder Baker was subsequently cast as Sherlock Holmes (as part that you could say is right up his street).

But it's largely thanks to David Daker that we buy Captain Rigg's acceptance of this grumpy interloper into his intergalactic disaster. His downplayed but sincere response to the Doctor's mention of Vraxoin eschews melodrama. Rigg (a decent man trying to stay in control of a difficult situation) looks like he's on his way to being the Doctor's trusted sidekick, but then, in a moment of cruel dramatic irony, talks of the Vrax smuggling being "the least of our worries" before swallowing a drink spiked with the stuff – it's an unexpected twist that wrong-foots the audience and puts the most likeable guest character in mortal peril.

Lewis Fiander is still sort-of working for me. Context means everything – stick him in the Hinchcliffe era or Season Seven, and I'd want to beat him about the face and neck with a heavy mallet. But here, I only want to kick him in the shins... and only every now and again. He seems quite at home amongst some of the lighter and bouncier scripting, and the self-conscious gag at the show's own expense when the Doctor goes through supposedly different carriages which all look the same, right down to the identically costumed passengers. Defenders of the Williams era could rightly claim this as some sort of postmodernism concerning the show's famous low budget, and I don't think I'd argue with them. What they'd say about the sparkly costumed customs men and their comedy haplessly-outwitted-acting might be more easily rebutted, though.

That said, let me actually be positive about even the least impressive aspects of this episode. Look at the way the poor actors have to give quite a protracted reaction to being locked in the control room by the escaping Doctor and Romana. Peter Craze (as Costa) at least has the control panel to play with, but once

Geoffrey Hinsliff (as Fisk) has looked at his subordinate exasperatedly and banged on the door, he's out of business... so he draws his gun. It's a little thing, but it gives the scene a little dramatic drive before the cut – in those days of minimal editing, you needed experienced actors to keep things lively and interesting, thus preventing potentially stodgy scenes from looking limp. These days, where performances are really made in the edit (such a scene would now be assembled from a number of set-ups and close-up cutaways), things aren't quite so important, which is why so many in TV production think anyone can act and that experience counts for nothing. Those people are wrong... or on drugs.

Nightmare of Eden (part three)

R: There's a lovely moment at the top of this which not only sums up my feelings about how this story is handled, but the state of latter day Graham Williams' Who. The Doctor and Romana are in Eden, and things are tense. The Doctor proposes they go east, and Romana demands to know how he can be sure it's east – maybe it's north? The Doctor agrees that it might be north, but why not call it east? And so the banter goes on, until there's the growl of a predatory monster, and with some urgent irritation the Doctor asks whether they can simply get on with the business of escaping.

There's a wit to the series, obviously. Watched in isolation, a lot of Nightmare of Eden in particular is very funny. It's no wonder that Lewis Fiander saw Tryst as a comedy part, and adopted an increasingly outrageous accent, because a lot of his dialogue is built around gags – they're funny gags, but they're also unnatural gags, gags that are there for the writer's cleverness not the character's truth. (My favourite, and I honestly do love it, is how he worked with Professor Stein until his mentor's death. Then he stopped.) But that's part of the difficulty right there. For a comedy writer, the Doctor is a gift; he can come out with silly jokes in the most unlikely of circumstances, because he's an alien – and, if you're lucky, and Tom's happy in studio that day, the comedy won't undermine the drama but actually enhances it. When other characters take on the same ability, to drop into inappropriate jokes

at random, the viewer is adrift. Even in a sitcom, the audience needs to understand which of the characters are supposed to be funny and which ones aren't – in a drama that plays about with death and drug addiction and high concept science fiction, it's all the more essential.

The scene from this episode that everybody always points at is the one where Captain Rigg watches the passengers being attacked by Mandrels and laughs at it uproariously. On the one hand, of course, this is wonderful black comedy; and it's the contrast between Rigg's delight and Costa's horror at the carnage that sells it. ("They're only economy!") But on the other, watching these rather naff monsters attack some badly acted extras, and laughing at it all on a television screen, Rigg is unconsciously mirroring the reaction of the audience at home, and their laughter will be one of contempt. And that's the problem. At what point do we take Doctor Who seriously, and when do we point at it and sneer? Both reactions can be entertaining. But when the programme invites us to switch between these reactions so quickly, is it asking too much of us? Or is it asking too little of itself?

City of Death knew it was a comedy, and like all good comedies, recognised that making people laugh was a precise and serious business. The Creature from the Pit wasn't so sure that it was a comedy, but its drama was postmodern and arch enough that the moments of silliness didn't seem to be breaking the house style. Nightmare of Eden wants to be a drama, and wants to have funny bits in – and there's nothing wrong with that in itself, so long as there's someone at the rudder who knows which is which. And no one is here. And scenes of potential power are squandered; when Fisk tells Costa how he plans to exploit the deaths of the passengers to get promotion, it ought to be shocking – but the moment is lost within the gaudiness around it. When the Doctor discovers that the Mandrel can be broken down into a deadly drug, it ought to be a big revelation – but we've been too busy chuckling at the things to take in the dramatic import.

I feel like I'm picking on Nightmare of Eden harshly, and that's a shame. Because I genuinely think that at the heart of this is Bob Baker's best script. And I'd rather watch a story of this ambition, even of this squandered ambition, than something bland and by the numbers. But of all the stories this season, Nightmare feels like a casualty of the wrong production team. Made a couple of years later, or made a couple of years before, this might have been a masterpiece.

T: I think it's *enjoyable*, at least – it transports me right back to a childhood of dark Saturday nights, inclement weather battering at the windows, open fires and boiled eggs and soldiers. Okay, so it looks a bit cheap and some of the performances are suspect, but has there ever been a better lit jungle in a TV studio in Doctor Who? It's all very well lauding those from Planet of Evil and The Creature from the Pit, which had time and film cameras lavished upon them, but this place is bathed in alien colours and shadows. It also highlights (or low lights?) the effectiveness of the Mandrel design when filmed properly. When one looms out of the darkness in pursuit of the Doctor and Romana, its green eyes glow with malevolence, and its skin exudes an alien phosphorescence. In this clammy, murky jungle, and amid the comedy banter, Tom Baker isn't all flippancy – he gets down and dirty as he incapacitates a carnivorous plant by biting through its root with his teeth, and getting sprayed with its goo. Later, when rewiring the ship, his face is awash with the sweat of fear and graft – despite his flamboyance, this Doctor has a saltiness that ensures that there's nothing vaguely bouffant about him so late in his reign.

The guest performances continue to be a mixed bag. I can see the advantage of casting Geoffrey Hinsliff as Fisk, as his slight stature and belligerent tone make him come across like a petty, little, power-crazed bureaucrat, but Hinsliff sells the comedic aspects of the role too hard. So while I do like the moment where Costa reads the casualty list, and Fisk responds with glee that this carnage will guarantee them promotion, it benefits more from the writing than the performance. And it may seem an odd thing to eulogise, but the relative dullness of Barry Andrews as Stott actually does the piece some favours – it makes him straightforward and unflappable, bringing a necessary solidity when others are showing off. His matter-of-fact announcement that he con-

sidered blowing his own brains out, and his delightful "*the* name's Stott" by way of introduction, are both delivered quite bluntly, and so his heroics aren't sent-up. (Though no one playing a goodie ever puts their hands on their hips anymore, and I for one think that's one of the tragedies of the modern era.)

The best acting comes from Lalla Ward and David Daker, in the scene where the now-addicted captain begs, bargains and ultimately threatens Romana to get his fix. It's a shame when he's rather perfunctorily dispatched, as it robs the piece of its best actor and most likeable character. So it's a good job that before Daker goes, he's awarded the most enjoyably postmodern moment when, having seen a guard nudged to death by an unwieldy creature, Rigg guffaws as any grown-up watching telly at the time might well have done. That he tops off this witty set piece with a gag about the slain passenger being economy class shows that the pursuit of humour isn't a lost cause during this period of the show... even if jokes of this quality aren't as frequent as the revisionists might claim.

But I've never been sure that I like the idea that Vraxoin eventually kills its addicts, because if death was inevitable, surely no-one but the *most* desperate and suicidal would take it in the first place? That said, I suppose no-one would logically dabble with heroin with the knowledge of the pain of addiction that follows – which surely every novice must have – and yet they still do. Still, if one of the definite side effects is *actual death*, that seems rather too inevitable and final – not everyone who smokes dies, and I know, for example, that this particular smoker is immortal and lung cancer only gets other people. But if I knew smoking would *definitely* kill me, I wouldn't have started; it just seems too simplistic. All of that said, I do like the discovery (via a nifty effect) that the decomposed remains of a Mandrel create Vraxoin – it's a neat sci-fi concept upon which the disparate plot elements all hang.

And talking of neat sci-fi concepts, *what* a cliffhanger as Romana, with grim conviction and at gunpoint, activates the switch which sees the Doctor's unstable image shimmer and then blink out of existence as the ships finally separate. I desperately want to know what happens next! Oh no, maybe I'm addicted!

August 26th

Nightmare of Eden (part four)

R: And in no other episode is the schizo-phrenic nature of this story made so clear. The scene where the Doctor can't even bring him-self to look at the captured Tryst, and inter-rupts his pleas for forgiveness with a whis-pered "Go away", is certainly very striking. But it follows on the heels of the sequence where the Doctor is attacked by the Mandrels off-screen in the bushes of Eden – "Oh, my fin-gers, my arms, my legs, my everything! Ouuugggaaa!" We'll get scenes of emotional realism, like the one where Della talks of her guilt in leaving her lover to die, and then there'll be extras being felled by Mandrels and even the people standing inches away from them show not the slightest reaction. And it's in this struggle between its humanitarian themes, and its dehumanising treatment of the characters, that Nightmare of Eden comes unstuck.

Terrance Dicks was churning out the nov-elisations by the bucketload at this stage, but when you read his take on Nightmare of Eden, divorcing it from all the production problems and acting excesses, its angry urgency is revealed. Tryst, in particular, comes across as a likeable scientist who has been corrupted by his belief that the end justifies the means – it's his very compromised banality that makes him work. Lewis Fiander is no slouch as an actor, and at times his comic affability serves that intention well – but saddling Tryst with such an accent is a mistake, fatally making him gro-tesque and unidentifiable.

This is Bob Baker's final script for Doctor Who, and he's been with us on this quest for ages now, his work with Dave Martin running like a spine through the seventies. And it seems sadly typical, after so many scripts that have smacked of crazy overambition, that when he finally turns in a well-paced, thought-ful and wholly practical tale, the production team ruin it anyway.

T: The more we've delved into this tale, the more I've felt torn between what my adult self appreciates (or doesn't appreciate) and the ghosts of what my youthful self recalls – all of which is perhaps fitting, because Nightmare of Eden too seems to be working against itself at times. It's a thoughtful tale, this one, but it's hampered by a slightly clunky pace in between the exciting bits that younger me appreciated (notably baddies in silver suits charging about zapping people). My upbringing is such that I love the straightforward pencil laser beams of the 1970s – they're the hallmarks of TV sci-fi for me, and I remember being excited by the different colours and thicknesses they came in. For that matter, to judge by Della's reaction, Dymond clearly has the very special capability of hurting someone's stomach when shooting them in the face – it must be the laser bolt equivalent of acupuncture, but less beneficial.

As a kid, I was quite chuffed that Dymond was one of the baddies – he'd seemed like a straightforward sort of chap, so his mendacity was an exciting twist. Whereas as a grown-up, I love that he does an evil profit calculation just to gloat (and provide an opportunity for the Doctor to learn of his villainy). It's a daft moment, as is the Doctor hiding directly behind Dymond on the shuttle, yet both bits are saved from total ludicrousness by... (sur-prise!) Tom Baker. Yes, the man who needs reigning in, and *should not* have been indulged with the (obviously dubbed in after the fact) "Oh, my arms! My legs! etc" nonsense, can, when he feels like it, either give weight to the silliness at hand, or do a piece of alien business that sells something that is clumsily staged. His rebuke to Tryst of "Go away" is rightly cele-brated, but we're paying for such excellence with Baker's insistence on occasionally enter-taining himself more than the rest of us. It's a curious experience, but I suppose that's what you get with a genius at the helm.

Lewis Fiander's performance, too, makes me vacillate. As you say, the slightly dotty comedy-foreigner shtick works when he plays the guileless bystander as he and Fisk discuss the situation. Fiander and Geoffrey Hinsliff have a nice dynamic, with the villainous scientist wrapping the arrogant customs man around his little finger. I also have mixed feelings about the Mandrels – I really like their faces and the way they keep turning around to attack the guards herding them towards the projection, as well as the cooing, keening noise they make in response to the Doctor's whistle. But they look very – well – frayed, and their stiff arms and flared feet aren't doing them any favours.

The script, at least, keeps shifting its moral stance more deliberately (at least, I'm guessing it's deliberate), even if this does create some odd results. When Tryst argues that the Mandrels would have gone extinct without his having become a Vraxoin dealer, Della snaps at him, "I think a few million people becoming extinct is rather more serious", which A) doesn't actually make any sense, and B) makes her somewhat callous to the defenceless creatures especially since, as Tryst points out, the humans had a choice in the matter. That the killer drug requires the slaughter of dumb animals adds an extra layer of complexity to the issue of recreational drug use, which probably couldn't have been explored too much further in a family show, but at least it's paying lip service to it.

So that's Nightmare of Eden: a story of enormous highs and terrible lows – which, seeing as it's about drug addiction, is probably quite apt. Let me finish, then, with a bit of delight from the credits watcher inside me, as I point out that Eden Phillips, playing a crewman, must have surely been the only actor cast because the story title contains part of his name. (I bet there are actors called Rupert Invasion, Keith Daleks and Mandragora Perkins really cursing their luck somewhere in a Soho drinking den... and if only Deep Roy had played the Weed Creature in 1968.)

The Horns of Nimon (part one)

R: There is the germ of a good story in here, but it's stymied by that opening scene. Imagine if we hadn't had it. The episode opens with the TARDIS incapacitated in space. The Doctor and Romana are alarmed to find that they're being sucked into the gravitational pull of a mysterious ship, alone, unmoving, hanging there. They crash into it, but are able to get onboard. There they are surprised to find there are people alive – and these people claim to be on their way to ritual sacrifice...

It's strange that The Horns of Nimon takes such pains to remove any mystery or intrigue – especially when you consider that the story it's telling is such a familiar one in the first place. That first scene with the two pilots on the Skonnan ship tells us everything we need to know, and nothing we wouldn't have learned more dramatically later on if only they'd just shut up. Doctor Who thrives on suspense, on the way that the Doctor's first job in a new story is to try to work out exactly what sort of adventure he's landed in this time. And the joy comes from making those discoveries with him – finding Davros when he finds Davros, finding the Mona Lisas when the revelation will be most effective, seeing a big green creature in a pit only after sifting through the evidence of other people's impressions and lies. In The Horns of Nimon, the viewer is uncomfortably situated at a point in the story at least half an hour in advance of the Doctor – and all we can do is sit about and watch as he catches up with us. You might think that this would make us feel clever. It does not make us feel clever. It makes us feel patronised, that we have to be spoonfed the information at the top of the show, because we're not capable of deducing the information alongside our heroes. It'd be the equivalent of watching an Agatha Christie movie, and being shown who the murderer was before Hercule Poirot shows up, because we're not smart enough to play detective too.

With no mystery to the episode – and there isn't any, there really isn't – it all becomes rather dull. We're only in the first week of the story, and already we're marking time with copious amounts of padding – because this isn't going to be a story about a spaceship at all, the spaceship is just a delaying tactic to stop us from getting to the actual plot. There's some pleasure to be taken from the broad comedy of the TARDIS scenes, especially when Tom Baker starts channelling Eric Morecambe ("It's uncanny!") – but don't they seem awfully long? We're used to sequences of mayhem in the TARDIS, and even the sight of the Doctor giving artificial respiration to a metal dog might be acceptable if it were just some comic shtick before the story began. But the story takes an age to begin, and even when it does, the script still needs to find time to waste. The scene where the Doctor steals Romana's screw-driver is quite sweet, but it's shoehorned into a bit where there's a pretence of urgency and the Doctor is being held at gunpoint. Look at Malcolm Terris' face during this whole business. He's been given no lines to interrupt the comedy with, he's been written no reaction at all, even though he'd clearly be impatient. Is he supposed to be interested by Romana's screwdriver or not? The poor chap clearly doesn't know.

And the episode ends with the Doctor stuck on the TARDIS again, still no closer to Skonnos, still no closer to the main plot – and hugging K-9 with fear because an utterly random aster-oid is about to hit them. It's almost as if the first episode hasn't happened at all. It may as well not even have been broadcast. You know, sod it, I'm going to pretend it wasn't. I'm going to pretend we start with episode two. I bet that the story doesn't even miss a beat for its absence.

T: My hope in rewatching this story was that it would unfold as a comedy classic – that beneath the surface tat, some gems would enliven a financially precarious production. So you can imagine my surprise that the design seems to be doing all the hard work. One of the things that leaps out at me is Romana's crimson costume – it's a smartly upper class, feminised parody of the Doctor's (albeit with added leather gloves) and is very stylish and swish; it's a vast improvement on the grey maternity tent she was saddled with last time. (No, I can't believe that I'm commenting on fashion either!) And the story, made during a time of hyper-inflation, tries to turn its cheap-ness into a virtue as the pilots take great pains to explain that their spaceship is clapped out. As a result, when the rackety control banks wobble as the thing careens out of control, it's actually reasonable that the whole thing looks as though it's about to come apart.

I have to focus on such things, because... well, most of this is curiously uninvolving, isn't it? We begin on the spaceship Exposition 3 before some nice comedy business aboard the TARDIS, but the plot is explained rather than told. (There's a crucial difference between the two – one is dramatic, the other isn't.) And we've arrived at the crux of Tom Baker think-

ing he can get away with *anything*, when he really can't. Although Baker and David Brierley have clearly worked out a lot of comedy busi-ness that was no doubt hilarious on the studio floor, it doesn't translate because – within the context of the story – it doesn't really make sense (notably the artificial respiration scene and the cliffhanger). It's slapstick in the middle of high drama and neither really helps the other. So thank God that Lalla Ward is all piss and vinegar – she's clearly decided to take charge in trying to drive the drama to a satisfy-ing place.

The guest cast, at least, is somewhat inter-esting. Bob Hornery, as the Pilot, claims some sort of fame as the first actor from Neighbours (he was a semi-regular there, as Carl Kennedy's dad) to appear in Doctor Who; Kylie is a major Johnny-Come-Lately compared to our Bob, who is also rather good in Sapphire and Steel's spooky tale of evil photographs. Sadly, he's not with us long, and once his character dies – and has a rare splash of blood daubed on his face for his pains – it's left to poor old Malcolm Terris (as the Co-Pilot) to shoulder the villainy. Terris was one of those actors who cropped up in everything when I was a nipper, and I remember being rather chuffed to realise that he'd done a couple of Whos. However, between his tiny turn in The Dominators and his hor-rible, bawling, one-note idiot of a part here, I fear he's been rather poorly served by the show – and so has repaid it in kind.

And while I appreciate Graham Crowden's efforts as Soldeed, and enjoy the gleeful bounce he gives to any production he graces, in isola-tion – and with Michael Osborne's Sorak steadfastly refusing to acknowledge he's talk-ing to a character with the diction of someone on a strict scenery-only diet – it just seems a bit odd. Simon Gipps-Kent does his best as Seth, as – I'm sure – does Janet Ellis. (Unfortunately, *her* best doesn't come terribly close to anything resembling good acting.)

In the Anethan scenes, I'm most drawn to the rather beguiling chap with the blond Michelangelo curls – the one we first see ren-dering his interpretation of ship-buffeting-act-ing in the hold, and wobbling his body so stiffly, he makes Matthew Waterhouse look like Mata Hari. Later, he flinches back when the Co-Pilot once again issues his unfunny, unthreatening "Weakling scum!" catchphrase, and then puts his hand to his mouth in fear. Finally, when the ship is in flight again, he springs to his feet and seems rather excited to get his circulation back. Look, I appreciate that being a background artist is hard – any actor worth his or her salt knows that the less you have to do, the more difficult it becomes. So, sure, Michaelangelo Curls isn't terribly good, but at least he's trying to be as convincing as possible... which in this episode, at least, puts him in a distinct minority.

The Horns of Nimon (part two)

R: The ever-changing walls of the labyrinth are really rather a smart idea, and works better if you can think back to the 1970s when the audience took for granted the way television was recorded. They understood implicitly that the scenes were filmed as if on a theatre stage, and so big changes to the set will only happen between takes. When you see Tom Baker double back and realise that a wall has shifted position whilst he was looking the other way, you're also invited to realise that just off camera an entire bevy of BBC staff have been moving it – it's the closest we get to a subtle form of pantomime in this Christmas episode, where if you could only call out "look behind you!" we'd see technicians trying to pull off a special effect.

Lalla Ward is allowed to shine as Romana at last. With the Doctor pratting about in the TARDIS with dog rosettes and exploding musical consoles, she's forced to take on the hero role, defending the underdog and annoying the Skonnan regime. With a new production team on the way, all set to stamp the comedy out of the show, her serious portrayal now feels like a portent of things to come – and leaves Tom Baker looking somewhat old-fashioned and out of touch.

But when Lalla Ward isn't there to rein things in, there's a desperation to proceedings. I know many fans who claim The Horns of Nimon is a comedy classic, and that a failure to appreciate it marks you out as someone who takes the show too seriously. For my part, I can't but help feel that that is a severe underestimate of what comedy actually is – if comedy were simply a matter of overacting and impre-

cision, we could all be Laurel and Hardy. The great shame of Horns is not that it's aiming for laughs, but that the script hasn't made much allowance for humour at all – if there were proper, well-constructed jokes in this, you wouldn't need the likes of Graham Crowden and Tom Baker making such an effort to put in their own. The Horns of Nimon as a concept isn't too silly – it's not silly *enough*. When a throwaway gag at the start of The Creature from the Pit has a wittier take on the Minotaur legend than a whole four-part story wallowing in it, then you've got problems – and the truth is, sticking a bull on a man's head isn't a reinvention of the myth, it's just an unimaginative retelling of it. Underworld was dreadful, but it still had more imagination than this, and a greater willingness to play fast and loose with the source material. With Nightmare of Eden, you saw a production team ruin a story because they treated it too flippantly. Here, they hope that the flippancy will disguise how dull and predictable it is, and it simply isn't enough.

And since episode two went out on 29th December, 1979, this is where the seventies end. The decade that brought us the series at its most popular, that brought us Inferno and Carnival of Monsters, that brought us Genesis and both Robots and City of Death. A bit of an anticlimax, isn't it? What do you reckon, Toby? Shall we end the second volume right here, or shall we struggle on a bit further?

T: End *now*, on one of the clearest memories of Doctor Who from my childhood? I remember this *working*. I remember that much of the excitement of a four-episode Doctor Who story was the anticipation – yes, we'd seen the Nimon at the end of episode one, but this week was building up to when one of the regulars encountered him. Tension and horror mounted in stages; I clearly remember the horrible man (the Co-Pilot) begging for his life and getting zapped, which entailed the first sight of the special effect used for the Nimon's lethal rays. Again, even that was something to be anticipated: when you saw a sci-fi gun, you'd wonder what colour ray it would emit in combat. The guns here are rather neat – a flash-bang *and* a laser bolt, belt and braces – whilst the Nimon horns and their twirly red spirals of doom are novel and exciting. These days, of course, we're encouraged to notice none of that, and to laugh at the fact that Terris' trousers split (although I think his wobbly cheeks as he shakes his head and pleads with the Nimon are pretty funny too).

So I know that The Horns of Nimon did its job, and I remember how excited I was watching it... which makes me rather sad that it's pretty slim pickings again this week. Yes, Baker and Crowden are entertaining enough, but they're not being especially funny, they're being *silly*. Their antics enliven the proceedings, but only to distract you from a general dullness, not to augment something apocalyptically awful with postmodern showboating. There's no context to the oddness of their performances, except they are in something that is otherwise a trifle underwhelming, or just not very good.

A couple of really good jokes aside (such as the fabulous exchange of Seth: "[The Nimon] lives in the Power Complex", Romana: "That fits"), this episode is actually enlivened by the bits people do properly rather than when they try to prop it up with indulgent hi-jinks. The mummified corpse that collapses to the touch is a genuine jump-out-of your skin moment, as is the concept that the Nimon feed off "the binding energy of organic compounds such as flesh". It's a pretty hideous concept, and the Anethans' intended fate as the contents of the Nimon larder is chilling stuff. A maze that physically changes is a nice twist on the legend, and the lighting within – at a low level and shadowy – at least tries to provide some moody atmosphere. Whilst Seth's vague revelation of his humble beginnings feels infodumped rather than built into the story, Simon Gipps-Kent at least plays it with sincerity. And he's ably supported by my blond cherubim, who looks terribly shocked in the hold when Seth warns that "no-one must know" his secret, and is still acting his socks off in the very last shot as the Nimon looms towards our heroes. He may be only a humble background artist, but he's a prince to me.

August 27th

The Horns of Nimon (part three)

R: Well, I'll say one thing for this. The extras are of a better quality than we've got used to all season. Some of those Anethans, in spite of all reasons for the contrary, seem positively terrified!

The Horns of Nimon serves a genuine and valuable contribution to Doctor Who. We're moving now into the fan age, when the incoming production team take great notice of what the fans think, and stories are shaped to meet their approval. An essential part of this is that there has to be a story that can be demonised, one against you can hurl all your brickbats – and that defines the low point that the series must never ever stoop to again. From this point on, and for several years afterwards, The Horns of Nimon serves that function. And in that way, its legacy is huge. When the new production team of John Nathan-Turner and Barry Letts react against the excesses of the seventeenth season, it's really The Horns of Nimon that acts as the lightning conductor. For the first time in the show's history, a new showrunner will seek not merely to succeed the previous regime, but to revolutionise it entirely.

And so when you read old interviews with Graham Williams, who talks with regret of the cancellation of the season finale Shada, and how he would never have wanted to end his tenure with a story as poor as Nimon, you can't but help feel that he's fighting a losing battle. Because Nimon not only ends his time on the series, for years it came to define it. Cheap and dull and silly and overacted – it's definitely not the template for three troubled seasons which have managed, in spite of problems with budget and temperamental actors, to be the most genuinely science-fiction stories Doctor Who has ever broadcast. Their ambitions may have often far exceeded their capabilities, but at least the show in its middle age was finding newer and bolder things to do.

Because I do think this has been an unexpectedly hard decade to get through on this quest of ours. If you'd told me when we were wading through all those missing episodes of the black and white years that they'd still be collectively more exciting than the colour ones, I wouldn't have believed you. But if the sixties were about a process of constant innovation, in which so much felt like it was a brave experiment, then the seventies have seemed to me largely reactionary. The Pertwee years were about finding a formula that was popular and sticking to it, rigidly; the Baker years under Hinchcliffe changed that formula, but adopted a repetitive formula of their own nonetheless. And unarguably over the past few months, we've been watching Doctor Who play out with its two most iconic Doctors – certainly of the "classic" years – and the appeal of Pertwee and Baker may have been directly because of its reliable predictability.

The Graham Williams seasons changed all that. There have been some duff stories – my God, yes – but The Horns of Nimon is the very first of them that actually feels stale. There's barely a thing in it we haven't seen before. And it doesn't matter that it's hot on the heels of a season that has tried to push the barriers of the show's storytelling in distinctively varied ways. As we slip out of the old decade, all the trappings of it look old too. The time tunnel opening sequence. The theme tune. Dudley Simpson. Tom Baker himself.

The Horns of Nimon was the perfect gift for the new production team. Shada wouldn't have given them anything to fight against. And they needed something to fight against – it was time for revolution, and Nimon provided the opportunity for revolution like no other. Because whatever one might feel about John Nathan-Turner's time on the show – and it's going to be a controversial time – it's also impossible to imagine it lasting the nine seasons it did if it had meekly followed the template set over the last few years. I dislike The Horns of Nimon very much. But I do honestly believe that without it, Doctor Who's future would have been a short and timid one. If The Horns of Nimon didn't exist, you'd have to invent it.

T: It's interesting... while the more appalling stories have prompted me to scribble reams and reams of notes, I've barely mustered half a page per episode for The Horns of Nimon. In context, it's just a rather shabby affair – neither the grand folly of legend nor the misunderstood comic tour-de-force of modern reinvention. It's a slightly drab adventure with some misjudged comedy, limp supporting performances and questionable design, but at least that features one particular extra trying very hard indeed, bless him.

It didn't have to be this way, because there's a fabulous concept to the Nimon: intergalactic marauding locusts that strip planets clean of their assets, then move on to the next one. Any premise that has an echo of the natural world automatically gains believability, and this gets a political dimension too, with the exploitation of the greed and gullibility of a power hungry leader (in this case, Soldeed). Also, welcome effort has been made with the bland hero figure, by having poor Seth as a slightly harassed sort, burdened by the weight of Teka's publicly enunciated certainty that he knows everything, and is terribly brave despite his protestations to the contrary. (It's a shame his secret was revealed on the Exposition 3 early on, as it could have made for a dramatic reveal at a crucial moment, and thereby served as a deliberate deflation of the story's classical roots.) So there's some potential here, yes, but not enough to keep my attention from wandering...

But what's this? An extra threatening to take Blondie's mantle? Look at Soldeed's crowd. They are a mixed bunch, but I'm especially drawn to the camp moustachioed fellow who's really going for it with gusto. He's not phoning it in, is he? The background artists in this story really do put the super into supernumery.

The Horns of Nimon (part four)

R: John Bailey turns up, just as he did all those years ago in The Sensorites, to add some weight to a dull story in its dying fall. As Sezom, a former supporter of the Nimon, Bailey disguises the fact that his character only exists as a handy expository device for Romana – someone to give info, then expire – by finding a guilt and a dignity that feel real and human. That he's the Crinoth counterpart of Soldeed only more emphasises the difference in approach, as Graham Crowden is truly running rampant by this stage.

And Sezom's sacrifice to save a girl he's only

just met and a planet he's only just heard of is lovely. In a story which puts a lot of emphasis on the nature of heroism (and Seth's obligation to live up to Teka's demands of him), this is the only moment when anybody really does anything that seems especially heroic. The Doctor spends the majority of the episode sending shuttles back and forth, acting less like a hero, more like a bus driver,

And there's a big explosion, and then it just sort of ends, really.

Enough of this. I don't know about you, but I'm just about ready for something different. Radiophonic music, star field credits, neon tube logos. And a renewed sense of purpose. What about you, Toby? Shall we strip off our flared trousers, and jump into the eighties?

T: This is the last outing for this combination of theme arrangement and opening titles. And do you know what? They've never been done better. The Hartnell, Troughton and Pertwee combos were all brilliant, but this one edges them, only just. I'll be surprised if anything to come ever gets quite as evocative, timeless or imaginative as the faultless work Bernard Lodge and Delia Derbyshire provided to the programme's first 16 years – if the curator of The Doctor Who Hall of Fame is reading, etch their names with pride. We shall not see nor hear their like again.

The best thing about this episode is, as you say, Sezom. As Anthony Read gets everyone to enunciate their character and backstory pretty much straight away, we learn as much about Sezom as anyone else in The Horns of Nimon, and he's only in it for about ten minutes. Indeed, I remember that I missed the beginning of this on broadcast, so didn't even know who he was, but still found myself rather moved by his sacrifice to save Romana. Bailey was a special actor – his wonderful diction and sympathetic, broken dignity compel me to mark this, his final of three fine contributions to the show (including, notably, Victoria's father in The Evil of the Daleks). Graham Crowden's dignity is an altogether more eccentric affair, but it's hard not to love a performer who consistently teeters on the edge of madness. The way he clasps Teka's hand and forces it aloft, to usher her in grotesque supplication to the Nimon, is effective. Equally notable is

his realisation that with *three* of the creatures appearing, his world has all-but crumbled (and his sanity quickly follows).

And you know, I rather like the Nimon. The heads don't quite work (a shame the budget didn't stretch to the reveal that they were masks hiding a real face underneath), but their bodies are very sturdy (dare I say beefy, even) and director Kenny McBain allows himself a late flourish by filming them – in their final marches around the tunnels – low, close and on the move. Also, one of the Nimon is played by Trevor St John Hacker, who has shot straight into my Top Ten of all-time favourite Doctor Who actor names.

[Toby's addendum, written June 2012: Since writing this entry, I have been shown a letter written to my friend and fellow fan called Ben Jolly from another Nimon, Robin Sherringham. It was very short and said, "I remember it being the least enjoyable job of my entire career in what I believe is generally considered the third worst Doctor Who story of all time" – which makes it my favourite-ever response to being asked what someone remembers about their time on Doctor Who!]

It's just hit me, though... incredible as it sounds, I think The Horns of Nimon is the last time I was wholly satisfied with Doctor Who. On first watch, I found Season Eighteen a bit stodgy – it was all confusing science and slow elegance rather than the earth-invading, explosion-generating, monster fests that the Target books and Doctor Who Magazine promised me the series had delivered back in the day. Suddenly, what had gone before had a lustre that what was currently being offered couldn't hope to match. And I must have come of age after The Horns of Nimon, because I remember the cliffhanger to episode three, not as it is to my adult eyes (comedy villain and mugging Doctor), but as the absolute dramatic climax to an exciting story of death and drama and laser beams. ("The bloke with the beard – the *main* villain – is pointing his laser stick *at the Doctor!!!* He is in so much trouble!!!!")

It was when I happened upon a copy of DWB at a Doctor Who convention, where it listed a poll of the All Time Classics and All Time Clunkers, that the idea that I could look at Doctor Who with an eye to *criticise* it first hit me. It was my loss of innocence. There it was, in all its glory, at the top of the All Time Clunkers, as voted by their readers... The Horns of Nimon. I was being educated that a story I'd watched and enjoyed as a kid was actually a load of old rubbish, and I began to enjoy the idea of being disappointed in the series I was supposed to like. It's taken me a long time to discover that a more honest and humble way of enjoying something is to remember why I liked it in the first place. After all, no matter how much we fans like to slag the show off, the reason we're fans in the first place is because *we actually like the bloody thing*.

I still loved Doctor Who with Season Eighteen, but there was a hankering for past glories that didn't exist when I watched Nimon. By The Leisure Hive, I'd become a fan. And whether I like it or not, being a fan means you look at things from a slightly jaundiced perspective (or I do, anyway). So actually, the next step in our marathon watch might be the most fascinating of all; because I saw the next stories go out, and when I did so, I was looking for faults and trying to recapture a past I had no right to invoke because I'd never seen it. It was a past that only actually existed in my imagination – an imagination which created images more impressive than could ever have been rendered in the corner of a TV studio. This time, I shall be viewing at them with fresh eyes, looking to see what positives can be gleaned from stories no longer hampered by the responsibility of securing the show's future. Now, *they'll* have nostalgia on their side, too. I've been surprised by many things on this journey of ours, but I think the biggest ones are just around the corner.

ACKNOWLEDGEMENTS

Toby Wishes to Thank: As ever, my close friend Peter Crocker has been an eye on my ham-fisted typing and is also my conduit to the world of all things Who, with whom I can compare notes and vent spleen about all the current Gallifreyan gossip.

I thanked most of the English speaking world in volume one (and many of them are due thanks again, but this isn't UK Gold, so I shall avoid repetition), but a notable absence was Bill Bruce, which is insane as he is a fellow Who-loving comedian who was kind enough to tech the second-ever performance of Moths Ate My Doctor Who Scarf at very short notice, and was then very patient when it overran by a decade or so. It was he who sacrificed a precious fringe slot one evening for a Doctor Who-themed charity night and asked me to perform at it, which resulted in my first direct encounter with David Tennant – the start of the path that led me here.

I probably wouldn't be on the internet were it not for Steve Wild, who answers stupid questions at midnight, whilst Shauno Eels always seems happy to drop everything to provide help and moral support – or even a Peppermint Tea at a train station. Also thanks for various Who-related matters to Elton Townend-Jones, Peter Ware, Chris Boyle, Melanie Ashcroft, James Worienecki, Chris Cassell, Kevin Davies and Ben Jolly.

And especial thanks to Louise Jameson, proof that sometimes you *should* meet your heroes (and heroines).

I should also acknowledge that the marriage chronicled in this volume hasn't, sadly, lasted the gestation period of this book. But if the process has taught me anything, it's to look back fondly, with appreciation and without regret. And so I do.

Rob Wishes to Thank: ... all those who read and enjoyed volume one, and were so patient waiting for the follow-up. I know for a long time this looked like becoming the Shada of Doctor Who Reference Books. But, yes, look, it's finally here, and it's shiny! (Sincere apologies it took so long.)

The Publisher Wishes to Thank: Rob and Toby, for devoting so much time and passion to this great diary of theirs, and letting us see *Doctor Who* through their eyes; Louise Jameson, for her gracious and gentle foreword; Lynne M. Thomas, for coming up with the title to this series; Katy Shuttleworth, for help with the "running men" graphics; Jack Bruner; Jim Boyd; Christa Dickson; Carrie Herndon; Adam Holt; Paul Kirkley; Shawne Kleckner; Braxton Pulley; Heather Riesenberg; Josh Wilson and the incomparable Robert Smith?.

Robert Shearman... is probably best known as a writer for Doctor Who, bringing back the Daleks for the BAFTA-winning first series, in an episode nominated for a Hugo Award. He's also written short stories and comic strips for the range, as well as several award winning audio plays for Big Finish, including *The Chimes of Midnight* and *Jubilee*. He has written five short story collections, and between them they have won the World Fantasy Award, the Shirley Jackson Award, the Edge Hill Readers Prize and three British Fantasy Awards. He began his career in the theatre, and was resident dramatist at the Northcott Theatre in Exeter, and regular writer for Alan Ayckbourn at the Stephen Joseph Theatre in Scarborough; his plays have won the Sunday Times Playwriting Award, the World Drama Trust Award, the inaugural Sophie Winter Memorial Prize and the Guinness Award for Ingenuity in association with the Royal National Theatre. He is a regular writer for BBC Radio, and his own interactive drama series *The Chain Gang* has won two Sony Awards.

Toby Hadoke...is an actor, writer and comedian. He is a regular compere at the award winning comedy clubs XS Malarkey, the Comedy Store and the 99 Club. His one man show *Moths Ate My Doctor Who Scarf* toured the world and spawned a Sony-nominated radio series. It was performed at London's West End (Garrick Theatre) alongside its critically acclaimed sequel (and official Edinburgh fringe sell-out show) *My Stepson Stole My Sonic Screwdriver*. His acting credits include *Holby City*, *Casualty 1907* and a cameo role in *An Adventure in Space and Time*, plus much theatre and radio. He writes obituaries for *The Guardian* and *The Independent* newspapers and has contributed to *Doctor Who Magazine* and *SFX*. His most recent radio play, *The Dad Who Fell To Earth* (which he wrote and starred in) was nominated for a BBC Audio Award. He presents *The 7th Dimension* on Radio 4 Extra and has moderated *Doctor Who* episode commentaries for both Fantom Films and the BBC's official DVD range (for which he has also presented several documentaries). His website is www.tobyhadoke.com and he indulges himself using 140 characters or less on Twitter at @tobyhadoke.

Publisher/ Editor-in-Chief
Lars Pearson

Senior Editor/ Design Manager
Christa Dickson

Associate Editor (MNP)
Joshua Wilson

Assistant Editor (Running)
Carrie Herndon

1150 46th Street
Des Moines, Iowa 50311
info@madnorwegian.com
www.madnorwegian.com